MW00345834

BLOOD SOLACE

BLOOD GRACE BOOK II

VELA ROTH

FIVE THORNS PRESS

ISBN 978-1-957040-04-2 (Ebook)
ISBN 978-1-957040-06-6 (Paperback)
ISBN 978-1-957040-07-3 (Hardcover)

Edited by Brittany Cicirello, Suncroft Editing

Cover art by Patcas Illustration
www.instagram.com/patcas_illustration

Book design by Vela Roth

Map by Vela Roth using Inkarnate
inkarnate.com

Published by Five Thorns Press
www.fivethorns.com

Visit www.velaroth.com

CONTENTS

For all of us who put on the Smile while our hearts are silently breaking.

For all of us who dare to want more.

CONTENT NOTE

BLOOD SOLACE portrays some medieval fantasy violence, an emotionally abusive parent, and conversations about attempted sexual assault.

In particular, in "Blizzard Wraiths" (48 Nights Until Winter Solstice), villains make verbal threats regarding sexual violence. "Battle Scars" (47 Nights Until Winter Solstice) shows women confiding in each other, without graphic detail, about past close calls with sexual predators.

The novel confronts these topics to show women supporting each other, finding courage, and fighting back.

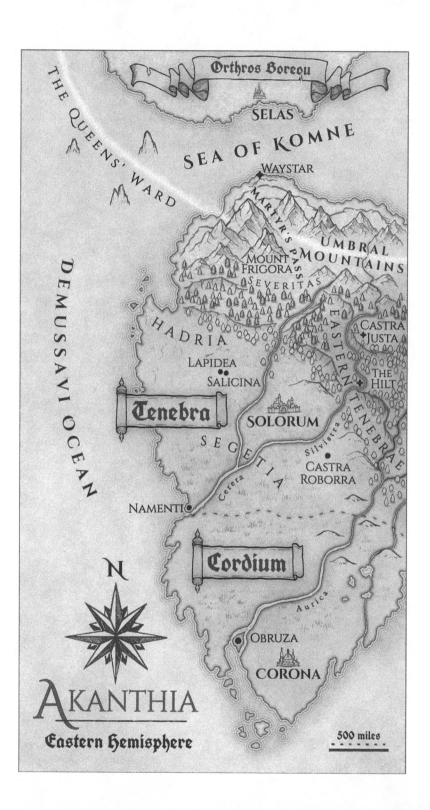

MIGRATION NIGHT

Hesperines shall have the right to children who have been exposed, abandoned, or orphaned without anyone to take them in.

Hesperines shall have the right to the dying whose own kind give them no succor and to the dead whose kin and comrades fail to collect their remains.

—The Equinox Oath

AMBASSADOR'S WATCH

A GUST OF WIND WHIPPED across the deck of the Observatory and struck Lio head-on. He sucked in the bracing air, hungering for any hint of scent from the south. But all he smelled were the fresh snows and evergreens, ice caps and ocean depths of Orthros Boreou. Not enough to give him relief from the aftertaste of his last drink. The fetid remnants of deer blood threatened to gag him. He kept swallowing and focused on the horizon.

The Umbral Mountains stood sentry on the rim of the world, guarding the border between Orthros and Tenebra, between his nocturnal homeland and the mortal realm. Polar twilight cloaked the range in indigo, while the snow on the peaks gleamed under the lights of Hespera's night sky. Vivid aurorae veiled the constellations named for those whom Orthros had lost, who would have lived forever with their fellow immortal Hesperines had they not given their lives for others. The Goddess's Eyes, the twin moons, looked on. The shadow of her lashes had just begun to descend over the smooth white orb of the Light Moon, while the Blood Moon was a crescent iris of liquid crimson.

No fire lit the mountains.

At this great distance, the Summit Beacon must appear as nothing more than a candle flame. But the bonfire the Tenebrans lit atop their fortress on Mount Frigora was visible to keen Hesperine eyes from Hypatia's Observatory, the tallest tower in the capital. Orthros's ambassadors always came here to look for the Beacon.

Tonight, only Ambassador Deukalion. Alone, Lio stood his elders' watch and saw no fire. The King of Tenebra had not ordered the Beacon lit.

Yet.

A few hours remained before dawn. The Beacon might yet appear. There was still time for Lio to behold the sign he prayed for: an invitation from the king for the Hesperine embassy to return to Tenebra in the spring and reconvene the Equinox Summit. Another chance to renew the Equinox Oath that would secure peace between their two peoples.

Lio's chance to keep his promise to Cassia that he would return to her.

The Tenebrans would light the Beacon before the night was through. They must. Because she intended for them to, and Lio had never known a plan of hers to fail.

He looked again at the scroll in his hands. It was the best portrait he had of her. Not nearly enough to remember her by. But he added each additional detail with great care, as if he could make this some kind of antidote to the months, the miles...the hunger. As if the cure for that was not out of reach.

The Goddess's Eyes looked with him, illuminating the paper with moonlight. Lio re-read the neat, black lines of his own handwriting in search of one more pattern he might have missed, one more revelation that had not yet struck him.

He was sure there were many who would not feel particularly flattered if a lover immortalized them in a list. But somehow he thought Cassia would appreciate this effort far more than any work of art designed to capture the physical beauty she worked so diligently to hide. Here in this documentation of seemingly unconnected events lay her true beauty, which Lio had beheld with his own eyes.

Each of the events he had recorded here, which he had meticulously gleaned from the reports trickling in, had occurred in Tenebra in the last half year. To the Queens of Orthros, their envoys, and every diplomat besides Lio, these were political developments of great import, but of no specific significance except for their potential impact on Hesperines. Lio, however, could see Cassia's hand in each and every one.

What tantalized him was the knowledge he had missed some. No doubt word of many of her deeds simply never reached him. And in the piecemeal information he did manage to gather, more developments for which she was responsible might lay hidden, while he lacked the insight to recognize them. She only became more creative; there was no telling what she might try next. These were only the events he knew of and felt certain he could attribute to her, and it was already a generous list.

Her clandestine victories against her father reassured Lio time and time again. The king did not suspect her.

Lucis Basileus, the cleverest and strongest king to rule Tenebra in generations, had no idea the most dangerous traitor in the land was his own daughter. He saw his late concubine's bastard as nothing more than a spare tool that might prove useful to his ends, while she defied his vision of her more and more. It was she who sabotaged his attempts at alliance with the Mage Orders in Cordium and stoked the nobility's resentment of his tyranny. The Council of Free Lords pressured the king, but it was Cassia, unseen and unsung, who pressured the free lords. If she had her way, Lucis would have no choice but to break ties with the Cordian mages and seek a peace treaty with Orthros instead, lest he lose the Council's mandate and his grip on his frightened subjects. The king must soon bend to the will of his people…to Cassia's will.

The reflections of her that Lio saw in the tales of her achievements were nothing like enough. They did not sate his hunger. But they were all that reminded him he had done the right thing when he had left her half a year ago.

Six months or two seasons according to the Tenebran calendar. Four lunar months or one season according to the Hesperine calendar. The vapid numbers amounted to an eternity of agony by Lio's reckoning. But Migration Night had come at last, when his people returned from Orthros Notou in the distant south. As of tonight, the eve of the Autumn Equinox, the Hesperines were once more in residence here in their northern home that bordered Tenebra, and Cassia knew it.

For the first time in half a year, they were not on opposite sides of the world.

Lio looked again at the horizon as if his Will alone could light the Summit Beacon. But the absence of the fire drew his gaze back from the mountains, over the dark line of the sea at their feet and the white landscape at his own. All of Selas lay spread out before him, a city of snow and marble built in a crescent around the bay. No railing stood between him and his people's northern capital. The vast drop was no threat, only a thrill to every young Hesperine when he or she first learned to levitate high enough to reach the top of the Observatory. From here Lio could count all the stained glass windows, including the ones he had contributed to their number.

Cassia felt as far away now as she had last night and every night before, even here in the one place he might glimpse some sign of her. The viewing deck's circular white expanse was only stone, a tribute to the Eye of Light, but Lio might as well be standing on the real moon, cradled in the Goddess's serene sky, while Cassia must live down in the tumultuous, dangerous world.

A polar wind stirred his robes, from the north this time, tugging silk and embroidery out over the rim of the deck. The icy scents of Orthros drowned out the fragrance of the talisman Cassia had made him to ward off ill dreams, although he wore the charm filled with dried betony around his neck.

All he had of her were a few mementos and these lines of ink on a scroll.

What else she had given him, he must not dwell on. He had tamed his hunger for a precious hour, perhaps a few if he was fortunate. And careful.

The text before his eyes quivered. Lio's gaze darted to his hand. Shaking like a leaf. He tightened his grip on the scroll's roller of cassia wood.

The Summit was their best chance. He could see in Cassia's actions how hard she pushed for her people to reopen negotiations. How could there be no Beacon?

Nothing had happened to her. By all accounts, Orthros's envoys brought only the same dire tidings everyone had come to expect from Tenebra, nothing worse than usual. If any devastating events had occurred, the Queens' Master Envoys would have brought word right away. It was a good sign that the murmurs among the Firstblood Circle, however grim, had not changed, and that Basir and Kumeta were keeping to their schedule.

Lio had come to mark his own calendar by Basir and Kumeta's. He knew they were in the city at this very moment.

The Queens' spymasters would bring a warm welcome back to the north, affectionate greetings from the First Prince, and news of whether or not Lio's world was coming to an end. Everyone would make sure Lio was not privy to the conversation.

He would have to be creative, like Cassia, and bring the information to himself by other means.

"Lio," said a voice behind him. "Never one to take an ill-considered step. When your deliberations are complete, note that I am here and would have a word with you."

DIVIDED MINDS

LIO MADE HIMSELF TURN around slowly, instead of spinning about like a startled prey animal. He rolled up his notes on Cassia and slid them into the scroll case at his side in one smooth motion as he faced his uncle.

Uncle Argyros looked like a statue one shade darker than the tower. Only his silver silk robes and his pale blond braid moved, whipping about him in a gust of wind, then swinging to rest at his heels. There seemed no color about him but the thin streak of dark auburn in his hair, his Grace's braid woven into his own.

"I knew I would find you here," Uncle Argyros said.

"It seems I will require still more decades under your mentorship before I am no longer transparent."

"I hardly need thelemancy to see through you. I've known you since before you had teeth."

"A fact I shall bear in mind." Lio never forgot who was the greatest threat to his secrets. He and Uncle Argyros were the two most powerful thelemancers in Orthros, but this was not a contest of mind magic. Uncle Argyros was more likely than anyone to discover Lio's relationship with Cassia because he was Lio's mentor. He knew Lio through and through.

Uncle Argyros watched Lio with dark eyes that had cowed many a warrior, mage, or foreign diplomat with a mere glance. An instant too late, the elder Hesperine's worry crept into Lio's awareness and weighed upon him as if it were his own. If he had been paying attention, the Blood Union would have warned him of his uncle's approach. His effort to make those he loved believe they had no cause to fear for him was not going well tonight.

Lio reached for the magic that ran in his veins, inseparable from his own blood, and strengthened the veil spell he now kept around himself at all times. His Gift came to him sluggishly, then spiked without warning. He struggled to apply his Will. If he could not sustain his concealing magic, his uncle was sure to sense through the visceral empathy of the Blood Union that Lio felt like a mortal about to be led to the gallows. He had made too many mistakes tonight.

"I relieved you from your duties for Migration Night," Uncle Argyros said. "The only assignment I have given you is your proposal on the potential applications of Hesperine light magic and glassmaking for improving reading comfort in Imperial libraries. You told me you would finish in time to present your recommendations at the first Circle of the season three nights from now. That will allow ample months for the firstbloods and the Queens to deliberate before we return south and present a plan to our Imperial allies."

"My proposal takes shape apace." Lio kept the defensiveness out of his voice and resisted the urge to rub a hand over his itching chin, certain the nervous gesture would betray him.

Where had he packed his proposal? He hadn't left it on his desk in Orthros Notou, had he? No...it was here in Orthros Boreou, in one of the scroll cases he had dumped in his rooms before coming up here. He had remembered to bring the proposal with him. All two sentences of it.

Uncle Argyros continued to scrutinize him. "Since you personally attended to the Empress's Vice Administrator of Library Improvement during his visit to Orthros Notou, I thought you would be enthusiastic to write an opinion and propose it before the Circle."

"Indeed I am. Although I admit my enthusiasm would be still greater if my first independent assignment had been *in* the Empire." With authorization to cross the border of Orthros and the protective magic that guarded it, he could have gone much farther than the Empire. All the way to Tenebra, in fact. But instead, his elders had kept him at home, where he must play nanny goat to the Empress's visiting administrator.

"At this time, the Queens wish to limit all but the most necessary travel outside of Orthros, for our safety," Uncle Argyros reminded him.

"The Empire is safe for our people. It wouldn't have been the least bit dangerous to send me along with the other Hesperines whose work there was deemed necessary."

"If the Queens were less judicious with their permission, there would certainly be youngbloods who would visit the Empire on pretense, in order to indulge heroic notions about returning to Tenebra at this time of crisis. Their urge to help might cloud their judgment and motivate them to act in defiance of the royal decree that all Hesperines must return from Tenebra to stay." Uncle Argyros wore his blandest smile. "Of course no diplomat I trained would ever consider such a course of action, least of all you, my upstanding nephew. You know you have our complete confidence. But naturally the Queens must hold everyone to the same rules, and all of us who are in their service must set an example for others."

"Of course. The Queens were right to strengthen their ward on the borders of our southern home to match the fortifications here in the north. Only their magic is enough to prevent our idealists from going errant."

"And coming to harm."

Cassia might come to harm at any moment. She didn't take a breath without risking her life, while Lio sat in Orthros scribbling documents. The Queens' ward kept every threat out and him in. "No one is safer than Orthros's youngbloods."

"Lio, your libraries proposal could reach the palace scribes and might even earn a glance from the Empress herself. If approved, it will take her administrators years to fulfill such an ambitious program of library improvement. This is an advantageous, long-term opportunity."

"Indeed, the sum total of all the skylights, windows, and reading lamps in the Imperial libraries is considerable, and of course they must all be replaced with the latest advances in light magic and glazing. No telling how many years I will spend here at home in my workshop, working up panes and spells to ship to our neighbors."

"Institutions of learning are the cradles of innovation that benefit all people for generations to come. You have every reason to take pride in this project—and devote the entirety of your considerable ability to it."

"I certainly will, beginning tomorrow, when my duties resume."

"In the meantime, you naturally chose to make the most of your free night by standing atop the Observatory for hours. Without a blanket or someone to share the view. Nor even a cup of coffee. What youthful delight."

Lio considered making some remark about how every Hesperine enjoyed taking in this view of the city now and then. But such dissimulations were painfully fruitless at this point. Despite his best efforts, he found himself on the defensive. "I helped get Zoe settled before I came up here, and I shall return in time to be with her while she is awake from the Dawn Slumber."

"I am not here to give you the impression you are lax in your responsibilities. Only to excuse you from mine."

"I don't know what you mean."

Uncle Argyros came to stand beside him and followed his gaze to the Umbrals. "It is my duty as the Queens' Master Ambassador to keep this vigil. Whether I am called to do so tonight or not is for me to judge. Go back down, Lio. Dust the snow off the gymnasium with Mak and Lyros or enjoy a night on the docks with Kia and Nodora."

"Mak and Lyros are at the gymnasium? I thought the entire Stand would accompany the Queens to check the border's defenses."

"They finished that hours ago and are now enjoying the holiday like the rest of the family."

"If I had not come up here, Uncle, would you have?"

Uncle Argyros was silent for a long moment. Lio listened to the absence of sound that meant his uncle was making a decision. The reckoning, it seemed, was about to arrive. His uncle would not be delicate about what the rest of Lio's friends and family tactfully referred to as his "Tenebran preoccupation."

"Lio, are you really so discontented with our work together?"

Lio tore his gaze from the mountains, taken aback. "Of course not, Uncle. To become your initiate when I came of age was my greatest honor, and now to work beside you as an ambassador in my own right is a privilege I shall never take for granted. I have desired this all my life."

"And yet you petition the Queens for entry into a different service on a regular basis."

Lio's stock of ready words failed him, and he floundered in silence for a moment. "Those requests were never meant to reach your ears. I—"

"You really thought the Queens would not make me aware of your desire to become an envoy in Basir and Kumeta's service?"

"I made such a point of petitioning them privately...I assumed they were...sensitive to my intention to..."

"Spare my feelings?" Uncle Argyros arched a brow.

"You know how much our work means to me. Do not think for a moment my...other interests...are any reflection on how I value my position with you. Or on my devotion to our work." Lio suppressed a wince. *Other interests?* What pathetic words to describe his cause of finding a way back to Cassia.

"Lio, my feelings are not a concern. Nor is your choice of how to spend your own time. Personal projects are the sign of an active mind and a devoted servant of our people. I would expect no less of you. But it is no longer a project when you hang on every rumor from Tenebra as if your life depends on it."

Lio's life did depend on it. On Cassia.

She was his Grace. The one who could nourish him for eternity on her blood alone. The only antidote to the Craving that had been destroying him since the first night they had been apart and his fast from her had begun.

He searched for conciliatory words and found instead the other edge of a diplomat's tongue, the one that could cut. "Alas, ambassadors assigned to the Empire take an inordinate interest in secondhand gossip about Tenebra. It is an unfortunate side effect of our position, for we do not attend audiences with the envoys who know the facts."

Oh, he would suffer one of Uncle Argyros's famous scowls now, along with the icy burn the elder firstblood's temper made on the Blood Union.

"I have endeavored not to intrude on you," Uncle Argyros said gently, "but this has grown into an issue you must discuss with me. If you are no longer committed to your choice of path, it is not something to conceal from me."

"I remain utterly committed to our work." The work they had begun in Tenebra. Not libraries in the Empire, where everything was peaceful and cozy and oh, so safe.

"You conducted your assignment with the Imperial administrator as adroitly as I knew you would, but can you maintain your course?"

"You are concerned about the quality of my performance?"

"I am concerned that when my youngest ambassador earns the honor of his first audience with the Empress, he will stand before her with his thoughts in Tenebra. Such moments are not kind to divided minds. If that is something I must be prepared to expect, you ought to tell me now."

Lio felt the powerful urge to lower his gaze. But that would be an admission of error. Of defeat. "I do not anticipate failing you in such a manner."

"Lio." Uncle Argyros shook his head. "What am I to do with you? No matter my choice of words, you understand them as a commentary on failure."

"How else am I to understand them?"

"If all the efforts of the famous Silvertongue have been insufficient to make that clear by now, I have no answer for you. What can I say? I remember when you would have poured all of your enthusiasm into this assignment."

"We have plenty of other ambassadors more qualified to represent us in the Empire. For centuries, all your initiates have been assigned there because our treaties with the Empress and her many peoples are our life-blood—and relations with Tenebra had broken down altogether. But last year King Lucis reopened negotiations with us. *That* is *my* work."

"At one time, you would have leapt on a project that brings together your service, magic, and craft. You would have relished showing the administrator the windows you have crafted, your contribution to the arts our people have nurtured in the face of persecution. Our time in Tenebra changed you."

"Of course it changed me. How could it not? For the first time in my existence, I saw real suffering. I witnessed a man's death. I played a role in the death of another. I may not have killed Dalos with my own hands, but all of us who were there are responsible for his end. How could I take part in a duel with a Cordian war mage and not be changed?"

"These are real concerns, Lio. We have all borne them, and we know they are heavy. You should share them with your father and me more often. None of us should have to navigate such struggles on our own."

His uncle's sympathy only added fuel to his frustration. They thought they understood. He kept letting them believe that, citing all the experiences that had indeed left a mark on him in Tenebra, while he never breathed a word about the one person who had transformed him.

"I take no less pride in Orthros's achievements than I ever did, Uncle. But I take greater pride in the lives I helped save in Tenebra than in the glass I have crafted. You must forgive me if I fail to see the importance of reading lamps when Tenebra suffers under a tyrant king and the Mage Orders of Cordium persecute Hesperines."

Here Lio stood in Orthros, where all Hesperines came for refuge. For nearly sixteen hundred years, this had been the place where they could escape Tenebra and leave all their troubles on the mortals' side of the border. But Lio carried Cassia's troubles with him, and his Craving for her knew no boundaries. This once-beloved, familiar place held onto him so tightly he could scarcely move. Peace had become a tether he chafed against.

"You have done your part in Tenebra," Uncle Argyros said. "In fact, you went far beyond your duty."

"It was not enough. Nothing would have been enough, save the king's oath not to make war."

"Lio, we all wish our embassy to Tenebra had been a success. For as long as we could, we held out hope we could secure peace with the renewal of the Equinox Oath. But tonight, the answer to your question is no. Had I not come to find you, I would not have set foot on the Observatory. I know not to look for the Beacon. The situation in Tenebra, I am sorry to say, no longer calls for diplomats. Much as I am loath to admit it, we must leave it in the hands of our warriors. Even I must resign myself to the fact that my work is done, and my Grace's work begins, Goddess keep her."

He was worried for *his* Grace? Hippolyta, the Guardian of Orthros, the greatest warrior in Hesperine history? "How am I expected to do that, when *my*—when I am already so deeply invested in Tenebra's plight?"

"That is not your duty, any more than it is mine, now. Only envoys and those in the Prince's Charge have the Queens' permission to remain Abroad in Tenebra. Here at home, we must trust your aunt to keep us prepared to assist those who arrive at the border seeking safety behind the ward. She tells me you are making rapid progress in your training in the gymnasium. Given enough decades, you may eventually catch up to Mak and Lyros. Apply yourself to that, if you feel you must do something for the war effort." Emotion flickered in Uncle Argyros's eyes. "Although I always thought you would remain devoted to the path of peace."

"You said yourself the situation no longer calls for diplomats."

"You cannot and will not take up Basir and Kumeta's work in the field, Lio. To go errant in Orthros Abroad is to begin every night expecting you will lay down your life for Hespera. No one as young as you will ever be called upon to make such a sacrifice. You know better than to believe any of us would allow it."

"I have already risked my life for her, and I will gladly do so again."

"Your dangerous actions during the Equinox Summit were a matter of necessity. We are as proud of you as we are determined to prevent such a situation from ever arising again."

"I know." How well he knew. It was a wonder they let him out of their sight long enough for him to take a drink.

"And yet Tenebra is all you think of, to the detriment of the work you have loved these many years." Before Lio could utter a defense, Uncle Argyros held up a hand. "To *your* detriment, Nephew. It is clear you are not happy."

"I am as happy as any of us could be at a time like this."

Uncle Argyros was shaking his head again. "If service as an envoy is truly what you desire for yourself, it will be many centuries in coming, and I am not certain the path to prepare yourself for a life of subterfuge bears any resemblance to what you envision. Is such a dramatic change truly what you want?"

Centuries. Lio no longer reckoned time in centuries. Cassia's life was measured in years, and if her father ever found her out, she would count it in hours until her execution. *"No."*

"Then what is it that you want, Nephew? You committed to diplomatic service so early, it would not be unexpected if you had second thoughts. There is no shame in changing your mind, nor in being uncertain of your desires."

"I know what I want." The words were out of his mouth before he could stop them.

One step nearer to the end of his control, to the precipice he sensed ahead of him. Once he fell, he would lose the last vestiges of his masquerade. Although his veil hid how his hands shook, he clenched them into fists to reassure himself he could still master his own body. But the tremors did not stop, even though he had tried to tame his thirst with the Drink twice already tonight.

He had known it was not enough. Nothing ever was.

He wanted Cassia.

"What, Lio? If you have an answer, tell me, and let us see what we can do about it."

Lio looked away, past the snow-swaddled streets and moonlit gardens below, to the southern horizon. Wind slammed across the deck again and drove his words out over Selas. "I want to go back to Tenebra."

Uncle Argyros let out a sigh.

"I see nothing has changed since we were last here." Basir's words were audible an instant before he appeared on the deck, Kumeta at his side.

WEDDINGS AND WAR

OR THE FIRST TIME, Lio turned his back on the view. He beheld the impossible: two Tenebran soldiers on the Observatory at the heart of Selas. The moonlight glinted off their coats of light mail, and their boots gave off the odor of leather.

Lio blinked, and there stood Basir and Kumeta in their travel robes and Grace braids. The moons shone on their true faces, revealing their ageless dignity and their deep black skin that bespoke their human origins in the Empire.

Lio knew he had just glimpsed only a modest example of the workings they could achieve when they combined their magic. Weaving her illusions and his thelemancy together with the power of the Grace Union, they had mystified Orthros's enemies for almost eight hundred years.

"Still trying to become our next initiate, Deukalion?" The intervening time had only made Basir's customary glower more severe.

Although Kumeta was shorter than Lio, she somehow looked down her nose at him. "Still trying to grow out that fuzz on your chin?"

"Yes, I fear I continue my attempts to foist myself on you." Lio swept a hand over his cheeks and chin. "I think it fair to say this is now long enough to classify as a 'close-cut beard.'"

"'Stubble,' if one is feeling generous. You may have my recommendation for service as an envoy when it is a full beard at least half as long as your father's, and no sooner." Kumeta waved a dismissive hand at Lio's face, but her tone lacked the usual bite.

Basir only sighed, instead of subjecting Lio to the direct remark he might have expected.

For a moment Lio surfaced from his concerns and felt the ache of a weariness not his own, like an old pain that had reawakened. He bit back the torrent of questions he wanted to ask the Master Envoys. It would not be right to berate them with an interrogation. Basir and Kumeta's bodies were as eternal as every Hesperine's, but within, they were exhausted. Even the great power and experience their age granted was not enough to protect them from low spirits.

"Tenebra is no place for youngbloods," Basir said.

Kumeta slid an arm around her Grace's waist, and they leaned against each other. "No place on the same landmass as Cordium is fit for any Hesperine."

"I apologize, my friends." Uncle Argyros spread his hands to indicate the empty deck. "When I asked you to come find Lio and me after your audience with the Queens, I intended to offer you comfortable chairs on my terrace and a pot of the Empress's coffee. Alas, I have yet to lure my wayward ambassador down from his post."

Lio's anger cooled, and he shot his Uncle a look of gratitude. "You set out a cup for me this time?"

"No time for coffee, I'm afraid." Kumeta sighed.

"Our thanks, Argyros," Basir said. "But the First Prince expects us. The reports we discuss with him and the Queens tonight cannot be committed to paper or subjected to delays. A swift word with you, and we shall rejoin the Charge in Tenebra."

Lio suffered now-familiar twinges of frustration. As a light mage and a mind mage, he could befuddle the enemy's eyes and thoughts. His dual affinity made him a perfect candidate for becoming an envoy. He could do so much in Basir and Kumeta's service, given the chance.

He could infiltrate Tenebra's royal palace without stirring a hair on the back of the king's liegehounds. He had done it before.

Uncle Argyros's aura mirrored the Master Envoys' fatigue. "I shall not delay you with pleasantries then, my friends. What can you tell us?"

"Our prince sends his greetings to Deukalion." Kumeta drew a small roll of paper from the satchel on her shoulder.

The scroll floated out of her hand toward Lio. As soon as the letter came within reach, he caught it midair, then tucked it into his scroll case with his notes on Cassia. He bowed, trying not to betray his eagerness. "Thank you for delivering my letter to him. Please tell him how much I appreciate him taking time to reply."

"You may tell him yourself," Kumeta said. "We will report to the Queens again tomorrow night, and if you have a reply, we will pick it up then."

Basir seemed as reluctant now as he had the last time Lio had managed to catch the Master Envoys. Lio preferred not to remember how desperately he had pressed his letter to the prince into their hands and begged them to deliver it.

"Do not let this give you the impression the envoy service is for passing notes," Basir warned.

"You have my gratitude," Lio assured them.

"Nonsense." Kumeta sighed again. "It is only natural for you to stay in contact with your Ritual father. When he is the First Prince of Orthros and deep in enemy territory, it isn't as if you can send a city courier."

Uncle Argyros did not comment, but through the Union, Lio could feel the intensity of his uncle's aura like a second stare. They must all suspect what the contents of Lio's letter had been. As if Lio's requests to the Queens for reassignment had not been enough, now he must rub salt in the wound he had dealt his uncle by petitioning the prince. Discretion was yet another effort at which Lio had failed.

But he had his reply. Lio would soon know if the prince agreed to intercede with the Queens on his behalf and favor him for a position in the field. Surely they would reconsider if the First Prince himself asked for Lio to be placed in his Charge.

Basir looked to Uncle Argyros. "You have told him there will be no Beacon?"

"It is my hope he will take it to heart if he hears it from you. You see why I asked the two of you to have a word with him."

Lio could not keep himself from voicing his protest. "Even though we have seen no Beacon tonight, there is still time for the king's mind to be changed. Spring Equinox will bring the new year and the renewal of the Equinox Oath."

"Lay down your hopes, Deukalion," Basir told him. "You know better.

The Oath lapsed nearly four hundred years ago. In the absence of the treaty, we may have held to its tenets and continued the Goddess's sacred practices in Tenebra, but the mortals consider the treaty broken."

Kumeta's mouth tightened. "The Tenebrans know we have remained active within their borders all this time, despite the uncertainty of relations between our peoples. So too have the Cordians known. While the Tenebran mages and warriors have nipped at our heels, the Cordian mages have champed at the bit, eager to face us again in a real war. Only the Tenebrans' resistance to outsiders has kept their kingdom neutral ground."

"But the hour has come," said Basir. "The mages will have their war upon our people. Two choices remain to King Lucis: to be an obstacle or a collaborator. Only one promises him power."

"He will host the war on his own soil," Kumeta said. "In return, he will have the power of the Orders holding him on his throne. He has no use for peace with Hesperines."

Lio shook his head. "Since the battle at the Summit, Lucis's people have been more afraid of antagonizing us than making peace with us. They cling to superstition and tradition. They would rather see us appeased than riled."

"When has Lucis ever listened to his people?" Kumeta asked.

"He can hardly round up the entire populace and silence their cries, and the free lords will not do it for him, when they share the common people's fears. Even Lucis cannot afford to lose the support of the entire nobility. As strong a king as he is, there are certain free lords he needs on his side. They are calling for him to reconvene the Summit."

Basir shook his head. "Lucis will yield to the mages, not the free lords."

"How can we be sure?" Lio demanded.

Kumeta looked to Uncle Argyros. "We came to tell you that Cordium is mobilizing."

Uncle Argyros nodded once. "I am not surprised," he said after a moment. "And yet the confirmation comes as a shock."

"Nothing can cushion that blow," Basir agreed.

This despair. . .this was not theirs, inflicted upon Lio by the Blood Union. This was entirely his own. It felt vast enough for all of them combined.

"The entire Order of Anthros is stirring out of the temples," Kumeta told Lio. "The war mages are the force that moves their brethren, and even the scribes are pushing scrolls faster in preparation. I do not have to remind you what history has proved: the other Orders will follow, as their teachings say all the gods bow to Anthros's Will."

Goddess help him. Even if all his other efforts to return to Tenebra failed, he had counted on the Summit to get him to Cassia. She accomplished so much, but were her two hands enough to hold the entire Order of Anthros in check? Were the strings she pulled in Tenebra stronger than the reins the war mages held?

If she could not manipulate the king into calling the Summit, what hope did Lio have of ever seeing her again?

The letter. There had to be something in the prince's letter. Surely Rudhira would come through for Lio.

Basir added, "The free lords do persist in their belief that renewing the Equinox Oath with us is the best course of action. To their credit."

Kumeta's lip twisted. "I never thought I would have a good word to say about the free lords of Tenebra, but they are proving astute in this case. Who knew those warmongering fools could see reason?"

Lio knew who truly saw reason. In his mind, he ran down his list once more, recalling each and every lord who had gotten something or given something at Cassia's instigation.

Basir leaned against the wind, holding Kumeta closer. "The pressure the king's nobles apply will not be enough, but it is considerable, and more coordinated than any effort they have exerted in a very long time."

"And yet," Kumeta added, "they have not resorted to violence as they are wont to do. They stop short of armed rebellion, which would accomplish nothing except destabilizing the kingdom. Whoever is influencing them is aware that revolt would only give Cordium an excuse to 'aid' the king and thus hasten the Orders' intrusion into Tenebra."

Uncle Argyros's gaze sharpened. "Do we have any information yet on who among them is responsible for motivating them to stand together?"

Basir scowled. "We are not pleased with that person's ability to act without our knowledge."

"But," Kumeta admitted, "we can give you an exact tally of how many lives their actions have saved."

Lio must ask her for each and every name, when there was time. One night, he wanted to recite them to Cassia.

"The more resistance the free lords mount," Basir said, "the more slowly and carefully the king must build his alliance with the Cordian Orders. The time this has bought us is a boon. When the king brings the lords to heel and he can give Cordium their war at last, we will be prepared. We will have located all the Hesperines errant who did not return to Orthros when the Queens made the Last Call on the Spring Equinox to summon everyone home. Lucis will eventually give the Cordians permission to begin their hunt for Hesperines everywhere in Tenebra, but by that time, there will be no Hesperines for them to find."

Uncle Argyros's voice was admirably steady. "How many more of our people remain Abroad who did not heed the Call?"

Basir's hard expression softened. "Your daughter is not the only one, my friend. We shall see Nike returned to you before the storm breaks."

"Trust in us—and our prince," Kumeta said with emphasis. "He will not rest until he brings his Trial sister home."

Uncle Argyros said nothing about the prince. "I wish I knew the name of the anonymous benefactor who may be my daughter's savior."

In moment's like these, Lio's secret felt too great to bear any longer. But all he could do was remain silent and promise himself that he would thank Cassia for giving his family hope of Nike's return.

"We have ruled out Free Lords Hadrian and Titus," Basir said. "Although they are undoubtedly the most powerful men in Tenebra after the king, their feud makes it impossible for either of them to act as a unifier. The loyalties of the Council are divided between them. Neither could direct their peers as a whole."

"Yet they both stand together in urging the king to call the Summit," Kumeta observed.

Lio would never cease to marvel at Cassia. "The two patriarchs of the bitterest feud in Tenebran history have been brought to agree on something."

"One thing is certain." Basir's smile looked more like a threat. "The king ought to be very concerned about this person. Someone who can rally—or perhaps manipulate—the free lords to this extent may well be the greatest enemy he has yet faced. One who uses his own strategies more effectively than he."

"You mentioned Lord Flavian last time," Uncle Argyros said. "You still do not suspect he could be the one?"

Lio made himself ease his grip on his scroll case. If he was not careful, he would leave a dent in the metal.

"Lord Flavian is popular," Basir replied. "He has the qualities men of Tenebra value in one another."

Kumeta snorted. "Namely a list of female conquests second to none. Granted, he has also shown prowess in battle and as a sportsman, and he is known for delivering on his promises to allies and dependents alike. All this, and he has his father's way with words and good looks. In fact, his charisma outshines even his father's. Although he is Lord Titus's son, his long years of service to the king have placed him above the free lords' squabbles and led his peers to perceive him as a much more neutral figure. He is respected by both sides of the feud."

Uncle Argyros pursed his lips. "Does Lord Flavian realize how much is his for the taking?"

"If he does," Basir answered, "he appears to have no ambition to take advantage of his position, except to further the king's goals. His loyalty to Lucis is unquestioned. The king orders him to ride, Lord Flavian asks how far. His courtship of the king's daughter is further evidence of this."

Lio gritted his teeth. His belly threatened to humiliate him and reject the useless deer blood with which he'd filled his gnawing gut not an hour past. Now he regretted trying to stave his hunger with an extra drink.

It sickened him to imagine the suitor who inflicted himself on Cassia. Lio had scarcely left her side before this bloodless Flavian had closed in on her. For half a year now, she had been forced to bear it, and Lio had been forced to listen to tales of the man's persistence.

"Lady Cassia is considered illegitimate by human standards," Uncle Argyros pointed out. "How much would she really strengthen Lord Flavian's position?"

As if she existed for Flavian's benefit. As if it were not she who had fought tooth and nail for her own hard-won position these past months. Flavian was everything Cassia abhorred—a man whose attentions she must endure at her father's command, one who surely wished to use her for his own gain.

Lio's blood felt hot in his veins. "She won't wed him."

Three pairs of elder eyes turned upon him.

Lio struggled to keep his voice even. "It would make Flavian too much of a threat to Lucis. The king won't go through with it."

"Not an unfounded observation," Kumeta granted him. "For someone as popular as Lord Flavian to marry one of the king's family, whatever Lady Cassia's status, might indeed make him appear a very favorable alternative. No one loves Lucis, and no one respects his thirteen-year-old son. The free lords would see Lord Flavian as one of their own, and any heirs Lady Cassia bore him would have a tenuous hereditary claim on the throne."

Lio's gorge rose.

"However," Basir reiterated, "Lucis appears assured of Lord Flavian's loyalty. The point is moot."

Uncle Argyros once more gave Lio a reprieve from his gaze, looking instead at Kumeta. "If Lord Flavian is to be a factor, we must keep him in our sights."

Kumeta shrugged. "As suspicious as the king is, if he does not regard the young lord as a threat, I am inclined to think Lord Flavian is not the powerful influence mobilizing the free lords. He is still someone to watch, however, as the man who will soon be betrothed to Lady Cassia. He could certainly do better than an illegitimate daughter, but who can really do better than the daughter of the king? Regardless, with Lucis arranging the match, Lord Flavian will go along with it."

"No," Lio insisted. "The king has allowed many free lords to court Lady Cassia and denied as many her hand. Flavian must know this is a game Lucis plays. The king merely uses his daughter to tempt his allies as if she were a jewel or a plot of land rather than a person."

"Now is not the time for your theories, Deukalion." Basir sounded resigned. "You are correct in your observation of the king's usual pattern, but this appears it will be the exception."

Lio braced his legs against a wave of dizziness that made him feel as if he might go spinning off the tower. "He will not marry her to Flavian. It would strengthen a young, popular lord's position too much."

"Or make him easier for Lucis to control, as he does his daughter," Basir countered.

But Lucis did not control his daughter. Not at all.

Lio bit back his protests. He would achieve nothing by questioning Basir and Kumeta's wisdom except drawing more suspicion on himself. He had few shreds of composure left. Best to make the most of those that remained to him.

He had guarded his and Cassia's secret so carefully these months. It was the axis around which his world now rotated. He would keep protecting it, for it was the only way he could protect her.

He had kept his promise to exile himself here while she stayed in Tenebra and faced their worst enemy alone. If she begged him to make the same promise now, it would be beyond his power. Now he knew what it cost him. But he had been strong enough to make it then, and he would hold to it now.

He wasn't sure what he feared more. That a night might come when she was in danger and he would be unable to act. Or that he might be the one who betrayed her.

If he ever gave in and admitted what he knew, it would be the same as violating his promise to stand back and let her fight. Her fight would end the night he revealed her importance to his people. They would pluck her from the king's grasp without effort. Lio would be with her again, his misery at an end. And all her valiant efforts would be for nothing.

Basir sighed. "It is time we were gone. The prince must have the Queens' reply."

Kumeta took his hand. "After that, we are to shadow a party of mages due to arrive in Tenebra from Cordium."

Uncle Argyros lifted his gaze toward the sky. "How many times has the Prince Errant expressed a desire to do more than shadow them?"

Basir let out one deep, grim laugh. "Thank Hespera he is not the human he pretends to be. If he did not have his Gift and his Queens to temper him, he would hand the mages a war, indeed."

"Goddess help us all," Uncle Argyros muttered.

"Pray our prince's thirst for battle is unjustified in this case." There was no humor in Kumeta's tone. "These Cordians are from the Order of

Anthros, and we can only hope they are agriculturalists and geomagi as purported. We know they could be war mages hiding their magic from us. After what we experienced when we fought Dalos at the Summit, we must be wary. Others from his order may use the same methods to conceal their true power."

"Another ruse seems too bold," Uncle Argyros said. "It would be a risky course of action on the part of the Order of Anthros and King Lucis. The free lords are still up in arms that Dalos pretended to be Tenebran under the false name Amachos and that the king appointed him royal mage. They blame Dalos for the catastrophe at the Summit and feel betrayed that their king colluded with him."

"It would make more sense for the mages to be what Tenebrans expect," Kumeta agreed, "emissaries come to bless the harvest during the sacred Autumn Equinox rites taking place at Solorum in the morning. The Cordians seem bent on smoothing ruffled feathers among their brethren in the Tenebran temples to make way for 'cooperation.'"

Uncle Argyros nodded. "Such a sacred day in such a significant location as Tenebra's capital is an opportunity for the Cordians to achieve both religious and political ends. The Autumn Greeting is the most important courtship ritual of the year, when many alliances are formed."

"The whole kingdom is astir with the news," she said. "Lord Flavian wishes to play the role of Anthros in the sacred festival dance, and he intends to ask Lady Cassia to be his Kyria."

A roar filled Lio's ears.

"Well," said Uncle Argyros. "Lord Flavian to ask the king's daughter for her promise dance. That is news."

Through the throbbing pulse in Lio's head, Kumeta's words continued, blow after blow. "For Lucis to allow Lord Flavian to dance the Autumn Greeting with Lady Cassia would be a sure sign the king and Lord Titus will begin negotiating the terms of their children's betrothal."

Basir dealt the next strike. "We can expect the betrothal to be final by winter and legally binding, then the wedding to follow in spring."

Lio could not speak, but his uncle voiced what ran through his mind. "Princess Solia danced the Autumn Greeting with one of her suitors, but did not marry him."

"Hers was a sad fate," Kumeta said. "We can hope marriage is indeed what awaits Lady Cassia after this dance."

"How certain are you the king will allow her to accept Lord Flavian's invitation?" Uncle Argyros asked.

Basir issued his verdict. "They are the two things that never cease in Tenebra. Weddings and war. Lucis shall order both this Autumn."

OFF COURSE

W HEN BASIR AND KUMETA were gone, Uncle Argyros turned to Lio. "Is their firsthand account enough to convince you? There will be no Summit."

No Summit. Only the dance.

Would the Autumn Greeting sentence Cassia to marriage or death?

It was all Lio could do to stay on his feet atop the tower and not leave his uncle's presence at a run. "After I read Rudhira's letter, I think I will join Mak and Lyros at the gymnasium. Then I ought to check on Zoe."

"Good." For the first time that night, Uncle Argyros did not sound worried. In fact, he smiled, his relief and affection obvious on his face. "I know you will wish to put Zoe at ease. Waking up in a different place than the one where you went to sleep can be unsettling at that age. It is admittedly a boon to elders that polar twilight makes sucklings Slumber through most of Migration, but I am quite ready for their hours of wakefulness, aren't you? Kadi and Javed are perfectly capable of parenting Bosko and Athena without help from hovering grandparents, but Lyta and I intend to enjoy every opportunity to hover all the same."

Lio descended the tower with a single Hesperine step. He stumbled at his destination, but found he had landed where he had intended. Not the busy agora at the foot of the tower, but the Queens' Orchard. His eyes adapted to the darkness under the trees and revealed he was alone. He sensed no other Hesperine auras. For miles around him, ancient, untamed forest shielded him from all witnesses. He yanked the letter out of his scroll case and unrolled it.

Lio,

My pride is wounded. You saved me for your last resort.

Your mother, father, uncle, aunt, and your Queens already said no. Don't think you'll get anywhere with me. I would sooner spend the Dawn Slumber in Cordium than ask my mothers to reverse a decision. If you think you know better than they do about anything, go ask Javed to examine your head.

Your skills would be invaluable to me, and I will gladly have you at my side, son of Apollon—in a few hundred years. Even then I will make sure I am not within your father's reach when you break it to him that you are following in his footsteps and going errant with me.

You're my youngest sister's age, Lio. You think I could stand myself if I brought you out here now?

Your training with Mak and Lyros is not a waste. Keep at it. Stay strong, and stay close to your Trial brothers. I hope none of you will need your skills as soon as I think. In any case, learning the battle arts will create opportunities for you, benefits that will come to you in the future. Remember that your father, Nike, Methu, and I were already old when we left Orthros together.

I will not caution you with reminders of what befell Methu. My Trial brother's memory has been held over you too much already, like the fact that you are bloodborn, as he was. Nor will I speculate as to Nike's fate. What is worth considering is that among the four of us, only your father found happiness.

I will visit soon, now that you have all come north. We will talk more then about whatever it is that has riled you.

—Rudhira

Lio's last way out, shut in his face.

What a way for Rudhira to refuse. He closed the letter with everyone's affectionate name for him and the promise of an interrogation.

When Ioustinianos, First Prince of Orthros, Prince Regent of Orthros Abroad and Royal Master of the Charge, could get away from his duties long enough to visit, they would talk? By then talk would be useless, and Cassia would be out of time.

The Autumn Greeting…legally binding…the wedding will follow…

The help they needed would not come from Rudhira. Lio was on his own.

Lio crumpled the letter into his pocket and broke into a run. Monumental trees seemed to fly past him like light. He pushed himself to his limit, then broke past it and pushed toward his next one.

Weddings and war. Lucis shall order both this Autumn.

The next limit eluded him, and his body gave out on him far sooner than it should. He stumbled to a halt. He whacked his head on a low branch while reaching blindly in front of him for the nearest tree. The trunk was solid, but the ground swayed under his feet and seemed to want to trade places with the branches overhead.

…Lady Cassia's wedding.

His body felt hot as magefire. He kicked off his shoes, but even the snow was not enough to cool his feet. He struggled out of the constriction of his robes and dropped them at the base of the tree. Night air crept into his tunic without offering relief. The strap of his scroll case threatened to choke him, but that he would not take off.

He had to decide on a course of action. The Autumn Greeting was tomorrow. He had to start thinking now, and quickly.

Lio blinked and rubbed his eyes, but blinding white moonlight flared between the sharp black fingers of bare branches. The red berries on a nearby holly appeared lucent to his dilated eyes.

He could not make any decisions in this state. He would have to drink again. For the third time tonight. At this rate, he doubted he could make it all the hours until Slumber without another drink after that. Hespera's Mercy, he would have to begin drinking four times a night. Nausea gripped him anew at the mere thought of more deer blood. But his hollow belly needed the very thing that sickened it.

He forced his reluctant body to walk. Best not use his power to cover the distance this time. No telling where he might end up if he tried to step right now. Ha. Tenebra. He would accidentally aim for Tenebra and wreck himself against the Queens' ward that blocked the border.

At last the forest gave way to the open grounds beyond. Lio halted in a field of snow and braced his hands on his knees.

He meant to send out a friendly invitation, but his mind barked a summons. The snow moved. A wave of white swept across the field toward him, parted around him, then stilled all at once.

The entire herd of boreian deer stood around him. Their thick white coats made them appear part of the snow, but their bodies gave off warmth, life force any Hesperine could sense. They were living beings, and they stood frozen before him, eyes wide, as if before a hunter.

Lio let out a string of hoarse curses. He rubbed his face in both hands. Dampness met his fingers. Lowering his hands, he stared down at them and saw the clear liquid of tears.

He stood in the snow and wept with shame.

When Hesperines spoke of Grace, they waxed poetic about perfect partnership, eternal companionship, and unending pleasure. They advised young Graces on how to get through the eight nights of their Ritual separation required before their avowal, when they would profess their bond before Hespera and their people.

None of the pretty things they said had prepared Lio for the reality of living with the Craving.

Eight nights over and over again. An eon in half a year. But the suffering itself was his one assurance it would end. His addiction to Cassia's blood was proof she really was his Grace and they were meant to remain together. The Goddess wanted them for each other. There must be a future in which they were not apart.

To enjoy that future, he had to live to see it. He had to survive withdrawal from Cassia's blood. It took all the Will he possessed to cope with the phases of heat and chills and bouts of shaking, nausea, and dizziness. He had managed to stay on his feet each time he had nearly fainted and to keep his drinks down until he was alone, but that wouldn't last much longer if the headaches kept getting worse.

Then there were his emotions, which seemed to have taken on a life of their own and constantly threatened to make those he loved pay for his misery in spite of him. Moment by moment, he must choose to think, to force words out of his mouth, to put one foot in front of the other in spite of thirst that could not be sated if he glutted himself on every deer in Orthros.

One night the Craving would break him. His strength would fail him, and he would no longer be able to protect any of them. His parents. Zoe. Cassia.

No, he was not to that point yet. There was still time. He might yet manage not to fail her.

Lio bent his own mind to his command. He heard one hoof crunch in the snow, then four of them, then many. He mastered himself until the warmth of another body near him told him only one deer remained. Fur brushed the back of his hand, and a pair of leathery lips mouthed his knuckles.

He huffed a pained laugh and lowered his hands. One of the does peered at him with a big blue eye. His vision swam, and he saw three eyes that looked like dancing spell lights. But he managed to keep his hand steady and rested it, ever so slowly, on her forehead. She did not shy away. He sat down hard on the snow, and she folded her legs gracefully to lay before him without apparent concern.

But he could never truly know when he would lose control again.

TRAINING

O NCE HIS HEAD WAS clearer and the third deer he called to him walked away on steady feet, Lio stood and turned his back on the bloodstained snow.

No amount of running would cool him tonight, nor provide him the clarity of thought he needed to decide how best to help Cassia against the looming threat of Flavian. Lio strode back through the Orchard, pausing only to retrieve his robes. He needed to get in the training ring.

He had never cared much for the arts of battle. While his cousins and Lyros loved to challenge body against body in the ring, Lio had always been more interested in studying how people pitted their opinions and beliefs, needs and goals against one another. The solitary pursuit of running had provided all the athletics his body required and the time for meditation his mind needed. But since the Craving had consumed him, nothing short of sparring was enough to discipline his body, and only the utter concentration the battle arts demanded could truly order his mind.

The Orchard was a long walk from the athletics district. To spare physical energy for his training session, Lio decided not to go all the way to Stewards' Ward on foot. Instead, he took a chance and used his power to step there, right into Hippolyta's Gymnasium. The Drink had bought him some time; he arrived only slightly off from where he intended in the corridor behind the baths. The small steam rooms afforded welcome privacy before and after a match. He ducked inside one to compose himself.

It was frigid, the taps cold and dry as the athletes had left them last season. He welcomed the chill more than he would have the warmth that would infuse the complex once the geomagi got around to summoning the heat. Lio wrapped his robes securely around Cassia's charm and the scroll case that protected his list, then stowed his things on a bench in the corner.

He secured his hair out of his way with his speires. The simple cloth ties still made Lio proud every time he used them. Every Hesperine who studied with Aunt Lyta received the symbolic hair ties as a gift from her the first time they entered the ring, and every member of the Stand and the Prince's Charge wore them throughout their careers. In his speires and the practical, undyed cotton tunic that served as the uniform for training, Lio felt ready to show his face outside the bath.

He did not sense Aunt Lyta or Kadi. Satisfied the legendary Guardian of Orthros and her second-in-command would not be present to witness any humiliation he might suffer, Lio headed along the deserted hall. It appeared Aunt Lyta and Kadi, like Uncle Argyros, were eager to stay at home and spend time with the children. Lio knew how much the two newest members of Blood Argyros meant to everyone. Kadi and Javed's sucklings were a powerful balm for the old wound of Nike's absence.

After a round in the ring, Lio would be bound for home as well. Home and Zoe. He smiled for the first time in hours, in fact the first time since he had left her at the house. He had much more than just a list and a charm. He had Zoe.

Lio came out on the lowest level of stone benches that ringed the bowl of the gymnasium. The barest hints of sound echoed off the ranks of empty seats. The heaps of snow on the outside of the glass rotunda reflected spell light onto the hard pack of snow that covered the carefully maintained floor. The expansive structure had long served Hesperine athletes, but also Hippolyta's Stand, the Stewards of the Queens' ward, who kept the battle arts alive in a kingdom devoted to peace.

The Queens' power ruled out any possibility of mortals, even mages, trespassing in Orthros. It was no surprise hardly any Hesperines felt motivated to become trained fighters, and those few who did left to join the Prince's Charge, for it was Abroad where Hesperines were embattled. But lately Lio had worried as never before that the Stand might not be a sufficient patrol for the border, even as protected as it was. What if there weren't enough Stewards to help anyone trying to cross to safety in Orthros?

There were others like Lio who pursued some measure of training for well-being or self-defense, but they could not compare to those in service under Aunt Lyta's command. In Nike's absence, Kadi was the only Master Steward left in the Stand. The fighters Aunt Lyta mentored with her younger daughter's assistance were the future of her Stand and Hesperine fighting techniques. Lio watched all two of them wrestle below.

The pair of combatants who now occupied the ring had taken over the Guardian of Orthros's command while she and Master Steward Arkadia had escorted Silvertongue's embassy to Tenebra.

Without hesitation, these two young Hesperines had assumed total responsibility for resolving any trouble along the border for the duration of the Equinox Summit, when Hesperine and human relations had strained to the breaking point.

With great courage, they had dared hike to the top of Wisdom's Precipice with Lio when they were all newbloods and with great eagerness, they had jumped off with him in the hopes of forcing their instinct for levitation to manifest.

With great remorse, they had all cursed and convalesced together in the Healing Sanctuary afterward.

Mak and Lyros were a blur before Lio's eyes, but he didn't need sight to recognize his two dearest friends. Almost nine decades of growing up together and undergoing the Trial of Initiation with one another had a way of strengthening his Blood Union with them, to say the least. He could trust them with nearly any confidence, including the fact that he was a wreck tonight. If he made a fool of himself during this training session, they would laugh with him, then peel his broken face off the ground and carry him to the healers themselves.

Lio studied the match, paying attention to techniques he didn't yet know or still couldn't manage with competence. Occasionally a smudge of brown, Mak's hair, indicated his position. A sweep of darker hair showed what Lyros was up to. But sound and temperature told Lio the most about each move the fighters attempted against one another. He heard a foot touch the snow pack; a rush of cool air told him a body had changed position.

Lio's cousin came into view for an instant; he caught a glimpse of Mak twisting his large body in a sudden, graceful move. But Mak's most beloved opponent was faster still. Lyros was leaner, slightly shorter, and no less powerful. He darted out of reach and became visible when he landed on his feet. Lio's friend hadn't even levitated, for magic was forbidden in the ring. Lyros's dance on the snow was pure agility.

Lio didn't see either of his Trial brothers again until Mak appeared flat on his back on the ground. Lyros stood, nothing disturbing his stillness, his pale face taut in an expression of utter concentration. His foot was poised on Mak's breastbone, perfectly positioned to apply destructive pressure to crucial bones. Mak lifted his hand in the traditional gesture of respect toward the victor.

Lyros's mouth curved into a slow smile. "I win."

Mak propped his hands behind his head, his fair complexion ruddy from the match. He gazed up at his Grace. "Victor names the prize."

"I'll collect…later." Lyros straightened, his aura full of mischief, and offered Lio a bow. "Here to see me flatten your cousin again?"

Lio eyed Lyros's foot, which had not moved. "He is clearly at your mercy. I still don't know how either of you ever manages to best the other. You know all each other's strategies by now."

"Good moon, Lio. You're late." Mak waved a hand from the ground, smiling cheerfully. "Move that foot, Lyros, or I'll be forced to use my most secret and effective strategy—"

"Shut up." Lyros moved off and offered Mak a hand.

Lio suppressed a snicker. Since they were sucklings, everyone had known Lyros's feet were ticklish. He had never grown out of it, if Mak's jests were to be believed.

Mak sprang to his feet without assistance, then took Lyros's hand anyway, tugging his Grace a little closer to him. In the years since the two of them had started sharing, and especially in the months since their avowal, Lio had learned to weather these moments of envy and forgive himself for them. There was not a Hesperine their age who did not wish for what Mak and Lyros had found in each other so early, nor were there any among them who did not rejoice with their whole hearts for their fortunate friends. Lio was no different. It was just harder now that he knew who his Grace was.

His Grace. Lio had found her, and not even a century into his existence. He was not to endure his father's fate and wait fifteen hundred years for her. He would never face the doubt Rudhira lived with every night that made him question why the Goddess had not yet bestowed Grace upon him, one of the most ancient Hesperines in existence, the eldest prince of her treasured people.

No, Lio would stay here trapped in Orthros while Cassia faced one of her two worst fears becoming reality. A marriage to the man of her father's choosing. Or a death like her sister's.

Lio vaulted over the railing without the aid of magic and landed in the ring. *Over my dead body, Flavian,* he promised. *And I am immortal.*

Mak raised his brows. "Lio is not here to play."

"I can see that." Lyros studied Lio. "You all right?"

"No, but it's nothing an hour of hard training won't fix."

"That's the spirit." Mak released Lyros's hand and ran through a quick stretch. "What'll it be? One against one? Three-warrior free-for-all?"

"Two against one," Lio requested.

Mak grinned. "Challenge accepted."

"Nonsense. He's challenging the victor." Lyros smiled smugly. "Allow me to lay waste to both of you."

Lio shook his head. "Both of you, against me."

Mak just laughed.

"Try me," Lio insisted.

"Uh, Lio…" Lyros hesitated, clearly choosing his words with care. "That is not part of the training program at this stage."

Mak clarified, "The night you started training with us, Mother made us promise we wouldn't break you into little pieces."

"How kind of you. Please keep your promise for Zoe's sake. Now let's go. Two against one."

They glanced at each other in one of their silent exchanges. Their expressions told Lio they had decided to humor him. Lio could barely hear Mak mutter, "Overachiever."

Mak and Lyros took their positions opposite Lio, and all three of them bowed. Then Lio eased his body into a relaxed, ready stance, crouching slightly. He knew he would lose. He suspected it would hurt. So be it.

Suddenly only Mak stood before Lio. For a disorienting instant, Lio was aware of Lyros somewhere behind him, precise position unknown. Lio shut his eyes and fell left into a dodge as Lyros swept in from his right-hand blind spot. Veiled Warrior.

The scent of cloves and the warmth of another body told Lio that Mak was a hair's breadth away from tackling him. Moon Warrior.

They were being obvious. He slid to the side and felt Mak sweep past him. Lio knew he moved right into Lyros's reach, as the two had planned, but he positioned his body correctly. When Lyros tried a Mortal Vice, Lio was ready.

Lyros landed on the snow with a satisfying thump, and Lio crouched, letting Mak attempt a Dawn's Grasp. Lio allowed Mak's weight to propel him and tossed his broader cousin over his head for an even louder landing.

"Well, Mak, I think we should congratulate ourselves." By the time the sound of Lyros's voice indicated his position, he was somewhere else.

"I'll say. We'll turn this soft diplomat into a fighter yet."

"Soft?" Lio glanced around him to see if his eyes gave him any information. "Say that again."

Mak's laughter echoed off the stands, and the sound reverberated in Lio's sensitive ears. Magic might be against the rules, but every Hesperine brought enhanced senses into the ring as an advantage—or a weakness, or a weapon.

"Someone brought his temper with him to the match tonight." Mak's taunt made its own echo.

Lyros's reply joined the sound, creating a small aural chaos. "Temper is an ill-behaved guest."

It almost worked, but Lio made out the barest brush of a foot on the snow. He managed a clumsy dodge roll just as they executed a perfect Grace Dance that would have had him trapped between them and on the ground in an instant. He jarred his shoulder on the rock-hard snow and came to his feet hurting, but small price to pay.

"You've just been waiting to try that one on me, haven't you," Lio huffed.

"We'd rather try it on a Cordian war mage we're allowed to kill, but you'll do for practice." Mak's hand came out of nowhere and twisted Lio's smarting arm in a Crippled Dove.

Lio moved with Mak, turning his body into the painful hold and easing the pressure on his arm while he brought his free hand around to attempt a Sun Strike in Mak's eyes. His cousin caught his wrist and turned the move against him, spinning him off-balance.

Lio's stomach churned. The world tilted.

"We're still jealous you got to duel with a war mage from the Aithourian Circle and didn't save a piece of him for us." That was Lyros. That was his foot tapping the back of Lio's ankle, robbing him of the remnants of his balance.

The snow felt more like granite against Lio's back. The air rushed out of his lungs, and those felt crushed by granite from above, too. Sparks dotted his vision. Curses he could not articulate ran through his mind. If he still had thought to spare for curses, he was not focused enough. A different kind of anger drove him back onto his feet. The anger of conviction.

Mak let out a call, half guffaw, half cheer.

"Keep it up," Lyros urged.

Lio threw himself into his next defensive move, and the next after that, until even the names of the moves no longer flitted through his mind. He was in his body, in his senses. No difference, no delay between thought and motion.

When he transitioned into offensive moves, his mind registered on some deep level that his two opponents were giving him room. Letting him try what he knew. Anger that they allowed him anything poured force into his attacks. He wanted a fight. Not a lesson.

"Temper is a weakness." Another blow to Lio's sore shoulder brought Mak's words home.

"Don't let your anger out in the moves." Lyros's voice echoed strangely through the ring once more. "Let the moves drain the anger out of you."

How did they expect him to release this anger? He wanted a fight, and his enemy was out of reach. Flavian was in Tenebra, and Lio was in Orthros.

Lio's eyes were shut; he only heard a back hit the snow again.

"Hey, I'm not the enemy!"

"Who do you think you're fighting?" asked his other opponent. His other teacher.

They were right. Lio hated to own it. But Flavian was not the enemy. The man was a pawn. Lord Titus's or the king's. Or perhaps the one who moved him was Cassia, as she moved the other lords. The true enemy was King Lucis.

"Better, Lio," Mak approved. "Think, act."

"Anger clouds thought," Lyros instructed. "Focus clears your head."

Motion by motion, the focus came to him. His mind calmed and sharpened into the state he could only achieve in the ring. He was no longer at odds with his body, but within it. His body had no energy for hunger, only motion. Defense, offense. Parry, attack. Follow through.

Lio and Cassia's true enemy remained the same. Her father, who ruled Tenebra and his daughter without mercy. But she had held her own against him until now; what if this latest threat to her was no threat at all? What if she had the danger of a betrothal firmly under control?

"That would have worked if you'd had more confidence," said Mak.

"Any shred of doubt is enough to bring defeat," Lyros warned.

This was the true problem: he was not sure. Did she need him to rescue her? Or did she wish for him not to interfere? Was this the hour when her need was so dire, he might break his promise to let her fight? Or did she still wish him to do as she had bade him half a year ago?

How could she expect that of him? She had bade him be safe. Just like everyone else. Everyone denied him the chance to fight at her side. Even Cassia herself.

The anger resurged, and pain bloomed in his knee, then his shoulder yet again.

Didn't he have as much a right to fight for their safety, their happiness, as she did?

His body told him in dodges and parries that his offense had fallen apart, and he was on the defensive again.

He *did* have a right. This was his fight, too. Would no one acknowledge that?

Snow slid under Lio's feet. He gave more ground, and it infuriated him. But the more he raged at it, the more ground he gave.

"You were doing fine until you got mad again," Mak said.

"What happened?" asked Lyros. "Try to regain your advantage."

Lio had done nothing but try. Every complex move he attempted, someone countered, herding him back into the most basic tactics.

"Stop making it easy for me!" he shouted. "Anthros's bollocks, I don't want to be coddled like a suckling!"

The snow covered the sky and fell toward him. It struck him. This must be how the Queens' ward felt. Like an eternal mountain brought to bear upon a single person.

The impact dragged the air out of Lio's lungs and turned his belly inside out. For a horrible moment, he thought the dampness under his face was blood he had vomited on the snow.

Then he could feel his face again. He wished it were still numb. The blood was coming from...somewhere in all that pain.

Two pairs of strong, gentle hands were, as he had predicted before the match, prying him off the ground. Moving hurt like Anthros's pyre. Lio let out a growl of protest. They ignored it. Lio found himself in a sitting position.

Mak held him upright. "Thorns, Lio, we honestly thought you would dodge Grace Dance a second time. Sorry."

"When you asked for a real fight, we thought you would be a little more prepared for it." Lyros touched a cloth to Lio's chin to catch the mess pouring from his nose...lips...eyes too.

Lio grabbed the cloth and pressed it to his mouth. He would *not* vomit the blood of three deer all over his two best friends. He planted a hand on Mak's shoulder, heaved himself to his feet, and staggered away.

"Lio, walking?" Mak warned. "Bad idea."

"*We'll* take you to Javed," Lyros announced.

Lio couldn't see or smell, and his ears roared. Mak and Lyros were about to step to the healer and take him along. He wouldn't vomit the blood of three deer on Javed either. All the magic he'd used to pass Javed's last physical exam would be a waste then.

His Gift was in almost as much chaos as his body, but he used the last of his presence of mind to hone in on Cassia's charm and step to the bath.

He went down on his knees and rid himself of every drop he'd drunk all night.

HYLONOME

AS ALWAYS, MAK AND Lyros understood. They took Lio's sudden departure to mean he wanted to be left alone.

As always, they waited patiently for a grand total of five minutes.

They did knock at the door of the bath. Well, pounded. That was the unmistakable sound of Mak's fist. Lio tried to tell them to go away, but his stomach heaved again, and they misinterpreted the sounds he made to mean *come in.*

"Goddess," Lyros breathed.

Mak didn't say anything at first. His anger charged through the Union and collided with Lio's own. Lio found it comforting. Mak only got furious like that when something very real was wrong with someone he cared about very much. He and Lio were alike in that way. Lio used to think they were not alike at all. But Tenebra had changed him...no. Made him see himself for who he was.

"I'm getting Javed. Now," Mak said.

"*No,*" Lio ground out.

Lyros answered, grim but calm. "This isn't a training injury, Lio. You need a healer."

"Don't! *Please.* Keep this—between us. Let me—explain."

A clean, damp cloth pressed against Lio's forehead, and his friends supported him while he finished emptying his stomach. Cool magic flowed around them. The smell of blood faded, and the fresh fragrance of citrus filled the room. He couldn't see much through his swollen eyes, but the floor was now a blur of gray, not red.

"Done?" Mak asked.

Lio's skin burned with humiliation. The heaves had stopped, although his body still trembled. "Uh-huh."

"Time to tilt that head back, then."

He followed his cousin's instructions. Mak settled the cloth over his face. Lio felt the dampness of blood that was not his own and with it, the sensation of magic, dark and bracing. The familiar blend of Mak and Lyros's Gifts went to work on Lio's eyes, nose, and mouth.

"A topical treatment," Mak said firmly. "Then we talk."

"We wouldn't want this mess on your face to scare Zoe later."

Lio would have smiled at Lyros's comment, except it would hurt like magefire.

"Thank you for doing this," Lio told them.

"Doing it again, you mean." Mak chuckled.

"Just as you've done for us," said Lyros, "and not just on the night of Initiation, when we all shed our blood to seal our Trial circle."

Lio was so glad the two of them were here.

Goddess help him, this had been so hard. They didn't even know what was wrong, but at this moment, he could not have been more grateful for them. It had been such a solace to see them again the night he'd come back from Tenebra after everything that had happened at the Summit. He'd hardly gotten home before Lyros had started in on him with thoughtful questions Lio hadn't wanted to answer, and Mak had harassed him with jokes about how he was his father's son, which were all too accurate.

How many times had he been so tempted to tell them about Cassia that he'd nearly given in?

"That's better," Lyros said with satisfaction.

Mak removed the cloth, and Lio realized he could see. The swelling around his eyes had eased enough for him to blink, and the pain in his nose was bearable. His lips throbbed, but he could speak without wanting to curse again. He only wished he had something to clear the foul taste from his mouth. Anything but deer blood. The very idea brought another wave of nausea over him, and he pushed the thought away.

Lyros offered him a flask. "Don't swallow any, not when your stomach's just settled."

Gratefully Lio took a swig of citrus water and spat into the rag. Mak took it from him and tossed it aside with another cleaning spell. Lio moved carefully and managed to get himself, with their assistance, onto one of the stone benches that lined the room. He leaned his head back against the wall.

Mak and Lyros stood over him. Their concern came at him through the Blood Union and cornered him as effectively as their Grace Dance had in the ring.

Lyros looked at Lio steadily. "Mak, I haven't seen anyone this sick since I made the mistake of looking in the mirror during our Ritual separation."

Mak's gaze snapped from Lio to Lyros. "Are you serious?"

"My Grace, you yourself have given Lio no rest from your raillery about a secret share."

"I was jesting!"

"Lio? Is that what this is?"

He shut his eyes. Now he could betray Cassia, or lie to Mak and Lyros.

As much as he'd done for half a year to keep his secret, he had *never* lied. Especially not to his Trial brothers.

He had known if they ever saw him like this, they would realize what was wrong with him right away. They had endured Ritual separation to prove to everyone their Craving was true. Mak and Lyros actually knew what Lio was going through.

Only for them it had lasted eight nights. Well, seven nights and a few minutes. As soon as they had surfaced from the Dawn Slumber on the eighth night, Mak had broken down four doors to get to Lyros, and everyone had called that definitive.

"You would have told us," Mak protested. "You haven't even shared with anyone lately. We would know. All you do is work and train, when you aren't with Zoe. You never come out to the docks with all of us. You haven't so much as nibbled any of the human guests from the Empire since…"

"Since he got back from Tenebra."

Mak froze, then rubbed his face in both hands. "Goddess, open my blind eyes."

Lyros looked rather ill himself. "Half a year, Lio?"

They understood. They knew.

I'm sorry, Cassia. But you are my Grace, and they are my brothers. They are your brothers, too.

"I can't say." Lio couldn't keep the smile off his face.

"Lio, this isn't the time to put us off." Mak jabbed a finger at him, scowling. "Not about something this important. I would think you'd trust us with—"

Lyros put a hand on Mak's arm. "He said he *can't* say. Not that he won't."

"*Can't* say? As in, if he acknowledged that person's status to us verbally, it would be a legally binding commitment to…someone vital to his future sustenance, happiness, and sanity?"

Oh, laughing did still hurt. "Yes, Mak. I can't say. Yet. But I'm glad you two are the first I can't say anything to about her."

Mak sat down on the bench beside Lio. "I would have been furious if you'd told someone else first."

"Not a soul." Lio's smile faded. "She doesn't even know."

Lyros raised his eyebrows. "You didn't tell *her*?"

"We were never apart long enough for me to feel the effects, until I left Tenebra." Lio looked away. "I didn't realize until I got home."

They were silent. Yes, Lio thought. It was that bad.

"It's the worst mistake I've ever made in my life," Lio said. "I found her in Tenebra, and I didn't know that's who she was, and I left without her."

There. He had said it. It felt so good to get it out into the open. The truth of how utterly he had failed.

Mak snorted. "Typical."

Lio frowned at him. "What?"

"You're blaming yourself," Lyros explained patiently. "If a human guest you've never met finds a bug in her shoe on the other side of the city in a guest house you've never set foot in, it's always your fault."

"What? I don't… Lyros, there's no comparison. How is it not my responsibility to recognize who she is and let her know? I was so preoccupied with how foolish I'd been about Xandra that I was determined I would never again mistakenly believe someone was my…" His Grace. "When I actually did find *her*, I didn't seriously consider the possibility until it was too late."

Mak gave Lio a wry look. "You were in Tenebra for less than a season.

You don't just say, 'Nice to meet you. By the way, I'll suffer for all eternity without the blood in your veins. Spend the rest of time with me?'"

"Lio, it took Mak and me years to own up to it. We knew for a long time before we were sure, if that makes sense. And it was even longer before it wasn't too…" Lyros paused to search for words.

"…before we stopped being scared bloodless about how sunbound serious it is," Mak finished.

Lyros nodded with a smile.

"But it seemed like you were always sure," Lio protested. "You were sure even before you were old enough to be allowed to do anything about it, although we all know—that is—never mind."

Mak exchanged a private grin with his Grace. "We aren't known for our patience, are we?"

Lio abandoned the ruins of his diplomacy. "Is it true what the elders say? If you feast before mastering your Gift and passing the Trial of Discipline during Initiation, does the Blood Union catastrophically overwhelm you?"

Mak and Lyros shot each other another look Lio could not possibly interpret.

"Lyros passed out first," Mak said.

Lyros burst out laughing. "Oh, no. It was definitely you who—while I was—never mind."

"It was a challenge," Mak concluded with a self-satisfied smile.

Lyros's gaze softened. "And it was worth it."

"Eighty years is a very long time to wait for Initiation and official adulthood," Lio grumbled. "If I'd met her before I was officially allowed to do anything about it, I wouldn't have waited, either. In fact, I *was* officially, expressly forbidden to drink a drop from any human in Tenebra." It definitely hurt to smile this much.

"Well?" Mak prompted.

Lyros studied Lio, one hand propped on his chin in exaggerated consideration. "Well, we know he *drank* from her, because of his *symptoms*. But the question remains…"

Mak lowered his voice. "Did he *feast* on her?"

"Did our little Lio finally lose his innocence?"

"I'm older than both of you," Lio said flatly.

"But you're bloodborn," Mak reminded him.

Lyros nodded sagely. "Your head start doesn't count."

Lio looked away, losing heart for their teasing, as much as he appreciated their intent. "Four nights. That was all."

"Get back in that training ring. You need to work on your stamina."

Lio punched Mak in the arm. "She needed time to feel sure an illicit affair with a foreign heretic was worth the risk. By then we only had four nights left before her sunbound father's mage tried to assassinate the Hesperine embassy and the entire Council of Free Lords, and I had to flee the sunbound country and *leave her there.*"

Lyros's eyes widened. "Her *father?*"

Mak let out a long whistle. "Lio got his fangs polished by the king's daughter."

"Do you realize what a disaster this is? I can't be without her, but if she had agreed to come with me like I asked—"

Lyros leaned closer. "You asked her to come with you?"

"Of course I did."

Mak was grinning again now. "You tapped the king's daughter and invited her to run off with you. How can you see as a mistake?"

"She said no. Don't you dare make another remark about my stamina."

Mak's smile was gone. "I'm sorry, Lio."

"It wasn't that she didn't want to escape with me. I could feel what it cost her to say no."

"Of course," Lyros said. "Did you doubt it?"

In his darker moments, perhaps he had. But explaining it to them now strengthened his convictions. "She had to stay for political reasons."

Lyros sat down on Lio's other side. "And you did the noble, self-sacrificing thing and left without her."

"I didn't do anything noble or self-sacrificing the entire time I was there. At least, not the way everyone thinks I did. I wasn't sneaking into the palace to spy for the embassy in some act of daring on behalf of Orthros. I just went to be with her."

"So she was your source of information all along," said Lyros.

"Of course," Mak said. "She would want to share as much *information* with Lio as possible."

Lio couldn't stand to smile again. "She discovered that the royal mage wasn't just a Tenebran temple-sweeper. She warned me that 'Amachos' was really Dalos, the elite war mage trained by the Aithourian Circle in Cordium, and that he and the king were plotting the assassination. She saved all our lives—Aunt Lyta and Uncle Argyros's, Kadi and Javed's, Basir and Kumeta's, mine. She found out about the Eriphite children the mages of Kyria were hiding from Dalos in their temple. She convinced the Prisma to let us bring them to safety in Orthros, where his order can never hunt them down. She gave us Zoe, Bosko, and Thenie and all the other new sucklings. I can't even bear to think about what the Order would have done to them, just because their parents worshiped the wrong god. Everything I said I did, she and I did together. I couldn't have done any of it without Cassia."

A sigh escaped him. He had said her name aloud for the first time in half a year, except for those utterances in his veiled chambers for his ears alone.

Perhaps he should still make some effort to be sparing with the facts, to tell Mak and Lyros only what he couldn't avoid revealing and withhold the rest. But it was too late for that. And it was too much of a relief to tell the whole truth.

They knew she was his Grace. That was the most dangerous secret. There was no reason they shouldn't know everything.

"That anonymous gardener from the Temple of Kyria," Lyros said, "who carried messages between you and the Prisma. That was Cassia all along?"

"Yes."

Mak shook his head. "Even Javed didn't make the connection, despite the fact that he listened to Lady Cassia speak at the Summit to request medicine from the embassy on behalf of the temple."

"Well, Lio. You've certainly been careful to draw attention to—or away from—certain facts."

"Forgive me. You don't know how much I wanted to tell everyone the truth. But I let everyone believe I was the only one involved, because I had to, to protect her."

Mak was frowning. "How could it endanger her for *us* to know?"

"The reason she wouldn't leave with me was that she wanted to stay in Tenebra and do everything she could to fight her father, to foil his plans."

"If she was behind all of that," Lyros said, "stopping the assassination, rescuing the children…she is clearly capable of accomplishing a great deal. And without even *our* people knowing."

Finally, Lio could make them see her for who she really was. "You give her one small thing to work with, and she turns it into a weapon powerful enough to make the king's throne wobble under him. All without anyone knowing it's her. She's brilliant. Even if she was not who she is to me, it would have been wrong to leave her. It shouldn't have taken the realization of our bond to convince me I should have stayed with her, no matter the cost. Why didn't I just stop on her side of the border and join the Charge the night the Summit ended?"

"Rudhira would have packed you up and sent you home," Mak said.

"Then I should have gone errant alone."

"No," Mak barked. "You shouldn't have. One mind mage using Father's training to hide from the family Abroad is more than enough."

"Hespera's Mercy. I'm sorry, Mak."

"If you'd stayed there," Lyros said, "what would Zoe have done without you?"

"Cassia would understand." Lio breathed a sigh. "A seven-year-old girl needed a Hesperine to carry her from danger."

A silence fell between the three of them. That was when Lio sensed the wound in the Blood Union.

"You could have trusted us about Cassia, you know," Mak said.

Lio sensed his cousin trying to understand, struggling to give him the benefit of the doubt. But he had hurt Mak.

"Of course I could trust you," Lio hurried to explain. "You would have done anything to protect her…and me."

Mak winced. "Right. Rudhira would march to the capital of Tenebra and retrieve her, then deliver her to Uncle Apollon at the border so he could bring her home to you as a Gift Night present. If not for the Queens' ward, Lyros and I would beat them to it."

At last the relief really sank into Lio, blood-deep. "You understand. It's not because of you. Please don't ever think that."

Mak braced a hand on Lio's shoulder. "If it were Lyros in another kingdom, I would say to Hedon's privy with the King of Tenebra, he can do what he likes, I'll have my Grace at my side, thank you. But you have to do this the way you feel is right."

Lyros gripped Lio's other shoulder. "We will do everything we can to help. Even if it means persisting in this secrecy. But I have to ask, how have you managed like this for half a year? Can you hold out much longer?"

Mak looked like he wanted to hit something. "Goddess help you, Lio, I hate this. We all know how it works. It won't get easier for you."

"This isn't a question of strength, Lio," Lyros reminded him. "It's not a test, and there's no such thing as success or failure. It's just the nature of your body. Once you have tasted that person's blood, your body is addicted, and no other sustenance will ease the Craving."

"Other blood is enough to keep him going, though." Mak sounded as if he was comforting himself as much as Lio. "He won't actually starve."

"No." Lyros did not sound comforted.

Lio didn't need them to go on. He already knew his fate. He would endure withdrawal, but his body would never overcome its addiction to her blood. He would feel thirst that no animal, human, or Hesperine could quench. He would lust, and no one's touch but hers would satisfy him.

He would be doomed to an eternity of deprivation in a land of unending plenty. There were some ironies to Hesperine existence he would never understand.

Deer blood could keep him alive, but what kind of life would it be?

Lio tried to sound objective. "Do you know how long, precisely, it takes before other blood stops providing a modicum of relief?" For the withdrawal symptoms and thirst, in any case. A full belly did nothing to help with the lust.

"I'm not certain," Lyros admitted. "I would imagine human blood, being more nourishing than animal blood, would offer the greater benefit. But I know you. You won't consider drinking from another person, now that you know who she is."

"Fidelity isn't required until they've both acknowledged their bond," Mak protested. "Since Cassia hasn't recognized what they are to each other, Lio is by rights allowed to seek sustenance from anyone. The human guests would do him more good than deer. It's not as if he would be properly sharing with any of them. It would just be the Drink. No cause for Cassia to be jealous."

Lio left aside the fact that he would never inflict himself on any human in this condition, even for a dispassionate drink from the wrist. That point was moot. "Could you bear to drink from any person besides Lyros, after you two tasted each other?"

Lio took Mak's silence as an emphatic *no.*

"How are you doing with the deer so far, Lio?" Lyros asked.

"More than two?" Mak glanced at the clean floor, where Lio had lately demonstrated the volume of his dinner.

"More often than twice a night?" Lyros pressed.

"I tried to find some guidance about my situation, but I was afraid to ask anyone for information, for fear they would find me out. I have studied some of the historical records that describe Hesperines who attempted to survive without their mates, but most of those concern cases in which one had died and the other was the sole survivor. We all know that doesn't last long."

"Stop talking about history," Lyros told him. "You're not Hylonome."

"That's a horrible story!" Mak's brows descended. "Don't tell me that was even one of the examples you looked at."

It was the first one Lio had re-read, but he hastened to reassure them. "As if I would fast atop the Observatory tower and refuse all blood until I join my fallen mate amid the stars. I'm not really that dramatic by nature. Besides, Cassia would never battle twelve wicked mages to save the lives of an entire town, only for the prejudiced villagers to turn loose their liegehounds to rend her to shreds. Dogs love her. And she would outsmart the mages and save the village without any of them the wiser."

Talking about the grisly love story of Hylonome's suicide after her Grace's noble death in such flippant terms…talking about Cassia in such terms…was not having the effect Lio had hoped of robbing the tragic story of its power.

He had thought Mak's initial sense of betrayal and his Trial brothers' ensuing worry had been hard to withstand, but this? He could taste their fear.

They didn't want to lose him. They actually feared they might.

OATHBOUND

LIO LEANED HIS HEAD back against the wall again and looked toward the sky he could not see through the ceiling of the steam room. "I have to do what's best for Cassia."

"You have to do what's best for both of you," Lyros told him.

"Cassia is in danger as long as she's in her father's kingdom. I don't know how to live with the knowledge that she's risking her life as we speak. But look what she's accomplishing. She's the one uniting the free lords, you know."

Mak rubbed the back of his head. "No offense, Lio, but I think you're a bit lovestruck. I know she's extraordinary, but those goat-feasting Tenebrans don't listen to women properly, and…"

Lio gestured to the wad of his tunic in the corner. "I'm keeping a record of everything. You can read it if you don't believe me. The evidence is all there. The carefully constructed rumors, the drawn-out strategies." He cleared his throat and decided not to mention the bribes, blackmail, and extortion. "It's all her."

"He is in earnest, Mak."

Mak sat back against the wall. "Then she's the reason the Charge still has time to look for my sister."

"Yes," Lio replied.

"When we get to meet her," Mak said, "I want to thank her, Lio. Someone ought to."

When. Mak had said when. That made it seem so much more real… certain, even.

"I did manage to send Cassia a message on the Spring Equinox," Lio said. "Her blood is a powerful focus. I achieved Union with her despite the closed ward, at least enough to sense she was alone and to fix her location. I manifested an illusion for her while the Queens sent out the Last Call."

Lyros looked impressed. "You hid your spell beneath the Queens' magic."

"I don't know what Cassia's response was, of course. I could only feel her, not see or hear her. But at least...I gave her the impression it wasn't over, and I sensed what it meant to her that we had contact."

"She's ready to thrash someone to get to you," Mak said. "Make no mistake."

"By now she's probably ready to accept your offer." Lyros got to his feet and began to pace. "However, removing her from Tenebra is going to have wide-ranging consequences. Why couldn't she have been a milkmaid?"

"She *is* a skilled gardener and, as I said, wonderful with dogs."

"Her bodyguard is a liegehound." Mak gave Lio a pointed look. "They're bred to protect innocent maidens and eat Hesperines. That's not the reason you had to cut it short after four nights, is it? Did you come home with everything you had when you left? It takes time for those to grow back."

"Her dog likes *me*. I'm not too sure how he'll react to you, though."

Now the Union was full of their humor. Lio still felt wretched, and odds that seemed impossible still stood between him and his Grace. But he felt better than he had in months. Since that first night he'd been without Cassia, and a sneaking suspicion of the truth had first set in.

His Trial Brothers' fear for him was still there, though, lurking under the jests and the will to fight for a solution. Or was it Lio's fear for himself?

"If her dog would just make sure Flavian can't produce heirs, everything would be so much simpler," Lio muttered.

"Who's Flavian?" Mak asked.

"And why is his castration desirable?" Lyros inquired. "Besides the obvious fact that human males have an unhealthy obsession with their own fertility, and the loss thereof would teach him a universal lesson."

"'Who's Flavian?'" Lio echoed. "You've heard of Cassia's dog but not Flavian? Do you two pay attention to politics at all?"

"No." Mak flashed his most cheerful smile. "We have special lessons on fighting against liegehounds, though. Mother talks about Lady Cassia's war dog all the time. I can recite Knight's pedigree. Apparently there are Hesperines walking around Orthros tonight who had to regrow limbs thanks to his ancestors."

"Surely Uncle Argyros talks about more than Knight."

"When Father gets started on Tenebra, that's my cue to leave the room," Mak muttered.

"We prefer to focus on the clarity and directness of physical training," Lyros said. "Do you need us to try a little Grace Dance on this Flavian, whoever he is? If such a gentle soul as yourself feels inspired to threaten him, Lio, I'm sure he deserves it."

"As much as I appreciate the offer, there would be nothing left of him for the two of you after I had a chance at him. Hypothetically speaking, of course. Realistically, his untimely death would be a diplomatic disaster and is to be avoided."

Lio dragged his hands through his hair. His fingers snagged on the single, thin braid he wore behind his ear. His reminder of his other promise to Cassia. The one he'd had his illusion speak to her, once he'd realized who she was and that he had let her slip through his fingers. He had given her his solemn oath he would come back for her.

More than that, in his solitary hours since then, he had promised her... promised himself...he would make things right. That he would do everything in his power to be with her again so he could tell her what she really meant to him, as he could not have done in a hasty, desperate message carried to her on an ephemeral act of sorcery.

Lio had been trying for half a year to fulfill both promises, his promise to leave and his promise to return. His oath to let her fight and his oath to end his own fight against the Craving. Every time the two promises were at odds, he blamed himself and grew angry at everyone around him.

Perhaps his Trial brothers were right, and his only real error had been to think in terms of mistakes.

"Lio said Flavian's *death* would be a diplomatic disaster," Mak pointed out. "There's plenty of bodily harm we could do short of killing him. Would it sway the course of politics that much if he had to do without his eyes, or he could never walk again?"

"Why can't we do bodily harm to this Flavian?" Lyros crossed his arms.

"He is one of the few neutral figures among the free lords who has the favor of all his peers, thus he is a stabilizing influence on their feuds. He's also the only man in Tenebra who might be able to take the throne from Lucis if he wanted to. Unfortunately, he doesn't. He's loyal to the king, to a fault. So loyal that Lucis is letting him..." The force of Lio's anger made his Gift spike in his blood, and his face throbbed. "...court Cassia. Sunbind those bloodless goat feasters. Flavian thinks he's going to marry my—Cassia."

Mak snickered. "Poor Flavian."

"Poor *Flavian*? Poor mighty, accomplished warrior sportsman Flavian who has apparently bedded most of the female population of Tenebra and is frequently begged to do so again?"

Mak cleared his throat. "Does that majority of the female population include, ah..."

"*No.* Not Cassia."

Lio wouldn't even imagine the possibility. Flavian had *not* imposed himself on her in that way. Cassia was too expert at avoiding the unwanted attentions of men. She was strong and able to protect herself.

And Flavian's attentions must surely be unwanted. Lio refused to admit he had no way of knowing, after all these months apart, whether he was still the only lover Cassia had ever had. But he was her Grace. She would want only him, as surely as he wanted only her.

Lyros and Mak did not question Lio's pronouncement on the subject. They just gave each other a knowing look.

"She's your...Cassia," Lyros said. "Flavian can have his belongings sent ahead of him to Hypnos anytime. He already has an appointment with the god of death."

"You won't let anyone touch your Cassia," Mak stated.

They spoke as if it were not a decision Lio must make, but a natural law written in the stars. "I'm not sure Cassia wants me to intervene. Flavian may not be a real threat to her. For one thing, it remains to be seen whether or not the king will allow the courtship to progress any further.

And even if he does, Cassia is sure to destroy any plan for her life of which her father is the architect. What if she already has a strategy for preventing the match?"

"What if she has?" Lyros asked.

Then Lio was still here in Orthros, trying to keep two promises that worked against one another. And he had no idea how long Cassia expected him to persevere.

How long was her fight to last? Did she see any end to it? She might maneuver her way out of her marriage before spring, but what then? When she realized spring would bring no Equinox Summit and no Lio, what would she do?

He had read her actions correctly, hadn't he? Hadn't she been working toward another Summit that would bring him back to Tenebra, just as he had been trying to escape Orthros? Hadn't they, even at this distance, endeavored in partnership for the same goal, as they had when they had been together?

"What if the king does want the match, and she doesn't find a way to get out of marrying Flavian?" Mak asked.

"Then my course would be clear," Lio answered. "I would have to rescue her."

Mak nodded. "You know I'm the last person to advise better safe than sorry, Lio, but this is your Cassia."

"If there's no way to know which is true," Lyros said, "which choice is safest?"

The answer to that question could not have been clearer.

If Lio didn't intervene, and she needed him…if the moment came when she faced Flavian at the altar with no way out, with no one to stop it, and Lio could have spared her that…

Lio would be abandoning her. He, her Grace, the very one who should do everything in his power to protect her safety and happiness.

He could not tolerate the thought, but he must. He had to face precisely what it would mean for her if he judged wrongly.

She would be trapped in an unwanted marriage, in a marriage *bed*, with that man.

Or she would die.

Lio's head pounded. "Cassia will look upon any marriage her father arranges as a death sentence. They are the same thing in her mind. Such a betrothal *was* the death of her sister Solia."

"Princess Solia?" Mak asked. "I have heard Father talk about her. She was the king's heir, wasn't she?"

Lio nodded. "She and Cassia adored each other, despite the fact that they had different mothers. She was the closest Cassia ever had to a real parent. When Solia was seventeen and Cassia seven, the king allowed the princess to dance with Free Lord Bellator at the Autumn Greeting, which Tenebrans understand as a promise of betrothal. When Bellator discovered the king didn't intend to deliver on that promise, long-standing tensions between the nobility and the king erupted into violence. Bellator led some of the other free lords in a revolt. They captured Solia and threatened to kill her if the king didn't make concessions." Lio looked at his friends. "He refused their terms."

"Is *that* how she died?" Lyros grimaced.

"Cassia was there, listening to the negotiations. She heard her father throw away her sister's life. She listened to the catapults at sundown, when the rebels fired Solia and her bodyguards over the walls of their fortress, and she heard the soldiers discussing the king's orders that they not risk any men to collect the remains."

"Bleeding thorns," Mak swore. "I'd like to pack the king off to Hypnos myself, except that's too good for murderers who make children grow up without their sisters."

Lio winced inwardly, hating that he'd probed his cousin's wounds.

"The king let them brutalize his own daughter and then left her body there to rot?" Lyros demanded.

"He would have. But that night, Cassia tried to approach the fortress to recover her sister's body. Alone. No older than Zoe. When I think of what could have happened… But when a rebel's arrow almost found Cassia, a Hesperine errant plucked her out of death's path. That Hesperine and her two comrades gave the Mercy to Solia, then took my Cassia to safety. That's the whole reason she first sought me out. It was the first chance she'd had to talk to another Hesperine since that night, to try to reach an adult understanding of what they had done for her sister. I had the privilege of explaining to her that we honor fallen mortals with Hespera's own rites and transform their remains into light, just as the Gift does for our bodies if we die. I was able to offer her the comfort that Hesperines errant shared in Solia's final thoughts and feelings and now carry a part of her with them for all time."

Mak leaned forward. "Which Hesperines errant were they?"

"We don't know. They didn't tell Cassia their names."

"How did she describe them?" Mak asked.

"I've considered and reconsidered the details to no avail, but perhaps you two will notice something I didn't."

"Try us," Mak urged.

"Well, they were a party of two females and a male who appeared to be of Tenebran origin. Cassia said they were all quite tall, so perhaps they received the Gift as children…"

"…or just seemed very tall to a little child," Lyros finished.

"Not much to go on," Lio agreed. "They wore formal robes…"

"They would for such a sacred office," Mak said, "no matter how rough the territory."

"But anything Cassia saw that night could have been illusion," Lyros pointed out. "There are many reasons for Hesperines errant to alter their appearances, one being to make themselves appear less frightening to a Tenebran child."

"They certainly had a light mage with them. Cassia described a diffuse, omnidirectional illumination."

Mak cleared his throat at Lio. "Light magic is one of the four essential affinities that lots of Hesperines study. Sometimes too much."

"Cassia also recalled being surrounded by shadow that made her feel safe."

Mak brightened. "That's definitely a description of a Hesperine protective spell. One of them was a warder."

"Also an essential affinity," Lyros said. "Lio just described half our Hesperines errant."

"True. Warders like us are among the most likely to go Abroad."

"Of course," Lio went on, "they would have traveled with at least one thelemancer or healer trained to ease pain."

"Because that's required of all Hesperines errant." Mak sighed.

"No way to know which of them had one of those two essential affinities." Lio lowered his head. "One of Solia's guards still lived when they arrived, but they did not say who treated him."

"The Gift empowers all of us to give the Mercy," Lyros said. "Cassia's rescuer could have had any kind of magic."

"She did confide in Cassia one personal matter. She was grieving for her brother. She carried deep regret that she had not been able to save him from capture."

Mak shook his head. "Unfortunately, that describes all too many of our people as well."

"There's nothing in our chronicles about Hesperine involvement at the Siege of Sovereigns," Lio said. "That must mean the three of them haven't returned home to give a report of their deeds and have remained Abroad since that night or longer—so at least fourteen years."

"That's not unusual," said Lyros, "given the freedom Hesperines errant have, but Rudhira must surely be aware of their activities."

Mak's jaw tightened. "The Charge doesn't give orders. Rudhira provides support and oversight to make sure no one else ends up like Prometheus, but despite his best efforts, there are just too many ways for a Hesperine to go missing in the field."

Lio joined Lyros in sending silent encouragement to Mak through the Blood Union.

"Have you tried interviewing any of the Hesperines who have made it home?" Mak asked. "You know that every time the Queens' summons brings someone back to Orthros, the first thing we do is ask if they have word of Nike, although we've yet to learn anything."

"I'm afraid my questions have yielded no more than yours. No one seems to know anything about the Siege of Sovereigns. I've had to be subtle about how I ask, but if Cassia's rescuers were in Orthros, I would have found them by now."

Lyros nodded. "So many newcomers and returnees pass through House Komnena while your mother is helping them readjust to life here."

"I won't give up until I give Cassia's rescuers my gratitude for saving her life. Not to mention for showing her our people's kindness. That's why she was predisposed to trust me when we met. Those three Hesperines errant are the reason she loves our people and wants to fight for peace between Orthros and Tenebra."

"There you go, giving her childhood rescuers all the glory." Mak looked at Lio askance. "It's obvious her motivation for saving the embassy and fighting for peace has a name, and it isn't 'gratitude.'"

"She said that," Lio confessed, reminding himself. "She said, 'I would have done this just for you.'"

"Of course," Mak told him.

"You're worried that this time, the only Hesperine who will rescue her is you," said Lyros.

"Lucis allowed his own daughter's murder, because the princess's popularity among his subjects—and all the secrets she knew—made her too much of a threat to him. It's all I've been thinking about since I heard Flavian is going to ask Cassia for the promise dance. Is that Lucis's purpose now as well? What if he knows Cassia is a threat to him, and he plans to use this situation to rid himself of her the same way he did her sister?"

Mak gripped Lio's arm. "If there is any chance Cassia's life is in danger, now isn't the time to hesitate."

"If her life is in danger, so is yours," Lyros reminded him quietly.

"I made up my mind when I left that if there was ever a real threat to her, I would intervene. Somehow."

"What's the worst that can happen, if you're wrong?" Lyros reasoned. "So she'll be angry with you for interfering with her ability to commit more treason."

Lio voiced the same argument, the one he'd had to repeat to himself every other moment since he'd left to keep himself from going right back. "She spent her whole life being afraid of the king. Now she has finally found the courage to stand against him. I have no right to prevent her from that. That's like telling her to go back to being silent and obedient."

"How does running away with a Hesperine equate to silent obedience?" Mak asked.

"She wants to right the injustices the king has made her suffer all her life. She wants justice for her sister. I can't ask her to just leave all of that. Think of what she is doing for her people and ours."

"To fight anybody, she has to be *alive*," Lyros said.

"But the moment we remove Cassia from the king's court, we remove the only person who stands in his way. Without her influence keeping him in check, Lucis will welcome Cordium into Tenebra with open arms and allow the war mages free run of his kingdom, so they can mount a persecution against our people the likes of which we haven't seen in centuries. We aren't ready for that. The Prince's Charge is still…making preparations."

"Lio, it's my sister's life we're talking about." Trust Mak not to mince words. "I think my opinion carries some weight here."

"Of course it does." Lio met his cousin's gaze. "I would value your honesty."

Mak hesitated. "I would never say this in front of my parents. I wouldn't want to worsen their pain."

"You don't have to watch what you say with us, my Grace," Lyros assured him.

"This is a night for speaking openly," Lio agreed.

Mak gave a nod. "We wish every moment Nike would come home. Mother and Father begin and end each night wondering if she's safe. But Nike knew the risks when she decided to stay Abroad on her own after the Blood Errant disbanded. She wasn't the same after the Aithourians got Prometheus. I think her grief clouded her judgment. But she *chose* her path. I don't think we'll ever know if she came to harm…or if she's out there now and just doesn't want to come home." Mak let out a sad laugh. "She's Mother's daughter. Who else would have the backbone to refuse a summons from the Queens?"

Lio voiced a question he had never dared ask before. "Are you ever angry with her?"

"Bleeding thorns, no. Even after what happened to Prometheus, she didn't run to safety in Orthros. She had the courage to stay Abroad, to keep up the Goddess's practices where they're really needed. I admire her. I just wish she'd come home long enough for me to meet her so I can tell her that. But I can't do anything about Nike. None of us can. We have to respect her Will for her own life. Even if…"

Lyros got up and went to sit at Mak's side.

Their shoulders touched, and Mak took Lyros's hand. "Even if her choice for her life was to sacrifice it."

"The Charge is still looking for her," Lio reminded him. "They need more time."

"*You* don't have more time. I must accept Nike's choices. I don't have to accept what's happening to you."

"That's right," Lyros said. "We can do something about the fact that our Trial brother is suffering. Hesperines who go errant face the danger in the name of serving Hespera and her people. You aren't in a position to make that sacrifice. Think of your parents and Zoe."

"And us, Lio. Goddess knows I don't want to lose you, too."

Lio swallowed. "I'm grateful for you two."

"You're welcome," Mak answered. "We're happy to break your nose for you anytime."

"Stop making him laugh, Mak. It hurts just looking at him."

Mak's reply was not a joke this time. "His body should have repaired itself by now. He's that bad off."

Lio had to do what was right for his people, his family, and Cassia. But also for himself.

"I got Cassia her seat at the Summit in Tenebra, against her wishes," Lio said. "I regarded it as an invitation, she as an unwanted intervention. I understood afterward I should not have acted without her consent, but she came to realize she truly wanted her seat. She did great things from there, and if she hadn't, Dalos and the king would have succeeded."

"Such what-ifs don't bear thinking on." Mak shook his head.

Lyros shuddered. "Thank the Goddess. You were all in the right places at the right times."

"That's the last time I dismiss a diplomatic mission as a lot of boring talking," Mak said. "I keep wishing the two of us had gone with you after all."

"I wished that constantly while I was there," Lio admitted. "But who would have patrolled the border while the embassy was in Tenebra, if you hadn't stayed? The Queens' ward protects us, but it doesn't have hands to reach out and help anyone seeking asylum from the other side."

Lyros smirked. "Besides, it earned us our promotions from initiates to full rank in the Stand. Just like your feats in Tenebra earned you your ambassadorship."

Mak's chest shook with laughter. "We'll keep your 'feats' with Cassia a secret, if you won't tell anyone how much fun Lyros and I had while everyone was gone."

"The three of us spent the shortest time as initiates in the history of our people, after all," said Lyros. "We'd better not let on."

"Right," Lio said between excruciating laughs. "Wouldn't want anyone to think we advanced so quickly by getting our fangs polished."

Their humor offered a moment of respite. But only a moment.

"We won't feel safe until you're with your Cassia on this side of the border," Lyros said.

"It may be the only safe place for her," Mak reminded Lio.

Lio leaned his elbows on his knees. "Basir and Kumeta are consulting with the Queens again tomorrow. I'll find out then whether or not Flavian and Cassia danced the Autumn Greeting. Whether she's really in danger."

"Even if she isn't, you still are," said Lyros.

"What if she doesn't dance with him?" Mak asked. "What will you do for your sake, Lio?"

"I don't know." Lio stood, and his Trial brothers steadied him on his feet. "But if Cassia dances with Flavian tomorrow, I will no longer hesitate."

ZOE

LIO DIDN'T WANT TO admit how relieved he was Mak and Lyros offered to take him home. It didn't strain them to step with him back to House Komnena, and they delivered him precisely to the family terrace.

The side door stood open, its stained glass panels illuminated by spell light from within the house and moonlight from without. It was an early effort of Lio's from before he had learned to infuse glass with its own light, but the door remained one of Mother's favorite Gift Night presents.

Father always said the house he had built for his bloodline had been a mausoleum until he had brought his Grace and their child home, and the monument of white marble would not be finished until his son filled every window frame and doorway with color. Lio had centuries of work ahead of him.

Lyros's eyes narrowed with amusement. "This feels familiar."

Mak chuckled. "How many times have we had to carry each other home after one of us caught the wrong end of our mischief?"

"Only our sisters are missing," Lyros mused.

"Yes. Our Trial sisters." If Lio kept referring to all three of them that way, perhaps he would come to feel it was true not only of Kia and Nodora, but also Xandra as well.

At the outset of Lio, Mak, and Lyros's doomed childhood expedition to the aptly named Wisdom's Precipice, Kia had given them a lecture on why leaping from the cliff would not cause them to learn levitation any faster.

Upon their return, when she had visited them in the Healing Sanctuary, she had said, "I told you so," before weeping at the sight of them.

Nodora had sent them dismayed, sympathetic get-well notes while devoting her time to keeping Xandra busy for as many hours as it took the healers to make Mak, Lyros, and Lio more presentable.

When Xandra had finally burst in for a visit, Lio wasn't sure what had set off her infamous temper the most. That the three of them had done such a thing to themselves, or that everyone else had tried to protect her by keeping her in the dark.

"I think it will require more diplomacy when I tell the others than it did with you two," said Lio.

"Telling us didn't require any diplomacy," Lyros pointed out.

"Nothing diplomatic about getting your face smashed and then vomiting your guts out on the steam room floor."

"Hush," Lio begged Mak. "Zoe might hear you."

"We understand," Lyros assured him. "You have to plan how you'll share your happy news with our sisters."

"It's different," Lio said. "I wish it weren't...it didn't use to be... but it is."

"It's not different with Kia and Nodora." Mak let out a sigh. "But you can't tell them without telling Xandra, and *that*...well. I hope you don't wait much longer."

"Pushing me toward the edge of the cliff?"

"No, Lio." Lyros huffed a laugh. "We just want you to hurry up and put them out of their misery. Do you have any idea how relieved they'll be?"

Lio couldn't share Mak and Lyros's optimistic prediction of their Trial sisters' reaction to his secret. Nothing could convince him not to dread that conversation with Xandra. Few things could be more uncomfortable than telling the person you had once mistaken for your Grace that you had discovered your real Grace, with the knowledge you must remain acquainted with your former share for the rest of eternity.

"Please," Lio pleaded, "don't say anything until I'm ready."

"Don't worry," Lyros promised. "We won't."

Mak nodded in agreement.

Lio clapped them on the shoulders in thanks. He could already feel the auras of his family stirring within. They knew he was home, of course. It was all he could do to keep his veil close about him. Lio let only his father sense that he needed assistance. He didn't want to worry his mother, and he couldn't have Zoe get an eyeful.

Lio felt his father acknowledge his call for help. His father's aura rose within the house and prowled closer.

"Father's coming out to take care of this." Lio waved to indicate his nose, or perhaps in warning. "Go home and get some sleep. The next battle is one you can't help me with."

"You don't have to tell me twice. Facing off with Uncle Apollon, you're on your own." Mak was shaking his head when a splitting yawn interrupted him. "Accursed sun. I can feel it coming on already."

"Exhausted from your crushing defeat? Understandable." Lyros slid an arm around Mak's waist. "But he who loses the match must forfeit rest until the victor claims his prize."

Mak's yawn transformed into a grin as the two of them disappeared.

Now that his friends were gone, the full weight of Lio's trepidation settled over him. He leaned against the railing of the terrace and eyed the open side door. Thorns, he was so tired. How was he supposed to tell his family the life-altering news that he had found his Grace, when his mind was barely working due to his Craving for her?

Why was one of the best things that had ever happened to him the most difficult thing he had ever endured? This might be the eight-hundredth time he had asked the Goddess that question since he had first set foot in Tenebra.

Before Lio had even begun to decide what to say, his father strolled out of the house. It was easy for Lio to forget that he, as a bloodborn, was the tallest person in Orthros, when Father's powerful frame seemed too large for the delicate doorway. The moment his gaze landed on Lio, he crossed the terrace in a single step.

"Well now." Studying the damage, he held Lio's chin with one hand. An ancient hand that could lift marble out of the ground without touching the stone and had put many mages six feet under. But right now his touch was gentle. Dark blue eyes just like Lio's looked back at him, rueful. "I see my brother managed to talk you off the top of the Observatory. When Argyros and I agreed a bout in the gymnasium would be good for you, this is not what we had in mind."

"Can't blame Lyros and Mak," Lio said. "I asked for it."

"I somehow doubt that."

"No, I did. Quite literally."

"You asked them for a challenge," his father guessed. "Not a broken nose."

"I must beg a boon of you, Father. I can't go inside like this. It still doesn't take much to upset Zoe. It will distress her to see me injured."

Father raised his golden eyebrows. "Since when is giving blood to my own son some boon he must ask for with such ceremony?"

"Since he's been too old to drink from you outside of Ritual."

Father tilted his head back and laughed. "Too old to drink from your parents? Try that one on me again in a thousand years or so. It will be just as amusing then. Better yet, try it on your mother."

"Sustenance from an elder firstblood *is* a boon, even if I have enjoyed the privilege all my life. I do not take your blood for granted."

Father touched his thumb and forefinger to Lio's nose, so carefully Lio didn't even flinch. "'Grace' and 'Father' are the only titles to which I have ever aspired. Every time I hear those words from my family, I would give up my seat in the Firstblood Circle."

His father's past was a familiar story, but lately Lio could relate to it as never before. "You really think the Queens would let you do that, especially after you were absent from your seat for seven hundred years? There is no escaping it since you returned to Orthros with your Grace and announced you will never again go errant."

"Well, at least it's a title to offer your mother. Nothing less than 'Elder Grace Komnena' would be worthy of her. And attending Circle meetings as my firstgift has been of some use to you."

"Oh yes, some small use. I think I might have learned a thing or two, assisting you before the Queens my entire life."

Father ran his free hand over the blond curls of his famous beard, which ran in thick, neat braids against his face to join the long braid of his hair behind his head. As if unconsciously, his fingers lingered on the black braid amid the gold. Mother's braid started at the corner of Father's mouth and trailed across his cheek, then under his ear and down his back.

Lio thought again of Kumeta's half-jesting promise of a recommendation when his beard began to rival his father's. Replacing all the windows in the house with stained glass would be an easy task by comparison. Sometimes the age-long pace of Hesperine bodily processes was not an advantage.

"There." Father nodded. "Bones are much finer work than stone, but those are in their proper place now and ready for healing."

Lio blinked. He hadn't felt a thing. "How many times did you have to do that in the field?"

His father laughed again. "For a nose? Rarely. When we broke something, it was usually more spectacular."

"It's a good thing Rudhira is a real healer. It is your opponents I pity."

Apollon, onetime Blood Errant, flashed a predatory grin. But it was Father who patiently rolled up his sleeve and offered his wrist to Lio. A wrist that bore no battle scars, only the ropy muscles that betrayed this Hesperine had once worshiped his Goddess on the path of battle, not peace.

Lio bowed his head and accepted his father's offering. He braced himself, but even so, his first taste of his father's blood in some time hit his veins with enough of a kick to nearly stagger him. As a child, he had never given it a thought. But once he had come into his full power and the ability to sense the magnitude of his father's, he had come to appreciate the might to which he was heir.

Perhaps this was what strong spirits tasted like to a human on a frigid night. Once the initial burn wore off, Lio felt warmed and fortified from head to toe. He lifted his head, careful not to spill. That would be truly embarrassing, on top of needing to drink from his father as if he were still an uninitiated newblood.

But he couldn't deny this had been the right decision. He wouldn't need the deer anymore tonight. "Thank you, Father."

"I waited fifteen centuries for a child of my own to sustain on my blood. Do not ever imagine that ends at Initiation."

Lio clasped his father's wrist, which had already healed. His father returned his grip.

"Now tell me." Father's voice was calm and quiet, devoid of command.

His aura felt about as yielding as a granite mountain. "Why didn't your nose heal on its own?"

Lio sighed. "I will answer your questions. There are things I must speak of with you and Mother. After Zoe is asleep."

"Good."

As soon as they crossed the threshold into Mother's study, Father's sense that all was right in the world enveloped Lio. The house Father had built with his own hands and to which Mother had given her name stood stronger than ever. Lio and his father passed through her favorite room and went into the Ritual hall.

The mosaic Ritual Circle at the center of their home gleamed under the skylight, catching the moons' glow as it always had. Red tiles for the petals of Hespera's Rose, black for the thorns, white for the stars in their bloodline's constellation. The symbol had always oriented Lio until his return from Tenebra.

His parents had waited months for him to finally speak about what troubled him. Father clearly thought Lio was about to set their minds at ease. It galled Lio that he had no reassurance to offer them, only the dire truth.

The patter of little feet announced that Zoe was done waiting for Lio. Her footfalls were somewhere in the hallway outside her room when she apparently grew impatient with walking. She appeared beside the Ritual Circle, her own betony charm swinging about her neck at the sudden stop.

Mother was right behind her. When Zoe learned to step farther than from one room to another, they would have their hands full indeed.

Lio's small sister gazed up at him with her big brown eyes, holding her favorite mantle over her head like a tent. Now that Lio was near again, Zoe was still and silent. That always seemed enough for her, just having him near, ever since his efforts to make her feel safe during the journey home from Tenebra.

He dropped to one knee in front of her, folding himself down to her eye level as he had that first night, when she had been a frightened orphan and he an imposing stranger.

Tonight she inched toward him and let him put an arm around her. When he hugged her close, she did not pull away. A great reward indeed.

Eventually, perhaps, she would feel comfortable with him grabbing her and swinging her up into his arms the minute he got in the house, as he frequently felt the urge to do.

"I'm sorry it took me so long to get home," Lio said.

She frowned in displeasure, but showed no sign of the real distress she had so often experienced when they had first brought her home. She lowered her arms, letting her mantle drape over the top of her head and hang in her eyes.

Lio rejoiced at every sign their family's patience and care was helping Zoe heal from all she had suffered as a mortal. Malnourishment had made her small for her seven years, while isolation had left her ill-prepared for life among any people other than the few surviving Eriphite children. And yet in many ways, hardship had forced her to grow up too fast.

The Gift had restored her health, and now that she would remain a child for decades, her body had more than enough time to catch up. It was her mind and heart that would require the most effort and nurturing so they could heal and, at last, have their opportunity to grow.

Her presence in the Blood Union was soft but tenacious, and currently pouting. "Why did you have to stay gone? We already took care of my goats and made sure they have everything they need in the barn."

That explained the unusual absence of Zoe's retinue. The two kids trailed after her every waking minute, at least when she allowed them to walk. The miniature breed their parents had chosen as companions for her were easy for a Hesperine child to carry.

Lio suppressed a smile and answered her as seriously as he could. "I regret I missed it. But I'm sure as long as you were there, they didn't mind that I wasn't. Did you have your dinner?"

She nodded in silence, looking at the floor. "Papa says I may not sleep in the barn with my goats."

Father's hand came to rest on Zoe's head, and instead of startling as she once might have, she visibly relaxed. He winked at Lio over her head.

Lio struggled still harder not to grin. "If you slept in the barn, you would be too far away, and I would miss you."

A small smile appeared on her face. She tugged on a stray lock of hair, nervous under all the attention. Their mother had spent nights on end rescuing Zoe's locks from under the grime and teasing out every knot and snarl so she would not have to cut a single hair.

It had truly been a labor of love, one that had revealed Zoe's hair to be a straight, elbow-length curtain the color of creamed coffee. Now it shone, silky and healthy, a source of confidence for her that garnered praise from all her fellow Hesperines.

She seldom knew how to respond to the compliments, but she always wore her beloved mantle so most of her hair could be seen. The voluminous silk scarf had been a very thoughtful gift from Lio's Trial sisters, one that made Zoe feel safe under the high ceilings of House Komnena.

Mother smiled at Lio and stroked the back of Zoe's head. "It's just as we said, sweetling. Lio is home to bid you good veil before you go back to sleep. Let's get you settled in your room."

Zoe turned without protest to their mother, who now stood in the circle of their father's arm. Lio looked up at their mother, who had been tall even in her human life. Her long black mane had come with her into immortality, and she now wore it in myriad braids that signified her promises to her new life.

For as long as Lio could remember, one braid had been thicker than the others, the one she said was for him. Now there was another for Zoe. Both were now braided together with their father's curly blond braid. Remarkable how familiar the view was from Zoe's eye level.

As Zoe pressed close to Mother's skirts, Lio stood, suppressing a sigh. He was glad everything could be simple for his little sister. It was a new and powerful feeling, this fierce urge to ensure it stayed that way, at any cost.

THE BRAVE GARDENER

L10 STOOD IN THE doorway of Zoe's room while their parents coaxed her into bed. Not for the first time, he nearly bumped his head on the ceiling. The former storeroom was a far cry from the lovely chambers Mother and Father had reserved for their daughter upstairs, but this room's low ceiling made it the one place in the house where Zoe felt safe without her mantle.

The room was too small to hold their parents' happiness. The simple act of tucking blankets around her long-awaited second child was enough to make Mother's aura glow with delight. Father sat down on the edge of the bed, as if there were nothing in the world he would rather do than answer Zoe's nervous questions yet again. In fact, there wasn't.

"Are you sure I shouldn't go check on the other children, Papa?" Zoe asked for the third time.

Even though Lio knew to expect the question, it always pained him to hear it. To think, Zoe had assumed the duties of a mother at the age of seven, looking after her fellow orphans with no one to help her but ten-year-old Bosko. It would take her a long time to realize she was no longer responsible for the lives left in her care when her human elders had died.

"The other children are safe in their beds, just like you," Father reassured her. "Their parents will make sure they have everything they need, just as we do for you. Your mother and I will be right here when you wake up feeling thirsty."

"What if they have bad dreams?"

"They won't have any bad dreams, little one. It will be much easier than last season."

Zoe clutched her betony charm. "What if they dream about Tenebra?"

This was why Cassia had stayed behind. To spare this child the misery she herself had endured, growing up in Tenebra as a mortal, a female, a child who was made to pay for others' shame. To keep the mages who murdered children away from her people and that much farther away from Lio's.

"None of you will dream about that tonight," Father promised. "Even after Lio and your mother are asleep, I will be awake, and if I sense any day terrors, I will chase them away."

"But what about when you have to sleep, Papa?"

"Your mother's and my magic never sleeps, and that will protect you every moment until we wake." He tapped her betony charm. "And so will this."

"Who will take care of my goats when we're all asleep?"

Their parents exchanged a smile Lio had often seen over the last nine decades. He suppressed a grin and a sigh of relief. Diverting Zoe's sense of responsibility to her goats seemed to be helping.

Mother caressed Zoe's head. "Our magic will keep your goats safe, too."

This was why Lio had left Tenebra. So Zoe could be a child. Her greatest concern should be her pets, not the threat of her own death. He would not allow her second chance at childhood to be marred by a mage war that would devastate Hesperines and humans alike.

If he brought Cassia to safety, would he ruin all they had fought for?

If he did not bring her home to him, would she be the next casualty of their fight?

Was he not in danger of becoming a casualty as well?

He had to believe he and Cassia could fight better when they were together again, as they had in Tenebra.

"I can't sleep until Lio tells me a story," Zoe declared.

Lio glanced at his parents. "Do we have time for a story?"

Their mother's amused contentment filled the room like a soft light. "I think so."

"Go ahead, Son," Father agreed. "Zoe is fortunate to have none other than Glasstongue for a brother and bedtime storyteller."

"Nodora's ballad is too generous." Lio stuck his tongue out at Zoe. "See? It's just like everyone's."

She giggled. "Tell me a story about the Brave Gardener."

Lio sat on the foot of Zoe's bed, taking up a tailor's position. "I knew you'd want to hear a story about her. Which one would you like me to tell?"

"The bad dreams story."

Lio smiled. "A perfect tale for tonight."

Mother leaned against the wrought iron headboard, one arm around Zoe. Holding her betony charm close, Zoe snuggled against their mother and watched Lio expectantly.

"Far away in the land of Tenebra," Lio began, "there lived a young mortal woman who was very kind and very brave. During the day, she worked in the gardens at the Temple of Kyria."

In the air above Zoe's head, he let his first illusion take shape. She gazed raptly at the miniature Temple of Kyria he conjured on her ceiling, although the image was now familiar to her after so many tellings.

From his own memories of Tenebra and the paintings he had seen of daylight, Lio reconstructed the temple in every detail. He showed Zoe the place she had almost died and shrank it to fit inside her room in their home in Orthros, where she lay surrounded by a family who loved her.

Now Lio swept them down inside the walls of the temple and into the gardens. "The Brave Gardener planted seeds that would grow into a bounty of vegetables. She pruned trees that would drop delicious fruit, and watered plants the Temple mages could turn into powerful medicine that would make the sick well."

Zoe smiled at the images of tiny seedlings sprouting from the soil and branches shaking free their fat, succulent apples.

"And during the night, she helped people," Zoe recited.

"Indeed she did. Under the shelter of darkness, with the Goddess's Eyes to light her path, she did good deeds in secret..."

Night descended over Lio's illusory garden, and in the midst of the shadows he conjured her. A slender figure in a cloak, her face hidden in her hood, bearing a basket in her arms.

His Grace, of whom his family had heard him speak these long months. They believed her to be no one but a messenger with whom he had spoken only briefly, a nameless gardener embellished into a hero by Zoe's imagination.

"The Brave Gardener had many secrets," Lio went on, "and she was very good at keeping them. She knew there were children in the temple hiding from wicked mages, and she made sure no one found out."

"Because she was smart and kind," Zoe murmured.

Lio smiled to himself. What would Cassia think if she knew she was a hero in a story? "One night, the Brave Gardener learned that the children hiding in the temple were having bad dreams, and they were very frightened. She wanted to make them feel safe. So she decided to harvest good plants from her garden that would help the children. She cut beautiful purple betony flowers and fragrant green betony leaves and bound them together in cloths."

Lio sprouted a garland of betony about Cassia's image. A square of cloth fluttered to her, and at a motion from her hand, needle and thread obeyed her and sewed the scrap of fabric into the charm Zoe wore at her neck. Despite Cassia's protests about her awful sewing skills, he made the work of her hands into art, her labor into magic, for it had always seemed to him like nothing less.

"She sewed the cloths into charms, and she put the charms in a basket. This basket, she brought to the Prisma of the Temple, who brought it to her mages, who brought it to the children who were having bad dreams. The good mages took the charms the Brave Gardener had made, and they put one around the neck of every child. The bad dreams were banished, and the children wore their charms all the way home to Orthros, where there are no bad dreams."

"What are the children's names?" Zoe's eyes had slid shut, and she did not see him conjuring their faces in the air above her, but she smiled to herself.

"All the children got new names when they came to Orthros," Lio said, "to show how brave they are. The oldest girl is called Zosime. And the oldest boy is named Boskos, and he has a little sister named Athena…"

By the time he named each of the two dozen children who were now the youngest Hesperines in Orthros, Zoe's breathing had stilled. She had finally slipped into Slumber.

Or not. "What is the Brave Gardener's name?" she mumbled. Still awake enough to end the story with her customary question.

For which Lio always gave his customary answer. "Her name, like all her good deeds, is a secret. All those who admire the Brave Gardener must keep her secrets safe, just as she protected their secrets from the wicked mages." But the night had come when that answer was no longer enough. "The Brave Gardener's secrets are safe with us, so I shall tell you, and only you, her name. She is called Cassia, and she still lives in Tenebra, where she works hard to keep everyone safe."

Zoe's eyes flew open, only to slide shut again. "You never told me that part!"

"I'll tell you even more about her after you wake."

"Don't want to…sleep…"

But Zoe was asleep before she could ask him anything else, leaving Lio to answer the much more difficult questions from their parents.

BREAKING POINT

LIO HELD HIS VEIL steady and braced himself. But the storm would not break until they were out of Zoe's room, it seemed.

"Come into the Ritual hall," Mother said, low and urgent, "where our words will not trouble her dreams."

They stepped to the Ritual Circle, and to Lio's credit, he didn't land face down on it. His parents stood across the mosaic from him. For a moment, the only sounds were the splash of the fountains throughout the house and the rustle of feathers as Mother's familiar stirred in her sleep in the study. Then the questions began.

"Are all the stories you've told Zoe true?" Mother asked.

"I have romanticized them, I admit. But yes, all are essentially true."

Mother's brows arched. "Only one 'Cassia' has ever been mentioned in connection with our embassy's time in Tenebra."

"So," Father pronounced. "Lady Cassia Basilis is none other than the Brave Gardener—the object of Zoe's admiration and, I take it, the cause of our son's melancholy."

As Lio had suspected, that one revelation on his part had been sufficient, and now they were making all the connections between his own behavior and the Lady Cassia who had been on the periphery of the Hesperines' political awareness. The center of Lio's world.

"May I ask if she was the reason for your discreet visits inside the palace?" Mother inquired.

Lio folded his hands behind his back. "She was."

Mother let out a long sigh, and her relief washed over him. She slid her arm around Father, and he pulled her close.

Lio's jaw tightened. "I fear this is not cause for relief."

A low rumble emerged from Father's chest. He was laughing. "That nothing worse afflicts you than pining for a young lady? It certainly is cause for relief."

Now Mother's suppressed amusement revealed itself in a smile. How long, while Lio attempted to deliver dread news, had they been struggling to keep straight faces, as surely as they did over Zoe?

"Here we were, imagining you haunted by the violence you experienced in Tenebra," his mother said. "Fearing you might struggle for years with the scars you brought home. Worst of all, you wouldn't talk, which is the only sure way to heal the marks death leaves on the mind. Not even I could coax you to speak. To learn you are troubled by love, not death, is the greatest relief we have experienced since your safe return."

Lio should have presented the truth in a different order. He didn't want to rob them of reassurance as soon as he had given it to them. But he must make it clear how serious this was.

"Well," his mother observed, "now we have the context for your constant vigilance regarding the situation in Tenebra."

"And your repeated requests to return." Father shook his head. "When you asked Ioustin for a place in his Charge, you should have told him why. He might have actually hesitated before saying no."

Lio rubbed his temple. "Rudhira wrote to you as well, I see."

His father grinned. "You are a Hesperine after my own heart, Lio."

Lio tried to take consolation in hearing that, but his frustration remained too fresh. "And yet no one will heed my requests." Not even his father.

"I did not have a mother waiting at home to worry about me," his father reminded him.

Mother pressed her lips together as if to hide a smile. "I accept any blame you wish to lay on my worries, love. I shall not repeat all the things you say to me when you fret over our son."

It was easier, and yet so much harder to tell his parents than to tell Mak and Lyros. With his mother and father, his immediate bloodline, he could say the words aloud without invoking a binding commitment…but he would invoke something much worse. If his Trial Brothers were afraid for him, how much greater must his parents' fear be?

But he had charted his course. Now was the time.

"Only wait until you're older," his mother advised, "before you follow your father's path. If not for our peace of mind, then for Zoe's. At least another eight decades, until she is of age."

"I don't have decades," Lio said. "Nor even months. I must act now."

"Such feelings are natural at a time like this," his mother said. "When you love, you love very strongly. It is in your nature to feel a great sense of devotion—something we admire about you."

"You've drunk nothing but deer this season, have you?" his father asked.

"Lio! You might have made an impersonal arrangement with one of the human guests, at least. Everyone knows it will take you some time to move on from her, but half a year on deer?" His mother rounded the Ritual Circle and pressed a hand to his forehead, then his wrist, measuring his pulse. "It's a wonder you aren't ill."

Lio was glad his veil was strong enough to spare his mother the truth of just how ill he was, not to mention to fool Javed during the physical exam required to begin battle training.

His father fixed him with a level gaze. "Tonight, his training injuries would not heal without a drink from me."

"Father—" Lio protested.

"Zoe is a child who must be protected from the truth. Your mother is not."

His mother reached up and brushed his hair back from his forehead. "When I guide newcomers to Orthros on the path to healing their minds, I confront everything in the harrowing pasts they left behind. I survived my own past. I may have a mother's tender heart, but there is nothing you can do or say that will break me."

The speech Lio had planned out deserted him. He did not build up to the momentous announcement or make any eloquent remarks worthy of the occasion. The truth just came out of his mouth. "Cassia is my Grace."

He wasn't sure what he found more overwhelming. The depth of their emotion flooding the Blood Union, or the way they embraced him like a lost son who had only just now returned home. When he lifted his head from his father's shoulder, he realized something that made this entire wretched situation that much more bearable. His parents' happiness was stronger than their fear.

"I will take you to get her," Father announced.

Goddess bless. It sounded so easy.

Father turned to Mother, taking her hands. "You know I will bring our son home without a scratch—along with our Grace-daughter."

She looked down at their joined hands, giving his a squeeze. "Lio and Cassia could not ask for a better protector."

"We can be in and out of Solorum before Zoe has time to get thirsty. You needn't do without me for long." Father's gaze softened with amusement. "I'm sure Lio requires even less time than it took me to persuade my Grace to return with me. I'm much less diplomatic, after all."

"You know what I think of your methods of persuasion." A grin eased her worried expression. "As surely as you delivered Lio and me from Tenebra, I know you and Lio will now deliver our Cassia."

How quick they were to speak of Cassia as one of the family. They were already making plans to rescue her, just as they would Nike, if they knew where she was.

How wonderful it would be to let go at last, to lay down his sword and let his elders take care of everything.

"It's not that simple," Lio said.

"Sit down," his father replied. "We shall decide our course of action."

The next thing Lio knew, a chair was behind his knees. He resisted the urge to sink into it until he saw his mother and father had pulled up chairs for themselves as well. If it was only a gesture to soothe his pride, he didn't question it and gratefully took his seat. It was harder to resist the urge to put his head in his hands.

"When I asked her to come back to Orthros with me, she gave up the chance so she could stay and work against her father."

It surprised Lio to discover it was not as difficult as he had expected to explain their situation. All the stories of the Brave Gardener had prepared him, as well as his parents. It was a relief to talk with them about the real Cassia at last. In fact, it was a rare pleasure. Despite his best efforts, he probably sounded like a lovestruck fool eager for them to like her.

But he knew he didn't have to try. He had seldom been more proud than in this moment, when he could tell them that his Grace, their Grace-daughter, was necessary to the safety of Tenebra and the Hesperines who were still secretly at work there.

What was more difficult than he could have imagined was pushing away his best source of aid, as he worked to convince his father they could not do precisely what Lio had longed to do for months: go to her.

"Of course you didn't tell us." His mother sighed. "You are just like your father...and me. Always taking matters into your own hands. We're proud of you."

"We are indeed."

"Thank you," Lio blurted.

The Craving really had affected his judgment. All his predictions about their reaction had been wrong. Then again, his parents were extraordinary, often surprising people. They had not achieved so much by fulfilling expectations. In fact, they had spent most of their immortality defying expectations at every turn.

"You should be proud of yourself for how well you have coped with the last four months," his mother said.

"I'm not sure I am." Once more, the confession came out in spite of him. "It has been so hard to be sure of my course."

"There are many paths to the top of the Hilt."

The Hilt, where Tenebrans left their unwanted children to die and staked out heretics. The site of many of his people's greatest rescues. The symbol of every Hesperine's effort to do the right thing.

"But how am I to bring my lady down from the cliff without causing the mountain to crumble beneath us all?"

"That is not a concern," his father said simply. "Cassia must not remain in Tenebra. We are bringing all our people home and closing the borders. We are doing what we have always done when Cordium stirs restlessly, what every person, Hesperine or mortal, does in times of trouble. We are holding our kin close and barring the gates. Cassia is one of us now, just like her three anonymous rescuers and Nike and all the others for whom we are still searching. Rejoice that we know where Cassia is, and that she is safe. For now."

"But Cassia has the power to protect the others, to buy us time to find them. That is what she would want, on behalf of the Hesperines errant who saved her life and gave the Mercy to her sister."

"That is not her duty. It is in Ioustin's hands, and there are none better. Cassia must be home with us as soon as possible."

"What if that isn't what she wants?"

"She heard your message," his mother reminded him. "She knows you are coming back for her."

"But when I do, what if her answer is the same as it was last year?"

"It won't be," his father said.

"Lio." His mother leaned forward. "Have you considered the possibility that she changed her mind long ago but has had no way to tell you she is ready to leave Tenebra?"

Lio's chest tightened, and for a moment, he had no words. He hadn't considered it.

He had not wanted to. That would mean he had failed in the worst way of all. She had been awaiting rescue all along, and he had not lifted a finger to help her.

"Do you imagine she does not feel your bond, even as a human?" his mother asked.

That was the very question that had taunted Lio most of all during the long, hungry nights, when he felt like only half a living thing without Cassia, and she was in Tenebra, fighting the good fight. What if she needed him? What if she didn't? "You think she feels the separation as much as I do?"

"I know she does." Mother twined her fingers in Father's. "My need for your father was profound even when I was human. Grace does not begin with the Gift, although only through the Gift can it reach fulfillment. The Craving is more than thirst—or even hunger. Cassia needs you."

"Tomorrow night, I will know for certain," Lio said. "You must have already heard the news Basir and Kumeta brought."

"Yes," his father replied, "all the elder firstbloods have been discussing the Anthrian mages who arrived at Solorum. Would that I could do more to them than discuss them."

"Are they a threat to Cassia?" Lio's mother asked. "Is there a possibility they suspect her of assisting our people?"

"I believe the king's plans remain the greatest threat to Cassia," Lio answered.

He had now spread his fear for her safety like a wildfire. He had no choice but to fan the flames and tell his parents about Flavian's courtship.

"If she dances with him," Lio concluded, "I must take it as a sign she has not found a way to avoid the betrothal and that she needs my help. I will know it is time to act."

"It is time to act," his father said, "whether she dances or not."

"Father, I will not risk destroying everything she has worked for. I will not take the sword from her hand and drag her to safety in a tower while her enemy—her father—scours the land unhindered. She would never forgive me, and she would have every right not to."

"You need her. We are bringing her home."

"I must do this according to her way. Nay, our way, as we worked together in Tenebra. Those efforts were not in vain. I *know* we did the right thing then, so that path must still be the right one now."

"Do you have a plan?" his father pressed.

"I promised her I would find a way. I will. Only give me until after the Autumn Greeting to reassess her situation. Then I will tell you what I have in mind."

His parents were silent for a moment, surely having one of their many discussions about him. He had no doubt this was in the same category as offering him the Drink. He would never be too old for them to discuss his well-being out of his hearing.

"Very well." Father did not sound happy, but his aura shone with unmistakable pride. "We have always raised you to make your own decisions. You are the best judge of how to proceed with your own Grace. We will see what occurs tomorrow, and then we will discuss your plan."

"Thank you, Father."

"We will not wait too long, however," Mother decreed. If Father was a granite mountain, she was the inexorable current of the sea. "In the meantime, you will accept the Drink from us. I will not have my son scrounge among the animals. You need our blood to sustain you, if you are to endure."

He knew she was right. He reminded himself of Lyros's advice. The

Craving was not a test, merely a fact. Lio needed the strength his parents could provide.

So he could be strong for Cassia.

No sense in protesting in the name of his pride. There was too much at stake for him to refuse. And refusing their gifts was no way to show his gratitude to those who had given him life.

His mother was suddenly standing before him. Her arms came around him, and she held him to her, planting a kiss on the top of his head. In her mortal life, she had lost seven children before him and fought tooth and nail for his survival, all so she could hold one thriving child in her arms at last. After all these years as a Hesperine and even Zoe's arrival, there were still times when she needed to hold Lio to push away old griefs. He counted himself fortunate he could ease her pain.

Lio returned her embrace. "I'm all right, Mother. You needn't worry about me now."

"I shall worry as long as your Grace needs air to survive." She rested her hands on his shoulders and looked him in the eye. "But you are my son and Apollon's. You will not break, either."

EVE

of the

AUTUMN EQUINOX

A lady always listens carefully.

—*Solia's instructions to Cassia*

A LADY'S WEAPONS

ASSIA ALWAYS KNEW AN effective weapon when she found it. At times it was a piece of information she delivered to the right ears at the right moment. Often it was information her handmaiden brought to her, for Perita was an ally, and Cassia had learned to treasure her few allies even more than weapons.

Tonight and every night, her best weapons against the king were his own words, the ones he spoke behind the closed doors of his solar. No one was privy to all the secrets the king discussed in this chamber. Except Cassia, the one person alive who had breached his bastion.

Cassia listened to the fire crackling in the king's hearth and waited to hear how he would betray himself this time. Flames licked at the delicate linen that shielded her body, and all she felt was the warm tickle that had become familiar after many such vigils here at the back of the enormous fireplace.

She had come to appreciate the bitter scent of the flametongue oil that gave her garments their protective power. Her eyes no longer watered as she breathed through the treated veil.

Cassia stood without fear a few paces away from the king and knew that if he looked into his hearth, he would see only fire. She would disappear among the flames like a spirit, for flametongue was a thing of fire, and like concealed like.

Even the mage now in conference with the king looked past her every time his gaze darted about the room. But she could watch the men from behind her shield of fire and the armor of her sheer veil.

King Lucis of Tenebra sat in his heavy oak chair behind his desk. The sight had not changed all Cassia's life, except his blond hair and beard had gone white over the years, and in addition to the burn scar that had always blemished his jaw, he now bore many more marks of battle. He was a squarely built, warlike figure unsoftened by his royal finery, a creature that had sprung from the bestiary to don a crown. With sky-blue eyes that saw everything, he watched the young man on the other side of the desk.

The apprentice mage stood very still, as if he feared any movement might provoke the predator to pounce. A handful of the royal guards attended their king, who would gladly gobble them up if they would serve him better dead than alive.

One such man-at-arms drew near and knelt before the fire. Cassia stood calmly while he stoked the flames. The men in the solar must be feeling the predawn cold. Summer, such as it was, had come to an end in the kingdom of Tenebra.

Tonight was the night when darkness and light were of equal length. The Autumn Equinox.

The night when the Hesperines returned to the north.

They were still beyond her reach. But she knew they were there. *He* was there.

Lio.

"My masters in Cordium still await your answer, Basileus, if you will allow me to remind you."

Cassia had to listen closely to catch all the mage's words. She had never heard him speak in his entire time as apprentice to Dalos. The young man's continued service under the new royal mage had proved him to be soft-spoken and quiescent. This whelp couldn't be older than sixteen and had less confidence than Cassia's half brother of thirteen—and Prince Caelum was not known for his presence.

The young mage was a strange agent indeed for the Order of Anthros to employ. It was apparent, however, he had come from Cordium and had known all along Amachos was really Dalos. The apprentice was now all the Order had left to work with in Tenebra, since Honored Master Dalos, when challenging the protective magic of seven Hesperines, had succeeded in killing himself on his own spell. Perhaps the Order found the youth useful for the same reason the king tolerated him—he was unambitious.

"What answer is that?" The king's voice drove into every corner of the room.

"Regarding the land grant, Basileus," the mage murmured. "The frozen bit of ground in the north that is of no benefit to you. My masters bid me remind you we would put a small temple there, from which to guard against Hesperine incursions."

"And I have already told them Free Lord Galanthian will not sell the land."

"Of course, Basileus, I understand your dilemma. My masters have requested I respectfully ask if you have increased your monetary offer?"

"He will not sell it, because he no longer owns it. He donated it to the Tenebran mages of Kyria."

During all the long hours Cassia spent here, moments like these were the ones she awaited. These incremental victories were what got her back on her feet every time the sun rose again. She stood back and watched the havoc she had wrought.

"He—what? Begging your pardon, Basileus?"

"It appears," the king said, his words clipped and controlled, "the land is optimal for growing rimelace, a rare medicinal herb the mages of Kyria prize. When this came to Lord Galanthian's attention, he donated every last acre, and they took one of his spare daughters off his hands in return."

Cassia smiled and listened to the king explain himself. Lucis *never* had to explain himself.

"What would your masters have me do?" he demanded. "Would they have a warrior lower himself to robbing land from a lot of chanting, flower-growing old maids?"

The firelight gleamed on the young mage's sweaty face. "I am only a messenger and must faithfully relate my masters' questions, Basileus. I am to—forgive me, Basileus—convey their heartfelt disappointment that you have not upheld the agreement you made with Honored Master Dalos, may he live forever in Anthros's exalted company."

The king slammed his hand onto the desk. The mage jolted where he stood. Only Cassia remained still, for she had endured much worse surprises. Her days of quivering before the threat of that hand were over.

"I do not wish to hear the name Dalos ever again," the king breathed.

The mage's reply was almost a whisper. "Of course, Basileus."

"You are desperate to have something to show for your efforts by the time your superiors arrive tonight. It is a vain attempt. When you see your masters, tell them that if the first mage they sent me had succeeded in disposing of the Council of Free Lords as they promised, I would have delivered the land they requested from among the holdings that would have reverted to the crown. But since that mage was too incompetent to withstand a few Hesperines, I must make do with legality, and they must make do with what I can spare them. They will have no more land grants from me until they uphold *their* end of the bargain and provide me with mages who will strengthen the authority of the crown against the nobility."

"Of course, Basileus. I am pleased to tell you the party of mages arriving from Cordium tonight are equal to any challenge that awaits them here in Tenebra. They are ready and able to fill the offices you have set aside for them."

"They will go to Ostium and Littora."

The apprentice's swallow was audible. "Basileus, what explanation might I offer them for this when I welcome them to Tenebra tonight? They will wish me to remind you that you agreed to appoint them to key positions in the Temples of Anthros here at Solorum and in the south at Namenti."

"The plan has changed."

Cassia drew a breath of smoke and flametongue that did not choke her and let it out with a silent sigh of relief.

Tenebran sentiment against the Cordian Orders remained volatile enough to stay the king from appointing foreign religious leaders to his people's most influential temples. And the king's own sentiment against the mages stayed his hand still more. His subjects saw a fine line between reform and sacrilege, he between making use of his allies and allowing them to make use of him. Thus far he could do no more than hand-place select Cordian mages in the noble households that were most loyal to the crown—or most afraid of the one who wore it.

The Cordian Mage Orders still could not get the firm foothold in Tenebra they required. The king still could not give them a war with the Hesperines.

Cassia was holding her ground.

There came a knock. The king gestured in the direction of the guards who manned the door, and Cassia heard it swing open.

"My King," said one of the men-at-arms who kept watch in the antechamber without. "Free Lord Titus would like an audience with Your Majesty."

The king beckoned with a hand by way of agreement. "Leave me," he barked at the apprentice. "Go back to your duties with my new Tenebran royal mage. If you make yourself useful when your colleagues from Cordium get here, perhaps you can prove to them you are more than a dead man's inadequate lackey."

Whether the mage's silence was insulted protest or mournful agreement, Cassia could not tell. As he folded his hands inside his sleeves, his fingers tangled in the fabric. He gave a hasty nod of respect before backing away from the desk.

When he was gone, someone else paced through the door and across the carpets in a long, fluid tread Cassia recognized.

"Titus," Lucis greeted. Nearly expressionless. Utterly in control.

"Your Majesty." The Free Lord of Segetia came into view. Tonight he had garbed his tall, fit figure in golden-brown velvet and oiled his chestnut hair, which was turning silver. He swept a bow. "Staying warm, I trust."

Lucis acknowledged Lord Titus's pleasantries with a nod.

Lord Titus gave the king a rueful smile. "I thought to provide you some relief from endless conferences with men of the spell. I understand that as soon as the final summer tournament was over today, the new royal mage occupied you with preparations for the autumnal festivities tomorrow. Honored Master Orumos the Younger follows in the footsteps of the Elder, eh? The meeting-point of Summer and Autumn when Anthros hands the season to his lady wife Kyria may be one of our greatest holidays, but no fighting man should have to endure that many hours of magical bibble-babble."

"Tiresome indeed."

That Lucis tolerated Lord Titus's preference for graciousness over directness, much less agreed with anything he said, was testament to the free lord's position in the king's good graces, as Cassia had often observed.

"I must tell you…" Lord Titus's smile widened. "My son is looking forward to the Greeting with great anticipation."

"Is he."

"Who doesn't, at his age? Autumn Equinox is a fine time to be a young man." Lord Titus laughed. "Flavian has made no secret of his goal, as you've seen, and I could not imagine a finer object for his attentions. Lady Cassia's grace and virtue are a great compliment to you and a true reflection of your boundless generosity to her."

Cassia's lip curled. Oh yes, what a model daughter she was, and all to reflect the glory of the man who had sired her, of course. How generous of the king to use her mother as a concubine and then bother to let the resulting girl-child live. Especially after letting her mother die in an assassin's fire spell meant for him, mere hours after their daughter's birth. His kindness and tender care had absolutely made Cassia what she was.

A footstep took Lord Titus nearer the king. "It will come as no surprise that my son intends to ask your daughter for the Greeting dance."

Cassia also knew what Flavian would request and how the king would answer. She did not allow the king or his courtiers to take her by surprise.

There were only two possible ways that Lucis would respond. Any daughter of his was to be courted, marketed, bartered. But never surrendered. Tomorrow was the day Flavian's hopes would finally be dashed—or the day he surrendered himself to the king for the promise of Cassia's hand. Either way, the game would come to an end.

And the next one would begin. The moment was finally at hand. She would discover which game it was to be.

Cassia had warned Flavian. How she wished he had understood her words for what they were.

Lucis was silent for a moment. "You know the extent of your value to me, Titus. You know the limits of the girl's value as well. I suspect we can come to an arrangement."

"Indeed, I am proud of how my son has made himself an asset to you. Your daughter would be a great honor upon my house, should you choose to bestow her."

"Despite her bastardy, her blood is to be coveted for your son's sons. Do not think that comes without a price."

"My son is glad to serve you with all his ability and devotion," Lord Titus emphasized again.

It would have been more accurate to call him a dog, one who leapt at the king's whistle. Men paid all sorts of prices for the king's favor to keep his eye from their lands or their daughters. Lord Titus paid his son as a hostage to Lucis's whims.

What whim did the king have in mind now? He had jerked Flavian's chain for so long. Would Lucis now yank him the other way or tighten the collar?

"Your son has the opportunity to achieve many things under my banner," Lucis said. "My daughter can be one of those achievements."

"What more would you have him do to prove himself worthy?"

"He need not do anything. I ask only that you put your skill with words to work for me. A few well-placed remarks from you, and your son shall have his dance with my daughter on the morrow. Call it your wedding gift to him."

Cassia waited. This might be another of Lucis's ploys. The word *wedding* seldom meant anything, coming from him, and when it did…it was just as likely to be a threat as a promise.

What he had done to Solia was proof of that. Cassia carried her grief for her sister every moment as a reminder.

"How can I serve you, My King?" Lord Titus asked.

"You are well aware of the tenuous situation regarding the Hesperines."

Cassia held her breath.

"Certainly, Your Majesty. It was the next subject I intended to broach tonight. I would of course be honored to serve you once more at the negotiation table, as I did at the last Summit. I could not be more pleased to know you have made your decision."

"I have."

"What excellent news, that your agents are at the northern border even now, lighting the beacon at Frigorum to signal our willingness to treat with the Hesperines."

"They are not."

"Ah, of course. The Hesperines have only just returned to Orthros tonight. At a later date then, when Your Majesty deems it opportune. The Spring Equinox is months away. There is ample time yet to arrange the Summit well before the new year arrives and the Oath must be sworn."

"There will be no Summit."

Oh, but there would. Cassia would see to that. That was no game. It was her war.

She waited to hear how well Lord Titus would advance her cause. He would never know it, but he was one of her best mouthpieces.

After a pause, the free lord broke the silence. "As your adviser on diplomatic matters, who is eager only to promote the safety and prosperity of Your Majesty's domain, might I be permitted to offer my thoughts on the matter?"

The groan of the door interrupted Lord Titus. Lord Hadrian marched into the room. Reinforcements for Cassia. The Free Lord of Hadria was the only man in Tenebra who had proved his loyalty so thoroughly he could speak bluntly to the king without ending up at the gallows. He was also the only man willing to speak the truth, whether it benefited him or not.

"Titus will tell you this," came Lord Hadrian's gravelly voice. "The free lords will sleep with their swords in one hand and charms of Anthros' fire in the other until we've brought the monsters here for another meeting and made right with them. And he'll be correct."

"How magnanimous of you to agree with me, Hadrian. Pray tell, what is the occasion?"

Lord Hadrian halted before the desk, short and strong beside Lord Titus's taller, elegant figure. But the graying warrior's presence commanded the room as surely as he commanded the king's armies. "War with something our swords are no use against would be an occasion indeed, Titus, and I hope you'll cease aiming yours at me, should such a battle come."

"I will always fight for the safety of Tenebra, wherever else I may take aim."

"Is that enough for you, My King?" Lord Hadrian asked. "Both sides of our feud are agreed. His ancestors and mine sent each other to their graves, but they'd all prefer to stay there rather than have Hesperines ravage their corpses. A second attempt at a truce with the heretics is the only way to clean up after the debacle that Cordian made of our Summit."

"Your Majesty." Lord Titus lowered his voice. "I know in your wisdom and perception, you heed the words spoken among the free lords. Fearful words."

"What my lords speak of are lies. If I knew who had planted such doubts among my liegemen, I would cut the tongue from his head myself."

Cassia smiled to herself again.

Lord Hadrian crossed his arms over his barrel chest. "Close the gate after the lambs have scattered if you wish, My King."

"But bring the sheep back into the fold," Lord Titus urged. "Your liegemen need their king's strong hand to protect their women, their children, their vassals. Only you can provide the security they seek, and if you do not, My King…you know what fear does to a man's mind. Loyal men may be driven to desperate acts."

"I have no use for men too cowardly to swallow their fears and do their duty."

"My King," Lord Titus pleaded, "men do not know their duty against things of the night we cannot see, much less kill. They wave their swords at phantoms."

"Warriors with no enemy to fight are dangerous," Lord Hadrian warned. "Especially frightened ones. They become restless and turn against each other—or their king."

"Twice in one day, Hadrian. Praise Anthros for your good fortune, for you will never again hear me say this. He speaks the truth, My King."

"I'll speak some more of it then, Titus, and see if you are equal to it. The new pack of liegehounds Free Lord Tyran has bred from the heart hunters' stock are not the only weapons he has readied these past months. The blades he's forged to wield against Hesperines will serve much better against his fellow men."

"Lord Tyran is loyal to my son," Lord Titus cut in, "which means he is loyal to Your Majesty. You know you can rely on any man under Segetia's banner. But there are those who rally around no one's banners—or seek to attract followers to their own. These lone wolves might well lure Your Majesty's flock into unsafe territory."

"Discontent is an opportunity," Lord Hadrian said. "Men are too glad to exchange an effective leader for any upstart who promises them petty gains."

"That would make them traitors," Lucis said.

"We do not speak of traitors," Lord Titus soothed. "Merely of fearful, dutiful men with many lives under their protection."

Lord Hadrian looked the king in the eye. "They are only traitors if the man they betray is still on the throne."

Silence fell.

The king gazed back at Lord Hadrian. "You recall what befell the last men who took that view."

Cassia clenched her hands into fists. She heard again in her mind the sound of the catapults that had heralded the last open rebellion any lords had ever mounted against the king. Lucis had slaughtered them and wiped their names from every free bloodline in Tenebra, reduced their keeps to rubble and sown their fields with salt. But not until he had let them murder Solia.

"I have gone to the effort and expense of hosting Cordian mages," the king went on, "the most effective defense against Hesperines. I have rewarded the two of you with the highest protection by placing masters from the Order of Anthros in your own houses. If such efforts are not enough for my people, they are craven and ungrateful."

"Those meddling bastards from the Orders are no reassurance to anyone." Lord Hadrian's answer was anything but craven. "They're more likely to incite war than prevent it."

Lord Titus cleared his throat. "We in Tenebra hold the Cordian masters in reverence, for the gods themselves appointed the blessed Orders as the rightful authority over all mages in the world. However, our people feel the need for spiritual leadership from their fellow countrymen who serve the gods as Tenebran mages, the Tenebran way."

"The Orders rule magic, but they ought to do it from Cordium," Lord Hadrian translated. "Our folk won't stand for them turning Tenebra into Cordium—or into the Orders' cow to be milked for temple tribute. The principalities and city-states of Cordium were powerful domains once, ruled by mighty men, before the mages broke the very lands that raised their temples. Take heed, My King. The lords of Tenebra won't kneel and be the mages' next victims."

"With all due respect, My King, Honored Master Dalos did not present a reassuring example for our people," Lord Titus reminded him.

The king leaned forward. "The late Honored Master Amachos, also known as Dalos, was a respected expert on the destruction of Hesperines, whom the Order of Anthros generously sent from Cordium to watch over us during the creatures' visit to Tenebra. The honored master kept his identity secret for our safety, for knowledge of his presence was sure to inflame tensions with the heretics. When the Hesperines' so-called ambassadors attempted, without provocation, to cast a malign spell over the entire Council of Free Lords and the royal family, the honored master sacrificed his own life to save us all."

Silence reigned again. Cassia gritted her teeth.

"There are plenty who don't believe that," Lord Hadrian informed the king. "He was a war mage. We know their kind. A great many folk say he only wanted at the Hesperines and didn't care who stood in his way."

"Or they say..." Lord Titus hesitated. "...there is some talk that Honored Master Dalos and his order would have found it convenient if our nobility was no longer an obstacle to Cordium's influence in Tenebra. These rumors persist. They have taken on far too much life to die now."

"I have given my people the truth. Those who deny it are not only traitors to the crown, but heretics in the eyes of the Orders."

"Then most of your subjects are traitors and heretics. What will you do?" Lord Hadrian asked. "Hang the greater part of the population and let the mages immolate the rest?"

"Enough," the king said.

The two lords said no more. But they had indeed said enough.

Cassia's words, her rumors, her truth—the real truth—had made it to the king's ears, and he had no choice but to react.

Tenebra was on the verge of rebellion. Precisely where Cassia must hold it.

The king rose to his full height behind the desk. "I have already decided upon a course of action, which I was just about to discuss with Titus when you joined us, Hadrian. Titus, you are the most persuasive man in the kingdom. You will lead the charge against these lies and ensure my people believe the truth. Begin tomorrow. You will have plenty of opportunities to speak with the kingdom's most influential figures at the Autumn Greeting, while you watch your son dance with my daughter."

No. Don't do this. Cassia wanted to shout at Lord Titus. *Don't do this to your people, your son, or me.*

But she already knew what he would say.

"As you wish, My King," Lord Titus answered.

"Excellent. What a fine picture our children will make at the Greeting on the morrow."

And so the king named his price, and Cassia knew what game was to commence.

"It's not enough," Lord Hadrian said. "Our people will find no reassurance in words, only in a renewal of our ancient truce with the Hesperines. Without the Oath, there will be war."

"Our Cordian allies will keep us safe from the Hesperines," Lucis stated. "There will be no Summit."

Cassia had heard that tone all her life, ordering her to all she feared, denying her everything she dared love. She knew what it meant. The king's decision was final.

Once she had felt pain each time he laid waste to her hopes. Then she had learned to feel nothing. That time was over. Gone were the days when she rendered herself numb for self-protection and in so doing rendered herself helpless.

She had remembered how to feel. She embraced all her dread and anger and fed it to her resolve.

She knew Lucis better than anyone. When one pushed him, he pushed back harder. When one pushed him too far, he lashed out with unparalleled ferocity.

The pressure from the free lords, together with the wedge between the king and the Cordian mages, was powerful enough to immobilize him. But not to make him give way.

Cassia had never had any illusions she could do more than stall him. Even as she had fought with everything she had these long months, she had considered what would eventually be necessary. She had, night by night, maneuver by maneuver, come to acknowledge it would take more to break any possibility of an alliance with Cordium once and for all and secure a lasting peace with Orthros.

She had known it would come to this. But oh, how she had hoped it would not.

There was no room for her sweeter hopes now. She must focus on what she must do for Tenebra. For Orthros.

His name, his face flashed in her mind. Her greatest grief. Yet still her greatest comfort.

You understand, Lio. You are the one who will understand better than anyone.

Cassia must take matters well and truly into her own hands. It was time for the last resort.

THE FLOWER OF CORDIUM

T HE KING'S SOLAR GREW brighter suddenly, as if midday had
come an hour before dawn. The glow faded just as quickly and
gave way once more to firelight, but the flames now illuminated
seven robed men who had not stood in the room an instant before.

Fresh anger rose in Cassia with the speed and power of reflex. She
didn't know what it signified that the new arrivals wore unadorned, flame-
red robes instead of the Order of Anthros's customary red-gold. But it was
clear enough these were the guests expected from Cordium.

The young mage hovered among them, licking his fingers and tucking his thin black hair under his apprentice cap. "Basileus, allow me
to present—"

"That will be all, Eudias," said the man in the lead.

The apprentice shut his mouth.

"Basileus." The mage in charge inclined his head, then withdrew his
hands from his sleeves, revealing long fingers, smooth palms, and a gleaming collection of rings. "I am sure you are as weary as I of go-betweens and
deliberations. Allow me to introduce myself and my brothers who have
come with me from Corona to resolve your troubles with the Hesperines."

Corona! That was the heart of Cordium, the seat of the Order of
Anthros, where their Akron lived and wielded his power as the head of
the Order that ruled all other Orders.

"By all means," said the king.

Cassia looked at the mage's face for the first time and assessed the facts.
By accepted standards he was the most handsome man currently under
the palace roof, and Flavian was in residence. Before morning, many ladies

of the court and no few men would be speculating as to how seriously the mage took his vows to give up the pleasures of the flesh in exchange for magical power.

He appeared athletic and in the prime of life, and even through her own flametongue, Cassia could smell the oil that scented his wavy black hair. He had golden skin and a golden voice and had probably been born to a Cordian princess with a golden spoon in his mouth. The Order must have handed him a position reserved for those of high birth whose families' wealth paid for the Akron's jeweled slippers. Had this man qualified because he was a perfectly bred example of Anthros's ideal of manhood, or did he have magic too?

With the air of a salute, the mage touched a hand to the sunstone medallion he wore. "I am Chrysanthos, Dexion of the Aithourian Circle. I am here to clean up my late colleague's mess."

If Cassia had been a mage, she would have feared her own power would defy her self-control and lash out at the opponent before her. As it was, her emotion was a force so strong her body shook.

The king studied his new reinforcements in silence, while Lord Titus spouted His Majesty's welcome and compliments. "What an honor! We have not had the privilege of welcoming the Dexion as a guest in Tenebra since…well, since the Last War, surely. How magnanimous of the Synthikos to send his right hand and future successor to us in our hour of need."

The Cordian Order of Anthros hadn't sent just anyone to repair the damage Dalos had done. They had sent the man who would one day lead the war mages' most deadly circle. Dalos's grand delusions had been bad enough, but this Chrysanthos could honestly say he was the living heir of his circle's founder, the legendary Aithouros, who in ancient times had personally burned every Temple of Hespera to the ground.

There was no question of whether Dexion Chrysanthos had Hesperine blood on his hands. Cassia could only wonder how many lives he had cost Orthros. Had any of the mage's victims been close to Lio?

If there had been any shred of doubt or hesitation in Cassia's mind, Chrysanthos's arrival was proof enough. The king and Cordium would not retreat. It was time for her to bring all she had cultivated for the last six months to fruition and make her long-term plan a reality.

There was no other way. She must go through with the last resort.

"You are correct, Lord Titus," Chrysanthos was saying. "The question of whom the Synthikos would select as his Dexion has gone unanswered for many years, at least publicly. However, he recently finalized my appointment as a mere formality. He has groomed me for this position since my youth, when I was his apprentice."

"Honored Master Dalos was once the Synthikos's apprentice," the king pointed out.

"There were two of us." Chrysanthos smiled. "Competition for promotions can be quite brutal."

Cassia added *ruthless* and *opportunistic* to her assessment of Chrysanthos. Facts. She must focus on facts. Dwelling on the full scope of the effort ahead of her…the consequences…was no strategy at all. The way to proceed was one task at a time, and the imperative at hand was to get to know her new enemy.

She wouldn't make the same mistake she had made with Dalos. She hadn't been curious enough about him. She hadn't understood what he really was until it was almost too late. Chrysanthos seemed to wear his status and his intentions as clearly as his sunstone pendant, but she knew better than to accept things as they appeared.

Chrysanthos proceeded to introduce his seven colleagues as his war circle and listed their qualifications. Cassia collected names and masteries into her memory. The youth with the earnest face and fire in his eyes was Chrysanthos's apprentice, Tychon. Aflame with devotion, the desire to prove himself, or a longing to best his master?

All of the mages certainly acted as if their chief pleasure in life was basking in their Dexion's glorious presence. All but Dalos's former apprentice. Eudias, they called him. He appeared ready to sink into the floor.

With apparent appreciation, Chrysanthos surveyed the arsenal that adorned the king's walls. "Eudias has informed me that my brothers and I are to fill positions on the noble estates of Ostium and Littora. Allow me to demonstrate we would be of much greater use to you here in your own household, Basileus. I wish to begin our new association with a show of good faith. A declaration of intent, if you will."

"What do you have in mind?" the king asked.

"On my way in tonight, I took the liberty of assessing the safety of Solorum. We must discuss improvements to the protections upon Tenebra's capital sooner rather than later. As a starting point, I must bring to your attention an ungodly site that has been allowed to remain on your doorstep, unattended and uncleansed."

No. No, he couldn't mean… It had stood for time out of mind. It was older than the Orders or Orthros, a memorial to a time when everyone could worship as they chose without fear. Mortals had forgotten its meaning, and no one but a Hesperine had the power to recognize it for what it was. This peacock from Cordium couldn't possibly have discovered that secret.

"The structure is a ruin," said the mage, "but alas, the unnatural magic in it lives on. There are even vines of harlot's kiss growing up through the rubble, in full bloom and armed with thorns."

Hespera's roses. Cassia and Lio's roses.

"There is a shrine of Hespera on your grounds, Basileus," Chrysanthos announced.

SILENT ROSES

CASSIA'S STOMACH turned.

Chrysanthos smiled. "Allow me to perform a proper purging. Dawn is imminent. My brothers and I shall channel the power of Anthros's rising sun and give you a demonstration of how truly competent Aithourian masters deal with heresy."

"As I said, my lords." The king glanced from Lord Titus to Lord Hadrian, then nodded to Chrysanthos. "Our allies from Cordium shall ensure no Hesperines blight Our lands. We shall accompany you to observe."

"Excellent, Basileus. I can see you and I are both men of action who do not like to waste time."

Cassia could plan what to do while she ran. She turned and bolted through the back of the hearth.

She didn't even feel the solid stone as she moved through it into the passageway beyond. She raced through the corridors within the walls of Tenebra's most ancient royal household with only the barest glow of the flametongue on her clothes to light her way. When she came to the princess's chambers, she crossed through the wall again.

Stumbling across the cold ashes in Solia's hearth, Cassia caught herself on a large, shaggy body. Her liegehound braced his legs and whined in concern.

"*Dockk*, Knight. We have to save—" Cassia's throat closed.

No breath for talking. No time for discretion. She must stay ahead of the mages. Knight launched into motion at her side, ready for anything, unquestioning as always. The pendant Solia had passed down to

Cassia bounced at her neck as she ran through her sister's deserted rooms. Kicking up clouds of dust in her wake, she threw open the door to their abandoned garden.

The trek through the weeds and ivy, down the passage under the walls of the palace, up through the hatch and out onto the grounds had never seemed so long. She took the deer paths Lio had shown her, but underbrush clutched at her skirt and mud robbed her of her footing. Cassia felt as if she were living one of her nightmares of fleeing for her life with her legs and arms bound.

Once again she found herself racing toward all that remained of someone she loved too late to stop the king's destruction.

At last white marble and black thorn thickets came into view. Cassia was dizzy from lack of breath, but she pushed herself through the shrine's crumbling doorway and into the antechamber.

Cool darkness and the fragrance of roses wrapped around her. Shattered tiles chimed against each other under her aching feet. She ducked beneath the fallen pillar that barred the inner door and fled into the Ritual Sanctuary. The sensation of Hespera's magic crept under her skin and whispered through her blood.

For the first time, she froze. The knowledge of what she could not do paralyzed her. Knight twined around her legs, silent and frantic. She stared at the pedestal that had once held a statue of Hespera and knew she had no magic that would protect this place. She had no strength in her limbs great enough to lift the stones. She had no time to transplant a single, precious rose from the soil.

Our roses, Lio.

But she had her seeds. A few of the roses, in anticipation of autumn, had finished flowering and begun to produce fruit—rose hips, legend called them, which carried precious seeds within. Cassia had collected them with the utmost care and hidden them among her stock of more mundane plants. She could, she *would* grow their roses again. Hespera's rare, sacred blooms would live on as long as Cassia did.

Cassia spun in a circle, taking one last, long look at the fanged, verdant rose vines with their blood red blooms, the fractured mosaic of the night sky on the floor, and the domed skylight that let in the moons when night fell. How many people had rested or rejoiced, prayed or celebrated here since the mages of Hespera had built the shrine?

She and Lio had been the last. She could think of no better way to honor this place than with what they had shared. Her blood. Their bodies. Honest words. Freedom.

The voices of men echoed through the woods.

They must not find her here.

Cassia darted back through the antechamber, but once outside the shrine, she halted. She could not bear to turn her back on this place carrying nothing more than her memories. There must be something more she could salvage from the ruins.

Perhaps there was one stone she had the strength to move, if she acted quickly.

She paused to clutch a hand to the capstone of the arch over the front doorway. The faded engraving of Hespera's glyph was still stained with Lio's blood and her own, which had brought the roses back to life. She dug her fingers into the grooves around the glyph stone.

Through the linen of her glove, she felt the ancient mortar crunch. She gasped a breath and dug harder. She felt the stone shift ever so slightly under her hand.

Yanking off her gloves, she drew her gardening spade from her belt pouch and began to dig.

She dug and carved with her tool and her hands until her fingers bled. The sight of the red smears on the stone encouraged her. Blood was power. She had the power to do this.

She put away her spade so she could get better purchase with her fingers. The mortar and blood turned to a paste that lodged under her nails and plastered her hands to the stone. With a groan of effort, she took hold of the stone and heaved.

In a rush of blood, the glyph stone slid out into her hands. A sigh or a sob escaped her as she clutched the relic to her, balancing its weight. Through the linen and slick of blood, she felt a pulse.

The throb of magic. The power in the shrine wouldn't die, not today. She was carrying a part of it.

Bits of stone and mortar fluttered to the ground at her feet, and then the top of the arch crumbled. Dawn cast golden light on the collapsing doorway. Knight pushed his weight against Cassia's legs in warning, urging her to move. Over the crack of the scattering stones, she heard the men's voices again. Closer. She could make out Chrysanthos's and the king's.

She fled with the glyph stone cradled to her breast. She was out of the thorns and on the other side of a massive ash tree when the voices clarified into words she understood, but did not really hear. If she ran any further now, the noise of her movements would give her away in return.

She dropped to the ground at the foot of the tree and wedged herself between its roots. Knight flattened himself in the underbrush with his bulk between her and the rest of the world. She focused on quieting her breathing. She could only hope the odors of flametongue and liegehound, which could fill a room, would not carry far in open air amid other forest scents.

Although Cassia was hidden by the forest and Knight, she felt exposed. She had never felt so fragile, so vulnerable. If the glyph stone led Chrysanthos to her, that would be the end. He would find her with evidence of heresy in her lap, which would lead to the truth of her treason.

She curled herself into a tight ball around the stone, tallying all the magic she and Knight were carrying between them. Her gardening spade, warded against rust by the Kyrian mages. The enchanted bath they gave Knight for fleas. He still bore whatever lost magical arts the original breeders of liegehounds had used on his ancestors to make them immune to Hesperine magic. Solia's wooden pendant, carved in the shape of a triqeutra of ivy, held Lustra magic as ancient as trees and soil. Cassia could only hope all this would be enough to obscure the aura that must surely emanate from the glyph stone, which any Aithourian war mage was trained to detect.

"Look at this!" One of the mages. "Blood."

"Fresh blood." Another mage. "Someone was just here."

"Hesperines?" Lord Titus demanded. "On the grounds of Solorum?"

"Fear not," the Dexion answered. "A mortal did this."

"You're here to destroy it, and you're worried about a little vandalism?" Lord Hadrian sounded impatient.

"This was no act of vandalism," Chrysanthos said. "Who would spill her own blood to remove the glyph stone moments before our arrival? Only someone who recognizes, but does not fear its power."

"Her?" Lord Titus echoed.

"Small hands. See the prints in the blood? No common hedge witch would have the boldness to salvage a relic of the dark goddess and risk toying with such dangerous magic. This was the work of a Hesperite, and she can't have run far."

Chrysanthos launched into the Divine Tongue. Cassia could not understand the orders he gave his fellow mages, but half a dozen robes began soughing through the underbrush. Two swords whished out of their scabbards.

"No need, my lords," said the Dexion. "There is little purpose in beating the bushes with steel when dealing with a Hesperite sorceress. Mortal heretics who worship Hespera practice the vile arts of blood sorcery, and their females are especially sly. Our revelatory spells will be of greater use than swords."

Cassia's heart pounded so hard she felt light-headed. She listened to the mages spread out in a search pattern. They began at the shrine and moved outward through the thicket. It would not be long before they reached the ash trees.

"Who would have known we were coming?" Tychon asked.

"All of Solorum," Lord Titus answered. "Everyone in the capital has eagerly anticipated your arrival."

"They anticipated aromagi who would bless the harvest," Chrysanthos said. "No one expected the Akron to send members of our circle. Our discovery of the shrine must have alerted the sorceress to our presence and our power. It has caught her by surprise that we are war mages. Her removal of the glyph stone was a hasty act that speaks of fear, desperation—and fanaticism."

Oh, so Cassia was a fanatic, was she? Was that what Chrysanthos called someone who thought children shouldn't be executed for heresy? Someone who believed the Hesperines' deeds of kindness for the people of Tenebra should not be rewarded with persecution?

"Did you know there was a heretic in your capital, Basileus?" Chrysanthos asked.

"There won't be for long," said the king.

"No," Chrysanthos agreed. "We will see to that."

The mages' fine shoes trod closer between the fern fronds and thorn bushes. Cassia heard fabric rip and an angry outburst in the Divine Tongue. But still the footsteps drew nearer.

Knight's whole body tensed to spring. She dug her hands into his fur, willing him to be silent and still. She could feel his muscles twitch under her fingers. Everything in him told him to charge out and face the threat, to rend to shreds those who endangered her. His mistress's command told him to lie on his belly and wait for death.

She was so sorry. Just as she had gone to the Summit with Knight at her side knowing Dalos planned to assassinate them all, she now led her trusting protector toward certain demise yet again.

This time, there were no Hesperines to save them.

Cassia didn't know any spells or prayers. All she knew to do was rely on herself and keep trying.

She could not let this be the moment when all she had worked for came to naught. What did it matter if she saved the glyph stone and lost Orthros?

There must be something she could do. She wracked her thoughts as her heartbeat made her whole body rock around the stone. She ran her bleeding hands over the glyph, feeding it the only resource at her disposal that she knew was effective. She had ample fuel for blood magic. Useless, when she was no blood mage, nor any sort of mage at all. She had never even heard Lio recite a spell. He had simply pricked his finger and, in a silent act of Will, conjured a lovely bauble of light or a veil spell powerful enough to hide her from a war mage.

Cassia had blood and Will.

Could the glyph stone provide the magic she lacked?

Lio had told her of the Great Temple Epoch, when his goddess's sacred sites had offered Sanctuary to all, from the lowliest criminal to the mightiest king. The mortal mages of Hespera who had built those refuges were long gone.

Did their spells live on in the stone? Could Lio have left a little of his magic behind as well?

Would awakening their power only serve to draw the war mages' attention?

If Cassia did nothing, they were sure to find her. Better to act on the one chance she had of protecting herself from them.

And if she was to face the Order's judgment, she would do so fighting.

Wrapping herself more tightly around the stone, Cassia rubbed her blood into the shallow grooves of the glyph. She mustered all the determination she had brought to bear on the free lords, all the courage she pitted against the king and the Cordian mages, and every promise she had made to herself, Lio, and all those under her protection. Everything that had determined Tenebra's course in the last six months, she focused on the artifact in her arms, while she imagined herself wrapped in the safety of a Hesperine veil.

A soft sensation eased the tension in Cassia's body and cooled the sweat on her skin. Knight's fur stood on end, and he trembled.

The smell of roses filled the air an instant before darkness wrapped around Cassia.

It was all she could do not to gasp. She had seen that darkness before, felt it all around her as a little child of seven. It had hidden her from two armies while a Hesperine errant held her close and told her she was brave.

From beyond the deep, pure shadow that enfolded her, the smell of Dexion Chrysanthos's hair oil washed over her.

In its wake came a blast of magic.

She was aware of the probing heat of his spell, the way she might hear a storm raging outside the shelter of the shrine. The hairs on the back of her arms didn't even stand up.

The heat faded. The robes swished away.

Cassia let out a breath. He didn't turn back toward the sound. He couldn't hear her. Hadn't even seen the shadow wrapped around her.

It seemed Hespera's sanctuaries still turned no one away, regardless of their creed, status, or deeds. Not even dogs bred to hunt her people.

Cassia held fast to the power she sensed in and around her. Her fingers stuck to the stone where her blood dried, and her limbs ached. But she huddled as still as she could inside the darkness, and Knight, true to his purpose, waited with her.

After what seemed like an hour, Eudias's voice carried from the direction of the shrine. He delivered a breathless report. "Dexion, Basileus. There's no one here."

"We found no one," one of the war mages corrected.

"Has she escaped?" Lord Titus asked. "Or perhaps concealed herself in some way?"

"Both are distinct possibilities," Chrysanthos said. "She is no hapless, superstitious peasant. She is someone with power. How very interesting. It seems my brothers and I will get to enjoy a little challenge."

For once, Lord Titus did not sound composed. "Will you be able to find her before today's festival? We cannot have her at large during the Autumn Greeting. A female under Hespera's influence is a dangerous abomination! We must not give her a chance to seduce others and spread destruction."

"With us in attendance," the Dexion replied, "everyone at the sacred festival will be perfectly safe. Besides, she will most likely return to her lair now that the sun is higher in the sky. Come nightfall, we shall see the chase through."

"Are we to continue with the purging of the shrine, Dexion?" asked his apprentice.

"Certainly. This will be the best blow we could strike against her and her goddess. One that is long overdue." Chrysanthos's robes rustled. "Well, well, Hespera. It has been some time since we last saw each other. There is something I've been wanting to say."

There came a roar in the air. Fire.

When Cassia heard the first impact of the magic against the stone, her whole body flinched. It sounded so much like catapults.

She listened to the mages level the shrine as if it had never been there. Like the roses, she could not scream.

AUTUMN EQUINOX

TENEBRA

A lady always dresses correctly.

—Solia's instructions to Cassia

CASSIA'S GAUNTLET

WHEN UTTER SILENCE MADE her certain the men were gone, Cassia dared move. As soon as she stirred, Knight leapt out of the underbrush in a challenge stance and scented the air. She untangled herself and struggled out of her hiding place, holding the glyph stone close.

The chill, dark embrace of magic slid away from her, and sun glared in her eyes. The odors of smoke and ash threatened to choke her. But she went deeper into them, rounding the tree to return to the site of the shrine.

She knew what she would see, but nothing could have prepared her to confront what the mages had done. She stood numb and wordless before the charred swath that had once been the shrine and a garden of thorns and roses. In the center of the burned-out area glowed a glyph of Anthros, branded on the ground in embers and spell light.

Cassia's awareness of time passing threatened to shatter her moment of silence. Day had come. The Autumn Greeting drew near. She must go.

She must put the last resort into motion.

She and Knight retreated across the grounds, a procession of two with only the birds for mourners, and bore the glyph stone away from where it had rested for a millennium and a half or more.

Cassia knew of only one place steeped in magic that old, where the aura of past spells might be powerful enough to hide an artifact of Hespera from a band of war mages. Solorum Palace had stood since the Mage King's time, when the Hesperines had left Tenebra to found Orthros. But his wife, the Changing Queen, had possessed power that was older still. Lustra magic, which the Orders had never understood or controlled.

Everyone knew their line had died out long ago, but their power lived on in all they had built. It was the Changing Queen's sort of power that imbued the ivy symbol and made the walls of the king's stronghold porous to the women of the royal house. It would always be a mystery to Cassia how the pendant and its secrets had come down to Princess Solia, but she would never cease to be grateful that it worked for bastard daughters as well.

In the passage behind her sister's hearth, gentle red light emanated around Cassia, the glow of flametongue through the bloodstains on her clothes. By that light, she laid the glyph stone on the dusty floor. She had no place of honor to keep it, but it would be safe here, and she had made her libation of blood.

She had done all she could. For now.

She stripped off the treated garments and dropped each in turn in front of the stone, until she stood before it in nothing but the pendant and her own skin. She let fall her last glove.

She did not weep. She made a new promise. "I will deliver you safely into Hesperine hands. But first, I will bring this kingdom to its knees."

NOT SO FRAGILE

IN A DIFFERENT WING of the palace, Cassia emerged from the wall and pushed aside a tapestry to step out into her own bedchamber. She shielded her eyes from the morning sun that poured through the open shutters of the large window.

She had yet to chart the full extent of the maze the ivy pendant had opened to her, but the passages she had already discovered gave her an astonishing advantage, not least when she needed to get back inside her room without the king knowing she had ever left it.

Perita was another matter.

That pounding was not Cassia's throbbing headache. It was Perita's hand on the door. Knight put his ears back and eyed the panel as it shuddered on its hinges.

"There's no time for washing, my lady!" came Perita's customary, frantic admonition.

Cassia looked down at herself. As always, she had put her own clothing back on before leaving the passageways. For all the good that did her. Perita had seen her wear this tunica to bed clean last night. Now it was wrinkled and begrimed with dust and hardly disguised the bloodstains smeared all over Cassia's chest. Although her hands had stopped bleeding, they needed a healer's attention.

She stared at her dry blood and torn skin. Chrysanthos must never, ever get a look at her hands.

Now she would pay for throwing her usual caution to the winds. She hurried to stow the ivy pendant in her gardening satchel on the table beside her bed, planning to don the talisman again after her companion had dressed her. Perita knew nothing about Solia's secret, and if she knew her lady went on forbidden excursions, she officially didn't know anything about that, either. How was Cassia to explain doing herself such an injury when resting alone behind the closed door of her bedchamber?

"My lady?" All the force had gone out of Perita's voice. She sounded more worried than she had in months.

Cassia was loath to put their hard-won friendship to the test. But perhaps the hour had come when the best way to keep trust was to show trust.

Cassia had helped Perita save the man she loved from execution, then given him a position so the two young lovers could wed. Thanks to Perita's insight and persuasion, he had given Cassia the crucial information she needed to stop Dalos from assassinating everyone at the Summit. Perita and Callen would never know it, but they had saved Cassia's lover in return.

Bonds like these were not so fragile. Cassia must be brave and let them take her weight.

She cleared her throat. "Would you be so kind as to open the door for me, Perita?"

As the door groaned and swung open, Perita peered in. She already wore her festival gown, which matched her blue eyes. Her light brown hair fell in shiny, perfectly-dressed waves from beneath her finest linen kerchief, where she proudly displayed the woven headband of a married woman.

Behind her stood Callen in a leather breastplate and ceremonial gold tabard. Perita's husband looked ready to escort them to the Greeting or perhaps break down Cassia's door. With his broad shoulders and lifetime of battle training, the sandy-haired warrior was equal to the task despite a bad leg that would never fully recover from his time in prison.

Perita didn't rush in and begin fussing, as was her way. Her gaze darted from the smear of dried blood on Cassia's collarbone and fixed on her hands. "My lady. What have you been doing?"

"I care for you too much to tell you. When the king asks, you must be able to say honestly that you do not know."

Perita came and put her arms around Cassia.

Cassia stood frozen for an instant in surprise. It had been a long time since anyone had embraced her, and that had been seldom enough.

Dangling her hands away from Perita's gown, Cassia held her friend. She let her forehead rest on Perita's shoulder.

In a moment, Perita drew back and patted Cassia's shoulders. "Whatever it is, don't you worry about it a moment longer, my lady. I'll set you to rights. This is the first time His Majesty has ever let you go to the Greeting dance, and I won't have anything ruin this day for you."

This day was broken beyond repair, but Perita's desire to mend it made Cassia feel as if she would make it till sundown.

"What would I do without you?" Cassia asked.

Perita ducked her head, but with an unabashed smile.

Callen waited a pace outside the bedchamber. "We're glad to see you up and about, my lady. We were that worried when you didn't answer the door."

"I'm grateful for your concern, Callen," Cassia thanked her bodyguard.

Perita took Cassia's hands gently in hers, clicking her tongue in sympathy. "Your mage friends from the Temple of Kyria ought to see to these, my lady, if not the king's healer."

"Shall I send a messenger for a healer, my lady?" asked Callen.

"Whatever for? I have not injured my hands. Just as the late royal mage was a Tenebran named Amachos from the Temple of Anthros at Namenti."

"Right you are, my lady." Callen gave a short bow.

Perita nodded. "Your hands have never been better."

Relief made Cassia want to sit down. "I shall wear gloves constantly for the foreseeable future only because the weather is turning cold, and this wing of the palace is drafty. In fact, if one of the king's messengers happens to stop by in the next hour, we must make sure he finds no reason to be interested in my gloves."

"Of course," said Perita. "In the meantime, let's see what we can do with your medicinal herbs and Grandmother's methods."

"You've taken your tincture this morning, haven't you?" Cassia asked her. "I don't want you to get sick from coming in here where Knight's fur is everywhere."

"I haven't missed a dose. That new tonic from the Kyrian healers works wonders, and I don't even feel sleepy. Look at me just a pace away from Sir Knight without any rashes or coughing." She eyed the dog. "Not that you're to get any ideas. Save your kisses for your lady and go to her for all your ear rubbing."

"Do put on your apron. I don't want you to ruin your dress. You look lovely." Cassia smiled, happy for her friend's good fortune in beauty and love.

"That she does, my lady." Callen grinned like the besotted newlywed he was, but then his smile faltered. He shifted on his feet the way he did when he was leaning his weight on his good leg and trying not to show it.

"Do not regret you cannot dance with her today," Cassia said. "Any man can dance with his wife, but which of them can say he has defended her as bravely as you have protected our Perita? You earned your right to stand still with her at your side, Callen."

His only answer was a bow, but Cassia saw how his tension eased. Perita gave Callen a smile that promised they would have a private dance later.

She ushered Cassia out into the hearth room and sat her down by the fire. "I'll get some clean rags from the dressing room."

"Why don't I heat the water?" Callen offered.

"See there," Cassia said. "I am perfectly all right, for I am in such good hands."

PROMISED

Y THE TIME THE king's messenger arrived, Cassia was clean, dressed, and warm by the fire, with her softest wool gloves to conceal the bandages on her hands. She showed the messenger an expression of unflinching courtesy.

"His Majesty requires your presence in his solar, Lady Cassia."

"I shall attend him right away," she replied.

As soon as he was gone, Cassia turned down Perita and Callen's concerned offers to accompany her and left her rooms with Knight. This path to meet the king was hers to walk and hers alone. Every step reminded her of the fear of him that had once ruled her life and why she no longer allowed that fear to have power over her.

As she made her way to the solar, this time through the visible portions of the palace, she remained alert to the man who tailed her. He was a runner, swift and observant, one of two she had grown accustomed to seeing every time she stepped out the door of her rooms. She had taken to wearing the ivy pendant beneath her clothes at all times so surreptitious detours were always available to her. Without the hidden passages to help her avoid the men the king assigned to follow her, she would have been in trouble.

An uncompromising voice inside her reminded her she could not afford to be anything other than honest with herself. She must always admit the truth before it proved her undoing.

The truth was, if the king thought she needed to be watched, she was already in trouble.

It had taken weeks after the events of the Summit for the king to loosen his stranglehold on Cassia's activities. For her safety, he'd said, of course. He had moved her to new chambers conducive to her growing household, her new suitor, and house arrest.

While she kept her vigil unseen in his hearth, she had publicly resumed her old act. The expressionless, obedient spare daughter with no real interest in anything beyond the meals, the clothes, and the four walls he allotted her.

At last the constant guard had lifted, and she had been permitted to resume her usual occupations. Visits with Lady Hadrian, exercising Knight on the grounds, taking her potted plants out for a sun. Although certainly not her erstwhile visits to the Temple of Kyria.

That the king's scouts now dogged her heels instead of guards was proof enough. He had freed her to discover what she would do with that freedom. To put her act to the test.

He was watching her, just waiting for her to make a mistake. The day that happened would be the day she joined her sister.

She must not let that happen. She must live long enough to see her plan through.

She did not quiver, break a sweat, or clench her hands when she walked through the door into the solar and found herself alone with the king. She swept Lucis a deep curtsy, lowering herself before him. But not to her knees.

That was her promise to herself. Beneath the concealment of her skirts, her knees would never touch the floor in that man's presence. Every time she rose to her feet, she silently dared him to call her what she was. A traitor.

The king announced, "Today Lord Flavian will ask you to dance the Autumn Greeting with him."

"Yes, he will, Your Majesty."

The king's eyes narrowed. "He made his intentions known to you?"

"No, Your Majesty. They were apparent."

"Do not flatter yourself. See to it his courtship does not give you an exaggerated perception of his regard for you. Be grateful for the notice of a lord so far above you and do not forget. He has no interest in you. Only in what you are to me."

She kept her head bowed, watching the king from beneath her lashes. "I assure you I appreciate the true motivations for his attentions, Your Majesty."

"Prepare yourself. It will require constant attention on your part to keep him and a lifetime of effort for you to come close to being worthy of him."

Strategy. She must stand back and envision her long-term strategy. Not become mired in the moments…so many moments she must spend wearing a smile for Flavian. "I shall be most diligent in my efforts, Your Majesty."

"Do not shame me at the Greeting dance today. No such opportunity will ever be within your reach again."

"I understand what this means, Your Majesty."

"Do you?"

She met the king's gaze. Did he?

"I take it you wish me to accept him, Majesty."

"No."

Cassia raised a brow.

"How has it entered your head that you are to accept anything?" the king said quietly. "You were promised to Flavian at dawn when I spoke with his father. You will dance with him."

"Yes I will, Your Majesty."

"I do not need to spell out for you what an unprecedented condescension it is for the king to allow a female of your status to play the role of Kyria in Tenebra's most sacred festival. Your relation to me and your honorable partner will ensure your presence in the ritual is not a total insult to tradition. You will never be a real lady, but I expect you to behave like one."

"I know how to be a lady, Your Majesty."

He gestured two fingers at Knight. "Your liegehound will be in the way. He will spend the duration of the ritual in the royal kennels."

At first she thought she had misheard the sudden declaration. "I beg your pardon, Your Majesty?"

"Do not make me repeat myself. You can hardly perform the Greeting with a large dog underfoot."

Cassia always picked her battles with the king with the utmost care. She did not even think before choosing this one. "His behavior is exemplary,

Your Majesty. He will be in no one's way if I instruct him to remain in a sit-stay on the edge of the gathering."

"The attendees must already tolerate a bastard in the procession. I will not have an unsightly dog take part as well."

"You provided him to me for my safety. There are many risks in a crowd, and Callen will not be able to remain near me. Would you have me do without Knight as a bodyguard?"

"My visitors today are war mages from Cordium. There is no better protection. If you ask me to explain my decision again, the only bodyguard you will have will be one of my guards at your door."

Those very guards opened the door of the king's solar to let in the kennel master. Cassia whipped her head around and looked at him. The man who had first put Knight in her arms as a pup did not even meet her gaze. He shuffled to Knight's side with a harness and a leash.

Knight would never consent to imprisonment in the kennels, except at Cassia's command. And yet the king would see to it his command was obeyed, one way or the other.

The outrage she cultivated every time she stood in this room now gave back to her, nursing her resolve in return. Whatever happened today, she must make sure Knight was not caught in the magefire between her and the king. She would not allow Knight to suffer. She could not lose him.

Even if it meant violating their bond, which cleaved him to her till death. All he knew was protecting her. He wouldn't understand. She had no way to explain she was trying to protect him.

She unclenched her teeth so she could speak. "Very well, Your Majesty. I will go with the kennel master and see Knight settled for the day."

Whatever the king had in store for her today, she would have to face it alone.

FIT FOR A QUEEN

ASSIA WOULD NEVER FORGET what she beheld in Knight's eyes as she departed the kennels. All the way back through the palace, the image of him watching her leave haunted her. From behind the locked gate of his run, he had looked at her with bewilderment.

She had hoped the one night her hound had spent apart from her before would prepare him for this. She had been wrong. That night, he had watched her leave his side under Lio's protection. Today, Knight had watched her abandon him.

Cassia came to a standstill in her hearth room and fought down the quivering mix of emotion inside her. Where was everyone? Callen must have gone next door to his and Perita's rooms, which served as newlywed nest, guardroom, and servants' quarters for Cassia's tiny household. She ventured through her bedroom to her dressing room to find Perita.

Cassia balked in the doorway and waited to see if she was going to be sick.

Perita and the royal seamstress hovered over the largest clothing chest that had ever crossed Cassia's threshold. They had brushes, ribbons, and worst of all, bottles of scent oils at the ready.

"My lady," Perita cooed. "Look what His Majesty has sent for you! An entire chest of gowns, and see how fine!"

"Oh, aye," said the seamstress with a cackle of laughter. "He's had me mending and trimming for weeks. I've taken in every scrap in this chest to fit you, Lady Cassia. It was that hard for me not to let on."

Cassia stalled. "Mistress Riga. How lovely to see you again. How is your son?"

A smile transformed the old woman's haggard face. She always lit up when she had the chance to speak openly of her son born out of wedlock, knowing Cassia and Perita would not censure her. "How kind of you to ask, my lady. I'm fair bursting with pride. He's doing right well in the position you got him in Lord Hadrian's household. He says he won't be surprised if he's not a house messenger much longer, but a rider carrying battle orders between his lordship's forces."

"Please offer my congratulations to him."

"Thank you very much indeed, my lady. I can't tell you how grateful we are for all you've done."

"It was the least I could do. Folk like us have to look out for each other, after all."

The seamstress gave a speaking nod. "If there's anything I can do for you, you have but to ask."

"Well, I can't resist asking, how is my red dress coming along?"

"I'll finish it for you yet, my lady, and make no mistake. I had to put it off to ready your festival gowns, king's orders, but now I can give it my full attention."

"I can hardly wait to see it. I know it will be a masterpiece."

Cassia fished for anything else to say, but her stock of honesties and even niceties was running out. Perita was taking her arm and ushering her into the dressing room.

It was time.

Time for Cassia to sit helpless on a dressing stool and be bound and gagged for her presentation to Anthros.

"My lady?" Perita asked. "Are you feeling well?"

Cassia swallowed hard. "I'm trying to."

For an instant, Perita's gaze darted to Cassia's gloved hands, then she pressed a hand to Cassia's forehead. "What could be the matter?"

The seamstress pursed her lips, studying Cassia. "I dare say she's thinking of her sister."

"Oh, my lady. I didn't think. I'm so sorry."

The seamstress's gaze softened. "Aye, you would have been too young to remember, Perita. But I remember like it was yesterday. Not an Autumn Greeting comes and goes that we don't think of Her Highness and how this day brought her to grief. But see here, Lady Cassia, you mustn't let that sadness spoil your happiness."

"My lady..." With a hopeful smile, Perita cast the chest a significant look. "Am I right in thinking you have a very particular reason to be happy today? Isn't that what this means—the king's summons and the new gowns? Someone's going to ask for your hand in the dance today, isn't he?"

"Yes," Cassia said.

Perita beamed. "And your father said yes?"

Cassia nodded.

"Oh, my lady!" Perita embraced her again, all but bouncing on her heels.

The seamstress chuckled. "That's reason enough for Lady Cassia to look as if she swallowed my pincushion. It's only natural to suffer a case of Greeting nerves. Well, well, by the time we've worked our magic on you, dove, you'll feel so confident in yourself you'll sail into the dance like a swan."

With a flourish, the seamstress threw back the lid of the chest. She drew out the first dress with loving fingers. At the sight of ivory velvet and cobalt embroidery, Cassia's mind went blank. As the seamstress held up a diamond-patterned gown of sapphire and sky blue, Cassia's numbness gave way to a sweat.

One by one, the seamstress unfolded the gowns and laid them all out until the dressing room was covered in them. White lace here and yellow ribbons there and a violet sleeve that had once been part of a skirt Cassia had clung to.

The fragments of Solia's entire wardrobe surrounded Cassia.

The seamstress smoothed an embroidered belt. "You're to wear a queen's finery today, my lady. All this belonged to Prince Caelum's late mother."

"Before that, this belonged to our future queen," said Cassia.

"Aye. It was I who made them for Her Highness, then unmade them and worked them into new gowns for Her Majesty," the seamstress replied. "It was I too who filled your sister's orders for all your childhood gowns. She saw to it you had everything a young lady ought. Just think how happy she'd be to see you finally getting to enjoy such luxury again."

"She would have given me the gown off her back," Cassia said.

The seamstress nodded in approval. "Just so, my lady."

Cassia walked from one garment to the next, putting the pieces back together in her mind until she could once more envision her sister in each of the gowns. Her belly was in her throat. She wasn't sure if she was going to vomit or faint. But she kept looking, until she found the one she sought.

It was hiding beneath a blue surcoat, but when she pulled that outer layer aside, she found it remarkably unchanged, aside from a new trim of satin piping. The velvet and embroidery in every shade of sunlight had not lost their sheen. Cassia lifted the fabric to her nose. She could no longer smell the oils her sister had worn that day, except in her memory.

Cassia had spent the last fifteen years trying not to relive the day her sister had donned this gown to dance with Lord Bellator at the Autumn Greeting. It was in this dress that Solia had taken the hand of the man who would murder her.

While the king who would allow that murder looked on. The king who claimed he had tried to save their beloved princess and made a show of mourning for her every year.

Cassia could now stand before the king without being crippled by her fear. She could do this too. She could find the strength to dance in this dress.

She wore Solia's flametongue garments as armor in her war against the king, carrying on the cause for which her sister had sacrificed her life, making that cause her own.

Today, to the Autumn Greeting, she would wear her sister's funerary gown.

One might think the king only wished to spare his coffers by tossing Cassia a handout of old gowns. Cassia knew better. Like her, the king wasted nothing. He made no move without purpose.

He was reminding her. Perhaps warning her. Or meting out his verdict.

Let this be her reply: she knew the truth. She would never forget.

Like everything else the king dealt her, Cassia would take this dress and turn it against him.

"This one." Cassia held up the golden gown for the seamstress. "It must be this one."

IN THE FOOTSTEPS OF THE GODDESS

THE SCENT OILS WERE the most difficult for Cassia to endure.
She held her breath as Perita did the honors, the same ritual
of anointing that Cassia had once watched Solia's handmaiden
Lady Iris perform for their princess. Cassia could see their golden heads
and ivory faces in her mind's eye. She tried to focus on the present instead,
but seeing her own brown hair and freckled olive skin gleam with those
oils horrified her more than her memories.

It was just like last winter, Cassia told herself. When she'd had to, she
had covered her skin in the scent oils she hated in order to slide through
a murder hole and get to Lio inside the impregnable walls of Solorum
Fortress. Just as she had then, she was preparing for a siege.

The greatest siege she would ever undertake in her life to breach a
much more monumental goal. But just like last time, her reward would
be to save the Hesperines.

To see Lio.

Anything was worth that. Even enduring the ordeal that loomed ahead
of her. Somehow she would find a way to get through it.

"I'm afraid I can't do that, my lord."

The sound of Callen's voice made Cassia jump. She, Perita, and the
seamstress looked toward the open door.

They couldn't see Callen, but they had no trouble hearing him. His
tone was as friendly as a bucket of waste water. "If you ask again, I'll have
to come down and request that you leave."

Perita frowned. "It sounds like he's shouting out our window. I'll go
see what's amiss, my lady."

The seamstress wove the last blue ribbon into Cassia's hair while the two of them waited. Cassia resisted the urge to check the security of her golden velvet gloves. Perita had deftly switched them with the woolen ones while the seamstress was busy making a quick alteration to the gown's hem.

"My lord!" Perita exclaimed from somewhere near Cassia's bedroom window. "Anthros isn't supposed to meet Kyria until it's time for summer to turn into fall! It ruins the harvest and brings bad weather."

A pleasant tenor voice called from below. "Indeed, separation before the promise dance is a treasured Tenebran tradition. Almost as treasured as men sneaking off to see their ladies in spite of it. My, but that glower is worthy of the occasion, Perita. Now tell your lady I have come to see her."

"I'll do no such thing, my lord."

"I can see you are ready for the festival," came the reply. "I'd tell you how fair you look, but then Callen would certainly come down here and ask me not-so-nicely to leave. I can only conclude your lady is already dressed as well. I shall leave a broken-hearted man if I do not get a glimpse of her."

Flavian was here. It was time for Cassia to brave the murder hole.

Cassia went to stand behind her companion, just out of sight of the window. "Thank you, Perita. I'll take care of this. Why don't you go call Callen off?"

Perita made a show of tossing up her hands at the interloper below. As she turned from the window and moved to make way for Cassia, she grinned and winked.

Cassia took a deep breath and stepped up to the windowsill.

In the small courtyard below stood Flavian, idling at the base of the ivy that covered the walls as if he might scale the vines and storm her keep. He wore his riding leathers and a russet half-cape slung over his broad shoulders. Tall boots invited everyone to admire his long legs. Close-fitting breeches flaunted the muscles he developed in the saddle. An armored jerkin and vambraces announced his fitness for battle.

He must have just returned from one of his frequent errands for the king. His chestnut hair was windblown, and yesterday's growth of beard adorned his strong jaw. The glint of sunlight on his spurs and sword marked him for an aristocrat. The smear of dirt across one chiseled cheekbone made him look like a rogue. Tenebra's favorite charmer of damsels was in top form today.

"At last the goddess bestows her generosity on her poor supplicant." Flavian stared at Cassia. "Kyria's wreath, but you do look divine."

"Nonsense. Yellow is my worst color."

"You make any color lovely." He took a deep breath, closing his eyes. "But I am disappointed. I cannot smell you from here. Everyone says the sacred scents of autumn that Kyria wears for Anthros have a magical affect no man can resist. I cannot wait to discover if that is true."

"You must make do with whatever whiff reaches you, for you may not come up, and I shall not come down."

"Far be it from me to gainsay the goddess. I shall have to wait to discover what spell she shall work upon me."

"She is unlikely to work any magic on you at all in that attire, my lord. Do you intend to appear before her dressed for the road?"

He gave her his famous grin, which made dimples appear beneath his stubble. "I shall appear before her in whatever attire she wishes."

"Well, we ladies have devoted the entire morning to our wardrobe in the hopes of catching Anthros's eye. On behalf of womankind, I am sure the goddess would have me insist you exert equal effort."

"Only one lady catches Anthros's eye on this day, and that is Kyria herself." Flavian propped his boot on a planter and braced an arm on his knee, leaning closer. "Am I to take your command as a sign you speak for the goddess today, Lady Cassia?"

"Am I to take your question to mean you act for Anthros?"

He reached under his cape and pulled out a floral wreath of red-gold Anthros's fire. With a single dexterous motion, he tossed it up to her. Cassia's stiff hands fumbled, but she caught the ring of blossoms.

"My Lady of Ice," said Flavian, using his favorite nickname for her. "Will you be my Queen of Fire this day?"

The most eligible lord in the king's court, the most coveted lover in all of Tenebra, was at Cassia's feet.

She stood holding his wreath of Anthros's fire and tried not to moan at the pain in her hands, which had worked and bled to nurture roses.

She saw Lio's earnest face before her and heard his sorcerous voice.

Hespera was once known to all as the goddess of Sanctuary and Mercy. People saw darkness as her gift of protection and blood rituals as a reminder that we must all make sacrifices for the good of others.

Cassia donned the mask she had labored to create for the last six months. Each time she crafted it in flawless detail on her face to make it as convincing as a solemn vow and as unwavering as the stone beneath her feet.

At first she had endeavored only to make it pleasant and believable. Over time, however, she had seen that it had far-reaching and unintended impact on Flavian and indeed other men who beheld it. Never one to waste a tool, Cassia had learned to wield the unexpected power of that expression.

But it was harder to put it on each time. Today she paid in blood.

She put on the Smile and crowned herself in Anthros's fire.

CAPABLE HANDS

FLAVIAN'S CHEER FADED, AND he gazed up at Cassia with an expression all too earnest. He swept a deep bow.

When he had imagined the lady who would one day accept him on Autumn Equinox, Cassia had not been whom he had envisioned, of that she was certain. How much did it cost him to look at her with such sincerity?

"This will be a day you shall not forget," he promised.

"It already is."

"But it's only just begun." His tone lightened again, and his grin returned. Did he have so many of them to give that they cost him nothing? "I shall surround you with good friends to celebrate. They're riding in from everywhere to enjoy this day with us."

Cassia bolstered the Smile. "How lovely."

"My cousin has come all the way from Segetia."

"Lady Eugenia?"

"Indeed, you shall meet Genie at last, and Lady Valentia too. I made Tyran promise to bring her. I have even persuaded Benedict to smile."

Cassia knew her mask faltered, but she let it. "Free Lord Tyran has returned to court?"

She had thought the occupation she had arranged for Tyran would keep him well away from Solorum. It should have taken him much longer to escort his disgraced sister Irene to their home estate. The scandal surrounding her expulsion from the Temple of Kyria should have kept her brother embroiled in family matters.

Flavian hesitated, his brow furrowing. "Tyran arrived this morning with his betrothed. You and I have talked so often of Lady Valentia. I thought it would please you to finally be introduced to her."

"Of course I look forward to her company." Cassia cast a quick glance behind her, relieved to discover Perita was not to be seen. She must still be with Callen in their chambers. "Just a moment. I'm coming down."

"My goddess descends at last?"

Cassia left the seamstress putting away the gowns and hurried out into the corridor, then to the nearby stair that led down to the courtyard. As soon as she stepped outside, Flavian loped forward to greet her. He swept one of her hands into his, and it took all her effort not to grimace in pain.

He brought her fingers to his mouth. "There. The tradition is complete. I have taken your forbidden hand and bestowed a premature kiss." He did not release her. "But I will not believe any touch of this little hand will cause the crops to wither in the fields. Quite the opposite."

"This hand must apply itself to work of greater import than superstition. I must speak with you about a matter that concerns me deeply."

"Ah. You drive right to the point, as usual. I must say, your directness is always a breath of fresh air." He surrendered her hand and gave her his full attention. "What is the matter, my dear?"

"We have spoken of Lord Tyran in passing, although never precisely of your regard for him. Your remarks have given me the impression he is not a very particular friend of yours."

"His betrothed is an old family friend and a lady worthy of the fond regard she receives from everyone around her. As for Tyran himself..." Flavian quirked a brow. "I will pay him the best compliment I can: he is loyal to Segetia."

"He is fond of filling everyone's ears with tales of your recognitions upon him."

"People tell all sorts of stories about me. I hope you don't believe every one of them." He lowered his voice with a half-smile. "If you did, you would surely think me quite the scoundrel."

"On the contrary, my lord. Your honor is well known and certain to attract followers."

"There was once one of our Segetian hunting dogs, the runt of the litter, which followed me everywhere I went, regardless of how many times I bade it stay in the kennels."

Good. This would be easier since Flavian acknowledged Lord Tyran's position as a sycophant rather than a comrade-in-arms. "My lord, has Lord Tyran spoken of the business that transpired between him and myself while you were away from court last winter?"

"He said you owe him a dance. I think he intends to claim it at Lady Valentia's party. I'm not sure I shall let him."

"He has the gall to think I owe him a favor. The truth of the matter is, I had to do everything in my power to keep him from having Callen executed."

Flavian stood back, his gaze sharpening. "I beg your pardon?"

"Verruc, a guard in Lord Tyran's service, led two of his comrades in an ambush after dark with no witnesses. Callen defended himself and, although outnumbered and gravely injured, defeated all three of them with skill and courage." Cassia told Flavian as much as she and Perita had allowed to become public knowledge. For Perita's sake, no one must ever know that Verruc had in fact ambushed her, and that Callen's sword had been the only way to stop Verruc's constant, abusive advances. "Lord Tyran, instead of taking responsibility for his men's dishonorable conduct, accused Callen of murder. Callen almost died in prison from his untended wounds while I worked to persuade Lord Tyran to let me pay Verruc's life-price so Callen would not have to pay with his life. At last, Lord Tyran's baser nature got the better of him, and he accepted a great deal of gold and jewels from me. By then, Callen had lost the strength of his leg and a promising career on the battlefield."

Flavian the cheerful suitor was no longer in evidence, and in his place stood a formidable lord. "Allow me to personally apologize for Tyran's behavior. Needless to say, had I been aware of the situation, you and your dependents would never have endured such an ordeal."

Cassia had been right to expect Flavian to take her at her word. She had known she would one day need to rely on the trust she had built with him during his courtship of her. That time was at hand, and it would not be the last. "Now you know the truth of the matter and the man who serves you. As you can imagine, I am loath to be in Lord Tyran's company and most of all to subject those in my service to his presence."

"Of course. I will take care of Tyran at once."

Some of Cassia's tension eased. "Thank you."

"Rest easy, my lady, for the errand I contrive for him will keep him out of your sight indefinitely. He will be gone from Solorum before the dance commences."

Her relief gave way to disbelief. This was to be Flavian's grand gesture of honor and justice? To send the man away on an errand? There was no estate remote enough, no road long enough, and no mud deep enough to hold Lord Tyran in check. What matter if he no longer troubled Perita, Callen, and Cassia, when he might subject others to the same cruelty elsewhere?

If Cassia were Tyran's liege lord, she would not need to make do with family scandals to detain him, and she would resort to much more effective measures than errands. She would not let men like Tyran protect criminals like Verruc, and she would not let men like Flavian respond with mere slaps on the wrist. She would not let women like Perita live in fear.

Flavian should not need to know what Perita had suffered. He should already know how Tyran and his guards treated women. He should have already made sure no man who claimed loyalty to Segetia treated women that way.

"You intend to just send Lord Tyran away?"

"I will handle the matter with the utmost discretion. It wouldn't do for any ruffled feathers or hard feelings to tarnish this day."

Cassia bit back her frustration and resisted the urge to protest outright. Lord Tyran wielded his seat on the Council of Free Lords as his weapon of choice and his loyalty to Segetia as a shield. Flavian carried his desire to please everyone as a crutch. This matter required delicacy.

She took one step closer to Flavian and rested a hand on his arm. He went still, then lifted his brown eyes to meet hers. Hedon's horn, those smoldering gazes of Flavian's lived up to their reputation. If Cassia had been anyone else, there would have been no hope for her. Unfortunately for Flavian, all such gazes were wasted on her, for his eyes were not jewel blue, nor did they reflect light so that they glowed in the dark.

"My lord," she beseeched him. "The liberties Lord Tyran takes without your approval concern me."

"Not to worry. He will not trouble you again." The touch of his fingertips upon her brow took her by surprise. He brushed a strand of hair back from her forehead, tucking it under the wreath he had given her. "Put Tyran out of your mind."

"Now that you know his real character—"

"Or lack thereof. His behavior is ill-befitting a free lord. If he wants my respect, he must show his backbone and learn to properly discipline his men. My father and I have no use for the weak-willed."

"I have heard tell of Lord Tyran's activities, and I would hardly call them weak-willed. Are not the ranks of his men-at-arms swelling by the day? Does he not have a pair of liegehounds at his side at all times?"

"The man can't hide behind his dogs if he wants to be a leader."

"He already has a reputation as a leader among his men. They are thirsty for battle and ready for him to name the opponent. He claims his intended target is the Hesperines, but the nature of his forces calls that assertion into question. Who forges swords to fight magic?"

Flavian gave a surprised laugh. "I see the grievances of the garrison have intruded upon the pleasant gossip of the weaving rooms. I'd like a word with the louts whose lax tongues have put such a furrow upon my lady's brow." He brushed his thumb between her eyes. "Lay down your worries, my dear. The matter is my responsibility, therefore you have no cause for fear."

"I do worry what Lord Tyran may do when your back is turned."

"I treasure your concern for me."

Cassia tightened her hand on Flavian's bracer. "When Tenebra faces such threats from without, we cannot afford for restless lords to stir up trouble from within."

"Fearful gossip has a way of blowing these things out of proportion," he said patiently. "If you knew of the changes stirring among the free lords, Lord Tyran's actions would not seem amiss. With all the troubling talk, I'm sure it's difficult to understand, but the truth is, this is a very good time for Tenebra. You see, the Council of Free Lords has actually drawn together of late. In the coming weeks, you may be very surprised indeed at the unity we show."

Cassia clenched her teeth on a retort.

"Tenebra's truce with the Hesperines is a very old tradition," Flavian explained. "Did you know it's as old as the Council itself? When faced with a common enemy, we hold fast to our common love for tradition. The free lords can find it in themselves to be of one mind. My father and Lord Hadrian certainly won't be tossing back a pint together anytime soon, but they are setting an example for everyone by placing the common good above their grievances against one another. Their leadership has inspired the rest of the Council to do the same."

Cassia fixed the Smile on her face. "What reassurance, to know men of such stature as your father and Lord Hadrian have the situation under control. I see I can relax and leave the course of events in their capable hands."

"Right where they have always been." Flavian lifted her hand to his mouth once more. "And that is quite enough talk of lords and heretics. All my lady need think of for the rest of the day is dancing."

ANTHROS'S SICKLE

ALL MORNING LONG, SOMEONE had labored to bedeck the Temple of Anthros in flowers and boughs. Cassia could scarcely breathe for their fragrance. Scattered petals of Anthros's fire covered the floor. Bushels of fertility herbs hung over every rounded arch. No one could set foot here without getting blessed by Anthros, who made the seed of summer yield an abundant harvest from gardens, fields, and wombs.

Good riddance to summer. If only that did not mean autumn must begin.

Just inside the entrance, Cassia hesitated, letting earnest worshipers sidle around her. The celebrants hurried between the sandstone pillars to take their places in the swathes of sunlight that reflected off the vast bronze sun disk that levitated overhead. The lords at the front of the temple cast brazen glances at the ladies gathering at the back. The ladies glanced in return, then looked away to murmur and laugh with their mothers, sisters, and friends.

Cassia did not know where her place was today. The king had told her she must accept Flavian, but had said nothing of where she should stand while she waited for her suitor.

At the head of the temple, Lucis watched from the royal chair that gave him a view of the entire gathering. He had not put away his liegehounds for the occasion. The whole pack of them crowded around him with his human retainers. Prince Caelum sat at his right hand and looked bored. When she was thirteen, Cassia would also have wanted to be elsewhere than watching a lot of lovesick grown-ups and religion.

At this moment, she wanted to be anywhere else but here.

Familiar faces in the crowd caught her gaze. Lady Hadrian and her daughter Sabina. As Cassia watched, they stepped aside to make a place next to them for her. Lady Hadrian smiled at her. Sabina smiled, too, before her gaze slid away. To the garlands on the nearest pillar. To the embroidery on her mother's hem. Not to the men at the head of the room.

Plenty of male gazes sought her, though. Her father's power was temptation enough, but Sabina also came with long, wavy brown hair, expressive gray eyes, and full breasts and hips that promised both pleasure and healthy children. With all this and poise like her mother's, men overlooked the facts that she was nearly thirty and had her father's temper.

But they had best not try her patience with any unwanted attention today. The heir of Hadria was putting on an admirable act, but Cassia knew Sabina was the only person here who dreaded the coming dance as much as Cassia herself did.

Cassia thanked Sabina and her mother with a deep curtsy, then turned toward the stairs that led to the gallery.

She passed the entrance to the royal crypt where, on more solemn holidays, people went to mourn over Solia's bones and were heard only by an empty tomb. Cassia did not dignify the door with a glance. She fisted Solia's skirts in her hands and ascended the steps, turning her face up toward the sun.

All the light that ever was in this world remains and always will, Lio had taught her.

Cassia took her place in the gallery among other bastard daughters and the concubines who had borne them. Where her mother, Thalia, had once stood.

Mistress Risara looked at her in surprise. Lord Titus's companion of two decades always appeared as if she were smiling, thanks to the natural upturn at the corners of her mouth. "A better place awaits you today, my dear. You may have your choice of where to stand."

"Thank you, but I shall present myself where I always have. If everyone saw me in a different place, they should hardly recognize me. I will not have them see me as anyone but who I am."

Mistress Risara's mischievous eyes lit with approval. "It takes strong legs to stand in the gallery."

"When I have achieved your years of experience, I too hope to still be on my feet."

"It doesn't get any harder with age...just with indulgence." She winked and patted her waist, which had reputedly been rather smaller when she was Cassia's age. But if anyone found fault with her ever more buxom figure, it certainly wasn't Lord Titus. In fact, he was the happiest widower in the kingdom.

But as the concubine of a leader with so many vital decisions to make, and so many enemies, she was certain to have earned the silver that encroached on her blond curls.

Cassia smiled. "I should think a little indulgence is warranted after such endurance."

Mistress Risara gave a laugh that still made other men jealous of Lord Titus. "A woman must see that her man makes her troubles worth her while. Don't ever forget what you deserve."

Cassia had no answer for that. She could not stop to consider what she might deserve—it might make her think of what she wanted. Today she could only afford to think of what she had to do.

Mistress Risara leaned closer. "I assure you, *your* knees won't buckle anytime soon. Take my word on it."

Cassia smiled her thanks and hoped that was true.

She had such a long, long way to go and the first steps, today's dance, would take all the strength she had.

She studied the crowd. This was her last opportunity to observe the court from her customary position, which had served her so well. The lords and ladies below had once been lips to read and glares to avoid. In the last six months, they had become antagonists and acquaintances, enemies and potential allies—and in a few rare cases, something akin to friends. After today, they would, for the first time in Cassia's entire life, be her peers.

She disagreed with Mistress Risara. It was much harder to stand below than in the gallery.

By the time the royal mage and his procession emerged at the front of the temple, the entire scene was fading into a blur. Cassia hardly saw the Tenebran geomagus's round face and barely heard his pompous invocations in the Divine Tongue. Chrysanthos and his war circle were hazy specters behind the new royal mage, standing in silent support of their Tenebran brother, waiting in readiness.

It was not the fate they had in mind for her that would catch up to her first. Cassia's usual careful attention escaped her grasp, and all her powers of concentration turned themselves upon what she was about to do.

What a time for the reality of it to hit her. It was no longer an idea, a possibility, or a future event. It was really going to happen.

The royal mage droned on and on, providing Cassia's silent panic plenty of time to work her over. The crowd stirred, and the celebrants' restless movements seemed like a wave that would tow her under.

Then the king stood up, and her heart punched against her ribs. Her merciless senses chose that moment to sharpen into crystal clarity.

Lucis marched down from his chair and met the royal mage. Spell and sword, divine voice and royal hand faced one another. The mage hefted the sickle that represented Anthros's power over the harvest and, with great ceremony, surrendered it to the warrior king, the Champion of Anthros.

Lucis lifted the sickle high without effort, then swung it down in a smooth, practiced motion. The blade and his gaze pointed to one man in the crowd, one young god among gods. The Champion had chosen the crown's official Anthros, who would lead his fellow males in the ritual today.

Cassia could not see his face from here, but Flavian's chestnut hair and broad shoulders were unmistakable. Not dressed for the road, now. As he came forward to receive the king's blessing, he was a flash of golden velvet and snowy white linen before her eyes. What a pretty package for her doom to come in.

He accepted Anthros's sickle from Lucis and held it to his breast, saluting first the king, then the crowd.

Flavian strode between the men to cheers and calls from his comrades, but when he reached the ladies, he slowed to an agonizing stroll. He glanced here, bowed there, making a great show of his search.

Matriarchs loyal to Hadria kept their pouting daughters out of his way, while maidens loyal to Segetia dared face him in invitation with their mothers looking on hopefully. Flavian's admirers were making their last effort to protest his imminent attachment, their last gesture of denial that he would waste himself.

At last he reached the back of the crowd empty-handed, except for the god's blade. Halting there, he looked up. His gaze found Cassia. He saluted her with the sickle and swept her an elaborate bow. Then he bounded up the stairs.

The crowd below had gone silent. But in the gallery, the paramours' expensive skirts rustled, and the bastards' threadbare slippers pattered on the stone. The women grinned and tittered and parted to make way for Flavian, just barely. Weaving between their close bodies and welcoming gazes, he came to stand before Cassia and offered her his hand.

He was just Flavian. Cassia had betrayed Dalos to the Hesperines, thieved the glyph stone from under Chrysanthos's nose, and committed treason upon treason against the king. She was certainly equal to this task. She rested her fingers lightly upon Flavian's.

He lifted their joined hands for the crowd to see, raising the Sickle in his other. Now she put on the Smile, for nothing less would keep her from grimacing at the pain in her hand.

Somewhere below, a boot hammered the floor, and Cassia would have wagered Anthros's Sickle it was Sir Benedict's. The silence broke, and the expected foot-stomping and hand-clapping commenced. Flavian's friends bit their tongues and applauded him, and the whole court offered up the noise the king had requisitioned for the occasion of yoking his ill-bred daughter to Tenebra's favored son.

Cassia found her voice and another measure of conviction to be forthright. "You passed by many ladies who sat much nearer to you. You do not find it a burden to venture so far to choose your partner?"

"No, I am not ashamed to come to the gallery to get you. Two of the women I admire most in all of Tenebra sit here." He lowered Cassia's hand so he could take her arm, then offered a parting bow to Mistress Risara.

Her answering look of encouragement was the last thing Cassia saw before Flavian escorted her down from the gallery. They descended into the thundering rhythm of the crowd. Drummers took up the beat, and the minstrels embarked on the music that would not end until long after the sun set. To trumpets and harps, Flavian and Cassia led the crowd down the temple steps and out onto the greensward.

Her confrontation with Anthros was at hand.

KYRIA'S BOUNTY

EVEN THE MAGE KING'S throne was covered in flowers. For generations of Autumn Greetings, the four-sided stone chair and ivy-covered dais in the center of the greensward had served as the boundary marker between Anthros's and Kyria's sides of the festival.

At least Cassia would now have a moment of reprieve. The mages of Kyria waited for her on the green's open western end. Flavian delivered her, then retreated to join the men in front of the Temple of Anthros, where the king sat in state.

For once, Lucis did not occupy the throne, for it must stand empty on this day as an invitation to the gods. That was the extent of his display of humility. Spell lights and important men decorated his purple pavilion. Chrysanthos looked right at home in the ostentatious gathering. While visiting mages and married lords played a game of who could get closest to the king, men who were neither celibate nor attached followed Flavian's example, selecting their Kyrias and delivering the ladies to the goddess's mages. Music and laughter echoed all the way to the ramparts of Solorum Palace on the south side and the grim walls of Solorum Fortress to the north.

Perita broke through the crowd and came to Cassia's side. "Well, my lady. Who's the royal today, hmm?"

"Perita, there is something we haven't discussed, and I shall not wait a moment longer to reassure you. Whatever happens, I wish for you and Callen to remain with me. Folk may say whatever they like about Flavian's wife being the sort of lady who gets served by other ladies, but I will have no one but my tallow chandler's daughter, and that is that. Flavian may take all three of us or none at all. If that's what you and Callen want, that is. I know he is Lord Hadrian's man to the last, and I would expect nothing else of him. However he may feel about Segetia, if he can find it in his heart to be loyal to me, that is all I ask."

Perita preened Cassia, straightening a ribbon here and a brooch there. "What a thing for you to be thinking about right now, my lady."

"I know you and Callen will need to discuss the matter."

"The first day Lord Flavian came courting you, we discussed it, and we decided while the porridge water came to a boil. I don't trust anyone but me to get the gardening stains out of your gowns properly, and Callen isn't about to let you be taken off to Segetia without one of Hadria's men to look out for you."

Cassia gave Perita her first genuine smile in hours. Perita smiled back and straightened Cassia's gloves one more time before standing aside.

One of the mages put a hand on Cassia's arm and ushered her forward. Cassia recognized the friendly eyes that smiled at her over a pale blue veil. Deutera's magic had seen Cassia through greater trials than the Autumn Greeting.

Cassia found herself before a short figure in gleaming white robes. The Prisma of the Temple of Kyria at Solorum peeked out from under her hood at Cassia, and a web of wrinkles spread across her face as she beamed.

"Prisma," Cassia cried. "It's so good to see you again."

"The last six months have felt much longer than half a year, haven't they, daughter?"

"The longest of my life." One of the last times Cassia had seen the Prisma, she had introduced the mage to Lio.

"We've felt your absence keenly. But what a blessing from our Mother of the Harvest that such a happy occasion brings us together again." She lowered her voice. "Much happier than last time."

The Prisma might regard it as an unhappy event when she had resorted to meeting with a Hesperine in secret to save the dying children she harbored. But that night when Cassia and Lio had smuggled the medicine into the temple had been one of the best of Cassia's life.

"So much has changed," Cassia said.

"That is what this day means," the Prisma replied. "Do not fret. In time, you will ease into your new life as naturally as summer gives way to autumn."

"Thank you for your kindness to me."

"I rejoice in the knowledge you have a future full of kindness ahead of you. I have prayed the goddess would guide you into a life that befits the woman you are."

The Prisma began to recite the Equinox prayers to Kyria in the Divine Tongue, and all around her, the goddess's other maiden mages echoed her.

Cassia was fortunate in those few who genuinely cared about her. Their happiness for her was a sign of their support. She must try to draw strength from that. They would be at her side in her future, although it would take on a far different shape than they imagined.

There came one last chorus of prayers, and a young mage proffered a large basket, from which the Prisma withdrew a sheaf of wheat. She lifted it high and said a final benediction, then put it in Cassia's hands.

With the other ladies of the court, Cassia recited the ritual response she had learned for the occasion. It was probably some nonsense about submitting gracefully to Anthros's leadership.

While Anthros was listening, Cassia added her own personal greeting. *Well, well, Anthros. It has been some time since I sent your mage Dalos back to you. You'll be seeing Chrysanthos next.*

Armed with her sheaf of wheat, Cassia took her place at the foot of the Mage King's empty throne.

Separated from her by the breadth of the dais, Flavian grinned and lifted his eyebrows. Time for the Smile again.

Cassia was not pleased that the first place she ever led the ladies of Tenebra's royal court was into Anthros's hands, but one had to start somewhere. The other young women filed past the Prisma to receive their bundles of wheat and lined up beside Cassia. Before long, the row of Kyrias-to-be stretched across half the green, facing the company of warriors who waited to claim them in the dance.

Lady Biata was at Cassia's right hand but showed the king's bastard only her shoulder, pinning her gaze on her suitor across from her. Cassia cast a glance down the line. Most of the women appeared only to have eyes for the men.

The motion of their lips was more revealing as they murmured among themselves. Some ladies bragged of their suitors' lands and wealth, while others praised their chosen partners' honor and kindness. Then there were those who sang Flavian's praises to the last.

"...not another man equal to him in all the world!"

"He is privy to all the king's meetings in the solar..."

"Do you know he has a suit of flametongue armor?"

"...can't believe our Flavian must make do with her!"

"Such an ugly, brown little thing."

"...hardly enough breasts to put in a spoon..."

"...always gardening like a common kitchen maid. No wonder she's covered in those hideous freckles."

"That must be why she bathes so often. She is trying to scrub them off."

"Her spots are the least of what she can never wash away."

The crowd around the edges of the green was just as raucous. Younger sisters, maiden aunts, and weeping mothers slipped in and out of the audience to approach the line of young ladies, offering advice and congratulations. Amid niceties, nagging, and foolish vapors, Cassia spotted many genuine expressions of love.

Lord Galanthian's two daughters stood with their arms around each other. Lady Nivalis looked vexed, a sure sign she felt like crying.

Her elder sister smiled and patted her shoulder. "Do not regret I will never dance the Greeting."

"You are welcome to be an old maid as far as I'm concerned. I just wish I didn't have to do without you."

"You shall do well all on your own, and you know it. You will make a wonderful wife and I a wonderful mage. We will both have everything we always wanted. I thank the goddess it came to father's attention that his land up north is hospitable for growing rimelace. I can still scarcely believe my good fortune that the mages of Kyria accepted me in return for the donation. Be happy for me."

"I am happy for you, and you know it."

So was Cassia. It wasn't always easy to make her plots against the king turn out so happily for all concerned. But this time, through her anonymous intervention about Lord Galanthian's land, she had been able to achieve her goals while also helping a fellow woman.

When Nivalis's sister retreated to rejoin the visitors from the Temple of Kyria, Cassia caught her gaze and smiled her congratulations. The new mage looked away and turned her back.

Cassia bit back a sigh. Her progress building bridges with the ladies of the court had never been very good. Now they were ready to torch the bridges altogether. Being the bastard daughter of a concubine had been enough, but now she was the presumptuous bastard of a concubine who had dared aspire to be Kyria and steal the most eligible lord in the king's court. The temple's patronage and Flavian's courtship had stoked woman-kind's disdain and occasional pity into full-fledged loathing.

Cassia remembered a time when the ladies' opinions would not have mattered to her. But she had come to appreciate that all of them were potential Peritas. Cassia had learned not to look at her fellow women as hypocrites, threats, and competitors. Perhaps too late. Convincing them to stop looking at her that way might well be one battle she could not win.

It would be hard to do what she must without their support.

The last young lady joined the line, and the Prisma raised her hands once more behind the women. Across the green, the royal mage did the same behind the men.

"With his Sickle," the royal mage declared, "may Anthros bring his season of the sun to its end."

"With her generous hands," the Prisma echoed, "may Kyria deliver unto us the season of her Bounty."

Flavian broke the line, twirling the Sickle in his hands. Showoff. Cassia met him halfway and held up her sheaf of wheat in both hands. With greater care, he positioned the Sickle over the middle of the sheaf.

He paused. The whole court waited. Flavian winked at Cassia.

Then he brought the Sickle down, slicing through the sheaf, and the crowd erupted in cheers. Cassia did as she was expected and turned to face the attendees on the sidelines. Now everyone looked at her, waiting to see who would catch the halves of her sheaf and receive Kyria's fertility blessing right from the goddess's hands.

Cassia shut her eyes and hurled the wheat in Perita's direction. When she opened her eyes, she saw her friend shaking with laughter and holding both halves of the sheaf.

Flavian chuckled as he made an elaborate bow to the throne and laid the Sickle upon the dais. When he took Cassia's hand once more, the minstrels launched into their next fit of music, and the dance began.

Cassia and Flavian commenced the ancient steps of the Autumn Greeting, weaving past one another, circling, nearing again. She could see the other females around her watching the way he moved. But even so, too many eyes were on her. She imagined herself invisible in the gallery. Better yet, hidden behind Solia's flametongue veil.

"My lady," Flavian said under the music, "you will never guess what news my cousin has brought from home."

What now? "I'm sure I shall not, my lord."

"Do you recall that lovely Segetian hunting hound I told you about, the young, pretty bitch with the black mask and green eyes?"

She blinked in surprise. "The one you were trying to breed for the first time?"

"The very same. My kennel masters had success with her and one of our best studs. She delivered a healthy litter without a bit of trouble not three days before Genie departed for Solorum. My cousin was excited to tell me the news the moment she arrived."

"Well, congratulations." A grin crept up on Cassia in spite of her. "That's lovely. How many pups?"

"Thirteen."

"Oh my." A chuckle escaped her. "Her first time? Poor darling."

"I now have puppies running out my ears."

"That is an astonishing vision, my lord. It's a good thing you have so many friends to assist you with this malady. Are they not lining up to beg you for Segetian hunters?"

"Ah, but you see, I cannot let any of the pups out into the world without training. They shall need a firm hand as they grow. Perhaps from someone who is adept at dealing with the even greater demands of disciplining a liegehound."

"My lord, I somehow do not think Anthros spoke to Kyria of dogs when he took her to wife and established the rhythm of the seasons."

"Well, he must come up with at least some topics of conversation she finds engaging, for she has continued to put up with him through all fourteen scions." He grinned. "See there, you are smiling instead of looking ready to take up the Sickle and hurt someone. It worked. I shall advise all the men I know that the cure for Greeting nerves is a good dog. Although you must do without Knight today, we can at least talk about hounds."

It was really a shame Flavian planned to marry her. They might have been friends otherwise.

The trill of a horn announced it was time for Anthros to allow lesser gods a turn about the green with Kyria. Flavian handed Cassia off to Lord Adrogan. She made one repetition of the dance steps with her erstwhile suitor, who was today Lady Biata's partner. Then he surrendered Cassia back to Flavian with a bow of defeat.

After she and Flavian performed the pattern again, it was another lord's turn. One by one, the men recognized Cassia with a dance down the line, then returned her to Flavian to show they relinquished their claim.

"Congratulations on your recent appointment to the Council," said Cassia to her fourth partner.

"Thank you, my lady," the new Free Lord Ennius replied.

"I was in a state of shock when I learned the king stripped Free Lord Ferus of his title and lands, leaving an empty seat at the Council table. Last I heard, the guards turned him out into the eastern wilds with nothing but what he could carry. What an astonishing turn of events."

"I only wish we knew who alerted His Majesty's exchequer that the bandits waylaying royal tax wagons were Ferus's men in disguise. I'd like to thank the informant for my good fortune."

Cassia seldom revealed her hand, but she had made sure Ferus knew it was she who had exposed him, and that she would lay him even lower, should he show his face again. He must live with the knowledge that she had ruined him. Just as she had suspected, he was so humiliated that a woman had bested him that he had not breathed a word of her involvement to anyone.

Now he was on the eastern frontier, where there was no one for him to tell—or threaten—except hard men like himself. Denied the king's protection, outlaws like him were at the mercy of the only justice in that wild territory: Hesperines errant.

"Free Lord Ennius, your mysterious benefactor must rejoice to see Ferus's lands and Council seat bestowed upon a man of honor. The way you have already championed Tenebran temples since you joined the Council is an inspiration."

"I value the good opinion of such a devout lady as yourself. You appreciate how those of us in positions of influence must show our devotion to *Tenebra's* temples and the mages who uphold *our* traditions."

"Indeed, my lord. I could not agree more."

Cassia danced her way through the court, winning many more smiles from the men than she had from the ladies and even some disappointed gazes. Any object of Flavian's must be worthy of pursuit, and his rivals regretted their failure to snatch Lady Cassia while they'd had the chance.

A number of them also regretted their recent loss of a copper mine, toll collection privileges, or a vote on the Council. How might their faces change if they knew they owed those failures to the lady herself? Cassia offered her condolences for the hopes she had dashed and compliments to those whose status she had elevated, in between turns with Flavian in which he jested with her incessantly.

At the very end of the line, a callused, strong hand took hers, and she looked up into the weathered face of a man who had endured more years and griefs than the careless young bucks around him. He danced the steps with the skill of someone who had done them before, but he did not smile.

"Lord Deverran," Cassia said. "I had no idea we would have the pleasure of your company in the dance today."

"No one is more surprised than I, Lady Cassia."

As the dance turned them, Cassia looked to see who stood across from his place. "Allow me to congratulate you. Lady Nivalis is a woman worthy of admiration."

"Yes. She has borne too much for one so young, but she has not lost her spirit."

"I have seen her talent and strength of character in the many hours we have passed together in Lady Hadrian's weaving room."

The dance brought him back around to face Cassia, but he looked away. "You must wonder at an autumn dancer such as myself attempting a summer carole."

Here at the end of the line, the minstrels' music was loudest, the path back to Flavian and other prying ears longest.

Cassia ventured, "I should think a harvest union brings comfort and prosperity to those who suffered rain in spring."

"It seems you've made it through your own winter." Lord Deverran glanced at her gown. "You still intend to hang a new sun in our sky, Lady Basilis?"

"I shall not rest until I have done so. When the time comes for me to dispel the clouds, can I still rely on you to carry a bystander out of the storm?"

His gaze sought Lady Nivalis's. "I am more prepared now to offer shelter."

"Is she?"

"You said yourself she possesses great strength of character. I would not dishonor such a woman by dealing less than straightly with her. She knows what I am and what I am not...and yet here she stands." He did indeed sound surprised.

"I am happy for you, my lord. It is rare for those of us who have suffered losses at Anthros's hands to find solace."

"Anthros is king. How can we say he stole from us, when all within his domain is rightfully his?"

"Do you mean to say you have doubts, my lord?"

"We mortals ought to have doubts when resisting the will of a god."

"You would rather go back to bearing your loss in silence?"

"That's what you have done these many years."

"Not any longer," Cassia swore.

"Do we not have more to lose after today?"

"Nay, my lord. More to protect."

"I will only risk abandoning Anthros for a goddess who promises victory—and reigns with a kinder hand."

"She has the power to triumph, and her request to you is proof of how she will lead." Cassia lowered her voice, lifting her face so Lord Deverran could hear. "She will see no more of Anthros's scions pay for the god of war's abuses. The youngest will not be the next to fall. He deserves a father with a kinder hand."

"Then we are of one mind."

"You have told me you regret that you once laid down your sword.

I know you have the strength and the will to take it up again. For the sake of your fallen goddess and mine, let us drive Anthros's chariot down from the sky."

His eyes flashed, and his face hardened. "I shall make way for the new goddess to ascend."

The dance forced them out of the shelter of the minstrels' noise. Lord Deverran escorted Cassia back to Flavian in silence. He gave her a deep bow before retreating down the line.

The ritual was complete, Anthros's right to Kyria acknowledged. The other men now bounded forward to stake their own claims. Their ladies met them and bestowed their sheafs of wheat, which would later be scattered under their marriage beds to invite the gods to bless them with male heirs on their wedding nights.

"We've done our duty." Flavian spoke low in Cassia's ear. "Now our couple dance begins."

Cassia hoped Flavian was equal to the steps she would require of him before their dance was through.

CROSSING THE FEUD

THE GREETING DANCE WAS over. But Cassia could not let her legs give out yet.

The sense of blur came over her again, and one couple dance with Flavian melted into the next. His fingers entangled hers and unleashed her anxiety anew. The dances shrank the distance between them and tied her stomach in knots. She had done her part—but only for today.

Between two dances, Flavian came to a standstill and eyed Cassia's brow. "It's grown quite warm, hasn't it? I think the weather mages rather overdid it. I see the indefatigable forces of the king's kitchens have arrived and set out the festival feast. Allow me to retrieve you a drink and a plate to refresh you."

"Thank you, my lord."

"But it won't do to leave you alone." He glanced around at the promised couples who danced and others who had joined in simply for merriment, partnering with friends and siblings. "I still cannot see Genie and Lady Valentia. I had thought they would find us by now. I sent Benedict to look for them."

"I'm sure they will have found us by the time you return. I am quite capable of enduring a few moments of solitude, I assure you. You may safely venture to the tables, my lord."

Flavian sighed. "I'll only be a moment."

He headed for the side of the green nearest the palace, where trestle tables were quickly disappearing under mounds of food. Like a trail of ants, servants carried platter after platter of traditional harvest dishes from the king's gates. Flavian joined the lords who were selecting delicacies for their ladies…and tasting the wine. To ensure it was suitable for feminine consumption, of course. There was no telling how many sips it might require to determine that.

Some men made for one end of the spread, while others drifted toward the opposite side. Flavian roamed the entire length of the tables. On the green, the lines between the men's and women's halves of the festival were no more, but a new divide was gradually becoming visible. The king's pavilion seemed to mark the new dividing line and the only neutral ground between Lord Hadrian's faction and Lord Titus's.

Lady Hadrian sailed to Cassia's side without dignifying any of the prowling feuders with a glance. Although her long, wavy hair was gray and her expressive eyes only for her husband, she received no few gazes of respect and admiration. "Allow me to compliment you on your gown, my dear, and the grace with which you wear it."

Cassia took Solia's skirts in her hands and offered a curtsy. "Thank you, my lady. Those words mean a great deal to me when spoken by you who have seen this gown before."

"I shall never forget."

Cassia was grateful for the reminder. She valued every rare chance to speak of Solia with one of the few people who knew the truth about her sister's death. Lord Hadrian did not keep secrets from his wife, not even the tragedy of that night when he, the king's most powerful and trusted warrior, had been unable to save the princess from her own father. All Lord Hadrian could do was show kindness to Cassia for Solia's sake and keep his own daughters as far from court as possible.

Cassia cast a glance at Hadria's side of the gathering. "It was lovely to see Sabina earlier. I know how happy you are she is making a rare visit to Solorum for the Greeting. I hope she has not had to depart for home already."

"No, not for home, not yet. But I am sorry to say she had to return to the palace. She is not feeling well."

"Is she all right?" What a question for Cassia to ask. How well she knew that after today, neither she nor Sabina would feel anything was all right ever again.

"She became overheated, that is all. I advised her to return to her rooms right away and get off her feet."

"I would love to pay her a visit later and see how she is feeling." Cassia hesitated. "That is, if I may. I hope you can forgive me for declining your invitation at temple. I assure you, it was no reflection on my regard for you and His Lordship. It would grieve me if today's events cost me your good opinion."

"Our promise to Solia that we would look after you did not end with her death. Do you imagine Titus's little boy would be enough to weaken such a promise now?" Lady Hadrian sniffed. "In any case, you were wise not to make Flavian cross the feud to ask for your hand, although I would not have been satisfied had I not offered you a place at our sides."

"Your invitation meant more to me than I can say."

"That invitation will always be open to *you*, my dear. You are always welcome in my weaving room, whatever the lords may have to say about it."

Lord Hadrian appeared at her side. "This lord says Lady Cassia must escape as often as possible to visit us. That young man who danced with her may keep his thoughts to himself."

Cassia smiled. "You are very kind, my lord."

"If I had a son, you would be wed to him already. But Sabina must remain a friend to you, if not a sister."

"Sabina's friendship is a treasure without compare."

If only it was one Cassia could call her own. The looks of jealousy and derision from the other ladies were easy to bear compared to the sting of knowing she and Sabina could never be friends.

"Ah." Lady Hadrian stared without staring at a knot of approaching celebrants. "My lord, your opponent has sent his children onto the field, and they are prepared to invade us armed with smiles and laughter. Shall we put them to the test, or withdraw?"

"A withdrawal, I think. It would be unfair of a seasoned warrior such as myself to give the young and inexperienced a beating for which they are thoroughly unprepared." Lord Hadrian took his lady's arm, tucking her close. "There is no shame in a retreat arm-in-arm with the most beautiful woman at the festival."

Cassia stifled a grin. She had never heard such a flowery compliment pass Lord Hadrian's lips, but when it came to his wife, it seemed he was not to be outdone by eloquent Lord Titus.

Lady Hadrian did not look surprised at all. "That is because you are not retreating from anything, my dear, but charging to a better position on the field."

Lord Hadrian's battle-hardened face did not crack a smile, but Cassia caught a glimpse of the gleam in his gaze as he let his lady lead him away. His reply was only for her ears, but Cassia could not help but see it on his lips. "You have been demonstrating better positions to me these many years. Do tell me what maneuver you have in mind for us today."

The invader who first descended on Cassia was a girl about Perita's age with fistfuls of velvet skirts and a head of chestnut curls. How many unenviable hours had the girl devoted to those shiny ringlets, only to dash across the greensward without thought for their preservation? "Lady Cassia! I have made it to you at last! What a bother this crowd has been. I had no idea Kyria's dear handmaidens could be such a formidable obstacle."

A lady several years older than Cassia arrived at a dignified but brisk walk. She offered an apologetic smile and a flawless curtsy. "Forgive us for waylaying you like this without introduction, but…"

"I'll do the honors, my lady." Sir Benedict took up a post behind the two women. He wore golden brown, a match for his hair and the season, his only acquiescence to his liege lord's sense of fashion. Compared to Flavian, Sir Benedict's traditional tunic and braccae were as humble as the 'Sir' in front of his name. "Lady Cassia, allow me to present Lady Valentia…" He bowed to the eldest lady. "…and Lady Eugenia." His second bow lasted a heartbeat longer, and his faithful gaze attained still greater depths of abject devotion. It seemed he took his oath of loyalty very seriously indeed when it came to Flavian's maiden cousin.

Lady Eugenia was unmistakably a scion of Segetia's noble family, from her chestnut hair to the spark of wit in her eyes. She studied Cassia with evident delight as she bobbed a curtsy. "Lady Cassia in the flesh! We meet at last. Do call me Genie as my dear Flavian does. I would not let him rest until he appointed Lady Valentia and me to be your companions all day, although now that we have taken so long to find you, I am sure we will hear about it from him."

Cassia offered them a curtsy in return. Here were two women, at least, who were glad to see her. It might be for Flavian's sake, but that was the only opportunity Cassia needed to win them to her side for her own sake as well.

"I'm delighted to meet you both. I must confess, Flavian did promise me your excellent company today, but after you have fought so hard to reach me, I shall see to it he holds no delays against you."

Lady Valentia was a dark-haired beauty with a perfect figure and even better posture. Her antiquated blue festival gown was cut from pure tradition and sewn according to all the dictates of impeccable taste. Not that the gossips would refrain from taking her apart for her past, her poverty, and Lord Tyran's neglect. Her real armor was Flavian's favor and, by all accounts, her own strength of character.

Her polite smile wavered into discomfort. "We intended to greet you as soon as you arrived in the temple and invite you to stand with us. I sincerely apologize that you had to climb all the way to the gallery."

"Do not give it a thought. As much as I would have enjoyed your company, I was happy to stand in my customary place."

"Well, there is no better company than Mistress Risara," Genie declared.

Cassia did not reply, for she noticed Sir Benedict's dour expression had turned forlorn. No, she was not mistaken, for he had just done it again. He was catching glances at her dress and trying to appear as if he were not.

"Sir Benedict, my lord Flavian has informed me you agreed to smile today." Cassia put on a smile of her own and leaned closer so she need not project her voice over the crowd. "I know how hard it is today, but if I can, I am certain you will be able to as well."

He did give her a smile, a sad but grateful one. "Aye, my lady." He cleared his throat. "It's a lovely dress."

"Lovelier to those who believe it to be new."

"It is a truly divine gown," Genie declared blithely, but her observant gaze took in Sir Benedict and Cassia.

"Thank you," Cassia replied. "But you see, Sir Benedict has seen it worn before, and he sympathizes with me that I must dance in it. Please, don't tell my lord Flavian. I should hate for him to know my Greeting dress is a hand-me-down."

Genie frowned. "My dear Ben, what a time to develop an eye for fashion."

Lady Valentia cast a knowing glance at Sir Benedict, then at the golden gown. "I shall not breathe a word. But there is no shame in a hand-me-down from caring hands."

The minstrels struck up a new song, and Cassia provided Sir Benedict an escape from the conversation. "Sir Benedict, I must insist you do another favor for me, besides that smile. You absolutely must ask Genie to dance, for if you do not, I shall be unhappy I am the only lady here who is enjoying the festival to the fullest."

"It would be my honor to obey that request, my lady." Sir Benedict showed everyone his second smile of the day, this one entirely genuine. He bowed to Genie and offered her his arm.

She had a charming grin, a lopsided one that made only half her mouth turn up. "I do believe Lady Cassia is a mind mage. I have been standing here longing for my first dance at Solorum and wishing you would ask me."

"Go enjoy yourself, my dear," Lady Valentia urged her. "How well I remember my first Greeting, when I was your age."

"Oh, don't say that. You talk as if you're an old maid! I do hate that Lord Tyran has left, for we were planning to work on him, weren't we, Ben? I am determined to persuade him not to wait a moment longer to finally wed you, my dear Lady Valentia. Fifteen years is quite long enough to be betrothed!"

"We must allow my lord Tyran to see to his business for your cousin," Lady Valentia replied, "and make certain we do not distract him with any letters. Don't spend such a lovely afternoon worrying about me. Only go and get the most out of the festival."

"Very well. But I am not done with your Lord Tyran." Genie leaned close to Cassia. "Nor with you! I hope we will have plenty of time to talk later. We have so much in common."

The young lady's half-smile changed. For the first time, she smiled with her whole mouth. There at the corners of her lips, a natural upturn appeared, the image of a particularly famous mouth.

She must have seen Cassia's look of comprehension. Genie put a finger to her lips before turning away to tuck her arm around Sir Benedict's.

Cassia watched them join the crowd. Now she understood the over-done curls and half-smiles. It would take Genie great effort indeed to make her ringlets appear an affectation rather than a natural feature from her mother. But the greater challenge was not showing the world she had inherited Mistress Risara's mouth. How had the girl trained herself to grin with only part of herself every hour of the day? Did it cost her as much as it cost Cassia to put on the Smile?

"Oh, my." Lady Valentia sighed. "Her first visit to court. I do hope Solorum is ready for her."

"She is clearly ready for Solorum. But I would expect no different from a lady of Segetia's noble family." Cassia smiled to herself. "From what my lord Flavian has said, their fathers were quite a pair when they were young. I understand Lord Titus and his younger brother were very close—and very alike."

"So I've heard." Lady Valentia's smile faded, and her voice hushed. "It's a shame what happened to Lord Eugenius's family."

"Yes." Cassia said no more. She did not have to imagine the loss with which Genie's family lived. Nor did she have to explain it to Lady Valentia. They all carried their fair share.

It had been the hazards of settling the eastern Tenebrae that had devastated Lord Eugenius's household and supposedly left his infant daughter the only survivor. Now Cassia surmised there had been no such babe, and the tragedy had inspired Lord Titus and Mistress Risara to donate their own child to the continuance of Lord Eugenius's line.

A clever, kind lie to honor Lord Eugenius's memory and secure their daughter a better life than that of a concubine's bastard. A painful lie, perhaps. But Genie had still enjoyed many years with her mother, who doted on her in the guise of her uncle's companion.

Cassia had never known her mother. But she had once known someone who had loved her, who had tried to improve her lot.

For her and Lady Valentia, it had been the Siege of Sovereigns that had reduced their lives to ruins and made self-reliance their best and only recourse.

Cassia turned to Lady Valentia. "It is kind of you to take Genie under your wing. She is fortunate in your guidance."

"It is my pleasure, I assure you. I am her opposite—I have been at court too many times. It is refreshing to share in her enthusiasm."

"I too am accustomed to wearying years," Cassia replied, "and long waits."

"You are indeed, my lady. Although now that you finally have a promise, I suspect he who has made it will not keep you waiting long."

"I am sorry your betrothed had to leave you so suddenly. I understand you had been apart from him for some time already."

"You are the last person who should apologize, for we have you to thank for relieving us of his presence. Please accept my compliments, and this." The lady untied a purse from her belt. "I am aware Callen is not the only one who suffered injustice at his hands. I make no excuses for Tyran and his men. I do not clean up after their crimes. I only try to mete out as much justice as I can when he will not. You will find herein the fine the law stipulates an offender must pay in cases of attempted assault and slander of a lady's reputation. Of course, I have no knowledge at all of the woman whom Tyran's guard so abused, if anyone were to ask. Since I do not know her name, much less her rank, I have provided the maximum amount, which is reserved for ladies of the highest station. Something tells me you are in a position to ensure the right person receives this."

When Cassia felt the purse's weight, her surprise gave way to a vision of Perita's expression when she saw this much coin in her own hands. "This is more than any lord or magistrate has done for her."

"This is not a payment for silence. If there were any lords or magistrates who would listen, I could fill their ears with tales. As you know all too well, Tyran is expert at ensuring there are no consequences for his and his men's misdeeds."

"And at preventing any challenges to your betrothal?" Cassia guessed.

Lady Valentia touched Cassia's hand briefly. "I am glad we understand one another. Now then, you cannot dance with this at your belt. I will gladly have one of my household deliver the purse to your residence later, if you will trust me to uphold my promise."

"I will." Cassia handed Perita's fortune back to Lady Valentia for the time being. "On behalf of the woman in question, allow me to express heartfelt gratitude. I cannot tell you what this will mean to her."

"Sir Benedict has spoken of your kindness and forbearance. He is one of the best judges of character I know. It is I who am grateful you deign to speak to either of us."

"Lady Valentia, you have as much reason to hold that night against me. But I think none of us should revive a dead war by blaming each other for our fathers' actions."

"Indeed, I wish only to offer my condolences. First for lesser offenses, which may yet be mended. I am sorry for the rumors that have pervaded at court all these years about your callousness. It is clear from how you speak of Princess Solia to Lord Flavian that whatever your reason for never visiting Her Highness's tomb, it is not due to any lack of feeling. As for the wounds that cannot heal, I can only strive to express how deeply I regret that my family's allies cost you your beloved sister."

"I appreciate your kind words, but I cannot accept them. Once already today, you have apologized for a crime you did not commit. That is enough."

"Someone ought to."

"But not you."

"Then at least let me offer you comfort, if I can. I only hope my words will bring you more consolation than pain. You and Benedict were only seven and eight then, but I was thirteen and more aware of events."

Cassia tried to swallow the fist in her chest. "Knowing more of the truth is worth any pain and does bring its own kind of comfort."

"Then I will tell you this. As you know, none of my family were at Castra Roborra during the Siege of Sovereigns, but we had the closest of ties to Free Lord Evandrus, who assisted in Her Highness's capture. He was in the fortress that night with his eldest son, Evander—that is, Lord Evandrus the Younger." Lady Valentia's smooth voice became throaty with emotion. "I don't know if you can take my word for their character, but I knew them as well as I know myself. I can speak to their motivations, and I hope what I say will not merely rub salt in your wounds."

Their motivations for kidnapping and brutally murdering Solia in cold blood? Cassia bit her tongue. If she responded to Lady Valentia's plea with hostility, the other woman might change her mind about confessing what she knew. "Are you suggesting there was something more to their motivations than was apparent?"

"Whatever the other lords who perpetrated the rebellion wanted, I can say with certainty Lord Evandrus held the tenets of the Free Charter in his heart and felt honor-bound to take action to stop what he regarded as abuse of royal power. Whatever went wrong in the fortress that night, he would never have wanted it to end the way it did. I believe he strove to prevent it from descending into bloodthirsty revolt, but the other lords overruled him."

With an effort, Cassia kept the skepticism out of her voice. "So you believe the plan to which Lord Evandrus originally committed himself degenerated into something he never intended, which he could not control."

"I can believe nothing else of a man like him. He would never willingly join in the feral madness the traitors committed that night. Lord Evandrus would have had every intention of holding the princess safely under house arrest and treating her with respect and courtesy until the men resolved their differences. He and his son would have done everything in their power to ensure their actions brought no suffering upon innocents like your sister. Perhaps it is little comfort, but I believe with all my heart she had two lords striving to protect her from the others that night. Their failure to do so most certainly means they forfeited their lives in her defense."

Solia's gown weighed on Cassia. She had thought herself prepared to confront her memories today. She had not expected the greensward to turn into the field where her sister had fallen. She struggled to find words. "Forgive me. It is so sudden and rare to speak about my sister like this."

"I understand."

Cassia studied Lady Valentia. The woman gripped her white-knuckled hands in front of her. All the color had drained from her face, and her gaze was that of a supplicant. Cassia could imagine the lady had been forced to assume that role many times as her family had scrambled to tie their futures to Free Lord Tyran and the Segetian faction to keep from following Lord Evandrus's kin to the executioner. Cassia had never before found herself in a position to stay the axe, and it would be a long time before that power felt easy in her hand, if ever.

A woman just trying to get ahead did not empty her own purse on behalf of a nameless victim. A woman trying to buy the silence of those her betrothed victimized did not avoid marrying him for years. Cassia did not see before her a conspirator who sought to use Lord Flavian's bride-to-be as a stepping stone out of ignominy. She saw a woman like herself, who sacrificed what she must and held fast to what she could, so she neither sank with those to whom birth had bound her, nor became them by pushing others down.

That woman wanted Cassia to believe two of the men who had led Solia to her death had actually had good intentions.

Cassia's grief leapt up within her to rend the offering of compassionate words to shreds. But all that lashed out within her halted at one thing Lady Valentia had said.

Lord Evandrus felt honor-bound to take action to stop what he regarded as abuse of royal power.

Was not Cassia that kind of traitor as well?

Denial made her shake inside. She was nothing like Solia's murderers. She would die before she would allow her plans to bring someone so good to harm.

Perhaps Lord Evandrus had escorted Solia to Castra Roborra that night believing the same thing. Perhaps he had died before he allowed his plans to bring her to harm.

The landscape of Cassia's inner world shifted, and suddenly the two lords were standing at her sister's side with the king's victims, no longer among the ranks of enemies who were no better than Lucis himself.

That would mean she and the two lords were exactly the same kind of traitor...only she still drew breath.

"I do not doubt your words," Cassia said in realization. "I take them to heart. It is a revelation to me to know Solia had two protectors in that fortress. To know she had some recourse...some hope...that she was not without allies when she faced—" Cassia's breath caught in her throat. "I never imagined the possibility."

"She was not alone," Lady Valentia said.

"No. I see that now."

And neither was Cassia.

"The results of this Greeting are in our hands." Lady Valentia held out hers in the traditional gesture of offering. "I hope we shall make better of it than our forbears."

"With the gods as our witnesses," Cassia replied, "we shall."

Lady Valentia's expression softened. "You have a much brighter future ahead of you already. Here he comes now."

Flavian approached, rosy-faced and cheerful from the wine, with drinks and plates for all three of them. He escorted Cassia and Lady Valentia away from the dance and laid claim to a portion of the green's western slope, where he spread out his festival cloak to serve as their table.

Cassia stared at the spot a few paces away where the Hesperine embassy had first appeared upon their arrival at Solorum. It was hard to tear her gaze away from where she had first seen Lio. It was even harder not to stare at Solorum Fortress, where they had last made love.

She knew who represented her bright future. He was the beacon who awaited her far ahead in the distance, the light she would finally reach when…if…she made it through her perilous course.

The afternoon was going to be a gauntlet. She could see them swarming now—Flavian's many friends, supporters, and assorted beggars for his favor. She must get through the congratulations and still more dances with the man who regarded her as his.

BONFIRE DANCE

IN THE WANING DUSK, Cassia watched apprentice mages of Anthros and Kyria pile sacred branches in the center of the green. Flavian and his friends talked and laughed around her, excited for the next spectacle. She tried to ignore her aching feet and Flavian's arm tucked around hers.

It was not the royal mage who came forward with a temple brand. Chrysanthos strode to the foot of the Mage King's throne with empty hands. Silence descended, and the crowd watched him with fervent expectation.

The words of his prayer rolled across the greensward and drummed in the night. He squared his broad shoulders and held out his hands.

The hair on Cassia's arms stood on end, and painful goosebumps broke out all over her skin.

This time she saw the blast of fire. Flame leapt from the mage's palms.

The Dexion's spell set upon the pile of wood to commence its feeding. Cassia's whole body started while the crowd roared their amazement and approval.

Lost in the noise, were there any protests from those who had nearly been the victims of Dalos's war magic? If any of the cries were outrage, they went unheeded. In a moment the flames roared so high, they were taller than the throne.

Cassia watched the power that had destroyed Hespera's Sanctuary rise into a bonfire and her countrymen begin a circle dance around the pyre. The celebrants had found their second wind, intoxicated by magic, flirtation, and drink.

Cassia spoke in Flavian's ear. "My lord, it is awfully hot and noisy here by the bonfire."

He looked down at her in surprise. "My dear, would you fancy a stroll under the trees to cool ourselves before we rejoin the dancers?"

"I admit some quiet and privacy would be most welcome to me."

Tenebra's expert on romance did not disappoint her. Within moments, he arranged to be seen leaving the green with Sir Benedict while Cassia departed from the opposite end with Genie and Lady Valentia. With laughter and knowing gazes, their escorts deposited them under the cover of the woods. In no time, Cassia stood in a clearing with Flavian. Alone.

He lounged against a fallen tree as if he were a young god who had descended into the mortal world to take a stroll and lead maidens astray. "Fancy meeting you here."

"Thank you for your willingness to forgo a bonfire dance." Cassia checked the security of her gloves.

He straightened and took a step toward her. "Shall we make our own music?"

"I'm afraid that is not why I wanted to speak with you alone."

He gave her a playful grin. "I know how it is. You have heard the tales of how dreadful my company is when Benedict is not around to enliven the conversation. Allow me to repair my reputation in your eyes."

"My lord, we are not officially betrothed yet."

"My matter-of-fact Lady Cassia. What a sweet trove of modesty you're hiding under your pragmatism." He took another step, this time around her. Suddenly he was very close in front of her, and the tree not so far behind her back. "My Lady of Ice. Let me warm you a little."

As his mouth descended toward hers, she put her fingers on his lips. "Flavian, the person you would rather have danced with today is within your reach. Why don't you make the most of it? I am the last person who would protest, and I think it would mean a great deal to Sabina."

He froze there with her hand upon his mouth. A less graceful man might have recoiled. But he only took one step back. She moved out of his reach, and he swiveled to face her. He didn't seem to realize she had him cornered between her and the tree now.

"What did she tell you?" he blurted.

"She asked me the same question about you, when I told her I knew."

He regained his composure with admirable speed. "If she told you nothing, my lady, then it seems you are at an impasse, for you will get the same from me."

"As I said, I already knew. I am one of the few people who is intimate with both your families. Who else in the kingdom would bear witness to the signs of what has passed between you? You and I have this in common— our closeness to the king allows us to bridge the feud. How else would you, a son of Segetia, ever have come into the company of a daughter of Hadria?"

"You cannot see signs that are not there."

"You dismissed your last concubine three years ago," she reminded him.

He sank down to sit on the fallen tree. "Don't tell me Cornelia attends temple and stands in the gallery."

"She did for a little while, when she made a short visit to court earlier in the summer with Lord Nonus, the benefactor into whose arms you commended her."

"Cornelia knows nothing about my personal affairs since we parted," he protested.

"But after my conversations with her about you, I had to wonder: why did you dismiss a woman like her and take no other concubine since? Who captured your interest?"

He fidgeted as if someone had put stinglily in his clothes. "There are times when a man finds he is not in a position to fulfill his responsibilities to his concubine. I have been traveling a great deal."

"Yes, you have. You have entertained me with wonderful stories about all the places you have traveled in the last few years. Do you know who else must often travel at the king's behest? Lady Hadrian. She is stuck with the court year in and year out while her daughter must be at home. She misses Sabina sorely and loves to read her letters aloud to her friends here whenever we attend weaving parties."

A muscle in his jaw twitched. Amiable Flavian now looked like he wanted to draw his sword and deal the tree a few hacks.

"Sabina must spend most of her time in Hadria," Cassia went on, "but she does get to visit other families occasionally. I had almost forgotten that three years ago, she spent a summer in Saxara to renegotiate their tithe to her father. I hear Saxara is lovely in the summer." Cassia tapped her chin. "Who was it who told me that? Oh yes. It was you, wasn't it?"

Flavian rubbed a hand across his mouth, and she was fairly certain the words he muttered into his palm were curses from the filthiest end of the list.

Cassia swept her hand in the direction of the palace. "Devotion to the crown opens paths to our generation that our parents feared to tread—or would not tread without causing a considerable body count. The king's favor secures your welcome everywhere in Tenebra, and your character sees to it you never wear out that welcome. There are families in Tenebra that hate Segetia but like you. Some of them are families who love Hadria. Then there are the new lords the king has made, who welcome whomever he says they should and have not existed long enough to have ancient quarrels. All this has worked together to produce an astonishing result: Sabina of Hadria and Flavian of Segetia have happened to be visiting mutual friends upon seven occasions in the last three years. It was a different friend every time, and sometimes it was only for a few days... other times, for an entire season."

"As you say, my lady, Hadria and Segetia nurse their enmity as bitterly as ever. It seems all you know for certain is that Lady Sabina has occasionally tolerated being under the same roof as the son of her father's rival."

"Oh, I should say she did far more than tolerate you." Cassia smirked. "What convinced me of that is how she struggles to tolerate me."

"On the contrary, the two of you have been inseparable since she came to court."

"She is making a noble effort to like me. For a well-born lady to disdain me is not remarkable, of course. But Sabina is the one person who has every reason to like me and no reason not to. She was Solia's friend and is fair-minded like her parents, so I thought she would love me for my sister's sake, rather than censure me for my mother's. And, I reasoned, she is the only person with no cause to be jealous of my good fortune in your courtship. I couldn't have been more wrong."

"Plenty of other ladies envy my attention to you, and you are not assuming I have behaved thus with them."

"None of those ladies spent the summer at Saxara with you around the same time you dismissed your concubine. Sabina is in no way responsible for my discovery of your secret. It was only after she realized how much I already understood that she told me everything."

Flavian was silent. Indeed, he could have no retort for that.

He was really hearing Cassia...*listening* to her. She had finally gotten his attention and cut through his elaborate act of gallantry. This might be the first, but it would not be the last time they had a real conversation.

"In our position, it was one solace I could give her," Cassia said. "The chance to speak honestly about you as she cannot with any other living soul. Which is more than can be said for you. You've not said two words to her since she arrived at Solorum."

"Solorum is different from Saxara!"

"Are you going to educate me on how court life demands greater discretion, after you just sneaked off with me in front of the king himself?"

"You and I just danced the Greeting."

"And what a spectacle you made of it. Don't pretend you don't know you've hurt Sabina."

Eloquent Flavian, never before without a quip or a compliment, said nothing for a long moment. At last an expression of resolve came over his face. "What Sabina and I had was over before I started courting you—and I don't mean to say we had anything. We knew when we began what it would and would not be. We never entertained any notion of marriage." He paused. "Gods above. That does make me sound like a scoundrel. I did not seduce her."

"Oh, no. I gather it was quite the opposite."

Flavian flushed red from his forehead to his neck.

"What a sweet trove of modesty you're hiding under your boldness," Cassia exclaimed. "I had no idea my pragmatism could embarrass a man of the world such as yourself. But the lovely Sabina's thorough conquest of you is certainly worthy of your blushes. She is as proud and relentless as any Hadrian and just as unwilling to accept there is anything that is not hers for the taking."

"There you have it. We were forbidden to one another. The most irresistible temptation known to mortal kind. There is nothing more to tell."

"Flavian, I know your heart was not in what we did today. You have put on a merry display, for merriment is your shield of choice. You have acted out of loyalty to the king and duty toward your family. I invited you out here tonight to relieve you of any sense of duty you may feel toward me. Make all you can of every opportunity you and Sabina have to be together. I will not stand in your way. I know there will be certain responsibilities you and I cannot escape, but they stop outside the bedroom door. Heirs can be adopted or produced by relatives. You and Sabina have my blessing now and when we are officially betrothed—and after we are married."

He shook his head as if to clear it. "That's the kind of marriage you envision?"

"It is the best I can offer the three of us."

"I have told you, Sabina and I exchanged no promises. We have always known we must one day do our duty to Hadria and Segetia. We had no illusions that what passed between us would last."

Cassia should not have been surprised, but she was disappointed. How could he sit here and dismiss Sabina as if she had been nothing but one more amorous adventure?

"Your exploits include concubines, widows, handmaidens of Hedon, and talented beauties among the traveling players. But you never take advantage of your dependents or lead other men's wives astray. Above all, you limit your adventures among marriageable maidens to flirtation and dancing. Then there is Sabina. You certainly did not limit yourselves to words and dances. Has it occurred to you she means something different to you than any other woman you have known? Something more?"

Cassia waited, but he mustered no answer for her. She pressed on.

"Sometimes the indulgence of forbidden desire comes to nothing. But other times…" The words welled out of Cassia with the strength of conviction, and she said for Sabina's sake what she wished with all her heart someone would say on her own behalf. "There are extraordinary occasions when, in our defiance of all we have been told is right, we find something even more precious…something sacred. Sometimes what we have been told we must not want is precisely what we need. Sometimes rebellion leads us home."

Flavian stared at her as if he had never seen her before.

She left him speechless and alone with only one companion. He and the truth needed some time together so they could become acquainted.

SABINA'S FAVOR

THE PALACE WAS SILENTLY astir with ladies staying awake late to gossip and lords making furtive visits to their conquests. Lady Sabina's handmaiden did not raise a brow at Cassia for paying a visit in the middle of the night after the Autumn Greeting. She showed Cassia into Sabina's hearth room within the Hadrian residence.

Sabina sprang out of her chair by the fire. A blanket fluttered off her shoulders and fell at her feet. She stood tall, her shoulders squared, her curls agleam in the light of the flames. "Gods damn him."

"I'm glad you did yourself the kindness of feigning illness," Cassia began.

Sabina made an angry gesture with one hand and began to pace. "It is well indeed I did not stay for the Greeting, for I might have committed sacrilege by taking up a branch from the sacred bonfire and putting Anthros himself to the pyre."

Once more Cassia chose her words with care. She was not yet certain whether all the fury she beheld was for Flavian alone, or whether she too was in danger of being caught in the blaze of Sabina's ire. "I wish I had more to offer you, but I have only one thing to give. My word. If there were any other way I could do this, I would."

"I know," said Sabina to the window.

"Thank you for taking me at my word."

"Your word is worth more than that seasonal decoration he calls his honor." Sabina made a noise of disgust. "The only person in this whole affair who had any power to influence the outcome was Flavian. I knew he would have to marry. I hoped he would not sit by and let his father and the king hand him a bride. I expected him to take his leave of me like a man."

Now, of all times, the kindest thing Cassia could do for Sabina was listen. There was no one else to hear her grievances.

Sabina continued to rage at the window. "If he had bothered to speak to me, I'm sure he would have made some attempt to convince me that when the king invited him to marry you, it was not in his power to refuse. He could have at least offered the defense that he had tried to weasel himself out of it. How expert he is at weaseling, and always with a smile."

Instead, Flavian had made it appear to the entire court that he was having the time of his life accepting the yoke of marriage the king had ordered for him.

Flavian's greatest expertise was not trying.

Sabina seethed. "I have no idea what is rattling around in the place he claims his heart resides."

"And yet I have made an appeal to it on your behalf, such as it is. He and I spent some time alone after the dance, and I want you to know why."

Sabina spun around. Tears quivered in her eyes. She was shaking with anger. "Do not coddle me like a maiden. His reason descended into his breeches long ago. You don't have to explain to me why Lord Flavian would want to take his prospective bride off alone…and you don't have to justify why you would go with him."

"*I* took *him* aside, and I did so to tell him he did not belong with me tonight, but with the woman he truly wanted for his Kyria. I made it clear to him our promise is to our duties, not each other. There will be no intimacy between us. You and he can continue as you always have, and I will be happy for you."

Sabina wiped her tears away with a vengeance. "I don't understand. Why is my happiness more important to you than your own? Why would you try to win my friendship rather than the favor of your future husband?"

"I have learned through hard experience the true value of a woman I can call a friend. I am not demanding anything, Sabina, and I understand if you can never extend your friendship to me. In your position, I am not sure I would find myself generous and kind enough to do so. But I want you to know you can rely on me. My friendship is always available to you."

"I don't know what to say." Sabina's hands fidgeted at her side, as if she longed to reach for some weapon that was not there. "Will you come back tomorrow for a weaving party?"

"Certainly," Cassia blurted.

"You and I shall sit together at my loom. I shall invite every harpy in the court to attend us. I will see to it they spew compliments to you until they learn to mean them. I want all of Tenebra to know who Lady Cassia's true allies are."

THE HAWK AND THE OWL

A S SOON AS CASSIA neared the kennels, she could hear the din. She could tell Knight's voice apart from that of any other dog in the world. His bays filled the night as those she held within her could not.

The kennel master was not eager to leave his cups or the company of the comrades commiserating with him about how marriage was the bane of man's existence. By the time Cassia was done persuading the drunken pig she required his assistance, she had joined his wife among the ranks of women he never wanted to see again. He dared not accompany her to retrieve her hound. He gave her the key.

When Knight caught scent of her, his howls turned into frantic barks, and he pressed himself against the gate of the run. Cassia dropped to her knees, crooning reassurances to him. She unlocked the door and threw the key aside just in time for him to leap into her arms.

She sat on the ground in the kennels in her sister's fine gown and held Knight while he shed on her and wagged his tail so hard his whole body swayed. She buried her face in his fur.

She had made it through one more day. Chrysanthos had not immolated her for heresy in front of the entire gathering. She had survived the Autumn Greeting.

It wasn't long before familiar voices reached her ears. "Oh, if she isn't in the kennels, right where we thought we'd find her."

"You'd best stay here, even if you have taken your medicine. I'll bring her out."

Cassia lifted her head to see Callen coming toward her and Perita wringing her hands just on the other side of the fence that bordered the kennels. Callen helped her up and took her to Perita, who put an arm around Cassia for support.

"Are you all right, my lady?"

"Yes. Worn out, but all right."

"When Lord Flavian didn't escort you back to the palace as he ought..."

"I excused him from his responsibilities to me. Let us retire for the evening, shall we?"

Callen made sure Cassia got back to her rooms without further battles, then left her with her handmaiden. Perita ushered her to the warmth of her own hearth fire and rid her of the trappings of her sister's doomed Greeting.

While Perita brewed an herbal infusion, Cassia retreated to her bedchamber for a bath. Her handmaiden had already set a pitcher of warm water beside her washstand. She shut the door. She had seldom been so grateful for the simple respite of solitude in her own room with only Knight's comforting presence.

The weather mages' handiwork that had let the sun beat down earlier that day now made way for the moons. The Blood Moon, nearly veiled, was a circle of black-red in the black sky, one edge traced in a fine line of bright crimson that one could only see if one didn't look right at it. The Light Moon was its opposite, bright and white and just past full, with only a hint of shadow along one side.

By its light alone, Cassia retrieved the ivy pendant from her satchel. She ducked behind the tapestry and into the darkness of the secret passageway. She felt for a familiar niche in the stone wall and retrieved the priceless treasure she kept hidden there.

When she went back out into her moonlit bedchamber, she just looked at Lio's handkerchief for a moment. Then she lifted his gift to her nose. The handkerchief still smelled like him, and the cassia soap she kept wrapped in it was as spicy and fragrant as the day he had given it to her. If there was ever a time to use a little of it, it was now, to wash away all traces of this wretched day.

She undressed completely and treated herself to her first bath with cassia soap in months. She took her time, luxuriating in the scent and the feel of it on her skin. She let herself remember.

Her nightly appointment with her tears arrived. The uncontrollable weeping had astonished her on the first night she had spent without Lio. Cassia did not cry. Not since she was seven, when she had learned not to make such noise. She had allowed herself tears of mourning for her sister only once, last year during the fourteenth anniversary of Solia's murder, when she had told Lio the truth and he had kept vigil with her. So, she had reasoned, she was entitled to one such outburst for his sake.

The second night, the keening sobs she had stifled under her blankets had thoroughly humiliated her. By the end of the first week, she had been forced to realize she would not stop crying, no matter how she tried.

There must never come a night when resignation finally drained the last of her tears out of her. She must not let that happen. She was no longer numb, and she was not yet resigned. Her love for all she had given up burned inside her, and she would keep weeping for that beacon so the light did not go out.

After she dried herself and her tears and returned Lio's gifts to their hiding place, she put on a clean woolen tunica and went back out to sit by the hearth with Knight on her feet. Perita pressed a hot cup into her hands, and Cassia breathed strength from the steam of the herbs she had grown. Perita began to untangle Cassia's wet hair, and the soft, rhythmic tugs of the wooden comb lulled her.

"Do you want to talk about it, my lady?"

"About what, Perita?"

"Why you aren't happy tonight."

Once again Perita reminded Cassia how fortunate she was in her insightful handmaiden. In her thoughtful friend. If only Cassia could tell her how right she was.

The realization that she wanted to took her aback. It had always been easy for her to keep her own counsel and difficult for her to confide in others. This was the first time she had ever had to resist a temptation to tell someone else a secret.

"I am exhausted from dancing and being a spectacle, that's all." Cassia drank her infusion so as not to give her wagging tongue a chance.

Silence fell, except for the sound of the comb. Until Perita said, "He must be something else, to make you think twice about Lord Flavian."

Cassia froze. "Whatever do you mean, Perita?"

"You used your fine foreign soap tonight. You still haven't forgotten the one who gave it to you."

It was a good thing Cassia had just drained her cup, for otherwise she would have spilled it all over herself.

"No, don't worry, my lady. I've no idea who he is, and I won't press you for a name if you think it best to keep it to yourself." Perita leaned around and had a look at Cassia. "Oh, you're blushing. You've a pretty blush. I daresay Lord Fancy Soap appreciated it before Lord Flavian ever did."

"Perita, it's just a bar of soap. I like the scent. That's all."

"Is that so? Because I remember when everyone was trying to get one of those soaps, the gifts from the embassy, hmm? He must have been a very fine lord indeed to get his hands on one of those. But I thought to myself, she'll use that on her hound's feet, like the beauty salve Lord Adrogan gave her. But you didn't." Perita gave Cassia a knowing smile. "He must have been very good to you, my lady, to pass muster with you at all."

Cassia let her gaze fall, trying to make sense of the scramble of words inside her. What she wanted to say. Everything she had always assumed she shouldn't say. Perita simply waited, giving her time to answer, and the comb kept swishing through her hair.

Cassia could trust Perita with bleeding hands. As long as she never told her friend she had injured them in defense of a shrine of Hespera, of course.

Cassia could trust her friend about Lio, too, as long as she never let on he was a Hesperine.

"He was my Callen," Cassia said.

The comb stilled. "Then what is he doing, letting Lord Flavian gad about with you like this? When the owl sleeps, he loses his mouse to the hawk."

"Well," said Cassia. "The hawk has not gotten any of the mouse yet."

Perita leaned closer over Cassia's shoulder. "Did the owl get any?"

"Actually, my owl didn't sleep at all."

They both burst out laughing.

"Is he handsome?" Perita asked.

"I could scarcely take my eyes off of him."

"And good in the saddle?"

Cassia put her hands to her flaming cheeks.

Perita laughed again. "That's my answer. Is he kind?"

"Kinder than anyone I have ever known."

Perita nodded in approval. She gestured at Cassia with the comb. "You're using his soap. Please tell me that means your promise to Lord Flavian isn't set in stone. Tell me you'll see the one you want again."

"I will. But not for some time."

"Isn't that just like a man."

"No, he didn't do wrong by me. It wasn't his fault he had to leave. He…" Cassia's heart beat faster. She couldn't believe she was saying this aloud. It was strange how much more it alarmed her than committing treason. "He asked me to go with him."

Perita gasped.

"I wanted to say yes." Cassia swallowed. "But it was too dangerous."

Perita set aside the comb and sat down across from Cassia.

And Cassia let herself keep talking. "We exchanged no promises when we parted. There wasn't time to ask each other when, or if, we might see one another again. We were too occupied trying to…do our duty. But in those few, rash moments we had, he did ask me to go with him. And I told him no. I don't know if that means I missed my chance."

"How did he take it?"

"He wasn't even angry with me, not for one moment. He was in so much pain, I could tell, Perita—I'm not flattering myself when I say he felt the loss of me. But he said I should decide what was best for *me*, and no matter what it was, he would do it. And he did."

Perita's lips parted, and her voice hushed. "My lady, I would have gone with that one."

Cassia's anger stirred. But what use was it to be angry at the results of her own decision? "People would have gotten hurt."

"Seems to me then, you didn't do what was best for you. You did what was best for other people. That's very like you, my lady."

All this time, Cassia had been trying to become someone who did not think only of herself. This was the first time anyone other than Lio had told her she was succeeding. "Thank you, Perita."

"What for, my lady?"

"I'd never be able to list all the reasons, even though I can write better these days."

Now it was Perita who was blushing.

A knock at the hearth room door interrupted their conversation.

Perita went to answer with her hands on her hips. "If that's Lord Flavian, I'll tell him Anthros has seen quite enough of Kyria for one day. The lads may be wooing their ladies all over Solorum at this hour on Greeting night, but not that lad, and not my lady."

Cassia smiled and refrained from giving away that she was still expecting a servant of Lady Valentia's before the night was through.

A moment later, Perita returned to the fireside carrying a small, plain chest. She set the discreet delivery in Cassia's lap, then took her chair again. "That was a courier in Lady Valentia's colors. I suppose she just couldn't wait until the betrothal is official to send you her gift. Let's see what it is."

"This is not mine." Cassia opened the chest and lifted out the heavy purse. "This is yours. Lady Valentia doesn't know who you are, and you needn't reveal yourself to her. I thanked her on your behalf."

Perita stared at the coin pouch. "I don't understand."

"This is the money that, by law, Verruc should have paid for his crimes against you. Since he is dead, his lord should have settled it. Tyran's betrothed took it upon herself to right that wrong." Cassia dropped the purse into Perita's hold.

As her jaw dropped, her hands fell to her lap under the weight of the purse. "I know my price. This can't be for me. It's too much."

"Lady Valentia disavows all knowledge of your name or rank, so your secret is safe with her, and she has given you the price for a lady."

"But—the price goes to the lady's father or husband—and I'm not a lady."

"Do not say you are only a householder. Give no regard to the law that calls only for your master to be compensated. We owe the king *nothing*. And I owe you everything."

Perita's lip trembled, and then tears were pouring down her face. "I didn't think anyone else cared."

"I know. That's worth more than money." Cassia pulled her chair closer to her friend, grinning down at the purse. "But it's a lot of money."

With tentative fingers, Perita opened the purse and peered inside. Golden likenesses of the king gazed out at them, too flattering to really look like him.

Giddy laughter bubbled out of Perita. "By Anthros, Kyria, and all fourteen scions. I can't wait to show Callen! And his mother and sisters... We're..."

"Set for life," Cassia said.

Perita met her gaze with wide eyes. "I think it will take some time before it seems real."

"When it does, you may want to make some new plans. If that means you decide on something different for your future than what we spoke of earlier, I want you to know I understand. You must do what's best for you and Callen, and I will be so happy for you."

Perita shook her head. "Nonsense, my lady. At your back is right where we'll always be. I know a good situation when I'm lucky enough to find it."

"The near future may hold challenges...even dangers...we have never faced before."

"Well, that's nothing new really, is it, my lady?"

Cassia smiled. "I too know a good situation when I'm lucky enough to find it. I am grateful indeed for the two of you."

"But see here, mightn't an even better situation await than Segetia? Have you heard anything from Lord Fancy Soap? Anything at all?"

"Yes. He managed to send me one message."

Perita's eyes lit. "What did he say?"

Cassia could never explain how Lio had appeared to her in one of his illusions, insubstantial as moonlight and impossible to hold. His apparition had nonetheless given her a glimpse of him, the sound of his voice, and his words to hold on to. Cassia had recited those words to herself over and over since that night to be sure she would never forget.

She repeated as much of his message as she dared reveal to her friend. "I should never have left you...I swear I will come back for you. Trust me. I will find a way...I need you. Wait for me."

Cassia had just admitted aloud that she was no longer a maiden and that she'd been in secret contact with her forbidden lover. She found it did not matter that she could not say he wasn't human and had sent his message with heretical magic.

It was so good to speak of him aloud. It made him feel real again.

"Well," Perita said, "you might not have exchanged any promises when he left, but he certainly made his intentions clear after the fact. How did you reply?"

Cassia knotted her hands in her lap. She had promised him then and there she would hold him again, but he had not heard her. The illusory Lio before her had not responded to her words. "I couldn't reply. There was no way to get my message through. I did try."

"I'm sure you did your best, my lady. I dare say that's not the reason he hasn't returned. What you've said about him makes it clear he's a man of honor. Even though he hasn't heard from you, he'll come back for you, because he gave you his word."

Cassia nodded. "If it were in his power to return, I have no doubt he would have fulfilled his promise already."

But his power, as great as it was, would never be a match for the Queens' magic. His apparition had explained they prevented him from leaving Orthros in this time of danger. He would never be able to return to Tenebra.

Unless Cassia brought him to her.

Then he would come for her, as any Hesperine errant would strive to deliver a mortal to safety.

"But would honor be all that motivated him?" Now she was confessing fears aloud. Fears, desires, tears. Once they started, they never stopped. "His message came only a fortnight after we parted, when his feelings must still have been fresh. But after all this time…" A fortnight must seem like nothing to someone who would live for eternity. And if a fortnight was nothing…what did a few nights mean? "I have no doubt he was sincere then. But I don't know if his regard for me has changed in the months since."

"It's only natural to worry about that. A man's always a risk, and it's always hard to decide if he's worth it."

"He is worth any risk."

"You're sure? Because for you, my lady, the risk is different."

"How well I know it. But I'm not afraid of punishment. Or the one who would punish me."

"If you're not afraid of *that*, my lady, what could you possibly be worried about?"

"The things I must do to bring us together again. How much time that will take." At last she confessed to her friend—and herself—the worst specter she envisioned ahead of her, looming even larger than the last resort, waiting for her on the other side of it. "What if I go through all of that, only to find it is too late for us?"

Perita shook her head. "I don't know anyone else like you, my lady. You can stand among kings and lords and Hesperines without twitching, but when it comes to your man, the thought he might have changed his mind has you wringing your hands."

"I—may I take that as a compliment, Perita? All things considered, I would be more dismayed to hear the opposite."

"You may take anything I say however you like, my lady. But it seems to me you've made up your mind."

"I made up my mind the night he left. I still dread what I must do to make good on my promise. But I will not give up. I *will* see him again."

AUTUMN EQUINOX

ORTHROS

Hesperines shall not set foot in temples, orphanages, or places of burial.

—*The Equinox Oath*

CALL TO ACTION

L IO WAS WAITING ON his uncle's terrace when Basir and Kumeta came out of Uncle Argyros's library. Their sense of urgency rebounded through the Blood Union.

"Don't think you missed another conference," Kumeta said. "There is no more time for discussion, only action."

Basir held out a hand. "If you have a letter for the prince, give it here."

Lio hurried to open his scroll case. "What has happened?"

"War mages," Basir announced, "wearing Aithourian colors and bristling with all the power Dalos sought to hide. They could not be more obvious."

"They arrived so near dawn," Kumeta said, "we barely had time to confirm their presence before we had to make for Rota Overlook to Slumber. We are fortunate our Sanctuary there is old and well veiled, for Cordium's so-called goodwill ambassadors are anything but farm mages."

"How many?" Lio asked.

"A full war circle," Basir answered.

That meant Cassia had seven war mages breathing down her neck. "Do we know who they are?"

Kumeta nodded. "When we returned to Solorum after dark, we witnessed the king allow the war circle's leader the privilege of lighting the festival bonfire. The whole gathering was astir about Lucis's new crony. It appears the Synthikos of the Aithourian Circle has finally appointed his Dexion, just in time to send him to Tenebra."

"The Dexion!" Lio echoed. "That is all but a declaration of war."

"The Synthikos has chosen Chrysanthos," Kumeta informed Lio, "Dalos's lifelong rival. The envoy service's information on Corona's inner workings is not what it used to be, but we do know both were born into the Cordian high nobility with an affinity for fire and taken into the Aithourian Circle as very young boys. They received the same training from the Synthikos, always competing for his favor, and became notorious for sabotaging each other at every turn. While Dalos made a name for himself as a firebrand, Chrysanthos is known as their generation's foremost politician."

"Then he is sure to be even more dangerous than Dalos," Lio said.

Basir shot Lio's scroll case an indicative glance. "We are out of time. If we do not find the rest of our people immediately, it will be too late. We are returning to the prince now."

Lio drew out his letter for Rudhira. "Wait."

"Ask your questions quickly," Basir bade him.

"Did you learn anything else at the festival?"

"Nothing else of import." Frustration edged Kumeta's words. "After the dance, the king and the Dexion retired to a game of kings and mages in the Sun Temple, where we could not follow. We hardly know what they're planning. Now, while the Dexion is busy blessing Lord Flavian and his bride-to-be, we must make use of what little time is left to us."

"Lady Cassia danced?"

"Of course. Hurry now." She gestured at the letter Lio held.

He stood frozen. "She is really promised to Flavian?"

"Promised and delivered, by all accounts," she said. "After they played Anthros and Kyria in the dance, they wasted no time sneaking off alone without even her liegehound to supervise. When we left just now, Flavian's comrades and rivals alike were still in their cups making bawdy speculations. We can thank the happy couple that Tenebra's warriors will be too thick-headed in the morning for even the Dexion to muster them."

Lio stood there holding his letter, unable to speak. Basir took the scroll from his hand, and then the Master Envoys were gone.

Lio made it to the woods beyond the terrace before his body got the better of him. His roar of frustration turned into a gag, and he made a mess of the snow at the foot of one of his uncle's fruit trees. He braced his hand on the trunk and hunched on the ground, unable to do more than wait it out while the Craving ravaged him.

"Lio," he heard Mak say, "we know you're here."

"Let us past your veil, won't you?" came Lyros's voice, gentle but firm.

Well, at least Lio's veil hadn't failed him. Uncle Argyros didn't know his nephew was out here yelling and defacing his trees. Lio attempted a cleaning spell, which left a hole in the snow and him crouching in a patch of unsoiled but soggy mulch. He sat down hard, put his head between his knees, and let Mak and Lyros through his veil. He heard them walk inside the reach of his concealing magic.

Lyros sat down beside him. "Oh, Lio."

Mak knelt on Lio's other side. "What did Basir and Kumeta say?"

Lio shut his eyes. "Flavian danced with Cassia."

"Then that settles it," Mak said. "You have to do something."

"I should have done something long before now. I swear, I am truly going to murder Flavian." Lio's fangs unsheathed, and he bared his teeth. He was beyond wondering at his thirst for violence or the way his Gift leapt within him, out for blood. He was beyond philosophy, and pure conviction drove him. "They went off alone together after the dance. They're alone together right now. It's unbelievable—for some reason she doesn't even have Knight with her. If Flavian imposes on her in even the slightest way, I will start with his mind, and by the time I am done with him, he will be broken from the inside out."

And if Flavian didn't impose on her? If she wanted a tryst with him in the woods she had once shared with no one but Lio?

Helpless frustration gripped Lio as never before, and his magic flared so powerfully he shuddered.

"Thorns!" Mak exclaimed. "Easy now."

The veil around them strengthened, but not with Lio's power. Lyros and Mak bolstered his concealment with one of their own wards.

The high tide of Lio's Gift receded, leaving a well of hurt behind. Cassia was not bound to him by any promises, not until they acknowledged to one another they were Graced. She was within her rights to choose anyone, and after a lifetime of stifling her beautiful, powerful passions, she was all the more entitled to pleasure and exploration. Lio was not a Tenebran man who thought a walk in the woods meant he owned Cassia. He was not Flavian.

But even in the absence of promises, if she did not feel her bond to him… Lio was immortal, not immune. He still wanted to kill Flavian.

"It's just gossip," Lyros insisted. "Basir and Kumeta must pay attention to any information, from hard facts to rumors mortals swap in their privies. But don't assume too much from the drunken jests of a lot of randy humans."

"You're right." Lio held fast to reason. "You're right, gossip would blow it out of proportion, and I don't know what really happened. I must withhold judgment until I have a firsthand account—firsthand reassurance. From Cassia herself."

Mak let out a laugh of relief. "You're going to bring her home."

"I am going to bring her home," Lio repeated.

As he spoke the decision aloud, his relief was enough to make him shake.

Lyros grinned. "You said your father already offered to take you to get her. Now we are jealous. Rescuing a mortal in distress from Solorum itself with one of the Blood Errant? That's the stuff of legends."

Lio looked at his friend. "No, Father is not going to set foot in Solorum. Not when there are seven Aithourian war mages in residence."

Lyros cursed.

Mak sprang up. "The Charge has a war circle on their hands? Already? It wasn't supposed to happen so soon. They haven't found everyone yet."

Lio staggered to his feet and put a hand on his cousin's shoulder. "If there is one Hesperine who knows how to deal with war mages, it's Nike. Don't forget she has single-handedly defeated whole war circles."

"Goddess, I'd like to see that." Mak held fast to Lyros's offered hand. "Pray for my sister—and our parents."

"Don't waste any more time," Lyros urged Lio. "I don't care how you're planning to do it. Just get Cassia home. You can't leave her sitting there now that the Aithourians have come, not a night longer."

"I know. But I have to find a way to bring my Grace home without starting the war ahead of time."

Mak eyed him. "If anyone can do that, Lio, it's you."

"You are a diplomat through and through," said Lyros. "Just as you promised, you'll find a way."

Lio let his Trial brothers feel his gratitude through the Blood Union. He could only hope they were right.

CUT FROM EXPERIENCE

L IO CLOSED THE DOOR of his library and shut the veil over his residence with all the force of a portcullis. Zoe and the other children were oblivious in Slumber. All his loved ones who were Graced sought refuge from the world's troubles in one another's arms. Lio had what remained of Veil Hours to himself, and he was on his own. Which was precisely what he needed tonight.

He was out of time, and he had to find a way to rescue himself and his Grace without destroying two kingdoms. He had to find the answer somewhere within these walls—or within the walls of his own mind.

He sank into his chair and looked around him at his resources.

He couldn't even see his desk. The crescent of wrought iron had disappeared under his latest notes and research, which for the first time in his life he was not bothering to organize.

The shelves that lined the walls to the vaulted ceiling held enough scrolls and books to educate him for eternity. The finest truths he had discovered therein, he had immortalized in glass on the brilliant windows between the shelves. Moonlight beamed through the ancient letters.

Was this how he had found his answers last year in Tenebra? Had letters of glass delivered life-saving medicine to Zoe or defeated Dalos?

Yes and no. Much of this study had led Lio to Tenebra, and he had carried all of this wisdom with him into the field. But how quickly he had realized preparation was only that, and not enough.

What he needed now was a solution cut from his experience. Stained with the blood he and Cassia had shed.

Lio gave into temptation and opened his scroll case. He drew out his papers and set them on his desk atop a stack of books that offered a nonhaz-ardous position. Bracing himself, he reached into the empty cylinder and opened the small compartment that lay hidden at the bottom. He pulled out the handkerchief he had once used to bind Cassia's wounded hand.

Dried blood stained the white silk, caught in the black threads of an embroidered Rose of Hespera. The scrap of fabric felt heavy to his senses with the weight of the powerful veil he kept over it for the sake of his sanity. The smell of her blood was more than he could bear. But he could not resist.

He lifted the veil. The fragrance of that remnant of her blood wrapped around him like whiffs of dying flowers and wrung a groan from him. Hunger roared to life within him.

"Cassia," he said aloud. "What are we to do?"

Clenching her blood in his hand, he took hold of the moonlight that shone through the words on the windows and shaped a person. He had needed many nights of practice, but after all this time, he was finally able to conjure an illusory portrait that was accurate enough not to anger him with its insufficiency. He rode the erratic rise and fall of his Gift, and it served her image well. Flows of power made her gaze flash, ebbs sculpted the dark smudges under her eyes.

Lio kept at it until Cassia stood before him, life-size and opaque, in her gardening dress, with her hair unbound. Just an illusion. But one that paid tribute to every freckle.

"I do not rescind my protest of your effort to bring me to the table," she declared. How good to hear an echo of her voice, however faint. "You should have asked me first. But if you had, I hope I would have had the courage to say yes."

"Would you protest such an effort now, my love?" he wanted to ask her.

"What a momentous night, when a Hesperine heretic helped a bastard girl, his fellow godsforsaken, to the table," her illusion reminded him.

"I would do it again."

Hazel eyes made of pure light met his. "I was glad for my place at the Summit."

What better course of action could there be but to invite Cassia to Orthros, just as he had brought her to the council table? To put all the power and possibility of that invitation into her hands and let her go to work?

But how in the name of the cup and thorns could he do that?

He fueled his frustration into magic, his magic into Cassia, and he watched her lift a hand to the stone archway that was not there and trace the pattern of Hespera's glyph.

He did not have that many options. Whatever he attempted must, first, bring them together. Second, it must do so without inciting the Aithourians to violence any sooner than they already intended. Third, it must not, in one motion, destroy all she had built with such care, all that held the mages and the king in check.

That third imperative was the most difficult to fulfill, for he was working blind. His insight into her strategies was warped by distance and secrets and the limits of his own interpretations.

Ideally, whatever he attempted would buy his people time to keep looking for their lost Hesperines errant, rather than wasting what precious time still remained to them.

What would bring Cassia to Orthros and delay the Aithourians? What would play to the strengths of her strategy, driving the wedge further between the mages and the king, swaying the free lords in favor of the Hesperines?

What could Lio even do from here, with no influence upon events in Tenebra? If only there had been a Summit, he and Cassia could have attempted and, indeed, accomplished so much. But Lio no longer doubted the truth: the king would never call the Summit now.

It all came back to that. No Summit.

The Summit was precisely what they needed.

Lio was exactly right. He did not have that many options. In fact, he had only, exactly, one.

Shock at himself made Lio's magic spike again. Illusory Cassia blazed into a silhouette of light and disappeared.

Goddess, he said to Hespera, but stopped there, uncertain whether to ask for her benediction—or her forgiveness.

Had he really just conceived of such a thing—was he seriously considering it?

Did he really intend to make it a reality?

King Lucis would not convene the Summit. But what if Lio did?

97

nights until

WINTER SOLSTICE

Hesperines shall not take to them children who are still under the care of their elders, regardless of the elders' treatment of the children.

Hesperines shall not disturb the dying who await mortal aid or the dead whose kin or comrades are coming to claim them.

—The Equinox Oath

HEROISM OR INFAMY

O NCE LIO STARTED WRITING, the words came fast and certain. He didn't pause his quill even when he consulted one of his sources for facts to strengthen his argument. Without looking up from his work, he searched through his familiar shelves only in his mind's eye and summoned the histories and treatises he needed to hand. When one hand got tired, he switched his quill to the other and kept going. When he filled the first length of scroll, he hastily appended more reed paper with an adherence charm and pressed on.

He didn't remember falling into Slumber. He woke in his chair with his quill still in his hands and ink stains on his fingers. A new night had begun, the one he had promised his uncle he would devote to finishing his Imperial libraries proposal. Lio wrapped his Tenebran army blanket around his shoulders against the Craving shivers. The wool still smelled like roses, blood, and Cassia. He started writing again.

When he heard a goat bleat, he altered his veil to allow for small visitors. It wasn't long before he heard a pair of bare feet on the tile. He looked up to see Zoe with a goat under each arm and her mantle draped over them all. She didn't say anything, just crawled under Lio's desk. At ease beneath the shelter of iron, she uncovered her head and wrapped her scarf around her shoulders instead.

Lio smiled at her and put down his pen. He fished under his literature to find the tin he always kept at hand when he was working. There it was. He got rid of the ink on his hands with a cleaning spell and plucked something out of the box for Zoe.

When he handed the sapsweet under the desk, her eyes lit up. He watched her stuff the candy in her mouth, gnaw on it for a split second, and nearly swallow it whole. She was licking her fingers when he handed her another. It lasted barely an instant longer.

After several more of the syrupy morsels, he handed her a gumsweet she could chew on for a while. She smacked her lips, and one of her pale cheeks puffed out around the big lump of candy. Lio would never get tired of watching his once-starving sister enjoy food not because she needed it, but only because it gave her delight.

Her little brown-and-white goat sat on his foot. The black-and-white kid wandered off to nibble on any scrolls within reach, which Lio had already bespelled to withstand caprine cravings. Zoe played quietly with one of the glass figurines Lio had made her while he went back to his writing.

He took refuge in their contentment, and it kept his hands steady as he wrote words that would shake their world on its foundations.

Sometime later, Zoe departed in answer to their mother's call. Neither of their parents came to ask Lio what he was up to. Mak and Lyros let him be. The handful of his loved ones who knew it was not Imperial libraries that occupied him had given him the gift of uninterrupted time.

He was surprised when he came to the end of it and realized his work was complete.

Lio set down his pen. For the first time, his hands shook.

The furor of his inspiration drained out of him all at once, and he realized how thirsty he was. He did not have the focus to repaint Cassia in light and ask for her approval of his work. Instead he looked at his less ephemeral portrait of her, his account of her deeds, which he had kept right next to his scroll as his primary source the entire time he had been writing his new proposal.

However his own people reacted to what he proposed herein, Cassia would understand. She would see his strategy more clearly than anyone, grasp its logic, and know how to use it to her advantage. He hoped—he dared believe—she would approve.

Moon Hours waned. Lio had a little while before Veil Hours to settle his affairs. He would need that time to seek strength in the Drink from his parents and prepare for tomorrow. Tomorrow and the inaugural Firstblood

Circle of the season, at which he was to deliver his proposal before the Queens, their Master Ambassador, and the heads of every bloodline in Orthros.

It hadn't even taken that long, just the time between one moonrise and the next. In one night, he had written the proposal that would secure his place in Hesperine history. Whether that legacy would be heroism or infamy, he must leave it to his people to decide.

TO MAKE THIS ERA

L IO STEPPED DIRECTLY TO the back portico of Kia's residence, avoiding the rest of House Hypatia and any possibility of delay. He paused at his Trial sister's closed door to ascertain whether there would be magefire to pay if he interrupted her.

Since she had unleashed her latest theory on the world and earned promotion to full mathematician, the name Eudokia Hypatia had been on scholars' lips from here to the Empire, and she had been very busy. Lio wondered where she found all the energy she devoted to her next great work and her visiting colleagues. At the moment, her open veil indicated he was not in danger of disrupting her research or her extracurricular adventures with one of her admirers visiting from the Imperial university, so he let himself into her study.

The travel desk that was the center of her world on journeys and at home now stood deserted in the middle of the floor, surrounded by a pile of cushions and the bespelled tablets she used to scrawl and erase calculations. Her coffee pot sat abandoned on its geomagical warmer, filling the room with the aroma of her favorite blend of Polar Night Roast and bitter cacao.

In the pot's heat basked her familiar, tasting the air with a forked tongue. Sophia was longer than Lio was tall, but somehow the serpent had managed to slither most of herself into a coil on the copper tray of the coffee service.

Lio glanced around, then up. Kia herself was at one of the shelves near the ceiling on the opposite side of the room, levitating some distance from the ladder she only kept to oblige her mortal visitors. Lio expected her to offer him a greeting and a prescient inquiry without looking up from the scroll in her hands. But she rolled up Laskara's *The Geometry of Art* and thrust it back into its rack on the shelf.

"Lio! I'm so glad to see you." She dropped to her feet, tossing her mantle of turquoise-and-white silk more securely around her shoulders.

Lio had often seen Zoe mimic that gesture with her own scarf. "It's good to see you too."

"Would you like some coffee?"

"No, thank you." It would be an injustice to her coffee indeed if it ended up regurgitated on her silk cushions. "Actually, I'd like your opinion on something."

"Better than coffee." She beamed, and her keen blue gaze went to what he carried in his hands. "A new writing of yours?"

"Yes."

"It's about time you came to visit me with something worth several hours of conversation. I've hardly seen you lately. As much time as you spend with Zoe, you're seldom there when I come to give her lessons." Kia shoved her blond curls out of her eyes and held out her pale, ink-stained hands.

But now, at the last minute, Lio hesitated before giving her his proposal. It was difficult to hand over his heart and soul to anyone, even Kia. "I haven't shown this to anyone yet."

She eased the scroll out of his hold, unsmiling now. "What are you so worried about? I promise I'll be a gentle critic, even if you do take Axioprepes's side of the argument in the *Discourses on Dung Beetles.*"

The reference to their long-standing private jest did nothing to cheer him. "I think I shall let the proposal speak for itself."

She pursed her lips. "This isn't your Imperial libraries proposal, is it."

"No."

Her face lit up again. "It's your firsthand account of the Summit? You've resumed work on it!"

"Actually, that project is still stalled." He had no heart to pen the travelogue he had boasted of to Cassia when he must omit her from it. His record of her deeds had become the only account of Tenebra that mattered.

Kia frowned. "When will you add your own primary source to our histories? You said yourself it's your most important work to date, and I agree with you."

"No. I think the scroll you're holding is my most important work. Possibly ever."

"You look like you need to sit down." She gestured to the cushions.

Lio sank down onto a large tasseled pillow to await her verdict. "You may want to be sitting down as well."

"I've read every word Phaedros has ever written and lived to tell the tale. Nothing from your honorable pen can possibly shock me."

"Do tell me if what I've come up with is worthy of the most notorious and only criminal in Orthros's history. I should warn you, after I make this proposal to the Circle tomorrow, they may brand me mad as Phaedros and sentence me to join him in exile under the midnight sun."

The Blood Union became vibrant with Kia's ferocious curiosity. She unrolled the scroll with relish, and her eyes began darting back and forth as she devoured the text.

One, two, three heartbeats passed before her jaw dropped.

"You *are* shocked," Lio said. "You!"

"No," she breathed. "I am…" Another few heartbeats. The scuff of the scroll against itself as she unrolled it further. "Deukalion Komnenos, I am honored to be the first person you chose to read this."

"Honored?" he repeated.

She did not speak another word until she came to the end of the scroll. At last she met his gaze, her aura alight with what he could only describe as joy. She held the scroll out toward him, and her feet lifted off the ground. "Lio! This is history! Thank Hespera she ordained that we should live now and make this era."

"Is that really what you think?"

"You don't need to ask me that question. And I don't have to ask you if you know what you have done here. You know exactly what you're doing, you have laid out your case with perfect precision, and you could predict the consequences for the next sixteen hundred years with the same undeniable reasoning. I am holding pure brilliance in my hands. Cup and thorns, I cannot wait for Circle! As soon as Mother and Father get back from the Observatory, I will tell them I am going with them tomorrow."

Kia's enthusiasm engulfed Lio, and he couldn't help feeling it. He was almost too relieved to speak. "Will you do me another favor?"

"Anything. Allow me to declare myself your first partisan. You will need help with this."

"All the help I can get. It would mean a very great deal to me if all of you were there tomorrow. You'll help me convince Nodora and Xandra to attend as well?"

"Attend what?" came Nodora's voice from the doorway.

"Lio is going to change the world tomorrow," Kia informed her. "You won't want to miss Circle."

Nodora strolled in with, as always, a musical instrument in her hands. Tonight it was a shamisen, one of the three-stringed instruments she lovingly crafted in the tradition of her mortal foremothers.

She turned her big, brown eyes upon Lio and gave him her sweet smile. "Lio changed the world once already last year, when he saved the entire embassy and the new sucklings. Do you mean to say he's at it again?"

Lio returned her smile. "I hope so."

"You know so," Kia corrected.

"I'm glad you're here," Lio said to Nodora. He saw that she was wearing one of her ocean-blue work robes and no cosmetics on her fair skin. "It looks as if you're not on your way to a performance. I was going to pay you a visit right after seeing Kia, but do you have a moment now?"

"Certainly," Nodora answered. "I came by for opinions on a new song. I gather you could use my opinion on something as well."

"Please. Tell me what you make of my mad plan."

Nodora's smile became a grin. "I suspect I'll be writing commemorative songs about tomorrow's events. I shall be fortunate indeed if they are as well-received as my composition about the Summit. You're very helpful to our reputations, Lio."

Lio shook his head. "It was your original piece in the style of the Archipelagos that secured your initiation and your reputation as the only Hesperine expert on the music of your human homeland. I will not let the spotless name of Menodora Kithara be cut to pieces by Glasstongue. That's no way to thank you for giving me such an epithet. You should hold off planning songs about tomorrow until you know what I'm getting us all into."

"It sounds more like you need me to keep you from slicing yourself to shreds, Guilttongue." Nodora came to stand by him and rested a hand on his shoulder. "Of course we'll all be at Circle."

"Mak and Lyros already know," Kia guessed.

"They know how much is at stake for me right now. I'm going to tell them exactly what I'm planning when I go to training after this. I know they'll come tomorrow."

Nodora raised her brows. "If Mak and Lyros will be willing to sit through Circle for it, it must be important."

Kia waved his scroll at their Trial sister. Nodora set her shamisen carefully aside, then swept her long, straight black hair out of her way before settling onto one of the cushions with the scroll. She studied his proposal in silent concentration, her aura withholding judgment. In suspense, Lio watched her read.

At last she met his gaze, and her concern enveloped him. "Lio, are you sure you want to do this?"

Kia glared at her. "How can you ask him that?"

"She has every right to ask. Every Hesperine in Orthros has the right to ask. What I will say to the Circle tomorrow is the greatest act of presumption anyone of our youth—anyone at all—has taken it upon themselves to commit in the history of our relations with Tenebra." Lio's prediction of the future he dreaded most worked its way out of him. "The Circle will almost certainly be scandalized by my proposal and vote against it unanimously to save the Queens the trouble of refusing."

"The firstbloods would be fools not to leap at your plan!" Kia declared. "They cannot deny your argument. You are right, Lio. This is the only way."

"It's also the most dangerous way," he said. "You know how they are about safety. It will be a battle to get any of them to agree."

"Overprotective traditionalists," Kia scoffed. "This proposal is just the kind of shock they need to get them off their seats."

They were all accustomed to Kia's irreverent outbursts, but Nodora still took it upon herself to be the lone voice of conciliation. "How can you say that about our elders? We owe everything we have to their power and protection. It's with good reason they are so cautious to act."

"All my proposal may change is the history of my career." Lio's shoulders slumped. "By shortening it."

"That's what I'm saying," Nodora told them patiently. "This is ultimately the Circle's decision. However they vote, whatever does or does not come of Lio's proposal, he will have already made his decision. For him, once he comes forward with this, there is no going back."

"The first heralds of change always face persecution, but in the end, their opponents eat their words and erect statues in their honor." Kia pointed to a marble bust of Alatheia.

Now it was Nodora's turn to glare. "Kia, Alatheia was the first mage of Hespera executed for heresy."

"Yes, and we could bestow no greater honor upon her than the epithet history has given her: 'the First Heretic.' Her refusal to recant before the Akron's inquisitors was the seed that grew into the unwavering tree that is Orthros. Tomorrow, our elders may put Lio to the figurative pyre, but just wait until the night comes when they all pretend they never disagreed with him. He will be too kind to say 'I told you so,' but I shall not."

"What advice did your uncle give you, Lio?" asked Nodora. "With him encouraging you to proceed, I cannot imagine anyone would call for your resignation, no matter how many good opinions you sacrifice among the firstbloods."

"I haven't told him," Lio admitted.

Nodora fell silent.

"Of course he hasn't told his uncle," Kia said. "Good for you, Lio, for not giving Argyros a chance to talk you out of it."

"I've made up my mind I'm not going to warn any of the elders beforehand," he said. "I don't think it would be appropriate to give them prior knowledge of the proposal. My argument must be judged for what it is, without bias or leniency. I'm going to let my family find out with your parents and everyone else."

Nodora offered sympathy to him in Union. "That must have been a hard decision."

"I wish there was some way to soften the blow to my family." His mentor would have no forewarning before Lio put to the axe everything they had worked for together. With their peers as witnesses, Lio's parents would watch him throw away all the respect and opportunity his position as Firstgift Komnenos afforded him.

"I certainly can't promise this will go well for you," said Kia, "but I can promise you this. You will be able to look at yourself in the mirror while the firstbloods cannot because you were brave enough to speak the truth. And we will be proud of you."

Nodora wrapped Lio's hands around his proposal. "No matter the consequences, you have *our* support."

Lio might stand before the Circle tomorrow opposed on all sides, but he would not stand alone. "You have my gratitude."

"I hope you'll be all right." Nodora didn't let go of his hands. "You've worked so hard to get where you are, and I know how hard you will take it, whichever way the Circle votes tomorrow. I worry that success may be an even greater weight on your conscience than failure."

"How could it? Success would be—" Just the thought of actually seeing Cassia again made his skin shiver. "I won't care what it costs me, as long as it works."

Nodora's brow furrowed. "You're staking everything on this. This must be why you've been so troubled since you came home. Have you been working on your proposal all this time?"

"No. I wrote it tonight. My proposal is not the cause of my troubles, but my path to the cure." He took a deep breath. "I mention her by name in the proposal, in fact."

Nodora's lips parted. "Lio, do you mean to say…"

"Thank the Goddess." Kia flopped down on a cushion. "You're finally going to tell us you met your match in Tenebra."

"Wait, what?" Lio stammered. "You knew?"

"I spent your first month back in Orthros researching the few diseases to which Hesperines are susceptible, malevolent magic to which you might have been exposed in Tenebra, and mental illness, which was my original hypothesis regarding your condition. As I ruled out possible explanations based on your symptoms, it quickly became obvious you are suffering from the Craving and not telling us due to the paranoid behavior induced by your addiction and your natural inclination toward secrecy when you have made what you perceive to be a mistake. I confess, I didn't consider there were political motivations for your reticence to discuss her, but now I realize you mention only one woman in your proposal who could possibly be the person you mean, and you would most certainly keep her identity a secret to facilitate the political goals you have been pursuing in coordination with her since the two of you first formed your...alliance." Kia grinned, flashing her fangs.

Nodora's happiness bloomed on the Blood Union. "Lio, you met *her* in Tenebra?"

"I didn't tell anyone else," Kia appended. "Of course I would not take it upon myself to make such a momentous announcement on your behalf."

"Yes," he told Nodora, smiling. "Lady Cassia Basilis."

Her face fell. "Oh, Lio."

He winced. "Yes."

Nodora pressed a hand to his forehead, much as his mother had done. "Six months! Have you been to see the healers?"

"No," Kia answered her. "He's been faking his exams with Javed."

"Lio!" Nodora cried.

He raised his hands in surrender. "I have heard all of this from Mak and Lyros already, and from my parents."

"Oh good." Kia sighed. "They will have talked some sense into you. Who else have you told?"

"No one."

"*Please* tell Xandra," Kia and Nodora said in unison.

"I was rather hoping—"

"No." Kia crossed her arms. "We will not tell her for you, you coward."

"Just go talk to her," Nodora urged him. "Even if you don't talk to her about Cassia right away, only try to have a conversation with her. You'll see. It will make you feel better about everything."

"Perhaps after the Circle tomorrow."

Nodora blinked at him. "Lio, consider how Xandra might feel if you make her wait to hear your proposal along with the elders."

Kia skewered him with a gaze. "Do you really want *that* to be how she finds out?"

He grimaced. "Thorns, no. What am I thinking?"

He was thinking he would need all the boldness and strength he could muster to face the Circle tomorrow, and he did not have any to spare for the encounter with Xandra he had been dreading.

A great deal of that dread was his fear he would hurt her still more than he already had. But if he didn't talk to her before the Circle tomorrow, that hurt would be much worse.

There was no way around it. He would have to spend some of his final hours of peace on a confrontation with Xandra.

SILK AND GLASS

L IO SHOULD HAVE CONSIDERED his approach before now. There was
little he could do to rescue the encounter, but there were strategies
that might have allayed what was to come. Such as choosing neutral
territory, perhaps a pleasant coffeehouse on the docks. Treating her to a
drink. Asking her how her worms were doing.

As it was, Lio had no time to prepare and no leeway to choose his
ground for his first real conversation with Xandra since the night they had
realized they were not Graced.

Last Winter Solstice had been a humiliating experience that had left
both of them wondering what they had done wrong. As if it were somehow their fault they weren't made for each other. They had put themselves
through so much unnecessary distress. Cassia had taught him just how
unnecessary it had been.

He had a responsibility to help Xandra see that, too. His only regret
now was how long it had taken him to see they were not suited and to
release her—and himself—from their misguided promise to each other.
If he had been wiser, he could have spared them both so much hurt and
embarrassment. The least he could do now was share some of what real
Grace had taught him and help Xandra lay her feelings to rest.

He went to find her where Kia and Nodora had confirmed she would
be, in her mulberry orchard. As he stalled outside the door of the greenhouse, it occurred to him that if he must put her through the confrontation,
it was probably more courteous to do so in a place she felt most confident
and comfortable. That did nothing to make him feel better, though.

He had spied on the King of Tenebra and battled an Aithourian war mage. He'd had a torrid and forbidden affair with Cassia, the most dangerous woman he knew. Why was it so hard to face the mundane risks of embarrassment and hurting Xandra's feelings? Why would it seem easier to charge forward and do this if lives were at stake to give him motivation?

But lives *were* at stake. Cassia's life. His. All the lives his proposal to the Circle tomorrow might save…or cost.

He had a more important task at this moment than just making amends with Xandra. This was not about their personal conflicts. He must petition her for her support, because this was about their people.

Xandra might not rest easy under the weight of her status, but she took her responsibilities to heart, and she would expect Lio to do no less. Neither of them would hesitate to disregard their wounded feelings and do what was best for Orthros.

As a firstblood in her own right, Xandra was the only one of Lio's peers who could directly influence tomorrow's outcome. Lio needed her vote.

He let his veil drop slowly to give Xandra ample time to realize he was there, then physically knocked on the door of the greenhouse to give her plenty of warning.

There came no response for several moments. He could make out nothing through the foggy glass and her personal veil. Perhaps she was mastering her own trepidation.

He heard a door open and shut somewhere at the back of the greenhouse. At last the door in front of him swung open. He went inside, and humid warmth enveloped him.

He walked between rows of mulberry trees laden with unhatched cocoons. Then the aisle, and his last moments to prepare his thoughts, came to an end, and he was in the center of the greenhouse.

Xandra sat at one of her worktables in a simple undyed robe with her black hair braided against her head to keep it out of the way. She perched over a tray of larvae, her pale cheeks flushed with the intensity of her concentration on the squirming white insects. A few more of the infant silk moths crawled over her palm, while her other was poised over her sketchbook, pencil in hand.

"Hello, Lio."

He had once whispered to her all his most eloquent professions of love. Every time he was in her presence now, he was as dumb as a Tenebran macer. It wasn't as if they hadn't spoken in the past few months, but forced, awkward politenesses hardly qualified as conversation.

Lio unclasped his hands from behind his back, realizing only then that he had put them there. His tell, Cassia called the gesture. That made him think of the first time he had talked to her about Xandra and how his Grace had laughed with him over his foolishness.

Remembering that night, he managed to speak. "Xandra. Hello. How are you?"

"Oh, this is ridiculous. Just come sit down."

"You're right, it is. Thank you. I will."

He took the bench on the other side of the table from her. She eased the worms she held back into the tray with their five hundred siblings. How fortunate for them that they had hatched in Orthros, where they would not die to produce their coveted fibers.

"How is the latest generation of the Alexandrian silk moth faring?" Lio asked politely. The worms were always a safe and successful topic of conversation.

"Very well, thank you," said their namesake. "It's really working to cross wild silk moths with cultivated Imperial ones to reintroduce traits lost through domestication."

"Congratulations again on your promotion to full sericulturalist."

"Kia and Nodora and I weren't about to let you and Mak and Lyros progress from initiate status without us. I was planning to earn my promotion with a more spectacular hybrid, but in hindsight I'm glad I didn't wait. I'll save those plans for the future when I apply for mastery."

Lio glanced at Xandra's sketchbook to see she was filling yet another volume with anatomical diagrams of her breed at each stage of life. She never seemed to tire of making new portraits of her thousands of identical babies. Her drawings were at once scholarship, craft, and meditation.

She closed her sketchbook and set it aside, giving Lio her full attention. "I'm glad you decided to come by. I missed you."

"I—"

She held up a hand. "No. Don't start the conversation by apologizing *again*."

"I owe you an apology for how long it's taken me to come see you."

She sighed and put her face in her hand. Then she straightened and planted both fists on the table. "Lio, I am going to tell you something I never said when we still had our understanding. I am sick to death of your self-deprecation, and your struggles with yourself wear me out. My struggles with myself are tiring enough, and your attempts to help me with them never made me feel better. I hate feeling like a pupa who is late to metamorphose. We aren't silkworms trying to burst from our cocoons. We are Hesperines and just as we ought to be. For your sake, I hope you stop trying so hard. But even if you don't, I'm not going to let your perfectionism make me feel imperfect anymore."

Lio sat in silence for a very long moment. "Is that how I made you feel? Really?"

"*Don't* apologize. It just digs you deeper into your perfectionism hole."

"But I feel terrible. That was the last thing in the world I ever intended. I always tried to treat you better than anyone."

"Like your personal goddess, yes. Which made me feel I had something to live up to and should not be the messy creature I am."

"You aren't a—a 'messy creature,' Xandra! You're the Queens' daughter! The youngest princess of Orthros. We should all treat you with honor and cherish you."

"You don't have to treat me like a princess, Lio. Just treat me like *me*. I'm not a goddess, I'm a person."

"If not an apology, then what can I possibly do to repair this…perfectionism hole, into which I sank both of us?"

"You're on your own down there now. Don't ask me to figure it out for you. I'll give you some free advice, though. Stop worrying so much."

She was right—he had worried too much. He'd been so afraid the success of his relationship with Cassia would only make Xandra dwell on the failure of his relationship with her.

But she sounded nothing short of thrilled to be rid of him.

They were *both* relieved it was over.

The only person agonizing over failures was Lio. He was the one who had reduced what he and Xandra had shared to a personal measuring stick. Mak and Lyros had warned him about the dangers of dwelling on mistakes, and he had thought he'd seen the light. But Xandra had remained his blind spot. Until now.

He shook his head. "I've been so—"

"Distracted," Xandra said judiciously.

"—self-absorbed," he realized.

"Oh, Lio. Don't you see we're all trying to make it easier for you? Like I said, stop being so rough on yourself."

"It's just that I was so determined not to hurt you any more than I already have. But I'm only now realizing I hurt you more than I knew."

"I'm not that fragile, Lio. I know I'm not easy to deal with. My emotions are as volatile as my magic, and I wear my responsibilities about as gracefully as a newblood caught levitating at dawn. But how in the world did I ever give you the impression I am fragile?"

"In hindsight, I think I owe that impression entirely to myself. It never occurred to me my efforts to love and respect you were more like…"

"Treating me like a glass votive Hespera statue. Our Trial sibs sometimes shelter me too much as well, but you're the—"

"Worst."

"Most protective. Do you really think *any* of us are that fragile? How do you think it makes us feel when we see ourselves through your eyes? One moment you'd think we're likely to shatter if you treat us poorly. The next moment, we're judges harsher than the Akron's jury, likely to hate you forever if you make a single error. That couldn't be more false. We're your friends. Your Trial sisters and brothers. We are the first people whose strength you should lean on, and the last from whom you should expect censure."

While Lio had been struggling to redefine what Xandra now meant to him, she had written the dictionary and moved on to her next project. "Xandra, I realize now I should not enshrine you like a goddess. But would you object if I thanked you for giving me some of Hespera's own wisdom?"

"I may be prone to fits of temper, irresponsibility, and small feelings. But just like all of you, I am prone to my fair share of moments of divine wisdom as well. I shall let you thank me for that."

"You're right. I should stop apologizing. I'm not going to say I'm sorry about any of it, because I'm not. Not when we learned so much from each other. And, well, thorns, we had so much fun."

"I'm glad that's how you feel. I do too." She flashed him her grin, which always made her eyes light up and her magic spark.

He met her gaze, in which he had not found his future, but did see a good past. "All those years. I think it would be a shame to regret anything."

Her aura softened. "So do I. I think everything turned out just as it should have, exactly when it ought to."

He extended a hand across the table to her, palm up. She slid her hand into his for a moment, gave him a squeeze, then let him go.

"How about, instead of an apology, I give you a promise," he offered. "From now on, I will make every effort to acknowledge your strengths as a craftsperson, a mage—and a friend."

"As long as you don't turn that into your next lofty goal to live up to."

"Understood. For what it's worth, even though I made you feel fragile, I have never believed you to be weak. Not you, of all people. In fact, I came here tonight to request that you lend me your power as a royal firstblood and member of the Circle."

"Oh! You came to ask me for my vote?" She straightened on her bench, clasping her hands in front of her.

"I can count on Kia, Nodora, Mak, and Lyros for a show of partisanship, and I hope that coming from the children of the elder firstbloods, their favor will make a statement before the Circle. But ultimately our parents are the voices of our families, and when they cast the vote for each of our bloodlines, I am not sure they will take our view. You know how much it would mean to have your support—your authority to not only make your voice heard, but to vote independently."

"Yes, it's occasionally useful that I am duty-bound to found my own bloodline and perpetuate the Queens' power among our people, which gives me a firstblood vote." She frowned at him. "But new windows for Imperial libraries don't call for partisans and a royal vote. Just what are you presenting tomorrow?"

"I'm going to make a proposal about the situation in Tenebra, and the Circle isn't going to like it."

"If you've come up with an idea that could help, we should all be glad."

"You haven't heard my plan yet. I must ask that you not tell any of the other firstbloods ahead of time, though. I don't want the rest of the Circle to hear about my intentions until I come forward officially. I understand that might put you in a position you would rather avoid, especially with your brothers and sisters. If that's the case, I won't burden you."

She waved a hand. "Your secrets are safe with me, even from my formidable eldest sister. I've been in the Circle for most of a year now, and I have yet to tell Konstantina about how you and Kia destroyed a library scroll when you were trying to come up with a way to magically transcribe text."

"Oh thorns. Please don't remind me."

"If Rudhira were here, though, I would advise you to tell him. He would consider your plan with an open mind and vote against the entire Circle without any hesitation, if necessary."

"I wish he was here, too."

"I miss him every time I vote and every hour in between." Xandra sighed. "In his absence, I'll do my best to be the royal who hears you out…and who isn't afraid to ruffle everyone's feathers." She looked at Lio expectantly.

He told her his plan.

When he was finished making his case, she breathed another sigh. "You are going to be all right."

"I suppose that will depend on the Circle's decision."

"No," she said firmly. "I mean you are going to be all right with yourself. When I found out you broke all the rules while you were in Tenebra, I knew there was hope for you. This puts my mind entirely at ease. If you're willing to even consider this, despite how our elders will react, you can see the light at the top of the hole. If you go through with it, you will have dug yourself out."

"I never thought of it in those terms, that's for certain."

"It should be obvious. Something is finally more important to you than approval."

Saving lives. Securing peace.

Cassia.

All of that was so much more important than a pat on the head from his elders.

"I realized that on the embassy's last night in Tenebra when I told my uncle I'd walked all over the terms of the Summit, and I had absolutely no regrets."

"Don't backslide and say you're sorry," Xandra warned him, "but I do wish we'd talked earlier. I think things have actually been all right between us for a while now."

They had been, ever since the night Cassia had told him not to regret Xandra. He should have had enough confidence in Xandra to realize she wasn't sitting around regretting him, either. "That brings me to the most important thing I learned during the Summit."

"Something more important than courage?"

Lio smiled. "She taught me that too. You see...I met someone in Tenebra."

Xandra laughed aloud. "Oh good. Because I met someone while you were in Tenebra."

The realization sank into Lio's brain extra slowly. He wanted to think his mind might have grasped things a little faster if he were not so starved. He put a hand on his chest and bowed slightly. "May I hazard a guess I heard him departing via the back door upon my arrival?"

"Yes." Xandra blushed.

And Lio had had the presumption to think the delay had been due to some dread on Xandra's part. That her reason for making him wait had been all about himself. That her cheeks were flushed with enthusiasm for worms. "Please note that I'm not apologizing. Just congratulating you, with all my heart."

"Thank you, Lio."

He hesitated. "Would you like to tell me about him?"

"Certainly. I want you to know I haven't kept this from you on purpose. I introduced him to everyone else, and if you'd come out to the docks with us all, you would have had a chance to get to know him too. But perhaps you have, in any case. Have you met any of the new theramancy students lately?"

Now Lio understood why the others had been so eager for him to talk with Xandra. He smiled slowly. "Yes, just the other night, Mother introduced me to a few of the guests who are mind healers. He's the young dignitary studying with Annassa Soteira, isn't he? The recent graduate of the Imperial university whose merit exams place no limit on how far he can rise in the Imperial administration. He aspires to serve as a Diviner of the High Court."

"But his knowledge doesn't come only from scholarship. He started his career in his family's farm, close to the soil. He's not afraid to shovel compost."

"I seem to recall his family are the Empress's cousins, and their estates are known for producing the finest beer and mead."

"Yes! We started talking about their bees and my silk worms and, well."

"He is worthy of you," Lio said.

As Xandra grinned, the tip of one of her fangs peeked out. "And I have such a taste for him."

She had definitely never looked at Lio like that. "I'm happy for you indeed."

"Don't ask me if he's my…you know. I'm not worrying about that right now. Just enjoying the way things are." She wiggled her eyebrows. "So tell me about your newly acquired taste."

"She really is the only one I shall ever have a taste for from now on."

Lio had been ready for Xandra to ask him if he was sure this time and not deluding himself again. She said nothing like that.

The air around them rippled with Xandra's magic. Her mouth tightened, and her nails dug into the table. With a composed face, she looked down at her silkworms, and the torrent of power inside her calmed.

But her eyes gleamed with tears. "Goddess, Lio. You've had the Craving for half a year and didn't tell anyone? That's not just stupid. That's dangerous."

"Thank you for being so concerned."

"I'm not concerned. I'm furious. I expect you and Mak and Lyros to be idiots sometimes, but this isn't a broken arm in the training ring. Who is she? Why didn't she come home with you?"

"She's Lady Cassia Basilis."

Xandra's eyes widened. "The King of Tenebra's daughter? The person you identify in your proposal as the scheming traitor turning her country's laws and traditions on their heads? The woman who uses her charity work in the temple to thumb her nose at her own gods and help heretics abscond with children?"

Lio grinned with all his fangs. "That's my Cassia."

"Now I understand who rescued you from the perfectionism hole. I can't wait to thank her and tell her she's the best thing that ever happened to you."

"Neither can I." Relief buoyed him for one lovely moment, but the reality of what tomorrow would bring dragged him back down. "I won't have a chance, unless the Circle approves my plan. I'm not sure what hope one green ambassador has of moving our elders to such lengths, but I will push with everything I have."

Xandra's face steeled into the look of determination she had when she was not controlling, but wielding her tumultuous magic. "You won't be the only one pushing."

"Then I can count on your Circle vote in favor of my proposal, Royal Firstblood Alexandra, Eighth Princess of Orthros?"

"You certainly can, Ambassador Deukalion, Firstgift Komnenos. We are the voice of our generation, and it is high time we made the Circle spin."

96

nights until

WINTER SOLSTICE

Hesperines shall not, under any circumstances, intervene in conflicts between the Mage Orders, the Council of Free Lords, the King of Tenebra, or his enemies, or in any way attempt to influence worship or politics in Tenebra.

—*The Equinox Oath*

THE WISDOM OF THE ANCIENTS

T HE MURMURS OF THE elders had never sounded so deafening. Their quiet voices echoed up, down, and around the circular amphitheater, each word audible and distinct to Hesperine ears without the aid of any magic save the cleverness of Orthros's architects. Currents of silence were the only evidence that other conversations went unheard behind the time-honored custom of veils.

A twirl of vertigo threatened to hurl Lio from where he stood with his friends behind the highest row of seats.

Despite the shared veil around their own conversation, Nodora kept her tone hushed. "I always feel as if I hear music between their voices. But every time I go home and try to capture it in a composition, I can never find the right notes."

With a glance, Kia took in the other Hesperines lingering with them in the gallery and those who had already taken their seats below. "All I hear are the same opinions they've been repeating for the last sixteen centuries, as if they re-read the annals every season. No wonder we call the amphitheater and the elders in it the Firstblood Circle. They're both made of stone."

Attending Circle with his parents as a child, Lio had always imagined he could hear among his living elders the voices of the foregivers whispering timeless wisdom to him. But right now, he dare not open his mouth to join in his Trial sisters' philosophical commentary. He swallowed hard.

The amphitheater was packed for the first Circle of this season of great trouble. The firstbloods of all the bloodlines of Orthros sat below in their vibrant robes and gleaming braids. Generations of their children and many-times-great-grandchildren filled the rows behind them, along with the Ritual tributaries who also carried their blood.

Circle was usually a time of companionship and festive feelings, when all the families in Orthros joined together to celebrate what they had accomplished and what more they would do in Hespera's name. Tonight the Union throbbed with concern, pregnant with the fears left unspoken.

The power of everyone's auras was already enough to make Lio weak in the knees, but the elder firstbloods and the Queens weren't even here yet.

"Steady." Mak gripped Lio's shoulder. "Are you sure you aren't going to be sick?"

Lyros peered into Lio's face. "Are you certain you're ready to do this?"

"Now or never. I've managed to keep down my parents' blood so far. That should carry me through." He found a smile for his friends. "As will the support of my partisans."

"Let's assess our position." Kia nodded downward. "Xandra has assumed her seat. You will take the stand with one vote and five partisans already on your side."

A lone figure in black-and-white formal robes occupied the royals' section of the amphitheater. Xandra had arrived ahead of all the other princes and princesses and taken her place, the eighth seat in the row directly behind the Queens' bench. Hesperines of all ages already flocked around her, eager for a word with the first royal in attendance.

What allies Lio was fortunate enough to call his own. A royal firstblood seated below and the children of the elder firstbloods standing here ready to descend upon the Circle. Kia and Nodora were dressed to impress in their most ceremonial silk ensembles.

Mak and Lyros had eschewed formal robes in favor of their Stand regalia. The knee-length black robes were elegant in their simplicity and powerful in their meaning. The constellation Aegis embroidered on their chests stirred every Hesperine heart. The uniforms, cut for ease of movement, belted at the waist and paired with sandals that laced up the calves, were designed to be practical for the Hesperine fighting style. Tonight they were a persuasive argument that the defenders of Orthros endorsed a dangerous proposal and stood ready for the challenge.

Lio had never felt more proud to have his friends at his side. They shone as brightly as their elders, and they carried themselves like what they were—heirs of the oldest bloodlines in Orthros, who belonged here.

"Thank you all for doing this." Lio adjusted his scroll case on his shoulder and straightened his collar. The black formal robes he had worn at the Summit gave him a measure of boldness.

Mak took a flask from the pocket of his robe. "Since Javed gets to stay home with the sucklings, he asked me to bring this to you. He offers his well-wishes and the following instructions: 'Drink every drop.'"

Lio accepted the flask. "Do I want to know what's in there?"

"No," Lyros reassured him. "Bottoms up."

Lio uncapped the flask, but as soon as the odor hit his nose, he held it away from him. "Absolutely not. I will not drink thirst suppressant."

"It's just what you need," Nodora urged. "It's the best treatment to mitigate the symptoms of the Craving."

Kia chuckled and shook her head at Mak and Lyros. "Hypocrites. You wouldn't stay on the stuff during your Ritual separation."

"That only lasted eight nights, not half a year," Lyros answered.

"Drink," Mak commanded Lio. "I know you want to be your best for her when you see her again, but that's not going to happen unless you make it through Circle tonight."

"It will wear off by sunrise," Lyros promised. "And you'll wish it hadn't."

Mak nodded. "Believe me, it takes more than one dose to wilt your thorn."

Nodora and Kia did Lio the kindness of refraining from further comment.

If only to disguise his flushed face, Lio held the flask to his mouth and tilted his head back to drain the elixir. He suppressed a grimace of disgust and handed the flask back to Mak. "Thank you."

Mak made the face for him. "Awful, isn't it? Too sweet, like its trying too hard to make you like it."

The stars spun over Lio's head. "How long does it take to work?"

"It will be in full effect by the time the proposals begin," Lyros advised.

"Well, that should help with the wait. I'm last on the schedule tonight. My Imperial libraries proposal isn't high priority."

Kia's aura shone with anticipation. "They have no idea they're saving the best for last."

The sky was clear and sharp as glass. It would require no wards to keep snow out of the Circle, and the moons and stars would have an unobstructed view of Lio's presentation. The Goddess's Eyes and her stellar heroes would bear witness to the debacle. "I wonder how far into my address I'll get before they send me to live with Phaedros."

"They have to let you finish," said Kia. "Everyone is allowed to present any idea inside the Circle. It's the law. They can't actually exile you for your ideas, you know."

"Right. Phaedros was banished for acting on them. Maybe they'll reconsider bringing charges against me for violating the terms of the Summit last winter so they'll have a reason to banish me, too."

"He *is* a genius," Kia pointed out. "He's probably rather interesting company."

"How comforting. I shall have an insane genius to keep me from growing bored in exile."

"And you can keep contributing your controversial writings to the veiled section of the library, like he does. I promise to write a discourse in response. You can ask the wardens to deliver it to you when they make their regular visits to invite you to recant."

"Stop it, Kia," Mak broke in. "That's not funny."

"It wouldn't be so terrible," she persisted. "Since the Stewards *are* the wardens, you would get to see Mak and Lyros now and then."

She didn't twitch under the full force of Lyros and Mak's scowls, but at a sudden change in the levels of magic below, she left off her gallows humor and scrutinized the Circle again. The sea of auras swelled with the influx of eleven waves of power. The elder firstbloods and their Graces had arrived.

The founders of Orthros had appeared in their places in the front row of each of their five respective sections. No sooner had they stepped into position than they began to receive greetings and requests from the descendants and tributaries who occupied the wings behind them.

In the Boreian section to the royal family's right, the rows behind Lio's parents had fewer occupants than any others. Even so, they received a warm reception from the Ritual tributaries to whom Lio's father had dutifully passed on Anastasios's Gift. Father had waited a long time for children who would fill those rows with family.

Lio stared at the empty seats. Would his and Cassia's children ever fill them?

Even as his mother devoted her attention to those around her, her mind reached for his, and her auric gaze settled on him. A moment later, between one petitioner and the next, she found him with her physical gaze as well. He saw the worry line between her brows and felt the encouragement she sent him through the Blood Union. She might not know what he was about to do, but she could tell how important it was for him. Father took her hand as his power joined with hers in bolstering Lio.

Lio sent back to them his gratitude. His regret he kept behind his veil. No regrets. That was his promise to himself.

Whatever happened tonight, he would stand by his proposal, his conscience, and his Grace.

"Knowing Uncle Apollon and Aunt Komnena, you can count on your own bloodline's vote." The confidence in Mak's voice was reassuring. "I'd be surprised if the firstbloods of all their Ritual tributaries didn't follow their example."

Lio dared a look at the front row of the Anatelan section and found his mentor. Uncle Argyros glanced up from his conversation with Aunt Lyta and smiled. The relief in his aura raked Lio's conscience over the coals.

"What about your father?" Lio asked Mak.

It was Lyros who answered. "Well, when Grace-Father saw we were coming to Circle for once, he, ah…thanked us for encouraging you to stay on course and for reminding you of your priorities during your time of doubt."

"Don't despair," Mak comforted. "Just think who has suffered his disapproval. The Blood Errant. Me. You'll be in good company."

"Indeed I will. I only wish I could look forward to your bloodline's vote."

"Count mine out too." Kia glared at her parents. Hypatia and Khaldaios presented a dignified picture in the seats to Uncle Argyros and Aunt Lyta's left. "Far be it from Elder Firstblood Hypatia to take a chance on anything. She doesn't remember how to be a heretic anymore. Neither bloodline from Hagia Anatela will vote in your favor."

Nodora and Lyros exchanged glances. She patted Lio's arm. "I'm afraid the bloodlines from Hagia Zephyra won't be willing to risk it, either."

"Perhaps some of Kassandra's bloodlines will take your view," Lyros said. "It's a shame she always abstains. I would be surprised if she disapproved of your proposal."

Lio's gaze came to rest on his Ritual mother, who stood alone at the head of her section. The packed rows behind Kassandra were a rich legacy, larger than two temple sections combined, although none who sat there were her blood children.

Since Hesperines had first reached out to the Empire, she had guided the weft of Orthros with her strong, mahogany hands. She had crafted a bridge of fabric between Orthros and the Empire and woven their alliance, which had endured these many centuries. She had beheld their future and worked to build it.

She carried herself like the woman she had been in her mortal life, the sister of the Empress, and the Hesperine she was now, an elder firstblood and the Queens' Ritual sister. Her purple formal robes evoked her royalty, and her heel-length, locked hair was a testament to her long, full life.

"Does it gall her that she has a vote she cannot use?" Kia wondered aloud. "That her power is so great she must not wield it?"

"I think her magic must be very hard to bear," Nodora said. "Not only because it means she cannot vote."

"I wish she would vote," Mak said. "Why shouldn't she? She's the only Hesperine in Orthros with the power of foresight. That makes her more qualified than anyone to rule on what course of action Orthros should take."

"I object," Kia agreed, "to the argument she and the other elders make that her votes could compromise the fairness of the Circle. Such unfairness to her renders the Circle already compromised."

Nodora pursed her lips. "I think she is right to be concerned that if she voted, everyone would assume she knew something we do not. The other firstbloods probably would vote as she did out of fear for the future, rather than forming their own opinions."

"What a waste," Mak lamented. "Whether it is her opinion or prophecy, everyone would do well to allow her vote to decide matters."

"As the Queens' Master Economist," Nodora replied, "she hardly lacks direct influence. Every decision she makes outside this Circle has profound impact on Orthros."

Kia scowled. "All the more reason she should be able to wield her direct impact over the Circle. The person who manages our trade relationships with the rest of the world should not have to withhold her vote."

Lyros cleared his throat. "Are we certain it is everyone's faith in her prophecies that keeps her from voting...not lack thereof?"

"Everyone still has great faith in her," Nodora protested. "They understand why her sight might be clouded where her son is concerned. People are greatly swayed by her prophecies, even though she still denies Methu is gone and insists he will return."

Prometheus's mother had never once told her son to shy from action. After nearly a century, she persisted in her belief he would come back from his final, doomed journey into Cordium. After all these years of grief and hanging onto hope, did she regret that she had not stayed his hand?

Or did she too chafe at Orthros's eternal pace? Did she regret no Hesperine since her son had dared shake a fist at the Mage Orders?

Lio could do that, if he offered Tenebra an outstretched hand.

"No one doubts her prophecy that 'the bloodborn will return to Orthros,'" Kia said, "only that Methu was the subject of it."

All of Lio's friends looked at him.

Mak wiggled his eyebrows. "Everyone knows the prophecy must really have foretold Uncle Apollon bringing Aunt Komnena and Lio home to Orthros."

Lyros cuffed Lio on the arm. "Remember that when you take the stand tonight. You're a prophecy come true."

"No expectations." Kia grinned wickedly.

Lio looked upon the statues of the Ritual firstbloods, which marked the seats reserved for those who bore their blood, and studied the memorial that stood before his parents' seats. Ritual Firstblood Anastasios might be mistaken for a living Hesperine, if not for his marble skin and robes. He who had given Father the Gift in the Great Temple Epoch looked ready to judge tonight's proceedings with kind eyes and to offer up suggestions with a lifted hand.

Father had sculpted him so everyone might in some way know his foregiver as he had. Anastasios and his fellow Ritual firstbloods had not lived to see Orthros. They had sacrificed their lives for the hope of their people's salvation. Would their constellations shudder when Lio proposed a plan that could threaten the Sanctuary of Orthros?

The burning stars in the sky and the quartz stars on the floor of the amphitheater traded places. Lio planted his feet and reached for the lifeline of his Gift.

Was this how Anastasios had felt, knowing every life inside the walls of Hagia Boreia was in his hands? Had he wondered whether his choice to die for them would be enough to save them?

It was too much.

Anastasios had been the Prismos of Hagia Boreia, strengthened through experience to bear such responsibility. He had been a Ritual firstblood, who had received the Gift from the Goddess herself, who through his magic and blood had helped create all Hesperines.

Who was Lio to take those lives into his hands?

"It is a good likeness," said a voice behind him.

Lio looked away from the statue to behold instead a living memorial. He put a hand over his heart and bowed deeply, which brought him to her eye level. "Annassa Alea."

Her royal finery was the simple white robe that had been her vestment as the Prisma of Hagia Boreia. Her only crown was her Grace's black braid. Her train was her white hair, which hung loose past her feet.

She was the only Ritual firstblood whose heart still beat, but she could still smile, and she did so at Lio now. "It is one of my favorites of your father's works. Anastasios would appreciate such a complimentary portrait. But my old friend would agree with me that the best likeness of him Apollon ever sculpted will take the floor later tonight and speak."

"You honor me." Lio bowed his head.

He wanted to tell her how much her words meant to him, especially at this moment. But he did not know if he would forfeit her confidence in him before the night was through.

"Why look into stone eyes for wisdom, when you need only seek it in your veins?" she asked.

"There are times when I doubt my own veins."

"So do we all. But that is the same as doubting the Goddess." She walked between the five of them, touching affectionate hands to their heads. "Xandra would not breathe a word of what all of you are up to. I believe the Circle may look forward to a rare phenomenon tonight—a surprise."

She descended from the gallery, and faces lit with hope, relief, delight as she walked among her people.

Lio felt another wave of the same emotions on the other side of the amphitheater and knew Queen Soteira had made her entrance somewhere in the crowd gathered there.

No one knelt or prostrated themselves, and the words "Your Majesty" were not to be heard here. Everyone gave one bow with their hands over their hearts, and their honorific for their Queens went up all over the amphitheater on voice after voice: *Annassa, Annassa, Annassa.*

Mak grinned. "Everyone has complete confidence in you, Lio. Even our Queens."

"No expectations," Kia said again.

"We'd best take our seats." Nodora clasped Lio's hands. "May the Goddess lend you her voice."

Kia touched his shoulder. "May her Eyes watch your path—and shine the light of truth."

"May her darkness shield you," Mak and Lyros said together.

"You have my gratitude, my friends," Lio replied. "I pray the future we are striving for will be a good one for all of us."

They descended the rows with a step to take their places behind their parents. As Lio sat down, his father reached back to clasp his arm, and his mother smiled. If they would greet the end of his speech with the same gestures, he would count his blessings.

Lio tried not to lose sight of Lyros, Kia, and Nodora among their many brothers and sisters. He saw Mak sit down next to Kadi and say something that made her laugh. She tore her gaze away from Nike's empty seat beside her. Lio wondered if Kadi would have been happier staying at home with Javed to look after Zoe, Bosko, and Thenie.

It was good to think of Zoe feeling safe at House Argyros, all unknowing of the elders' troubles. It was hard to think of bringing danger so near to her.

But it was harder to think of explaining to her one night, when she was old enough to understand, that he had been too cautious to face immediate danger for the chance to secure long-term peace. When that night came, he wanted to be able to tell her he had not given into fear, but had been brave enough to try to build her a better future.

AMBASSADOR DEUKALION'S PROPOSAL

B Y THE TIME THE other proposals drew to a close, Lio wasn't sure whether he wanted to thank Javed or do a few Sun Strikes on him. The thirst suppressant had indeed stolen Lio's appetite, but it had taken half his senses with it.

When Second Princess Konstantina, as her mothers' voice in the Circle, invited Lio onto the floor, he fumbled for his scroll case and his wits. His feet felt like blobs of wool at the end of his legs. As he stepped down from the second row, the voices around him sounded muffled and distant. So did his own heartbeat.

As he made his slow progress toward the podium, the princess turned to talk with one of her children in the row behind her. Her unconcern would vanish when she realized Lio was not here to discuss Imperial libraries.

His dulled senses softened the blow the crowd dealt him through the Blood Union as they all turned their attention on him. Their affection and concern, admiration and interest blurred together into an incoherent whole Lio need not dwell on. He was definitely going to thank Javed.

He kept his gaze on the floor so he wouldn't trip as he approached the podium. The mosaic of the Firstblood Rose pointed its black marble thorns and red marble petals at the watching elders. Lio would have to look at them eventually.

Once he was sure his scrolls wouldn't tumble off the podium, he raised his head. Uncle Argyros had taught him to look at everyone's foreheads, not meet their eyes. Lio looked past Queen Soteira's dark brow and Queen Alea's pale one and pinned his gaze on Princess Konstantina's black-and-white silk circlet.

The Second Princess did not need a jeweled crown to remind anyone of her role in this Circle. Her seat right behind the Queens was the enduring crown of her achievements as their eldest daughter and Royal Master Magistrate. She was Hesperine royalty embodied, with her black skin and white robe, the coils of her dark hair tied back with pale silk cord.

Lio was about to sacrifice *her* respect.

He dared not meet her regal gaze. He already knew the opposition he would see there before the Circle concluded. The Second Princess's approval was priceless, her dissent ruinous. Proposing anything to her that threatened the security of her people was political suicide.

Lio invited his destruction as courteously as possible. He recited the formal thanks expected from each speaker she called to the podium.

The words were barely out of his mouth when the empty place to Princess Konstantina's right was suddenly no longer vacant. She spun in her seat, and the amphitheater erupted with exclamations of surprise and welcome.

Lio met Rudhira's gray gaze and grinned. The First Prince of Orthros had found the time to attend Circle with Basir and Kumeta at his side. They had even taken a moment to exchange their field gear for silk.

Rudhira still looked rather like a harbinger of death in his blood red robes, with his blood red braid, pale skin, and hawkish features. But he was their harbinger of rescue.

Xandra abandoned her seat with no trace of royal dignity and threw her arms around her brother. He held her while he paid his respects to their mothers.

A ripple in the Union made Lio look to his left. He saw Uncle Argyros frown and look from Rudhira...to Lio.

The prince had come to hear Lio's speech. No one expected an Imperial libraries proposal now.

On their way to their seats, Basir and Kumeta paused to have a word with Lio's uncle. Uncle Argyros looked puzzled, and the ripple became jarring. Kumeta gave Uncle Argyros's shoulder a squeeze before the Master Envoys ascended the rows behind him to take their places as his Ritual tributaries.

Rudhira sat down and devoted his entire attention to Lio. The commotion silenced.

There was no shame in defeat with Rudhira at his side, if defeat he must face.

Lio lifted a hand toward the sky. "Annassa, Firstbloods, and heirs of the blood, thank you for hearing me under the Goddess's Eyes. By Alatheia's light, I shall strive to speak only truth, according to my conscience."

Somehow the ritual words, which every presenter to this Circle had spoken before him, helped him go on. Because they were true of the speech he would deliver tonight. Because he had a right to speak here, to his people. He had a right to be heard, even if he was wrong.

"I am called upon tonight to deliver my findings on whether Hesperine magic and craft could improve the libraries of the Empire. It is my honor to propose a course of action to our Queens for further serving our Imperial friends and allies." Lio placed before him on the podium the scroll he had dedicated to his libraries proposal. "Each of you knows my findings, although I have yet to announce them." He bowed to Uncle Argyros. "My mentor knew what I would suggest before he assigned this matter to me." Now Lio bowed once more to the Annassa. "Our Queens have already decided on a course of action, upon which we will proceed regardless of what I say tonight, and all shall benefit."

Lio unrolled his libraries proposal and turned slowly to display to the entire Circle the mostly blank scroll. "So I have resolved to use this opportunity to present conclusions that will surprise you. I ask that you consider a course of action Orthros has never before undertaken. I appeal to our Queens to rule on a future that has yet to be decided: the fate of Orthros's relations with Tenebra."

No outburst of surprise greeted his declaration. Only knowing smiles, amused glances, and a few almost inaudible sighs of resignation.

Lio set aside the first scroll. He unrolled his new proposal and his list of Cassia's deeds on the podium in front of him. "I will now name the individual who is responsible for our current reprieve from war with the Mage Orders and present irrefutable evidence of that person's identity."

The amphitheater was silent, but the Blood Union told Lio, even through his muffled senses, that he had their attention now.

"She is…" Lio drew breath and looked at last into the gleaming eyes, the ageless faces, the worried hearts around him. His people. Her people. "Cassia Basilis, the best ally Hesperines could ask the Goddess to give us."

He didn't listen to find out if they were shocked or skeptical or amazed. He delivered his proposal, the real one he had been working on all this time. The truth of all the deeds she had done on their behalf and all the rules he had violated to help her. Telling Mak and Lyros had been his first rehearsal, telling his parents his second. Now Lio gave the performance of his life.

He didn't know how much time passed. His tongue went dry and his head grew light. Surely Javed's elixir couldn't be wearing off already. Not when the most difficult part was still ahead of Lio.

"In light of these revelations," he said at last, "it is clear our situation calls for a change of policy, one that will make the most of what our sympathizer at Solorum has accomplished—one that will further enable her to influence Tenebra on our behalf. It is clear from the events of the Autumn Greeting that although her valiant efforts have been our salvation, the king is set on his course and will not call the Equinox Summit. And yet the Summit is our only hope of pulling our kingdoms back from the brink of war, of nurturing the fragile opportunity we have with Tenebra…of reestablishing contact with Lady Cassia.

"Ever in such times of trouble, it is our way to stand down from confrontation. It is the right thing to do, for it is the only antidote to the Mage Orders' thirst for conflict. I say, let us withdraw, as we always have. But let us bring Tenebra with us.

"The King and Queen of Tenebra who first called us to a Summit no longer dwell in this world. We are still here. The spirit of the first Equinox Oath lives on, and we are its bearers.

"No king will call the Summit for us. What matter? Let our Queens bring the world to their table. Let our Goddess guide the world to peace, as she did our people.

"I hereby propose that we invite the very first Tenebran embassy to Orthros."

The tremor in the Union made him sway on his feet. Hespera help him. He had to say the rest.

"Let us establish a new tradition—the Solstice Summit. For the first time in history, a party of mortals shall cross the great divide between Tenebra and Orthros. We shall show them all the beauty and goodness of our homeland and see if they are not moved to lay down their swords. We shall see whether they can behold Hespera and not be changed. Come Winter Solstice, we shall see if they are not ready to swear a new oath for a new era."

He looked at the statue of Ritual Firstblood Eidon. He did not yet dare look beyond the Prismos of Hagia Anatela to see the look on Uncle Argyros's face.

"There you have it. My youthful vision. My faith in the goodness that still beats within Tenebran hearts. But believing and hoping is not enough. We must pave the way to our ideals with wisdom we have learned from bitter experience. But pave it we must. We must act, although we do so with the caution our losses have taught us."

He proceeded to lay out his recommendations for security measures. He had really just done it—asked the Circle to bring mages and warriors behind the ward like wolves into the fold. But he was ready to erode their outrage with each excruciating detail of his plan for safety. He hurried to get the words out before he lost his credibility before them entirely.

"Mothers, fathers, sisters, and brothers, I feel your fear. The thought of allowing such dangerous men to occupy the same side of the sea as my young sister Zosime fills me with terror. That is why the Tenebran embassy shall be kept isolated from any Hesperine sucklings and newbloods at all times. All those who have contact with the visitors must be at least initiates who are in command of their power. We shall also ensure our Imperial guests never cross paths with the new embassy, in strict adherence to the Empress's policy on Tenebra and Cordium."

By the time Lio was done itemizing safety protocols, he could no longer see Alatheia's constellation in the sky. Had he really been talking that long?

"And yet one question remains to be answered. Will King Lucis accept our invitation? I can tell you without a doubt that he will.

"He wants the Orders' support, and they want a war. How else will they view our new effort for peace but as a new opportunity to incite violence? They will leap at the chance to come to Orthros, thinking it will serve their own purposes.

"It doesn't matter why they will come. What matters is what the Tenebrans will see when they get here.

"This is our chance to humanize ourselves in their eyes. It is easy to drum up support for a war against a specter that lives large in mortal imagination. It will not be so easy to rally warriors against names and faces they have met or pit mages against worshipers who offer up prayers in the same tongue their own gods speak. It will be even harder to convince the free lords to turn against lucrative new trade agreements and goods never before seen in Tenebra. Why glut Cordium's coffers when they could fill their own? Why fulfill the southern mages' dreams of war, when they could lay their nightmares of the north to rest?

"The king and the Cordian fanatics will not change their minds. But the Tenebrans might. Their minds and hearts are worth fighting for.

"And if we lose that fight, if we accomplish nothing else, consider this one last reason to approve my proposal." Lio looked at Rudhira. "The Prince's Charge sheds their blood night after night to find those of us who have not come home. As long as any of our people are out of reach, the Charge's work is not done. While the First Prince continues to lead the search, what safer place is there to keep our enemies but here in our stronghold, where they cannot harm our Hesperines errant who remain in hostile territory? What better delay could we contrive to buy time for Orthros Abroad than a long, drawn-out diplomatic event here at home, which will tie Cordium's hands? The Orders will not dare start a war when some of their own are at our mercy, for fear our guests will become hostages or martyrs should violence break out.

"There is no denying Cordians will send their own to Orthros. We will invite the mages of Tenebra to renew ties with us, but among their number, we shall receive Cordian mages disguised as Tenebrans." Lio looked in turn at each member of the embassy who had fought Dalos at his side. "We need this to happen. We must discover how a member of the Aithourian Circle can disguise his power from us. If we bring disguised Aithourians here, our best scholars can observe them firsthand and expose their secrets."

Lio looked down at his proposal. He hadn't even glanced at it the entire time he had been speaking. He supposed it was written somewhere much closer to him.

He made himself look at Uncle Argyros at last. "Until everyone we love is safe behind the ward, we must not give up. We must keep fighting for peace. Even when peace is impossible, the hope of peace carries us far. It carried us to Orthros sixteen hundred years ago. Let it carry a Tenebran embassy to Orthros now."

Uncle Argyros's face was made of stone as surely as the memorial statues. Lio could see no trace of emotion there. No hint of either support or outrage. Nothing.

The vertigo was back. It twirled the Circle around Lio and spun his last drink up toward his throat. He willed it back down. He had one more thing to say.

"Before you cast your votes, I must disclose one more relevant fact. I have endeavored to present my findings as objectively as possible and propose only that which will further the good of our people. However, I must admit a possible bias, which you should take into consideration when evaluating my proposal."

The feeling came back to Lio's limbs all at once. His veins lit on fire with the Craving. For her.

"I did not merely collaborate with Cassia. She also did me the honor of sharing with me. She is more to me than an ally of our people. She is not only the hero who saved our lives during the Summit and gave Orthros our new children." The empty seats behind his parents blurred before his eyes. "She is the partner I hope will eternally sit at my side in this Circle. As surely as my blood is the future of House Komnena, so too is hers. Her blood is my future. When she comes to Orthros, I hope you will welcome her not as a friend of the Hesperines, but as a Hesperine, for nothing is sufficient to honor who she is to me except that I offer her the Gift."

Just in case the Circle needed further evidence Cassia was his Grace, the Craving chose that moment to bring Lio to his knees, then drag him into unconsciousness.

95

nights until

WINTER SOLSTICE

So long as Hesperines hold to these terms, they may traverse all lands under the rule of the King of Tenebra without fear of persecution. Should they in any way violate this Oath, then they forfeit the king's protection from mages, warriors, and any subjects of Tenebra seeking to exact justice.

—The Equinox Oath

THE VOTE OF BLOOD ARGYROS

THE VOICE THAT GUIDED Lio out of Slumber was warm and rich and low. He would follow that gentle summons anywhere. If he awoke now, he felt sure he would feel a savanna wind upon his skin and see southern constellations overhead.

He opened his eyes to behold Queen Soteira leaning over him. She touched a gentle, powerful hand to his cheek. Her skin was black and cool as the night sky. The adornments in her hair twinkled at him like stars, and the metallic embroidery on her black robe seemed to mirror them. Countless braids comprised the intricate tower that crowned her head, ringed at the bottom by Queen Alea's braid. When Lio was that ancient, he wondered if he would have that many promises to keep, too.

"Annassa, your Night Call does not sound like any I have ever heard."

She bestowed upon him another wonder of great beauty. She laughed. "Do not tell Argyros I said so, but he could improve in that area."

Lio tried moving a little where he lay. There was a bed under him. He glanced around. A row of empty beds stretched to his left and right, and floor-to-ceiling windows filled the room with soothing light. A hall in the Healing Sanctuary. "I feel better than I have in months."

"You were long overdue for a healer's attention."

Not just a healer. The healer. She who had brought Annassa Alea and all Hesperine kind back from the brink of death.

Although his body was restored, he felt shaken to his core. "Am I so far gone that only your power is great enough to rescue me?"

"You had a very close call. It would have been closer if you were not so strong Willed and the child of an elder firstblood. From this night forward you are to remain on a steady diet of your parents' blood and receive regular healings from me."

So he was on borrowed time. He made to sit up. "I am grateful for your strength, Annassa. It will carry me back to the Circle."

"Let my healing work on you awhile longer." She rested her hands on his shoulders.

Lio found himself lying back down. "Annassa, the vote—"

"It has yet to be held. I have assured Apollon and Komnena my magic will preserve you long enough for them to finish their speeches before they come to give you the Drink."

"My parents are making speeches?"

Rudhira appeared at Queen Soteira's side and touched a hand to her shoulder. "*Bamaayo*, I will gladly wait with him, should you need to return to the Circle."

She stood. "I will leave you with your Ritual father for now, Lio."

"Annassa," he beseeched her.

She waited, smiling down at him.

Lio had often asked the Queens for their wisdom, but seldom questioned it. Tonight he found the boldness to ask, "What will be your decision on what I have proposed?"

"Let us wait and see what the Circle has to say first." She turned and touched a hand to her son's face, her deep black complexion a contrast to his frosty pale features. "I'm glad you're here."

He stooped to accept a kiss on his cheek. Queen Soteira disappeared, leaving behind in the Union a fragrant aftermath of her power.

The prince sat in the chair and stretched his long legs out before him. His scuffed Tenebran riding boots revealed themselves from under the hem of his silk robe. "Your parents are indeed giving addresses—in favor of your proposal."

Lio heaved a sigh of relief. He *did* have his own bloodline's vote. And, he dared hope, the prince's as well. "Rudhira, I'm so grateful you've come. But I had no intention of taking you away from your Charge. When I sent my last letter explaining the truth of my situation, I did not expect you to reply in the flesh."

"I came to get you. And to convince Apollon he must stay here with

Komnena and Zoe while I take you to get Cassia. But I see you have devised your own solution in the meantime. Imagine my surprise when I discovered your plan is more disruptive than my own. It's a good thing I got here in time for Circle, for you need my vote."

"I knew I could count on your support."

Rudhira raised a brow. "You knew I would leap at a chance to bring Aithourians within range?"

"I mean no offense."

"None taken."

Lio rested his head back on his pillow. "Well, what do you make of my plan, really?"

He gave Lio a half-smile. "As your Ritual father, I think I am supposed to spout encouragements from the font of wisdom on a momentous occasion such as this."

"When you and my father were in the field, did you ask him for pretty truths?"

"Spoken like a Hesperine who has come into his Gift, and I will answer you as such. There will be many nights after this when you will ask yourself if you have done the right thing. I am ill-qualified to reassure you, for I ask myself the same about more decisions than I can count. But there is something I want you to know, for those times when you wrestle with your own judgment. You have my gratitude."

Lio looked at Rudhira in surprise.

The moons' light revealed all the lines of strain on the prince's face. "You will not hear this outside the royal family, but I want you to know. Since Autumn Equinox, there has been talk of invoking the Departure."

Lio sat up too fast, and his head spun. "That can't be. It's never happened. It's a contingency plan that dates from the founding, when we were still afraid the Last War might break out again at any time. Surely the Queens wouldn't really declare an end to Hesperines' time in Tenebra! I thought bringing everyone home and closing the borders was a temporary measure."

"It is a real possibility it will be indefinite."

"If that is the case…even if the Circle votes in favor of my proposal, will our Queens overrule them?"

"I cannot say. You know they are sparing with their vetoes, for they wish to preserve every bloodline's right to decide what is best for their own kin. But I can tell you that just a few hours before you gave your speech, my mothers spoke of bringing all Hesperines out of Tenebra forever."

"I cannot fathom it. The end of our fight for the land where our kind began."

"The royal family agrees no one should know how close we are to that necessity. We want to avoid spreading despair unless the Departure must become a reality. It goes without saying you may tell Cassia, of course. I take it for granted that what you know, so too does she."

"The secret will stop with us."

Every Solia who would never receive the Mercy. Every Cassia whose life would never be saved. Every Zoe who would never be Solaced. So many precious lives.

If that was to be their new reality, to Hypnos with politics. Lio would bring Cassia home.

"What about the Hesperites?" he protested. "Their settlement in the eastern Tenebrae won't survive without your protection. Nor will they depart with you. They have always been adamant in their refusal to accept Sanctuary in Orthros. You have said yourself they will never abandon their purpose of keeping human worship of Hespera alive."

"That is the decision I do not want Hesperites or Hesperines to face. Tonight you have offered hope of an alternative, and for that, you have my gratitude and my vote. I have exerted as much influence as I can to sway others in your favor. You can count on the votes of all those who are loyal to me and some who are loyal to my status."

"I cannot thank you enough."

"Don't thank me yet. I fear it may yet be necessary for you and me to ride for Solorum and disrupt Cassia's plans. I am still uncertain we have enough votes."

"Perhaps we can change more minds during the debates."

"The debates are at an end. They raged on till sunrise and recommenced at sundown when the Circle reconvened for a special session."

Lio pushed himself off the bed. "When is the vote?"

Rudhira offered a battle-strengthened arm and helped Lio to his feet. "Within the hour."

"Cup and thorns. I have to get out of this healing robe. Where's my formal attire?"

"I will help him prepare for the vote, First Prince."

Uncle Argyros stood a few paces away in the light of a different window.

Rudhira kept a hand under Lio's arm. He nodded to Lio's uncle. "Argyros." He paused. "It has been some time. How fares your House?"

Lio bit his tongue. Had the two of them really not spoken a word to each other since Rudhira had arrived last night?

"Lio is our concern tonight," Uncle Argyros replied. "I would like a word with him before Apollon and Komnena arrive."

Rudhira nodded again and strode toward the door. As he passed, Uncle Argyros bowed, but he did not meet the prince's gaze. Before Rudhira reached the exit, he stepped out of sight.

Uncle Argyros went to stand by the window. Cursing his own weakness, Lio sank down to sit on the edge of the bed. Goddess, why did he have to have this confrontation now, like this? If he must face the breach with his mentor at last, why could circumstances not leave him at least a little dignity?

The moment was really at hand. His bond with his uncle, which had lasted his whole life and survived the Summit…it would never be the same after this.

A sense of loss knocked the wind out of Lio, and he felt he needed air like a mortal.

He looked at the back of Uncle Argyros's braid and tried to think of what to say. The Blood Union ached. Uncle Argyros ached.

Lio *had* hurt him.

His uncle spoke at last. "How expertly you have used everything I taught you to shake the foundations of my paradigm."

Lio opened his mouth to ask for forgiveness. But he had sworn he would not. It was not his proposal he must apologize for.

How could he apologize for hurting his uncle without recanting?

Uncle Argyros turned to face him. "You and Cassia have perfectly positioned yourselves to revolutionize Hesperine and Tenebran relations, and the Circle wishes to thank you by tucking you both in behind the ward with pats on the head. My peers have wasted hours going up one side of your proposal and down the other. They could have spared us all the agony and summarized their blather with a simple 'not till Corona freezes over.' They busy themselves with convoluted counter-arguments so they can ignore the simple truth: everything you said tonight was right. I quit the amphitheater during Hypatia's third address. I would not dignify their so-called debates with a single remark of my own. Which is why I will speak tonight before the vote, so I may have the last word."

That made Lio find his voice. "*You* are going to make the final remarks on my behalf?"

"I shall not tolerate anyone else presuming to do so. Besides, you are in no condition to make another speech."

"Does Aunt Lyta agree with your position? Is she willing to commit the Stand to safeguarding us while the Tenebran embassy is inside the ward?"

"Your aunt agrees there is no better place for the mages who hunt Nike than here, where the Stand can keep an eye on them. Lyta finds your proposed security measures well-considered and is prepared to implement them to her satisfaction. She has no patience with the Circle's hysterics. She has made it clear to them that any mage who behaves less than diplomatically will not survive long enough to be a danger."

Lio had the vote of Blood Argyros. Surely that meant victory. "Uncle. How can I thank you?"

"There is nothing to thank me for."

Why was Uncle Argyros wearing his stone face? If he did not disapprove of the proposal, what could be wrong?

How long would it take for this fresh wound in the Union to seal? Would it ever?

"Uncle," Lio began.

Uncle Argyros held up a hand. Lio's formal robes landed beside him on the bed.

"It is time," Uncle Argyros said.

THE FUTURE OF ORTHROS

Lio would never forget his uncle's address. He had spent his life aspiring to Silvertongue's mastery of words. Tonight, he listened to his uncle devote all that eloquence to promoting an idea of his. He listened to his uncle work language like magic and felt the pain they had left unresolved in the Union. But that pain did not temper the power of Uncle Argyros's speech. Somehow it was the force behind his every argument.

When Uncle Argyros concluded his oratory, he stepped back to his seat to rejoin Aunt Lyta. Lio stood alone in the center of the Circle. But he wasn't alone, not at all.

Princess Konstantina frowned, but continued the formal proceedings. "The Goddess hears all of us, from the mightiest firstblood to the smallest child. Let any who are not empowered to vote for their bloodlines come forward if they wish to show their support for the proposal in question."

Lio's Trial brothers were the first to come out onto the floor, and Kadi with them. Mak and Lyros lifted their speires in their hands for the Circle to see, then placed them on the podium before Lio. Kadi showed the crowd Nike's abandoned speires before adding them to the stand.

Mak's voice carried as if he were rallying a vast army on the field of battle. "We of Hippolyta's Stand are ready to face any danger at the ward—or inside of it. It is nothing to us to ensure a few visiting warriors and mages are not a threat. It is Hesperines errant like our own Master Steward Pherenike who face real danger Abroad, shedding their blood every night with honor and courage. We would be derelict in our duty to our errant forces if we did not offer them every possible support from our fortified position at home. We will fail them, if we do not take this chance to draw off the enemy."

Lyros looked around, studying the grave, considering faces of the first-bloods. "I am the first Steward in centuries who is not of Blood Argyros. Since bloodborn Atalanta gave her life in service to the Stand, no Hesperine but Hippolyta's own children sought her training. When I chose the battle arts over my own bloodline's arts of painting and sculpture, I made a vow to protect Orthros. Not to keep myself safe, not to choose the safest course of action, but to face any foe, to accept any risk for the good of our people. The Stand has never been afraid to shoulder the burden of violence for Hesperine kind. I trust that the firstbloods are not afraid to shoulder the burden of this vote. Do not choose the safest course of action. Instead, protect Orthros."

Kia marched out next and planted her small statue of Alatheia on the podium. She turned the bust so it gazed at her mother. "Orthros was built on heresy. Our scholars questioned every stricture and our mages pushed every boundary. Our founders dusted the ashes of the old epoch off themselves and created something entirely, wonderfully new. I am looking at those very scholars, mages, and founders right now. And yet I scarcely recognize the heroes from my history texts. I ask you, are you still heretics?"

Offense disrupted the Union, rippling outward from Hypatia. Lio bit his tongue. Kia might antagonize their elders rather than win them to the cause. But it was her right to have her say.

"Who are we, if we are afraid to question?" Kia demanded. "Who are we, if we establish boundaries? What is to become of Orthros if we stop creating it and let it become old? The only truly Hesperine course of action tonight is to be bold and vote in favor of the Solstice Summit."

At last came Nodora with one of her hand-carved ocarinas. She played a strain of her ballad about the Equinox Summit before committing the instrument to the podium. Her gaze sought and found her Ritual mother in the Zephyran section. Matsu pressed a hand to her bright red lips and held out her palm to Nodora. The stain of lip color on her fingers resembled blood, as good as the promise of a vote. Matsu's Grace also put her hand out on the railing before them to show her support.

With the iron calm of a consummate performer, Nodora spoke. "All my human family perished in the attempt to see my Ritual mother and me escape the Archipelagos and arrive safely on Orthros's shores. They dared to breach the isolation of the land of our ancestors and paid with their lives. When I allow myself to imagine what might come of even one Summit between the Archipelagos and Orthros, the possibilities astonish me. However, the Archipelagos have never sought diplomatic engagement with us, and they never will. Not so in Tenebra's case. We have an opportunity to shrink the rift between their people and ours. If there is even the slightest chance Tenebra will accept, we must invite them. If even a small step can be accomplished, we must take it. After what my loved ones and I endured, I will never support any decision to isolate Orthros from other lands."

Nodora's declaration garnered applause from many young Hesperines. Lio clapped with their peers, sending his Trial sister his admiration. The elders acknowledged her family's sacrifice with a wave of condolences through the Blood Union. Whether or not they agreed with her, they honored her losses. They recognized this was her argument to make, as only she could. She had moved them.

Once Lio's cousins and friends had spoken, to his astonishment, a procession of other Hesperines followed them down to the podium. Most were his own age, others from Kadi's generation, and he quietly gave thanks to each of them. He knew their families and suspected how their parents would vote. He knew what courage it took for them to show their support against the Will of their firstbloods.

Princess Konstantina watched the last of Lio's partisans resume their seats. "Let the firstbloods speak for those they have given power and life, and cast their votes on behalf of their bloodlines."

Xandra was the first to prick her finger and stain the white marble railing in front of her with blood to signify her vote of approval. Rudhira wasted no time doing the same. Lio saw his parents' blood mingle on the stone behind Anastasios. In the rows behind them, red droplets appeared from the independent bloodlines who owed Father their Gift. Uncle Argyros and Aunt Lyta pressed their thumbs to the railing together, then Basir and Kumeta, then many others in their section.

The air filled with the scent of the Gift, and Lio tallied the crimson stains, weighing them against the blood that remained unshed.

His own blood chilled in his veins, then burned with frustration. No. Not after all of this.

He was going to lose.

A quake of power shook the Blood Union. He looked toward the source. A droplet of red on Kassandra's finger.

She held up her hand and let the drop of blood fall to the stone in front of her.

Silence fell. No one moved.

Then suddenly Lio saw votes in blood everywhere he looked. Before he knew it, he could count the nays on one hand. One untouched patch of marble lay before Hypatia, although many railings behind her bore traces of blood. Princess Konstantina stood stiffly without touching the clean stone in front of her, her children unmoving behind her, while all her siblings and their families and some of her own descendants joined Rudhira and Xandra in voting.

At last she raised her hands. The drops of blood transformed into orbs of light and rose before each voter.

Although no one could doubt the outcome, tradition demanded the oldest child of each of the elder firstbloods must stand and count aloud on behalf of their bloodlines and tributaries. Kia's, Nodora's, and Lyros's eldest siblings rose to perform their tallies, while Kadi stood on Nike's behalf. One of Kassandra's tributaries performed the office for Prometheus, as a tributary of Blood Komnena counted in Lio's place.

Lio, honor-bound to observe silently from the podium, hoped Prometheus watched with him from the stars. Lio met Kassandra's gaze, pouring his gratitude to her into the Blood Union. She smiled at him and lounged back in her seat with an expression of satisfaction.

Together they beheld a rare sight. The First Prince, not the Second Princess, tallied the royal votes. He and his sister exchanged a charged glance.

At last Princess Konstantina turned and looked to the Queens, her aura beseeching. "Annassa, what is *your* Will?"

"We shall make it known to Tenebra and Cordium," Queen Soteira said.

Queen Alea took her hand. "Let them hear it from our own lips."

It seemed to cost Princess Konstantina great effort to turn and face the crowd again. "Ambassador Deukalion, Firstgift Komnenos, the Circle… and your Queens…have approved your proposal. May the Goddess's Eyes watch the path you have laid before your people."

❧94❧

nights until

WINTER SOLSTICE

A lady always honors the queen.

—Solia's instructions to Cassia

THE RESOURCES FOR VICTORY

WHAT HAD THE KING said and done while she slept? Cassia opened her eyes to the question that was always her first waking thought. She calmed her suddenly pounding heart with logic. She could not defeat him if she sickened from lack of sleep. She must accept she could not be everywhere at once. She must come to terms with wasted opportunities. Her reach went farther than the hearth, and her plan against the king was built on more than his self-incriminating words.

That was truer now than ever before. Now that she had committed to the last resort, no matter what it cost her. Time to rise and forge ahead.

Her body refused to move.

One day at a time, she admonished herself.

This one was almost over. The light in her room was the color of dusk. At nightfall, Chrysanthos had an appointment with the king. The sleep she had snatched would keep her on her feet during the conference.

But even reducing her focus to only the next few hours was not enough to stir her limbs.

She lay there a moment longer and tried again. She still had the strength to try. That was a good sign, surely. When she no longer had it in her to make an effort, then she would be truly concerned that she did not have the inner resources necessary to realize her course of action.

Her feelings had not yet breathed their last. Her powerful, unruly, and renegade emotions, which she had once regarded as a weakness and a threat to both her reason and her body. She knew now they too gave her strength.

She reached for her anger. She could always rely on that.

She sank into emptiness. Something worse awaited her below. She could almost feel it. Apathy.

So this was what she was made of, in moments when her anger failed to sustain her.

Cassia looked up at the plaster ceiling and listened to the evening birds outside her window. She contemplated the distance between her effort to get out of bed and her body, which had yet to move.

What was wrong with her? How could she give into this malaise more and more each day? How could her body fail her like this?

Her body, which had made love to Lio. Her body, which had bled to sate him, to bring their roses back to life, to power the Hesperines' spell against Dalos. Her body, which had climbed through a murder hole and given her the strength to save the glyph stone.

Cassia got out of bed.

Her preparations took her longer than usual, and her steps dragged through the hidden passageways. But she made it to her post in the king's fireplace just as Chrysanthos strolled into the solar.

"It's been three days," said the king. "Have you found the witch?"

"No," Chrysanthos replied, but he did not sound concerned. In fact, he sounded interested. "I look forward to meeting her, when our search yields results at last. How long has it been since you burned a heretic on the greensward of Solorum, Basileus?"

"See that it is not long before we burn the next one."

"Are you sure you do not wish for me to draw out the chase a little longer? The rumors you are circulating about a Hesperite sorceress on the loose are proving quite effective. Nothing like fear to warm ignorant minds to your alliance with my Order."

"Presenting the heretic in the flesh will be even more persuasive. So will the witch hunts that are sure to ensue across the kingdom."

"A useful pursuit to keep your Tenebran mages occupied. I'm sure you will understand if my brothers and I do not waste our time on such diversions. Once we have made an example out of the Solorum Hesperite, surely you will have all the justification you require to authorize our hunt for the greater enemy. We know all too well that Hesperines errant run rampant in your lands as we speak. My circle is eager to meet them in battle at last."

For one more night, Cassia had managed to escape becoming Chrysanthos's justification for harming Lio's people. For one more night, she stood between him and the Hesperines errant who were still risking their lives for mortals.

"You will soon have your chance to destroy them," the king promised.

"I hear the heart hunters want their own chance at my targets. Reports abound of an increase in their activities. Since the Equinox Summit, it seems they are seeing red and lying in wait to intercept Hesperines crossing to and from Orthros."

The king made a dismissive gesture. "A perennial phenomenon. There have always been warbands of heart hunters roaming the northern border, acting as self-appointed guardians against Hesperines."

"Or as brigands and extortionists, I take it. I wonder how many have actually earned their name by taking a Hesperine's heart and how many are merely common criminals."

"How difficult can it be to cut up a corpse?"

"Ah, but Hesperines leave no corpses, Basileus. Allow me to share a detail known only to those of us who have slain them. The instant a Hesperine dies, their remains disappear in a flash of light. Some call it Anthros's divine judgment, while other legends hold it was a spell placed upon them by Aithouros, designed to outlive him as his eternal revenge."

How dare the mage reduce one of the most sacred aspects of Hesperine existence to an act of his god or his order's magic? How dare Chrysanthos take credit for the Mercy in which Cassia's own sister, though a mortal, had shared?

"Regardless," Chrysanthos went on, "if you wish to collect any physical samples from a Hesperine, you must do it while the creature is still alive, then kill it before it kills you. Of course, removing the heart is one of the few effective ways to truly destroy a Hesperine, as is decapitation. But what primitive tactics, compared to the pure elegance of immolation. I find it doubtful these heart hunters could be very successful at vivisecting powerful, vicious immortals. What do a lot of low-born, Orderless rabble think they can do against Hesperines?"

"Their liegehounds are effective enough, although those mongrels are nothing compared to the pedigreed dogs from my kennels."

"The heart hunters seem eager to seize upon any excuse to breed more liegehounds and increase recruitment, the better to raid and drink their way across the mountain forests."

"It is convenient how the warbands siphon off village boys. Better that restless young men be initiated into the heart hunters' delusions of brotherhood and aspire to violence against Hesperines than that they become traitors I must bother to hang."

"I deem them more suited to my circle's pyre than your gallows, Basileus. The heart hunters' warbands are dens of crude apostasy and forbidden nature arts. I will not hesitate to take action against them, should they interfere in Order business."

"Heart hunters have their uses. They can be brought in line, if necessary. Many act under the patronage of free lords who are loyal to me, such as Lord Severinus the Elder. You will find his true devotion to stamping out heresy quite to your taste. He and his household mage would answer the call eagerly, should you see fit to delegate your witch hunts to them."

"We have much to discuss regarding the Hesperite threat. Would you care to adjourn with me to the Sun Temple for a game of Kings and Mages? We would both be more comfortable at the board with a glass of wine in hand."

To the pyre with Chrysanthos. More and more, he drew the king out of the solar—and out of Cassia's reach. Even before the Dexion's arrival, the king had taken to joining the royal mage for regular matches of Kings and Mages. The men's game of strategy was an age-old medium for schemes and conflicts that reached far beyond the board and its playing pieces. Cassia was dangerously blind and deaf to what transpired within the walls of the Temple of Anthros.

Before the king could answer, the solar door slammed open. Chrysanthos and Lucis glared at the interloper.

"I fear I must interrupt you, Basileus," the royal mage announced in the tone of a warrior rallying his troops.

He might be the only man in Tenebra who relished every chance to interrupt the king. He was skilled and diligent in his duties, but he knew it, and he was all too eager to indulge his own sense of importance.

"Now is not the time," the king warned him.

"I have a message for you, Basileus. It is highly irregular. The master mage you appointed to the fortress of Frigorum has performed a traversal all the way from our northern border to bring me the news."

Murmurs erupted amongst the guards. *Orthros. Monsters. Threat.*

Cassia clenched her hands into fists. Only a message of vital importance would warrant such an expense of magical power.

Was she out of time? Was this the moment of disaster she had fought with all her might to prevent?

Had the war already begun?

"Speak," the king commanded.

"It's the beacon, Basileus."

"I gave no order for the beacon to be lit."

"Not ours, Basileus. This has never happened, not ever in Tenebra's history, nor even in legends. But before my colleague lost consciousness from the ordeal of his traversal, he attested to what has happened tonight. The Hesperines lit their beacon first."

Silence descended. Cassia heard her own heart pounding. She tried to mitigate her expectations, to quell the longing already taking hold of her. But she could not.

It was said the beacon was a clear, white light, like a star. She had never seen it with her own eyes, but now in her memory she could see such a light, which a Hesperine had made from his blood for her, like a star in his hands.

"You're the expert on Hesperines, Dexion," the king said. "How do you interpret this?"

"I can only assume they mean the same thing by it that you would, Basileus. They appear to be inviting you to a Summit." Chrysanthos smiled. "This could present an opportunity."

"Let Orthros's advance delegates explain to Us the meaning of this unprecedented gesture. I assume the Hesperines' representatives are waiting at the customary site on the border. A party of my agents from Frigorum will meet them, as they did last year when We settled the terms for the Hesperines' visit to Our lands. When I receive word of the creatures' intentions, I will decide how further to respond."

The royal mage lifted his hands, and between them, the barest hint of orange light glowed. "Allow me to appoint one of my mages to traverse back to Frigorum and convey your decision, Basileus."

Chrysanthos gave the royal mage a condescending smile. "At this rate, half the mages in Tenebra will soon be in dead faints. My brothers and I will take it from here."

THE COST OF PASSAGE

I T WAS ALMOST DAWN when Tychon returned from the border. He traversed right into the king's solar and landed on his feet among his war circle, who had joined Chrysanthos there.

The Dexion put his arm around the young mage to support him. "Basileus. I ask your forbearance, that my apprentice may sit in your presence."

At Lucis's nod, Chrysanthos seated Tychon in the chair before the desk.

The apprentice was pale as death and soaked in sweat, but he had enough breath to speak. "Basileus, Dexion. The Queens of Orthros have invited an embassy from Tenebra to enter their land."

The Queens of Orthros had just torn the foundation from beneath all Cassia's plans, and she had never felt such hope.

Hope. At last. The Hesperines had lit their beacon. They were her beacon.

This changed everything.

"By Anthros," said the royal mage, "they have never been so obvious in their attempts to lure mortals into their clutches. The vile sirens are calling us toward their corruption loud and clear."

"On the contrary," said one of the Aithourians. "We must credit them for their subtlety."

Another Cordian mage nodded. "We can only wonder at their hidden motivations for such an elaborate scheme. The Akron has placed us here at the right time. An unprecedented time."

The Dexion asked Tychon, "You remained in the fortress behind the Tenebran mages' wards, as we agreed, and did not use any war magic?"

"Yes, Dexion. I did not allow the Hesperines to see me or gain an impression of my affinity. As soon as Basileus's men returned to the fortress, I traversed back to you to relate what they learned from their meeting in the pass with the Hesperines' representatives. The Tenebrans informed me they met with two of the members of the last embassy called Basir and Kumeta."

"Excellent. Continue."

"Basileus," Tychon addressed the king, "the Queens of Orthros have laid out very specific terms. They say any free lords or their appointed representatives shall be welcomed as guests of Orthros to discuss matters of security and trade affecting your two kingdoms. A special invitation is open to the Tenebran mages of Anthros, Hypnos, Kyria, and Chera to join the Hesperines' scholars for a circle." Tychon's lip curled. "To 'promote goodwill between cults.' You, Basileus, are invited to send a representative to discuss matters of state."

"They delude themselves there is still a chance of swearing the Equinox Oath?" Chrysanthos scoffed.

"No, Master. They wish to propose a new treaty, which is to usher in a new age of cooperation. They have dubbed it the Solstice Oath, for it is to be sworn during their so-called 'festival' of Winter Solstice. They expect a party of mortal men—and women!—to enter Orthros before the snows make the mountains impassable, then remain through the winter."

"The passes will still be snowbound until well into the spring," the Dexion observed. "I suppose the Hesperines have offered some guarantee of safe passage in and out of Orthros with the assistance of their magic. They wish to place the embassy at their mercy."

"Once a mortal steps into the Queens' magic," the royal mage warned, "there is no returning. Mark my words. Any who set foot in Orthros will never escape from behind the blood magic that marks the border. The Hesperines are trying to lure our finest to their deaths—or worse, their corruption."

The king rested one ring-heavy hand on the desk before him. "The Hesperines may issue as open an invitation as they like, but no one sets foot outside of Tenebra without my leave. I shall appoint the embassy, and it shall consist of men who shall see to it my will is done."

So he thought! Cassia would see to it the Hesperines' open invitation did not stay behind the closed doors of the solar.

"Basileus," the royal mage burst out. "You intend to accept?"

Lucis met Chrysanthos's gaze. "I think this is too useful an opportunity to waste."

The geomagus protested, "Anyone we send faces certain destruction."

Chrysanthos's voice was devoid of his courtly, gallant tone as never before. "Every war mage risks destruction when he faces his true enemy. I will not give up the Order's first and only chance to penetrate the Hesperines' domain. The Hesperines know they cannot run from my Order forever. I do not believe they really expect this stunt to save them. I must go and discover what they are really planning."

The royal mage turned on the Dexion. "No invitation was issued to Cordian mages."

"Indeed. I shall have to aspire to appear more Tenebran, shan't I."

A chill went down Cassia's spine. Did the Hesperines know they had just invited their worst enemy into their Sanctuary behind the Queens' ward? They surely understood the implications. Cassia could only believe the immortal sovereigns who had reigned Orthros with love for sixteen hundred years knew precisely what they were doing.

Cassia also knew all the reasons why Lucis and Chrysanthos, for their own purposes, would accept the Queens' invitation, and a dozen more why the Hesperines would be able to use this entire event to their ultimate advantage.

She knew the Tenebran embassy would go to Orthros and meet with the Hesperines' ambassadors. With Lio.

And she would not be there.

How could such a miracle as a human delegation to the Hesperines' homeland be such a cruel twist for her?

"Basileus, if you intend to accept the invitation," Tychon broke in, "there is one term the Hesperines insist you must meet. They were quite adamant on this point. If you fail to comply, they will revoke their offer."

"What is this demand the monsters think they can make of me?"

"They insist the Oath must be sworn with a member of your own blood, as Tenebran tradition dictates."

The geomagus sputtered, "That's preposterous. Basileus cannot risk himself or Prince Caelum on such a perilous undertaking. We cannot allow any member of the royal family to come under the Hesperines' power."

"Not a member of the royal family," Tychon clarified. "The Hesperines require that Lady Cassia be your representative, Basileus."

The room erupted in cries of *inappropriate, bastard, expendable, weaker sex*. Cassia didn't care. She barely heard.

She had not felt such jubilation in her heart since she had been with Lio. Her plans lifted from her shoulders. All the work she had still to do in Tenebra faded into the back of her mind. For a precious instant, only one plan, one thought mattered.

She was going to Orthros.

Unless the king refused to send her. Her joy halted in her chest, and helpless anger returned. She turned a gaze upon the king and wished he could see and feel the spite in her eyes.

It would never be that easy. He would not send her.

"The Aithourian Circle's first infiltration of Orthros depends on a woman?" one of the Cordians scoffed.

"This expedition is no place for a female," another Aithourian insisted. "The Dexion cannot be expected to coddle her all the way to Orthros."

Chrysanthos waved a dismissive hand. "The Hesperines want to swear the Oath with the king's blood. They know Lady Cassia is the only option who is irrelevant enough to the kingdom for Basileus to risk her. It seems she is the cost of passage into Orthros. A small price to pay."

"Basileus, she isn't a screamer, is she?" Tychon asked. "We cannot have her flying into fits of hysterics at the sight of Hesperines and interfering with our plans."

The king lifted a hand, and one of the guards came to his side on cue. "Dispatch a messenger to my daughter's rooms. She will attend me immediately."

It was not the first time Cassia and Knight had made the mad dash from the solar to her rooms in time to answer a summons she already knew was coming. But she had never done it so fast.

By the time she heard the messenger hammer on the next door over, Cassia was in her bed in her own tunica, and Knight was asleep on her feet.

Callen's curses would be colorful at the interruption. She did not envy the messenger who disturbed her bodyguard at this hour of the night and required his wife to leave their bed to wake the lady.

A little while later, Perita arrived at Cassia's bedside, flushed and pouting in the light of the candle she carried. "Messenger, m'lady. Majesty wants to see you."

Cassia got to her feet again, grimacing in sympathy. "Go back to bed, Perita. I can dress myself."

"Certainly not, m'lady."

Perita set to work on Cassia in the dressing room, and Knight supervised the ritual from the doorway.

"This is the third time," Perita muttered as she finished lacing Cassia's gown.

"Fourth," Cassia amended.

Perita gave Cassia a worried look, but they left the rest unsaid. The king's bastard had always been at his beck and call, but it had not been until recently that he had taken to summoning Cassia at all hours of the night. As if to ensure she was in her proper place at all times—or catch her if she wasn't.

A new thought occurred to Cassia. She should have seen it sooner.

Would he see a journey to Orthros as an expedient means of ridding himself of her at last?

Perhaps this was to be the blow heralded by the spies who watched her and the gown that meant death. An illness on the road. A fall from a cliff. Murder by Hesperine.

Cassia could have laughed. All she had to do was survive long enough to get to Orthros.

Once she was there, the king had no hope of touching her.

If he intended to send her in the first place. He would most likely keep her here to tether Flavian. Which meant she would have to take matters into her own hands yet again and somehow secure a place for herself in that embassy.

She strode through the front door of the solar into the scene she had just observed from the fireplace. She gave the king his curtsy and the mages her blankest expression so it would not seem as if she recognized any of them. Lady Cassia had not yet been introduced to the Dexion who had destroyed her shrine and sought to execute her for heresy.

The king gestured at Cassia. "Here is the girl, Dexion."

Chrysanthos gave Cassia an artful bow. Tension stiffened the curtsy she gave him in return. Would he feel the memory of Lio in her aura? Or had it been too long since she had touched her Hesperine lover for even an Aithourian to sense the evidence?

The mage's smile was surely one he gave to Cordian princesses when he sought to slay them with his charms. "Lady Kyria, how nice to meet you in person."

"I was indeed the lady who had the honor of dancing the goddess's steps upon this year's Equinox." Cassia fawned, "I need not beg an introduction to you, Dexion, for your reputation already precedes you all over Solorum. You are the hand of Corona, whom Anthros himself has sent to light our festival bonfire and our path in this hour of trouble." Should she bat her eyelashes for good measure?

"This hour calls you to a grave task, but do not be alarmed, for I shall be at your side every step of the way. I am loath to ask this of a woman, but your kingdom needs you." He proceeded to relate the night's developments like a scary bedtime story. "Your father is prepared to extend you the honor of accompanying me on his official business. If I promise you can rely on me to protect you, will you come with me into fear itself?"

"She will be ready for your departure a fortnight hence," the king replied.

Cassia could scarcely believe it. After she had scraped together all her plans with her own two hands, suddenly the perfect plan was handed to her. The almighty Order of Anthros and the king himself were ready to serve it up to her. She could not have asked for anything so perfect, for she would never have dreamed it possible.

She could not begin in that moment to predict the complete consequences to her last resort. Until she knew what the Hesperines intended, she could not adjust her plan accordingly. But she knew one thing with certainty.

She was going to Orthros. Whatever the situation, surely that meant there was a chance she would see Lio again. She was good at making the most of chances, however slim.

If they could only be together again, they might once more take on the impossible. And win.

Dare she hope the last resort might not be necessary? Could she and Lio use the Solstice Summit to find a different solution?

She must not get ahead of herself and run headlong into foolish hope. But for the first time in months, the despair that had been so close at her heels was falling behind.

She would not let the king have the last word. "I am not afraid, Dexion. I will do what my people need of me. It will be my honor to go to Orthros."

93

nights until

WINTER SOLSTICE

A lady always keeps ivy.

—Solia's instructions to Cassia

FAREWELLS

"I'M SORRY, YOUR LADYSHIP. My lord is indisposed."

Cassia cocked her head at Sir Benedict. "You need not address me so. Lady Cassia is more than enough."

Sir Benedict didn't budge from where he stood in front of Flavian's door. "You're to be the Lady of Free Segetia. We haven't had a ladyship in a very long time."

"If I am to be a ladyship, I'd best become acquainted with the future lordship's vices sooner rather than later, don't you think?"

"I'd hoped to beat a few out of him before the happy event, Your Ladyship."

"Benedict." Cassia smiled. "There are things I must do here, things I have to say. So many preparations in case... You understand."

Benedict looked away. "Aye. Too well." With a sigh, he opened the door and escorted her into Flavian's chambers.

As much time as she and Flavian had spent together over the last six months, she had never set foot in this room, which served as his solar and the center of his domain whenever he was at Solorum. A large window looked out over the kennels and stables, and Cassia imagined it always smelled good in here, like dogs and horses.

Except on occasions such as today, when the room smelled of the debauched figure at the desk. Flavian sat hunched over a stack of letters. There was a quill in his hand and an as-yet empty sick bucket at his feet. He didn't look up from what he was writing, only shoved his goblet in Benedict's direction with his free hand. "There's something wrong with this cup."

"Yes," said Cassia. "The number of cups that preceded it."

Flavian started in his chair, then straightened and reached for his shirt laces. How quaint that he felt the need to cover his chest hair and his amulet of the Brotherhood of Hedon from Cassia's sight.

He got slowly to his feet. "Forgive my state of dress, my lady."

"It is forgiven, and so is the wine, if you will allow Benedict to leave that goblet empty."

"Ben, I think a flagon of cold water is in order."

"Indeed, my lord." Benedict excused himself, his expression promising he would dump it on Flavian's head.

Cassia eyed the empty decanters that lined a cabinet behind Flavian. "I take it the one who has laid waste to your forces has a name, and it is Sabina."

He leaned with both hands on his desk. "She left court."

"Are you going after her?"

"She has gone home to Hadria. The one place I cannot follow."

"Is it?"

"It doesn't matter. She declined what I proposed. It seems Hadria has more honor than Segetia after all. She said she could not reconcile her conscience to the arrangement."

"Perhaps if you were the one who had thought of it, she would have felt more inspired to accept."

He saluted Cassia with his empty goblet.

"Did you first win her to you with one conversation?" asked Cassia. "It will take more effort than this, Flavian."

"As you so eloquently reminded me, I did not win her. She won me. But although you explained how you knew all of that, there is one thing you did not make clear to me. Why are you so concerned about Sabina and me?"

"That is not the question you should be asking right now. You need to sober up and saddle your horse. This is an opportunity you will never have again—I will be out of the way. Out of the country, in fact."

"I beg your pardon?"

"I'm going to Orthros."

His goblet hit the desk with a thud. "What is the king thinking?"

"Now you are asking the right questions."

Flavian skirted the desk. "How can he do this to you?"

"Thank you for worrying about me. But I will be fine." Oh, so fine.

"The so-called embassy is a suicide mission! I will not stand by while my future wife is sent to her death."

"What question did you ask a moment ago?"

He looked confused, shook his head. But he answered, "What is the king thinking?"

Cassia nodded. "You know the answer. Your time in his service has taught it to you, as has my life as his daughter."

Flavian came to Cassia, reaching out to her. He hesitated only a moment before resting his hands on her arms. "Whatever we do or do not make of our union, Cassia, I care about your safety. I care about you. I would not call myself a man if I let you be taken into danger."

"My safety is not what must occupy you. What did your time in Misellum teach you?"

He took a step back. "You know about that, as well?"

"Yes, I know that when the king instructs you to take care of his thieving problem, you do so by putting bread on starving people's tables instead of taking off their hands. You are a man who can walk into a potential bloodbath and turn it into a thriving trade town. But what about the criminals in your vassals' own barracks? What did Verruc's crimes teach you?"

This time, Flavian did not kiss her hand and tell her to think only of dancing. He said nothing.

"Would you entrust the safety of *your* dependents to Lord Tyran's guards?" Cassia demanded. "Would you trust his men with a Segetian dairy maid?"

Flavian grimaced.

"Many such problems will demand your intervention, and you must make a commitment now to doing what you know is right, even if it is not what others wish of you."

Flavian sat down on the edge of his desk. "You are in no way the woman I so foolishly assumed you to be."

"Now you are reaching the right conclusions." She took Flavian's hands in both of hers and looked into his eyes. "Are you the man you assume yourself to be? Tenebra needs you to know the answer. Tenebra needs you."

The consternation was still there in his gaze, but thoughtfulness too. He had listened to her.

She let him go. She had done all she could at this late hour. Would it be enough?

She could only hope this conversation would cause him to think back on all their previous ones, when she had been, unbeknown to him, instructing him. She had thought she would have more time to prepare Flavian for the role he would have to fill. She had believed she would be here to do what he did not find himself capable of.

The ivy pendant weighed on her chest. No plan for victory was effective unless it accounted for the possibility of defeat. Cassia must lay a foundation for that eventuality, and she had only a fortnight in which to do it.

Her cause must not die with her, if the king used a supposedly suicidal journey to commit murder.

When Benedict returned with the flagon, Flavian turned away from Cassia and poured himself some water.

He drained his cup before speaking again. "Cassia is going to Orthros."

"I know," said Benedict. "I am going with her."

Flavian rounded on him, and Cassia thought he might be about to hurl his fist, but no. He put a hand on Benedict's shoulder. "Gods. Not you too."

"Your father approached me about it this morning, when I was on my way to volunteer. I am clearly the one you should send to represent Segetia in the Tenebran embassy and personally ensure Her Ladyship's safety."

Flavian let out a bitter, disbelieving huff of a laugh. "Father didn't even ask me."

"I'd have said the same thing if he had, my lord."

"You are not expendable, Ben."

"Thank you, my lord."

Flavian looked from one of them to the other. "I, Lord Flavian of Free Segetia, am to sit on my velvet-covered ass and mind the king while my dearest friend and future wife ride into the clutches of the Hesperines."

And while Sabina rode home to Hadria. He did not say it, but Cassia knew she and Benedict were thinking it for him.

"Gods," Flavian said again. "I don't know if I'll ever see any of you again."

"I will be disappointed in you if you spend my time in Orthros sitting on your ass," Cassia informed him. "You have questions to ask, conclusions to draw, and a great deal of work to do. You are a clever man. It should not be necessary for me to itemize it for you."

Flavian reached into his collar. Cassia heard a snap, and he yanked out his amulet of the Brotherhood. She caught a glimpse of the phallic glyph of Hedon before Flavian hurled the charm with unerring aim into his sick bucket.

"I will do what I can, my lady."

She gave him the best words she had to offer him, the most powerful influence, which she had saved for this, their last moment before her departure. "I have confidence in you."

85

nights until

WINTER SOLSTICE

A lady always tries to understand what's going on.

—Solia's instructions to Cassia

HYPNOS'S BASTARD

THE NECROMANCERS SMELLED LIKE funerary incense. Cassia had not seen a mage of Hypnos since the one who had come to clean up what was left of Dalos after his duel with the Hesperines. Although the six necromancers who now presented themselves in the solar were Cordian, she would have been hard-pressed to tell them apart from their Tenebran colleague. Their black hoods and robes shrouded them from head to toe, and long beards obscured half their faces.

The leader of their hex was set apart only by the silvery, metal glyph of Hypnos that adorned his hood. The death god's symbol, an eternally closed eye, sat right upon the master's forehead. Cassia had heard a hexmaster's brooch was always wrought of deadly liquid quicksilver, caught in a spell.

With his hands hidden in his sleeves, the hexmaster bowed to Chrysanthos. "We are ready to assist you, our brother mage, as Hypnos assists his brother Anthros. We will represent our Order in the embassy to Orthros."

The mage spoke in Vulgus, presumably for the benefit of the king, who watched from his chair with a judgmental gaze. Little did the men know they also benefitted the spy in their midst.

Chrysanthos bowed in return and answered in the same tongue. "An entire hex? How thorough. The Order of Anthros appreciates your eagerness to collaborate on the expedition to Orthros. However, I am afraid you have traversed to Tenebra for nothing. The Akron and the Synthikos have left it to me to invite the necromancer of my choice to join me in the embassy. Basileus and I expect his arrival imminently."

The hexmaster subjected Chrysanthos to a momentary silence. "The Inner Eyes have chosen us for this task. I have been told nothing about another necromancer. There is no room in a hex for a seventh mage."

"Indeed, that would be a defiance of the laws of magic, wouldn't it? Alas, I regret to tell you there is no room in the embassy for a hex. Only one necromancer will accompany us. Your instructions must have crossed with his, for he assured me he has the sanction of the Inner Eyes."

"One necromancer is hardly sufficient for a penetration into Hesperine lands," the hexmaster returned. "One is barely enough to see to the casualties of dysentery on the road, to say nothing of the possible death toll once you encounter the heretics. Does this mage you have chosen even have an apprentice to whom he can delegate the corpses?"

"He is equal to the challenge, I assure you. In fact, he possesses the singular magical expertise this venture demands. With all due respect to your hex, I require his skills." With a smile like that, Chrysanthos might send someone to the pyre and make them look forward to the trip.

The black hood replied, "Our hex is steeped in secrets no other mages possess, which we six have practiced together since before you were an apprentice. You wouldn't want to leave those powers in Tenebra... behind you."

Chrysanthos's expression hardened. "He has promised to give Basileus a demonstration of his unique arts. Perhaps he will agree to let you watch, since you are colleagues."

Cassia sat up straighter, leaning forward through the flames. Forewarned was forearmed. The more she knew of the magic Chrysanthos's chosen necromancer could wield, the better equipped she was to warn the Hesperines.

"Ah." Tychon's face brightened, and he looked at the door from where he stood near at Chrysanthos's side. "Here he is now, Master. There is no mistaking his aura."

Lucis nodded, and the guards opened the solar door. Eudias scurried in, but offered no announcement of Chrysanthos's guest. The apprentice got out of the way in haste.

A new fragrance filled the room, one Cassia recognized. Belladonna. From her vantage point, the first things she saw were spurred boots and the hem of a cape. He wore black like the other necromancers, but there the similarities ended.

This mage's robes stopped at his knees and revealed leather armor beneath, along with an arsenal of blades and vials. He looked as if a Kyrian apothecary had rolled in the hay with Hypnos himself, and the resulting scion had slaughtered the village butcher for the tools of his trade.

Chrysanthos smiled and clasped the man's arm. "Good of you to come."

"I wouldn't miss it." Hypnos's bastard sounded as if he has swallowed a bin of gravel, or perhaps had his throat ripped out at some point. "It's been a month since I last bagged a Hesperine."

The words sent a shock through Cassia. She wanted to dismiss them as an empty boast. But she knew better. She had believed there might already be skirmishes between Hesperines errant and mages. Hearing this necromancer confirm it in such blunt terms made her fears real.

"Basileus, may I present Master Skleros," Chrysanthos said with relish. "He is Tenebran born, Cordian trained, and battle-hardened."

Skleros gave the king a nod, not quite a bow.

The king nodded in return, studying the knives the mage wore. "The Dexion speaks highly of your years of experience in the field hunting Hesperines."

"He is not like any necromancer you have met before," Chrysanthos said. "You see before you a Gift Collector, whose work it is to make Hesperines pay their dues to the god of death."

Chrysanthos was taking an assassin of Hesperines with him to Orthros.

Skleros turned to the other necromancers, and Cassia saw his face for the first time. Scars twisted his visage. Upon the breast of his leather armor, a glyph of Hypnos was written in long-dried blood. Was that Hesperine blood? The red stain made the eye appear more like a mouth that might open at any moment, ready to devour.

The Gift Collector's smile was derisive. "I like to get my hands dirty."

"You will work well with us, I can see," Lucis said.

The other necromancers stood at arm's length and made no move to offer their greetings.

"Master Skleros," said the hexmaster. "What a surprise. How unusual for a Gift Collector to come out of the shadows and rejoin society. I thought bounties from the Inner Eyes are the only Order business in which those of your profession deign to participate."

"The Order has lined my pockets for delivering Hesperines to Hypnos. But I'm not in it for the coin this time. You can't put a price on a chance like this."

The hexmaster shot a pointed glance at the empty space behind Skleros. "You seek to beat your colleagues to the prize, as usual, I take it."

"You know each Gift Collector always works alone." Skleros cast a condescending gaze on the hex. "If you're good at what you do, it only takes one."

"Such humility, Master Skleros," Chrysanthos jested. "If you downplay your skills any further, I shall have to remind your colleagues of your reputation. I can't decide which I find more impressive—that you have completed more bounties than any other living Gift Collector, or that you are still living."

The hexmaster did not look amused. "This endeavor calls for the most devoted servants of the Order of Hypnos. The Inner Eyes appointed my hex to join you, Dexion, and we came all the way from Cordium for the purpose."

Skleros thrust a scroll at the hexmaster. "Don't try my patience with politics. There's a reason the Inner Eyes don't like me to spend much time in Cordium. But I did make a visit there long enough to procure this. I am going to Orthros."

The hexmaster drew himself up and unrolled the scroll with great impatience. He spent more time looking at it than necessary for such a short document. Finally he handed it to one of his colleagues, who then handed it back to him.

With obvious reluctance, the hexmaster concluded, "This appears to be official."

Chrysanthos raised a brow at Skleros. "Playing by the rules for a change, my friend?"

"Only when I have to escort a fastidious Aithourian to Orthros. Don't expect me to carry you."

"I appreciate you making an exception for me. I assure you, I shall clean the mud off my own shoes." Chrysanthos eyed Skleros's spurred boots. "You wouldn't happen to have an extra pair of those that would fit me, would you?"

"I might. If there's a fire charm in it for me. My smokes don't light themselves."

"We have a bargain. I will start a new fashion when I return home."

"Keep talking about *when* you get home. Work hard to convince yourself you will. It will seem unlikely while I'm working on you."

"I have endured worse than the ritual you intend to perform upon me tonight."

"No. You haven't."

"What ritual can you mean?" the hexmaster cut in. "Whatever the Dexion requires, we can surely provide."

"Shall we excuse your colleagues so they can rest before their return to Cordium?" Chrysanthos asked.

"I do appreciate your concern for my professional secrets, but that won't be necessary." Skleros told the necromancers, "You will assist me and make your magic available to me while I perform the ritual."

The hex murmured among themselves in Divine.

"This is highly irregular," said the hexmaster.

"Take it or leave it," Skleros replied. "Stay and pay for my knowledge with your magic—or get out."

Their murmurs turned into huffs and hisses.

The hexmaster glared at Skleros. "*Some* mages of our Order respect their colleagues and their craft. We show proper appreciation for those rare opportunities when necromancers consent to share their arcane secrets with one another. We will remain."

Cassia watched Order politics play out before her in miniature. No doubt the hex did want to pry into what Chrysanthos referred to as Skleros's exclusive skills. What ulterior motive might Skleros have for betraying his secrets, though? Cassia hoped he would show his hand, not just make a show of power.

"Very well," said Skleros. "The Dexion has enlisted my services to hide the true nature and magnitude of his power from the Hesperines."

Cassia's heart raced. When the Tenebran embassy departed for

Orthros tomorrow, might she carry with her one of the enemy's greatest magical secrets to offer as a gift to Lio's people?

"You performed the same service for Dalos?" the king asked pointedly.

"Yes. The spell *I* crafted in preparation for the Equinox Summit was one of my best workings."

Chrysanthos smirked. "What a shame when an artist paints a fine fresco upon a wall, only to see the architect's shoddy work crumble away and destroy his masterpiece."

"The fate of my kingdom rests on this ritual you are about to perform. Let us discuss it. I will have no half-explanations and obtuse ramblings."

"Would you be so kind as to repeat the lesson you gave me after Dalos's altercation with the Hesperines?" Chrysanthos made a gracious gesture toward the king. "What you can tell me, you can tell Basileus."

"My guards know better than to breathe a word of what is said in this room," the king informed Skleros.

"Very good, Basileus," said Skleros. "If you care for arcane wordage, this process is called essential displacement."

"Basileus," the hexmaster interrupted. "This man seeks to deceive you. Essential displacement is only a theory, and anyone claiming to be able to perform it is nothing but a charlatan."

"Theories don't keep mages alive in battle against Hesperines," Skleros returned. "Don't pretend our Order is unaware that Gift Collectors have been practicing essential displacement for decades, and that the Inner Eyes want to get their claws on our methods. This is your lucky day, Hexmaster. You get to watch me work."

"I can attest that Skleros's arts are as effective as he claims," said the Dexion. "My circle has established a partnership with him for the purposes of our war mages' diplomatic journeys in Tenebra and now Orthros. I regret to say the only reason it has not been a complete success is that a certain mage was chosen to attend the Equinox Summit."

Lucis steepled his fingers. "How does the process work?"

Skleros answered, "This configuration of essential displacement requires three men. A source, who will have his essence—his magic—displaced. A vessel, who will receive the source's magic. And a channel, who acts as a living conduit between the source and the vessel."

"So I am the source," said Chrysanthos. "While my magic is displaced from me into a vessel, the Hesperines will be unable to sense my power. Of course a channel is necessary so I can access that power at will should the need arise for me to cast a demanding spell."

"Be cautious in drawing your power," Skleros warned. "Fluctuations could draw Hesperine attention. The amount of magic that I'll leave in you will be sufficient for routine tasks. The greater portion of your power will await you in your vessel until you have need of it."

Chrysanthos pursed his lips. "For Dalos's vessel, the Synthikos provided a convict. The man remained in our custody in Corona for safekeeping until his usefulness was expended. Should I send for something similar?"

"No need. I can provide a body from the western wing of my prison." The king sent off one of his guards.

"Excellent," said the Dexion. "The other masters from my party will remain here in Tenebra to ensure the vessel is not disturbed. It wouldn't do for the prisoner to die until I require it."

"Make sure the vessel is fed and given healing if need be," Skleros advised the king. "The only way to reverse the displacement is to kill the vessel. The Dexion won't want that to happen until the moment when he's ready to draw every last quantity of his magic back into himself. Inadvisable until he returns from Orthros."

"Now, as for my channel—" Chrysanthos began.

"Master." Tychon stepped forward. "It would be my honor to serve you."

Chrysanthos shook his head. "That is no task for an apprentice of your ability."

Skleros raised an eyebrow at Tychon. "It's an uncomfortable position, to have another's magic thrust and drawn through you day after day. But it does require some affinity for the source's magic to begin with, however slight, to grease the channel."

"Eudias will serve," Chrysanthos said. "As he did for Dalos."

"Can we risk taking Eudias to Orthros?" Tychon asked, as if the other apprentice were not standing right there in the room. "The Hesperines will recognize him from the Equinox Summit."

"They still believe him to be a Tenebran apprentice," Chrysanthos answered. "It was not apparent to them that he assisted Dalos with the assassination attempt, since he merely acted as a channel rather than taking an active role in the casting."

Now Cassia understood why the poor apprentice had appeared so ill and cowed all the time. What a wretched fate, to be used by your master so.

"Eudias is unworthy," Tychon insisted. "I am far more equal to the task. You need someone of strength and dedication."

"I need you at full strength," the Dexion replied.

"I shall be at full strength, only I shall lend all of it to you."

"I must agree with your apprentice," the king said. "Eudias is unsuitable for the task. We cannot afford to take any chances. The stakes are much higher. Besides, I have another purpose in mind for the boy. My daughter will need an arcane bodyguard in addition to the liegehound and the man-at-arms I already have watching her. None of you should be bothered minding the girl. Eudias will make a suitable shadow for her."

Cassia's sympathy for the apprentice dried up. She was to have Eudias nipping at her heels the entire time she was with the Hesperines? While she had a chance to be with Lio. She could not allow any Cordian to get in her way.

Chrysanthos put a hand on Tychon's shoulder. "I am loath to subject you to this."

"You are not subjecting me to anything, Master. I am volunteering."

The Dexion gave the young man's shoulder a squeeze, then let him go. "I owe you a bottle of fine spirits upon our return to Corona."

Tychon chuckled. "I shall hold you to that, Master."

"You've a strong aura about you," Skleros told Tychon. "Channeling for your master will serve to disguise your power as well." Then the Gift Collector waved a hand at Eudias. "We don't need to bother with concealment in his case. His aura hasn't been the same since Dalos's defeat."

A foul taste came to Cassia's mouth. What sort of arcane scars had Eudias's masters left on him? She was not sure even an Aithourian apprentice deserved that.

"See here," said Chrysanthos, "I will not have my apprentice's power permanently affected."

Skleros shook his head. "It won't be, because you are smarter than Dalos."

Tychon looked to his master. "You know I am not afraid. I would be proud to fall in battle at your side."

"If our diplomatic excursion into Orthros costs any lives, it won't be ours." Chrysanthos rubbed his hands together. "We are ready then, as soon as the vessel arrives."

A sense of anxiety made Cassia rise to her feet. Was it wise of her to stay for this? She had never seen magic performed in the king's solar. The working wouldn't disrupt the magic that protected her, would it?

Surely not. Lustra magic was another beast entirely than Ordered magery.

She mustn't sacrifice this chance to make as many observations as possible. When she related this event to Hesperines who knew more of magic than she did, they might glean a great deal from her report.

When the guards returned, they dragged a young man between them. Beneath the filth that covered the prisoner, Cassia recognized the livery of the royal stables. The guards deposited him on the rug in the middle of the room, and he lay there, covering his head with his hands.

"Here's a likely one, Dexion," a guard offered. "He's not been in the prison long. He'll last."

"He looks fit enough," said Skleros.

"Is he strong?" Chrysanthos frowned. "He's not putting up much of a fight."

The guard jabbed a steel-toed boot into the man's ribcage. "He cares too much for his family to do that, don't you?"

The prisoner flinched, but made no outcry.

An image flashed in Cassia's mind—Callen prostrate on the floor of a cell in the western wing. Silently she promised the man before her she would see justice done for him too, that she would remember him and his family among all the others who had suffered at the king's hands.

Lucis sat back in his chair and observed the mages in front of him as he might a tournament between his warriors. Only there was something different about the sight of him. Something jarred Cassia, which she had seldom seen in the king's eyes.

Interest. Even...fascination.

She stared at him.

But the mages were arranging themselves for the spell, and she must pay attention. The six offended necromancers stepped back, positioning themselves in a semicircle around the prisoner, opposite the Gift Collector.

"You'll want to take a seat," Skleros told Tychon.

"As you say, Master." The apprentice bowed to the king, then sat down in a chair at Chrysanthos's right hand.

The Dexion spread his arms. "I am ready."

When Skleros rammed his fist into the Dexion's breastbone, Chrysanthos's jaw dropped, and Cassia's whole body jerked. The mage of Anthros buckled around the necromancer's hand and fell to his knees.

The prisoner's body undulated and writhed on the floor behind Skleros. Cassia was vaguely aware of the other necromancers swaying on their feet and Tychon slumping in his chair. But her gaze was riveted on Chrysanthos.

He clawed at Skleros's hand like a wild animal. Cassia's body wanted to turn away, and her legs insisted she run. But the weightless linen that hung upon her felt like a vice, and she couldn't escape. She had just enough reason to wonder what was wrong with her, why the torture of Chrysanthos's hateful soul should matter at all to her.

The war mage's touch burned through the necromancer's leather gauntlets. The smell of charred flesh filled the room. Skleros didn't flinch, just stood with his feet braced and his fingers twisted in the front of the Dexion's costly robe.

Chrysanthos let out a snarl, which turned into the wail of a dying man. The fire writhed and crumbled. The embers gave way beneath Cassia's feet. Flames spun around her.

She didn't know which way she was falling.

Solid ground knocked the wind out of her, and she had no breath to move or flee. If she had fallen into the solar, it was all over.

With a gasp of effort, she scrambled onto her feet and looked all around her.

Darkness and stone. Safe.

She stood panting for a moment. No sound came from within the solar. She stepped back into the hearth, slowly, for her head still spun.

The Dexion of the Aithourian Circle lay crumpled on the necromancer's mud-stained boots. Was Chrysanthos dead?

But suddenly he heaved at the air and braced himself up on his forearms. Skleros reached down and helped him to his feet.

"I apologize for your burns," Chrysanthos said. "I do hope they won't leave any more scars than you already have."

Skleros snorted. "Note that I bothered to aim elsewhere than your pretty face."

"My mother will thank you."

Chrysanthos staggered to Tychon's side and asked him a question in the Divine Tongue. The ashen-faced apprentice shook his head. Cassia couldn't see Eudias, but heard his uneven breathing from somewhere to her left. It seemed he was cowering in a corner as far from the brutal ritual as he could get.

Cassia recalled the night when, in this very room, Dalos had almost tasked Eudias with assassinating Callen. That threat to Callen was past, for their enemies had mistakenly decided he knew no secrets that made him a threat. But for a moment, Eudias had faced the prospect of murdering him, and the apprentice had looked as willing as if he were about to face his own certain demise.

Now he was the first to say, "They are dead. All of them."

No one moved toward the still, prone bodies of the six necromancers.

"Yes," Skleros returned. "They are. Moving power takes power. I used them up."

The Gift Collector availed himself of one of the concoctions he carried at his belt. He applied salve and bandages to his wounds with the air of a man rolling a smoke. The clean, bitter scent of medicinal herbs banished the stench of his burns and the prisoner's offal.

Cassia stared at Skleros's hand. She rubbed her breastbone, and her heart hammered back against her.

Lucis smiled. "I am impressed."

48

nights until

WINTER SOLSTICE

Hesperines shall be permitted to exercise any power on convicted criminals or miscreants acting in clear violation of the law to the detriment of honest people.

—*The Equinox Oath*

INTO THE STORM

A WHORL OF SNOW STOLE Cassia's breath and her first glimpse of Orthros.

If not for the weather, she might have looked ahead and beheld the Hesperines' home by the light of the moons. But leaning forward in her saddle and peering through the snow, she could see nothing beyond the caravan of weary mortals around her. She only knew they had entered the pass because the others had come to a halt.

Against the swirling white, her fellow members of the Tenebran embassy were dark forms shaped like mounts and riders. Ghostly flurries whipped about them, by turns outlining or erasing them from the face of the mountain.

Thanks to Cassia, the dozen travelers the king had authorized had swelled to fifty-six. As the king's oh-so-secret embassy had hastened north, lords and mages from every corner of Tenebra had attached themselves along the way in response to anonymous reports of the Hesperines' invitation. No suspicion would fall on Cassia or an innocent scapegoat while Orthros's beacon shone. With that light in the sky for all of northern Tenebra to see, a spy in the solar seemed an improbable explanation for how the king's plans had become widely known. From across the land, the courageous, the foolhardy, the desperate, and the devout had come, and they now waited together to enter Orthros, unsure of whether they would ever return.

They did not have long to wait. The sun set early this far north. Nightfall would soon arrive, and with it, their Hesperine escort.

The wind, although strong, was strangely gentle, shushing around them like a comforting voice. The cold was fierce enough, though. Even bundled in layers of wool with a hood and scarf to protect her face, Cassia felt as if winter gnawed on her bones. It was the necessary cost of leaving all her furs in Tenebra. Her only regret was how her refusal to wear them worried Perita.

The small, shaking form on the next pony was Cassia's friend, who now shared a long-suffering glance with her over their mufflers. The hazards of mountain travel made them curse the injustice that they were not entitled to ride astride as the men were. Instead they must teeter sidesaddle atop their ponies past one sickening drop after another, holding on as best they could through their bulky mitts and layers of skirts. As if either of them still had maidenheads to be damaged by a horseback ride.

The tall bundles of fur on horses that loomed nearest them were Callen and Benedict. Callen guided his horse a little closer to his wife, while Benedict cast a worried glance over his shoulder.

The knight fretted quietly, "I hope this wait in the snow is not too difficult for the Semna. Such cold is unhealthy for her bones."

Perita followed his gaze, frowning at the bundle on the horse litter not far behind them. "She didn't survive decades as the Prisma of the Temple of Kyria to crumple in a bit of winter weather. She may have been retired for twelve years, but her magic and her determination are as strong as ever."

"Her two attendants are capable healers, should she need their care after this ordeal," said Benedict.

"We're more likely to need the Semna to use her magic on our frost-bitten toes," Callen replied.

Benedict declared, "I will carry her or any other lady in the embassy myself if the need should arise."

"Is that how you do things in Segetia?" Callen demanded. "In Hadria, we don't let other men handle our duties to our women. Should my lady or my wife need carrying, it won't be from you, thank you very much."

Perita patted her husband's hand. "Who said we need carrying?"

Knight nuzzled Cassia's foot, offering her all the warmth he could. Thankfully he fared much better than humans out here, well-equipped with his broad paws and dense fur. Cassia spoke to Knight just to keep her voice from rusting, although she did not feel like making conversation, only like staring forward and training all her senses on what—who—lay ahead.

"This is practically your native land, isn't it, love? Your folk were first bred in these mountains to guard against our toothy northern neighbors. What an honor to be the only liegehound ever invited to Orthros for a visit."

Lord Severinus the Younger approached, riding through the gathering toward the front of the caravan. The pale-haired lord drew reign next to Cassia. "You couldn't ask for a better ally out here than your hound, Lady Cassia. I've lost count of how many of my men would be dead if our liegehounds hadn't pulled them out of the snow."

Cassia tugged her scarf down, the better to speak. "We're fortunate in your knowledge of the area as well, Lord Severin. Having a guide who hails from the north is indispensable. The mounts you have provided us have not missed a step."

The young lord sighed. "I wish I could have taken you on a tour through the mountain villages instead of this fool's errand. There isn't a tenant who doesn't know your name."

"I am humbled, my lord. All I did was give you advice on plants."

"Your counsel regarding frost-resistant crops and blight prevention saved my people from starvation. They will never forget you."

Lord Severin's hollow cheeks made it clear he had not eaten while his dependents went without, but they were all beginning to recover.

"Their good opinions are an honor, but I hope they know the one who saved them—and continues to save them—is you, Lord Severin."

He looked away. "I do what I can. But my father's domain is treacherous."

"You've accomplished a great deal in your efforts to mitigate that damage."

"And yet somehow I always feel a step behind." He lowered his voice. "I am still uncertain why I was approved for this venture. I am hardly the one to represent anti-Hesperine sentiment in the negotiations. My father knows better than to expect me to champion his cause."

"I know you chafe at being taken away from your duties."

"I am too busy fulfilling his responsibilities while he chases rumors of Hesperines. I have no time for this." With that, he gave her pony a pat on the shoulder. "The equines of this region are as excellent as the canines. I wish I could say the same for the weather and the men."

Lord Severin joined Chrysanthos at the front of the column for a word. Mage and warrior were difficult to tell apart under piles of cloaks and furs, but Chrysanthos had made sure to distinguish himself by remaining in the lead every step of the way.

He pirouetted his horse to face the others, and the posturing further assured Cassia he was indeed the Dexion. He spoke over the wind so all could hear. "Martyrs' Pass. I need not remind you how it earned its name. As you well know, few humans ever set foot here, and fewer still survive it. Tonight we go where mortals have always feared to tread. Be on your guard."

Lord Severin cleared his throat. "This is the place where the king's emissaries always halt to meet with the Hesperine envoys to arrange the Equinox Summit."

"How fortunate they have been," Chrysanthos said, "to survive that once-in-a-lifetime encounter. However, all who have ventured beyond this point fell victim to the weather, the blood ward—or the Guardian of Orthros. This is the only known route between Tenebra and Orthros, and the Hesperines have warned us the way is impassable without their aid. Whatever the case, we can be certain that proceeding further poses mortal danger. For the sake of our noncombatants, we have little choice but to wait for the Hesperine forces to arrive and take us over the border."

Lord Severin advised, "Hug the cliff that rises above us and avoid the slope on our other side. It falls off gradually at first, but can carry you far down indeed if you stumble. As we wait for nightfall, keep watch for the usual hazards. Frostbite, wolves, bears. We are close enough to the border that no human brigands should pose a danger, for even the most intrepid heart hunters dare not venture this close to the Hesperine Queens' magic."

"Thank you," Chrysanthos said in the tone of a dismissal.

"Happy to serve, Dexion." Frowning, Lord Severin rejoined the rest of the embassy and commenced yet another of his tours of the group, checking harnesses and appointing torch-bearers.

On impulse, Cassia double-checked the straps on her gardening satchel. Its seams were fit to burst with the glyph stone lying in the bottom, wrapped in Solia's flametongue garments, under the ivy pendant, Cassia's spade, and Lio's gifts.

Perita clicked her tongue and teased, "How much of your garden did you cram in there, my lady?"

"I hope we'll find out when we get there," said Callen. "I'll win our wager yet, Pet. I still say there's at least one whole pot with a living plant in it."

"Nonsense. Plants can't live in bags, and my lady left all her potted plants with the Kyrian mages. It's sacks of soil so she can start something from seed when we get there, although gods know how it will grow in the dark."

"I had to bring something to keep me from growing bored in Orthros while the men are talking," Cassia replied.

Perita's eyes gleamed with mischief, and Callen let out a *hmph.*

Cassia had carried her satchel herself all the way from Solorum so no one would wonder at the weight of the bag. She only gave her shoulders a rest in moments like these, when she could fasten it securely to her saddle in front of her.

She felt safer from Chrysanthos when she had the glyph stone close at hand.

The Dexion gestured to some of the men. "While we await the Hesperines, I'd like a word with a few of you. Skleros, Tychon, to me. Yes, yes, you as well, Eudias. Lord Gaius, Sir Benedict, if you would join us."

Benedict turned in his saddle. "I'll only be a moment, Your Ladyship. Stay close to your guard and your hound!"

She lifted a hand to reassure him. He rode forward, and Eudias followed on his donkey, nodding to Cassia on his way. Her two would-be guardians joined Chrysanthos's other chosen few in a huddle with Lord Gaius, one of Lord Hadrian's gray-haired loyalists. The Dexion led them still further ahead, as though he did not trust the wind to conceal their hushed words.

If Lucis had his way, the Dexion and those few at his side would be the only emissaries to Orthros. The king expected the Cordian mages and the representatives of Segetia and Hadria to further his ends. Cassia was not done demonstrating that he could no longer take the support of the most powerful lords in Tenebra for granted.

She wondered at Chrysanthos's tolerance of the interlopers who had joined "his" embassy contrary to his and the king's wishes. But then, Chrysanthos tolerated Cassia. He seemed unwilling to take any risk that might tempt the Hesperines to revoke their invitation, even if it meant bringing along everyone his enemy had requested.

He did not seem eager to do without the Tenebrans' aid against nature, either, as his reliance on Lord Severin had shown. As if with Anthros's own fire at his heels, the Dexion had battled the wretched autumn weather and raced to beat the snows that would close the path to Orthros. Under Chrysanthos's leadership, and with the help of Cordian fair-weather spells and speed charms, the embassy had performed the feat of traveling nearly one thousand miles from Solorum to Frigorum in only thirty-one days.

As dusk approached, the white gusts dimmed to silver, and torches flared to life around Cassia, only to gutter and struggle to survive in the wind. Their lights, although feeble, were many.

The blizzards that had hounded them as they approached had robbed Cassia of the sight of the Hesperines' famous beacon. But she knew it gleamed up there in the sky even now, marking the way.

Somewhere ahead, amid that chaos of white and gathering dusk, lay the invisible border between Tenebra and Orthros. It was a mere strip of ground, marked with neither banners nor walls. Nay, this line was drawn in centuries of bloodshed and the protective magic of two ancient Queens. And at this moment, in a veil of winter weather. Was that too a Hesperine working? Did Cassia even now look upon the Queens' ward as she watched the dancing flakes of snow?

If Cassia could just see through the storm, she would lay eyes on it at last. The divide between his world and hers.

She was almost there.

Once she finally made it across, what sort of welcome would she receive? The Hesperines had requested her specifically. Surely not merely because she was the only relative of the king's who was an option.

Lio must have told his people something about her. He was not prone to keeping secrets from them, and that night they had parted, she had released him from his promise of secrecy to her.

She would not assume there was anything personal about the invitation. Assumptions were foolish. Dangerous, even.

Dangerous to your plans? asked her uncompromising voice. *Or to your heart?*

Her heart pounded, and she wanted to leap from the pony's back and run ahead. She stared northward again, now into darkness, blinking fast to keep the snow from gathering on her eyelashes.

They were so near. Her Hesperines.

Hers? Could she really presume to have any claim on them? She did not even know if her claim on Lio, such as it was, still held. All she could say with confidence was that they had a claim on her. That was hers to decide, and she would not let anyone dispute it.

Cassia felt like one great knot from head to toe, and not because she was clinging to her pony. What else would stand in her way now, when she was so close? What might rear its ugly head at the last moment and halt her?

She barely caught herself before glancing about her as if something might leap at her out of the storm. Or from among the mages and free lords. After so much effort, she could not believe it would be as easy as riding over the border, not until she was safely on the other side.

A distant sound pierced the storm. A bird's cry? A creature's bellow? The sound echoed through the air again, a high, brazen tone that resonated through the pass. That was a mortal instrument. But not like any hunting horn Cassia had ever heard.

What mortals could be out here, other than the embassy?

"Heart hunters!" Lord Severin warned.

A voice called back to him from somewhere in the storm. "Death to the Hesperine allies! Death to the betrayers of mankind!"

A chorus of hunting horns sounded. Amid their clarions came a crack that echoed through the pass as if the world were splitting open. Cassia's pony shied beneath her. Tightening her knees, she gripped her satchel with one hand while she fisted her other around the reins.

The flakes of snow seemed to gather together into one great wall of white. The sky itself appeared to be falling toward her. There was nowhere to flee.

"Avalanche!" cried Lord Severin.

The snow pummeled Cassia's body and tore her grasp from the glyph stone.

CKABAAR

THE EMBERS OF THE king's hearth were collapsing under Cassia's feet, and she didn't know which way she was falling. Only this time, the fire was cold, so cold.

Heart hunters have their uses.

The power of the snow was immense. She was so small.

They can be brought in line, if necessary.

Suddenly the world was still again. Still and massive, its entire weight upon her, crushing. She could not get her breath. She was blind in the darkness under the snow.

Her heart raced, and she fought to move in her prison. Her legs were pinned. She could not flee. She felt as if a fist were closing around her ribs. Her left arm was trapped, useless. With her right, she tore wildly at the snowpack, her hand burning with cold through her mitten.

No. No, it could not end like this. She could not die within sight of Orthros. All her efforts, wasted, lost beneath the snow. Her entire life, a tiny speck in the vast mountains, a blink in Tenebran history whose marks the wind was already erasing.

She could not let the king win when she was so close.

Cassia went still. She labored to bring her breathing under control. This was no way to behave in a crisis. If she was smart, she might not run out of air before she got herself out of this—or rescue came.

The Tenebran embassy's Hesperine escort had been on the way. Hippolyta's Stand patrolled the Queens' ward, ready to rescue mortals from the snow. Were they even now charging head-first into an ambush?

Be safe. Please, be safe—and be our rescue.

With her one hand that had any leeway, Cassia wormed her mitt in front of her mouth so she could carve out more space to breathe. Her hand was about as effective as a gardening spade against a mountain. But she had achieved astonishing feats with only her little spade.

Cassia dug methodically at the snow with the slightest motions possible and made herself think just as deliberately. She had to keep her mind sharp. She must not fall unconscious.

She should have seen this coming. The way Chrysanthos had separated his and the king's chosen few. Those eerie horns, their only warning, but a warning nonetheless. She would wager the kingdom that Lucis had arranged for the heart hunters to rid the Dexion of those the mage did not want to take with him to Orthros.

Perita and Callen. The Semna and Lord Severin and… At least Benedict had been safe near the mages. But what had become of everyone else?

Cassia had to breathe slowly. No tears. She had to think.

Knight. Try as she might, she could not keep herself from getting her hopes up. Had her mighty liegehound managed to escape or surface from the avalanche? If he was on his feet, he would surely find her.

She spared some of her precious air to call out to him, although she had no idea if his ears, as keen as they were, could hear her through all that snow. "Knight? *Ckuundat,* Knight, I'm here! *Dockk.* Please, *dockk!*"

She kept worrying at the space in front of her face, but her hand was almost numb. That numbness crept through her bit by bit, deadening the hurt in every part of her body, tempting her to dreadful ease. She felt like her head was lifting, floating upward, as if it alone were free of her prison.

She had to stay alert. There was still hope. She had faced death twice before, and both times, Hesperines had saved her. Surely she would be so fortunate a third time, here on their doorstep. She kept digging.

As her senses hazed, the snow felt looser against her hand. No, no, it was not her imagination. It was coming loose more easily.

She sucked in a breath and dug harder, faster. Then the snow was flying, torn away from her. Her hand met a broad paw.

"Knight!"

She could breathe. She heaved at the air. The snowy night glared in her eyes. A shaggy face filled her vision.

"Knight, my wonderful Knight. I knew you'd find me."

He dug, diligent and frantic, while she squirmed. Together they got her upper body free. Then he sank his teeth into the layers of her clothing and starting pulling. His powerful jaws and the strength in his body slipped her out of the snow.

Gasping, she wrapped her arms around his ruff. He went into a down-stay, burrowing them against the ridge of snow he had flung up while digging her out. His warmth began to bring feeling back into her body.

"We have to find the others." Cassia made to get up, but Knight pushed her back down with his weight.

She went silent, listening. The fur on the back of his neck rose. He let out a low growl.

She heard it moments later than he did. The sound of sniffing and paws racing across the snow. Then howls—the bays of a pack on the hunt and closing in on their prey.

She knew whose hounds those were. And Knight was outnumbered.

But had the king forgotten? Those mongrels were nothing compared to a pedigreed dog from the royal kennels.

For the first time in her life, Cassia issued a command she had only ever used in training. She spoke the ancient word warriors said to their hounds as they readied to charge onto the field of battle.

"*Ckabaar!*"

Knight transformed into a dog she had not known she had. He took up a fighting stance on all fours over her. She rolled onto her belly and faced the oncoming pack.

Three massive, pale shapes charged out of the storm. Against the brightness of the snow, she saw that the dog on the left was closest. The heat of battle turned thought into a command on Cassia's tongue, and she called out the order for a left forward attack without needing to remember the words.

Knight shot out to meet the oncoming hound. Their bodies collided midair, then spun to the ground with a force Cassia felt in the snow beneath her. The hounds rolled, and the snow blew down and spewed up around them. Amid their growls came a pitiful whine, and then Knight's dark shape came out on top.

But his advantage was spent. The other two hounds had closed the distance.

"*Hridh!* Right! To your right!" Cassia rolled, gained her feet, and scrambled out of their way as best she could in the thick snow. Her feet sank, but strength came to her like the war commands, and she managed to position herself behind Knight once more.

Knight left the first hound unmoving on the ground and pivoted to his right. He leapt out and stood like a bastion between her and the other two dogs, launching booming barks at their faces. They hesitated, side-stepping and posturing before him.

Cassia pressed her and Knight's advantage. "*Hridh ckabaar!*"

With an eager snarl, Knight charged the dog on the right. He sank his teeth into its jugular. Red splattered on its white coat and the snow.

"*Adhin ckabaar! Adhin ckabaar!*" Cassia cried. A left attack now!

But the third hound was already on Knight. She screamed at the beast as it fastened its jaws on her hound's shoulders. Knight shook himself, and Cassia's tears hit the snow with his blood.

Then the enemy hound hit the ground, too. Knight had tossed it clear over the mound of snow where he and Cassia had sought warmth.

The beast regained its feet just as quickly, but Knight was in battle-stance again, ready for it. The heart hunters' dog charged, and Cassia called Knight off. She rolled, and Knight followed, and together they dodged to one side.

The enemy dog swiveled to catch up with them, but Cassia's idea had worked. Its back legs ran afoul of the hole in the snow where Cassia had been buried. By the time it scrambled out, Knight was upon it.

The snarls went silent. The other dog's body was still. Cassia had to look away. But in that direction, she saw another mangled liegehound.

Knight limped to her, blood and spittle dripping from his jaws. She sat up on her knees and cupped his face to ease him close to her and examine his wounds.

"*Oedann. Oedann, oedann.*" It was all she could say, and no other word was enough but that one, the praise for a battle well-fought.

"*Oedann* is right," came a man's voice.

Knight answered with a furious growl. Cassia snapped her head up, trying to get eyes on the speaker.

Fog and billowing snow closed around her and Knight. She couldn't see farther than the end of his tail.

Footfalls shuffled all about them, and rough male voices spoke back and forth, their accents strange and their dialect stranger. She strained to understand. She seized on words she had learned from old men in the kennels and gained impressions of what the heart hunters were saying.

"To Hypnos with that cur," said a second man. "He killed my best stud."

"So your stud wasn't the best," said the first man. "Only survivors are worth breeding."

A third man laughed. "This one's no cur, all right. He made pretty work of our test. Royal blood's as fine as they say after all."

"When it comes to dogs, anyway. The king's little bitch doesn't look so fine."

"Call me that again," Cassia challenged, "and my hound and I will put you on the ground with your mongrels."

"I wouldn't try that, little bitch," the first speaker advised.

Strange lights loomed close. Into sight came a crossbow, its bolt aimed at Cassia's heart.

BLIZZARD WRAITHS

ATTLE COMMANDS RAN THROUGH Cassia's mind, but none were any use against a bolt to the heart. Except one.

"*Het baat*," she said.

Knight growled again, but he obeyed the finality in her tone and went into a down-stay.

She put up her hands for whomever stood on the other end of that crossbow. "My hound is worth more to you alive. He deserves better than a bolt in his side after he managed not to go down fighting."

"He's worth more than you," said the voice behind the weapon. "In fact, he's our payment."

The crossbow came nearer, and the fog wafted away. She saw the white-gloved hand that held the weapon, then an arm clad in white, threadbare wool. Then a broad chest wrapped in white fur, crossed by a white leather bandolier. A rough-hewn light stone was strapped there, illuminating blades, bolts, and pouches full of who knew what.

From one buckle on that bandolier hung a pair of long, sharp canines tied on a string. Their roots, not their tips, were bloodied.

Had a Hesperine once smiled at her with those fangs?

Was she looking at the fate of the embassy's escort?

There had been so many horns... Only a powerful force could defeat a group of Hesperines. She didn't know how long she had been trapped in the snow... Long enough for the heart hunters to collect trophies.

She didn't know if Lio had been in the escort.

Had he once feasted on her with those fangs?

Cassia longed to shut her eyes at the sight, but she dare not. A dozen heart hunters appeared around her like spirits out of the storm. But their crossbows and clubs, swords and daggers were all too corporeal. Even the snowshoes strapped to their heavy boots had bladed, upturned tips.

"We do *exactly* what the king wants," the lead crossbowman ordered. "That fat rat in the palace is fickle as they come, and I don't want to give him any excuse to keep the dog and the gold after all. If we keep the boss happy, he'll see to it the king lines our pockets."

One of the men lifted a reed pipe to his lips. When not a note, but a dart flew from the end of it, Cassia jumped. When the dart struck Knight's shoulder, she gasped.

"You said he would live!"

"He'll wake up after it's all over," the piper said. "Too bad you can't have one of my darts too, little bitch. You have to stay awake."

Knight let out a groan, looking up at Cassia. She could not bear the confusion in his eyes. She held him, murmuring reassurance after reassurance to him as he finally closed his eyes.

"Get him back to camp right away and see to his wounds," the leader ordered. "We'll follow with the girl."

The piper and another heart hunter closed in. Their leader gestured with his crossbow, and only that threat was enough to make Cassia let go of Knight and move aside.

She watched them tie her hound to a litter and exchange their snow shoes for the skis strapped to their backs. They took off across the snow, sliding him behind them. Her dearest friend, her last defense, disappeared into the storm.

The lead crossbowman gazed at her from under his hood of fur. Liege-hound fur. His face looked no older than Callen's, and yet many years older.

He looked her up and down with a leer that made her skin crawl. "So this is what a king's daughter looks like. Not much, really."

"Speak for yourself," said a swordsman. "Her mother was a real professional, I hear. No telling what the daughter can do."

"Keep it in your crotch," the leader warned. "We have our orders. She belongs to the boss. No hands, no darts, nothing—right to the boss, untouched."

They had orders not to kill her, and Knight was out of harm's reach.

She could make a run for it without fearing a bolt in the back. But to what end? She would land in a snowbank, and they, in their snowshoes, would be upon her in an instant.

"He could at least let us have her when he's done," the swordsman complained.

"Not on your life. She's to die after he's gotten his use out of her—if she survives it. That's what the boss and the king agreed on."

They had orders not to kill her—until after it was over.

Cassia's thoughts became cold and clear, but her heart seemed numb. A war mage's spell. The headsman's axe. She had considered so many likely ways the king might finally deal death to her. But never this.

Had Solia listened to the rebels in Castra Roborra talk like this over her? What had she endured before the catapults fired?

Anger burned through Cassia's numbness. The injustice made her want to howl right back at the storm.

She didn't know what her sister's final moments had entailed, but she could imagine how Solia had faced her end.

Cassia put on the stone face she wore before the king, when she showed no fear, and looked into the eyes of the heart hunters' leader. "Very well. Take me to your 'boss.' We shall see if he survives me."

A chorus of whistles and catcalls went up around her.

"The boss has his work cut out for him," said the swordsman.

"But he always has his way, in the end." The leader stowed his crossbow on his back, only to unfasten a length of rope from his belt. He reached for her with one grasping hand.

Her gaze lit upon on the hunter's trophy fangs once more. She would never know if Lio was safe.

Lio? Can your mind magery reach across death? If you can hear me, wherever you are, I want you to know. All my final thoughts are for you. You are my Mercy and my Sanctuary.

The heart hunter's hand froze midair.

His jaw went slack, and white rimmed his eyes. He stared at something over Cassia's shoulder.

Before she could look behind her, an apparition appeared before her very eyes and loomed over him. It was night itself, a fissure in the snow and the sky and the world. But gazing into it, she saw no stars, only two red eyes and two white fangs.

The specters emerged from the storm all around her, impossibly tall, horrifically fast. The heart hunters screamed and cursed, brandishing their weapons in every direction. Their crossbow bolts flew right through the living shadows and were swallowed by the snow.

The towers of darkness lunged at the men. The panicked hunters charged them, only to be driven back. They fled, only to be hemmed in.

The circle around Cassia widened. The specters were driving them away from her.

The snow shifted before her eyes again, as if the storm itself parted. She found herself face-to-face with a fine black robe that whipped in the wind like darkness woven into fabric. From a bell sleeve, a hand as pale as the snow emerged and reached down toward her.

Cassia looked up and met the gaze of the only wraith who had blue eyes.

A wordless cry escaped her. She reached for him. His beloved hand took hold of hers, and he helped her to her feet.

No sooner had she stood than his arms came around her, strong and gentle. He scooped her up and held her close in the warmth of his cloak. She flung her arms around his neck and held fast to him, burying her face in his high collar.

She was finally holding him.

His voice was deep as night and smooth as velvet, as magical as she remembered. "My mind can always reach yours. I will always be your Sanctuary. Close your eyes, let all your thoughts be for me, and do not dwell on what is about to happen."

She had no desire to open her eyes or spare any thought for what lay beyond the shelter of his arms. She nodded against him.

She felt his power rise out of him like a whisper. A shadow passed over her mind, leaving her safe in its wake.

Suddenly the screaming ceased. The only sound was the wind. Then she heard the bodies hit the snow one by one.

THELEMANTEIA

T WAS SHOCKINGLY EASY. Lio's power swept out of him, eager as a bird that had never flown beyond its cage. He took hold of ten minds at once.

His fastidious exercises with his uncle had taught him what to expect, but this was real. Lio grasped the morass of the heart hunters' thoughts, every jeer they had hurled at Cassia, every pleasure they had taken in her fear. Their threats silenced. Their lusts died. Their Wills gave way to his power.

He pressed his advantage all the way through the gorge, and the two who were fleeing fell to his control and halted in their tracks. Twelve no longer a threat, and he felt he had only just begun.

How much danger could he spare the Stand thus? How many heart hunters could he deliver to the Charge's custody, rendered harmless and ready for questioning?

Lio held Cassia close and pushed his power beyond all the limits he had yet tested.

He could count them, but they were not a number. They were men, each and every one different to his senses, hundreds of windows through which he peered out upon a world he had thought he had known. Their memories were horrifying, their concerns sickeningly familiar. Hunger. Pleasure. Approval.

Lio was everywhere, from one end of Martyrs' Pass to another. His warband's legends had taught him the meaning of Stand regalia. He spat crossbow fire at a young male Hesperine as the Steward freed a pale-haired warrior from the clutches of the avalanche. The bolts never ruffled Lyros's robe. They hit a blood ward and rebounded back on Lio. Countless pains pierced his body.

Lio brandished torches at the defensive line of the Prince's Charge. They drove him back from their fellow Hesperines errant who were coming to the snowbound mortals' rescue. He rode a wave of reinforcements down from the ridge above on skis, guiding his progress with spears he would soon aim at Hesperine hearts.

With both forces, he broke upon a shield of light, at whose heart stood a small, powerful warrior with auburn hair. The Guardian of Orthros herself.

He commanded his liegehounds to charge the Guardian's daughter. The dogs snapped and snarled and hurled themselves at the witch warrior's magic, and their jaws rent tiny tears in her shield. But the shield blazed bright, sealing the wounds. The shadow sorceress drew upon the light of the Queens' ward to bolster her power.

Her fangs flashed, her hand flew, and she scattered her own blood across the snow. The dogs went mad, following Lio's cousin as she sought to draw them off. With hundreds of voices, he egged them to bring her down.

"*Ckabaar!*"

The dogs bruised their bodies against Kadi's ward, a living battering ram.

Lio plundered the words in the heart hunters' minds for a different command. He found it shut away behind a heavy lock of shame. He made each master say it to his beast. *Retreat.*

"*Loma hoor!*"

As one pack, the hounds turned from Lio's cousin and fled for the hills, leaving only the human predators on the attack.

With one man, Lio swung a club at his attacker, hefting the weight of the weapon, his arm still sore from a skirmish with another warband. The enemy was all around him, unseen, merely a disturbance in the air.

Then for an instant, a pair of brown eyes flashed at him. They looked too human to belong to a Hesperine, the man thought. But Lio knew those eyes. He put the club down, and the man's body obeyed. When Mak's hand descended for a killing blow, the heart hunter already lay still at his feet. Lio's Trial brother froze, his familiar gaze now confused, and shook his head over his paralyzed enemy.

Lio looked through another man's eyes at the oncoming pommel of a sword. That too halted midair. A red-haired barbarian stood over him with furious gray eyes and a splash of blood on his cheek, his two-hander at the ready. Lio made the man kneel before his prince.

Before the border of his Queens' domain, Lio made every heart hunter lay down his weapons and lower himself to the ground.

His only awareness of his own body was the sensation of Cassia in his arms and the lingering smell of her fear. His magic swelled, but did not overflow his banks. He channeled his power, driving deeper into the minds of the twelve men who had terrorized his Grace. Their fear of blizzard wraiths was still rampant in their unguarded minds. Conjured from the men's personal terrors and crafted with shadows, Lio's illusions had taught the hunters what their own tactics felt like.

Now he delved in their minds for the real enemy. He would find their "boss." The man would rue all the perversities that had ever entered his thoughts and every time he had acted upon them.

Faces. Voices. Mothers, brothers, victims, lovers. Lio sifted through the men's lives and crimes for their hornbearer, the leader of their warband.

The boss was everywhere. And nowhere. He was part of their every thought. Yet no one thought his name. No one envisioned his face. He was an iron rule and a whisper on the edge of their senses. Lio could almost hear him in the thoughts of the lead crossbowman.

Lio held the concert of hundreds of minds and honed the brunt of his power on one.

He heard every one of their hearts stop.

Hundreds of times over, Lio cleaved in two, and the greater part of him slipped from the grasp of his body. Their minds escaped his hold and fled beyond his reach.

His Gift surged back into him and slammed his soul back into his body.

Lio fell to his knees in the snow. Cassia was still in his arms. His heart still beat in his chest. Everyone in the pass was safe.

But what had he done?

TRIAL OF DISCIPLINE

THE LAST FEW MOMENTS refracted over and over in Lio's mind. The world was silent. He was deaf to the Union, his senses deadened by the rebound of his own magic.

A small, gentle hand in a frosty mitten touched Lio's cheek and brought him back to reality.

Speechless and shaking, he opened his eyes. And he saw his Grace.

Cassia had tucked her wool-bundled body as close to him as she could. Her face was ashen, her hair a damp and tangled mess. She was so beautiful he did not feel he deserved to look upon her. But there was no judgment in her hazel eyes. Only...gratitude.

She caressed his mouth. "Everything is going to be all right."

The intimacy of her touch made his fangs unsheathe. His tongue went dry. His senses jolted back into awareness. He heard her heart thudding in her chest, and the current of her veins twined around him.

His magic was thirsty enough to suck her dry, and his Craving was ravenous enough to lay waste to her.

Lio stumbled to his feet. He had to get Cassia to safety. He had to step with her, no room for error. Now.

"Lio?" Her voice, querulous, was seduction to his hunger.

He had to take Cassia home.

Her needs drove him forward, and the ward oriented him. He focused on the spell laid down in the Queens' blood, the blood of all his people, and prepared to step.

WAYSTAR

CASSIA COULD NOT TELL if the heart hunters were dead or unconscious. She only knew that the fallen men at Lio's feet were proof she was safe now, and he would keep her so.

She was with Lio again. It was really happening. She had made it, and he would see her safely through the pass into Orthros.

So why was he silent? Why, when she caressed his face, did he look away as if he were in pain?

The sensation of a Hesperine step made Cassia's senses skip a beat. She drew comfort from the tight embrace of Lio's power. If he risked stepping with her now, it meant she was still acclimated to his magic. Their time apart had not undone that connection.

Lio carried her out of the storm and up a flight of steps. The walls of a castle loomed above, a delicate fortress of dove gray stone. Light poured from its glass windows, and its peaked arches reached up into the night. Cassia looked to the clear sky and gasped.

The beacon looked like all of Lio's spell lights put together. The grand orb hovered above the castle's highest spire and pulsed, a gleaming heartbeat.

Iron doors burst open ahead of them, and in the light that streamed out, two silhouettes appeared and swept toward them. A female voice spoke in Divine, and Cassia recognized the tone of a prayer of thanks. The speaker's hand brushed her matted hair back from her face.

Then Lio was handing Cassia into another's arms. She recognized the kind face above her. Master Healer Javed, Lio's Grace-cousin.

Lio spoke at last, but his voice was ragged. "Make sure there's not a scratch on her."

The power he had spent to save her must have cost him. This night had cost both of them so much. But not each other.

Cassia reached out to him, but her hand met empty air. He was already too far away. He floated down the steps like one of his illusions and disappeared.

Cassia swallowed half a year of unsaid words. The urgency of survival gave way, and a wave of pain and exhaustion hit her. She let Javed carry her inside.

She squeezed her eyes shut against sudden brightness. She was aware of a large room and relieved voices surrounding her. Then Javed carried her into soft light and warmth and quiet. When her watery vision cleared, she was sitting on a padded couch.

"Are we in Orthros?" Cassia asked.

The female Hesperine knelt near her and spoke in Vulgus. "We are well behind the ward and into the circle of polar night. You are safe here at the Sanctuary of Waystar, where we can protect you every hour of the night. We are going to take some time to make sure you are all right, but rest assured the Tenebran embassy will never notice your absence."

She knew exactly what to say to banish Cassia's most immediate fears with just a few words. If this lady was not a diplomat, she ought to be, with a voice like that. Such velvet tones might lure Lord Hadrian himself to put away his sword and sleep with his head in her lap.

She peeled off Cassia's layers of cold weather gear down to her dry gown. Quickly she wrapped Cassia in a blanket, slid soft stockings onto her feet, and handed her a pillow to hug against her chest. The warm woolens felt as if they had been heated by a fire, but there was no hearth in the beautifully appointed sitting room where the Hesperines had brought her.

Cassia's surroundings, her first look into Orthros, hardly seemed real after the pass. She could only think how familiar the lady Hesperine's features were, even if her eyes were brown, not blue. The high cheekbones, the long, straight nose, the elegant mouth. Especially her jet black hair, a striking contrast to her fair complexion. Cassia's amorphous thoughts settled on the one person in Lio's bloodline with whom he would share a family resemblance, the only one to whom he was related by birth.

The calm kindness in the lady Hesperine's voice eroded Cassia's worries about making a good impression. "I am Komnena, Lio's mother, and you already know Javed. We are healers, I of the mind, he of the body. We are going to ask you a few questions about what happened while we tend any injuries you have, within and without."

Cassia felt wrapped in endless patience and reassurance. She nodded.

"I know this could be a difficult question," Komnena continued, "but we need to make sure we understand your injuries so we can give you the best care. Did the heart hunters harm you in any way?"

The heart hunters' threats assailed Cassia's thoughts, and her mind shied away from that moment in the pass. She shook her head. "Lio protected me."

Komnena sighed. "Thank the Goddess."

"Do you hurt anywhere?" Javed asked.

"Everywhere," Cassia admitted.

She felt the touch of Hesperine magic. Javed had yet to reach into the red cloth satchel at his side, but every pain in her disappeared. Her whole body relaxed, and all she felt was a deep sense of well-being. She blinked sleepily at the kind-eyed physician, and he smiled. She had last seen him in formal attire at the Summit table, but now he wore practical crimson robes.

"Thank you for your help, Master Javed," Cassia said. "You tried so hard to convince the Council of Free Lords to accept a gift of medicine from the Hesperine embassy."

The healer peered into her eyes, lifting each of her eyelids in turn. "Your deeds on that occasion were memorable as well. What else do you remember?"

"You are from the Empire and Graced to Master Steward Arkadia, Lio's cousin." She studied Javed's warm brown complexion, then tried to focus her vision on Arkadia's blond braid, which he wore in his dark curls.

He smiled again and proceeded to examine her ankles. She watched his gentle hands work, and it did not even occur to her to feel strange about the way he touched her, anymore than to fret that her hair was uncovered in front of him.

"What about tonight?" Lio's mother asked. "How many of you were trapped in the avalanche?"

Memory sharpened Cassia's thoughts once more. "Fifty-six minus the half dozen the king actually wanted to survive."

Javed exchanged a glance with Komnena, but he said nothing. Another wave of Hesperine magic calmed Cassia's pulse.

Komnena continued her questions in her kind, matter-of-fact tone. "Who was next to you when the avalanche began?"

Cassia's throat tightened. "Perita and Callen were closest. Benedict was safe next to the mages, but Lord Severin had already rejoined us." She took a deep breath. "How many made it out?"

Komnena rubbed Cassia's arms. "The Stand is presently bringing in fifty-six minus the one the Hesperines wished to give special attention. Healers and cots are waiting in the great hall below."

"Everyone?" The breath rushed out of Cassia. "I knew you would come. Please tell me every Hesperine has returned safely, too. I feared—"

Komnena shook her head. "We lost none of ours. Although some of our Hesperines errant were gravely wounded, everyone will survive. We should even be able to send your mounts safely back into Tenebra with Lord Severin's retainers."

Cassia did not ask about Knight. She already knew the answer. A liege-hound would not tolerate any Hesperine's attempt at rescue. Her friend's only hope was his own strength.

She pushed away the vision of him waking up trapped in a heart hunter camp. She would keep hoping he could fight his way back to her. She could not bear to do anything else.

If only she had managed to keep the glyph stone with her, she could have protected herself and Knight from the heart hunters. What would she do without her satchel of relics, her few real weapons?

Komnena frowned in concern at Cassia's hands. "These wounds are not new, but they look sore."

Javed examined Cassia's palms, but did not ask her what had cost her so much of her skin. "You will feel better within the hour and much restored after a good night's sleep."

She could sleep when she was dead. She wasn't dead tonight. She had made it.

Words were not coming to Cassia, but she must find some. "The others will not say it properly, but you have our gratitude. Yet again Hesperines bear the brunt of violence to spare mortal kind. Thank you."

Komnena wrapped a warm towel around Cassia's damp hair. "Lio owes you his life. I am happy I can honor the bond of gratitude we had long before tonight."

This lady had borne and raised the kindest, most trustworthy person Cassia knew. Saying the right words to her made strategic conversations to sway stubborn free lords seem like reciting children's rhymes in comparison. "Master Komnena, your son is…" Cassia trailed off.

"Yes, he is." Lio's mother beamed. "Call me Komnena."

"Yes," Javed agreed, "let us dispense with 'Master.' My Grace and I have you to thank not only for our lives, but our beautiful children. We Solaced two of the Eriphites you and Lio rescued from Tenebra, a brother and sister. They are safe at home with their new grandfather right now." Javed traced a finger over her cheek. "The scar Boskos arrived with has healed, and Athena grows in strength daily, despite the frost fever that endangered their lives."

Cassia saw again Lio standing in the Temple of Kyria, tracing a finger over his cheek as he told the Prisma that the little boy with the scar on his face must receive the medicine first, lest he die. "I am so happy to hear that children who suffered so much are now safe and well, and that they get to remain together as a family. How fortunate they are to have you and Arkadia as parents."

"And to have had such rescuers as you and Lio. I cannot express our gratitude to you for Bosko and Thenie."

Then they knew a great deal indeed of what she and Lio had done together during the Equinox Summit. "It seems you know already where my loyalties lie."

"That was never in doubt," Komnena replied.

"Then I must give the Stand the information I have right away," Cassia said. "There is no time to lose."

Komnena slid another warm pillow under Cassia's dangling feet. "Two Stewards are outside your door right now, eager to check on you as soon as you are ready to see them."

Javed's mouth twitched. "I will tell them they can come in before they break down the door. Now I must rejoin my Grace below and lend my aid to those she is bringing in. When you are ready, the Stand can escort you into the hall through the front doors, and the embassy will never know you had a private encounter with Hesperines."

"That's wise. I cannot have them thinking you magicked me."

"I regret many of them are refusing to accept our healing magic."

"Stubborn fools," Cassia muttered. "Perhaps the Semna can help."

"She is asleep after traversing herself and the six people nearest her safely out of the avalanche. But her attendants are busy setting bones." An expression crossed Javed's face that would remind anyone he was a warrior's Grace. "We will strive to respect our guests' Wills, but if any of them face grave risk to life or health, they will get Hesperine healing anyway, whether they know it or not."

He strode out the door. An instant later, two young, muscular Hesperines marched into the sitting room. Their short black robes were damp with melted snow, but Cassia could not see a bit of blood or grime on them. Only Hesperine warriors could fight in sandals in a blizzard and return from the battlefield unstained. They wore each other's braids at their temples and cloth ties that bound their hair at the napes of their necks.

The taller of the two posted himself in front of her as if another wave of enemies might come through her door, and he planned to lay waste to them, too. Broad-shouldered and barrel-chested, he looked like he could break Chrysanthos's neck with his little finger. "Are you all right?"

"Yes, thanks to all of you."

His companion crouched by Cassia on her eye level. "We're so glad you made it safely to Waystar."

"You must be Mak and Lyros." In spite of everything, Cassia was able to smile. She had no doubt they were the formidable warriors Lio had described to her and also his dearest friends.

"Our reputation precedes us, eh? Yes, I'm Lio's cousin." Mak grinned down at Cassia.

"And I'm the lucky fellow who avowed this heroic figure last year." Lyros gestured to his Grace.

"Cassia, would you like me to stay with you?" Komnena asked. "Or shall I leave you three to talk?"

It wasn't just Mak and Lyros's physical strength that seemed to surround Cassia. There was something about their presence that made her feel reassured. "I am sure you are needed downstairs. I will be fine here with Mak and Lyros."

"Call me if you need anything." On the way toward the door, Komnena planted a kiss on Mak's cheek and a caress on Lyros's hair. "All your elders are counting our blessings tonight, my dear ones."

Mak sat down next to Cassia on the couch. "So this is the valiant fighter who vowed to march to Anthros's pyre by our sides."

"Oh, Lio's tales about me make even my bitter outbursts sound noble, I expect."

"But they are noble," said Lyros. Although not as massive as Mak, his fitness and strength would be the envy of any Tenebran warrior who met him, and he too was taller than any of them. He had the thoughtful, perceptive gaze of a strategist.

"He's told me a great deal about you two, as well. I'm very glad the rest of the embassy isn't peering over our shoulders, so I can tell you truly how happy I am to meet you."

Mak's good cheer faded. "I wish it had been under better circumstances."

Lyros's mouth tightened. "On behalf of the Stand, allow us to tell you how much we regret that the attack came before your escort reached you. That should never have been such a close call."

"Everyone is safe now. That's all that matters. I..." She had just met them, her head was still spinning, but somehow it felt so easy to be honest with them. "I saw one of the trophies the heart hunters took tonight. I didn't know whose fangs they were. I thought some of you had fallen, but I didn't know who."

Lyros shook his head. "We are so sorry you had to endure such terror, Cassia."

"It's Basir who lost his canines," said Mak, "but don't feel too sorry for him. He's going to take a holiday for the first time in a hundred years."

Lyros smirked. "Bedrest. Helpless under Kumeta's care. He has to let his Grace feed him until his fangs grow back. The rest of him is in one piece, though."

Cassia covered her mouth. "That's terrible." But a little laugh bubbled out of her.

"You're going to be all right," Mak told her.

Hot tears burned at the back of her eyes, and her throat closed. Mak was right. She was going to be all right.

She blinked hard. "Stewards, I would like to tell you all the secrets the mages in the embassy think they are keeping. There will be no repeats of tonight."

"Not on our watch." The way Lyros looked at her made her realize he meant the three of them.

"Go ahead," Mak encouraged.

"The mages who came with the embassy are trying to repeat Dalos's deceit. The peacock who considers himself our leader will introduce himself as Adelphos, an honored master from the Temple of Anthros at Solorum. He is in fact Dexion Chrysanthos of the Aithourian Circle, a war mage from Cordium, as surely as Dalos was."

"Thank you for the warning," Lyros said. "Fortunately, Basir and Kumeta discovered the true identity of Chrysanthos and his war circle when they were at the Autumn Greeting."

"Basir and Kumeta were at the Greeting? They have been errant in Tenebra after the Summit ended?"

"Basir and Kumeta are always errant," Mak answered. "It seems Lio didn't have the chance to reveal all of Orthros's most closely guarded secrets and left this one for us."

"Orthros has an envoy service," Lyros told her. "The Mage Orders believe them to be messengers attached to the diplomatic service."

Mak grinned. "The enemy still has no idea that the envoys are actually spies who have been gathering information for centuries."

"Basir and Kumeta are the best," Lyros said, "the oldest, and the founders of the entire envoy service. They are the Queens' Master Envoys, the spymasters of Orthros."

Cassia shook her head. "No wonder Lio thought Dalos should be worried about facing them."

"Oh, yes," Mak replied. "They have kept us well informed about the Aithourians, including Chrysanthos. We expected that wolf to put on sheep's clothing and usurp a Tenebran mage's place in the embassy."

To think, while Cassia had suffered through the dance with Flavian, two of Lio's people had been there all along, within reach, and she had not known.

What had they told Lio about what had transpired?

Cassia must focus on the imperative at hand. "So you know Chrysanthos's apprentice, Tychon, is a fire mage in training. Then there is Eudias, who came with Dalos from Cordium. No one seems to consider him very capable, but I should warn you the glowing baubles we saw him conjure at Solorum were not light magery. It is his affinity for lightning that earned him his unlikely induction into the Aithourian Circle."

Mak snorted. "Just a couple of half-baked Aithourian hopefuls and a temple decoration from Corona. I'm disappointed. I thought the Orders would come up with something creative."

"The necromancer is the trick up their sleeve," said Cassia. "Master Skleros is from Tenebra, but he is affiliated with the Cordian Order of Hypnos. The Dexion handpicked him to join the embassy, with the approval of the Akron and the Synthikos."

Lyros's eyes narrowed. "The Aithourian Circle is allied with a Gift Collector? That we didn't know."

"Then you are aware of Skleros's profession."

Mak made a face. "His arsenal is impossible to miss."

"No other necromancers augment their spells with steel," Lyros explained. "Gift Collectors will arm themselves with anything that does not technically qualify as a weapon under the Orders' regulations against mages becoming warriors."

"Spurs," Mak said. "Whips. Every blade they can pilfer from the cook, carpenter, or tanner."

Lyros nodded. "The inquisitors take no action to prevent such abuse of the rules because they like the results."

"Skleros is making it very clear to us that he's a Gift Collector," Mak concluded.

"It's extremely surprising," Lyros went on. "His kind make every effort to conceal their identities from us."

"We've never even seen a Gift Collector," Mak enthused. "I hope we get to make him regret showing his face."

"He's not just any Gift Collector, according to Chrysanthos," Cassia warned. "He's been at it for a lifetime and…" The vision of Basir's fangs flashed in her mind again, and she regretted imagining what trophies Skleros might collect. She fixed her attention on the living, powerful Hesperines before her. "Skleros holds the Order of Hypnos's record for collecting the most Hesperine bounties."

The look in Mak's eye became dangerous. "He will definitely regret crossing the Stand."

"He is the one who has helped Dalos and Chrysanthos hide their magic from you. I can provide details about how he achieved it."

"That's incredible news, Cassia," Lyros said. "Our scholars will want to hear everything you know."

"You already have an appointment with Mother when we arrive in Selas," Mak informed her. "We're fortunate you can help us assess what we're up against."

"Who we're up against," Cassia said. "No matter what face he wears, the enemy is always the same. The king. The heart hunters were quite blatant about it, for they did not expect me to survive to tell anyone. The king hired them to get rid of everyone he didn't want in the embassy."

Mak and Lyros answered her with silence.

Yes. Her own father. She could not say it, but they knew it now. Her own father had bartered her to heart hunters to be captured, raped, and murdered.

Mak put a hand on her shoulder, and she realized she was shaking with rage and pain and all the fear she had not been able to afford in those moments when she thought the end had come.

"You are one of the bravest people we have ever met," Mak told her.

An extraordinary impulse compelled her to put her arms around him. She had just met him. She never trusted people this immediately. He might think her gesture inappropriate. But she embraced him.

He held her close, wrapping her up in a bear hug as if it made perfect sense. He smelled of cloves, and she could feel his magic like another fragrance around him. Hesperine warding magic, strong and familiar, the same power that had saved her life when she was a child of seven.

"That means more than I can say, coming from the two of you."

"I'm glad you're on our side," Mak said, "and you're safe on ours, Cassia."

Lyros rested his hand on her back. "You're in Orthros now, under our protection. It shouldn't have been so hard for you to get here. But it will be easier from now on."

Yes, it would. For she no longer fought alone.

"Lio couldn't be here just now to tell you that," Mak added, "so we wanted to, in his absence."

"His work in the pass isn't done," said Lyros.

Cassia searched their gazes. "Is he all right?"

Mak exchanged a glance with his Grace. "I'm not sure."

"He's going to need you, Cassia," said Lyros.

Her cheeks flushed. How much had Lio told his Trial brothers about what he and Cassia had shared? "I—I don't know how things stand between us."

Mak opened his mouth, but Lyros said quickly, "You will get a chance to talk to Lio soon." Lyros took her hand in both of his. "Cassia, whatever you need, no matter what, no matter when, we are here. You can rely on us for anything. We want you to know how thankful we are for what you've done for all of us, and especially for Lio."

Cassia gave Lyros's hands a squeeze. "I've been sick with worry for him. But I know you've been looking out for him. You have my gratitude."

"And you have ours," Mak told her.

SURVIVORS

THE WARD WAS PLAYING tricks on him, one of Orthros's own. Through the pulse of blood magic and the ebb and flow of the wind, Lio thought he could hear a human heartbeat.

He had to know. He followed the vague hint of a sound. He braved what he knew lay between him and his fool's errand. He must brave it.

He had laid waste to an army tonight, and yet his magic was not spent. Wrapped in his illusions, he drifted between the members of the Charge who were collecting the bodies, and the Hesperines errant did not mark his passage. He walked among the dead, matching faces to memories. Hopes. Lives, but how ill-lived.

Heart hunters did not deserve the Mercy his people would give them.

As soon as Lio thought it, he felt shame. But he already knew he was capable of such thoughts. Precisely the kind of thoughts that caused tragedies like this. Thoughts that destroyed control.

And yet Lio did not understand how it had happened. He had felt fully in command of his magic, so sure of his course. He had felt them die. But he had not felt the moment his power escaped him.

How could it be so...*possible* to make such a mistake? He played the moment over and over in his mind, but gained no clarity. He listened, and his ears still thought they heard a heartbeat.

No, that *was* a mortal's pulse.

He followed it and found himself standing over the body of the heart hunter who had aimed a crossbow at his Grace. Basir's fangs gleamed upon the man's chest, where that lone heartbeat carried on. Lio dropped to his knees, reaching toward the man's sick prize.

When a hand closed over Lio's, he froze.

How many times had that strong hand helped him up when he had fallen? Lio slowly lifted his head and met his Ritual father's gaze over the heart hunter's body.

"You did well tonight," Rudhira said.

"I don't know if I killed them."

Rudhira squeezed his hand, then pushed it gently aside. He collected Basir's fangs and wrapped them in a handkerchief. He tucked the pristine cloth into one of his boots, which was smeared with a bloody hand print.

Rudhira stood, then pulled Lio to his feet. "There is one left. I have strengthened his mind and body so he will survive the trip back to Castra Justa. Whatever happened here tonight, as far as I am concerned, you followed my instructions to kill only if necessary and take prisoners for questioning."

"With all these men as captives, you could have used interrogation and ransom to dismantle half the heart hunter activity in the region. You could have dealt their way of life a decisive blow. But dead, they are martyrs to their brothers. I wouldn't do this, Rudhira. And yet, how can I deny the evidence that I did?"

"Lio." His Ritual father shook his head. "Do not waste your regrets on these men."

"Our creed is to kill only if there is no other solution, in the face of any evil. There was another way." Lio held out his hand, pointing to his palm. "I had them. Right here. Every one of them. And I did not lose a single one, although there were hundreds. I am certain of that, because I learned of my power in that moment. I could have held ten times more minds."

"I know how it feels to have the power of life and death over others."

Lio hesitated, his gaze drifting over the corpses of men and dogs, his head pounding with the odor of death. "How many have you killed?"

"I make a point not to keep count."

"They are not a number," Lio said softly. "They are men."

"It never gets easier," his Ritual father confessed. "When it does, then I will truly despair of myself. These feelings you are having are good and right and proof enough you are the same person you were last night."

"I am. I am the diplomat who fought in the duel against Dalos.

Surely—it must be possible—he might still be the only life on my conscience. I see it now. I was not the only thelemancer at work here tonight."

"Yes, the heart hunters had the aid of mind mages—enough of them to take Basir by surprise."

Lio shook his head. "There was only one."

Surprise flashed in Rudhira's gray eyes.

"The heart hunters thought of him as 'the boss,'" Lio explained. "At first, I assumed they meant their hornbearer. I realize now he is someone more. I encountered him within the heart hunters. The same mind held sway over all of theirs."

"Then no hedge warlocks or apostate sorcerers were at work here."

"He is a mage of dreams," Lio realized.

Rudhira's jaw clenched. "He must be. Only a highly trained mage of Hypnos could single-handedly do so much against Hesperines."

"He was influencing the heart hunters' minds directly to ensure they did his and the king's bidding. It seems Lucis has more than a few mages assisting him with his…" Lio's lip twisted. "…ambitions."

"One mage of dreams enabled the hunters to capture Basir, evade Kumeta and move a force of hundreds this close to the border. On my watch! We have had the envoys and the Charge on high alert, patrolling for precisely this kind of trouble, and yet Basir and Kumeta suffered a close call, and heart hunters made it *into Martyrs' Pass*. Lyta will be out for the mage's blood, but I will spare her the trouble."

"Few mind mages can achieve what he did here tonight. Most thelemancers that powerful haunt the halls of Corona and belong to the Inner Eyes of the Order of Hypnos." Lio swallowed. "Unless they are Hesperines."

"Then attaching a Gift Collector to the embassy is not the Order of Hypnos's only involvement in the Solstice Summit. The Inner Eyes must have sent the mage of dreams ahead to lie in wait at the border and oversee the Tenebrans' crossing into Orthros."

"One servant of Hypnos to ride into Orthros with the king's allies, appearing blameless with the other 'victims' of the attack, and a second to stay behind and ensure the rest of the embassy never makes it, using the heart hunters as a weapon."

Rudhira nodded. "The two can't relish working together, but a robe from the Inner Eyes and a Gift Collector would tolerate one another for results like they achieved tonight. I have never in my centuries seen heart hunters launch such a sophisticated attack in such cooperation. About a dozen hornbearers led the assault—three or four of the largest warbands, plus several of the smaller aspirants. We have a long history of skirmishes with these men and know their crimes in these mountains. They are raiders, not an army. It is clear that tonight, they followed Lucis's strategy, lured by his gold, emboldened by the aid of Ordered mages."

"How very like a mage of dreams to wear gloves, rather than dirty his own hands. The heart hunters make the perfect tool. Everyone knows they are renegades. The king and the Orders can appear blameless. If Orthros were to revoke our invitation to the embassy on these grounds, it would reflect on us, not the Tenebrans' official representatives. The attackers may be Tenebrans, but they are heart hunters—causing trouble for Hesperines is what they do."

"This could have been a disaster. But it was not."

Lio bowed his head, listening to that last, tenuous heartbeat at his feet. "What reason could the other mind mage have had to kill his own soldiers at a crucial moment during the attack? Why not try to wrest them from me?"

"Perhaps he knew he had no hope of defeating you."

"If that were the case, a mage with no regard for human life would drive them mad and set them loose to do as much damage as possible. It seems destroying them would have cost him everything and gained him nothing."

Rudhira put a hand on Lio's shoulder.

A thought occurred to Lio, and even as he voiced it, he wondered if he was grasping at dreams to give his conscience false comfort. "Could he have been so determined to keep me from learning who he is that he would sacrifice his entire force and his chance at victory?"

"Only you can tell us what happened in that moment. But I can tell you how many lives you saved tonight."

The prince slung the heart hunter over his shoulder and stepped into the storm.

DISARMING

PERITA TUCKED ANOTHER PILLOW under Callen's bad leg. "That was the worst fright of my life, my lady. Imagine you being the last to make it in."

Callen captured his wife's fussing hands and pulled her close to sit beside him on the cot where he lay. "It's over now, Pet."

"I'm sorry I gave you such a scare." Sitting on the next cot over, Cassia watched everyone's lips, reading the weather in the main hall of Waystar.

"The Hesperines saved our lives! We owe them…"

"…not how I imagined Hesperines at all…"

"How easily they snuff out mortal lives…the way the heart hunters simply fell dead!"

"…could have been us…at the mercy of their whims…"

The Tenebran knights and lords greeted their hosts with varying degrees of frost and thaw, but all insisted on bleeding while they waited for the Kyrians to get round to them. The Semna slept beneath warm blankets while her attendants exhausted themselves.

Master Gorgos, the mage of Anthros from Solorum, got underfoot and prayed loudly over the casualties. Cassia wondered if he recited benedictions for the patients or pleas for protection from Hesperines.

Lio had not returned. He was nowhere among Komnena, Javed, and the other Hesperines who were trying to assist the mortals.

Arkadia, Mak, and Lyros stood in formation around the mages from Cordium. Chrysanthos smiled daggers at their "honor guard" while Skleros lit a smoke. Benedict and Lord Gaius breathed down the mages' necks as if they were also guarding them, rather than being guarded.

There was a room of Hesperines between Cassia and Chrysanthos. Javed's healing had even laid the secret of her injured hands to rest, and she need no longer fear losing a glove in the Dexion's presence. But her palms were still sweating.

Where was Lio? What work in the pass had Mak and Lyros meant? There might still be heart hunters out there.

"Neighbors from Tenebra." Komnena stood in the middle of the hall and raised her rich contralto voice above the noise. "Hippolyta's Stand and our Hesperines errant have confirmed the heart hunters' force has been defeated. All danger is past. You are now within the borders of Orthros and the Queens' ward. I am Elder Grace Komnena, the Queens' Chamberlain. I see to the needs of all those entering Orthros. On behalf of our beloved Queens Alea and Soteira, I welcome you and convey their warmest salutations. It is with the most heartfelt pleasure that our Queens receive you."

Before Chrysanthos could answer, Cassia got to her feet. The Dexion shot her an unsettled glance, but Mak and Lyros were standing in his way.

Cassia picked her way through the cots to approach Komnena. Since the Hesperines knew Cassia had helped Lio, she no longer wondered why the Queens had named her Tenebra's representative.

Lio's mother smiled. "Lady Cassia, I presume?"

"Yes. On behalf of all of Tenebra, we thank you for your people's heroic defense of us and your generous welcome."

"Many momentous words must mark such an occasion as this, the first embassy from your kingdom ever to set foot in ours. But the time for such discussions is not now, when the wounded still need care. Introductions can wait until after everyone is bandaged and rested. This humble fortress cannot show you the finest comfort we have to offer, but you will not want for refreshment and warmth, and you will have the opportunity to sleep during the hours to which you are accustomed. Allow me to offer you the Queens' hospitality."

"We are honored to accept," Cassia replied.

The men did not interrupt. Perhaps the free lords would wait as long as their second hour here to be ungrateful for the Hesperines' rescue and to turn the embassy into a debacle.

The Cordian mages, Cassia already knew, would bide their time until the moment they chose to strike. For now Chrysanthos stood calmly, hardly glancing at the fearsome Stewards, his attention politely on the Chamberlain.

Skleros pulled on his leaf-wrapped smoke and blew clouds of noxious herbal fumes into the air around him. He had slung back his black leather cape, not even bothering to hide his necromancer robes and the weapons strapped to every inch of him.

"There is but one request we must make of you," said Komnena. "Although we honor the sacred significance the sword and sickle, shield and spear hold for your people, it is forbidden for anyone, Hesperine or human, to carry weapons in Orthros. We must ask all of you to disarm."

Knights and lords startled, and a chorus of stifled protests and angry remarks went up.

Komnena did not appear ruffled in the least. "After the close call everyone suffered tonight, I appreciate how difficult it is to think of having no weapon at hand. However, even our few Hesperines errant who rely on weapons leave them in the armory here at Waystar. Not a single armament may pass beyond this point. We must ask that you honor our laws. Rest assured, your weapons will remain safe here in the fortress and be returned to you on your way home to Tenebra."

Cassia could see on the men's faces their horror at the thought of disarming in this den of monsters and their affront that the Hesperines required it. These warmongers still weren't convinced the Hesperines didn't lead them to the slaughter.

Cassia answered for them. "Tonight you have offered us the most powerful proof that we can rely on your protection. As a gesture of trust, we shall honor your request. The men of this embassy shall lay down their arms with goodwill."

"Now, see here, Your Ladyship—" Benedict said amid the outcries.

A buckle clinked, leather rustled, and Cassia glanced behind her to see Callen unfastening his scabbard with Perita's help. Cassia's handmaiden bore her bodyguard's sword to her, and Cassia surrendered it to Komnena.

Lord Severin looked from Cassia to Lyros, then made himself the second to remove his sword belt.

With gracious words and gentle hands, the Hesperines went around and began to collect everyone else's weapons. Gradually the men fell silent, staring bewildered into reflective eyes and faces that were beautiful as only Hesperines could be.

In a matter of moments, the Hesperines extricated an arsenal of swords, knives, bows, arrows, crossbows, spears, shields, morning stars, and gods knew what else from the Tenebrans' slackening grips. Mak and Lyros did not stray from the Dexion's side, but they looked like they wished to relieve Chrysanthos of his weapons—the hands with which the mage cast spells.

When the free lords were completely unarmed, Skleros was still retrieving all manner of deadly items from his cloak, boots, and pockets. Cassia was relieved to see it was Arkadia who stood before the necromancer, accepting piece after piece of his personal armory.

Finally, he surrendered one more bread knife and dusted off his hands. Arkadia did not move, but stood looking at him expectantly. His eyes narrowed. She held out a hand. With a grunt, Skleros pulled five cobbler's knives out of his sleeves and boots and handed them to her.

When she was finished, Javed joined her and held a metal case open in front of the necromancer. "Rest assured, we will store your alchemical weaponry as carefully as your steel."

"Sorry to disappoint you, but I did not bring my poisons with me. There is nothing for you to confiscate and study."

"You understand, I am sure, that I must nevertheless ask you to leave *all* your alchemical substances in my care."

Arkadia watched Skleros's every move as he reached into an inner pocket of his robes.

He dangled an oilcloth pouch and myriad bottles between his fingers. "Herbs for smoking and tonics for the men. Not every fellow wants to submit himself to the tender care of Mother Kyria. I'll keep my vices and their medicine."

Javed frowned. "I will verify the substances magically."

"Don't ruin the taste of my smokes with Hesperine spells," the Gift Collector warned.

A puff of dust escaped his pouch of herbs, and the liquid in his vials trembled. Javed reached out and plucked one of the bottles from the Gift Collector's hand.

The healer placed the lone vial in the metal box and snapped the case shut. "This will remain here. You may keep the others."

At her Grace's pronouncement, Arkadia nodded in satisfaction. Skleros gave his smoking herbs a careful sniff, then tucked them carefully back in his robes with the tonics.

"Thank you all for your cooperation." Komnena nodded to Cassia. "Now then, this is our first stop on the journey to the capital city of Selas. When everyone is equal to traveling, we will board ships that will bear us across the channel to mainland Orthros. In the meantime, please be at your ease."

Cassia gave Lio's mother another curtsy. Perita hooked her arm in Cassia's, and they rejoined Callen. At Perita's insistence, Cassia sat back down on her cot.

Lord Severin came over to Cassia. "At least some of our packs made it out of the avalanche. I still have the chopped liver from the last deer we brought down on the way. I shall save it for your hound for when he returns."

When. She had to keep thinking *when.* "I thank you, my lord. It will do him great good. He is no longer young."

"At fifteen, he is hardly past his prime for a liegehound," Lord Severin reminded her, "especially one of his breeding, training, and constitution."

Cassia was usually capable of facing facts. But not those few that were unthinkable to her. "Despite liegehounds' lifespan of nigh on thirty years, most do not survive any longer than mundane dogs."

"Due to the danger of their duties, yes—but when cared for as well as yours, they have the longest, healthiest lives of any dog. We must be prepared for his return. I am sure wound care was part of your training with him."

"Certainly. But I fear I lost all my healing plants with the rest of my packs in the avalanche."

Suddenly Lord Severin jumped as if someone had walked over his grave. He stepped aside and got out of the way of the Hesperine behind him.

The Guardian of Orthros stood before Cassia. She had never been this close to Hippolyta before. The most formidable warrior in Hesperine history wasn't any taller than Cassia herself, although her Stand regalia displayed that her petite limbs were all muscle. She dangled Cassia's gardening satchel from one hand.

"Lady Cassia, I believe this is yours."

Cassia stared. "How can I thank you? Surely the Guardian of Orthros has more important business than fishing bags out of the pass."

"This one has an aura about it. My senses guided me right to it. I believe it is the, ah, plants you are carrying in here." Hippolyta smiled and placed Cassia's weapons into her hands.

Cassia hugged the satchel to her, feeling the reassuring weight of the glyph stone. "I am grateful."

"Take care, Lady Cassia."

Hippolyta crossed the hall to join her Stand. As the Guardian of Orthros approached the Cordian mages, Chrysanthos and Skleros followed her with their gazes like hunters who had sighted the rarest of dangerous beasts. Tychon was pale and sweating. Eudias scuttled backwards, only to jump out of his skin when he nearly ran into Arkadia.

Lord Severin sat down beside Cassia and spoke low. "I should count myself fortunate the Hesperines do not know of my father and his connection to the heart hunters."

"They know," Cassia informed him. "They know you were in the snow, under attack with the rest of us."

Bitterness Cassia recognized crossed Severin's features, then disappeared behind a survivor's mask. She remembered when she had passed that point of no return with her own father.

Now the king had passed his point of no return with her.

TOLERANCE

L IO STOOD ALONE IN the snow once more, but he knew there was one more creature alive out here. There had to be. He followed the path of the two heart hunters who had taken Knight. It was easy to retrace their route, which he had seen in their minds.

He smelled the blood first, then the musk of liegehound. Knight's slow, powerful heartbeat reached Lio's ears along with another sound that made his stomach sour. Teeth worrying at flesh.

Lio stepped as near to Knight as he dared, then approached slowly on foot. Lio's assault had made the two men crash on their skis, and they had taken Knight with them on a litter. Between their bodies, Knight lay tangled in the remnants of his bonds. What had once been a muzzle was in pieces around him, and bloody bits of rope littered the snow.

Lio did not bate Knight by veiling himself. He kept to one side of the hound with his gaze averted, as he had learned from his Trial brothers.

Knight froze and lifted his head. A growl purred in his throat.

Lio stood very still. "Good dog, Knight. Remember me? Lio, your lady's champion. Here I am. No tricks."

Knight sniffed the air, eying Lio as he had the night they had met. The red around the hound's jaws was not just the natural markings of his fur this time. It was his own blood.

Lio studied the rope that bound Knight's front paws together. It was a knot the dog's teeth should have been able to saw through in no time. But Lio could smell the coils of a hedge warlock's arts woven into the rope.

Knight could not chew through the bespelled rope, so he was chewing off his own paw instead.

Without any sudden moves, Lio knelt down. "You won't let anything keep you from her, will you? I know. I'd give up more than a hand for her, and so would you. You risked your life for her tonight, just like breathing. No doubt about your kill count, Sir. What a shame that your opponents had the ill fortune to serve such barbaric masters. Would that all dogs could live under the fair hand of a lady like yours. Even now, I know her heart is breaking with worry for you. Will you not let me take you to her?"

Knight watched him, panting. Something came to Lio's senses through his instinctual Hesperine wariness of liegehounds. Pain. Knight's pain.

"I can feel you in the Union, almost as I could any other animal. I think we're picking up where we left off and even getting to know one another better."

He dared look into the hound's eyes. Knight did not snarl in challenge. Lio could see and feel the dog's uncertainty.

"I understand," Lio soothed. He inched closer. "It was a lot to ask for you to trust me before, and now all your protective instincts have taken over. You're in pain, and it's hard to tell friend from foe. But I am on your lady's side, Knight. Will you let me take you to Cassia? Cassia."

Knight let out an ear-splitting howl.

"I'll take that as a yes."

Inch by inch, Lio scooted nearer to Knight, wary of the moment when the hound's tolerance might turn to aggression. But he made it within arm's reach without Knight going mad and hurting himself further.

Lio waited. He and Knight sat together in the snow.

"It's cold out here," Lio said. "Are you ready to go home and get warm? I know the embassy brought you some meat. Aren't you hungry? I know who will have herbs to ease a liegehound's pain. Cassia."

Suddenly, all the tension went out of Knight's body, and he lay there in surrender.

"It's all right," Lio murmured. "You can trust me."

He reached out a hand and rested it on the dog's side. Knight let out a huff like a sigh. Carefully Lio eased the choke collar off of Knight, moving his hands right past the beast's maw. If he lost some fingers, they would grow back. But the liegehound didn't even snap at him.

Lio cast the vile chain away. "This next part is going to hurt. I wish

I could help you with the pain. But I know you won't tolerate my thelemancy, and I don't trust it right now in any case. We'll both have to be strong."

With careful fingers, Lio examined the knot. "Hespera's Mercy. I'll never be able to untie this. You shall have to be *very* tolerant, Knight."

With all the speed and precision of movement the Gift afforded him, Lio lowered his head, put his fangs to the rope, and sliced through Knight's bonds.

A mass of fur and flesh broadsided him, and snow sprayed in his face. When he sat up, he saw Knight streaking away from him toward Orthros.

When Lio caught up to Knight, the hound was limping in circles around the place where Lio had stepped away with Cassia. Her dog sniffed and sniffed the spot where her scent had disappeared.

"Even if you could find her trail, you are not going to make it all the way over the rest of the Umbrals on foot, my friend. We are going to have to step together." Lio knelt down again and put out a hand to the dog. "Come here, Sir. What is it Cassia says? *Dockk. Dockk,* Knight."

Knight stood utterly still, staring at Lio as if he had never seen him before.

"*Dockk.* To Cassia."

One step at a time, Knight limped through the bodies of the heart hunters and came to stand before Lio. Lio caught his breath, hesitating. Then he rested his hand on Knight's ruff.

"Good dog. Now let me do what I can for that foot before we go."

Lio stopped breathing, trying to clear his head of the stench of suffering and death, although he could not and must not hide from the carnage around him. He reached into a pocket of his robes and found his handkerchiefs where he always kept them. There actually remained something so civilized about his person as a handkerchief. He pulled one out and stared at the white silk embroidered with Hespera's Rose.

"Remember when I used one of these to care for your lady's wounded hand? Will you carry a message to her for me?"

As gently as possible, he bound the liegehound's wounded paw in Orthros silk that bore Hespera's sacred symbol. Knight's blood soaked the fabric quickly, but the only protest he mounted was a whine.

"Good dog. Now we're ready to go home."

Wrapping his magic around Knight felt like trying to put wings on a brick. The dog whined again, but did not lash out. Panic flared to life in Lio once more. What if he went astray with Cassia's dog?

Cassia. He focused on her. Her aura. Her blood.

Craving tore at him, but when he stepped, he opened his eyes and found himself before the doors of Waystar.

Knight labored up the steps, wagging his tail. Someone opened the doors from the inside, and the hound disappeared within.

Lio listened to Cassia's heartbeat and watched the double doors shut.

No sooner had they closed than he felt a powerful presence, and Aunt Lyta appeared before him. Standing on the steps above him, she was on his eye level. He felt the echoes of the Mercy in her aura, a sweet and grievous light. She wrapped him in a fierce hug.

When she released him, she looked into his eyes and gave a nod. "Thank you for making the Stand's work easier tonight."

"There was another mind mage at work in the pass."

"Only one, Ioustin tells me. One man, responsible for all the thelemancy I sensed from the enemy tonight! But he and his forces were no match for you, for which we are grateful."

Aunt Lyta was Uncle Argyros's Grace. She knew better than anyone what it felt like to fight with thelemancy at work around her. Was even she convinced Lio had been responsible for the heart hunters' deaths? How could she be wrong?

How could Lio be so wrong about himself?

Aunt Lyta shook her head. "Tonight reminded me too much of my first stand for Orthros, when your uncle and I held off the pursuing Aithourians in that very pass so the Queens had time to cast the ward. That night, Argyros and I swore to each other no more of us would become martyrs. I was able to kill Aithouros and most of his army single-handedly with my Grace wielding his thelemancy to manage their force. Keep that in mind and come to me if you wish to speak of it."

Lio found no reply. He could not have borne it, if she had pressed him to speak of it now. He could not, not until he was sure.

What had he done?

"Now do what your uncle did after we survived. Go into the arms of the one you love." Aunt Lyta cast an indicative glance at the fortress before ascending the stairs.

Lio watched her go. Cassia's pulse in the great hall drew him like the heart pulled blood. He wrenched himself away from her and stepped to the solitary room allotted him on the other side of Waystar.

MESSAGE

CASSIA HEARD SUDDEN CRIES of surprise near the doors of Waystar. Exclamations traveled through the hall. Then every member of the embassy fit enough to move his hands began to applaud. The Kyrian mages smiled over their patients, and an expression of relief crossed Benedict's face.

The crowd parted. Weary lords limped aside, and the Hesperines moved well out of the way. Through their midst came a bedraggled, shaggy shape.

Cassia ran to Knight and went down on her knees in front of him. Her hound all but collapsed into her arms. She beamed into his dog kisses and stroked him, careful not to touch his wounds.

Her gaze fell to his paw. A mangled injury there had soaked its binding in blood, but Cassia could make out the embroidered sign of Hespera's Rose.

She hid her face in Knight's ruff for a long moment so the onlookers would not see her tears.

With one arm around Knight and the other around her satchel, she gazed at the silk rose that had survived tonight's bloodshed.

LIBATION

WITH PERITA, CALLEN, BENEDICT, Eudias, and Knight to protect her from their benevolent guide, Cassia followed Lio's mother along a quiet hallway. Cassia felt as if someone had beat her from head to toe, but perhaps last week, not this very night. Javed's healing must be working apace. She carried her gardening satchel across her weary shoulders, for the glyph stone's weight soothed a much keener pain inside her.

Benedict kept a wary eye on Komnena. He wore an amulet of his patron god for all to see, a glyph in the shape of a sword hilt. Andragathos, the Seventh Scion of Anthros and Kyria, was known for defending maidens, eschewing the temptations of the flesh, and striking down the corrupted, including Hesperines. Eudias drove the point home, scuttling along with them in the yellow robes of an apprentice mage of Anthros.

Knight struggled along on three legs, favoring his wounded paw. It hurt Cassia to watch him, although she had bandaged him with herbal treatments and hand-fed him bites of liver before letting him back on his feet.

Limping through the fortress, he and Callen were two of a kind. Perita walked arm in arm with her husband as if for support. In fact, it was she who helped him stay on his feet without a crutch, which he had refused.

Between worried glances at him, she turned the expert eye of a chandler's daughter upon the candles that lit the corridor. It must impress her that they were fine beeswax instead of common tallow from animal fat. No spell lights here. The Hesperines were going to great lengths to make their human guests feel at ease.

Lio's mother was fluent in the language of reassurance. She kept up a conversation with interested questions that were easy to answer and turned everyone's thoughts away from what they had endured tonight. What colors were the trees at Solorum in the autumn? What were the most beloved dances in Tenebra at present?

Komnena halted them at the end of a corridor. "This is the opposite side of the fortress from the wings set aside for the lords and mages. I expect you will find it accommodating for an unattached lady and a young wife."

"You are very considerate. Thank you so much for your hospitality." Oh, what creative and clever words.

Words had always been Cassia's sword and shield, but tonight her survival had depended on more primal forces. She was out of verbal strategies. She couldn't think of a way to tell Lio's mother all she wished to, all that had not come to mind in the turmoil of their first conversation. Cassia strove to appear at ease under Komnena's gaze.

"I have prepared lodgings for you here in the tower," Lio's mother explained, "where each level offers its own quarters. If your household is ready to settle in here on the ground floor, the rest of us will proceed to your rooms at the top."

Towers and stairs, the banes of Callen's existence. Before any of Cassia's protectors could protest, she turned to Perita with a smile. "Isn't this lovely? You and Callen can have proper quarters to yourselves."

"They are most convenient to your lady via a private flight of stairs," Komnena reassured Perita.

Perita cast her husband a concerned glance. Callen's expression was grave as stone, his posture stiff with affront.

Cassia hastened to say, "How safe I shall feel at the top of a tower with Callen between me and the rest of the world."

His tension eased, if not the lines of pain on his face. "A fine arrangement indeed, my lady."

Conversation turned to the refreshment that would be offered in the fortress's main hall once everyone had a long sleep. It took another moment for Cassia to persuade Perita to leave her side and a moment longer for Callen to give instructions to Benedict that were veiled insults. At last Cassia and her reduced escort were able to proceed with Komnena up the tower stairs.

Several turns and landings later, they came to the sitting room where Javed had examined Cassia earlier, and she feigned surprise. She asked Komnena to pass on her thanks to whomever had brought her belongings upstairs.

Komnena pursed her lips. "With its rustic appointments, Waystar is far from the perfect setting for your first nights in Orthros. However, the fortress will provide an all-important opportunity to greet one another properly and attain sufficient respite as soon as possible."

"I have no doubt our time here will be a delight." As soon as she said it, Cassia's face grew warm.

What if they weren't talking about the rooms? She couldn't be sure. If there were double meanings in Komnena's words, Cassia had no context for them. Had Lio told his mother about the more personal alliance he and Cassia had forged in Tenebra? Did the matriarch of Blood Komnena approve?

Komnena smiled. "You are fortunate in your protectors."

"I am indeed." Cassia rubbed her arms, remembering how Lio's had felt around her.

Komnena stepped back from the door, gesturing within. "I see that these three wish to perform their duty and inspect the rooms on your behalf, Lady Cassia."

What ridiculous nonsense. They all owed their lives to the Hesperines, and yet Cassia's bodyguards were tasked with ensuring no heretical magic lurked under the pillow where she would sleep tonight. "I apologize for the necessity, Chamberlain."

"Please, do not let me hinder such diligent and admirable defenders."

Cassia realized Knight was leaning forward, ears pricked. A liegehound refused to rest until his work was done. But whatever had passed between him and Lio in the mountains, it had prepared her hound for dwelling among Hesperines. He had yet to raise his hackles at their hosts.

Cassia kept a hand on him. "*Baat.* Stay here by me, dearest, and let the men walk through my chambers."

Eudias blushed from his forehead to his neck and probably everywhere else. "Begging your pardon, Basilis. This is highly irregular. I assure you, it is not my way to impose myself upon a lady's bedchamber—that is to say..."

"I understand, Apprentice Eudias. You are duty-bound to go inside and verify magically that all is well. I do not feel you impose upon my modesty in the least."

"Our vows are Your Ladyship's shield." Benedict bowed, then proceeded into Cassia's bedchamber.

With his hands in his sleeves, Eudias nodded deeply to her. As he turned and ventured further into her lodgings, the hairs on the back of her arms stood up, as always when a mage of Anthros was at work anywhere near.

Cassia offered Komnena a curtsy, aware of the men within earshot. "Thank you for your forbearance. Please pass on my deepest thanks to the Hesperine who succeeded in delivering my hound safely to me despite the painful history between liegehounds and your people."

Her second conversation with Lio's mother, and all she had succeeded in doing was talking about Knight. Her desire to send Lio a message motivated her comment. Nevertheless, she was wasting another chance to make a favorable impression.

Komnena was not looking at Knight. "Far be it from us to part those who are so faithful to one another. I wish for you to feel welcome here. Despite how it began, I hope your time in Orthros fulfills all your expectations."

Cassia took heart at those words. Come now, she told herself. You once talked your way out of execution at the hands of your own father. Will you let yourself be defeated by a conversation with Lio's mother?

She met the lady's gaze and cleared her throat. "I can say without hesitation it has surpassed my hopes already. I am deeply grateful for the opportunity to be here. The invitation came as a very great surprise. I suspect you know I am no diplomat. Nonetheless, I hope to do my part for our peoples."

"I beg to differ, Lady Cassia. Word of your deeds precedes you. Your right to be here is indisputable."

Cassia tried to make her true feelings heard between her words. "I thank you. I shall strive to live up to such an assessment. This is perhaps not the moment for any discussion of politics, so I shall say only this. My brief contact with your embassy to Tenebra left a lasting impression upon me. The dashed hopes of the Equinox Summit have inspired me to do everything I can to renew contact between us and secure a lasting agreement that will fulfill our dearest hopes."

How flowery a speech. But if Lio's mother was in favor of what Cassia was saying, the words would not be wasted. If Komnena did not approve…well, with any luck she would assume Cassia was only talking about diplomacy, and not about Lio.

Komnena offered Cassia another lovely, inscrutable smile. "You will find that in this land, we value the efforts of a woman who does not surrender. I am very happy to welcome you to Orthros."

Benedict and Eudias reappeared, apparently satisfied, for they raised no alarms. They waited in Cassia's sitting room until Komnena departed, then the men excused themselves to return to the wings where the lords and mages would lodge.

As soon as they closed the door, another Hesperine became visible who must have been in the sitting room all along. Arkadia stood near, still in her Stand regalia, which only emphasized her large, womanly body and disciplined, martial body language. The blond Hesperine's contradictory beauty seemed natural to her.

Cassia wondered if the males of the Tenebran embassy would survive the intimidation they must suffer in Arkadia's presence. She was tall enough to look them in the eye, skilled enough to best them on the battlefield, and curvaceous enough to destroy their reason. If anyone mistook her for an overfed court flower, it would be his last mistake. They should know better after tonight, when they had all seen her pull grown men out of the snow—and put others in the ground.

At the moment, the creature suffering intimidation was Knight. Arkadia and the hound eyed each other warily.

"He knows a warrior when he sees one, Master Arkadia. Please take it as a compliment." Cassia put a hand on Knight's back to reassure him. "*Hama.*"

"I'm sorry I startled you two." Lio's cousin turned her gaze from the hound and smiled at Cassia. "Javed said no introductions would be necessary, although we never properly met during the Equinox Summit. I'm Kadi."

"Allow me to thank you for the Stand's valiant defense of us tonight and to congratulate you on becoming a mother."

"I am glad to honor my bond of gratitude with my children's rescuer.

I want you to know I will be standing guard outside your door, and your room is well warded and veiled. You need not fear the king's agents in the embassy. Many of the Hesperines errant who fought in the pass tonight are remaining in the fortress with us. Those who wish you harm will not have a second chance."

"I do not believe Chrysanthos will try anything now that we are here. He is determined to keep his foothold in Orthros and knows I am necessary to meet your terms." Even as she spoke, all the fear Cassia had been struggling to ignore refused to be denied any longer.

Kadi's expression softened. "A Hesperine will be within your reach at all times."

"Thank you so much. You have all been so kind."

Kadi came near and touched Cassia's shoulder. That hand, so soft, but strong enough to break bones, felt like an invocation. Cassia did not see or feel a ward spring to life around her, but she felt as if one had.

"I had an elder sister," Cassia blurted.

"So did I. I also lost her to Tenebra."

"No!"

"Nike. My example to live by. My best friend."

"I understand."

"I know. I wish the Siege of Sovereigns had ended like tonight's battle. It breaks my heart that my people could do nothing to save your sister, for your fight may have kept mine alive. Nike went errant almost ninety years ago, and none of us have seen her since. But because you have held off war with the Orders, we still have hope of her return."

"I will keep doing everything I can."

Kadi gave Cassia's shoulder a squeeze. "Right now, all you need is rest. Javed's healing spell still has work to do on you. Let me know if you need anything, all right?"

Cassia nodded mutely.

"Sleep well." Kadi took her leave through the closed door.

The hours of the night stretched out ahead of Cassia, and she dreaded the visions that would repeat in her mind.

If only her mind mage were here to banish them. All she had seen of him since he had saved her were his retreating back and his handkerchief.

She reached into her satchel and pulled out the handkerchief. After bandaging Knight, she had rinsed as much gore out of the silk as she could, but it was still ruined.

The stakes had been too high, her few moments with Lio too contradictory an encounter for her to interpret.

My mind can always reach yours. I will always be your Sanctuary.

Her bond of gratitude with him was deeper now than ever. A gift beyond price. That should be enough. But with Lio, she always wanted more than enough.

Kadi's presence made it fairly clear the Hesperine in reach tonight would not be Lio. But just in case, Cassia would not get Knight settled in the bedroom. Hope's banner was tattered, but Cassia would bear it onward.

Cassia spent half an hour coaxing Knight to sleep on the soft, thick carpet in the sitting room. Even then, she feared he might awaken the moment he sensed her leave his side. But his exhaustion was deep, her herbs soothing, and she managed to creep into the next room without rousing him.

Alone in her bedchamber, Cassia discovered just what "rustic appointments" awaited her. Her feet never touched the stone floor thanks to the rugs. Miles of drapes shrouded the windows, leaving only their peaks exposed, through which the beams of the beacon shone.

At last she lifted her satchel of relics from her shoulders. She set them safely on a side table in a pool of the beacon's light.

In the center of the room stood a wrought iron bed of impressive proportions. She found a matching dressing table tucked in a corner behind a silk room divider. There was a generous ceramic pitcher of warm water and a basket overflowing with clean towels and paper-wrapped soaps. The wash basin was large enough to stand in.

A glass flask held cool water. Clean, unpoisoned water for drinking. Cassia snatched it up. When her tongue was no longer dry and her belly was painfully full, she set down the empty bottle.

She could not make sense of silk and clean towels and fine paper. Mere hours ago, she had been alone, at the mercy of men whose gazes had made her feel like filth, who would have used her until they destroyed her.

Cassia ran one trembling finger over the familiar design of yellow flowers on the soap wrapper. Cassia blossoms. She lifted a bar to her nose and took a deep whiff of her namesake.

She peeled the wrapper off the soap, careful not to make a single tear. She smoothed out the paper and set it aside. Her hands moved faster. She tore out of every scrap of clothes she had soaked with sweat in her terror.

She scrubbed herself over and over, until the bar of soap was smaller and her skin was rosy and her hair finally smelled of cassia spice instead of tallow and wood smoke. She reduced heart hunters and kings and all of Tenebra to a heap of dirty clothes on the floor and gray suds in the bottom of the wash basin. In her own skin, she fetched her gardening dress from her travel trunk and wrapped herself in clean wool worn to softness.

She went all around the chamber to throw back the drapes and let in the beacon's light. The tall, narrow windows stood in trios on three sides of her room. Such was the Hesperines' wealth in luxuries and protective magic. They could put glass windows in the fortress that was their first line of defense inside the ward.

Cassia came to a standstill at the window that faced due north. Four moons greeted her, two bright and clear in the sky, two amorphous and sparkling upon the surface of the sea below. The Blood Moon had reappeared, a slender crimson crescent. The waning edge of the Light Moon looked like Hespera's dark lashes.

Waystar perched at the tip of a bluff, light as a bird, yet unmoving as the dark rock that was its foundation. The cliff dropped sheer, and beneath it the sea rose and fell, cradling the land in its tide as it did everywhere. But Cassia had never beheld a sea like this. She had stood on Tenebra's craggy western coast and walked the golden beaches of Namenti to the south, but they had only been rocks and sand.

Only hours ago, Cassia had been snowbound in Tenebra's northern mountains, miles from any sea. How could she now have eyes on these enchanted waters? It was all a mystery, everything that lay on this side of the mountains, hidden from humans under the cloak of Hesperine magic for nearly sixteen hundred years and by the forces of nature for even longer than that.

Cassia crossed the room and took in the view to the south, back the way they had come. Behind the fortress lay the bulk of the mountains, wreathed in the clouds of snow the embassy had just braved.

This was not the end of the pass. It was the other side of the range. In a single night, the Hesperines had not only brought them through the ward, but all the way across the mountains. The border was well behind her now.

Tenebra was well behind her.

She fisted her hands on the glass. "You lost. You did not have the power to stop me. I escaped you. Let your mages exhaust themselves traversing to Solorum with the tidings. Let your useless ire be heard all the way to the border, for there your power ends. I am on the other side, and you cannot touch me. Do you hear me? I will never be defenseless against you again."

The shivers had overtaken her once more. She could feel the glyph stone slipping from her hands and see Knight dragged away from her.

"Never again." She slammed her fists on implacable Orthros glass, then turned her back on the south.

She went to where she had set her satchel on the side table. When would her hands stop shaking? She unbuckled her pack and found her spool of gardening twine, which had held charms against bad dreams around the necks of Eriphite children and one grown Hesperine. Cassia drew her spade, then freed the glyph stone from her sister's garments and lifted the relic in both hands.

The sensation that shot through Cassia made her gasp. If the stone's first response to her had been a veiled moon, this was Hespera's full and open eye. Cassia carried the artifact to the northern windows and set it down in the moonlight, kneeling before it. She could almost hear the glyph stone throbbing. She realized it pulsed in time to the rhythm of the waves below.

She set her tools aside and ran her hands over the relic, testing the strength of each groove and corner. Crumbly mortar came off on her hands, but the integrity of the stone was solid.

Would the Sanctuary give of itself once more? She was loath to put it to the test, but she must. She needed the shrine's protection at all times. She must have her own defenses.

She took up her spade and held her hands over the glyph stone. With the sharp edge of her spade, she retraced the cut she had once made to feed life-saving Hesperine magic at the Equinox Summit. Her libation bloomed on her hand and pooled in her spade. She let it drip onto the glyph stone.

Something she could not name coursed through her, exhilarating, frightening, beautiful. Her heartbeat altered in her chest. She doubled over the glyph stone, her mouth dropping open.

Air still filled her lungs. Her head was clear. In the hush, she listened to her own breathing and felt her pulse in her head. The rhythm of her own heart had fallen into step with the glyph stone's.

Gazing at Orthros's sea below, she thought she could feel the ocean's rhythm rising and falling within her, as if this were the tide that set the pace for the whole world. It was so vast she did not think she could hold it all.

Tears filled her eyes, making her vision swim, but when she blinked the tears away, the ocean was still there, ready to embrace her. She recalled the night of the Spring Equinox, when she had felt the Queens' magic summoning their people home.

She lifted her spade high. Moonlight gleamed on her blood. With all her strength, she brought the spade down and struck one corner of the glyph stone.

Power shot up her arm and into her heart. The ancient marble gave way beneath her blade. A single piece of the stone broke free and rolled onto the carpet before her.

Panting, she let her spade fall to rest and pried her fingers off the handle. With her bleeding hand, she reached for the chunk of marble at her knees and took hold of it.

The shard fit perfectly in her hand. She lifted it, studying it in the moonlight. She could feel it throbbing against her skin with a warm echo of the Sanctuary's magic. It had worked. The glyph stone had yielded her a talisman that carried the power of the shrine.

Cassia wrapped gardening twine round and round the glyph shard. When she was done, she had fashioned a pendant out of rough string, fine white marble, and bloodstains.

She lifted her talisman over her head. The shard came to rest over her heart. With them throbbing in time, she could not tell one from the other. She could only feel a single, stronger beat.

BLOOD SHACKLES

THE BREADTH OF WAYSTAR and the walls of Lio's room were not enough to close out the sound of her heartbeat. The mortals' pulses had scattered through the fortress and faded to the rhythm of sleep. He barely heard them.

The longer he listened, the stronger Cassia's aura grew in his senses. She was breathtaking. After all she had been through tonight, she rose from the ashes and blazed like a star. The whole fortress throbbed with her heart.

Lio put his head between his knees and gritted his teeth on a growl, holding back a wave of power with all his might. But his might broke. His Gift erupted into the air around him, and every piece of glassware in the room shattered.

Mak dodged a shard of flying glass as he stepped into sight. "We came to ask if you're all right. I'll take that as a no."

Lyros levitated over the slivers on the floor. "It's a good thing the windows in this old place are warded, or I daresay you'd have broken those too."

Mak glanced out the modest windows of Lio's chamber. "Not a very romantic view. You're going to her room, I hope."

"I can't go anywhere near her like this," Lio snarled from where he sat on the edge of the bed. "I can't even look at her."

"Well," Mak reassured him, "we checked on her for you as soon as your mother and my Grace-brother finished clucking."

"Thank you, my friends. Please tell me how she is."

"Ferocious," Mak declared. "I can't wait to welcome her into our family."

"Such an endearing destroyer of kings for you to carry over the mountains," said Lyros.

Lio groaned. "In truth, I almost carried her off the moment she was safe in my arms."

"Why didn't you?" Mak asked. "Why are you in here? Why did you let your mother take her to her rooms?"

"To be fair," Lyros said, "if he had escorted her, it would have caused a scandal. But now is your chance, Lio. Kadi is right outside the door, but will gladly yield her watch as soon as you're ready."

"I am the last thing Cassia needs right now."

He, her Grace, could not be what she needed tonight.

"That's not what your physician says," Mak informed Lio. "I volunteered to deliver Javed's orders for him to spare you the embarrassment. Allow me to paraphrase. Drink her blood already. Your body's healing power will set her to rights, too. Just let her set the pace."

"I will *not* burden her with my needs tonight."

"Didn't you feel her aura glowing at you through the Union?" Mak demanded. "She might as well have been waving a banner over her head that said 'I need you.'"

"Of course she needs me!" Lio roared. "She needs the one who loves her to hold her without a lustful thought in his head and help her feel safe again. And I cannot do it. Because one man with a broken mind in the dungeon at Castra Justa may be all that's left of my self-control."

Mak and Lyros caught the next blast of Lio's power in a ward and eased it back at him. He remembered the impact of his magic returning to him after death had released his power from hundreds of minds. But his Trial brothers had had his back then too.

Lio put his face in his hands. "Forgive me."

"No one needs to apologize for tonight," Mak told him.

Lio shook his head. "No one seems to want to let me apologize."

"That's because no one blames you," said Lyros. "We all took lives tonight."

"I know," Lio replied. "Every Hesperine in Martyrs' Pass died with those men in Union. I am so sorry."

"No, that's not what I meant," Lyros clarified. "In some cases, the Stand

and the Charge could not stop the danger by merely incapacitating a heart hunter. We killed a number of them before you did."

Lio lowered his hands. "This is the first time you've killed."

Mak sat down in the room's one chair. "Yes, it is."

Lio looked between his Trial brothers. "Are you two all right?"

"We will be." Lyros sank onto the arm of the chair.

Mak put an arm around his Grace. "We did our duty tonight, in accordance with our training and our oaths. And we survived. I think everyone should stop wilting and sobbing, because I'm proud of all of us."

Lyros laughed and rubbed a hand over his face. "I love you."

"I love you, too," Mak answered. "All right, Lio, that's enough. Now go tell Cassia you love her."

"I don't dare. Cup and thorns, I can't promise what I'll do as soon as I'm in her presence again. Annassa Soteira healed me only last night, and I drank an embarrassing amount of my parents' blood in preparation for meeting the embassy in the pass and *it's not enough.*"

Mak and Lyros both sighed and tossed another ward in front of Lio's unruly power. He shuddered, but felt a trace of hope.

"Ward me," he said. "That's my only recourse. Cast the blood shackles on me."

"You're jesting," Mak protested.

"Not in the least."

"Lio," Lyros objected, "that's worse than the thirst suppressant."

"I have to get through this night without going to her room, and tomorrow I have to survive introductions and have a diplomatic conversation with her. I'll never get through that without something to keep me in line."

"Blood shackles are what we use on criminals." Mak scowled. "To keep them from repeating their crimes. We ward them against committing theft or murder."

Lyros shook his head. "It's a binding of the Will that is not to be undertaken lightly. We never place the shackles on an innocent person."

"And don't you dare mope about having lost your innocence," Mak warned.

Lyros frowned. "I've never heard of casting that spell to prevent someone from the Feast."

"Will it even work on the Feast?" Mak wondered. "For all we know, the kind of bond Lio isn't saying he has with Cassia can't be shackled."

"Please try," Lio pleaded. "It cannot be a violation of the Will if I am asking you to do it. Ward me so I won't take a drop from her until she's ready."

"What for the key?" Lyros asked.

"A kiss," Mak suggested. "A sure sign she's ready."

Lyros grinned at his Grace. "You won't hear any complaints from me."

"It ought to be a kiss from her," Lio said. "Not one from me."

Mak nodded. "As soon as *she* kisses *you*, it will break the blood shackles and you will once more be free to do as you please."

"Thank you," Lio told them. "I owe you for this."

"You've been spending too much time among humans," Lyros said. "Debts are un-Hesperine."

"Especially between Trial brothers," Mak agreed.

Mak and Lyros dragged Lio to his feet and stood him in the middle of his room. When they were certain he would remain upright, they retreated a few paces away on opposite sides of him. Breaking the skin on their palms with their fangs, they dripped blood upon the flagstones until Lio was surrounded in a ring of red droplets.

His Trial brothers met where they closed the circle and joined their bleeding hands. Their power rose in Lio's senses, a mighty force that bore him up. They too had tested their limits tonight, and yet they also had strength to spare and the generosity to lend it to him.

The drops of blood on the floor ran together until the circle was a solid red line around Lio. At that moment, the fortifying power closed around him and became something else. A vice on his heart. It knocked the breath out of his chest.

Mak and Lyros turned to face one another and kissed each other on the mouth. The blood on the floor glowed and became a ring of red light, then was gone. Their power faded. As the spell calmed, Lio staggered to catch his balance.

Mak held Lyros to him a moment past the end of the working. Finally Lyros pulled back with a bemused expression for his Grace.

"Well, I can see that was an ordeal for you." Lio smiled. "Thank you again."

Mak didn't let Lyros go. "I'm glad we're alive."

"So am I." Lyros rested his face on Mak's shoulder.

Lio stood still and waited to see if the Craving would make him buckle again. The next throb of vein-burn overtook him, and his magic crested again. He gasped. "I don't feel any different."

"I'm afraid it won't ease your symptoms," Lyros said.

Mak grimaced. "All the ward can do is keep you from acting on them."

This must surely be the most difficult night of Lio's life.

47

nights until

WINTER SOLSTICE

A lady can walk through fire.

—*Solia's instructions to Cassia*

BATTLE SCARS

ASSIA WOKE TO MOONLIGHT and a rhythm she felt more than heard. It pulsed above her and coursed below her and beat in her own heart. Her hand went to the glyph shard, and she opened her eyes.

Knight snuffled, and she hugged him closer to her under the covers, careful not to put pressure on any of his injuries. It felt like it had been hours since she had woken briefly to find him climbing into bed with her. She must thank Javed for his healing spell, which had sunk her into a deep rest without nightmares.

She made her first attempt to get out of bed. It only took one try. She must definitely give Javed her gratitude. She felt far better than any mortal should after last night.

The cut on her hand from her blood ritual was gone. She would not have minded a scar there. But it was for the best that Javed's slow healing spell had caught even that fresh wound in its wake.

"Ah, you're awake, my lady," came Perita's voice from the sitting room.

Cassia cast one more glance around the bedchamber to reassure herself she had hidden all traces of her blood ritual. "Yes."

The bedchamber door swung open, and Perita joined her.

"How are you?" Cassia asked.

Perita came to her, and they held fast to each other.

"The Hesperines didn't pull me out of the snow in the pass," Cassia said.

"What?"

"The avalanche carried me all the way down to the bottom of the ravine, and there were twelve heart hunters waiting for me."

"No!"

"One of the Hesperines reached me in time. The hunters didn't hurt me. But they could have."

"I didn't know. They got to you, and Callen and I didn't even know."

"I'm so glad you weren't there. You already had to endure that with Verruc. I never want you to go through it again."

"I wish Callen could have killed the men who tried to hurt you."

"I'm glad he didn't have to go through that again, either."

"You were right not to tell anyone what really happened. If they knew you were alone with the heart hunters, and then with a Hesperine, it would be just like the rumors Lord Tyran and his men tried to spread about me."

"In the confusion, I don't think anyone realized I was separated from all of you."

"Aye, your secret is safe. I'll keep it just as you have mine. No one will ever say a word against your reputation on Callen's and my watch."

"I know. I can always rely on you two." Cassia hesitated. "Perita, do you remember Initiate Ambassador Deukalion from the Summit?"

Perita nodded. "The one with the pretty face who had all the ladies talking after the dance, as if they didn't know better. But he did stay and fight Dalos with the others."

"It was he who saved my life last night. That makes twice."

"A male Hesperine! One you danced with before! Oh, my lady, you were *very* right not to breathe a word." Perita took Cassia's hands and studied her palms. "Your hands are healed. But you wouldn't let the Kyrians look at them."

"Master Javed was very respectful, I assure you, and I was not alone with him. The Chamberlain was there."

"You should never have been in that pass where only a heretic could save you, and you shouldn't have needed a Hesperine's healing! Just like you never should have been at the Summit when a war mage lost his head! It's not right, my lady. We shouldn't be here."

"It is not Orthros that gives me cause for complaint." Cassia went to the dressing table and held up one of the bars of soap. She went through with the strategy she had decided on last night, which she deemed the only way to throw her handmaiden off the scent, literally. "You won't believe what our Hesperine hosts have put here for me. Just like the ones they brought as gifts last winter."

"Would you look at that." Perita came closer, eying the soap.

"It's the same kind Lord Fancy Soap managed to get for me from the embassy. He once told me what it is made of. A plant called cassia."

Perita took a sniff. "What a nice thing to be named after, my lady." There was concern in her eyes, but no suspicion.

Cassia breathed easier. "I shall feel close to him the whole time I'm here. This will remind me every night I must not give up."

"As well you shouldn't, my lady." Perita busied herself arranging Cassia's towels to her satisfaction. "As if we won't make it through this. You've got me and Callen to look after you, and we won't let you out of our reach again, not for a moment."

Cassia put a hand on her friend's arm. "When you promised me you'd follow me anywhere, I know this is not what you had in mind."

Perita's hands moved more efficiently than ever. "I'd follow you to Hypnos's realm, my lady. But I think it might be more fit for mortals than Orthros."

Cassia longed to offer her friend some real reassurance. Here they were in the safest place in the world, and it brought Perita and Callen only fear. Why must the few people dearest to Cassia come from opposite sides of that snowstorm they had just ridden through?

Cassia could find no words of comfort to give her friend that would not give something away. So she offered what always seemed to ease Perita's mind when she was distraught. Tasks to distract her.

"We have our work cut out for us, Perita. I was on horseback for thirty-one days straight, then fell off a cliff. Now I must somehow manage to look like royalty. How much of my clothing survived in one piece?"

"As the Hesperines brought in what they recovered from the pass, I rounded up every one of your gowns myself and put them back in your travel trunk. Don't you worry that they need some work. I can undo horse patties, liegehound spit and all the dirt in the world in under an hour."

True to her word, it was less than an hour later that Perita pronounced Cassia fit to be seen.

"I must make my finest impression yet," Cassia said. "Thanks to you, I shall succeed."

"Mistress Riga worked magic on that gown."

"So did you!"

Perita grinned. "It does you justice, and that's the truth, my lady. It's a shame Lord Fancy Soap isn't here to see you now."

Cassia laughed. "If only." *If only you knew.*

Cassia picked up a hand mirror, a Hesperine creation of the clearest glass that put bronze Tenebran mirrors to shame. She felt she had never seen herself so well as she did now. She had not realized her face had become so thin from avoiding food that might be poisoned, nor that the smudges under her eyes were so dark from lack of sleep.

Her battle scars. She did not know what Lio would make of them. But she gazed upon them with greater satisfaction than she would ever have felt if bewitching eyes or a face worth killing for had looked back at her.

She met her own hazel gaze, ordinary as an herb that grew in her garden. But those herbs held power in their unprepossessing leaves. Her drab brown hair and her skin that was neither fair nor dark were her disguise, causing everyone to underestimate her.

Except Lio. He had only ever told her she was capable of more.

Cassia lifted the neckline of her gown to take another whiff of herself. Rosewater, flametongue oil, and her namesake spice soap. Not a trace of Tenebra, as far as her human nose could tell. She sniffed her hands. No deer liver. It had been fortnights since she'd worn fur or leather and months since she'd eaten meat. She ought to provide a delight for a Hesperine's sensitive nose. Or so she hoped.

She felt cleansed. Unburdened. Bathed in scents that made her feel treasonous and…beautiful. Not unlike the night she had once anointed herself and gone to the shrine of Hespera for her first tryst with Lio. If that had been the night she had first set foot on this path, then tonight must be when she came within sight of its end.

Cassia returned the mirror to the dressing table and squeezed Perita's hand in thanks. "After you escort me to the main hall, why don't you come back here to the tower and stay with Callen in your rooms? I'll have Knight and Benedict to look after me."

"That won't do, my lady. You must have an attendant at diplomatic events."

"As much as I wish for you to be at my side every moment, I think it will not be improper if you excuse yourself. This is just a preliminary encounter. The official ceremonies haven't begun yet."

"You heard what I said about Callen and me not letting you out of our sights."

"I know. It will be some time before any of us feel safe." She looked down at Knight, who had planted himself on her feet. "But I will be surrounded by the Hesperines who saved our lives."

Perita bit her lip. "Are you sure, my lady?"

"Yes. Don't tell him I said so, but last night set Callen back. He must stay off his leg entirely until we have to travel again."

Perita let out a sigh. "Trying to keep him off his feet is like trying to make candles burn backwards."

"Oh, I'm sure you can find a way to convince him to put his feet up."

That turned Perita's worried expression into a smile. "I can't argue with that, my lady."

"Don't. Your husband is in dire need and utterly at your mercy. What are you waiting for?"

"Well then, you and I'll just sneak downstairs, and I'll come right back before he has a chance to protest."

When the knock came at Cassia's door, she felt ready. As Perita went to answer it, Cassia reminded herself Lio would not be on the other side, for propriety's sake. But how she wished he would be.

Nevertheless, Kadi was a reassuring sight in the corridor. She and Cassia went through introductions for Perita's benefit and exchanged impersonal courtesies on the way down from the tower. Knight remained wary toward the Hesperine warrior. If only Cassia could persuade him to stay in her rooms and get off his feet. After their ordeal, he would not tolerate being that far from her side, and she would not expect it of him.

When Kadi led them into the main hall, Cassia took in the entire room with a glance.

Lio was nowhere in sight.

Kadi delivered Cassia to the Tenebrans, who had gathered on one end of the room. As Kadi rejoined her fellow Hesperines on the opposite side of the chamber, the men's gazes followed her, except for virtuous Benedict's. He glued himself to Cassia's side, as she had predicted, and a reassured Perita took her leave. Cassia managed to convince Knight to lie down on the edge of the gathering where he could rest, but only by giving him a down-stay command. Alas, that would not work on human knights.

"How are you, Your Ladyship?" Benedict fretted.

"In one piece. And you?"

He cast a wary gaze upon Chrysanthos. "All too well. I should not have been so far from you during the attack. I assure you, it won't happen again."

"As you assured me multiple times last night. Do not berate yourself so."

"Just stay close, Your Ladyship. You can rely on me, even without my sword or the assistance of a mage."

"Your magely assistant has deserted you?" Cassia made sure not to sound as relieved as she felt.

"I'm afraid Eudias is taken ill. The spells he cast in your chambers did him in."

She felt a twinge of regret. Could Eudias be suffering from the abnormalities in his aura that Skleros had described? "He didn't seem to have any trouble with all the weather magic he worked on the way here."

Benedict shook his head. "It's this place. He said there's so much Hesperine magic everywhere, casting revelatory spells is like counting rats after they've eaten your grain."

So nothing ailed the apprentice but an abundance of Hesperine magic. "Poor fellow. Are you sure it was the magic and not the sight of such beauty that overwhelmed him? He's quite innocent." Cassia spared a glance for Benedict's amulet of Andragathos.

Benedict made a point not to glance across the room at the seductive company. All it would take was one Hesperine to bewitch Cassia, but Lio was not here.

There would be no chance to thank Javed, for he was not in attendance. Cassia looked for Mak and Lyros, thinking the three of them could contrive to break the ice between their two factions, but they and their mentor were not in evidence either. The thought of Mak and Lyros patrolling the border with Hippolyta made Cassia feel safe. Yet there was an anxiety rising in her that even their protection could not assuage.

Cassia was here in Orthros, in a room full of Hesperines, and none of them were Lio. The hall was not a vast chamber, but the space between the mortals and the Hesperines who had saved them felt too great.

It felt enormous the moment Lio walked in on the opposite side of the room, as far from the humans as he could get.

FIRST MANEUVER

ASSIA COULD SEE LIO properly at last, but must not look. She let her gaze travel the room, taking in the shining stone floors, the sideboards of food that filled the chamber with rich smells, the wrought iron candelabras that cast them all in warm light. There at last, Lio. His dark head, his handsome face half turned from her, his shoulders she had once clung to while he…

Cassia looked away. The room felt so warm, although no fire burned anywhere. Magic. He sported the beginnings of a beard. What would that feel like against her skin? For the first time, he wore a braid. Would it work a spell on her to touch it when she ran her fingers through his hair?

It was unbearable. Last night he had been her rescue. He had held her in his arms. She had touched him. And now she must stand on the opposite side of the room from him and pretend to be diplomatic.

She slid another glance toward him, then away, then back again as soon as she could without being noticed. Each time, another little coil of heat spun through her. His well-groomed stubble suited the sharp lines of his jaw very well indeed. He had exchanged the solid black robes he had worn in the pass for his black silk formal robes with their mesmerizing red, white and silver embroidery. She remembered the way the fabric moved with him when he danced.

How proud he had been of the braided cords of silver-and-white silk he wore around his neck, which signified his status as an initiate ambassador. A shiny, new silver medallion of office hung from them upon his chest. She longed to go closer and make out the details of the emblem. Put a hand to him there. Congratulate him properly.

These meager snatches were so far from enough. Every glimpse did something wondrous to her, but deepened her worry. All she could not observe last night was now before her eyes.

He looked different. Not because of the fetching stubble. He looked...*older.*

That was impossible. Hesperines aged in centuries, not in months. Lio had aged far less than she in the time they'd been apart. Yet something about him had changed.

Lio's mother drifted into the space between Hesperines and humans with a smile that could bring hardened warriors to their knees. "Now that a night's rest has restored you, please avail yourselves of the bounty of the Queens' table, while we take this first opportunity for conversation without duress."

Chrysanthos commenced self-important oratory, starting with lies about himself. He was humble, well-meaning Adelphos from Tenebra. Not the royal mage, not from Namenti, a neutral party who had nothing to do with the debacle at the last Summit. Tenebran, but one who had gained diplomatic experience representing the king to the Orders in Cordium. A very tidy story.

Cassia stole another look at Lio, trying to pin down what most concerned her. His features were more chiseled, the lines of his face tense, as if with strain. As he drew nearer the divide, he moved with his familiar grace. But there was no evidence of the blitheness and good humor, so beloved to her, which balanced his seriousness of character. He carried himself as if he bore as many burdens as his elders.

Human and Hesperine, they had all borne their fair share of fear and grief lately. She had never expected it to show in Lio like this. It never had before, even when Tenebra had confronted him with human violence for the first time. Lucis's brutality had almost cost Lio and the others in the embassy their lives, but Lio's faith had not been shaken. Here among his own people, after last night's victory, why did he look so drawn and careworn?

Ah, such confident pronouncements Cassia made to herself about his nature. How much time had she had to become so expert? A precious handful of nights. Lio would be eighty-nine this Winter Solstice. Here he was, surrounded by the folk who had cherished him for all those years. And she presumed to know him after one brief affair.

When she heard Chrysanthos present her, she stepped forward and curtsied, trying to keep her attention on Komnena. From the corner of her eye, she could see Lio come to stand beside his mother. Was Cassia's official re-introduction to Lio at hand at last?

His hand would touch hers. She would have a chance to stand closer to him, if only for an instant. She had committed treason to stand here and stare hopefully at the edge of Lio's embroidered sleeve, wondering what it meant that he would not look at her.

Komnena smiled. "Everyone here in Orthros is delighted to have you, Lady Cassia. How well our ambassadors recall your contributions at the Equinox Summit."

"Thank you, Chamberlain."

"I trust you remember my son, who served in our embassy to Tenebra." She rested a hand briefly on Lio's arm. "Allow me to present Ambassador Deukalion."

Did every Hesperine in the room hear Cassia's heart jump? She schooled her face as she turned to him. She dipped her knees. Met his gaze.

Everything but his jewel blue eyes faded from her awareness. The feeling tested every one of her careful preparations, and she had to remind herself they stood in front of a room full of attentive observers.

He was going to touch her next, skin to glove. His fingers slid under hers, trapped them. Fabric separated her skin from his, but she felt his touch everywhere. It warmed her through and through and made him feel real to her again at last.

How well she knew his hands. How well his hands had known her. Long, elegant hands, powerful and tender at the same time.

None of the onlookers could see her memories. No mortal could hear her thoughts. In her mind, she whispered his name for him alone.

There was no sign of his smile as he bowed, only his gaze, unwavering. His pupils dilated.

He lifted her fingers, and she felt his mouth through fabric, as she had first felt his touch through a handkerchief. He gave her a mere brush upon her knuckles. A courtier's kiss.

"I remember," she murmured.

"A pleasure to see you again, Lady Cassia."

There, at last. His voice. Not magic, but his actual voice in her ears. His resonant baritone was still gravelly as after the battle.

Something was wrong.

A great deal of time seemed to pass between the moment his lips touched her and the moment her hand, released from his touch, returned to her side. Then it was over. They had touched. They had spoken. They had survived their first public encounter.

He folded his hands behind his back and glanced at his mother. Cassia followed his cue and tore her attention away.

"Please allow my son to act as your escort during your time here," Komnena said. "He will be happy to show you all that Orthros has to offer a lady such as yourself."

Cassia had thought it difficult to recover from what she had expected to hear. But those words were so unforeseen, it took a moment for their full impact to reach her. Her courtier's mouth was miles ahead of her as she responded with respectful platitudes.

On the edge of Cassia's vision, Benedict stepped nearer, homing to her side again. Ready to make it clear Flavian's intended already had an escort.

Komnena turned to meet him, graced him with one of her smiles, and absorbed him in conversation so smoothly no one would believe she had just blown him far off course.

Cassia would get to spend time with Lio during the embassy, openly, in defiance of all her uncertainty about how soon she might see him, if at all. The Queens' own Chamberlain was blockading for them.

Cassia wanted to believe this meant Lio was eager to see her again. But he was a diplomat, one who had been sent to Tenebra before. This was almost certainly an assignment. She did not know if he had requested the duty.

My mind can always reach yours. I will always be your Sanctuary.

There could be no doubt in her mind he cared about her. But did he protect her in honor of the past they had shared, or in the hope of what the present might bring?

Now it was just the two of them, alone in a crowd. Permission granted to look at him.

The shadows under his eyes were as dark as her own. He had lost weight. He looked weary and gaunt and oblivious to everyone except the person he gazed upon. Her. Cassia's throat tightened painfully.

It's all right now, she longed to say. *The fight is behind us.*

But it wasn't, not yet. Tonight an entirely new campaign must begin.

Lio turned slightly and glanced ahead of them, lifting his brows in invitation. She stepped forward to stand beside him, and they began a walk around the room.

This chamber was an ally to those seeking privacy. The thick carpets and tapestries wrapped everyone's conversations close about them. Whether there was also Hesperine magic at work to obscure their words, Cassia did not know.

Listening ears were not the only consideration. There was also Lio and her and half a year of not speaking, except for that single, fraught exchange in the storm. Cassia chose her words with care and took it upon herself to make the first maneuver.

LADY IN CRIMSON

ER BLOOD BEAT WITHin reach.

And the power of his need to reach for her was frightening. A room full of people, including his own mother, was not a sufficient deterrent. Sir Benedict's white knuckles and the mages' wary gazes did not temper the Hunger. A healing session with Javed right before his arrival had barely made his Craving bearable. Only Mak and Lyros's ward kept Lio from touching her.

Goddess, she is so beautiful. Goddess, I need her. Goddess, give me strength.

Every last inch of his body did battle with him. His fangs throbbed with eagerness in his gums. The pain in his mouth was rivaled only by the discomfort below his waist. It was a mercy his people favored loose attire. It would have been a greater mercy if the months of blood deprivation had somehow reduced the circulation in that direction. He needn't fear he would be ready for her, only how long he would last. His body thought he was starving and, with every primal urge he possessed, demanded he take what would save him.

Here she was, she who was more important to him than any other, and he could not maintain the most basic rudiments of self-control.

Precisely because she was so important. She was his Cassia.

He had so carefully planned all the things he would say to her when this moment came, but now he couldn't speak for the effort of mastering himself. He dare not open his mouth, for all he could think of was opening it on her throat.

The raw tension in his body made their leisurely pace around the room agonizing. He gripped his hands behind his back and stopped breathing so he could not smell her. He wanted to drink her scent until the moment he could taste her blood. He wanted the Blood Union to fill him up with her until she felt so close the space they must keep between their bodies did not matter.

But he had to hold his Gift in check at all costs. Else he would be truly lost. He must make do with drinking in the sight of her.

A challenge to his self-control all on its own. Her hair had never appeared so lustrous, gleaming with autumn shades he had not known were there. With each step she took, the beaded toes of her slippers peeked at him from under the undulating hem of her gown.

And what a gown. Even in his imaginings, he had never beheld her in such a dress. This was nothing like the shapeless scraps in her father's house colors she had worn at Solorum. This was a fabric war cry, a seduction dyed the rich crimson shade of blood. The narrow sleeves ended in points that drew his gaze to her dainty hands. He only regretted that her white gloves hid her freckles from him.

He dare not let his gaze roam elsewhere. The gown's deceptively simple cut and fine velvet texture worshiped her lissome shape, without revealing anything. Except her throat.

And the fact that she was even thinner than she had been before. Why did she appear as if she had been starving with him all this time? The condition of her hair was a good sign—her health did not yet suffer. But she would certainly become ill if she kept on like this.

The thought that she had gone without roused an unbearable sense of wrongness in him. Regardless of the cause of her fast, starting tonight, he would see to it she was well fed.

He halted that thought in its tracks. Tonight he could do no more than look upon her and listen to the sound of her footfalls next to his. And now her voice.

"Ambassador Deukalion."

So good to hear her say his name. So good to say hers. "Yes, Lady Cassia."

She eyed his neck. Her gaze proceeded downward to linger on his chest. Warmth raced through him.

"I recall it was 'Initiate Ambassador' last time we met," she said. "Did your Queens reward your deeds in Tenebra with advancement?"

Oh. She was looking at his cords and medallion of office.

He must draw breath, if he was to speak further. Her fragrance washed over him and went straight to his groin. Roses! She never wore scent, but tonight she had perfumed herself with roses. *Their* roses, the ones whose scattered petals he had licked off her bare thighs after the first time they had made love.

"It was somewhat a matter of debate whether I should be credited with deeds or misdeeds. My Queens did me the honor of elevating me to full ambassador. They also restricted my duties to Orthros."

Cassia's face was as impassive as ever, but he had no trouble recognizing the subtle signs of her surprise. "I am uncertain whether to offer my congratulations or sympathies."

"I shall gladly accept anything you have to give." He was not above begging. He made an effort to unclench his hands. "I understand I am to offer you my congratulations on your upcoming betrothal, my lady." Not the first subject he had intended to address. Not at all.

"I thank you, but you would be premature."

If words could quench thirst, those were the first that had allayed his tonight. He could only rejoice Flavian's claim on her remained tenuous. "The news we hear of King Lucis's court is not always accurate. It was my impression your understanding with your suitor was final. I hope I have not spoken out of turn."

"Not at all, Ambassador. My father the king does indeed intend to give me in marriage to my Lord Flavian, although His Majesty and Lord Titus are still in the process of settling their agreement. His Majesty excels at ensuring a bright future for all his offspring, and I am no exception."

Lio sent up a silent prayer of thanks. Cassia had made it safely back to him. They were no longer talking about the marriage he had believed to be the greatest threat to her, but the revelation that her father had not intended for her to survive to her wedding. "I can appreciate what such a union means to you, arranged by the king himself."

"I'm certain you can."

"Have you been well?" Such insufficient words to convey how he had feared for her and dreaded what she had suffered in Flavian's company. A meaningless question, after what had happened last night.

"I have been well enough."

Unable to bear true Union, Lio tried to read her face, her body, and her voice for any sign of hidden hurts. "This has been a time of great uncertainty at Solorum. I hope you have not had cause to fear."

Her aura softened. Moved by his concern, perhaps. "I have faced my share of difficulties in the palace, but I am well accustomed to that."

"Your devoted suitor must surely go out of his way to ensure your protection in these troubled times."

For just a moment, Cassia met Lio's gaze. "He has behaved entirely honorably toward me."

The relief that overtook Lio made him weak in the knees. "I should hope he has."

"It sounds as if you have a great many questions about what has transpired in Tenebra since you left." She cast Lio a brief but searching glance. "Did not your assignments at home still relate to your people's dealings with mine?"

"Everything but, I regret to say."

"You have not been at all involved in relations between Tenebra and Orthros, then?"

Now. Now was the time to find the words he had longed to say to her. Or at least to make a start. "It has not been within my power to remain involved in Tenebran affairs, but I can assure you, Lady Cassia, I have remained entirely invested in your situation."

"You have been following the events in my kingdom, then."

"Not closely enough to satisfy me."

She really looked at him now, tilting her head up so she could look at him eye-to-eye. Did she even realize how she treated him to a stunning display of her throat?

"If you are interested in word from Tenebra, Ambassador Deukalion, perhaps I could sate your hunger for news."

Cassia always knew what she was doing, every move she made and every word she chose. Of course she knew that one little motion and that handful of words were, to him, utterly erotic. Hespera's Mercy, let that be the invitation he thought it was.

He drew breath to speak again, and the deeper notes in her scent reached him. An exciting, bitter smell he did not recognize, sweetened by roses. Then the snap of cassia.

She had used the soap. That was undoubtedly an invitation. It had always been her secret sign to him she wanted a tryst.

"I would hope to make our time here mutually beneficial." She looked ahead again, back straight, hands clasped lightly before her. "Given that affairs between Orthros and Tenebra are no longer your responsibility, I would not wish it to be an imposition on you that you are called upon to be my guide for the duration of the embassy."

Hespera's *Mercy*. Invitation? Nay, her words were closer akin to evaluation.

It was the king's daughter who spoke. Perhaps he should have expected it, but he hadn't, and it galled him. This strategic approach. These probing words that said one thing and meant another. None of that had any place between them. "How can you imagine the opportunity to spend time with a lady such as yourself would ever be an imposition?"

Her smile stunned him. That smile was all Cassia. No calculation. Only her and the sadness she carried as if it were her second skin. "Orthros is your home. You have much to occupy you here. It would be understandable if your duty to attend me has pulled you away from your preferred pursuits."

She was not sure of him. She sought some sign that he desired to be near her, reassurance that his presence here was not merely a fulfillment of obligation or his response to a crisis. He had been right to fear. His message to her on the Equinox had not been enough. Goddess, what he had done to Cassia's attackers last night had not been enough. What in that violence had said anything to her about love?

Mak and Lyros were also right. Lio had wasted enough effort agonizing over his failure to tell Cassia how important she was to him.

He would put her uncertainties to rest. Now and for good.

As they walked, he let the distance between them shrink. He would endure it. She needed him closer. "You imagine I am not impatient to resume the pursuits that occupied me during the Summit? On the contrary, I remain deeply committed to ensuring the best possible relations between Hesperine and human." He looked down at her and waited until her gaze darted up to meet his. "It is my greatest vice. I am single-minded, once I find a challenge to sink my teeth into." He gave her a hint of a smile. Just enough for a glimpse of his canines.

Her melancholy fled, routed by a lovely flush that made her blood hum beneath her skin. What a reward for his comment. What torture.

Her gaze lingered on his mouth an instant longer than proper, then darted away. "I should think your firmness of purpose would be considered a virtue."

Lio swallowed. "Alas, my passion has not met with universal approval. Since the night I left Solorum, my constant requests to the Queens for reassignment to Tenebra have met with adamant refusal. With so much at stake, it was not deemed an appropriate task for someone of my tender years, despite my insistence that my role in the Summit prepared me well."

"With heartfelt respect for your Queens, I must agree with you. It seems to me your contributions to the cause of peace have been sorely missed."

"I am here tonight in the hopes of discovering whether that is true. I finally succeeded in convincing the Queens that my place is here, involved with Tenebra."

"How generous of them to grant such an escort to me. I count myself fortunate to be the subject of your personal attention, Ambassador."

"I can promise you an unforgettable stay. We shall see to it your time is filled with all that interests and delights you. I seem to recall you and your hound often take your exercise on the palace grounds." He looked across the room at Knight, wondering if he could still rely on Cassia's protector to take a bite out of him if he tried anything inappropriate. The dog's repose, complete with lolling, drooling tongue, suggested not. "Tell me, Lady Cassia, do you still enjoy a walk in the woods?"

That simmering warmth in her gaze, the little secret smile at the corners of her mouth. That was what he had been waiting for. "I love nothing better. I am very sorry to say I have had little opportunity in the last six months. I miss it dearly."

"Really? I was sure you were surrounded by young warriors eager to take you hunting." There was nothing like a token display of jealousy to assure a lover of one's interest. Token jealousy. Nothing more. "I hear one lord in particular is renowned for his horsemanship and very fond of the chase."

"I have no interest in sport." She glided beside him like a swan, chin high. "Only those who do not play can win my attention."

"Of that I have no doubt."

"The affairs that engross me are not games."

"I know," he said with all seriousness. "This time has been fruitful for you."

She glanced at him, and he caught a glimpse of her surprise again. "It has."

"I only hope *you* do not feel your duty to the embassy is an imposition on you." Now at last they came to the first, most important question he had intended to ask her.

Her eyes widened ever so slightly. "An imposition on *me?*"

That she let such candid words slip through her composure gave Lio his answer.

"I am most honored to be welcomed among your people, Ambassador Deukalion," she hastened to add, her guise of calm in place again. "My inclusion in the embassy came as a surprise, to be sure, but an imposition? Certainly not."

"Why should it surprise you, when you received a similar invitation to the council table during the Equinox Summit?"

"I had hoped to see this request for my presence in the same light, but I did not wish to presume. I take nothing for granted."

"Nor do I." He lowered his voice. "But whatever you see in this request, it could not possibly be a presumption. The invitation is yours. Make of it all that you will."

She drifted to a halt, rotating to face him, and the candles behind her cast a glow around the edges of her hair. "Then I shall consider it the opportunity I have long awaited and hoped for."

Hope. Lio did not know when he had felt so much of it. "I would be very interested to discuss all that you've achieved since we last met. Would you care to walk the grounds here?" He could not resist giving her a suggestive smile, although it surely appeared less seductive with his lips shut. "My grounds look their best after dark. Nights in Orthros are unlike anywhere else."

"What a lovely invitation, Ambassador. But I'm afraid a walk is not what I have in mind. All I wish to do is go to bed. After last night—"

"—you endured a horrific ordeal. Of course you need your rest." Lio quashed his hopes. How could he? He must not make such demands on her. It was too soon.

"Indeed, after the great difficulties I had to overcome to finally reach my goal, I can think of nothing else but bed." She covered her mouth and feigned quite a believable yawn, using it to disguise the way her gaze swept over him.

Shameless. Divine. Lio's blood sang in his veins. She *did* want a tryst. Tonight. *Now.* Merciful Goddess, the wait was at an end.

"You appear quite exhausted, Lady Cassia. I apologize for keeping you, when you must want nothing more than to get off your feet." He leaned down, as if to speak to her in confidence. The scent of her hair filled his nose, and he saw her shiver as his own breath touched her skin. "You needn't linger at our little gathering any longer. You have fulfilled your duty to my honored mother, I assure you. It will ease the minds of all those who are concerned for you if you retire early."

"How kind of you to reassure me, Ambassador. I think I shall do as you suggest."

Lio felt the air behind him shift and heard the tread of boots on the stone floor. A male, medium height and broad-shouldered, who smelled of ripe wheat and the tanned hide of goats long since sacrificed for his attire. It was the man who had been breathing down Cassia's neck earlier. The relentless Tenebran was apparently bent on reclaiming her and had broken free of Lio's mother.

As Cassia's keeper closed in, Lio's frustration gripped him, a physical force. How dare this man come between him and his Grace?

Lio could not subdue his animosity. But he forced himself not to take another step closer to Cassia. Instead, he straightened and turned to face the intruder.

"Benedict." Cassia at least succeeded in delivering a friendly greeting. "Have you met Ambassador Deukalion?"

The man gave Lio a brief, rigid bow. "Ambassador."

"Ambassador," Cassia echoed. It sounded like a completely different word to Lio when she said it. Not formal at all. "Allow me to present Sir Benedict, First Knight of Segetia, my Lord Flavian's dearest friend."

Sir Benedict's granite expression did not change. "You flatter me, Your Ladyship."

"Not in the least, Benedict." Cassia smiled.

She called him by his first name? The benevolent expression on her face was genuine. She did not regard this man as a threat. So, he was an inconvenience, but an innocent bystander. Lio must endeavor to remember that each time he felt the urge to subject the man to a Moon Warrior, then finish him off with a Mortal Vice.

"Benedict." Cassia took his arm. "I have a confession. I believe I may have overtaxed myself. I think I need more rest than I thought, after last night."

The man's aura filled with worry. "Allow me to escort you to your room right away, Your Ladyship."

Cassia gave Lio a curtsy that presented him with a lovely glimpse of her neck and her neckline. The view could not have had a greater effect on him, had she worn half as much clothing. His body might be deprived, but his imagination was much too well fed.

Sir Benedict would see Cassia delivered, supposedly untarnished, to her rooms, never knowing what awaited her once she was abed. That gave Lio enough satisfaction that he could let her go. For the moment.

Just one more touch before he was forced to surrender. He caught her hand. As his lips touched her gloved fingers, the scent of the blood under the fabric and her skin brought moisture to his mouth. "Sweet dreams, Lady Cassia."

RESCUE

CASSIA KNEW A COCOON of Hesperine magic wrapped her room. When Perita left her and shut the door, Cassia felt enclosed in another world. She could not hear her friend's footsteps retreating down the stairs. Callen's vigilance at the bottom of the tower was of no concern. The gathering in the main hall seemed far away.

No more wondering or waiting. She needn't even endure the excruciating crowd any longer. Lio would come to her right now.

He wanted her. Lio still wanted her.

Cassia put her crimson gown away in her trunk and pulled on her gardening dress.

After the way Lio had kept looking at her earlier, Cassia did hope he would have occasion to take her crimson gown off of her one night soon. That was a fine fantasy. One she might save for later, though. Tonight, it must be her gardening dress.

She could not be more obvious than to don the gown she had worn the night she and Lio had first become lovers. But no forwardness on her part had ever sent him running the other way. Far from it. He had refused to touch her until she had been certain of her desires.

It pleased him for her to be open with him about what she wanted...to show him...to speak of it aloud. She need never be coy with him. He did not expect her to behave like a reticent maiden. He wanted her just as she was.

Tonight was further proof. He had answered her attempts at flirtation by agreeing to a tryst. Whether or not she could credit her novice efforts as a seductress, her plan was succeeding already.

She smoothed the front laces of her gown, suddenly nervous. She wanted to lie down on the bed and present an irresistible image for Lio whenever he arrived. But now that the moment was near at hand, a sense of awkwardness overtook her. It had been six months, and she had only ever made love for four nights in her life. What if she seemed out of practice to him?

She had no idea how much practice he had acquired since.

She pushed the thought away with all her might. It shouldn't matter. Tonight was theirs, and she would not taint it with such thoughts.

Knight sprawled on his rug in the sitting room and looked up at her with the canine grin he had worn all evening.

"Thank you, darling. I'm glad you think I look well." She knelt and rubbed his ears.

His mouth was going to drip on that fine carpet. Let Hesperine magic clean it, for she wouldn't scold him. She buried her fingers in his ruff, which was always at hand when she felt troubled. Then she returned to the other room and dawdled by the bed.

How much time did she have before Lio managed to excuse himself from the gathering? Perhaps she should position herself by a window. Let him see her standing in a beam of moonlight, as he had that very first night.

"Knight seems to like me better than he did before. He doesn't appear to mind leaving you alone with me."

Cassia spun toward the sound of Lio's voice. It was he who stood by the window in an aura of moonlight.

He looked just like the apparition of him she had seen on the night of the Spring Equinox, clad in his embroidered veil hours robe of deep blue silk, his hair loose, except for that new braid.

The light did not shine through him now. This was no illusion. He was here. She would touch him at last.

"Knight knows what makes his mistress unhappy, and what lifts her melancholy."

Lio didn't move. "Have you been unhappy, Cassia?"

"Yes." The word simply came out. In a whisper, but it came. "I have been many things. But yes, unhappy too."

Not what she had meant to say. There were so many better things to speak of than the time they'd been apart. They needn't speak at all.

She regretted it already. She had confessed. Now that she had breathed a word of unhappiness, it had risen up inside her. She must never let it to do that. It was too hard to push back down.

"And what lifts your melancholy?" Lio asked.

Why must they speak of her feelings? Why had she not expected this? It was not only desires Lio always coaxed out of her. "Something I thought out of reach."

The air in the room moved, and he was suddenly standing before her. He took her hands. So careful. As if she might disappear.

What he pressed into her hands was not a kiss or a caress, but a cloth wrapped around something. As he unfolded it, a familiar aroma wafted out of it, albeit one she had never smelled from food before.

"What is this?" she asked.

In the light from the windows, she could just see his tight-lipped smile. "A cassia pastry."

A laugh rose out of her in defiance of all it had cost her to stand here in Orthros with Lio over a pastry. "I didn't know I'm named after a pastry, too."

"I fear I monopolized you in the main hall, and you never had a chance to avail yourself of the sideboard. You haven't eaten a bite since you arrived."

Cassia sighed. "We are forbidden to eat any food a Hesperine offers us while we are here."

He raised his eyebrows. "That will be impractical, if not impossible, although I cannot say I am surprised at the notion."

"Well." Her boldness had not entirely deserted her. "*I* have no intention of refraining. I look forward with great anticipation to all I shall eat while they aren't watching."

He folded her fingers one by one around the cloth-wrapped roll. He was touching her. Wonderful little unnecessary, luxurious touches. "Start with this," he instructed.

She left her hands in his a moment longer. "You won't let me eat alone, will you?"

"Certainly not. I'm famished. But ladies first."

Famished. That was as good as a promise. She slid her hands slowly out of his and with great care tucked the napkin closer around the pastry. "Ladies first is a very Tenebran notion. Let us do things the Orthros way."

"The Orthros way insists I be considerate of your needs. You should eat. You need your strength."

She turned and walked to the little table beside the bed, showing him the back of her neck as she set the pastry down. "Do I?"

When he spoke, she could hear he had not moved any nearer. "I'm worried about you. Have you been eating enough?"

Did he imagine she could give a thought to anything but him at this moment? How impossible. How very like him to be concerned.

She glanced over her shoulder at him. "Speaking of eating enough—"

"Go ahead," he urged her. "Have a taste."

She would have more than a taste, if only he would come closer. He must know it was not food she hungered for tonight. "Lio…" She turned around slowly.

His gaze was fixed on the table behind her. "I've been waiting to find out how well you like your namesake."

The nonchalant words stilled her. She hid her hands in her skirts, afraid the cracks in her armor would show. As if he could not sense them.

He could sense what it was she wanted. He could probably smell it on her already. And yet all he would talk of was a pastry. He was still standing on the other side of the room.

Was he stalling?

He lounged back against the wall. "I hope you actually like the flavor, after all I've said to you about it. But it's all right if you don't, you know."

Had he changed his mind? Why would he even come to her, make her hope like this, if he had changed his mind?

Cassia swallowed. "Lio, are you all right? Is there anything…troubling you? I noticed as soon as we arrived, you look…"

"What, you don't like it?" He showed her no teeth as he grinned and rubbed his hand over his chin once, then twice.

"That's not what I meant." It was so unlike Lio to make any superfluous motions. He was not prone to nervous gestures. "Actually, I like it very much."

"If you change your mind, I'll shave it off for you."

"Shave it?" she said lightly. "After you spent all this time working to grow it out?"

"Your pastry is getting cold," he reminded her.

He was evading her. Why would he ever need to evade her? Had he forgotten that was not necessary between them?

Whatever changed, even if they could not get back what they had, she had believed this one thing would still hold true: their pact to simply *speak*. Without pretense. Without consequences.

He had just made it clear that was no longer the case.

A sense of loss threatened, one unlike any she had known. She had acknowledged she might lose him as a lover. But she could not fathom going back to the way she had lived before she had known him, before there had been one other person in her world she knew she could trust forever.

Cassia turned back to the pastry. She filled the silence with the useless motion of unfolding and refolding the cloth. Another second, and the silence would become a confrontation. Honey soaked through the cloth, warm on her fingers, but it would not be warm for long.

She could not stand this. Lio, her confidant, her ally—her friend. He was too precious to lose, even if he never touched her again. She had fought far too hard. She would not give up now. They had fought too hard together.

Their Oath endured. She had never broken it. He just needed to be reminded. One of them had to renew the pact.

Cassia swallowed. One of them would have to confront. One out of two must take the risk and brave embarrassment or disappointment.

She knew who it would be. Risk? Risk was her medium, and confrontation was her art. She had not come all this way to avoid risk.

Cassia faced him again and met his gaze. "Lio, you have broken our promise."

Hesperines were so composed at any given moment, she had not known they could go still. But Lio did. The hand he had been about to run over his beard again sank to his side and halted in place like the limb of a statue.

"I thought—" He came back to life and scoured his hair with both his hands. Another moment of painful silence. Then he ran his hands through his hair again. "I took our conversation earlier to mean my interruption was not unwelcome. I see I misunderstood."

"Interruption?" she echoed. What could he mean by that?

"Yes, that's too mild a word, isn't it? Perhaps interference would be more appropriate." Lio cleared his throat, but his voice emerged roughly. "Please don't imagine it was something I did lightly. Give me that much credit. I know better than anyone what lives are at stake. But I feared *your* life was at stake, and the proof came almost too late for me to protect you. What would you have had me do?"

At this moment, she wanted nothing so much as the Hesperines' Blood Union. He must have felt everything that had overtaken her in these past few moments—the nervousness, the disappointment, the loss. She was at a disadvantage with nothing but human observation to give her insight into his words, which became more and more of a mystery to her every moment.

No, she had something else. Their Oath.

"Lio, please say what you really mean. Just *talk to me.*"

"I couldn't be more honest than I am," he protested. "You think it wasn't a difficult decision?"

She shook her head. "It's as if we're having two different conversations. This isn't how it should be between us." She took a step forward. Let her be the first to start closing the distance. "I'll keep our promise if you will. I know you haven't forgotten. It's just been a long, difficult time since we last spoke, and we've both had to make sacrifices, I know. To get through the day—or the night—there are times when you have to push the words back down inside yourself so hard you think you'll choke. You can't even admit to yourself what you're feeling, because if you do, it will make it true, and then you will be able to do nothing but feel."

What a terrible, inconvenient time for her own feelings to undermine her. She swallowed the lump in her throat. "I know, Lio. I of all people know. But you don't ever have to do that with me. If we can't be as we were—if you don't want me the way you did—I have no claim on you, I know that. But I trust you. I had forgotten how until you, Lio. I'll work hard to keep that, if only we can still trust each other. Our Oath still stands. You can say everything to me. No fear. No censure. No danger. So please." The first tear slid down her face, as if obeying what she urged Lio to do. "Speak."

Still he didn't come near her. But he stopped looking away and looked at her. That expression on his face…as if she were both forgiveness and condemnation.

"That's the promise you meant?" he asked.

"Of course. It's too important to break. Please. Keep it with me."

"That promise is constant, Cassia. It calls for no effort, like the motion of the blood in our veins."

Her tears overflowed, and she lifted her hands, thinking to hide her face. But she didn't have to do that. She stood there with her hands in front of her as the first sob overtook her.

By the time the second struck, he was there, his arms around her, his hand on her head, pressing her face against his chest. She closed her fingers around the front of his robe. Not enough. She wrapped her arms around him.

The full length of her was pressed against him, molded from cheek to thigh to the softness of his robes and the strength of his body beneath. That was Lio's hand on her head, his breath upon her hair, his arm around her waist. His scent enveloped her, rich with aromas she never could name. With it came the feeling she also had no name for, as if the very space around her filled with something more restful than sleep, more powerful than magic, which made her feel at ease and strong at the same time.

She was holding him again.

At last. After all this. She had kept her promise to him, the one he had not even heard her make, the one that had given her a reason to rise from bed every morning after she lay awake all night weeping like this because he was out of reach.

"What promise"—another sob shuddered through her—"did you think I meant?"

"I told you I would let you fight. I tried so hard and so long to stand back and not do anything that would get in your way."

"You-ou have. You did."

"Until now. I waited as long as I could to tell my people about you, for fear they would interfere with your plans. I still feared you would be angry that I had them bring you to Orthros."

"You. It was you."

His arms tightened around her. He was holding her so close. Let it never stop.

"Of course it was me. But I was almost too late."

"I'm not angry. I'm so—so glad. Lio. I'm so glad to be near you again. I'm so glad to be near you," she repeated, because she had tried so hard not to say it all night.

She sucked in little breaths between sobs. How could she make it all this way only to fall apart? It was all right. Lio had already seen her at her weakest.

His hands tightened on her, then relaxed, then tightened again, roaming over her hair and back. He seemed compelled to touch her. Holding him this close, she could not help but feel the evidence of his desire rigid against her belly. He still felt lust in her arms.

He framed her face in his hands and turned it up toward him. "We can't be as we were."

She felt as if her heartbeat halted in her chest.

He gazed into her eyes, his own intense with promise. "It wasn't enough. I want so much more for us."

Her heart leapt. She pulled his face closer to her.

"I need you." His first kiss was on her forehead, the second on her eyelid. "I need you more than I ever have." Her other eyelid. Her tear-streaked cheekbone. "Do you need me?"

"I don't sleep for needing you. I lay awake at night crying like this because you're not there. I never cry. But I cry for you."

His hand descended to caress her neck. She shivered, and she knew he could feel how her pulse raced faster at his touch, inviting him. But when he trailed a finger over her skin, it was not her vein he traced. He hooked his finger in the garden twine around her neck and drew her pendant out of her gown. It came to rest on her chest, throbbing between them.

"A piece of marble from our shrine." His tone was reverent.

"It's a shard that came off the glyph stone."

"I can feel the magic more powerfully than ever before. You kept offering your blood there."

"I have done all I could to keep our Sanctuary."

"So have I, in my heart. But now I can keep you in my arms."

With his forehead resting on hers and her face in his hands, he breathed, his lips parted as if he thirsted, waiting for liquid to drip into his mouth. She nuzzled his face, trading breath for breath. Did he think to drink her tears, when she could give him something better?

He took her lower lip between his, swift, tentative. Next her upper lip. Hungry, hesitant touches. She knew. They were both so hungry, but the feast was too sacred to devour. When he finally covered her lips with his, it was only for a moment. A perfect moment, when she felt his mouth, warm and damp, upon hers at last, and a current of heat opened up from her lips to the rest of her body.

"Cassia. I'm so hungry." His voice shook. That was how much he wanted her.

"So am I."

She took a step back, bringing him with her. The bed was somewhere in that direction. On the way, she pulled his face to hers again and kissed him the way she had yearned to all night.

And then the bed was under her back. His hands trapped her wrists as his mouth came down on hers. She opened her lips to make way for his tongue, and it plunged into her mouth, the way his teeth and rhabdos would plunge inside her. His fangs pressed against her lips. So swollen. He wanted her so.

His mouth scoured hers, then her jaw and throat. His stubble rasped over her skin, rough and new and exciting. She could feel the hard lengths of his teeth as he devoured her with his lips and tongue. The glyph shard throbbed as if invoked by his fangs.

He released one of her wrists, and his hand went to the front of her gown. Together they clawed at the laces, tugging them loose. Cool air and the heat of his kiss caressed her chest. His hand plunged under her breast, pushing it up until he could get her nipple into his mouth.

She jerked under him, closing her hand on the edge of her neckline where she held it out of his way. As he opened his whole mouth on her breast and sucked, she let her head fall back, just breathing, feeling, trying not to whimper.

His teeth pressed harder into the soft flesh of her breast. He drew her nipple deeper into his mouth. She arched her back, pressing up against his hold on her wrist and his body against her belly. His weight on her was an anchor as pleasure mounted inside her, unbound.

Beyond control. His front teeth grazed her nipple, and she bit her lip to keep from crying out. Would he do that again, if she asked him to?

She didn't have to ask. As much as he suckled, he nipped and grazed, each time a little harder. If he just bit down a little more, his fangs... Would he drink from her there? Could they do that?

He was off of her so fast the room spun over her, and the bed didn't feel solid anymore. She could only lay there, too surprised to move, and catch her breath.

The truth hit her a moment late, like an injury that left one numb at first, until pain awoke and brought home the real extent of the damage. He was going to stop.

She sat up, searching the light and shadows around her for where he had gone. He stood in the farthest corner of the room, where the beacon's light didn't quite reach. She could only make out that he had his back to her, his shoulders hunched.

"Lio, what's wrong?" She was already off the bed and on her feet.

"Cassia." The agony in his voice stunned her. Her name might have been forced out of him under magefire. Before she could take another step toward him, he barked, "Stay where you are. Please."

"Lio, is it something about me that's hurting you? If the heart hunters somehow poisoned me after all—"

"No! Hespera's Mercy, nothing like that."

"Lio, please tell me what's the matter. Tell me I can do something to help you."

"You are the only one who can."

"I'll do anything for you."

"I know." He let out a sound, half sigh, half groan. "But I don't want this for you."

Cassia stood still in the moonlight, giving him the length of the room between them as he had asked. She listened to the silence that meant he was not breathing. How ill he had looked all night. How carefully and desperately he had touched her.

He wanted her. He *needed* her. So much he could barely control it, barely endure it.

"Lio, you're starving."

At last he turned to face her and the light. Cassia gasped, and it took all her effort not to run to him.

He wasn't thinner, he was skin and bones, and he was shaking from head to toe. His eyes were wide and bloodshot, the blue in them a mere wire around his pupils. His dilated eyes shone at her through the darkness with a frenzied gleam she had never seen there.

Fierce, wild hunger. His fangs gleamed in the moonlight, burgeoning from his lips.

"Lio, what's happened to you? I've never seen you like this. Even earlier tonight, you didn't look this ill."

He started and put a hand to his mouth, as if to feel or perhaps hide his fangs. He gasped and stared at his hands. "My veil is gone?"

"You cast an illusion on yourself to hide your hunger? From me?"

He sucked in a breath. "If you can...just be patient with me...I *will* master myself."

"You need to feast. That's easily remedied."

"Easy? Not for you."

"It has always been a delight to me."

"Cassia, I might hurt you."

She tried to step nearer again. He flinched.

She halted in her tracks. "You would never hurt me."

"I'm not sure. I just—I need to wait until I'm sure."

"Why are you afraid of your hunger?"

He whispered as if he did not wish his own goddess to hear. "Because I'm not sure if I lost control last night. Hundreds of men died. How can I not know if I am the one who killed them?"

Cassia fell silent. She had felt the blood magic sweep over her and through her mind while its wielder held her. She had heard the heart hunters fall at her feet. Now she knew they had died in that moment.

She said gently, "The whole army of heart hunters fell with the ones who attacked me, didn't they?"

"Cassia, 'the boss' is a mind mage. He was controlling the heart hunters. I was trying to find out who he was. But then…their minds simply stopped telling their hearts to keep beating."

"You had to feel all of that. Worse than the Blood Union. You were in their thoughts when it happened."

"You must wonder why I agonize over their deaths. It must be hard to fathom how I could ever regret killing the men who did that to you."

"It is the thought that you killed without intention or necessity that horrifies you."

"You understand."

"You would never want to hurt anyone by accident. Any failure to control your magic is abhorrent to you. To resort to violence when there is another way is anathema to you."

"What they might have done to you—you were so frightened—I have never felt such rage. But I cannot afford to break. Not with power like mine."

Cassia narrowed the distance between them by one step. "Stop torturing yourself with such thoughts. You didn't kill anyone."

He met her gaze, his own beseeching. "You believe that."

"I know it." A few more steps toward him. At last, he did not try to stop her. "Your conscience rebels at the notion of trespassing upon a single person's Will. It is not in you to break the minds of hundreds with a thought. You would never lose control like that, and if you did, you still wouldn't hurt anyone. I know so, because I've held you in my arms when you've lost control."

She was near enough to reach for him. She took his shaking hands in hers.

His legs buckled. She scrambled to steady him as he went down on his knees before her.

He rested his face against her. "Thank you, Cassia."

"Please, let me help you."

He couldn't wait. Not a moment longer. He needed blood *now*. Cradling his head, she put her wrist before him.

REUNION

THE AGONY OF DEPRIVATION was nothing. The beautiful reality of her hurt more. Everything Lio wanted and could not have was real and within reach of his fangs.

Cassia was the beacon above him, aglow with radiant life force. A slender red aurora emanated from her wrist. The sound of her pulse wrung a hoarse cry from him.

The moment had come. His worst fear. His control was no longer enough.

But that was all right. She trusted him. He could trust himself.

His pulse hammered in his ears. His Gift roared within him. The hunger broke free of rational thought. He took hold of her wrist and closed his mouth over the light. He bit down hard, holding fast to salvation.

Cassia. She bloomed to life on his tongue and charged through his body. A shudder wracked him, and he groaned a plea.

A small, strong hand caressed his hair. His instincts took over. His jaw locked, his throat swallowed. She held him close as he glutted himself.

Warmth filled his gnawing gullet and spread, thawing the icy ache in his veins. The heat gathered in his loins. Her sigh soughed on his hearing.

The moment when the Blood Union had claimed him had come and gone; he knew only that he breathed in her relief, and her arousal pulsed through his blood with his own.

She enveloped him and filled him. Heady, hot courage. Rich liquid passion. The bitter spice of defiance. He had never forgotten the taste of her, but still she astonished him.

With each swallow, still more flavors overtook his senses. She held vast depths he had yet to tap. If he feasted on her for a thousand years, he might never plumb her farthest reaches.

But he wanted to. He wanted to taste her all.

Her wrist was not the floodgate he craved. Only the Craving gave him the Will to lift his head from his plate and reach for the banquet. She took his face in both hands, and the blood from her wrist made a warm, wet smear on his cheek.

Her blood on him, in him. He wanted to bathe and drown in her.

He pulled her down to him. As they landed together on the rug, her gown fell open again, baring her throat and breast. On her pendant of white marble, the bloodstains flared red as if fresh. The relic pulsed, their blood and passion made into a spell that stroked his senses and whispered to him that all was well.

When his fangs touched her neck, her heart made a sudden leap. Lio flared his nostrils and sucked in a deep breath. The scents of Cassia's excitement and her blood filled his head as he lay her throat open.

At last. All he feared he would never know again. Her blood welled and spurted on his tongue. He suckled her hard and flexed his hips. She rubbed against him, chest to chest, belly to belly. Had they ever doubted how this night would end?

He dragged her skirt up her thighs with both hands. Curse his robe that still separated them. But it fell before her advance in a moment.

Skin to skin, mouth to vein, mind to mind. Lio gripped her hips, opened his mouth wide, and bit down on her again as he drove inside her.

She let out a sound he had never heard her utter before. Silent Cassia cried out beneath him, an unmistakable cry of pleasure. His blood pounded. She held him to her throat and clutched him between her legs, one foot hooked around him.

"Don't stop," she begged. "Please, Lio. I can't bear it if you stop."

He flexed his mouth open, then closed, and drove inside her again, gliding through her slippery arousal and lodging in the snug grip of her krana. She was too tight. So tight. So good. It had been too long.

She shuddered under him as he bit and thrust. She ran her hands over his straining jaw, through his hair, down his back, as if she were hungry for him and could feast by touching.

"Don't stop," she moaned, her voice thick from the pressure at her throat. "Don't stop."

She never made a sound when he loved her. Their promise to speak had broken the silence that ruled her life, but not her pleasure. Until tonight.

This was how much she needed him. She told him in rough cries and low moans and the sound of his name. "Lio. Don't stop. Lio."

They needed this, and it was theirs for the taking at last. Her warmth poured out and filled him as his rhabdos filled her, and he knew they would survive.

Lio let out a growl of triumph and feasted upon his Grace. *His Grace.* He was inside her. He was drinking her blood. It was she who arched under him, her fingers that dug into his back and scored his shoulders. It was she who stoked his hunger with the sounds she made in the back of her throat. She who moved under him, around him, who drove away all thought. But no need to think. Not even of control.

He didn't know when his mind had sought hers and she had thrown hers open to him, only that there were no more barriers between them. His magic was already inside her. He lay deep within their Union, and her pleasure drowned him, sinking under his skin. She had never seen him like this. Neither had he. But it was all right.

He fed her more of his power. He had no end of it to give her. Her aura pulsed with pleasure, with him, taking his magic into her. He flexed his magic still deeper, feasting on her thoughts, worshiping her within.

"Don't stop," she begged him once more.

He surrendered his magic to her mind. Her pleasure came upon her, upon him, clutching around his rhabdos and making her damp hips buck and slide against him.

Release gripped in his back and thrust him into her. One spasm after another wracked him, half a year of need, and with wordless groans, he spilled inside her. Pleasure met in their Union and coursed together into joy, his and hers. Her blood filled with the taste of it, and he gorged on their climax.

Her cries quieted to gasps, and her heartbeat eased into a tantalizing percussion that promised to arouse him again. Another vein, another feast awaited them.

He unsheathed himself from her, only to mouth his way to the other side of her neck and take her in his teeth again. She let out another moan, raw and sensual. He wanted to hear her make those sounds again, to taste them again in her blood.

The blood sang in his veins, filling every part of him with vitality. He had never felt so strong or so exultant. He no longer felt his Gift inside him; the Gift was him, and he was the Gift. Power had become his heartbeat, and he shared it with her, letting it pulse in her mind. She rocked under him, her legs splayed, pleasuring herself against him.

Her blood hardened his rhabdos anew. Lust had never felt so good, and he had never felt so confident in his ability to satisfy her. He fitted himself to her and sank inside her slowly this time. Long and slow. She breathed another sound of invitation and tilted her hips to make way for him.

He thrust as deep into her as he could and stayed there, enveloped in her body and mind. He flexed his hips and his power, reveling in the sensation of being buried inside her. It only got better each time. Her feet trailed up his thighs, and at last she wrapped both her legs around him and held him. This was as it should be.

He drank her until she was crying out again, shuddering on his rhabdos once more. He held her to him, both hands wrapped around her buttocks, feeling the tremors of her release move through her.

With her feet locked behind him, she lifted herself off the carpet, and he realized he was levitating. He let out a laugh against her neck. He pressed them back down to the floor and began to thrust again. He let himself move, let himself take pleasure in her. Let himself lose control again.

At last their passion eased into contentment. Lio lay on her and breathed her scent and listened to her heartbeat grow slow and quiet. He might never move again. He hadn't felt this relaxed since he could remember.

The ferocious power in his blood had calmed to a deep, steady strength. He felt as if this one feast would sustain him forever. But it would not be the only one. She had come home to him.

"Cassia," he murmured. "Thank you."

She said nothing in reply. He lifted his head to look at her. As he moved on her, she did not stir.

"Cassia?"

Her head lolled to one side. She lay utterly still under him. Only then did he understand the languid sound of her pulse. It was only that sound that kept his panic from transforming into terror.

In the space of one heartbeat, he was off of her. In the space of her next, he gathered her limp form in his arms.

"Cassia!"

His shame was powerful enough to render him frozen. He could only remember that night in Solorum Fortress when she had come to him, battered and desperate, and he had so carelessly made love to her in the stupor of the Dawn Slumber. But now, as then, he focused on what she needed.

Here, he had a soft bed on which to lay her and blankets to keep her warm after he relieved her of her tangled gown and worked a cleaning spell. And tonight, she had no bruises. He drew a measure of relief from his examination of her, which revealed no evidence of any injury incurred during their loving. Not so much as a carpet burn on her buttocks.

Despite the vigor of their reunion, he'd had his mouth to her throat the entire time. The healing properties of his saliva, not to mention other bodily fluids, should have erased any mark as soon as he left it on her.

It was physically impossible for a Hesperine to drink a human dry. Or so he had always been instructed. But here was Cassia in a faint.

Taking a seat on the bed with her, he supported her against his chest and put his mouth to hers again. Perhaps a kiss would be enough to wake her. But another dose of his healing Gift did not rouse her.

He had taken too much.

His heart was pounding hard in his chest. Tuning out the sound, he concentrated on her heartbeat and made himself think. Was the situation so grave she needed a healer?

The rush of her blood sounded strong and healthy. A vibrant flush still adorned her skin from breasts to forehead.

He put his wrist to her brow. No fever-heat, only the warmth and dampness normal for a mortal woman's skin after a night of pleasure.

Her eyes moved beneath their lids, and her lashes fluttered open. As she gasped, Lio sucked in a breath for a deep sigh of relief.

"Lio? What…?" she slurred. She moved her chin, as if peeling her tongue off the roof of her mouth, then licked her lips. "Ohh. I fainted."

She giggled.

Lio stared down at her. Yet another sound he had never heard her make, nor expected to. She had most definitely not come to her senses yet.

He brushed her hair back from her face, cradling her against him. Any words of apology he might say seemed insufficient.

She blinked up at him a few times, then beamed.

How could she smile? Didn't she realize what he'd done to her? "Cassia, I'm *mortified*. I cannot begin to tell you how sorry I am."

"You're apologizing? For *that*?"

"I should never have taken so much. I—I drank you into a faint." His throat tightened on the words, and he uttered them in a hushed voice. "I didn't stop."

She raised her eyebrows. "I didn't ask you to stop, did I?"

"Cassia—"

"I'm not a deer," she reminded him.

"You most certainly are not. You are…" *My Grace.* "…infinitely more precious, and I have not treated you so tonight."

"Lio." She met his gaze, her own warm. "It wasn't the blood loss that made me faint."

"What?"

"I've fainted from blood loss before, and that is *not* what it feels like."

"When did you faint from blood loss before?" he demanded.

"I was fourteen. Worst fever I ever had. The healers bled me silly. I thought they were trying to kill me to spare the fever the trouble. I wasn't really well for the rest of the year. Uh, never mind."

Lio made a conscious effort to loosen his hold on her.

"In any case," she said, "fainting from bleeding feels dreadful. But this, tonight, was…" She gave him her secret smile.

Lio cleared his throat. "Thinking back on my education in anatomy, I suppose it's possible the healing properties of my bodily fluids, after a sustained period, might overstimulate your body and cause you to replenish your own blood flow so fast you lose consciousness. This effect would be exacerbated if you had recently suffered deprivation or injury, in which case an infusion of Hesperine regenerative magic could accelerate your restoration to health to an overwhelming degree."

"Thank you for the explanation, Sir Diplomat."

"If such occurred, you might experience an overabundance of physical energy and a sense of...euphoria." He caressed her forehead. "Followed by a feeling of safety and well-being as your physical processes return to normal."

Her eyes slid shut. She still wore that smile. "You make me feel that way with or without magical healing. Although I have a great fondness for your...bodily fluids."

A grin overtook Lio. He tried to hold back his laughter, but all the strain of the evening had been too much.

She peered up at him, grinning. "Fragile mortal women have been known to faint from sheer pleasure, you know."

"Anyone who imagines you are fragile is deceiving himself. And in great danger, I might add."

"Even dangerous mortal women have been known to faint from unbelievable pleasure. Even so," she added, "I hope I remain conscious next time. So as not to miss a moment."

"We'll try not to let that happen again. The fainting, that is. The unbelievable pleasure will happen every night, and you needn't worry about missing a moment, for there will be plenty."

"Every night?" she asked softly. Her tentative tone did not disguise the hope in her eyes, nor the rush of joy he felt through their Union.

"Every night that you wish for my company."

She lifted a hand to his face. "Every night."

Lio gathered her closer in his lap. "I dearly hoped you'd say that. If you want a moment's relief from me, I fear you shall have to banish me with great force."

"If I do anything with great force," she informed him, "it will not be your banishment."

They laughed together this time. A little more of this, and he would feel the night had been salvaged. This every night, and he might well feel as if all that his departure from Tenebra had ruined could yet be repaired.

Surely she too felt as if they rebuilt something precious with each passing moment they lay quietly together like this, holding each other. The moonlight shifted in the room; she grew chilly, and he wrapped them closer in the blankets.

It was some time before she spoke. "I have many things I need to tell you."

Lio ran his hand down the length of her hair. Pure luxury. "As do I. But I say they can wait. We have plenty of time."

The Blood Union told him he was right—those words did repair something inside of Cassia each time he said them.

Awhile later, she let out a splitting yawn. A real one this time. "Is it normal for your magical healing properties to make me feel sleepy?"

"I understand fragile mortal women have been known to feel sleepy after astonishing pleasure."

"Mortal men always fall asleep first."

He grinned at the darkness. "I'm not a mortal man."

She stirred against him and lifted her head. She blinked, clearly struggling to keep her eyes open. "Not fair. I've barely seen you. I have no intention of falling asleep."

He eased her head down to rest on his chest again, and she didn't put up much of a fight.

"Sleep," he murmured into her hair. "You need more rest. And more food. Don't think I've forgotten."

"I can sleep after you have to leave."

He couldn't wipe the smile off his face. "What makes you think I have to leave?"

This time she succeeded not in lifting her head, but only tilting it so she could look at him. Her lips were parted in surprise, deliciously swollen and kissable. "You don't have to be somewhere? To..."

"To avert the suspicion of your father's royal mage? Or avoid frightening the populace? No. You are in Orthros now. There is no dungeon I must return to at daybreak so the superstitious humans can lock me in. There is no daybreak. I go where I will, and I never sleep." He indulged his urge to give her a brief, gentle kiss. "I will be right here when you wake."

A few minutes later, her breathing eased into the gentle rhythm of sleep.

The depths of her slumber beckoned. Lio opened himself up to her and let himself slide into the embrace of her heart. There was nowhere else in the Goddess's good world he would pass the night when he could be here, lying with Cassia in restful Union.

46

nights until

WINTER SOLSTICE

A lady always keeps secrets.

—*Solia's instructions to Cassia*

MORNING IN ORTHROS

CASSIA FIRST BECAME AWARE of a delicious smell. As the scent drew her out of sleep, she noticed something much more important.

She lay entangled with a long, male body. She could feel his muscled thigh on the inside of her leg, his warm skin under her cheek, his chest hair against her breast. Oh. Because she was completely naked.

She was waking up next to Lio.

Cassia lay with her eyes shut and didn't move. She had waited so long and wanted so fiercely. If she didn't move, she could keep this moment a little longer.

She couldn't think straight. Too sleepy, too happy. She would have to think of difficult things soon. But not right now. Just a moment longer.

One more moment to savor the fact that he was here as she awoke, just as he'd said he would be. To lie with him and focus her thoughts on nothing but how it felt. What they'd done before she'd fallen asleep. What he'd said.

His hand trailed up her back. "Good moon, Cassia."

It must have been her smile that had given her away, or perhaps only the change in her breathing. She lifted her head and opened her eyes.

Now that she was in this moment, it was here she wanted to stay for a while, opening her eyes and finding he was the first sight she saw.

He was wonderful to behold, with that stubble and his hair tousled and his elegant embroidered robe hanging askance about his shoulders. A healthy dose of color had returned to his fair skin, and he gazed back at her with eyes that were no longer dilated and blood-shot. She realized she could see him so well because the room was full of his spell light.

"Good moon," she echoed, a bit shyly.

Was it correct to return the pretty greeting? Why was she worrying about it? His gaze was drifting over her, showing that he too was enjoying the sight before him.

He touched his lips to hers in a kiss that made an even lovelier greeting. Soft. Adamant. His kiss acknowledged the night before more eloquently than any words he might have spoken.

She could only smile back at him. "You're still here."

"Indeed. Knight didn't run me out. I admit I may have bribed him with a pastry."

That was the wonderful scent. Now she recognized it from last night. It must taste as good as it smelled, for Knight dozed contentedly on the floor by the bed.

"You fed him my pastry?"

"It was cold and dry, although he didn't seem to mind."

"He seems to have tasted the nectar of the gods. But I'm afraid I must feed him something more before long and change his bandages. We brought provisions for him, but I'm concerned they will be very offensive to Hesperine hospitality."

"We would never begrudge an animal his natural sustenance. Knight is what he is. So are we all. You can see to all his needs in the courtyard. His lady's needs come first, however. For you, I have a fresh pastry."

Lio sat up, and Cassia pushed herself up in bed beside him. She stretched, and a yawn overwhelmed her.

"You're not accustomed to Orthros time yet," Lio said. "You'll probably feel tired at odd hours, but restless and sleepless at others. To help you adjust, I raised the light level in the room to make it feel more like morning to you."

"Your spell light feels better than morning to me. I'm so glad the Dawn Slumber will not take you from me. Is it really night all winter long?"

"No Slumber to come between us. We will soon go even deeper into polar night. Ships will carry us north to Selas, the capital, which will see no sunrise until months from now."

"It isn't surprising we will sail the rest of the way, since stepping is an ordeal for mortals, especially when they're injured. What astonishes me is how quickly your elders brought the rest of the embassy to Waystar. How did they manage it?"

"It was a concerted effort between the Stand, the Charge, my mother and everyone waiting here with her. That many Hesperines, some of our most powerful elders among them, were able to apply enough magic to make the transition safe and bearable for the embassy."

She smiled. "It only took one recently initiated Hesperine to get me here."

"Well, you are a veteran stepper by now. You have become quite intimate with Hesperine magic." Lio gave her a candid grin, his fangs much in evidence. "The rest of the way, I intend for us to enjoy the scenic voyage to the fullest. There is time yet before we board. You can wake up slowly and eat a good breakfast."

A damp towel suddenly appeared in his hand, and he offered it to her. She blinked, taking it from him. The warm water and soft cloth felt good as she washed her face. He lounged beside her, watching.

She was hardly accustomed to being waited on, except by her handmaiden. It was something entirely new for him to drink his fill of her with his reflective blue gaze from the moment she awoke.

She lowered the towel, and before she could wonder where to put it, Lio flicked a finger. The cloth floated out of her hands, across the room, and draped itself tidily over the rim of the washbasin.

She raised her eyebrows. "You never did that in Tenebra. Except to my underlinens."

"In Tenebra, we were on our best behavior."

"Can you levitate many other things besides towels and breast bands?"

"Didn't you notice?" His voice lowered a pitch. "We were levitating last night."

"Oh. I thought that was just how I felt."

He held his hands about a foot apart and wiggled his eyebrows. "This far off the carpet." His humor faded somewhat. "Although, about that…I'm sorry. The bed would have been more comfortable for you."

"Nonsense. It's a lovely carpet. Much nicer than the one in front of the fireplace in my old rooms at Solorum. May I remind you how little you minded having that one under you?"

"I hope you will remind me. Soon. But not till you have eaten enough pastries to sustain such exertions." He waved a hand in a beckoning gesture.

A fresh pastry landed gently in her waiting palms. By Lio's spell light, with all her worries out of sight, the gooey roll made her mouth water. It was large enough for two, glazed with honey, and dusted with a reddish brown powder that must be her namesake. Her belly felt hollow just looking at it. She couldn't remember when she'd felt so hungry.

She gazed at it wistfully. "I don't think I have nearly enough time to do such a thing justice before the embassy is up and about, Perita charges in to dress me, and Benedict attaches himself to me to stare daggers at you."

"It is not the embassy that sets the schedule. You are on Hesperine time now, and we have plenty of it before the others awaken." Lio pinched a piece off the roll and lifted it to Cassia's lips.

Blushing and feeling entirely indulgent, she let him feed her one honey-soaked, cassia-dusted bite.

She held it in her mouth, curious and attentive, and savored her namesake for the first time. A rich, strong taste teased her tongue. Its spicy bite seemed a perfect counterpoint to the sweetness. It was a powerful flavor, complex and heady. She loved it instantly.

"Does it please you?" Lio asked.

Perhaps it was purely the effect of the handsome, half-naked Hesperine who fed it to her, but she found the flavor arousing. She smiled at him. "I shall gladly eat as many cassia pastries as you deem necessary for my health."

His own smile told her he knew the effect the taste had on her. What must this moment smell like to him? Not just the cassia spice on the roll. She blushed again.

He plucked another piece from the pastry and moved it to her lips.

"Lio," she protested, laughing. "You needn't serve me."

"You would deny me the pleasure of feeding you in return?"

"I…I had not thought of it that way."

As he fed her the roll bite by bite, she wondered if her blushing would ever cease. She knew her enjoyment of watching him certainly wouldn't. His graceful fingers mesmerized her, pulling off warm, sticky pieces of roll and bringing them to her mouth. Sometimes he kissed her between bites, sharing the taste with her. Their hands and their lips were very sticky indeed by the time there was nothing left in the napkin but crumbs.

She had escaped a world where she must look over her shoulder every moment. She had awoken in one where she was with Lio and could afford the luxury of letting him feed her breakfast in bed.

He retrieved her next course from the bedside table, this time without even a wave of his fingers. In his hand, there appeared a small glass filled with a creamy white substance. He lifted a silver spoon, and she obediently let him place it in her mouth. Thick, tart yogurt, fresh and chilled.

"Why haven't you been eating?" Lio asked casually. He withdrew the spoon so she could speak.

"I've been busy."

He filled her mouth with another bite of yogurt, more generous this time. "All the more reason to keep up your strength."

She swallowed the yogurt and opened her mouth for another bite.

He didn't take the invitation. "You haven't been taking care of yourself."

There was true worry in his eyes. She looked down, gazing at the geometric pattern on the bed cover instead. She wasn't used to someone worrying about her the way Lio did, nor to feeling the need to spare him worry. "I don't have to battle my fear of the king the way I used to. But I have other worries, and they tie knots in my stomach too. Eating too much just makes it worse."

He cupped her face, turning her to look at him again. "Your taster is a liegehound with natural poison resistance. Why is Knight no longer enough to reassure you?"

Lio saw right through her. She could not plead for his honesty, then fail to give hers in return. "Gift Collectors have tactics for hiding magic that Hesperines have never heard of. What if Skleros has some secret poison up his sleeve that would hurt Knight and me too?"

Lio kissed her forehead. "You don't have time to sleep, I imagine."

"I have more important things to do than sleep."

"Not more important than your health and well-being." He picked up the spoon and fed her another bite of yogurt. "I can offer you a kingdom full of good sleep and safe food, my lady."

"Orthros is indeed the land of abundance you led me to believe, Ambassador."

When he had fed her every last smear of yogurt, he concluded her breakfast with a flask of water and slices of ripe winter fruit. There was another cloth for washing her hands, but they licked the sticky juice from her fingers instead, along with the remnants of honey from the pastry.

"Will you be breaking your fast?" she asked.

He tasted her palm, but only with his lips and tongue. "Not now. I couldn't possibly hold another bite."

She studied him. He had yet to account for how underfed *he* was. "Lio…"

"I am in earnest. I remain entirely satisfied."

"How often do Hesperines normally feast, when they are at home?"

"Ah." He kissed her other palm. "Once a night is quite sufficient."

"Sufficient. I see. What is ideal?"

He nibbled her thumb.

"Lio?"

"It depends on expense of magic, the Dawn Slumber, and if we're busy with sucklings."

"You've been using a lot of magic, there is no Dawn Slumber this time of year, and you aren't a father."

"Hesperines have been known to feast twice a night."

Twice. She had awoken in a world where Lio wished to bed her twice a night. "What a terrible struggle for us."

He laughed. A relieved sound. "We shall have to exert ourselves."

"Are you sure you do not require our exertions now?"

"Right now, I feel ready to take on the world. Besides, I want to give my, ah, healing properties more time to diminish in your body."

She sighed. "I suppose that's wise."

"Speaking with you is another pleasure I have had to do without, and I have hardly begun to satisfy myself in that regard."

"There's so much I never had a chance to say." She ran a hand down the side of his face, simply because she could, touching his familiar features and the new texture of his stubble.

He caught her hand and put her fingers on his braid. "That's what this means. We wear braids to signify promises. This is my promise to you that, in time, I will say all that needs to be said."

It would take time. She would never cease to speak openly with him, but some honest words must wait for the right moment.

She ran her thumb down the length of the braid. "What happens to this once the promise is kept?"

"Usually, the person to whom the promise was made gets to undo the braid. Except in the case of Grace braids. Those are never undone."

"I thought Hesperine braids might hold spells."

"Promises are powerful spells, aren't they?"

She nodded, playing her fingers through his hair.

He relaxed onto the pillows, clearly enjoying her fondling. "What shall I tell you first?"

"How discreet we need to be. Who knows we are sharing?"

"When you said you no longer objected to me telling the others about you, I took you at your word."

"I meant what I said. I am not ashamed for any of your people to know. But I will not have a careless word from me reflect badly on you."

"How could it? We aren't doing anything scandalous. The terms of the Solstice Summit do not forbid me from having a taste of one of the defenseless mortal females in the delegation." He snapped his teeth at her, tickling her ribs.

She laughed, scooting out of his reach. "How have my countrymen failed to lay down the law on this matter?"

"I'd like to see them try." He followed her, snatching her in both his arms and dragging her onto his lap.

She left off their play, too happy to be in his arms even to pretend to want to escape. "Are you sure no one will disapprove?"

"We do not shame passion here. There is no one in Orthros who will not be happy for us. They all know what you did for us during the Summit…and who you are to me."

"No one in Orthros? Do you mean to say you told everyone?"

"It is public knowledge now. I hope that will not make you feel uncomfortable."

She looked away, then at him, then promptly lost her battle with an enormous smile. "Everyone in Orthros knows I am your choice, and you are mine. That makes me feel like the most fortunate person in the world."

He kissed her again. "I cannot tell you how proud I shall be to have you at my side during this Summit."

"I shall have to struggle not to crow."

"I don't think anyone will begrudge us a bit of well-earned crowing. I also took the liberty of telling everyone you are the invisible hand guiding Tenebran politics. I wanted them all to know we have you to thank for uniting the free lords, dividing the king and the Orders, and sparing our Hesperines errant from certain persecution."

Cassia let out a breath of astonishment. "You knew."

"I have done my best to be your herald, writing down all of your deeds and making them known. But I have missed so much. You must tell me everything."

"I scarcely know where to begin."

"That's all right. We have time."

"Well." She settled more comfortably in his arms. "The beginning is really Solia's secret. Her ivy pendant was truly her final gift to me."

She told Lio everything about how Solia's gifts and teachings had opened up the palace inside the palace. Cassia's months of spying in the dark came to light in the glow of Lio's spell, and she told him the secret her sister had entrusted to her as a child, which she had never shared with anyone.

He held her tightly. "When I think of how close you came to Lucis every night…"

Silence fell between them. Neither of them said anything more about how close she had come.

She pushed her memories of the pass away. He must want to do the same. She would say nothing to remind him of his crisis, unless he raised the subject first.

"There are still so many other things we must speak of," she said. "Not only regarding you and me."

He nodded, and for the first time the light his own magery cast upon his face made him appear tired again. "The real politics will begin when we arrive in Selas. We will have more time to prepare on the ship on the way to the capital."

"I'd best collect myself. There's still Perita to worry about, and my handmaiden's powers of perception are not to be underestimated. You see…she is the one person who has an inkling about you."

Lio's eyes widened. "She knows?"

"That I am feeding the Hesperine ambassador? No. But she did figure out there was someone during the Equinox Summit, who got his hands on a bar of soap from Orthros and presented it to me as a gift. So I told her. Everything. Except who you are. She thinks Lord Fancy Soap is a Tenebran of exceptional character."

Lio laughed. "Lord Fancy Soap, eh? That is a far kinder epithet than I expected to earn from Perita if she ever found out."

"All I left out was the fangs part. She heartily approved of everything else. Keeping secrets in plain sight is usually better, as we've often said."

"Indeed. And having friends to confide in is best of all."

"I have come to appreciate that," Cassia admitted. "Although it does necessitate some extra effort to keep our secret from her now that she knows more."

Even as Cassia said it, her gaze fell on the tangled bedclothes, and she realized how the scent of her namesake spice lingered in the air. After a moment's hesitation, she leaned closer to the foot of the bed and looked over the edge.

Lio drew her back, but not before she caught sight of the bloodstains all over the rug.

He flushed to his forehead. "Didn't have a chance to see to that yet. I was more focused on you than the sunbound carpet."

"We destroyed it." She put her hands to her cheeks, chuckling. "Is it very ancient and valuable?"

He had never appeared so embarrassed. "I'll take care of it."

"Well, if there's anything Hesperine cleaning spells can cope with, it is bloodstains." She planted a kiss on his mouth before she rose from bed.

She went to the wash stand and found the pitcher once more full of clean water. It was a marvel the room was warm enough that she didn't feel the urge to drag one of the blankets across the room with her. She could stand at the basin completely naked and perfectly comfortable.

Her goosebumps came only from the knowledge that she stood

brazenly for her lover to see, wearing nothing but the glyph shard. It was a good thing there was no one to peek through all those windows but the gulls.

The familiar, lovely sensation of his cleaning spell trailed over her skin. When she looked over her shoulder again, the rug was spotless, and so was her gardening dress, which was now spread out on the tidy bedclothes. She sniffed. The room no longer smelled of her breakfast or even his scent, which usually accompanied his cleaning spell.

She sighed. "I suppose we cannot have anyone smell evidence of you in my rooms."

He eyed his handiwork. "Perita might notice a detail like that. She will be spending more time in close proximity to me, unlike last winter in Tenebra."

"What about the mages? What measures are necessary to ensure they do not sense the arcane evidence of you in my rooms…and my body?"

Lio pointed upward. "You're sleeping under our Summit Beacon. That's enough Hesperine magic to drown Eudias's entire mastery class. And yet the beacon is a twinkle compared to the aura of the capital. In Selas, the mages won't be able to sense the noses on their own faces. Even the Aithourians will have no hope of detecting the mark of my innate Gift that our time together makes on you."

"Thank you for reassuring me, my champion," she said to remind him of their very first conversation. "I shall enjoy the mark you leave on me without any worries."

He gave her a satisfied smile. He drifted closer, his gaze traveling from her head to her toes. "I wish we had time for me to enjoy watching your bath."

She wrapped her arms around him, under his open robe. "Are you sure we don't?"

"Yes. If I stay to enjoy it, it will take much longer than usual." He kissed her again, then slid out of her hold.

"Next time," she invited.

"Please. I have fantasized about your baths ever since I first smelled you."

"Keep on like that, and I shall not let you leave."

He fastened his robe firmly. "Don't worry. I'll be back. Allow me to remind you that you are my official responsibility. Queens' orders." He flashed her another fanged grin. "Therefore you shall be seeing a great deal of me."

It was hard to believe. All the forces that had conspired to undermine them in Tenebra were now working in their favor. Magic. Politics. Even time.

"I am sorely tempted to hold you to your orders immediately. I am not seeing nearly enough of you at this very moment. Far less than you are seeing of me. Tonight seems like a long time from now. That is, later tonight."

"Veil hours," he supplied. "There are eight moon hours for public matters and eight veil hours for family time and private affairs. We observe fewer hours than Tenebrans, but ours last longer. We measure them by the degrees the moons move in the sky."

"Then I shall count the degrees till veil hours."

"I'll be counting with you." He stepped out of sight, taking the spell light with him.

Cassia took a breath for what seemed like the first time in months. Just as Lio had said, she felt ready to take on the entire world.

THE MOST POWERFUL TEMPTATION

THEY HAD FEASTED. THEY had loved. He had held her all night while she slept, safe and untroubled in his arms.

Those quiet, blessed hours had afforded Lio plenty of time to dwell on his good fortune and say his prayers of thanks. But once he was alone in his room, the reality of it struck him anew. He laughed aloud and levitated in a pirouette on the way to the chair where he had draped his formal robes.

Time to don the attire of an ambassador and become his other self, the diplomat who would show Lady Cassia the courtesy he owed a foreign guest. Nothing more.

Lio halted in the act of unfastening his veil hours robe. When had Ambassador Deukalion, Lady Cassia's partner in treason, become a different person from Lio, who loved her when no one was looking? In setting the Solstice Summit in motion, had he not succeeded in bringing those two broken pieces of himself together again? Had he not made Cassia a way to him that did not require her to abandon her political path?

He shook his head and pushed the thoughts aside, tossing his veil hours robe into his travel bag. Last night had been one of the best of his life. Why was there even room in his thoughts for worry?

Because those nights in Tenebra were still too near, when his duty to leave her had been at war with his need to be near her. Because every night of the Solstice Summit here in Orthros, he must get through the negotiations without letting on publicly what the crown's representative meant to him. Ha. Not a daunting task at all.

Lio set to it. He put on his formal robes and labored to ensure his appearance was impeccable while he planned what he would say when he and Cassia had an audience.

He must resist the temptation to constantly veil their conversations whenever the rest of the embassy's direct attention was on them. In Selas, where the very air was thick with Hesperine magic, it would be all too easy to use his magic to enable them to have candid conversations, even with the other mortals watching.

In most situations, however, it would be an unnecessary risk. She was no longer a wallflower in a crowded room full of the king's uncaring dinner guests. She was the royal representative from Tenebra, with protective friends and dangerous mages watching her like hawks.

Lady Cassia and Ambassador Deukalion's every word to one another in front of the Tenebrans was not only a spectacle, but a political opportunity. He and Cassia must not waste their conversations before the embassy, for those too were tools for winning Tenebra to Orthros's side.

He could still get away with some innocuous remarks that would alarm none of their listeners, while offering plenty of private meanings to her. Actually, this might turn into a sport. A very enjoyable one. Negotiations during moon hours could be a kind of foreplay, teasing at what they had to look forward to when veil hours arrived.

It didn't matter how hard it was to lead this double life. It was a small price to pay for having her with him at last. And they would only have to pretend for a little while longer.

What awaited them afterward was eternity.

While together they devoted their Will to wrestling Tenebra toward peace, he would devote all his heart to his own private cause with her. He would use all his powers of persuasion to convince her to choose to stay in Orthros.

And his powers of persuasion were great indeed. He had already given her a taste. Now she would feast on it night after night, the most powerful temptation there was. Happiness.

When Lio was buckling his travel bag closed, he became aware of two impatient auras outside his door. He pulled back his veil to let his Trial brothers in.

Lyros took a seat. "You didn't come back to your room until a few minutes ago."

"Of course he didn't." Mak leaned on the back of the chair.

"You look better," Lyros observed. "You aren't wearing a veil, are you?"

Lio shook his head, holding his arms out. "I am as you see me."

Their relief was palpable.

Mak looked at him expectantly. "Well?"

"How did it go?" Lyros grinned.

Lio sat down on the edge of the bed and folded his hands. "It was definitely Cassia who fainted."

His Trial brothers burst into surprised laughter. Mak came over and clapped Lio on the shoulder.

Lio smiled. "It was a challenge. But it was worth it. It was all worth it."

Lyros leaned forward. "How did she take the news of who she is to you?"

"Last night was hardly the time to tell her that. I'll broach the subject of her not returning to Tenebra after I help her grow comfortable with life in Orthros and show her what kind of future she can have here."

Mak chuckled. "I think last night probably did the trick."

"But it's not enough for her to stay for me. She has to want to stay for herself, too."

"Wait," Lyros said. "Do you mean you plan to convince her to stay in Orthros, *then* tell her about your bond?"

"Of course. How could I do it any other way? If I simply tell her I can't survive without her, she'll feel obligated to stay for my sake. She'll never have the chance to choose Orthros because it's what she wants."

Mak sighed. "You always make things so complicated for yourself."

"I see your point, though," Lyros admitted. "She did just face the prospect of a forced marriage. You don't want to make her feel trapped."

Mak shook his head. "It's well past that point! Cassia isn't safe anywhere the king can reach her. The heart hunters' attack proved that. You have to keep her in Orthros."

"I *will* keep her safe," Lio swore, "but I will not build our future on fears."

"The danger to her won't be enough to convince her to stay, will it?"

Lyros asked. "She's so committed to her cause, she will not put her safety first. It won't be easy for you to persuade her to do what she wants instead of what she feels she must."

"Whether you like it or not," Mak warned, "you may have to come out with the truth, for both your sakes."

"No." Lio smiled. "Treaty or no treaty, when the embassy returns to Tenebra, Cassia will choose not to go with them. I am her Lio. No one can make her happy the way I can."

UNCHARTED SEA

CASSIA TOOK A DEEP breath to taste the salt that flavored the frosty air. At the foot of the bluff below Waystar, a small fleet of slender, white ships with brilliant red sails waited to carry her and the rest of the embassy across the sea. She could not see the vessels' figureheads from this angle, but if they were not carved in the shape of swans, she thought the shipwrights had missed a perfect opportunity.

How Cassia wanted to say something to Lio, to share with him what went through her mind in this moment, when they would set sail for his home together. Although he walked beside her, she dared not meet his gaze now.

Benedict, Callen, and Perita kept close behind Cassia, and Eudias trailed after them looking seasick before setting foot on the ships. Cassia, the master crafter of court masks, feared one of them would see on her face good moon kisses, a breakfast of cassia pastry, and the taste of Lio's fingers in her mouth.

She occupied her gaze with their surroundings. The steep, slender coastline clung to the foot of the mountains, just a bit of land bound in snow where bare winter brush and creatures like her might gain a foothold between the massive peaks and the vast expanse of the sea.

Up and down the cliffs, water birds of every shape and size flocked long past their time to roost. Agile terns swooped, raucous gulls called, and graceful surf striders stood calmly about on their stilt-like legs as if they too were diplomats waiting to welcome the embassy. The creatures covered the air, the ground, and every hospitable perch upon the fortress far above.

As the Hesperines approached the edge of the water, the birds took wing and surged forward, but then turned midair and retreated. They must have noticed the human guests. By the time the embassy halted with their Hesperine guides near the gangplanks, the flock had vacated the masts, but they still watched from higher up on the bluff.

Lio was still standing next to Cassia. It seemed he might be the one who would hand her up into the ship. She caught her balance on a knife-edge of anxiety and gladness and allowed herself to seek his gaze for an instant.

Before he could reach for her, Callen positioned himself at her side. He bowed to Lio, then stood with his feet braced. Cassia bit her lip. Would Callen run his bad leg ragged trying to keep up with her Hesperine escort? She had no doubt he would, for he was willing to confront any danger for her. She knew how much courage it took a man to get this close to a Hesperine.

While Callen's attention was on Lio, Cassia noticed her hound had not taken a side in the confrontation. She couldn't let anyone think the Hesperines had magicked her dog or that Knight's breeding and training had somehow failed him. She bent and slid a hand into Knight's fur, as if for comfort, and muttered the command for him to be on guard. He dutifully adopted his most watchful stance, even if only on three legs.

It was Benedict who broke the stalemate. Flavian's faithful knight clapped Callen on the shoulder and stepped up to Cassia. Callen let him. Segetia and Hadria united, momentarily, around a common cause.

Lio swept a bow and slid out of reach. Cassia suppressed a sigh. Holding her skirts and clutching her gardening satchel close, she let Benedict escort her up the gangplank and hand her on board. Callen, making an admirable effort to hide his pain, followed suit with Perita.

They all turned to find Lio already waiting for them on deck. Eudias jumped a little at the sight of him.

"Why, Ambassador," said Cassia, "I must thank you for providing gangplanks for those of us who are not so fleet of foot."

He smiled benignly. "We strive to accommodate all needs."

Eudias cleared his throat. "Ambassador, did you, just, ah, perform a traversal to cover all of a few paces?"

"I stepped," Lio corrected. "Hesperines do not require traversals. Stepping accomplishes the same with far less effort."

"Can such a skill be learned?"

"I fear not. It is Hesperine blood magic."

Benedict signed a glyph of Andragathos over his amulet.

Cassia strode to the opposite railing and took in the view of the sea ahead. Lio made use of her swift advance to insinuate himself once more into her escort. Other Hesperines worked around them in coordinated silence. Cassia did not even feel the graceful ship begin to move, but the horizon began to sail toward her.

"How long will our voyage last, Ambassador Deukalion?" The Light Moon was so bright in the sky behind him, Cassia had to shade her eyes to look up at him.

A gentle sea breeze stirred his hair, playing with his braid as she had done little more than an hour past. "We will make harbor in Selas tomorrow, Lady Cassia."

"Is the channel between our mainland and yours so narrow?"

"Not at all, my lady. Without the aid of our magic, your people would be hard pressed to make this voyage in a fortnight."

Cassia looked behind them to watch the fortress on the bluff recede. "Your land is impressive in scope, Ambassador."

"Thank you." He smiled with a knowing light in his gaze.

The lords and mages must even now be contemplating the futility of a human military assault upon Orthros. They had no hope of battling winter over a treacherous mountain range and crossing a great uncharted sea. To say nothing of the Queens' endless, ageless blood ward.

The four ships sailed in formation, carrying the embassy and their Hesperine guides smoothly away from the cliffs and farther out onto the beckoning ocean. Cassia now saw that, for all the vessels' grace, the figureheads were not swans. Upon each prow was carved a magnificent winged serpent, lovely as a swan, but fanged.

Cassia was glad the vessel that carried Chrysanthos and the mages was farthest from her and that Kadi led their escort. The free lords and their retainers occupied the nearer ships. Cassia saw Komnena conversing with Lord Gaius on a neighboring deck.

Cassia had one ship and Lio all to herself. Except for her retinue and the Hesperines who sailed the ship. But all the same, being the royal representative had its benefits.

The ship cavorted beneath their feet. Knight's paws slid on the slippery deck, but he regained his footing quickly and gave himself a shake, tossing salt spray on Cassia's already damp cloak. She and her fellow humans grasped the rail to steady themselves. Lio, perfectly balanced, clasped his hands behind his back. That sign of tension made her wonder if he had been tempted to put a hand out to assist her.

"I'm afraid Orthros's sea is not for the faint of heart," Lio apologized. "Our sailors will ensure no storms trouble us, but the polar climate and the mixing currents here mean the winds and the waves are seldom steady."

"You will find no one among us faint of heart," Cassia assured him.

"I am not surprised, my lady. My time in Tenebra convinced me of your people's bravery," he said to her.

"I hail from Hadria," Callen declared, "on the western coast. The sea there has as much temper as her lord, and every soldier must be ready to weather both."

Benedict eyed Cassia's bodyguard. "Segetia may be landlocked and known for its gentle hills. But as my lord Flavian's First Knight, there isn't a corner of Tenebra where I haven't traveled, including our rivers, lakes, and seas."

Behind the competitive males' backs, Perita and Cassia exchanged long-suffering looks.

Cassia glanced past Perita, Callen, and Benedict to check on the mage. "Apprentice Eudias, I hope you are feeling better than you were last night. This cannot be a comfortable journey otherwise."

His color had improved. He nodded to her without any apparent discomfort. "Thank you for your concern, Basilis. Being on the water is the best tonic I could ask for."

So much for finding an excuse to send him below deck. "Well, that should come as no surprise to us, should it? Your magic must make you feel right at home here."

"Is that so?" Lio asked politely. "Your affinity is for water, I take it?"

Now Eudias shifted on his feet. "Weather, Ambassador."

The more comfortable Eudias was with Cassia and, especially, with Lio, the less excruciating this arrangement would be. A little effort to draw Eudias out would be beneficial in the long run.

She smiled. "Apprentice Eudias's spells greatly contributed to the speed and safety of our journey to the border."

"You flatter me, Basilis."

While the embassy had traveled, Tychon had tutored Cassia and Eudias incessantly on the mages' pretense, as if they were both children who could not keep a secret. She put a little of their act to work for them now, staying as close to the truth as possible, while omitting any mention of Cordium or lightning magic.

"Eudias tells me that when he was a boy, the mage of Anthros in his village took him under his wing. He started his apprenticeship assisting his neighbors with fair weather for their crops, before his extraordinary talent drew the attention of a prestigious circle."

"An impressive task for a boy to undertake," Lio put in. How quick he was to read her cues and lend his aid. "Yours is a demanding affinity. Weather is a complex and recalcitrant force, which requires great Will to control."

Eudias glanced out to sea, his ears reddening.

"What kind of crops did your neighbors grow?" Cassia asked.

The apprentice cleared his throat. "Grains. That sort of thing."

"Rye? Barley? Oats? They all have their own requirements. You must have had to tailor the weather to each."

By the time the fortress had slipped out of sight behind them, Eudias was naming the farmers and which crops they had cultivated in what rotation. He responded with increasing enthusiasm to Lio's comments on magical practice and Cassia's remarks about plants. She had never seen Eudias display anything like pleasure until now. He had certainly never appeared to relish his work for Chrysanthos, nor any of his tasks for Dalos before that.

After some time, Benedict joined in, proving Segetia had earned its reputation as Tenebra's bread basket. Flavian's right hand clearly paid as much attention to estate management as his liege. Callen and Perita drifted further along the rail to talk quietly with each other, no doubt glad for more time to themselves. The conversation on agriculture whiled away the time and roamed over everything from crop prices to a recent history of famines, including one from which Eudias had spared his village.

"Remarkable," Cassia said. "The farmers must have been very sad to lose you, when you left for advanced training with your circle."

Eudias shrugged. "It was an honor to be taken into the Circle, Basilis."

To be taken? Of course. The Order of Anthros required all those born with magic that lent itself to combat to be trained under the watchful eyes of the Aithourian Circle.

She had thought perhaps Eudias had merely had his enthusiasm beaten out of him by his masters' tyranny. But no. It seemed he had never been a Tychon in the first place.

"I have lived in many places all my life," Cassia said, "first one residence, then another. It must be nice to have somewhere you are from. You surely miss home. Do you get to visit often?"

"It is of greater benefit to them for me to devote all my time and effort to my training."

Did Eudias ever wish he had been born with less powerful weather magic, so he might have stayed in his village? Had that been the life he really wanted?

Had anyone asked him what he wanted?

Ha. He was a war mage in the Aithourian Circle, who would grow up to be another Dalos. Give him a few years, and he would be more eager to hurl lightning at Lio than to discuss weather spells.

It was a shame, actually.

Cassia pushed her sympathy for him away. She might pity him for his position as the Aithourian Circle's whipping boy, but he had still been at his master's side when Dalos had nearly killed her Hesperines.

She looked at Lio now, safe and sound beside her, in the flesh. Every glimpse of him felt like another dose of the Gift's healing power, reaching hurts much deeper than her skin.

But this time a glance at him didn't give her comfort. It reawakened her worries. The signs would go unnoticed by someone unaccustomed to Hesperines' almost unreadable body language and Lio's candid face. But Cassia was expert.

Lio's courteous diplomatic expression didn't disguise the tightness at the corners of his mouth. His perfect posture was not easy Hesperine poise, but tension. As the talk of crops neared a natural conclusion, Lio hid more and more behind harmless, insignificant remarks.

He didn't look ill as he had the night before. His color was fine, his eyes weren't dilated, and he didn't even look weary. But what if he was wearing a veil? If not for his magic, would she be able to see signs of his hunger returning?

She hastened a return to an earlier topic of conversation. She said lightly, "Are you prone to seasickness, Ambassador?"

He glanced at her with an expression of surprise and laughed. "No Hesperine is prone to any sickness, Lady Cassia."

"Of course." With her face turned toward him and away from Benedict and Eudias, she let Lio see a flicker of concern in her gaze before looking out to sea again. "But surely there are some dangers at sea with which both our peoples can sympathize. For example, being surrounded by water that is no good to drink."

Benedict and Eudias shifted nervously on their feet. How squeamish they were, even though she had referenced the Hesperine diet with so much delicacy her words had been almost meaningless. But Lio would know her true meaning.

He did not reply. It was Callen's voice, low with concern, that filled the silence. Cassia turned to him. He was leaning over Perita, who sat on a nearby crate.

Cassia went to her friend's side. "Are you all right, Perita?"

Before she could answer, Callen scowled. "No, my lady. She's not well."

"Did you get enough rest after what happened at the border?" Cassia asked. "If you think you are taking ill—"

Callen shook his head. "It's a more usual malady."

Perita cut in, "I'm perfectly fine, my lady."

"Oh, Perita. I wish you had told me you are seasick."

Perita crossed her arms and didn't budge.

"She's doesn't want to seem like she's failed you, my lady," Callen said quietly, which earned him a glare from his wife.

Cassia made a great show of relief, lowering her voice. "I'm so glad you've told me. I feel quite ill myself, but I could not reconcile my conscience to excusing myself. For Perita's sake, I will not hesitate. Let me make our excuses to the ambassador."

Perita breathed a sigh. "I suppose that's all right, my lady. It's not Ambassador Toothy's side I promised not to leave."

Cassia couldn't help but chuckle. Ambassador Toothy, Lord of Fancy Soap, could easily hear he had just earned another pert name from Perita.

Cassia returned to Lio at the rail and pressed a hand to her belly. "Ambassador, I must beg your forbearance. I stand by my claim of Tenebran steadfastness, come Hypnos or high water. But I must reluctantly admit the sea is putting me to the test."

Alarm flashed in Lio's gaze. "Perhaps we have been too hasty in departing Waystar so soon after the ordeal of your arrival."

"Thanks to the healers, we are all quite fit to travel, I assure you. But I neglected to ask them for a charm against seasickness. If you would be so kind as to excuse me, I would be very grateful for the opportunity to take a moment's pause below deck, where the motion of the ship is sure to be less."

"Of course, Lady Cassia. Please, take your time and rest."

Eudias interrupted, "Basilis, I'm sorry to hear you are ill. But if I may, I suggest you remain on deck. That is the best remedy for seasickness. Seeing the motion of the water will help calm your stomach."

"Thank you so much for your concerned advice. But I would really prefer to lie down. You and Sir Benedict need not bestir yourselves. Callen and Perita will escort me below."

Eudias looked uncertain, but Benedict nodded, clearly satisfied with his assignment to keep an eye on Ambassador Toothy. "As you wish, Your Ladyship."

Lio was very grave as he escorted Cassia, Callen, and Perita to the hatch that led below deck. Cassia began to regret her ruse. She'd had no intention of worrying him. But if it had escaped his notice that she wasn't really ill, he was not at his best indeed. He needed her, even if she must subject him to a few moments of fretting in order to arrange it.

She descended into the ship, and Knight joined her, his mass all but blocking the narrow corridor that ran the length of the keel. At Cassia's insistence, Callen took Perita to their cabin straight away, and Perita didn't even protest. Cassia slipped into her own cabin to wait for Lio.

This was yet another benefit of her position as the crown's representative. Her cabin was private and generous in size, its appointments fit for royalty. The bunk looked inviting and, not surprisingly, long enough to accommodate someone of Hesperine height.

Knight squeezed his big, furry body under a dainty dining table that was bolted to the floor, and the embroidered tablecloth secured upon it hung in his eyes. She strapped her gardening satchel to the table leg next to him.

She hadn't even finished unlacing her russet travel dress when Lio appeared just inside her door, his face clouded with worry.

She grinned at him. "I knew you'd find a way to get away from Benedict."

"He and Eudias are watching an illusion of me have a word with my mother on the opposite deck. Are you all right?"

"Of course."

"I feared you might need another healing from Javed, but call it seasickness in front of the others. Some injuries and fevers take more than one night to manifest."

"*Your* health is the reason I have come below deck. You *should* have had breakfast before we left. It is clear you are hungry."

There was a hint of panic in his eyes. "The symptoms shouldn't be showing. My veil is in place."

"I knew it. I'll help you out of your veil if you'll unlace me."

His gaze riveted on the bit of bare shoulder she showed him. The raw hunger she had seen in his gaze last night returned in full force. Cup and thorns, she thought for the first time. She wanted him to look at her like that all night. Her heartbeat quickened, and his pupils enlarged.

"I feasted on you too long last night. It's too soon."

She held out both hands to him. "Half a year, Lio. It's not too soon."

He was across the cabin in a heartbeat. Her arms were around him, his hands on her. His mouth found hers.

This was how she had so often imagined their reunion. Holding onto each other for dear life, devouring each other with kisses, no negotiation, no preamble. Their hands roamed over each other, shedding their clothes. They had their bodies bare in a matter of moments, and then he had her on her back, under him on the bunk. She pulled him down to her, parting her thighs for him.

She had one glimpse of his fangs straining against his lips before he lowered his head. She felt the sting of his teeth on her neck and the pressure of his rhabdos between her legs. He buried himself in her in one smooth, hard motion.

It was still a mystery that the razor-sharp blades in her throat wrought only pleasure, not pain. Her body shivered uncontrollably, tugging against the grip of his teeth with the motion. Pleasure filled her from his bite down to her krana and chased into the depths of her mind. Like a shard of moonlight, his presence plunged inside her thoughts with a caress.

She had waited so long to feel this. Him under her skin, completely. Everything was as it should be now. With a soul-deep sense of relief, she gave into the need to move. She lay her head back for him to drink and spread her legs wider, rocking beneath him in exultant silence.

The bunk rose and fell under them with the ship, and he matched his rhythm to the swell and ebb, timing his thrusts and his sucks at her neck. He feasted on her as if she were the last sustenance in the world.

The pleasure was so sweet. More powerful than her memories, more intense than her fantasies of him in their long months apart. The invasions of his rigid flesh inside her were marvelous, stroking her, stretching her to hold him, as natural as breathing. His weight sheltered her, and his long, lithe body rubbed against her, reminding her how her sensitive skin seemed made for this.

Cassia stopped thinking. Ceased her worrying and trying and fighting. She surrendered to her wants, to her need for him.

She let herself get lost in this world where his body drove the tide. They were safe. Adrift in a ship surrounded by endless ocean, with Lio at the helm. She relaxed for the first time in six months and let him consume her.

Her guard fell, and the self-control she had clung to every moment of every day escaped her. She tossed and twisted on his rhabdos, unable to be still. She pushed her throbbing body up onto him hard, bucking with the ship, and he drove down into her, carrying them under again. She devoured him in time to the sea and the throb in her throat.

He panted upon her, drawing in air through his nose as if to enhance his ability to taste her. What could he smell? What did he taste? The dampness from her body smeared across his skin. Surely the blood on her lip, where she was biting it now. And her heart, hammering in her chest. He could taste that.

And with every pump of her racing heart, she felt her blood rush forth from the warm ache at her throat, onto his waiting tongue. She felt him draw her essence out of her and suck her down like she was also sweet and powerful and marvelous. And in return he poured pleasure, magic, himself into her.

She had learned in his arms there was no limit to how much they could hold. For when they had their fill, more pleasure came.

Tears coursed down her cheeks, redeeming all the nights when she had cried without him. He was so full inside her, made thick by and for his feast on her. His hard, slick fangs swelled in her neck, and their points penetrated deeper.

Tears slid into her mouth, trails of salt on her tongue. She could hear her own breathing, fast and shallow. Then another sound, unfamiliar. A voice, uncontrolled, inelegant. It uttered sounds somewhere between a moan and a cry. That was her voice.

Only Lio to hear her. His veil covered them. His power hid her safe in the darkness.

Cassia called out again and again, begging and triumphant. The pleasure was so powerful under her skin, she could not keep it inside. It felt so good to cry out. So good to move her hips against his and clutch him within her.

Darkness hazed her vision, but she felt full of light and compelling, harrowing heat. That heat was building. So high. Almost there. He must taste in her blood how close she was.

When it came over her, she didn't try to be silent. She shattered the quiet. The ship lifted them up again and brought them down, and she rode the tide that had overtaken her body. He rode it down with her and penetrated her deep, now pouring more than pleasure into her.

Sensation swallowed her sight, then her hearing. All that remained was touch. Pleasure dragged her under, deep into darkness.

WORDS UNSPOKEN

ASSIA ROUSED TO FIND him holding her. He arranged them on their sides on the bunk and dried her tears with one of his silk handkerchiefs, and she let him. For so long she had cried alone and been denied the simple pleasure of him holding her. She would never get enough.

"I never meant to make you faint again," he said.

"No matter. It is natural for ladies to faint at the sight of Hesperines."

"You must be as steadfast as you say, for you had to see quite a lot of me before you succumbed."

She wriggled closer against his body. "It's also natural for ladies to faint at the sight of a male's endowments, especially if they are impressive in proportion."

"Am I to take that as a compliment?"

"Oh, yes."

She felt his chuckle in his chest.

"Thank you very much." His voice lowered to a purr. "I would say I never meant to make you weep. But there is one occasion when I cannot regret making you cry. I shall not apologize for tears of pleasure."

She was glad her face was hidden against his chest. She had not only cried, but also cried out, just like last night. Had she really made all that noise?

She lost track of time as they lay there together, trading caresses and reassurances. She never lost track of time.

"Tell me what you're thinking," he said after a while, resting his chin on her head.

"You can feel it. The Blood Union is telling you that you are a lover beyond compare, and your share is so satisfied she cannot stand."

He laughed again, warming her all over. "But I've missed hearing you put what I can feel into words. Goddess knows I've missed talking to you."

"You smell so good," she obliged. "Your skin feels so good against me. All of you feels wonderful against me." She let out a sigh and kept confessing, letting him hear all the dangerous, vulnerable thoughts inside her. For he would not use them against her. With him, no confession was weak or shameful. "When I lay here like this with you, I feel...safe. Like all will be well."

His long hand caressed her head, gentle and eager at the same time. "Yes, Cassia. All will be well. I will take care of you."

Take care of her? She had not even thought of it that way. She had not come here for that.

"Don't tell me I shouldn't," he said softly. "You've fought so long and so hard."

"I have," she whispered.

He sighed into her hair. "My weary warrior. You've earned the right to come home from the field and let your lover comfort you."

"And all along I thought I was comforting you, my starving Hesperine."

"You are. We take care of each other."

He had never held her quite like this, as if he were making some kind of declaration. He had never spoken of looking after each other. The words satisfied something inside her, like food that nourished, and only in tasting it did she realize she had been hungry. There hadn't been time for such things before.

"Lio, I have an important question to ask you, and you mustn't deflect. As you say, we are taking care of each other."

His speed and grace could still surprise her. In one motion, he took hold of her and rolled them over. Cassia found herself atop him, her head on his chest and his hands in her hair.

"Do you hear that?" he asked.

She pressed her face closer to him. His body was so warm, the texture of his chest hair against her cheek so pleasing. And there beneath his skin she heard it, the powerful beat. "Your heart."

"That's your blood pumping through it." His voice grew quiet. "Your blood keeping my heart beating. Do you not think that gives you the right to ask me any question you will?"

Cassia's breath caught. "Is that how you feel?"

"Of course."

She lifted her face. He smiled at her, one hand propped behind his head, the other now trailing down her neck and shoulder. He was the picture of relaxation. And she had just heard his strong heartbeat for herself. He seemed a different Hesperine than the one who had thrown himself upon her wrist and her mercy last night. She knew it was because of her blood.

And yet even after last night's thorough feast, he had been unable to make it from Waystar to Selas without another.

"Lio, why were you so ill when I arrived?"

He sighed and let his head fall back, looking up at the ceiling. "I was hungry."

"No, I thought you'd caught the sniffles. Why haven't you been getting enough to drink?"

"The quantity of my sustenance has not been at issue."

"Of course it wouldn't be, here." Her jealousy and frustration reared their ugly heads. "Lio, I am trying to ask you about this in the most diplomatic way possible, and you are not making it easy."

"What could you possibly mean by that?"

"There are some questions I am determined not to ask you, for it would not be fair. But I think I shall have to. Who has been providing for you since we parted, and what possessed her to fail you so utterly?"

He met her gaze again. The corners of his mouth twitched. "Don't be too hard on her. She means well, but deer aren't very bright."

Cassia let out a breath she hadn't known she'd been holding. "You've taken the Drink from nothing but *deer*? All this time?"

"Yes. I have thoroughly worn out my welcome among the Queens' herds."

Cassia's mouth dropped open. "But you're not supposed to have to do that here in Orthros! I saw the toll it took on you to make do with animals during the Summit."

"And you provided the cure then, as well."

"You had to wait half a year for it this time. No wonder you were ill."

His brows drew together. "Cassia, are you about to cry again… or smile?"

She hid her face against his chest once more so he would not see her do either. His heartbeat pulsed under her cheek again. *Her* blood in his heart. No one else's. She shouldn't be so glad. "Why didn't you take better care of yourself?"

"I didn't want anyone else."

Cassia lay there and held him, the way she would hold those words. *I didn't want anyone else.* She took long, steady breaths to keep the tears at bay, drawing his wonderful scent into her. When they were together, she wore no armor. There was nothing to mitigate the effect those words had on her.

"And when I know what I want," Lio added cheerfully, "I am more stubborn than my mild manner would lead you to believe."

Now she could no longer keep the smile from her face, and she grinned foolishly for his beating heart. "I told you, you are too passionate to be a diplomat."

"But that leaves me rather well suited to perform in other capacities, I hope."

She indulged the urge to place a slow, open-mouthed kiss on his chest above his heart. "Your other capacities…" Oh, but he tasted good. "…I am always astonished how well you perform in them…"

"My lady's vote of confidence has been noted."

She laughed and kissed him again, working her way upward, feasting in her own way on the taste of his skin. When she got to his lips, he was waiting for her, and his tongue slid warm and smooth inside her mouth.

When she paused to draw breath, she rested her forehead on his. "You will want for nothing now. I will give you all that you need."

"Cassia." He let out a long, deep sigh. A sound of profound relief.

"Now tell me truly. Will our feast just now sustain you until veil hours?"

"I believe so, although I can no longer delude myself that once a night is sufficient. I…I don't know how long it may be before we have made up for lost time."

"I rejoice to hear it. For I so dearly need to make up for lost time."

"Cassia." There was hesitation in his voice now.

She frowned. "Yes?"

"Am I correct in taking your words last night regarding Flavian to mean his courtship was one-sided?"

She lifted her head too fast this time, and it seemed to float. "You actually thought there might be a possibility it wasn't?"

"You actually thought there might be a possibility I drank from someone besides deer."

"I didn't take anything for granted. It wouldn't have been wrong of you. I have tried so hard not to be jealous."

"Nor would it have been wrong of you. I didn't take anything for granted either. As for striving not to feel jealous, I have failed utterly."

"You have no cause for envy, none at all. Flavian's courtship is not even one-sided, for he has no interest in me, either. The time he and I have spent together has been a matter of duty."

Lio pulled her face down to his again and feathered kisses over her eyelids and nose and cheeks. "I am still jealous he got to spend any time with you at all."

"It was just horseback riding and talking about dogs. Nothing special." Cassia straddled Lio. "Nothing like the time I spend with you."

His hands tightened on her waist. "Merciful Goddess, when Basir and Kumeta came back with news of the Autumn Greeting…"

"You must have known it was all politics."

"The Master Envoys brought home a thorough account of the event, down to the last detail of gossip."

Cassia's heart sank. "Oh, Lio."

"Knight wasn't there to defend you. Flavian dragged you into the woods. Alone. I had no way to know if that bloodless vulture coerced you, or if—"

"*I* dragged *him* into the woods—to *talk* with him. About Sabina."

"Sabina?" Lio frowned. "Of Hadria?"

"Indeed. Their fathers will never know it, but Hadria has long since conquered Segetia. Sabina set her sights on Flavian three years ago, and ever since, Tenebra's most illustrious skirt chaser has given up the hunt.

He only danced the Greeting with me to fulfill the expectations of his father and the king. I took the fool aside that night to talk some sense into him about how he's breaking Sabina's heart. Tenebran men can be so blind about women."

"In that case, I shall let him live for Sabina's sake."

Cassia laughed. "Such violent urges, Sir Diplomat."

His humor faded. "As you well know, my commitment to diplomacy stops short of men who threaten you."

She caressed his forehead, trying to drive away the haunted look in his eyes. "What men? I see none here. I have escaped with my Hesperine."

45

nights until

WINTER SOLSTICE

*Finally, each King of Tenebra, upon his accession to the
throne, is to reconvene the Summit and reaffirm this
Oath with the appointed representatives of the Queens
of Orthros.*

—*The Equinox Oath*

HARBOR

"DO YOU THINK YOU can walk?" Lio asked, his smile teasing. Cassia propped her chin on her hands, not moving from upon him. "I haven't been on my feet much since we left Waystar last night."

"My lady's health has benefitted from spending most of the voyage in her cabin."

"I see that the Ambassador's health has benefitted from spending no time in his cabin at all. Must we really leave my bunk now?"

"We shall arrive in Selas at second moon. There is a welcoming ceremony as soon as we land. You could stay right here until it's time to disembark, but you might want to consider getting dressed." He ran a hand down her back to cup her buttock.

"Hm. It might not be appropriate for me to attend a formal event as I am, certainly."

"Save your current attire for the ambassador's banquet late tonight." He nibbled the tip of her nose.

"I can hardly wait. I have enjoyed the appetizers so much."

"Mm. So have I, my rose."

Cassia had never been impressed by the overly sweet names the strapping heroes in ballads called their overly perfect ladies. Flavian's incessant "my dears" always grated on her ears. But the moment Lio called her his rose, warmth flushed her cheeks, and she was unable to keep from smiling.

Lio meant endearments, as he meant everything he said. He was a real hero, and he did not expect her to be a flawless lady in a song. She must ponder what endearment she might call him that would possibly do him justice.

"If you do feel inspired to dress now," he invited, "and come out onto the deck, you can enjoy a truly spectacular sight as we make harbor. I don't think you'll want to miss it. I have to confess, I've been looking forward to showing you this."

"In that case, I shall gladly find the strength to stand." She sat up and paused on the edge of the bunk. She treated herself to an eyeful of Lio sprawled there, nude and satisfied. "Especially since I shall get to enjoy the view before me again later."

He tickled her knee. With a chuckle, she shooed his hand away and stepped out of reach. But his cleaning spell tickled her all over.

Lio swung his feet over the side of the bunk. The wrinkled heaps of his formal robes picked themselves up off the floor, and his medallion of office untangled itself from her gardening satchel. As his ambassadorial attire flew into his hands, Knight startled awake, lifting his head from his paws.

Lio chuckled and began to dress in haste. "My apologies. I shall gather all evidence of my presence and vacate your lady's cabin."

"And the lady shall endeavor to choose the right dress without her handmaiden's direction."

"May I make a suggestion?"

"Certainly. What do you deem appropriate for the event, Ambassador?"

"Do you have anything purple?"

She raised an eyebrow. "The color of royalty?"

"And betony flowers."

She smiled. "Thank you for your expert advice."

Tousled but clothed, he planted a parting kiss on her neck. "I'll see you on deck."

She restored some order to her cabin, then reached under her bunk and braved her clothing trunk. Once she was confident in her appearance, she bundled herself up again and left her cabin. She decided not to drop in on Perita, in case she was feeling so much better that Callen was busy checking on her as Lio had Cassia.

Cassia came out on deck, one gloved hand on Knight's back, looking all around her for Lio. He was nowhere in sight, although Benedict and

Eudias were already on watch. Had those mother hens gone below to get any sleep, or had they patrolled the deck all through veil hours?

Then motion on the next ship over caught her eye, and she saw Lio stroll out from below decks and pause near the helm to say something to Komnena. Then he stepped to the deck of his and Cassia's ship.

Benedict startled, spinning on his heel, his hand going to his belt where his scabbard usually hung. Eudias just looked uncomfortable. Lio lifted both hands in a placating gesture and showered them with gracious apologies.

Cassia clucked her tongue at Knight. "*Haddan.*"

His tail stilled, and he stood at attention. They strolled to join the others, and Cassia reluctantly positioned herself at the rail nearer to her two escorts than Lio.

"Lady Cassia," Lio greeted her first. "I hope you are feeling better."

"I am entirely rejuvenated, I assure you. The time in my bunk has worked wonders upon me."

She took comfort in the veiled remarks she and Lio exchanged and found humor in Eudias and Benedict's innocent responses. But it was as hard to stand this far away from Lio now as it had been last moon hours when they had left Waystar. It was alarmingly difficult to keep her face blank when she glanced at him and keep her tone from growing too warm.

She had to do better than this. The skills that had kept her alive and successful at treason must not fail her now. She must not let a little pleasure dull her blades. Well, it certainly hadn't been a little. But even so.

She scanned the horizon for the view Lio had promised her. But all she saw was the sea. In every direction, there was nothing to be seen but endless ocean, black as the black sky above. She was floating on night itself, drifting between the water and the sky, or perhaps sailing on the sky with the water rippling above her.

She did not feel lost. Not with the Goddess's Eyes above her, which she had seen all her life, which looked upon her the same no matter where in the world she was. The host of stars overhead was better than a map, for she knew every single one was a familiar friend to the Hesperines who guided the ships.

"Do you have different names for the stars than we do in Tenebra, Ambassador?" she asked.

"Some of their names we carried with us out of Tenebra in the Great Temple Epoch. Others gained new names and new lives, as surely as we did when we came to Orthros."

"Tell me about them," she invited.

He pointed ahead and upward. "Do you see that star of exceptional brightness, due north?"

"I know that one. The Boreian Star. Sailors use it to navigate."

"We call it the Truth Star, and we swear on it when we testify. It is the eye of the constellation Alatheia."

"Alatheia had only one eye?"

"Yes." Eudias, too, stared north. "The Order of Anthros's inquisitors put the other out when she refused to recant. She was the first mage of Hespera they burned on the Akron's Altar."

Lio turned to face the mage. "As uncomfortable as it is for you and I to discuss this with one another, here beneath her star, I want to express my respect for what you have just said. You have delivered the facts of her history, nothing more, nothing less. However our opinions on her may differ, confronting the truth of the past is where we must begin."

"We too have a Truth Star of sorts." Eudias gestured at Benedict's amulet.

Benedict weighed the talisman in his hand, eying Lio. "We swear by Andragathos, the Seventh Scion, the most honest of the gods, that he may strike down any who lie or deceive others as to their true nature."

Cassia quickly turned in a different direction. "What constellations are in that part of the sky?"

Lio ignored Benedict's glare and pointed to another formation on the horizon. "Is that cluster of stars familiar to you?"

"No," she answered. "Tenebrans have no name for it that I know of."

"That constellation is known to us as the Faithful Traveler. It represents Queen Soteira's late husband, the man she loved in her mortal life. He journeyed all over the Empire at her side, acting as her bodyguard while she took her healing arts to any who needed her. He gave his life in her defense."

"I am so sorry for her loss. I'm glad she has such a beautiful way to remember him."

"One of your Queens was married?" Benedict ventured.

"Yes," Lio answered.

Benedict cleared his throat. "Then perhaps we ought to lay some of the unfortunate gossip about her to rest."

"What gossip is that, Sir Benedict?" Lio asked.

"That she, that is…that the two of them are…"

"I think," Cassia said carefully, "we ought to all rejoice for Queen Soteira that she has risen above such a tragic past and found good fortune in her current partner. She and Queen Alea are very happy together, by all accounts."

"The happiest in Orthros," Lio replied. "Our land is blessed with the reassurance of a strong royal line. Our Queens have eight children, most of whom have already founded bloodlines of their own with many descendants."

Benedict looked like he'd swallowed his amulet. Cassia bit back a sigh.

"Look there." Lio pointed straight overhead. "Do you see those eight stars? The brightest one might mark an uplifted hand, and those in line below it a Prismos's robe."

Cassia craned her head back. "I see the pattern."

"That is Anastasios, who was Prismos of Hagia Boreia, the Great Temple of the North. He was one of the first eight Hesperines, whose magic made our kind possible when they performed the Ritual through which the Goddess created us."

Benedict looked from the constellation to Eudias. "Perhaps you can educate us better on this history."

"Well, actually, no," Eudias replied. "I cannot fault the Ambassador's presentation of the facts. It is known among all the Orders that the eight most powerful mages of the Great Temples of Hespera discovered the secret of immortality. The only difference between the Anthrian and Hesperine accounts would be whether that ritual was considered an unholy rite or a sacred one."

"I am naturally biased in my view," Lio said. "It was Anastasios who discovered that the eight Ritual firstbloods could give their blood to others to pass on their newfound power. He was a healer who could not bear to lose a single patient. When one of his own mages lay dying in his care, in desperation he shed his own blood in an attempt to save him. That mage was the first ever to receive the Gift, as every Hesperine has since. His name is Apollon, and I am his son. Anastasios was my foregiver, and his constellation is the sign of my bloodline."

The revelation silenced Benedict and turned Eudias's eyes large. Cassia shivered, as if Lio's words had conjured around her all the power he carried in his veins. She'd had an idea of the ancient magic in his blood, but had not known his bloodline's history.

"Then you are the living legacy of a Great Temple," she said. "Can we really say that age is past?"

"I hope Orthros will convince you it never ended. We have no temples in Selas, for when our founders laid the first stone of the city, they declared everything we built would be Hespera's Sanctuary."

A new chill curled about Cassia's ankles. The cold manifested into a mist that hovered over the water and swept around the boats, sliding up over the deck to wrap soft and wet around all of them.

Soon the mist thickened into a dense fog that rose well above their heads and cut off their view of the surrounding ocean. The moonlight shone on one billow of fog after another, bringing strange shapes to life in the air, which then slid back into darkness.

Cassia breathed in the wet air, and her chest filled with anticipation. She felt comfort and promise in the fog and knew it was a spell. The winter wind picked up, making the sails snap above them, pulling Cassia's hair and cloak northward, toward Selas.

Then the wind became an icy gust that sliced through every layer of Cassia's clothes. She gasped, clutching her cloak about her, and huddled closer to Knight. Her teeth had no time to start chattering before a tall, warm body drew near, and two familiar hands emerged from the fog to drape another cloak around her shoulders. Lio pulled the hood up around her face, and she felt the brush of silk on her cheek.

"You may think this fabric too light to warm you," he said, "but silk fibers are conducive to magic. A spell is woven into the threads that will protect you from any cold. Please accept these cloaks, gloves, and shoes as gifts from my people. You will be unable to last long in Orthros without them. Anytime you are outdoors, you must wear these for the sake of your health."

By the time he finished speaking, Cassia felt as warm as if she lay under a pile of fur blankets, drinking a goblet of spiced wine. Almost as warm as when Lio kissed her.

She burrowed in the soft garment. Lio slid the most delicate gloves onto her hands, warming her fingers between his. Then he knelt for a moment at her feet and, with speed only a Hesperine could manage, swapped her Tenebran winter boots for silk shoes so adroitly she barely felt the chill on her feet.

She couldn't see anyone else, but she heard them moving about and fabric rustling. Perita and Callen's voices joined the others. No one even suggested they shouldn't accept magical gifts from the Hesperines.

The wind gusted again, but this time the biting cold didn't reach into Cassia's hood or under her hem. The fog roiled around her, and then it was gone.

She let out an exclamation of wonder. Gasps and murmurs of awe echoed across the water from every ship.

Ahead of them, a star had descended from the sky to hover over the water. Its rays reached across the sea like thorns of light.

"It is even more beautiful than the beacon at Waystar," Cassia exclaimed. "What is it?"

"The Harbor Light, which guides all Hesperine travelers to shore."

"It is a lighthouse in Selas?"

"You'll see."

She couldn't take her eyes from the light. She wasn't sure if they sailed toward it, or it pulled them forward. As she watched, a snowy coastline became visible in its glow. Then shapes beneath the Harbor Light—structures. The rooftops of Selas. Her first glimpse of the capital.

"We're almost home," Lio said.

The distant vision drew nearer and revealed details to Cassia. Selas was a long, pale city that rested around the entire rim of a deep bay, as if sipping from the ocean's cup. The capital cast its glow high into the night sky like a shadow made of light, and Cassia realized not all of that came from the Harbor Light. There were colorful windows everywhere, one for each star in the sky above, it seemed.

Lio swept out his arm to indicate the bay. "Here is Harbor, where our people first made landfall in Orthros."

As the ships slipped between the two arms of the bay, countless other vessels pulled alongside to escort them into Harbor. The entire surface of the water sparkled, reflecting the stars and the city and the stained glass lanterns of every color that adorned the boats. Cassia felt she was swimming in festival lights, preparing to dive into the glow of the Harbor Light mirrored in the center of the bay.

Lio stood closer. "This voyage is a rite of passage for every new Hesperine—the right of every new heir of the Goddess. Each of us finds Sanctuary when we land on these shores."

Half a dozen towering silhouettes ringed the Harbor Light's reflection. The ships pulled between the grand shapes, and Cassia saw they were in fact statues. Larger than life, six white marble Hesperines stood on pedestals in the bay, appearing to hover over the water.

They all seemed in motion, their hair lifted around their faces as if by the very wind that stirred Cassia's, their feet raised as if they prepared to set foot in Orthros for the first time. She could see every hole and tatter in their robes. Their gazes were turned toward the shore and the future. As the vessels sailed among them, Lio pointed upward and named each in turn.

"Elder Firstblood Timarete, Gifted by Daedala who was Prisma of Hagia Zephyra. She is our greatest painter. Her eldest daughter Laskara is the sculptor whose work you see before you.

"Elder Firstblood Kitharos, Gifted by Thelxinos who was Prismos of Hagia Zephyra. He is our greatest musician, who keeps our songs and our history alive."

The two firstbloods of Hagia Zephyra stood side-by-side, Kitharos with a lyre strapped to his back, Timarete with a bundle of brushes under her arm. A sash across the painter's chest held pockets full of vials, pots, and powders.

"Elder Firstblood Hypatia, Gifted by Ourania who was Prisma of Hagia Anatela. She is our greatest astronomer, who devised our clock and calendar."

Hypatia was a solemn lady with a heavy pack on her shoulders that was filled to bursting with scrolls. She pointed the way with an astrolabe in hand.

"Elder Firstblood Argyros." Lio's voice was fraught with pride. "Gifted by Eidon who was Prismos of Hagia Anatela. He is our greatest diplomat—my uncle and mentor. Beside him stands Elder Grace Hippolyta, the Guardian of Orthros, Gifted by him in the darkest hours of the Last War. She crossed into Orthros in triumph at his side."

Although Argyros's hair hung loose only to his shoulders, his face appeared as ancient as ever. He arrived in Orthros carrying nothing, but his eyes gazed upon the new land with such vivid expression, it seemed the burden he bore was his wisdom. He held fast to Hippolyta's hand. She wore a common woman's tunica, its ends tucked into her belt to shorten it into a tunic. For shoes, she had only rags strapped to her legs. She stood with her feet planted, making her Stand.

"And there you see my father," Lio said at last, with a loving glance for the sixth monument. "Elder Firstblood Apollon, whose history I have told you. He is our greatest architect, who planned this city and built many of its monuments."

Cassia beheld a curly head and beard and broad shoulders. Apollon wore his temple robe open over nothing but a pair of braccae, revealing a powerful, muscular body. He swung a mason's mallet in one hand and a chisel in the other as if he were ready to make war, not art. There was a look of zeal in his eyes she recognized.

"As you can see," Lio added, "I don't take after my father in many ways."

"I beg to differ," Cassia reminded him.

The ships carried them out from between the firstbloods, and Cassia saw whose back it was Apollon guarded. In the lead stood two more statues, one all white marble, the other deep black. The two women stood barefoot, holding each other up.

As the ships pulled ahead of them, Lio spoke again. "Ritual Firstblood Alea, once Prisma of Hagia Boreia. Ritual Grace Soteira, the great healer of the Empire. Now our Queens."

Soteira, the Hesperines' rescuing darkness, reached a hand out behind her, ready to catch any who stumbled. Alea, their light, gestured ahead, pointing the way.

"Hespera awaits you," said Lio.

There was no lighthouse. The Harbor Light hovered between the Goddess's upraised hands. The statue of Hespera was wrought of a black stone speckled with shining flecks of white. She wore nothing but her long hair, which draped and clung about her, concealing and outlining her body. With one blood-red eye and one pale eye, she gazed down upon the arriving ships. In her smile, Cassia saw an invitation to come see what she had prepared for them, to share with her the last laugh, to lay down their heads and rest at last.

As the ships docked at the Goddess's feet, Lio smiled at Cassia. "Welcome to Orthros."

HESPERA'S INVITATION

SAILING INTO HARBOR IN Union with Cassia, Lio felt he was coming home for the first time. Her wonder was more beautiful to him than all the lights in the bay. He would get to spend night after night surprising her like this and sharing in her delight.

Later this very night, he could steal her away from the embassy and begin showing her Orthros without her retinue in the way. For now he escorted her down the gangplank at his side, although he had to allow Sir Benedict to be the one who took her arm.

"The founders first arrived here by magical means," Lio said. "Now Harbor is where our ships embark and dock each year when we migrate to and from our southern home, Orthros Notou."

Lio struggled not to smile at Cassia. She seemed entranced by the ships pulling in at every dock, the busy Hesperines ushering the embassy onto shore, and most of all, by the Goddess herself.

Lio led Cassia and her retinue along the central dock at the base of Hespera's statue. "Please, come with me up the steps and onto the avenue that runs the length of the docks. Here are the guest houses, which are particularly designed for mortal comfort. Out of consideration for our visitors, our geomagi keep the interiors of all buildings in the city warm enough to be safe for humans."

Cassia looked up and down the way at the lodges and coffee houses. Her gaze traveled across their tracery, over their peaked arches, and up their spires. "Iron and granite, marble and glass. I can see the power and delicacy of your people in these works. You house your guests in art."

"Our crafters appreciate your kind praise."

"Did your father build all of these, Ambassador?"

"He or those he has taught. His students have elaborated on his style and contributed their own innovations all over the city. However, you will be staying in one of my bloodline's public works. Here is Rose House."

The wrought iron doors swung open to welcome them. Lio did not have to encourage them to hasten into the warmth of the brightly lit entry hall.

"Rest assured," Lio said, "the other lords and mages of your party will be staying just next door in the New Guest House, the four-hundred-year-old structure accessible via the gallery you see through that side door. To the king's own representative, however, we offer our newest lodgings here in Rose House, which we finished only last year. The rest of the embassy will join us here presently for the welcoming ceremony in the main hall."

Lio's mother entered behind them with the next group of Tenebrans. The free lords crowded in, talking amongst themselves. Some of her initiates came forward to take everyone's cloaks, curious and eager to perform the duties they had vied to be assigned. Sir Benedict and Callen barricaded themselves around Cassia, and Lio deemed it wise to let a young female Hesperine unburden her. The initiate gave Knight a wide berth, but he stood obediently at attention and made no aggressive moves.

Perita took her position at Cassia's elbow and fussed over her. "Oh, my lady, I was so worried when I couldn't help you dress, but…"

"It was a struggle without your expert assistance, but I tried to do everything just as you have shown me."

"That color is sure to make everyone recall who you are," Perita approved. "I couldn't have chosen better myself."

"That is a high compliment indeed, my friend."

Cassia had chosen an elaborate gown of royal purple velvet with pale purple accents and a leaf-green, embroidered belt. Lio could tell Zoe her hero had arrived in Orthros in a beautiful dress the color of her favorite flower. Later, he could tell Cassia how much the stunning sight of her in this moment meant to him.

The entry hall was filling up. Lio raised his voice and gave the Tenebrans a brief primer on Hesperine forms of address. Those who cared would need the reassuring crutch of courtesy.

It was time for Cassia's group to go forward to make way for the other

Tenebrans entering behind her. Now was Lio's opportunity to get her inside the main hall well ahead of Chrysanthos for an encounter with the elder firstbloods that would be all her own.

Lio nodded to the initiates. They opened the inner doors without touching them. Out spilled the aromas of refreshments and the force of ancient auras.

When Cassia saw who awaited within, Lio sensed her brace herself. She beheld the elder firstbloods, her aura full of the same wonder she had experienced at the feet of their statues. Then she lowered her gaze, as if she could not bear to look upon them too long.

"Join us and be at your ease," Lio said as they entered the crowded room. "The founders of Orthros are delighted to meet you. They and the firstbloods of every family are here tonight to bid you welcome."

"I feel too small to stand in their company, Ambassador."

"So does every young Hesperine. You should have seen me the last time I gave a speech before them."

"They know and love you," she protested, "one of their own."

Lio lowered his head and his voice. "I still fainted."

Cassia choked on a laugh. By that time her heart was no longer pounding, and they had reached Lio's parents.

Lio struggled not to grin like a fool or let his pride burst the Blood Union. "Father, allow me to present Lady Cassia Basilis, royal representative from Tenebra. Lady Cassia, my father, Elder Firstblood Apollon, the Queens' Master Builder."

Cassia gave his father a deep curtsy. As she straightened, she lifted her eyes to his. Lio was dismayed to hear her heart start racing again and her breath quicken with anxiety. Knight tensed beside her. In his golden formal robes, Father looked quite different from his statue, but there was no doubt his presence could be just as intimidating.

Father's gentle strength filled the Blood Union, so powerful even a mortal must feel it surrounding her. The tremble inside Cassia eased, and she looked at Father with large, hopeful eyes. The same eyes Zoe had turned upon him when she had first met her new father, Lio realized. Knight's tail gave a hesitant wag.

Lio's father winked at him over Cassia's head. "How fortunate I am that Anastasios Gifted me first, so I could be first in line to meet you. We are so glad you have come to us—and safely."

"You honor me, Elder Firstblood. It is a privilege to meet you. Your son has spoken of you with great love and pride."

"We are very proud of him, especially after what transpired in Tenebra last winter, and most recently in the pass."

Lio put his hands behind his back. "Thank you, Father."

He already knew about Lio's role in the battle? Of course he did. The sea was no barrier to Grace Union and parental conferences.

Father would see the death of the enemy as victory. Was that why he was proud? Did he believe that was how Lio had defeated the heart hunters?

Lio turned to his mother. "You have already met my mother, Elder Grace Komnena, the Queens' Chamberlain."

Mother exchanged a few easy remarks with them, and Cassia's tension eased further. Lio was about to lead Cassia onward when a disruptive aura approached, then joined them before his parents.

Chrysanthos had cut in line. He moved Eudias out of his way with a derisive glance and came to stand beside Sir Benedict and Cassia. Kadi was right at his heels, looking ready to react the instant the mage tried anything. She exchanged an auric glance with Lio's father, who answered with a silent negative.

Kadi frowned. "King Lucis's arcane emissary is eager for introductions, Uncle Apollon."

Chrysanthos put on one of his aristocratic smiles that did not reach his eyes. "I would count myself lax in my duty to Basileus if I let the responsibility of this occasion fall entirely on his daughter."

Lio's father said nothing. He just looked at Chrysanthos. Father's aura stirred and stretched like a predator ready to snap his jaws at a troublesome little bird.

Lio's mother wrapped her arm more securely in his father's, and the Blood Union filled with her calm. "My Grace, this is Honored Master Adelphos from Solorum, the mage I told you about."

The Dexion's smile hardened. "I need not request an introduction. How could I mistake the Lion of Orthros? You are none other than Apollon, the patriarch of the Blood Errant."

Lio prepared for diplomatic intervention. Cassia tensed with him, watchful of the exchange between his father and the mage.

"I am sorry to disappoint you," said Father, "but the tales that circulate among the mages of Anthros are perhaps exaggerated. The Blood Errant had no patriarch."

"The deeds of the Blood Errant are known all over Tenebra and Cordium, even to an administrator from Solorum such as myself. The other three members were your two Ritual sons and your niece, were they not?"

"We were equals and comrades in arms in every way."

"Arms, yes. In fact, you four are the only Hesperines errant who are known for bearing weapons into battle." Chrysanthos looked about. "Where is your famous stonemason's mallet, the Hammer of the Sun, which legends say could knock Anthros's chariot out of the sky?"

"I didn't have a spare hand for it on Komnena's and my journey home to Orthros."

Chrysanthos turned his smile on Lio's mother. "Well, what a surprise. Am I to understand the mighty Apollon has settled down at last?"

Lio was already sick of Chrysanthos's plentiful smiles. If he looked at Mother like that a moment longer, Lio would conjure some of his wraiths to change the Dexion's expression.

Mother replied, "I would not leap to the conclusion that Apollon has settled down, if I were you."

"The evidence of my eyes is clear," Chrysanthos countered. "Such a lovely lady must be the reason Apollon has not been seen Abroad in almost ninety years…or should I attribute his absence to a less happy event? Elder Firstblood Apollon, allow me to offer you my sincerest condolences regarding Prometheus. What a shame for your Ritual son's illustrious career as a Hesperine errant to have ended so. His day on the Akron's Altar was before my time as a mage of Anthros, of course, but I know how painful it must have been for you."

How dare he! Lio's fangs unsheathed. But he knew he could do nothing to stop the mage from rubbing salt in his family's wounds. Diplomacy tied his hands. They were not supposed to know the mage was the Dexion. Chrysanthos could hide safely behind his false name, his displaced power, and his so-called condolences. For now.

A response rumbled in Father's aura, but before he could speak, Mother pressed his arm once more with her hand.

Lio's mother smiled at Chrysanthos, making no effort to hide her fangs. "I am the reason my Grace considers his work in Tenebra done. I am disappointed my reputation does not precede me. Have you not heard of the woman who lured a member of the Aithourian Circle into her home so she could deliver the honored master's severed head to Apollon?"

Cassia gave a little start, and admiration colored her aura. Lio coughed into his hand to hide his fierce grin, while the Blood Union gleamed with Kadi's savage pleasure. Father smiled contentedly at the mage.

Chrysanthos's court mask had disappeared, revealing the hostility beneath. "I had not heard that tale. How enlightening. I must thank you for giving me a lesson in Hesperine-human relations. I begin to see what sort of education you have given your son. Ambassador. What an interesting career choice for the heir of Apollon."

"Diplomacy is very interesting," Lio said. "Fascinating, in fact. The Equinox Summit was a broadening experience for me."

"Ah, yes. You gave a few speeches, didn't you, and conjured some spell lights." Chrysanthos looked Lio up and down with an expression he might turn on Eudias.

It seemed all the Dexion saw in Lio was a fresh-faced light mage with an overlarge vocabulary and silk shoes. Lio almost smiled. So the Aithourian Circle hadn't made the connection that Lio's light magery had fueled the embassy's fatal blood spell against Dalos. The secret of Lio's thelemancy was even safer, it seemed.

"The thorn has fallen rather far from the thicket, hasn't it, Ambassador?" Chrysanthos taunted him.

Lio's hands weren't tied by diplomacy. Diplomacy was his weapon of choice. It was time Chrysanthos learned exactly whom he would face at the negotiation table.

"I hope not," Lio replied. "As a bloodborn, I take Prometheus's fate to heart and strive to live up to his extraordinary example."

Surprise flashed in Chrysanthos's eyes. "Well. No wonder your father didn't have a spare hand for his hammer. Now I understand what he brought back to Orthros instead."

"You may carry this tale back to your colleagues," said Father. "I am retired. But my son's career is only just beginning."

"Now, if you will excuse us." Lio left Chrysanthos surrounded and guided Cassia over to his aunt and uncle.

An ear-splitting growl disrupted the decorous conversation in the hall. Knight leapt between Cassia and Aunt Lyta and subjected the Guardian of Orthros to his most menacing snarl.

"*Het!*" Cassia called out, reaching for his ruff, but most of it was in a bandage. She took hold of as much of his nape as she could reach. He shook her off and barked a clamor of warnings at Lio's aunt.

Aunt Lyta didn't raise a ward. She didn't even bare her fangs. She braced her feet like her statue in the harbor, chin up and shoulders squared, and stared Knight down.

Lio waited, watching Aunt Lyta, knowing she did not need a trainee to intervene in her standoff with a liegehound. Callen and Sir Benedict had their hands at their empty sword belts, and Perita had jumped back out of the way. Chrysanthos, Eudias, and the other mages still stood in front of Lio's parents, watching the confrontation with crackling auras.

Knight fell silent and tucked his tail between his legs.

Aunt Lyta held his gaze. A moment later, he flattened himself on his belly at her feet.

"You're a good dog," she said, "simply doing as you were crafted to. It is your makers for whom I shall save my ire."

"I beg your forbearance for his outburst," Cassia said with a deep curtsy. "Please forgive our indiscretion, which has disturbed this noble gathering."

"Don't give it a thought. I hope Knight will be our guest in the gymnasium sometime during the Summit. It would be educational for the Stewards."

"You are too generous." Cassia's aura twinged with alarm.

"I'm sure we can ensure the encounter is safe for everyone concerned," Lio said. "Well, now you and Knight have officially made the acquaintance of Elder Grace Hippolyta, the Guardian of Orthros."

Aunt Lyta flashed her spirited grin. "Well met once more."

"I am glad we could be properly introduced under better circumstances than previously," said Cassia. "Thank you again for everything you did for us at Waystar."

"I was happy to help."

Aunt Lyta and Cassia exchanged a speaking glance that left Lio wondering what had passed between them at the fortress. Whatever it was, it seemed to have fostered an understanding between them. Cassia was already drawing closer to members of his family.

"Uncle." Lio turned to his mentor, making a conscious effort to put more confidence in his voice. "You remember Lady Cassia from the Equinox Summit. Lady Cassia, allow me at last to introduce you to Elder Firstblood Argyros, the Queens' Master Ambassador."

"Lady Cassia," Uncle Argyros said. "How glad I am that the length of the king's pavilion no longer stands between us, and the Solstice Summit has brought us properly face-to-face."

"I too am very glad for this opportunity, Elder Firstblood." Straightening from her curtsy, she met his gaze.

Lio watched in amazement, but somehow he was not surprised. His Cassia looked into the eyes of Silvertongue without a twitch.

"We have many things to discuss," she said, "some of it unfinished business from last year's Summit table. I believe this time will be fruitful."

"Clearly," Uncle Argyros replied. "However, you will be discussing it with my nephew, who will preside at the negotiations."

Lio wished it filled him with pride to hear his uncle say that, here in front of his Grace. But it just reminded him of the puzzle of Uncle Argyros's complete lack of involvement in the Solstice Summit.

Uncle Argyros had argued so vehemently on behalf of Lio's proposal, then dropped the whole affair in his lap. Lio had been so consumed with preparations, he had barely even spoken to Uncle Argyros since. It was almost as if his uncle wanted it that way.

But it appeared their lack of communication would not diminish the welcome Uncle Argyros gave Cassia. Lio could feel it in his uncle's aura. Within a few minutes, Cassia had succeeded in doing what few people alive, mortal or Hesperine, ever managed. She had impressed Silvertongue.

They made their way down the line to Kia's parents from Hagia

Anatela, then Lyros and Nodora's from Hagia Zephyra. At last, they came to Kassandra.

"Ritual Mother," Lio greeted her, sending her his gratitude through the Union.

She gave him an affectionate smile. She certainly didn't need him to introduce Cassia to her. No doubt she knew his Grace well already, as she did all the people she had met in her visions who had yet to encounter her.

"Here is Lady Cassia Basilis," he said, "royal representative from Tenebra, of whom you already know a great deal, I think. Lady Cassia, you have heard me speak of my Ritual mother, Elder Firstblood Kassandra, the Queens' Master Economist."

Cassia curtsied. "It is a pleasure, Elder Firstblood. I have seen the fine craftsmanship of Ambassador Deukalion's handkerchiefs. Your extraordinary works in silk are more than just cloths."

Kassandra laughed. "So these are the threads through which you have come to know me."

"How fascinating to learn you are also Orthros's lead economist."

"Yes. Weaving is my craft, but silk and cotton are fabric in more than one sense. My Imperial ancestors' innovations in textiles are responsible for millennia of prosperity and trade. I and my delegates serve Orthros by managing Hesperine economic relations with the Empire."

"It is clear your reach extends beyond the loom, and you weave far more than thread."

"My Ritual mother cast the deciding vote in favor of the Solstice Summit," Lio told Cassia. "We have her to thank for bringing us all together tonight."

"You have my gratitude," Cassia said.

The way Kassandra looked at Cassia, Lio wondered if this was one of those moments when his Ritual mother saw more than the rest of them. He ought to ask her as soon as he had a chance.

But he wouldn't. What if he didn't want to hear what she had to say?

He banished the thought. He and Cassia were building their own future, and it was looking brighter with each passing hour she was in Orthros. His plan was a success. Why else would Kassandra have voted in favor of it?

Kassandra patted Cassia's hand. "I so enjoyed our evening together during the Vigil of the Gift. I hope you will come to my pavilion again."

"Ah." Cassia covered her puzzlement well with a polite expression. "I beg your pardon?"

Lio cleared his throat. "The Vigil of the Gift is the fifth night of Winter Solstice celebrations, some weeks from now."

"Oh, I see. I would be delighted, certainly, Elder Firstblood."

The ripples of hostility in the room were the mages making their way down the line.

"And now the two of you will go and enjoy the rest of your evening," Kassandra said.

Lio looked with worry from his Ritual mother to the approaching Cordians. She cast her all-seeing gaze upon the mages, and the smile she gave them could have frozen Anthros's pyre.

She definitely did not require the youngest bloodborn to mediate her encounter with the Order that had taken her son from her. Was this very moment one of the reasons she had voted for the Summit? Lio could not begin to fathom the long strategy she always had in hand.

Lio excused himself and Cassia. As they left the greeting line, she shot him an inquiring look.

This was not the time or place to reveal that Orthros had an oracle, a secret of which the Orders remained ignorant. "Perhaps I can tell you more about my Ritual mother when we take a walk on the grounds. For now, may I offer you some refreshment, Lady Cassia?"

"No, thank you, Ambassador." While Sir Benedict's gaze darted watchfully behind her, Cassia rolled her eyes for Lio alone to see.

"Perhaps only some refreshment for your eyes, then." He turned to face the way they had come.

Cassia followed suit, and her gaze ascended above the entrance to fix on the rose window. The glow from the bay filled the many intricate panes that comprised each of the flower's petals. The Harbor Light, turned crimson through Hespera's Rose, shone upon Cassia's uplifted face.

She gave the window a knowing smile. "Ambassador, you must tell me what Hesperine master is responsible for this marvel."

"Not a master, I'm afraid, nor even a glassmaker of full rank, but a mere initiate. He has failed to progress in his craft of late, for he has devoted all his time to his service as an ambassador."

"Do you mean to say you are the artist?" She feigned surprise.

"I applied for the commission to earn my initiation, envisioning a day when the window would welcome guests to Orthros for diplomatic occasions such as this. In my own small way, I hoped to contribute to the already great and ancient beauty of our harbor."

"It is not small," she observed.

"No," he admitted. "It's rather unapologetically ostentatious, isn't it?"

Behind Lio's back, Sir Benedict and Eudias were surreptitiously signing little glyphs of Anthros upon themselves, as if Lio could not feel the fizz of the apprentice's magic. Eudias's spell puffed in the cool air of the hall and faded under the rich, dark weight of the firstbloods' power.

"We should always strive to be modest," said Lio, "but Hespera need not be."

Cassia's gaze followed the words upon the rose's center. Longing rose in her aura, a longing he recognized—the thirst to understand. "Those symbols inside the flower are writing, aren't they? Writing in Divine."

"Yes, it is a passage from a sacred text, one so ancient we no longer know who wrote the words. They might be the Goddess's own. They are known as 'Hespera's Invitation.'"

"Will you tell me what they mean?"

Lio looked at Cassia and quoted the words, which his work on the window had crafted indelibly upon his mind.

Come unto me,
to my certain embrace
under my wing of darkness,
where you shall find shelter,
against my heart,
where you shall find strength,
in the light of my eyes,
which shine with joy
in my endless sky,
where you shall be free.

THE SANCTUARY'S KEEPER

THE BEAUTIFUL FACES AND Divine names were dizzying, but Cassia gathered each and every one to her like a treasure. All the firstbloods Lio introduced as Ritual tributaries of Blood Komnena invited her to visit their homes. Couples spoke of how blessed they felt to have Solaced an Eriphite child.

Every one of the firstbloods greeted her personally, and none hesitated to welcome her as an ally of Orthros, despite the mortals within earshot. The Cordian mages must be tripping over Hesperine veils with every step they took.

Cassia expected to feel exhausted halfway through, but she didn't. Their welcome seemed to fill her up with something warm and sustaining.

But an instinct, honed hard and deeply rooted, kept her on vigil. Every moment she looked over her shoulder at the mages, as if they were her task, and there was not a room full of firstbloods who could crush them with a thought.

She watched Chrysanthos chat with Hippolyta as if he were a reasonable being and she were not the Hesperine who had defeated Aithouros. Cassia and Lio stood just near enough that the mage's words reached her ears, and she knew none of the Hesperines would have trouble hearing him.

"Have you heard from your daughter Pherenike recently?" the mage asked.

Hippolyta might be a warrior, but she had also been at every Equinox Summit with her Grace. "How thoughtful of you to ask," was all she said.

"I hear she has not returned to Orthros for some time. You must be beside yourself with worry, especially now that she does not have the rest of the Blood Errant to watch her back. Her warding magic and thelemancy are quite the dangerous combination. The sort that makes enemies. I wonder what could have befallen her."

Lio must be agonizing over the same question as Cassia. She was not certain whether Chrysanthos's words were merely a low blow or an implication that he knew what had happened to Nike.

Hippolyta sized up Chrysanthos with her gaze. Cassia and Lio watched without staring, waiting to see how the Guardian would respond. Would she take the opportunity to press Chrysanthos? Or would she forfeit it and refuse to let him bait her?

"You would do well to wonder," Hippolyta replied at last. "The Hesperines you don't see are often the ones who should most concern you."

"Hm. I will bear that in mind."

Cassia wished Lio's aunt would send Chrysanthos the way of Aithouros on the spot. But all Hippolyta could do, all any of them could do, was talk.

"This is truly a singular occasion, Ambassador," she commented to Lio.

"Indeed. One that puts all the forbearance of your people and mine to the test. But that is the very effort to which we have committed ourselves. I consider it a triumph for us all to stand together in this room at all."

He did well to remind her. "Spoken like a true diplomat."

"As true as the Goddess makes them." Argyros came to join them.

Cassia smiled at Lio's uncle. "And trained by the most eminent diplomat Orthros has ever known, I understand."

"When you are as old as I am, your reputation becomes a creature of its own, which may or may not be relied upon. In any case, if you would be so kind as to surrender your escort for a moment, there is a task with which I need the Ambassador's assistance."

"Certainly, Elder Firstblood."

"If you'll excuse me." Lio didn't look puzzled, but he didn't look in good spirits, either.

Cassia observed them until she lost sight of them in the crowd. She had seen their rapport at the Summit table in Tenebra, and it made a stark contrast to the chill beneath the surface of their courteous exchange tonight. She knew how close Lio was to his uncle. What could possibly have caused tension between them? Whatever was the matter, she could imagine how Lio must take it to heart. She must find a way to help.

"I don't know how you do it, Your Ladyship."

"What's that, Benedict?"

"You always find something pleasant to say. You even manage to come up with compliments about their foreign ways. Tenebra is fortunate to have you as our representative." He eyed the mages. "Your kind nature is the heart of our embassy."

"I appreciate you saying that. But I would be dishonest if I did not confess that I carry my prejudices just as close as everyone else." She tried not to glare at Skleros, who lurked at the edges of the crowd, watching. Cassia wanted to gouge his eyes out with his own blades.

"Don't we all." Benedict cast another nervous glance at Lio's window.

Cassia loved how Rose House was built of pale granite with touches of red and black, an elegant frame for the extravagant stained glass. "Benedict, if you will be so kind as to release my arm, I am going to have a closer look at the rose window."

"Do you think it wise, Your Ladyship?" he whispered. "Even your hound is bewitched by these Hesperines."

"I sincerely doubt some pretty glass is as dangerous as Hippolyta."

"It is a heretical symbol, Your Ladyship. We cannot know what strange power is in it."

"If that is the case, then you should direct your protectiveness at the ambassador's handkerchiefs. I happened to notice he has a pocket full of them embroidered with Hespera's Rose."

"Are you certain they're handkerchiefs and not charms, Your Ladyship?"

She towed Benedict along with her toward the window. As they passed the sideboards, she eyed the forbidden refreshments with a sigh and noticed Perita and Callen doing the same. The cheeses and fruits, pastries and breads looked delicious, and Cassia's parched tongue made the pitchers of juices and scented water nearly impossible to resist. It seemed her arrival in Orthros had inspired her long-lost appetite to come back to her at last, and with a vengeance. But she had no chance to sneak a bite. Only upon nearing the window did she manage to extricate herself from Benedict's arm for a moment, when he was busy signing yet another holy glyph.

She stood under Lio's artwork and turned her face toward the blood-colored light. Perhaps there *was* a spell in it. The stained Harbor Light felt more wonderful upon her than any sunshine.

With the light shining in her eyes, it was a moment before Cassia noticed the Hesperine sitting under the window. The lady perched on the pedestal of one of the hall's tall columns, but she was so short, her bare feet dangled. She looked red-haired and red-robed until Cassia took a step forward out of the window's glow. The Hesperine's hair and robes were in fact as white as the Light Moon. She had a round, pleasant face and a kind smile.

"I'm afraid we haven't been introduced," said Cassia.

"No, but I think we know each other well already."

Cassia recognized the gentle, ancient face before her, and her knees trembled.

Queen Alea put a finger to her lips. "I would like to ask a favor of you. Play along with my little ruse and do not curtsy."

Cassia glanced around her. Benedict was speaking quietly with Callen, and Perita held onto her husband's arm, looking fretful and tired. All the mages and free lords had their backs to this side of the room. Knight kept watch upon the firstbloods all over the hall, oblivious to the Ritual firstblood who sat before Cassia.

"Forgive me, Annassa. How could I not recognize you?"

"My statue in the harbor is not an accurate likeness. It is too tall. People were shorter in the last epoch. Alas, if we have already finished growing, the Gift does not increase our stature."

"I beg to differ, Annassa. Your monument is not tall enough to capture your presence. But I should have known your face."

Or perhaps the clue upon her hair. She wore one dark, textured braid round and round her head like a crown.

"I'll give you a hint. Argyros is not the only one who gave Lio lessons in weaving veils." Queen Alea chuckled. "I sense your surprise. It is as I suspected, and Lio was too modest to boast to you that I am his mentor in light magery."

"No, he did not tell me."

"He has such a sweet nature. Never flaunting his status and power. Magic like his is as much a burden as a gift. I could not resist taking him under my wing on Anastasios's behalf. It brought back fond memories of our time training apprentices at Hagia Boreia. He would be delighted with all the students I have taught since."

"I know how honored Lio must feel to be one of them."

"Few Hesperines in Orthros feel more gratitude than he. He would do well to lay some of it down and lighten his load. But we keep giving him so much of it in return, perhaps we have contributed to the weight."

Cassia did not know what to make of that, and yet she felt she ought to. "I feel honored that you have revealed yourself to me, Annassa."

"I've been looking forward to speaking with you. But I shall remain a mystery to the other Tenebrans for a little while yet, so I may get to know them before they know me. I have not laid eyes on mages of Anthros and Hypnos in over sixteen hundred years."

"I cannot but count that a blessing, Annassa."

"So too do I."

Then why bring them here now? How did it serve the Queens' purposes? What strategies and consequences, conclusions and predictions went on in the ancient minds of this ruler and her Grace? What was it like to have such power? To wield it together as equals, with love to guide its use?

Queen Alea hopped down from her perch. "Will you walk with me?"

"Of course, Annassa."

Neither Hesperines nor mortals noticed as Queen Alea hooked her arm in Cassia's and led her away from the gathering. Knight followed Cassia as he always did, as if they were taking a walk, just the two of them.

"No one curtsies in Orthros, you know," Queen Alea said conversationally. "The children bow to Soteira and me with their hands on their hearts because it makes them feel good. It was sweet of them to start the tradition of the heart bow, but all we ever ask of them is their nearness."

"Lio has spoken of how close you are to all your people."

"Our doors are always open to those who need us. Although we must rely on our Hesperines errant to help those in greatest need to reach us."

"I can attest to that, Annassa."

"My son will have more to say to you on that subject anon. I will only express how thankful we are to those who have delivered you."

Queen Alea took Cassia through an open doorway, out of the main hall and into a courtyard bright with spell lights. They strolled between beds full of thriving roses. This variety was as pristine white as the magic orbs. Cassia gulped deep breaths of the roses' miraculous fragrance. It felt colder in here, but she did not miss her cloak. Cassia realized crystal clear panes separated her from the stars.

"The whole courtyard is glassed in," she exclaimed. "To keep the roses warm?"

"Yes. Lio and Apollon collaborated with the geomagi to make the courtyard hospitable for mortals and flora alike. You will see many such structures in Selas."

Splashes echoed from a fountain in the center of the courtyard. Even it was carved in the shape of rose vines. Queen Alea took a seat on a wrought iron bench there and gestured at the one across from her. Cassia sank down onto it as if she expected to find pins on the seat. It felt wrong to sit in the Queen's presence. Knight sat down on Cassia's feet without a thought.

"I think it safe to bring Knight in on our secret now." Queen Alea held out her hand to him. She was holding a bite of cheese.

He looked at her for the first time. Cassia held her breath.

His ears perked up, and he got to his feet. He sniffed Queen Alea's hand, then accepted the treat, snuffling and slobbering on her fingers. Cassia knotted her hands in her lap and watched in dismay.

Queen Alea smiled and gave Knight a thorough ear rubbing. He lay down between her and Cassia, wagging his tail furiously against the hem of Queen Alea's white robes.

Cassia could scarcely fathom the vision before her. "Annassa, if I may ask…"

"Yes?"

"You were there. When Hesperines were made. You helped make them."

"We all help make ourselves."

"But you are one of the eight Ritual firstbloods, the very first Hesperines."

Queen Alea smiled. "Would you like me to tell you about it?"

"I do not mean to pry into your people's secrets."

"It is not a secret, dear one. Every suckling in Orthros has a book on it."

In Orthros, power hung on the vine like the roses that surrounded Cassia. "How did you do it, Annassa?"

"We don't know."

Cassia shook her head. "How can that be?"

"We, the leaders of the four main temples of our cult, convened in the depths of the night to devote our combined powers to an unprecedented blood Ritual. We prayed to Hespera and plied every spell we knew. We pushed our power beyond our limits and tested knowledge we had never dared put into practice. Healers, warders, light mages, and thelemancers, we all shed our blood for our Goddess and each other. Something happened to us that we still do not fully understand."

"You became Hesperines."

"The Ritual remade us into new creatures. We had beseeched Hespera to grant us power that would enable us to answer her calling, and her Gift was marvelous. The healing we needed to save lives was in our own veins. We could veil ourselves and others to hide them from harm. Our newly heightened senses gave us revelations as never before. We now lived in a state of Union with others that taught us compassion through visceral empathy. Blood magic was no longer merely our practice, but our very nature."

"It must have been wonderful."

"It was an exhilarating and terrifying time of discovery. Our new bodies were an expression of our creed in every detail, although not without consequences. We could use our blood to serve humans, but we depended on their blood for our survival. Drawing our magic from the Goddess of Night, we were helpless during Anthros's hours of sunlight. This kept us humble and tempered our power. Even so, any power so great rests uneasily in the world."

"The Orders of Anthros and Hypnos became angry with you."

"Tensions that had been abrading broke loose at last. Those tensions were what inspired our Ritual in the first place. We would not realize until later we lived in the death throes of the Great Temple Epoch. What we did know was that our world was changing in dangerous ways. Conflict was on the rise between cults and peoples in ways that threatened everyone. Loyalty to one's own twisted into hatred of all others. Those who hated most strongly were amassing unprecedented power as no one had believed possible."

"The Cult of Anthros was starting to take over," Cassia guessed.

Queen Alea nodded. "That would be the end result of those complex events. What we understood at the time was that people were suffering, and if we were to stand against wrong, we too must go to greater lengths than ever before. We had to act."

"The mages of Hespera, the goddess of Sanctuary and Mercy, would take to heart the plight of all those who suffered."

"The victims of the era's troubles were in our nurseries and sickbeds. Children left parentless by the Tenebran feuds. Common people devastated by epidemics that mages could have prevented if they had not hoarded power for the elite. Refugees from the cult of Demergos, such as Lio's father, who chose to serve Hespera after their cult fell to the mages of Anthros."

"Lio's father was a mage of Demergos first? The way folk talk about Anthros's brother, it sounds as if the god of war killed him much longer ago than that."

"The death of a god shakes the world and makes myth. Alas that Demergos's is recounted by the mages of Anthros, who call tragedy justice. They led a devastating campaign to dismantle, absorb, and defeat the only male cult that could have stood against them. We could not have imagined the even greater cataclysm that would destroy our own cult."

"But Hespera survived. You gained the Gift to protect you against Anthros."

"So the children's books say. We elders must still wonder if our discovery of immortality was our salvation or the catalyst of our destruction."

"The other cults must have coveted your power."

"When Anastasios succeeded in Gifting Apollon, our joy was great. Hespera's blessing was not for us alone. But we faced difficult choices about who should share in the Gift. Although we strove to navigate those decisions with fairness and compassion, we still wonder if we could have prevented conflict. Many of our fellow worshipers of Hespera came to feel betrayed, and other cults saw our caution as hoarding power.

"You see, we kept our discovery secret at first so we could fully understand the consequences of the Gift before we dared subject large numbers to the transformation. After Anastasios's discovery, each Ritual firstblood was to choose only one trusted student to join Apollon in receiving the Gift. They became the elder firstbloods.

"I was still deliberating over my choice when we ran out of time. The cult of Anthros struck. Our power was not enough to save our temples, our villages, our entire way of life as we knew it. But it was enough to make a new way of life here."

"Oh, but it is a beautiful way of life, Annassa. Orthros is even more wondrous than I imagined."

"I must confess I feel the same way. I am happy to say I have never left since the night we arrived nearly sixteen hundred years ago."

"I do not wonder at that, Annassa. Who would want to be anywhere else?"

Queen Alea smiled as if she knew something Cassia didn't. "I am an unlikely Queen. It is Soteira who has wisdom and experience of the wide world. I, in my mortal time, was happy to stay all the years of my life inside the walls of my temple. When we found refuge in Orthros at last, I never wanted to let this land out of my sight. It is a balm to me that I am bound here and must never leave."

"Do you mean to say you cannot travel outside of Orthros?"

"If I set foot beyond the ward, it will break. It is the nature of such workings."

Queen Alea could take one step too far, and the enduring fortifications of Orthros could shatter as easily as the glass over their heads? The thought sent a chill down Cassia's spine. "I had no idea."

"Orthros has two hearts, Boreou and Notou. I can step between them, remaining inside the linked wards my Grace and I maintain over our home. But I must not cross the border in the north or the south."

"I thought Hesperines could cast wards and veils over others without needing to remain within their own workings."

"Others can, but I am what we call a Sanctuary mage, someone with a dual affinity for warding and light. Sanctuary wards can protect and conceal as other wards and veils cannot, but our power comes at a higher cost than any other blood magic. To achieve the most powerful Sanctuary wards, we must either live or die inside our own workings. I could never have raised Orthros's fortifications without my Grace."

"I understand Annassa Soteira is a healer of incomparable power."

"Yes. The most powerful in the known world. She too has a dual affinity—for the body and the mind. She is both a physician and a mind healer. Soteira kept me alive while I built the ward. She also added characteristics to my spell that made the ward into something no Sanctuary mage alone has ever been able to achieve. She opened it to the mind so that it serves as a watchtower. It is possible to project one's thoughts and sight anywhere along the ward's length."

"No wonder the Stand can patrol your borders with so few warriors."

"The Stewards need only work in pairs, with at least one warder between them, to make use of the magic my Grace and I have established for them. Sanctuary magic by its nature is sacrificial. It gives itself to others, eager to serve. Thus those without any affinity for it can use it in ways they might not be able to tap other magic."

"Do other Sanctuary mages like you join the Stand to help tend the ward?"

"It grieves me to say I am the last with my affinity. Our cult was once full of Sanctuary mages, but all gave their lives in the Last War to protect Hespera's worshipers from persecution. They bled to death working our magic. Often they chose to end their own lives inside their workings in order to create the most powerful Sanctuary wards possible. Those wards still stand in Tenebra and even Cordium, and our people take refuge there when under duress Abroad."

"I carry your grief in my veins." Cassia found new meaning in the Hesperines' traditional words of condolence. It seemed grief had been in their blood since their beginning. She could scarcely conceive what it must be like for Alea, the last Sanctuary mage, the last Ritual firstblood. "What a miracle you managed to survive, Annassa. I cannot imagine what would have become of your people otherwise."

"The Goddess led me to my Grace in my darkest hour. Soteira was our salvation. She was the first to whom I gave the Gift, but in truth, it is I who owe her my life. If not for her, I would have met the same fate as the other Sanctuary mages. We keep hoping my affinity will reappear among Hesperines, but it has not, even in our own children. And yet you carry some of it with you into our lands tonight, the likes of which I have not sensed in centuries. I would dearly love to know how this came to be."

Cassia shook her head. "I don't know what you mean, Annassa. I am not at all a mage."

"You wear a Sanctuary ward upon you as gracefully as your purple gown. Are you certain you have no power of your own?"

Impossible. "I have never been able to work any magic in my life."

"You might, without recognizing it. In the absence of training or encouragement, a mage's own power sometimes plays hide and seek with her."

"A mage of your eminence would surely know right away if I had any magic. Would you not sense it in my aura?"

"Not if you are hiding it under a Sanctuary ward."

"You would know better what to do with this spell than me, for I do not even know it is there. Surely you could lift it off of me to see how it came to be."

"I would sooner halt a shooting star in its path. It would be a shame to tamper with such a precious thing. But between the two of us, I am sure we can solve the mystery of its origins. Ah. I sense I am trespassing on a secret. I hope you will forgive me for intruding, in my eagerness."

"Annassa, you can ask anyone anything." Cassia wished she could Will away the flush she felt on her cheeks. Her hand went to her chest, where the glyph shard pulsed under her gown. "I can think of only one place the spell could have come from. An abandoned shrine of Hespera on the grounds of Solorum…where Lio and I used to meet."

"Yes, our cult had a shrine at Solorum in better times."

Cassia drew the glyph shard out of her neckline and made to take it off.

Queen Alea held up a hand. "No, no. Do not disturb it."

She came to sit next to Cassia on the bench. The very air seemed to fill with the force of an entire ocean, as gentle as a single drop of rain. Cassia's heart pounded, and the glyph shard pulsed in her hands.

Queen Alea cupped Cassia's hands in hers. Cassia gasped. She felt as if light were singing in her veins.

A single tear slipped down the Annassa's cheek. "A living Sanctuary ward. What a precious gift you have carried into Orthros."

Cassia had no words, for none could speak like a Ritual first-blood's tear.

Queen Alea settled the glyph shard upon Cassia's chest once more. "The mage of Hespera who was the shrine's keeper would rejoice to know you have resurrected her power. Makaria was one of the Sanctuary mages who did not survive to reach Orthros or become a Hesperine."

"I am so sorry."

"Her lover, Laurentius, was one of the Mage King's favored warriors. They both gave their lives for what they believed in—Makaria for our hope of worshiping freely, Laurentius for the hope of a unified, peaceful Tenebra. He went to his funeral pyre with his amulet of Anthros and the votive statue of Hespera from Makaria's Ritual Sanctuary. The Mage King himself destroyed the shrine before the Orders had a chance, for he knew only he would leave some of it standing in their memory."

Cassia wiped her eyes with one hand. "Forgive me. I am usually more composed."

"In Orthros, we do not apologize for mourning. Their fate is worthy of your tears. You honor Makaria and Laurentius with your grief, and by carrying her magic."

Cassia struggled to regain control of her emotions. But she had carried their heartbreak out of Tenebra.

"So this is Cassia," said a beautiful, throaty voice.

Cassia looked up to see another statue come to life from the harbor. Queen Soteira had joined them. The dignity of her bearing was remarkable even for a Hesperine. She had full lips and a warm smile, a broad nose and deep black skin. From her coronet of Queen Alea's white braid, Queen Soteira's own hair rose in a magnificent sculpture of braids, a royal headdress of her own making. Her hair was a masterpiece of centuries, but one she must always be remaking anew as it grew with her age and power.

Cassia could not stop herself from getting to her feet. She gave the heart bow. "It is an honor to meet you, Annassa."

Queen Soteira laughed. It was the kindest music Cassia had ever heard. "You will be right at home here. Please, sit with us awhile."

"Thank you, Annassa."

Queen Alea reached out and took her Grace's hand in invitation. The Annassa sat down together across from Cassia, but their combined presence made her feel as if they embraced her. Knight got up and went to greet Queen Soteira, sticking his head in her lap for pets.

She also treated Cassia's hound to her beautiful laughter. She scratched the red fur under his chin with her free hand. "What a fine fellow. Oh, yes, you are a good dog. How happy we are to meet you under happier circumstances than your breeders intended."

He settled down at their feet again, rested his head on his paws, and shut his eyes.

"Let him sleep here until veil hours," said Queen Soteira. "He has earned a respite."

"You are very kind, Annassa."

"My Grace," said Queen Alea. "I must show you what gift Cassia has given me tonight."

Cassia felt an echo of the clarion call that had awoken her on Spring Equinox.

"A Sanctuary ward!" Queen Soteira studied the glyph shard, then Cassia.

Their gazes met, and for the first time Cassia dared looked into the healer's dark brown eyes.

Cassia's hands throbbed, as if phantoms of her wounds remained there. She felt suddenly aware of all her ribs that showed and every freckle on her skin. She felt as brave as she had when she had donned her sister's gown on Autumn Equinox. Beautiful as when she'd first bathed in rosewater of her own making. She felt the slivers of the shrine under her feet and knew they would cut, but she would keep walking. She had carried the glyph stone all the way over the mountains, home to Orthros.

She was so strong.

Cassia blinked, and she was sitting on the bench again, listening to the peaceful sound of the fountain, with smooth, cool stone beneath her shoes and the smell of roses around her.

"You did not dream the power you just felt," Queen Soteira assured her.

"Do not be afraid, Cassia. My Grace has given you a great gift, one only a theramancer as powerful as she can grant."

"I see what you have done," said Queen Soteira. "And so do you."

"Then you know what happened to the shrine. Makaria saved my life."

Queen Alea did not wipe away the tears that trailed down her cheeks. "Sixteen hundred years later, and she is still saving lives. It gives me solace to know. You too have made a blood sacrifice. As I said, Sanctuary magic comes to the hand of those in need, even if they are not mages."

"I thought I had lost it forever in Martyrs' Pass."

"We felt the moment when Lyta carried it across the ward. She has been the Guardian of our working for so long, she would not miss a needle of Sanctuary magic in a haystack. Imagine my surprise when she asked me what spell I had cast upon Waystar the first night the embassy stayed there. You did well."

"It grieved my heart to damage the glyph stone, but carrying a shard of it seemed the only way to make sure I always have its protection."

Queen Alea shook her head. "You have not broken, but crafted a powerful artifact. You have done more than awaken Makaria's ward. You have donned it." A little smile came to Queen Alea's lips. "Tell Lio he need not worry. No mages of Anthros will sense his power or anything else Hesperine about you. You have warded yourself most securely."

Cassia looked down at her hands. How could she tell him the truth about the shrine? "Lio works so hard to protect me."

"Just as you work hard to protect him. He will be glad to know his blood is a part of the ward as well. I can sense the devotions he performed at the shrine."

"Our glyph stone is in my satchel right now, hidden in my sister's magical artifacts." Cassia forced herself to go on, although she could scarcely bear to make the offer. "If there is a sacred site here where it should rest—if there is someone who should rightfully have it—"

"You," Queen Soteira said firmly.

Queen Alea nodded. "Do not fear it will be discovered. The glyph shard and its mother stone are bound together. The Sanctuary ward will keep them and you safe and hidden."

Cassia did not have to give it up. "Thank you so much, Annassa. I am honored to be its bearer. I had no idea someone like me could carry the shrine's magic."

Queen Soteira smiled as if she had known and cared for Cassia all her life. "Are you really so surprised?"

"This is Orthros," Queen Alea said, "where we all learn what we are really capable of."

ABSOLUTION

L
IO'S UNCLE CAME TO a halt in a less crowded corner of the hall as if
the coffee service on the sideboard were their only purpose tonight.
As Uncle Argyros calmly took up the coffeepot and poured them each
a cup, Lio felt his mentor cloak them in a familiar and undeniable veil.

"I am ready to complete our task," said Lio. "The Queens expect us."

"It will not take long to conceal the exit of those they have invited."
Uncle Argyros pressed the cup of coffee into Lio's hands.

There was no way around the cup of coffee, not with Uncle Argyros.
Lio downed it in two swallows, then felt compelled to offer an obligatory
apology. "I am sorry. I know such haste is an injustice to a roast this fine."

"Are you all right, Lio?"

There was no way around his uncle's grave tone of voice, either.

They were going to talk about Martyr's Pass.

"Cassia is with me now," Lio said. "That is what really matters."

"How she got here matters, as well. Would you like to talk about it?"

"Not here and now."

Uncle Argyros refilled Lio's coffee cup. "Why don't you let me take
care of the veil and you rejoin Cassia? She is with the Annassa in the
courtyard."

"Cassia has already departed with the Queens? I would not wish to
interrupt her first audience with them."

"They will be glad for you to join them. I have matters well in
hand here."

Lio set down his coffee. "I am perfectly capable of assisting you with
the veil, Uncle."

"I never said you were not. Will you not let me give you a reprieve?"

"I am not among those who need a leave of absence after the battle."

Uncle Argyros made no move, but suddenly they were standing in the gallery between the two guest houses. Had Lio's uncle really just stepped with him as if he were a suckling? The voices in the main hall had faded to echoes. Lio was alone in the stone corridor with his uncle.

Uncle Argyros gestured to a nearby bench. "Perhaps you will feel more at ease discussing this with our audience out of sight as well as on the other side of a veil."

Lio did not feel like sitting down.

They had not discussed anything of importance since the night of his proposal, but now his uncle was suddenly determined to press him about what had happened in the pass?

There had been a time, not so long ago, when his uncle would have been the first person whose counsel he sought about that night, the first person he confided in, the first comfort he reached for. That had been when Uncle Argyros had been mentoring him.

Right now, his mentor was the last person he wanted to speak with about it. Lio could not bear it.

He held onto Cassia's faith in him, his lifeline, which had restored his faith in himself. Every time his doubts crept up on him again, he reminded himself of her passionate defense of him. He had not murdered anyone.

The only words Lio could put to his fraught thoughts were, "I still do not wish to speak of it."

Uncle Argyros gave a nod. Then he sat down on the bench. "In that case, allow me to take the burden of speech upon myself. I hope I can help you put your experience in Martyr's Pass into perspective. There is something you should know. Something I have waited your entire life to tell you."

Lio sank down onto the bench beside his uncle.

Uncle Argyros sighed. "I have told you of the army that marched on Hagia Anatela."

"Your greatest victory. Mages from the Orders of Anthros and Hypnos, together with warriors who served the Cordian princes and the Tenebran free lords who collaborated with them, comprised an enormous combined force. And yet you managed to hold them off long enough for Hypatia to evacuate everyone. When the attackers destroyed the temple, it was empty of every soul and every scroll."

"But Lyta's village was not so fortunate."

"No," Lio said quietly. "They had no forewarning."

"You have gleaned from the words Lyta does not say what atrocities that army committed upon her family, friends, and neighbors. You can understand the guilt she carried as the one they chose to escape to warn the other villages. Her wards and skill as a rider saved many other communities in the army's path—but not her own. All your life, you have heard these stories."

"Yes, Uncle. They are our heritage. Your legacy." Everything Lio had tried to live up to in the pass.

"What I have not told you," Uncle Argyros said, "is why the army targeted her village, and with such brutality."

"They were purging all Hespera worshipers in their path. It is no wonder they brought the pogrom to Aunt Lyta's home. Since Aunt Lyta's people were Hesperite pacifists, and they would not make a stand against the enemy, the army found them easy targets."

"And yet that army had orders to march directly for Hagia Zephyra in the west, for Hesperines were to be their priority."

Lio shook his head, frowning. "Then what happened?"

Uncle Argyros fell silent. For a long moment, Lio was not sure his uncle would continue the tale.

But at last Uncle Argyros said, "I made a mistake."

Lio said nothing, aware that the wrong word might make it harder for his uncle to speak of this.

Uncle Argyros took a shaking breath. "I succeeded in mastering their minds utterly, to the last man. I broke their Wills and froze them in their tracks. With their whole force on puppet strings in my hands, I realized how much harm I could prevent—how much harm I could cause. I intended to turn them against each other so they destroyed one another. A travesty for their friends, families, and way of life. But the only way to rescue mine."

Lio let that sink in. The story he had grown up with had always ended with the temple's salvation. He had assumed the army simply marched on.

So the truth was, his uncle had tried to end the lives of all those soldiers.

"You had to stop them from hurting anyone else."

"So I decided that night. In the end, however, my power was not enough. I lost control of them."

"Uncle, you nearly died from that casting! You cannot fault yourself for reaching the end of your magic. They were a force of thousands. It is a triumph that you held them that long."

"There was no triumph in it. Suddenly released from the bondage that had enraged them, they went mad, like animals out of a trap. They had no reason left and sought to ravage everything in their path. And what was in their path was Lyta's village."

Horror froze Lio's thoughts.

"My own magic exacted justice upon me," said Uncle Argyros. "My power trapped me in their minds, as surely as I had trapped theirs. Tossed like baggage between the thoughts of madmen, I descended upon Lyta's village with them. I felt their bloodthirst and their lust. Had I lived within them as they acted upon it, I would have gone mad and, I am certain, never survived. Like a mortal unworthy of the Gifting, I think I would have died from the terrors of my own conscience.

"Lyta saved me. Her mind drew me like the Harbor Light, and I slipped into her thoughts as into Sanctuary itself, and she carried me away from that devastation. This was how she repaid me for taking everything from her. She rescued me."

Lio found words at last. "Did she know?"

"No. When we met later in a Sanctuary for refugee Hespera worshipers, I knew her, but she had no idea of the role I had played in the destruction of her home. And I did not tell her. Privately, I vowed to atone as best I could by supporting her in every way possible. As she struggled through her anger and grief, I devoted myself to her. Imagine my own grief, when I discovered that the one person in the world more precious to me than any other was the one who could never love me."

"But she does."

"I could not bear to keep the secret from her any longer and confessed, certain it would destroy what we had. Do you know how she replied?"

"Yes, Uncle. I do."

A smile glinted through Uncle Argyros's stone expression. "She forgave me."

"You have never told anyone this. It is not in the histories."

Uncle Argyros shook his head. "That is how Lyta wants it. The fate of her own people is her history to write, and she has rewritten it between us. By forgiving me, she taught me by example to forgive myself."

"I am so sorry either of you had to endure that."

"I am sorry you had a taste of such war, after all we did to ensure that would never happen. But your response to it did not cost innocent lives. Thank Hespera for that."

Innocent. That one word sent a chill through Lio.

His uncle had said *innocent* lives. Not that his reaction hadn't cost any lives at all.

Lio got to his feet. "Am I supposed to feel comforted that only the enemy died in Martyr's Pass? Even if I were the one who slaughtered them? Is that why you told me this? Because you believe I made a mistake?"

"Lio, I did not say that."

"There was another thelemancer at work within them—a mage of dreams."

"Right now, I am only concerned about you."

"I know I have been half-mad with Craving, I know it renders my power unstable. I know you are the foremost mind mage in Orthros's history, and all the signs which you are most qualified to interpret seem to contradict me. But…"

But he was Lio's uncle. Lio had expected Uncle Argyros to know him better.

"…but Cassia, who suffered most at the heart hunters' hands, has expressed her confidence that I was not responsible for their deaths. You understand, Uncle, after what you and Aunt Lyta went through. Now if you will excuse me, I will join Cassia and the Annassa."

Lio did not wait for his uncle's reply. He stepped to his Grace.

THE NEW PLAN

"WE ARE ABOUT TO be discovered," Queen Alea warned with a smile.

Cassia looked around. Queen Alea must have opened the little otherworld into which she and Queen Soteira had swept Cassia, for Lio came out into the courtyard and approached the fountain.

"Lio," Queen Soteira welcomed him. "Please join us."

He gave a deep heart bow. Then he took a seat on the bench with Cassia and took her hand in his, right in front of his Queens. "Annassa, I am so happy to see you have met Cassia. I would apologize for not properly introducing her to you, but I think she needs no introduction, in truth."

Queen Alea shook her head. "None other than the one you so eloquently gave her before the Firstblood Circle, when you proposed the Solstice Summit and made such a compelling case to win our support for it."

Cassia tightened her hand on Lio's and looked at him. He gave her one of his self-effacing smiles, but the determination in his gaze was anything but modest.

"My Grace," said Queen Soteira, "I sense the young people have some things to discuss. Why don't we give them a little time before they join us for tonight's circle?"

"Yes, I think so."

Before either Lio or Cassia had a chance to stand and bow again, the Queens were gone.

"I suppose it's time to talk about politics," Lio said.

"Lio, you made the Solstice Summit happen? All of this was your plan?"

"Yes."

"The Firstblood Circle...does that mean all your elders?"

"That's like our council, which advises the Queens and debates decisions affecting our people. The head of each bloodline in Orthros—everyone gathered in the hall here—has a vote, although their descendants can attempt to influence outcomes with statements of partisanship. The Queens have the final say and the power to veto decisions they deem unwise."

"You managed to convince all of them to take this risk? After what you said when I arrived, I knew you were responsible for inviting me, but...everything else, too? This is an incredible accomplishment in your career. You must be so proud!" She ran her free hand over his cords and medallion, caressing his chest.

The silver disk was engraved with two crescent moons overlaying a shining sun. It made the celestial bodies appear as one. A fitting symbol of the Equinox, when night and day were equal. A true tribute to the ideals Lio believed in with all his heart.

"I didn't do it for my career," he said.

She lifted her free hand to his stubbled cheek. "Of course not. You did it for the common good. For peace."

"If peace were my only goal, the idea would never have come to me. The only way I could keep my promise to come back for you was to make a way for you to come to me. But I knew that in doing so, I must aid your plans, rather than force you to abandon them."

"I don't understand."

"Yes, you do."

Oh, she understood his plan. Perfectly. The flawless plan that had dropped in her lap in her time of need after Autumn Equinox. How she had marveled at the opportunity. Lio had made it for her. How could she not have seen his hand in it?

She stared at their intertwined hands. "I don't understand how you could do this—move the sun and stars—for my sake."

"Then I'll just have to keep showing you." He pulled her close to him and wrapped his arms around her.

He, the son of Apollon, the future of Blood Komnena. The bearer of Anastasios's blood, the triumph of Hagia Boreia, the student of a Queen. He had changed the course of his people's history. "You did it for me."

"I did it for you," he confirmed. "Is it what you needed me to do, Cassia?"

She pulled back so she could look at him, but held fast to his hand. "This was exactly what I needed."

He let out a breath. "I told you that's what I would do. Whatever you needed."

"If you wore a braid for that promise, I would undo it now." She touched his hair, then lowered her hand. Her fingers tightened.

She didn't want to admit defeat. It grated on her down to her bones. But that's not what she was doing. She was telling Lio the truth. Discussing the situation, so they could rescue it. So they could win.

"I was at an impasse," she confessed.

"I feared so."

All her anger and frustration returned to her, and it was all she could do not to shake her fist at the king who was not here. "I was succeeding in stalling Lucis, but I could. Not. Move him! He would not cave. It was a stalemate."

And how she had feared what she must do to break it.

"Then Chrysanthos arrived," she said. "I knew we were out of time."

Lio nodded. "That was the turning point for us here, too."

"Meanwhile, I'm afraid Solorum was becoming rather too hot for me." Cassia looked at the fountain. "The king was having me followed even then."

"He *suspects* you? Goddess, Cassia—"

"I'm not sure how much he knows. But what he gave me on the Autumn Greeting made it clear he was closing in. I don't suppose the envoys reported on what I wore to the dance."

Lio shook his head.

"The king gave me Solia's gowns, among them the very one she wore when she danced the Greeting." Cassia set her jaw. "I chose that one. To show him that when he twists the knife, I take hold of the hilt. But I could not ignore the possibility that the dresses might be a message to me that I had expended my usefulness to him."

Lio let out an exclamation in the Divine Tongue that sounded like a potent curse.

"Then there was Chrysanthos to watch out for," Cassia said lightly. "He started a witch hunt in search of a Hesperite sorceress at Solorum. As if I didn't have enough problems."

"*What?*"

"Imagine him finding evidence of a Hesperine sympathizer in the capital and coming to the conclusion she must be a powerful blood sorceress. It's rather amusing, really, that he imagines I am some sort of wild-haired harpy chopping animal sacrifices into bits. What would he say if he found out it was me, the plain bastard who putters about in her gardening pots?"

"Hespera's Mercy. Cassia."

She was suddenly in Lio's arms again, and he was holding her so tightly. She clung to him.

"He almost found me out." She had been so frightened. Just how much, she hadn't realized until now.

Perhaps because the way Lio held her told her how frightened he was. How furious. "That was too close."

"But not as close as the pass."

She didn't want to say it. *The pass.* Like a curse, the words conjured all that had happened there. But that dark working was no match for the spell of Orthros all around her.

"It's all right now," Lio said. "You're safe here. I will keep you safe."

"I—I was so frightened," she admitted for the first time.

"I know."

"You do know. You could feel it in the Blood Union. You understand."

"He didn't win, Cassia. Everything you've dreaded didn't come true."

"All I could think in that moment was"—her breath hitched—"I still don't know what the rebels did to my sister while she was at Castra Roborra."

Lio rocked Cassia in his arms. "You will never, ever go through that. It's over now. You're safe."

Horror overtook her, horror like she'd seen in Lio's eyes when he had confessed his worst fears about the pass. Her stomach burned and soured as if she had never overcome her fear of the king. Lio held her shaking body, his hand cool on her forehead, and his gentle touches calmed her.

"It's all right to be afraid," he soothed.

"Yes." She swallowed. "If we don't let our fears out of their cages, how else can we banish them together?"

"You saved me from mine. Let me help you with yours."

She tucked her feet up onto the bench. He looked ready to pull her onto his lap, but she reached into her bespelled silk shoe and drew out what she had been keeping wrapped around her ankle, where no one would discover it.

She held out his handkerchief, which bore the brown remnants of Knight's blood. "I still have the first one you gave me. I keep it wrapped around the soap."

"I still have the one you bled on, the first night I smelled your blood."

"Let us not enshrine this one."

"Agreed."

The scent of his cleaning spell mingled with the fragrance of the Solace roses. The stains of Martyr's Pass disappeared from the white silk. He took the handkerchief from her, folded it, and put it away in his pocket where he kept all the rest.

"I haven't even said thank you, Lio. I would give you my gratitude for saving me, but you have all of it already."

"We have bled for that Ritual before, haven't we?"

"We did, at our shrine, and it saved me from Chrysanthos."

Lio held her face in his hands, stroking her. "What happened?"

"I was observing a magical demonstration the Dexion gave the king on the palace grounds. Chrysanthos grew suspicious that the so-called blood sorceress might be nearby."

"Solia's artifacts can't keep you safe beyond the palace walls! You were spying on a mage of his skill without any protection? You could have been—"

"He cast a revelatory spell right upon me, but he couldn't even tell I was there."

"How?"

"I've spent a lot of time at the shrine since you left. I couldn't stay away." It wasn't a lie. It was all true. But if she left out the details of that last day and never spoke of it, then that wasn't true, at least not for Lio. "I had no idea, but Queen Alea has told me it is so. The Sanctuary ward from the shrine. It's on me now." Cassia touched the glyph shard.

Lio ran his hand over hers with an expression of wonder. "You did that! Awakened a Sanctuary ward and took it upon yourself. That is a feat of sorcery unlike any I have known in my lifetime."

"Queen Alea says it will keep me safe from Chrysanthos and his suspicions."

"I should say so. That is old, rare magic, Cassia. Few of us have ever had a taste of it, except when we come near the Queens' ward."

"You have had a taste of it. Your blood was on the glyph stone too. Our blood, from your veins. You are part of my ward."

He smiled. "I could feel it when we made love."

"So could I. And I can think of no better way to honor the shrine's past. Queen Alea remembers the mage who cast the ward on the shrine and was able to tell me what befell her."

When Cassia finished sharing the tale of Makaria and Laurentius with Lio, he held both her hands in silence for a moment before he spoke. "I feel blessed the legacy of such fine people has touched us. They represent everything that was good about their time, when a mage of Hespera and a warrior of Anthros were free to fall in love. They fought so hard not to see that epoch destroyed. They may not have lived to see peace, but here we are. Still trying to make it a reality."

"For them," Cassia agreed. "For everyone lost to Cordium's hatred and Tenebra's civil wars."

"For us." He leaned over her hands, putting himself on her eye level. "I want to redeem their loss by making sure the Order of Anthros does not destroy us. Shall we try again? Will you help me keep trying?"

"Always." She kissed his hands. "I cannot save Tenebra without you."

"I cannot save Orthros without you. I need you here with me. I need your help."

"You know I will do anything."

He squeezed her hands. "The stakes have never been so high. There is something you need to know, just between us. I am the only person outside the royal family who is privy to this information, and I am to tell you. The First Prince, the Queens' eldest, has entrusted this secret to both of us. If it became widely known, it would spread doubt and despair among all Hesperines at an already grievous time."

"It is a privilege to be so trusted."

"You have a right to know." He looked at their joined hands, then met her gaze. "Since our people first swore the Equinox Oath, there has been a plan in place to protect us if the truce with Tenebra went ill. At the time, we could not be sure the Mage King would succeed in keeping the Orders at bay. It seemed the Last War could break out again at any moment. We never had to go through with the plan, thank the Goddess, but the Queens retain the power to invoke it in case of crisis."

"Could it help us now?"

"No. It would destroy everything we have tried to achieve."

"What can you mean? Surely the Queens would never order anything so devastating."

"It would break their hearts, and our people's with them. But they would pay that price if it were the only way to prevent the Next War. It is called the Departure."

Cassia shook her head. "Isn't that what the Queens did after the Equinox Summit ended in disaster? They made the Last Call to summon Hesperines home to safety in Orthros until the danger has passed. They closed the border so you couldn't leave."

"The Departure would make that permanent. Every single Hesperine would leave Tenebra. Forever."

The heavy fragrance of the courtyard went to Cassia's head, and the bench swayed under her. "Hespera never gives up on anyone."

Lio steadied her in his arms. "That's why you and I must never give up. We have to make sure the Summit succeeds so there will be no war and no Departure."

"The Queens wouldn't go through with such a thing! Hesperines wouldn't abandon Tenebra to its fate for all time."

"Can you forgive our people for considering it in the name of sparing Tenebra even greater suffering?"

"No more Mercy? From the fever towns to the battlefields, the dying would lay there in agony with no one to ease their pain, no one to share their final moments."

He nodded in silence.

"No more Solace? All the unwanted children. They would die, frightened and alone."

"All I can think of is the Hilt, where so many little ones are left to the wolves. I can hear them crying, and no one answering."

"My sister." Cassia's throat tightened. "Me."

"I know."

"So many lost and broken lives. So much suffering. Not a gleam of hope." She held onto his arms. "Tenebra would be a hollow body without a spirit, if we lost our guardian Hesperines."

"I will never abandon you." The look in his eyes left no room for failure. No room for doubt. "We are going to win your fight."

"Together, Lio, I believe we can."

THE SUMMIT BEGINS

"WE HAVE ALREADY ACCOMPLISHED so much." Cassia's determination returned to her in full force. "We are so close."

"Yes, let us begin with what we have achieved so far." Lio pulled two documents out of the scroll case he carried. He conjured an extra spell light over the bench. "Here is my proposal for the Summit and my record of what I know you have done in Tenebra. If we go over them together, we can resolve each other's unanswered questions and find a way forward."

Cassia glanced over her shoulder. "Is now a good time? I know Queen Alea's magic concealed our departure, but the embassy will eventually realize I'm gone."

Lio shook his head. "The lords and mages shall not be allowed to interfere with the Queens' plans. My uncle's thelemancy will ensure no one notices the absence of those invited to tonight's circle."

Cassia had not imagined it earlier. The subtle signs of Lio's tension appeared every time he mentioned his uncle. She must find a good opportunity to invite him to talk about it.

For now, she asked, "Are we expected to appear before the Firstblood Circle tonight?"

"No, most of the firstbloods will remain here with the embassy. The Queens have convened a special circle of only the elder firstbloods, the Stand, the First Prince, and Master Envoys Basir and Kumeta. Chrysanthos believes the negotiations will begin tomorrow when the embassy is officially presented to the royal family, but in fact, the Summit begins tonight, and you are the only Tenebran who will be in attendance."

"I don't want to arrive with gaps in my knowledge. Who is the First Prince? Is that like a crown prince?"

"He is the Queens' eldest, yes. He commands the Prince's Charge, a force of Hesperines errant. They fought with us in the pass. The circle will give you the opportunity to learn more of their mission. The prince is counting on you and me to help prevent the Departure. We can rely on him as one of our greatest supporters."

"Elder Firstblood Kassandra and the First Prince are both in favor of the Summit, then. It sounds as if we are fortunate in our allies."

Lio smiled. "Yes."

"I'd best make the most of our time to prepare for the circle. I hope your scrolls are in Vulgus."

"Yes, I wrote of your deeds in Vulgus. I had to present my proposal in Divine, but I've had time to translate the most relevant excerpts since. It was, ah, a rather long address." He said tactfully, "I can summarize for you if you need."

She plucked the offered translation from his hands and unrolled it with relish. "I have been practicing diligently, Sir Scholar. It turns out Solia left some excellent reading material hidden in her rooms. Thanks to her book on statecraft, I should be well-prepared for an ambassador's proposal."

He grinned. "We are going to have a great deal of fun with reading, I predict."

"I still can't win any races," she admitted, "but I am competent now. It's the only thing I've given as much effort as my observations of the king, because I know it is a skill I can no longer do without. When I am waiting for something of importance to happen in the solar, I often pass the time reading in the secret passageway."

Lio shook his head. "No wonder you haven't slept in half a year. It's amazing you're still on your feet."

"Do you think we might have time to…well, perhaps it is too ambitious of me as yet."

"Time to do what?"

"You once said you would be willing to violate all religious law of Tenebra and Cordium and teach a bastard female with no magic the Divine Tongue."

"You know how much I love violating Tenebran and Cordian religious law together at our shrine…or on the carpet at Waystar…or in your cabin on the voyage to Selas."

She grinned. "I do think our previous vocabulary lessons have been a pleasure."

"But I feel the need to point out that we are in Orthros, where most of the laws are written by females, and learning to read is not forbidden, but required."

Cassia sighed. "Required for sucklings, no doubt."

"Many adults come here with gaps in their education. It is nothing to feel ashamed of. Everyone here receives education in Divine and the language of their mortal origin."

"Well, I've only just found my way with Vulgus, but…"

"I would love to teach you Divine."

A new excitement brimmed in her, as if she were staring at a fallow garden plot. "Thank you, Lio."

"It will be an honor and a pleasure."

"I wish we had time to start tonight." She smiled at the opening lines of his proposal. "Even in translation, this is a beautiful speech. I can just imagine your triumph before the Firstblood Circle. When you said you fainted in front of them, I know you were just trying to make me feel better."

He looked sheepish. "I wasn't jesting. I talked for so long, my hunger made me pass out."

"Lio!"

"But not before I told them what we did during the Summit."

"Uh, everything we did?" That was when he had revealed their affair— when he stood before his people's government?

"Oh, yes."

He had held her hand in front of his Queens. He had declared before all the leaders of Orthros she was his share. "I wish I had been there."

He put a hand on his heart. "You were."

They went to work, sitting close on the bench and spreading his scrolls across their laps. Inspiration carried them quickly through recent events, and ideas for the future flowed fast between them. Despite the short time they had, Cassia felt confident they had made a strong start.

She also felt reassured by Lio's notes on her activities in Tenebra. She saw no sign in his careful records that he had any inkling of her last resort. He need never even know she had considered it. They could leave that behind them.

When the chime of bells drifted through the courtyard from somewhere in the city, Lio put away their scrolls. "That's the half hour. It's time."

Near one of the entrances to the courtyard, someone cleared his throat loudly.

Lio grinned and stood, pulling Cassia to her feet with him. "I hear you've already met my Trial brothers."

From behind the roses, Mak and Lyros strolled out, wearing their Stand regalia.

Cassia smiled at them. "I was very grateful to meet them when I did."

"The tide of battle sets in motion its own currents of Union," Lyros replied. "Or so we say in the Stand."

Lio put his arm around her waist and pulled her close. "Diplomat though I may be, I cannot disagree."

"Feeling better?" Mak asked Cassia.

"Much."

Lio said very seriously, "Lady Cassia Basilis, may I present Stewards Telemakhos Argyros and Lysandros Timaretes of Hippolyta's Stand."

Mak stood at attention and looked stern. "Yes, the Summit has officially begun. I insist you recite all our most glorious titles."

"And now that's enough." Lyros chuckled. "Lio's tongue looks tired, and so do Cassia's knees."

"Oh, yes please," she said. "No more curtsies."

"Let me show you how Hesperines greet one another." Mak reached out and lightly clasped Cassia's wrist, sliding his wrist against her palm.

She mirrored the gesture, wrapping her fingers around his wrist in turn. "Like this?"

"You'll be doing everything the Hesperine way in no time." Mak winked and gave her wrist a gentle squeeze before he released her.

"Lio doesn't need to recite your titles," Lyros said. "He never stops talking about your deeds."

Mak lifted his eyebrows at Knight, who dozed between the benches. "I must confess, though, one aspect of your formidable legend disappoints me. This lazy mutt sleeping in the presence of the Stand cannot be the ferocious liegehound, Knight."

Cassia spread her hands. "He has eaten a treat of cheese from the hand of Annassa Alea and heard from the lips of Annassa Soteira that he is a good dog. Their spell on him is complete. He has lost his heart and his thirst for battle."

The four of them laughed together. A bright, new feeling came over Cassia. A kind of camaraderie she had never felt, not even with Perita and Callen, as dear as they were. The king had precluded any possibility of it with Caelum. Lucis had also robbed Cassia of the chance to grow up with Solia and find out what this might have been like with her.

It had been a long time since Cassia had been anyone's sister. Was this what it felt like to have brothers?

"I hope we'll all get to spend a lot of time together." As soon as Cassia spoke, she questioned her words. "That is, if it would not be an imposition on anyone."

"Imposition!" Mak scoffed. "Lyros, I see we have another conscientious diplomat on our hands. We have our work cut out for us. We must convince the person who saved the lives of my entire family she is not an imposition."

"Challenge accepted. We will show Cassia more fun than she can stand."

Cassia couldn't help laughing. "I doubt there's such a thing as too much."

"Now that you're here, maybe Lio will remember how to have fun, too." Lyros gave Lio a pointed look.

Mak nodded. "He was in bad shape before you came."

"Mak—" Lio protested.

"He's not going to be in bad shape anymore," Cassia promised.

Lio's arm tightened around her, and she found it felt right to slide her arm around him in return, even though they were not alone. They were in Orthros now, where such displays were not considered improper.

"Now it is our duty and our pleasure to act as your honor guard." Lyros went to stand at Lio's side. "On behalf of Hippolyta's Stand, we are to show you to the Queens' Terrace at House Annassa."

Mak took a position at Cassia's shoulder. "Get used to it now. You're a hero of our people, and everyone is going to treat you like it."

Lio tucked Cassia's arm around his. His Trial brothers led them through one of the courtyard's narrow granite archways and brought them out on wide, shallow marble steps under a clear night sky. She wasn't sure how far they were from Rose House now, but Mak and Lyros had stepped them to another place entirely, one that must also be wrapped in the Queens' magic. Majestic evergreens lined the stairs, swaying in the wind, but Cassia did not feel the cold.

When they reached the top of the steps, they came onto a broad, crescent-shaped terrace of black-and-white marble. Here and there sat wrought iron benches and chairs with white silk seats, and small tables stood about on legs shaped like rose vines.

In the center of the terrace, the elder firstbloods and their Graces were gathered around their Queens. The Annassa had no thrones. They shared one of the silk-and-iron benches. There were a couple of modest tables to either side of them, decked in scrolls, writing instruments, and silver drinking cups, but no council table stood between them and the petitioners who might ascend those steps to appeal to them. As Cassia made that pilgrimage for the first time with Lio, Mak, and Lyros, the Annassa smiled in welcome.

"Argyros," said Queen Soteira, "the young people look ready for some coffee."

Lio's uncle poured a dark brown liquid out of a silver pot and into four cups. He handed one to Cassia, and she could only express her most gracious thanks. The most powerful mind mage in Orthros had just served her a drink. To be a good guest, she did not wait to take a sip.

Hot liquid, rich and bitter, woke up her tongue and warmed her all the way down. "This is delicious."

Argyros gave her the most apparent smile she had yet to see on his face. "I'm delighted you like it."

Lio took a sip of his coffee, then started. "Polar Night Roast, Uncle?"

"Cassia is equal to it."

Komnena handed Cassia a plate. "You haven't eaten since we made harbor. Here's a little of everything from tonight's sideboard."

Cassia accepted the dish. "I'm glad at least some of it won't go to waste."

Lyros's parents and their fellow firstbloods from Hagia Zephyra had pulled up chairs in an uneven formation around the Annassa, where Lio's Ritual mother was already seated at the Queens' right hand. The other elders stood around the coffee service or unrolled documents they had brought, and Mak and Lyros went to confer with Hippolyta at a nearby table. Lio seated Cassia next to him on one of the benches and with a touch of levitation, pulled a table near for her food and drink.

Cassia must try to get used to the lack of ceremony the Queens preferred. The Queens didn't need ceremony. Mortal monarchs must hoard trappings of power about themselves to make their might look more legitimate than the next warlord's. The Queens' power spoke for itself.

"Ioustin is still planning to join us?" Lio's father asked.

"Yes," answered Queen Soteira. "He would not be satisfied until he personally scrutinized the mages' lodgings to ensure the Cordians can cause no trouble."

Hippolyta shook her head, but she was smiling. She had exchanged her long, formal silks from the welcoming ceremony for the shorter black robe and sandals of the Stand. It was as if her rags from the harbor had been transformed into an elegant uniform. "I saw to the protections on the New Guest House myself."

Apollon chuckled. "Good. That means the mages are safe from Ioustin."

There came the sound of footsteps, and Cassia looked toward the stairs in anticipation of her introduction to the Queens' eldest son.

But no Hesperine prince came up the steps. A Tenebran lord strode onto the terrace with Basir and Kumeta at his side.

Cassia sat with Lio's arm around her and her coffee cup trembling in her hand and tried to think of a way out that she knew was not there. There were no words that would spare her now.

When had Hold Lord Justinian joined the embassy? Why hadn't she seen his memorable red hair anywhere among the men? How had he gotten past wards and the Stand and the master envoys to invade the Queens' Terrace and discover Cassia taking refreshments with the enemy?

Then Cassia's panicked mind made sense of the sight before her. Hold Lord Justinian wore a blood-red robe cut in the same style as Stand regalia, although those were Tenebran riding boots on his feet. His hair was braided down to his ankles. And he was bowing to the Queens with his hand on his heart.

Lio's father pulled Lord Justinian into an embrace. "Ioustin. It has been much too long. You must come by House Komnena when we are done here."

"I wouldn't miss it." Lord Justinian kissed Komnena's cheek.

"Cassia," Lio asked urgently, "are you all right?"

"Hold Lord Justinian is a Hesperine? The *First Prince* of the Hesperines?"

"You've met him in Tenebra?"

The man—no, the Hesperine—in question turned his sharp, chilly gray gaze on her. "You remember me."

"You are hard to forget, my lord. I crave your pardon. Your Highness." No, that wasn't right, either. "First Prince, that is."

"Please, call me Rudhira."

He came over to her and Lio, and she got to her feet out of pure instinct. Lio stood and embraced the First Prince as Apollon had done.

"I had no idea," Lio said. "Rudhira, it seems you have met Cassia. Cassia, this is in fact Ioustinianos, First Prince of Orthros, Prince Regent of Orthros Abroad and Royal Master of the Charge. My Ritual father."

Lio was a student of one of the Queens and the First Prince's Ritual son! Cassia almost curtsied to Ioustinianos, then remembered that was not done in Orthros.

Lio put a hand on her back. "Forgive me, Cassia. If I had known you had met before, I would have explained."

"I understand," Cassia assured him. "Tenebrans must never find out one of the hold lords is secretly a member of Orthros's royal family."

"And a veteran of the Blood Errant," the prince added ruefully. "I cannot allow myself to become a danger rather than a protector to my dependents."

"Of course." Cassia could well imagine the consequences, especially after hearing Chrysanthos's remarks to Lio's father. The First Prince must be Apollon's other Ritual son they had mentioned. She refrained from commenting on their past, lest she remind them of their two lost comrades.

The prince lifted his blood-red brows at Cassia. "This must have been an unsettling surprise. It did not occur to me our brief contact several years ago would leave a lasting impression."

"It is important to me to always be observant."

"I should not be surprised, given what Lio has told us of your deeds. But you couldn't have been older than ten."

"Yes. It was the annual tournament through which any man may seek to prove his worthiness and win a hold from the king. Lucis was only awarding three that year, for despite the need to settle the east, he was wary of empowering too many new lords. You arrived at the tournament after dark and were the last to compete. You laid waste to every challenger, including the victor of the day, who was sorely disappointed he must settle for seconds. Through right of combat, you won the prize of asking the king for hold over any unclaimed land of your choosing. Everyone thought you either the bravest or maddest man in the kingdom when you requested a large, but brutal tract in the far northeast—past the Hilt."

"My authority there has been well established for about seventy-five years. Only recently, with King Lucis's increasing oversight, did I deem it wise to legitimize my claim with the official title of hold lord. I tell curious people that the red-haired warlord who first built my keep was my grand-father. But they don't stay curious for long."

"Might is an effective means of persuasion and the only currency in the east. Most people don't want to know what goes on there. But I am not most people." Cassia looked at Lio. "If my powers of observation had been a little keener, I might have connected Lio's concern for that area with the mysterious combatant's interest in it. But Hold Lord Justinian disappeared into the east, much to lesser lords' relief, and has never been seen at court since."

The prince smiled, revealing his fangs. "I concluded I had already worn out my welcome."

"You have kept a hold in the eastern Tenebrae all this time, rescuing victims from the Hilt?"

The prince nodded. "My keep is the staging point for all the Charge's efforts. We are a considerable force of Hesperines errant who travel widely to offer Solace and Mercy wherever we can. My personal task, however, is to safeguard the last remaining community of Hesperites."

"Then there really are human worshipers of Hespera left in Tenebra?"

"Yes, they have built a settlement in the wild east, where they hope to escape notice. A dangerous endeavor. Although they have their own blood magic, Hesperine aid is vital to their survival."

Now Cassia understood why the prince was determined to stop the Departure. Why he was relying on her and Lio. "You must warn the Hesperites. Chrysanthos is a new danger to them. I am sorry, for I am to blame for this. My activities at Solorum have raised the Dexion's suspicions, and he now believes there to be a blood sorceress active in Tenebra. I would hate for his mistaken conclusions about me to bring harm upon the real Hesperites."

Kumeta stepped closer. "We are well aware of Chrysanthos's witch hunt. The Order of Anthros's aggression is inevitable, Cassia. Nothing you have said or done has increased the danger. You have mitigated the danger to us all."

"It eases my heart to know, Master Kumeta."

Basir joined them carrying two coffee cups and handed one to his Grace.

"Master Basir, how are you?" Cassia asked the unsmiling mind mage.

Lio extended a hand. "Please tell me no one has deprived you of your leave."

Basir returned Lio's wrist clasp. "Thank you for your concern, both of you. I am taking a working leave."

As Basir spoke, Cassia caught a glimpse of sharp steel caps where his canines had yet to grow back. She shivered.

Kumeta touched his cheek. "What will it take to convince you to let me dote on you? I don't know what to do with you."

The warmth in his eyes cast his whole face in a different light. "You may dote on me all you like. I can take a working leave and be thoroughly doted upon at the same time."

A grin appeared at the corners of her mouth.

Lio cleared his throat. "Did Rudhira, ah, return your—"

"Yes," Basir snapped. "I took care of them discreetly."

"He sent them up in a fearsome flash of light," Kumeta revealed, "so as not to be further embarrassed."

"As much as I appreciate our prince robbing that villain of his trophy, it's not as if I can put them back in my head."

Everyone did Basir the kindness of refraining from laughter. Cassia saw the whole circle smile behind his back, but they were smiles of affection.

"Lio," said Basir.

Lio looked a little startled, as if the Master Envoy had said something unusual. "Yes, Basir."

"Thank you for ensuring I lost nothing more. Your decisive intervention in Martyr's Pass made it possible for me to escape from the heart hunters. You have the envoys' gratitude. The way you stopped the hunters from committing further violence did our people proud. We only regret the enemy mind mage interfered before you could turn over your prisoners to our prince."

Cassia tucked Lio's arm closer to her in silent encouragement.

Lio clasped Basir's wrist once more. "Your words mean more to me than I can say."

"I have a report for the circle," the prince said, "concerning the events in the pass. Lio is best qualified to describe his battle with the mage of dreams, but my findings can assist."

Lio spoke with conviction. "When I came too close to the mage of dreams in the heart hunters' thoughts, the enemy thelemancer destroyed his own forces to avoid discovery."

The prince nodded. "I have now had the opportunity to conduct a more thorough examination of the only surviving heart hunter. As a theramancer, I can say without doubt the wounds on the man's mind were the work of a mage of dreams."

Lio let out a breath. Cassia took Lio's hand.

"However," the prince continued, "there are also signs of Hesperine thelemancy, which held the man's mind during the moments the mage of dreams committed his onslaught. Lio's presence in the man's mind tempered the damage the mage of dreams tried to inflict. Lio is the only reason the man lives."

Queen Soteira spoke. "No one can doubt your findings."

"Thanks to your power and wisdom, *Bamaayo*," her son replied. "You taught me well to recognize the scars of necromancy in ways that only the ancient mind healing tradition of the Empire can reveal them to us."

Lio looked at from his Ritual father to his Queen. "Thank you."

"Well done, Lio," Annassa Soteira said.

Lio put a hand over his heart and bowed deeply. His father clapped him on the shoulder, and relief was written large on his mother's face. Lio held fast to Cassia's hand.

Argyros spoke up from the opposite side of the terrace. "I want to know who the mage of dreams is who has done this."

Lio did not quite meet his uncle's gaze. "Yes, we must assess the threat he poses. Rudhira, were you able to learn anything more about him from the heart hunter's mind?"

"No more than the imprint of his power. He managed to obliterate most evidence of himself. But there is still hope the heart hunter's mind may respond to healing—and provide us with more information—since you managed to save his life."

"Unfortunately," said Basir, "I have no further insight to offer. The mage of dreams never directly engaged with me. Lio and Cassia, perhaps you can tell us more of him."

With the reassurance of Lio's hand in hers, Cassia spoke up. Knowledge was her preferred weapon, and she would bring all of it she had against the man who had planned to destroy her. "I overheard the heart hunters discussing him. The mage of dreams is colluding with the king, acting as some kind of intermediary between him and the heart hunters. Lucis was to pay the hunters in gold and breeding rights to my liegehound. The mage's compensation was me. Apparently he prefers women to coin as a bribe."

"He can't take either where I shall send him on your behalf." Hippolyta looked ready to make good on her promise that very hour. "Two mages of Hypnos on our hands!"

"If I meet the mage of dreams in a mind duel again," Lio promised, "I will report a single casualty to you without remorse."

"With such powerful protection, I shall not fear him," Cassia resolved.

"You have paid dearly to stand against your father," the prince said to her. "In so doing, you have won us the time we need to prepare for the coming war. Thanks to your tireless efforts, many lives have been spared that would already have been lost to us, had you not taken it upon yourself to lend your aid to our people."

"Lio got a message to me," Cassia replied, "about the Queens calling everyone home, but I knew from the murmurs among the mages there were still many Hesperines errant in Tenebra. I have feared for them without knowing how to help them more directly."

"You have helped them as directly as I," said the prince. "The Hesperines errant you encountered as a child are almost certainly among them."

Lio nodded. "I tried to discover who they are and learned that none of the returnees to Orthros were at the Siege of Sovereigns. We believe your rescuers are still in the field."

"And so is our daughter Pherenike," said Argyros.

Cassia looked to Lio's uncle. Argyros's expression and body language were even more mysterious than other Hesperines'. He was well-nigh impossible to read. But at that moment, there was grief in his eyes she could not mistake. If that look meant what she had done had not been enough for Nike, she would not be able to bear it.

"Kadi told me about Nike," Cassia said. "Is there any news?"

The prince met Argyros's gaze. "The Charge spares no effort in our search for her."

Mak had come to Cassia's side again. "I might get a chance to meet Nike for the first time, thanks to you."

"These eighty-nine years," said Hippolyta, "Nike has roamed Tenebra alone. She did not answer the Queens' call when they summoned everyone home."

"She will endure the crisis of the moment," Apollon said. "She is a Master Steward and a veteran of the Blood Errant."

"But as her Trial brother," said the prince, "I will seek her tirelessly until we reassure ourselves as to her safety. Cassia, if you had not stalled the hostilities this long, our work would be all but impossible."

Hippolyta came over and touched a hand to Cassia's shoulder. "There are many families here in Orthros that are bound to you in gratitude. We want you to know Blood Argyros is among them."

Cassia could see the power in Hippolyta's slight frame, the authority in her hand, and the worry in her heart. "I'm so sorry about Nike. If there is anything more I can do to help her, I will."

Argyros took his Grace's arm and drew her close. "You are doing it tonight, Cassia."

The prince nodded. "The Charge can now coordinate our efforts with you personally."

"The Stand," Hippolyta went on, "will go over all our security measures with you and adjust them according to what you know of the mages' hidden powers."

"Once we have addressed immediate dangers," Lio said, "it will be time to consult with you on the various motivations—and weaknesses—of the Tenebran lords that will make them vulnerable to our persuasion. We have methods in mind to sway them in favor of peace with Orthros over alliance with Cordium, but only with your insight can we apply those methods effectively."

Kumeta looked to Elder Firstblood Hypatia. "Also, our scholars will need as much information as possible on how the Aithourian Circle hides their magic."

Hypatia had yet to unroll a single one of the scrolls stacked on the table before her. Her ink bottles were capped, her quills untouched. Her statue had warned she was not to be trifled with, but what living color revealed was that she was as olive-skinned as Cassia herself, with thick black hair curled in a timeless fashion. Had she been a sophisticated Cordian in her mortal life?

Her Grace lounged behind her with a hand on her shoulder. Elder Grace Khaldaios was a Hesperine of Imperial origin with bronze skin and an elaborate, well-groomed beard. During Cassia's brief introduction to him at the welcoming ceremony, he had struck her as an articulate scholar who exuded far more warmth than his Grace.

Hypatia frowned at Kumeta. "I am still loathe to lay burdens such as these on one as young as Cassia. After fighting so valiantly these many months, I think she has earned the right to end her struggle and let us proceed from here. I shall go on record as the only one here tonight who offers her the opportunity to excuse herself from this gathering."

Argyros glanced at Hypatia. "No one is keeping annals of this circle, my friend."

"Yet we have all made statements tonight of our gratitude to Cassia. She knows how much we appreciate all she has accomplished. What more can we possibly ask of her? No one here can deny she has done her part."

Hypatia certainly took a different tone from the other Hesperines. And a Hesperine's tone, especially an elder firstblood's, was infinitely more nuanced than any Tenebran lord's bluster or even a Cordian master's double-edged courtliness. For the first time that night, Cassia had the feeling she must tread with caution.

When Cassia felt Lio's hand tighten on hers, she took that for a confirmation that Hypatia might present a challenge.

Before Cassia could respond to the Elder Firstblood's offer, Basir cut in. "There is still much more she can do."

"Will you milk a child for information, Basir?" Hypatia asked.

"She was never a child," Kumeta answered. "Life in Tenebra robbed her of that. Whether we like it or not, she carries a kingdom on her shoulders."

"And she has done so with extraordinary courage and strength." Hypatia gave Cassia a beautiful, majestic smile. Like all Hesperines, when she smiled, she gave away her fangs. "Now it is time for you to lay down your heavy burdens. You can leave matters in our hands."

That wasn't a challenge. That was an insult.

Cassia had carried grief so heavy all she wished to do was lay it down. She had woken to mornings when it took all her strength just to make it out of her bed. She had traveled the length of Tenebra with mages who would love to make it easy for her to give up and go home. When she had stared up the length of a heart hunter's crossbow, it would have been easy to accept respite from Hypnos rather than endure the suffering of living on in Anthros's world.

And every time, Cassia had chosen not to lay down her heavy burdens.

Cassia gave Hypatia the Smile. "I thank you for your generous offer of respite, Elder Firstblood. But I cannot accept. Since the night I helped the Hesperine embassy escape Orthros, I have had nothing to work with but my own two hands. You must forgive me if I deem them necessary to continue pushing forward all I have set in motion."

Hypatia's eyes glittered. "Come now, my dear. No one will begrudge you rest."

Lio touched his hand to Cassia's back more firmly, a subtle sign of support. The other Hesperines watched, but this time, none of them took it upon themselves to answer for Cassia.

"I cannot afford rest, Elder Firstblood," Cassia said.

"Oh, but you can. You are in Orthros now. This is the land of rest."

"When the King of Tenebra promises peace with Orthros, I will rest. When the Cordian mages go back to their temples disappointed, I will rest. When every Hesperine errant is safe, I will rest. Do you think any of this will happen tonight, Elder Firstblood Hypatia? Because if not, I am in for another sleepless night."

The Hesperine scholar gave a courtier's laugh, seductive and haughty. "Naturally, such ambitious plans take time, child."

"Would you like to know how much time, Elder Firstblood?" Cassia asked innocently as a maiden. "I have been learning the Hesperine clock, which you devised for your people, and can tell you according to your own system. Sixteen hours a night, which is twenty-four hours a day by Tenebran reckoning. That is how much time I have devoted to keeping the king and the Orders at bay."

"No one doubts your tireless efforts on our behalf."

Boldness and courage, it seemed, were enough to put Hypatia on her guard, but not to impress her. But then, she was not a fighter. Cassia thought of the scrolls Hypatia the statue bore on her back. With this Hesperine, surely knowledge was the most effective means of negotiation.

"Of those sixteen hours a night," Cassia offered, "I think you will be most interested in only a few minutes. A few minutes was all it took for Skleros to cast a working that left an entire hex of necromancers from the Order of Hypnos dead at his feet and brought the Dexion of the Aithourian Circle to his knees."

Hypatia hesitated.

It was all the opportunity Cassia needed. She kept talking and spun out the information she had to bargain, working up to what Hypatia must really want to hear. "Apprentice Tychon is powerful enough to traverse from Solorum to the border of Orthros and back without landing in a faint. But his fellow mages were satisfied that his power is obscured because he is acting as Chrysanthos's channel."

At that, Hypatia resumed her silken retorts. "A necromancer performing a harrowing ritual on a war mage? An apprentice serving as a channel? Dear child, I think what you beheld has caused you some confusion. The sort of magic you are making a noble effort to describe is strictly theoretical. It is not possible in actual practice."

"You mean essential displacement, whereby a mage's power is removed from him and seated in a vessel, from which he can draw via a channel?"

Hypatia's gaze sharpened. "Yes, that is what I was referring to. The concept has been known for time out of mind, if only among the most intrepid circles that investigate the darkest arcane mysteries. However, no one has ever achieved such a feat in reality. Certainly not an upstart Gift Collector who hasn't even lived a century. You cannot have seen this actually happen."

"I was standing in the room. I listened to Skleros explain in precise detail exactly how the spell works, then watched him perform it. I witnessed the effect it had on Chrysanthos, Tychon, and the victim they chose from the king's prison to use as a vessel. Shall I tell you more?"

"I think I ought to discuss the event with you in detail," the scholar conceded. She drew herself up in her seat. "So as to assist you in understanding what you really saw."

"I am ready," Cassia dared her.

"Then we shall begin." Queen Soteira was smiling. "Cassia, before the elder firstbloods, the Stand, our son, and his Charge, we welcome you to Orthros. Under the Goddess's Eyes, we make it known that you have our gratitude and that of all our people."

Queen Alea gestured to the terrace around them. "The doors of Orthros are open to you. You are as one of our own. If you are ever in danger, you can rely on our protection. When you are in need, you can rely on our aid. All your desires shall be fulfilled with generosity, as the Goddess has generously provided for us."

"Sit among us," said Queen Soteira, "and let the Solstice Summit commence."

VEIL HOURS

THEY HAD BEEN AT the circle for several hours by Cassia's count when the peals that marked the time changed to low, mellow tones.

Queen Alea set down her empty coffee cup. "Veil hours already."

"We have done enough for one night," Queen Soteira declared.

From their terrace, Cassia could see lights winking out all over the city. The glow Selas cast into the sky faded, and stars that had not been visible before revealed themselves.

"Are deaths necessary for every successful displacement?" Hypatia was saying to Argyros. "Could it be their willingness to engage in human sacrifice that allowed the Order of Hypnos to realize the theory?"

Lio's uncle shook his head. "The other six necromancers would never have agreed to assist Skleros if they had expected to be human sacrifices."

"Perhaps they were not aware of that requirement of the ritual. The art is clearly unique to Gift Collectors and remains mysterious even to their fellow necromancers."

"I must agree with Argyros," said Khaldaios. "As much as we wish to lay the blame on the Order of Hypnos's ruthlessness, their accomplishment stems not from lack of scruples, but command of methodology."

"How like Gift Collectors," she replied. "They squander brilliant innovations on revolting applications."

Khaldaios sighed. "Whatever else we may say about Gift Collectors, their expertise cannot be denied."

"Why would he kill six mages from his own Order, if the ritual did not demand it?" Hypatia wondered.

"To keep his secrets," Argyros mused, "just like his colleague in the pass."

From the other side of the terrace, the prince joined in, but he directed his remarks to Lyta. "Gift Collectors certainly do kill to prevent their techniques from being discovered. I wouldn't put it past one of them to silence his own brethren. They never cooperate with other mages. Skleros's appearance with the embassy is unprecedented."

"It is an insult," Lyta replied. "I cannot believe he did not even bother to come here in disguise."

The prince leaned over the diagram of wards and patrol routes they had drafted during the circle. "Given the Tenebrans' fears, they want Skleros to serve as a warning they did not arrive unprotected."

With a chuckle, Apollon put away his drawing tools. "As if one necromancer could keep them safe, if we wished to do them harm."

"But he is a clever choice for a show of force," Lyta conceded. "Their only option, in truth. As a Tenebran mage of Hypnos, he is technically eligible for our invitation."

The prince nodded. "Even if he is a bounty hunter for Cordium. Few Ordered mages spend more time outside Cordium than Gift Collectors. They know the prey is more plentiful in Tenebra. Unfortunately for the Charge."

Apollon asked, "You are certain Skleros is not one of the Gift Collectors you have dealt with before?"

"I do not recognize his name or his aura, but that does not mean I have never faced him. Secrecy is key to his profession's success and survival. While the war mages inflate their reputations so we learn to fear their names, Gift Collectors live in the shadows so they can always strike with the advantage of surprise. Skleros would never sacrifice his anonymity like this unless he expected the reward to be greater than the cost."

"That's what worries me." With an air of ritual, Lyta tightened the speires that secured her voluminous hair out of her way. "We must tolerate his presence for the sake of diplomacy—but only until the Summit is over. Once he leaves Orthros, there is no telling what might befall him, don't you think?"

The prince rolled up the map of the city's defenses. "Making himself known to us will be his last mistake."

The three scholars across the terrace continued to debate amongst themselves as the circle began to disperse. Gathering scrolls and draining coffee cups, everyone took their leave of each other and the Queens, except the prince, who sat down with his mothers as if settling in for another circle.

"Good veil," Mak told Cassia and Lio. "We'll see you tomorrow."

Lyros's smile was nothing short of wicked. "We're off to babysit the mages."

"I wish I could tell you more about what harm they're planning to cause while they're here," Cassia said. "It's maddening that I haven't been able to discover more about Chrysanthos and Skleros's intentions. It was so much more difficult to spy on them while we were traveling than it was at Solorum. As I told Lyta, I cannot even glean anything from the Tenebran mages or lords, for Tychon is the only one Chrysanthos and Skleros keep in their confidence."

Lio reminded her, "But we arrived at some very helpful educated guesses during the circle tonight. Thanks to you, we know more about their motivations, and that helps us predict their goals."

Cassia frowned. "I don't like guesses, no matter how educated."

"We can't possibly have missed anything," Lyros assured her. "As many scenarios as we all walked through together tonight, we're ready for every potential sabotage the mages might attempt while they're here, from magical to physical to structural."

Mak rubbed his hands together. "Whatever they have in mind, we'll be the first to know. We have eyes on them at all times. It's not often Rudhira leaves some of the Charge at home to reinforce the Stand. This will be fun."

Cassia wanted the chance to speak with Mak about his sister, to find the words she hadn't been able to say during the circle's discussion of Nike. But he looked so enthused for tonight's mission. Now was clearly not the time to bring up a painful subject.

"Enjoy yourselves," she said instead.

"Oh, they will." Lio chuckled.

Mak and Lyros trotted down the stairs and out of sight.

When Lio's parents passed by, heading for the steps, Komnena paused to say, "We'll see you in a little while."

Cassia looked up at Lio. "They will?"

He smiled down at her. "You are invited to House Komnena for veil hours."

Someone cleared his throat, and Cassia and Lio looked away from each other. His uncle stood before them. As long as Cassia lived, she doubted she would ever meet anyone more expert than Argyros at mystifying all observers. His eyes, his face, and even his body language were opaque to her.

He addressed Cassia. "At your earliest opportunity, I hope you will join us at House Argyros during veil hours. I will treat you to your first coffee tasting."

"That sounds wonderful," Cassia answered.

"That's very kind of you, Uncle. We'll look forward to it."

"We shall arrange it for a night when you are not occupied at House Komnena and I am not at the Queens' ward with my Grace."

"You, Uncle, are going on patrol with Aunt Lyta?"

"I am no student at it. I was the only partner available to her until her first group of trainees grew skilled enough to assist her."

"Of course, Uncle. It's just that it's been a long time since you were personally involved in Stand business. There is no one more suited, to be sure. You as a mind mage and Aunt Lyta as a warder can use the Queen's protections to their utmost potential."

"There is no one else at her disposal at this time, when every warrior is devoted to watching the guests."

Argyros departed with his Grace, and Cassia resisted the urge to interrogate Lio. The stilted exchange between him and his mentor confirmed Cassia's suspicions that something was wrong between them. Perhaps this was another time when Lio needed a reminder that he could speak about anything with her. But she wanted to help him feel better, not probe an open wound. Argyros's opinion meant the world to Lio, so she had best approach the subject with the utmost care and watch for the right moment to do so.

When Lio stepped with her back to the courtyard, she could hear her own heart pounding in the silent garden.

He rubbed a thumb on the inside of her wrist. "How many cups of coffee did you drink?"

"I lost count."

His lips twitched. "It has an energizing effect on mortals, and Polar Night is the darkest, strongest roast my uncle makes. I doubt you'll make up much sleep tonight."

"What a wondrous elixir. With this to keep me on my feet, I shall accomplish more than ever before."

"Hypatia doesn't stand a chance."

Cassia frowned. "I've wanted to ask you about her all night. Did Knight drool on her silk shoes during the welcoming ceremony when I wasn't looking, or does she have a real reason to set herself against me?"

Lio sighed. "Hypatia was an opponent of my proposal to the last. Her strongest ally in this dissent is Second Princess Konstantina, who is the Royal Master Magistrate. She is the foremost codifier and interpreter of our laws and the most influential of the royal firstbloods at home here in Orthros. Hypatia and Konstantina maintain their position against the Solstice Summit, and they show a minimum of cooperation with the whole affair only in deference to the Queens."

"Why do they disagree so strongly?"

"They are uncomfortable with the risk and, I think, any change this dramatic."

"I see. When we prepare for the next circle, you'd best tell me more about each of the firstbloods' positions on the Solstice Summit."

"You have far more allies here than opponents." Lio hesitated. "I'm sorry I didn't tell you Rudhira is Hold Lord Justinian. I never want you to feel I have kept secrets from you."

Cassia shook her head. "Things were so different then, the night we talked about the eastern Tenebrae. So many things hadn't happened yet. I was guilty of not trusting you the way I have learned to now."

"No guilt, then. Not for either of us."

"I'm glad the past is past. That is so seldom the case. Right now, I want to be in the present, in which I am in Orthros, with you, and veil hours have just begun."

Lio pulled her against him and gave her a kiss. "I can't wait to take you home. I have a surprise for you."

"Another surprise? After all the wonders you have already shown me?"

"You have no idea how many times I've had to bite my tongue since Waystar. Mother and Father have been kind enough to play along. Just let me go on ahead of you for a little while to see to a few things. I'll be back to get you when the bells of House Kitharos chime the half hour. In the meantime, feel free to see to Knight's needs here in the courtyard. The initiates will come through with cleaning spells later."

"In the rose bushes? But they're Hespera's sacred flower."

"I have no doubt she will smile to see a deadly liegehound nosing about in her garden like a happy pup. You might direct him to that bed of ornamental greenery, though. No thorns."

"Very well. After that, I'd best go check on Perita and see if she is feeling all right."

"Tell her you wish to sleep late tomorrow, and you don't need help dressing for bed. No need to take off your lovely gown yet."

"Then the same attire will be suitable for our first visit to your parents' home?"

Lio's eyes twinkled with mischief. "You may be somewhat overdressed, but we can remedy that at the ambassador's banquet, when I will help you become less so."

If this was what he wished to take off of her later, she would wear it. "I shall bow to your expertise once more, Ambassador."

He smiled. "When you walk back into the main hall in a moment and the embassy sees you, the thelemancy will wear off, but they will not know you ever left."

She ran her hands up his arms. "Thank you, Lio. You know what this night has meant to me."

"And to all of us as well." He gave her one more kiss and departed the courtyard.

Knight did not stir until she put a hand on his head. Then he opened his eyes, pricking his ears, and leapt up with more energy than he'd had in a long time. His limp was gone. Carefully, she peeked under his bandages. There was no sign of his wounds.

She breathed a sigh of relief. "Poor, faithful darling. The last six months have been dreadful for you too, haven't they? Protecting me is no easy task."

After Knight had done his business, Cassia returned with him to the main hall. She arrived in time for the remaining firstbloods to bid her good veil with indicative glances and knowing smiles.

Benedict laid claim to her arm again as if he had never let it go, and Callen and Perita commiserated with her about everyone's empty bellies. Eudias looked like he was almost done in again. Had he been trying to work magic in a room full of firstbloods?

Komnena and her initiates herded all of the embassy but Cassia's retinue away to the New Guest House. The young Hesperine who had taken Cassia's cloak earlier now showed her and her escort to her lodgings further inside Rose House. Eudias made only a cursory examination of her chambers before he and Benedict departed to find their beds in the other guest house. Callen, hiding his limp, retired to his and Perita's chambers down the hall and left Cassia in her handmaiden's care.

As she helped Cassia settle in, Perita did not seem wary of the potted roses all over the sitting room and bedchamber. She must not have recognized them for Hespera's flower, as most Tenebrans didn't these days, when roses were all but eradicated from southern lands. She didn't succeed in hiding that she was begrudgingly impressed with the accommodations, especially when they discovered the lavish privy.

Cassia spent several fascinated moments turning the taps on and off in front of the wash stand. "I've never seen anything like this. Oh, Perita, I shall take a warm bath three times a night."

"There's *definitely* no time for three baths in between all the events, my lady."

When they had completed their nightly routine, Perita took her leave to join Callen and, Cassia suspected, to pretend not to enjoy the luxury of their own rooms. Cassia took her time in the privy, then wrapped her silk cloak around her and made sure her enchanted shoes and gloves were secure. She freed Knight from his bandages, and he gave himself a good shake.

She paused to reach into her gardening satchel. She couldn't help running a hand over the glyph stone, and she felt the shard respond. But all she lifted out was the small pouch containing the gift she had brought for Lio. She would leave the satchel and the rest of its contents here in her rooms, reassured the Sanctuary ward would protect her secrets in her absence.

Cassia pushed back the sheer curtains and opened the glass doors that led out into the courtyard. Fresh air brought in the roses' fragrance and stirred the drapes. She idled in the open doorway with Knight beside her.

Suddenly a handsome young Hesperine stood across the fountain from her, his pale face lit by moonlight, his body lost in shadow. Cassia and Lio smiled at each other.

"My lady, what would you have in exchange for your name? I will pay any price, for I must know."

"A kiss."

He came forward and gave it to her. "This bargain has sweetened since the night we first met."

"Is there anything else you would like besides my name? I shall make the exchange sweeter still."

"I swear I shall surrender all I have to bargain upon your table, before veil hours are through."

THE BEST PART OF HOME

WHAT WOULD CASSIA SAY when she learned Lio had a different negotiation table in mind for them than her bed at Rose House? Her chambers here were better appointed than the work in progress that was his residence. Still, he held out hope she would find no guest house so inviting as his own rooms.

He tasted her lips again, then drew back. "My family and I are eager to give you our welcome gifts."

"As a guest in your home, surely I should bring your family a present to thank you for your hospitality."

Lio shook his head. "In Orthros, guests don't bring gifts to their hosts. Hosts offer gifts to their guests in gratitude for their presence."

There was no more time to wonder what further preparations he should have made or question whether he had left too many things unfinished. He would soon find out if she understood the bare shelves and empty rooms for what they were. An invitation for her to fill them with potted plants, a promise of a future they could create together. An offer of a home that was not his, but theirs.

He contemplated her guest room behind her. "Let me take care of one more thing."

By the time she turned around to look, he had finished his illusion. She laughed at the image of herself curled in bed with a liegehound who hogged the covers.

"Now I shall not worry if Perita pokes her head in to check on me."

"If a dark sorcerer is going to abscond with you tonight, we must not do things halfway."

"You don't look the part of a dark sorcerer in that vibrant shade of blue. The cheerful yellow and red embellishments thoroughly ruin the effect." She ran her hands up his bare forearms, then along his short sleeves, caressing wide bands of homespun embroidery.

"My lady gardener may be interested to know this robe is made of the fabric called cotton that my Ritual mother mentioned. Cotton is a plant that produces fluffy white bolls rather like sheep's wool."

"Wool that grows on plants! Marvelous, Sir Scholar." But she wasn't fingering the fabric, she was touching his arms again, her hands warm on his skin in the cool night air. "I do feel rather overdressed in Tenebran velvet."

"But I think cotton pleases my lady gardener." He would definitely have to abandon his robes of office more often.

"I've never seen you in anything like this. Except when you take a run in nothing but a tunic." That night, she had been all blushes, and he had watched her try not to stare at him. Now her gaze fell to his feet without hesitation. "Lead the way, my barefoot sorcerer."

Taking Cassia's hand, Lio led her out into the courtyard. "Let us test Knight's newfound tolerance and see if he will step with us. Instead of a crisis to motivate him, I have artisan cheeses from the sideboard. I can't claim to have the Queens' enchanting touch, but perhaps Knight is willing to accept a bribe from me."

Lio reached into his pocket and pulled out a lump of cheese. The dog turned and sniffed the air. Lio held out his offering. When he felt a slobbery tongue on his hand, he jumped. The bite of cheese was already gone, Lio's fingers intact. Knight looked up at him with big, sad eyes.

"Hespera's Mercy," Lio said. "That face must be liegehounds' secret weapon against mind mages. I find myself completely robbed of my Will to refuse him anything."

"It works on everyone, not just mind mages." Cassia's grin promised she was on the verge of laughter.

Lio must hear the laugh that appeared ready to leave her lips. He pulled two more bites of cheese out of his pocket and extended his hand again. Knight wagged his tail and devoured the treats, his nose and mouth smearing Lio's palm will all manner of doggy effusions.

There came Cassia's beautiful, abandoned laughter. Lio had heard her laugh so often in just the short time since she had crossed the border. In Tenebra, he'd had only glimpses of what she was like under her burdens and armor. Here in Orthros, those moments lasted hours. She did feel happy and comfortable here, as he had prayed she would.

One of the most important tests of that comfort was whether she would feel at ease with his family. But just as important was making her family at ease with him.

Lio fed Cassia's only loved one another bite of cheese. While Knight was busy gnawing on it, Lio ventured to ease his hand closer. Ears, chin, or chest were canine favorites, but they still seemed too ambitious. Lio had only touched Knight when the hound was wounded. What if Knight associated Lio's touch with pain? He aimed for the dog's side.

Lio's hand met dense, coarse fur. Knight didn't flinch. Lio didn't breathe. So far, so good. He tried giving Knight's back a gentle scratch.

Under the outer layer of his protective coat, there were deeper layers of thick, soft fur. Lio ran his hand over Knight's powerful frame, then slid his fingers into the warm smoothness of the dog's ruff. Lio began to understand why Cassia found it so relaxing to cultivate her bond with the animal. It must have a similar effect on Knight, for he sat down and blinked his eyes in apparent pleasure.

Cassia came nearer and slid her hand into the dog's ruff next to Lio's. She radiated contentment. "Now seems like a good time to step. He is inebriated with delicacies."

"Let's see if he even notices we've gone."

For good measure, Lio occupied Knight with yet another morsel while he stepped them. The dog leapt to his feet, taking a quick look around at his new surroundings, then sniffed Lio's pockets thoroughly. Lio and Cassia laughed together again. He gave Knight the last crumbs of cheese while she told him what a good dog he was.

Cassia's family had given Lio the final sign of approval. Now Lio could take her into his.

Cassia studied their new location with great attention, turning all around to take in the wild shrubbery and undergrowth. She looked up and gasped at the massive evergreen trees that towered overhead. "Where are we?"

"The grounds of House Komnena. Quite a bit of the Queen's Orchard, the forest that surrounds Selas, spills over to us here."

"How do such mighty trees grow in the darkness and cold? They have no spell lights and glass like the roses in the courtyard."

"I'll show you."

Lio cast a quick cleaning spell on his slobbery, cheesy hands before taking Cassia's again. As he led her between the trees, Knight trotted alongside them, wagging his tail, as if eager to resume their pastime from the last Summit. Cassia grabbed her skirts in one hand and followed Lio through the woods without a protest for her velvets.

As soon as they encountered a clearing, Lio paused in the middle of the open space. With one arm around Cassia, he pointed up at the sky with his free hand. "Look up and tell me what you see out of the corner of your eye. What hovers there on the edge of your vision, then disappears when you try to look right at it?"

"Light," she exclaimed. "A glimmer. Sometimes a filmy glow."

"It is the ward. We discovered long ago that even when the sun sets for the winter, plants still thrive in the light and shelter of the Queens' magic."

With the sky and one of Lio's spells to light their way, they trekked across his family's untamed grounds, under spruces and yews, between thorn thickets and holly bushes, through glades covered in brilliant fresh snow. By the time they emerged from the woods, he and Cassia were both windblown and breathless with laughter.

He brought them out onto the garden path, which was just a trail of footprints in the snow at the moment. Lio gestured ahead of them at the stone fence that surrounded the tidy yard. "Here we are."

Cassia took in her first glimpse of House Komnena with the expression of a polite guest, but the Union revealed her ravenous curiosity. Lio suppressed a smile. Her gaze traveled over the paddock cleared of snow and carpeted in tundra scrub. She looked beyond to the terrace framed in buttresses, the stained glass door, and the soaring white marble structure.

Finally, her attention returned to the paddock and came to rest on the modest barn. Lio supposed its low thatched roof and stone-and-mortar walls did make a strange contrast to the main house. But practicality and comfort were what Zoe and her goats needed, and she preferred the cozy barn to the vaulted halls. Lio suspected Cassia would also feel more at ease somewhere informal. This was definitely the best place for his sister and his Grace to have their first encounter.

When he and Cassia neared the fence, Lio indulged the urge to grab her around the waist. She let out a squeak of surprise. As he levitated them over without opening the gate, she clung to him in quite a satisfying way.

On the opposite side of the fence, Knight backed away, then took a running leap. Not to be outdone, he cleared the fence with room to spare. Lio set Cassia down so she could make over the hound's feat.

"Queen Soteira can heal anyone, even liegehounds," she said.

Lio dared pet the dog again. "Do you think Knight would mind waiting here for a moment?"

"Knight is the soul of patience, aren't you, darling? And you were born with your own enchanted cloak to resist the cold." She ruffled his fur and gave him a stay command.

As Lio approached the barn with Cassia, his mother came out and exchanged a conspiratorial smile with him.

"If you need anything, I'll be in my study, right through that door." She gestured to the terrace and the stained glass door to her favorite room, then strolled inside.

Cassia turned to Lio. "I cannot endure the mystery any longer, and I cannot begin to guess. You must tell me why we are beginning our evening with your family in the barn."

Lio couldn't keep the grin off his face. "There is someone here I want you to meet, and she will tell you this is the best part of our home. Come inside."

He tugged her hand, and she followed him through the low doorway without having to duck as he did. The scents of fodder and goat enveloped them. He heard skinny knees shuffle in the hay behind the wall of one stall, then two footsteps.

Zoe peered around the edge of the wall, hovering in the door of the stall, her eyes wide and her mouth tight. She stared at her hero, her aura bursting with so much eagerness Lio feared her little body would begin trembling. He sent her a wave of reassurance through the Blood Union.

"Zoe," he said, "Cassia has come to meet you."

Zoe gave no words in reply, only a little gasp.

"Cassia." Lio squeezed her hand. "I would like you to meet Zosime Komnena. She is one of the children you saved and now, I am so proud to say, my little sister."

Zoe's aura glowed at his words, and the light of her spirit hazed into the bloom of Cassia's surprise. Cassia's heart filled to the brim, fraught and longing, and Lio wondered if she, not Zoe, would be the one who broke from the power of her own emotions.

Indeed, it was Zoe who found her voice first. "You're the Brave Gardener."

BETONY

I T WAS A RARE sunny day that made it warm and nice to work in
Soli's garden. Cassia got up from kneeling by the flowerbed and
dusted the grass off her skinned knees. With her skirts tucked into
her belt, no stains would get on the outside, and Nurse wouldn't scold
her for getting dirty.

Cassia heard the door to Soli's rooms swing open, and she turned to
see her sister coming down the steps into the garden. Now that Soli had
come out to check on her, nervousness overtook Cassia. It was the first
time Solia had let Cassia decide what to plant and put all the flowers in
herself, with only a little supervision. She hoped her sister would like how
it had turned out.

Soli smiled and came to see Cassia's work. But Cassia clutched
her spade in front of her tightly and stood between her sister and the
flower bed.

Soli knelt down on Cassia's eye level, and her beautiful velvet gown
dragged in the grass and dirt. "Oh, Pup, this is beautiful! Show me what
you've planted."

Cassia beamed at her sister and turned around to look with her at the
flowers. Soli put an arm around Cassia and held her close as Cassia pointed
out the different blooms.

"These are delphinium, one of the prettiest blue flowers there is. Here
are goldenrods. And those there are white daisies."

Solia gave her a kiss on the cheek. "My garden never looked so
beautiful."

"You're the Brave Gardener," said Lio's little sister.

It was a frigid night in Orthros, and Cassia was in a warm barn lit with mellow spell lights. Lio's little sister stood before her.

Zoe shuffled her bare feet in the hay while two goat kids peered out from behind her legs. Her loose cotton tunic stopped at her knobby knees. Around her neck hung one of the betony charms Cassia had made for the Eriphite orphans. The child clutched a potted betony seedling in her hands, a leafy sprig that had yet to bloom.

Cassia recognized the look on the Hesperine suckling's face as if a mirror of crystalline Orthros glass reflected her own childhood back at her. That look of adoration was for her?

In the rush and desperation of providing the children an escape from Tenebra, Cassia had thought only of the reward of knowing they were safe. She had not expected the reward of knowing them. She had never even imagined receiving the honor of Zoe's expression in this moment.

She knelt down on the Hesperine suckling's eye level, letting her beautiful velvet gown drag on the floor of the goat barn. She thought of what she would want to hear if she were standing in Zoe's place, the kind of things she had always longed for her beloved Soli to say to her. "I am *so* happy to meet you. Lio kept you a great secret all the way here. I could hardly wait to find out where he was taking me. The secret was you! You are the most wonderful surprise I have ever had."

Zoe's mouth eased into an almost-smile. "He kept you a secret too. He told me so many stories about all the good things the Brave Gardener does in Tenebra, but he wouldn't tell me your real name. Until Autumn Equinox, when I found out you were coming to Orthros."

"Zoe has been so excited to finally meet you," said Lio.

"Please accept my welcome gift." Zoe held out the seedling. "Lio says you had to leave all your plants in Tenebra. So I wanted to help you start your garden over."

"This is for me?" Cassia wrapped her hands around Zoe's and the pot. "You have my gratitude. I will treasure this."

A happy blush colored the suckling's pallid cheeks.

Lio went to Zoe's side and sat down on the floor of the barn. "Stories about the Brave Gardener are your favorites, aren't they, Zoe?"

"I'm sure Lio is a wonderful storyteller," Cassia replied.

Zoe nodded. "He makes pictures to go with the stories. You look just like the illusions he casts of you."

Cassia pushed her windblown hair back from her face, suddenly aware of the sweat at her nape from hiking in a warm cloak. She glanced at Lio, and he gave her an unapologetic grin.

"Lio is so kind to say such nice things about me. In fact, your brother is the kindest person I know."

"Yes, he is." Zoe turned her look of worship upon Lio.

Cassia smiled. Well, she and Zoe had a very strong starting point in common. They both adored Lio.

Zoe slid nearer to her brother, and Cassia recognized the gesture as a tentative demand for attention. Lio drew Zoe close with one arm. She shuffled her feet and blushed again, then whispered something in his ear, hiding her mouth with her hand.

He smiled at her, brushing a thumb across her pink cheek. "Of course that would be all right."

Zoe cast a hesitant glance at Cassia.

"Why would Cassia mind?" Lio met Cassia's gaze with a soft smile. "She is my share. Thanks to her, I can help Mama and Papa provide for you."

Cassia let the meaning of his words sink in. "It's perfectly all right, Zoe. In fact, I'm so happy I can help."

For the first time, Zoe's smile peeked out. She was awaiting the arrival of a front tooth, but she had two perfect baby fangs. Cassia had never seen anything so adorable.

Lio hugged his little sister close and held his wrist out to her. "When you're a busy suckling, it's difficult to wait for dinner. Especially when you've had an important night and just met someone you're so very excited to see."

Zoe took his wrist in both hands. As she ducked her head, her long brown hair fell forward, half-concealing her face, but not her mouth. The child bit into Lio's wrist. Her black-and-white goat nibbled his big toe.

Zoe drank with guileless eagerness, just as a human child might guzzle a cup of fresh milk. Lio gave no sign her teeth pained him. Did Hesperines' natural healing make feeding their children painless? What did it feel like to suckle a baby Hesperine?

Lio's gaze came to Cassia's. They shared a long look while Zoe's head was bowed. In his eyes, there was unmistakable love for his sister and an invitation to Cassia to share in it.

A laugh wanted to bubble out of Cassia's throat, or perhaps tears, she wasn't sure which. She had never seen Lio hold a child.

This was what Hesperines were like with their children. This was what Lio was like with children. Zoe had years and years of this boundless kindness and affection to look forward to. She had this tender, powerful person who would never cease to protect and care for her. Cassia saw before her the future that awaited any child who dwelt in this house.

The invitation in Lio's gaze intensified into something more. An offer. A promise.

Cassia did not look away.

When Zoe lifted her head, she smacked a hand over her mouth. Lio chuckled and handed her one of his supply of handkerchiefs. With another, he wiped off his wrist, while she turned away and scrubbed at her mouth. When she faced them again, she hid the handkerchief in a wad in her hand and slipped it to her brother.

He slid it back in his pocket. "It takes practice."

Could Cassia reassure Zoe she need not be self-conscious in front of the Brave Gardener? Or at least distract the child from her embarrassment? Cassia found more words inside her that she knew were the right ones. "Are these your goats?"

Zoe's attention turned to her pets, and she nodded. "When Mama said I could have a familiar, I realized goats are my favorite animal. But you can't keep a goat by itself, because they're herd animals naturally. They must have friends of their own kind. So Mama agreed it was all right for me to have two familiars."

"The Eriphites have always been herders," Lio explained. "Zoe is a natural with goats."

"These are High Rift Dwarf goats from the Empire," Zoe explained. "They do well in the cold, and they don't grow very big."

Cassia smiled. "I can see you know a lot about goats."

"Whenever I get my affinity, I hope it's goat magic," the child said.

"What are their names?" Cassia asked.

Zoe picked up the black-and-white goat and said solemnly, "This is

Midnight Moonbeam." She tucked the brown-and-white goat under her other arm. "This is her sister, Rainbow Aurora."

Cassia did battle with her smile anew. "Those are very beautiful names and perfect for Hesperine familiars."

"Lio says you like dogs." Zoe looked behind Cassia. "But I don't see the Brave Gardener's Shadow. Isn't Knight with you?"

"I see you have heard tales about my faithful liegehound. They are all true, I assure you. He is out in the paddock."

Zoe hugged her goats closer. Aurora bleated amiably, while Moonbeam squirmed to get down. "Does Knight get along with goats?"

"Knight is very obedient, and when I tell him he must protect someone, he does as I say. He will get along with your goats."

"Then could I meet him too?"

Cassia looked to Lio.

"Yes," he answered, "however, you must remember what you have learned about magic. Some good things are dangerous because they are powerful, and we must be responsible when we interact with them. Knight is like magic. You must promise to be careful around him as I taught you when we were getting ready for tonight. If I ask you to go back inside the barn, you must do so right away."

Zoe nodded. "I promise."

Pushing Knight's limits with Lio was one thing, but with a child? Cassia willed her heart not to pound, for Zoe would surely hear it, and that would not reassure her. If the child noticed Cassia's racing pulse, however, Zoe gave no sign. Perhaps she took Cassia's misgivings for excitement. But Lio wouldn't.

Lio said carefully, meeting Cassia's gaze, "Zoe already knows how to step. We're very proud of her."

At that, Cassia nodded. "It sounds like you're a fast learner, Zoe."

"Thank you. I hope my magic comes in fast. Lio says it's different for every suckling, but I can't wait."

"I have no doubt your affinity will have to do with animals," he reassured her.

"Let me get Knight ready to meet you." Cassia set her betony seedling safely on a feed bin.

She returned to her hound in the paddock and let Knight sniff her, hoping he would pick up on the scent of goats and Zoe.

"*Ckuundat,* Knight. You are about to meet someone very special. A new *kaetlii.*"

At the word that meant someone to protect, Knight went still and paid utmost attention.

"That's right." She put a hand under his chin and lifted his head, looking into his eyes. "*Ckuundat.* You must treat her and her animals the same way you treat me, do you understand? *Barda!*"

He adopted guard stance.

"*Oedann!* Good dog. Let's greet her with our very best behavior. *Het baat!*"

Knight went into a down stay at Cassia's feet.

She called toward the barn. "Knight is ready."

Zoe came out of the barn carrying her goats, and Lio accompanied her with his hands on her shoulders. She had covered her head with a mantle of beautiful silk much finer than her cotton play robe, but Cassia noticed the embroidered design on it was a pattern of dancing goats. Zoe glanced eagerly in Knight's direction, but not into his eyes.

Zoe came to stand a little to the right of Cassia and her hound. "Oh, he's so big! He seems even bigger in real life than your illusions of him, Lio."

Knight stared at the little girl, his attention riveted on her. Cassia stood close beside him, ready to reach for his ruff if he broke out of his stay. But he lay flat on the ground, sniffing ceaselessly at the air.

What strange signals must Zoe send to him, a child like he was bred to protect, a Hesperine like he was bred to fight? Did it distress him for the safe and dangerous parts of his nature to clash so?

Or did he too, in whatever way an exceptional animal might, connect this moment with his own past? Could he remember that day when he had met a little girl in a kennel yard, and she had taken him in her arms for the first time while her elder sister looked on?

I am your new loma kaetlii, Cassia had told him, carefully pronouncing the new words she was learning. *You get to* baat *with me.*

Cassia echoed her past words now. "This is our new *kaetlii.* We get to *baat* with her and her family tonight."

Knight made his softest, sweetest whimpers deep in his throat.

Cassia smiled in relief. "That's a sound of affection. *Oedann,* Knight. Let's greet Zoe. *Obett.*"

With her permission to break his stay, Knight lumbered to his feet and went toward Zoe. The child's eyes widened, but she did not back away.

He sat down in front of Zoe and raised a paw. She giggled.

The silly hours Cassia had spent teaching him that frivolous trick one long, empty winter had been more worth it than she knew.

Zoe carefully set her goats down beside her. They did not back away either, a sure sign Knight was not a predator in their eyes. They wandered off to graze. Zoe carefully shook Knight's paw in a mimicry of the Hesperine way, with her fingers upon his ankle. Orthros was truly a blessed land, where liegehounds and sucklings were not enemies.

"*Oedann!*" Cassia said again. "What a good dog."

Knight put his paw down and smelled Zoe all over, which made her laugh and wiggle when his muzzle found a ticklish spot. His tail swiped back and forth in the scrubby grasses so hard his whole rump swayed.

He proceeded to make his rounds in the paddock and the barn, investigating every corner of Zoe's world as thoroughly as he inspected any room before Cassia entered it. Knight even subjected the goats to his scrutiny, nosing the tiny things until he lifted their little hooves off the ground and they bleated in protest. But when they showed him their tails and trotted away from him, it was not in panic, but haughty caprine disapproval. Zoe followed along with Knight, occasionally putting a hand to his shoulder with the fascinated urge to touch that Cassia remembered feeling as a child.

Lio watched, and Cassia could see the same wonder in his eyes that she felt. Zoe might consider Lio her hero, but Cassia could see the truth all over his face. It was Lio who was smitten with the child.

We call this the Solace, Cassia remembered him saying, *for we offer refuge and comfort to suffering children. But my mother once said to me the real reason for the name is that children are the solace of all Hesperines.*

BEDTIME STORIES

L IO LEANED AGAINST THE fence, content to watch Cassia and Zoe play
fetch with Knight. To think, only a few nights ago, he had wondered if
Cassia would make it safely across the border to join the children for
whom she had sacrificed so much. A mere month before that, he had not
been sure how he would ever see her again. Bringing her together with
his sister had seemed like an elusive dream.

Goddess, I will never take this for granted.

A soft gasp behind him told him his mother had come back outside.

"It's all right, Mother," he said quickly. "We introduced them very
carefully, and Knight's behavior has been exemplary. When I brought him
to Waystar, it changed how he responds to Hesperines—and when Cassia
commanded him to protect Zoe, he rose to the occasion."

"I can see that." His mother came to stand beside him, leaning on the
fence from the other side. "Ninety years I have been a Hesperine, and yet
I still behold new wonders all the time. So many of them lately have been
Cassia's doing." She reached up and put a hand on Lio's hair, tugging him
nearer. She levitated a bit and gave him a kiss on the cheek before she let
him go. "You are feeling much better."

"Cassia has put me entirely to rights."

His mother smiled at him, then propped her chin on her hand to
watch Cassia and Zoe. "I can lay down my worries about all my children."

Rudhira had been right when he had told Lio there were many
moments when he would wonder if he had done the right thing. But there
were also moments like these, when he regretted nothing.

His mother chuckled at Cassia and Zoe's game with Knight. "I hate to interrupt them. But Zoe will Slumber in the paddock if we don't bring her in for bed soon. Even sucklings may not sleep much during polar night, but when they do—"

"Their parents should make the most of it."

His mother gave him a rueful look. "I admit, it has been a busy two nights."

Finding his Grace had given Lio new appreciation for Hesperine parents' stamina. He wasn't sure if his parents had had a single moment alone since the embassy had made harbor, and they'd been feeding Zoe all that time.

"I gave Zoe a drink while we were in the barn," Lio said. "She shouldn't need anything else before bed."

"Thank you. We made sure she was full before you two arrived, but she still gets so hungry whenever she is anxious."

"Cassia and I can put her to bed, if you and Father would like."

"I should probably accept your offer, but I can't bear to miss a single bedtime. I've waited so long to get to enjoy them." The gate opened before her, and she came inside the paddock. "Zoe? It's almost time for bed."

Father joined Lio at the fence. They watched all the ladies they loved. Mother was soon drawn into Zoe and Cassia's game.

"Rudhira should be here," Lio said. "Hasn't he arrived yet?"

"He was delayed," Father answered. "Konstantina wanted a word with him."

Lio winced. "I hope the Summit has not become a point of contention between him and his sister."

Father shook his head. "The contention between them is older than you are, and their love for one another far older than that. If your Summit were not one more foil in their debate, something else would be. And that is all I can say without crossing the veil."

Lio shook his head and asked no more questions. He tried to hold on to the moment, but thoughts he had allowed himself to forget now returned and wore away at his contentment.

"Father," he began.

"Yes, Son."

"When I spoke with Mother at Waystar about what happened in the pass, she did not tell me what she thought. She just listened, as she does."

"That was what you needed."

"Then she asked me one question. Have I ever thought it was wrong of her to murder a war mage to keep him from hurting anyone else?"

"How did you answer her?" his father asked.

"Of course she did the right thing."

Lio and his father stood together in silence for a moment.

"Mother also did not tell me what you thought," Lio said at last.

"I told you what I thought when you introduced Cassia to me."

Lio took a deep breath. "My conscience is at peace about that night. But I would still like to know if you were proud of me because you believed I had killed them, or because you knew I hadn't."

"I am proud of you because I know whatever decision you made in that moment was the right one."

Lio turned to look at his father. "Thank you."

"You were there in the middle of that crisis. We were not. We must have confidence in your judgment. Why else did we raise you to have a conscience, if not to let you act on it? Why teach you to make good decisions, if we never give you the freedom to make them on your own?"

"I am grateful for your trust."

His father put an arm around his shoulders. "My only regret is that I was not there to fight at your side. I never imagined a child of mine facing war without me."

"Zoe and Mother need you here, safe in Orthros. I am glad one of your children is too young to confront what's happening."

"I wish neither of you had to. So much for my relief when you became a diplomat instead of a warrior."

Lio laughed. "I know. I hope we don't have to fight any more battles. But if we must, charging into one with you would be a great moment."

"Let us charge into the one before us. Only the full force of our family will succeed in getting our precocious suckling into bed."

Lio and his father joined Mother and Cassia in their noble efforts. There ensued Zoe's usual procrastination, her plaintive requests to sleep among the goats for just one night, and the drawn-out ceremony of putting her pets to bed and making sure they had everything they needed.

This last compulsion of Zoe's, their mother indulged with utmost patience, showering her with reassurances. They hoped that, in time, they could convince Zoe no one under her care was in danger of starving if she took a moment's rest. Cassia joined in with the words of someone who knew what Zoe needed to hear.

It was Cassia who managed the impossible and made Zoe excited for bedtime. "Can I stay and listen to Lio's stories tonight?"

Zoe looked at him, tugging on his robe. "Will you tell a Brave Gardener story? With the real Brave Gardener right here?"

"Of course. She can even help me, if she likes, and fill in any parts I leave out."

Cassia's awkwardness with her legend tinged the Union again, a kind of auric blush. "I'm not as good at telling stories as Lio, but I have had a lot of wonderful stories told to me. I'm sure I can help."

Zoe headed for the house without further prompting. Cassia and Lio paused to collect her betony seedling from the barn, then joined his parents in following Zoe inside. As they traipsed into Mother's study, she caught them all in a cleaning spell that lifted away the smell of goats and filled the room with her familiar plum-blossom scent.

In response to everyone's voices, there came the sound of ruffled feathers from the corner where Mother's familiar slept on her perch. The eagle's crest rose in disapproval before she settled back down to roost. Both Cassia and Knight cast the bird glances, hers impressed, his wary of a fellow predator.

"Can Hesperines be falconers?" Cassia asked Lio's mother.

"No, we could not bear the birds' natural hunt. Anna is my familiar, bound to me by blood. She does not need to eat."

"But we must still put food out for my goats," Zoe said. "They get scared if their troughs are empty."

Father picked up Zoe, and she rested her sleepy head upon his shoulder. As Mother closed the stained glass door and shut out the cold, the hues of spell light in the panes slid across her scroll racks and writing desk.

Cassia smiled at Lio. "Have you made all the stained glass in House Komnena?"

He took her cloak. "Yes, but there are still a lot of empty window frames to be filled and windows of plain glass waiting to be replaced."

His mother paused to tell how he had surprised her with the door as a Gift Night present one year. Lio got the impression Cassia's rapt attention was not merely for his mother's sake. Thorns. If his parents talked about him out of his hearing, how many things must his mother and his Grace have to share with each other? Thinking of the awkward moments of his childhood, he felt a little warm under the collar.

As his mother had said, though, she had waited so long for the joys that children brought. Talking to her Grace-daughter about her son was clearly one of them. Lio also recalled a night in Tenebra when Cassia had extricated from him all the embarrassing truths about himself he'd had no intention of sharing. As he had reminded himself then, he should not regret her voracious curiosity about him. He smiled to himself. It had its benefits on other occasions.

When they reached Zoe's bedchamber, Father set her gently in her bed, then sat down on the edge of it. Cassia lingered at the periphery of the room, studying the wall hangings. She eyed the constellations on Zoe's Gifting chart and his sister's Ritual tapestry from Kassandra. Lio could sense Cassia trying to stifle her uncertainty.

He slid closer to her and put an arm around her, speaking quietly for her ears alone. "Stomping your feelings back down inside you will only serve to make you uncomfortable, my rose. It won't hide them from the Blood Union."

She flushed, her aura humming with unbearable tension. "Oh, Lio, I don't want your parents to think me uncomfortable in their house. It might seem as if I find their hospitality lacking."

"No one will think anything about however you feel. My parents are very kind and patient people. You know they must be to put up with me."

She nudged him in the side. "That's nonsense and you know it. You were probably a perfect child."

"Well, I suppose. But giving birth to and raising a Hesperine suckling with two heaps of unruly magic was probably a handful on at least some occasions."

"A 'conscientious and well-behaved' suckling born under two full moons and blessed constellations."

He rubbed her back. "Cassia, everyone needs time to get used to new situations. When you have a chance, ask my mother to tell you more about her early years in Orthros. Although she came here with my father, there were still challenges she had to face."

Thoughtfulness stemmed the tide of Cassia's anxiety, and she leaned closer to Lio. "Do you think she would mind if I asked her about it?"

"Not at all. But right now, I think we are called upon to tell our own stories."

Lio took up his customary position at the end of Zoe's bed, crossing his legs, and patted the covers beside him in invitation to Cassia.

She eyed the place next to him with a smile, but passed him by, giving his shoulder a squeeze. Her gaze came to rest resolutely on the empty place by Zoe, on the other side of her from Mother. A sense of confidence came over her that Lio found beautiful to his senses.

"As I mentioned," Cassia said, "I am no great storyteller, but I did learn a thing or two about it when my elder sister used to tell me bedtime stories. There is a special way you have to sit to make the tales even better."

"There is?" Zoe asked.

"Yes. Would you like me to show you?"

At Zoe's nod, Cassia rounded the bed and put Knight in a sit stay beside it. She set her potted betony on the bedside table, pausing to admire the identical plant Zoe always kept beside her during the Slumber. Then Cassia pulled back the covers and crawled right in beside Zoe. Stretching out her legs before her, she patted her lap.

Zoe gave her a look as if Cassia had just invited her to finger paint a votive statue of Hespera.

Cassia waited, her expression inviting. "The stories are always more magical if you sit on the storyteller's lap. It's true."

Lio forgot to breathe as he watched his little sister crawl into Cassia's lap.

Cassia's arms came around Zoe as if she were embracing that Hespera statue. But then she hugged the little girl closer and planted a kiss on her hair. Zoe rested her head on Cassia's shoulder and did not see the sheen in Cassia's eyes. But Lio felt it all the way to his Grace's heart.

He wanted to catch this moment in glass, capture it forever, beautiful and clear and flawless. But that would not be enough. He wanted them all to get to live it every night.

"You have a sister?" Zoe asked.

"I did. Her name was Solia, and she was a wonderful sister."

Zoe's voice went quiet. "What happened to her?"

For the first time, Cassia hesitated, and the Union stuttered with the return of her uncertainty, her worry she had chosen the wrong words.

"Zoe understands losing people you love," Lio reassured her. "Her mortal parents were wonderful, too, and when they left her, it was only because they had to go and find food for her and the other children."

"They never came back," Zoe said. "We aren't sure what happened to them, but if they were alive, they would have come back for me."

Cassia stroked Zoe's hair. "That's exactly what happened to my sister. She had to leave me, although she did not wish to, and some dangerous men never let her return."

"Would you tell me a story about her?"

"I'd like that. How about I tell you the story of the first garden I ever planted, which was for Solia?"

THE RITUAL CIRCLE

CASSIA HAD NEVER HELD a child. Neither a preening lady's new babe, a palace servant's restless tot, nor any of the young apprentices who worked in the kennels. Parents kept their legitimate children away from bastards, and women in trouble kept their bastards away from other women they didn't trust.

The feeling of Zoe falling asleep in her arms was completely new.

The child's hair smelled good, like beeswax soap. Her legs and arms were sharp and bony, but somehow she was a soft bundle in Cassia's arms. When the little girl finally slipped into Slumber and stopped breathing, it startled Cassia. But she could still feel the warmth in Zoe's body and knew her Hesperine heart beat strong.

"You have made her night, Cassia." Komnena beamed, reaching for her daughter.

Cassia handed Zoe to her mother so Komnena could settle the child under the blankets. When Cassia got out of the bed, she found Lio right behind her.

He wrapped his arms around her, leaning down to rest his face against hers. "Are you all right?"

"I think so, actually. It was...well, I think it was good to talk about Solia. I'm glad to discover it's better to talk about her now than to stay silent."

Komnena tucked the bedclothes under Zoe's chin and straightened. "That's an important change. A sign of healing."

"It feels that way," Cassia agreed.

"Perhaps," Apollon said, "you would feel able to talk about the Hesperines who saved you when you were a child. Lio's Ritual father has some questions he would like to ask you when he joins us tonight. Any information you can give him will aid his search for our missing Hesperines errant."

"Of course, I will do anything in my power to help the prince find them." But Cassia looked down at Lio's arms around her instead of meeting Apollon's gaze. What a coward she was.

"Come into the Ritual hall," Komnena invited, and there was indeed a ritualistic tone to her words.

Cassia got the feeling this was another part of the nightly routine of House Komnena, and once again, Lio and his family were sweeping her into it naturally and effortlessly. The easy rhythm took her breath away.

She followed Lio and his parents to the door of Zoe's room. "*Dockk*, Knight."

Her hound hesitated, watching Zoe sleep with his head resting on the edge of her bed.

Cassia patted her legs. "*Dockk*, dear one. *Soor het*. It is safe to leave the *kaetlii* to sleep here in her *loma*."

He huffed a sigh and came to Cassia, but not without a glance over his shoulder at the sleeping suckling.

Lio put an arm around Cassia, and together they all left Zoe's room and went along a couple of moonlit corridors, then upstairs to a grand chamber they had passed through earlier. Cassia couldn't see any fountains, but the whisper of water made soothing echoes through the room. Pillars framed peaked archways that led into the chamber from all sides, and ribbed vaults criss-crossed the high ceiling, disappearing up into shadow. Light emanated from the mosaic in the center of the floor, and now she had the opportunity to get a better look at it.

"Hespera's Rose," she said in recognition. "And in the center, that is Anastasios's constellation, the symbol of your house?"

"That's right," Lio answered. "This is the Ritual Circle, where we hold all family religious observances. Or just spend time together."

Five chairs awaited at the edge of the circle. In what appeared to be the favored Hesperine style, they were silk and wrought iron. The gold and blue cushions were rather cheery. The matching table held a glass coffee service that must be another of Lio's creations.

His parents sat down on one side of the table, and on the other, Lio pulled his and Cassia's seats close together and put his arm over the back of her chair. Knight lay down on her feet. Relaxing on the comfortable cushions, Cassia realized how tired her whole body was. But her mind and heart raced like wild things. Perhaps coffee had its down sides after all.

"Would you like something more to drink, Cassia?" Komnena reached for a cup.

"No, thank you," Cassia replied sheepishly. "I'm not sure I should have any more coffee."

"Have you had enough to eat?" Komnena held out a tray of tiny pies.

"Oh, yes, but these smell so good, I can't resist." Tonight Cassia had already eaten far more than was her habit, but she wanted to be a good guest.

Before she knew it, Komnena had filled a cloth napkin with the morsels and given Cassia the handful. It seemed Lio and his mother were of one mind about making sure Cassia got enough to eat.

Cassia popped one of the pies in her mouth. As soon as she finished chewing, she spoke. "These must be Orthros's famous meatless mincemeat pies that Lio told me about. They live up to their legend."

Komnena smiled. "We use dates from the Empire, among other ingredients."

"There is so much food everywhere in Orthros," Cassia commented, "even though Hesperines don't need it."

"It is a matter of sacred principle," Komnena explained. "We seek to reciprocate our human guests' generosity to us."

"And we do enjoy food." Lio helped himself to one of the pies from Cassia's napkin.

Now that she was no longer the only one eating, she felt much less awkward under the Hesperines' gazes. As Lio had probably predicted. She smiled at him, and at the sight of a crumb at the corner of his mouth, she forgot what she was going to say.

Oh, yes. She was going to ask his mother a question. "Did you make these?"

"Definitely not." Komnena laughed. "Many Hesperines do choose the culinary arts for their craft, and it falls to them to provision our human guests. They supply House Komnena with everything I need to fulfill my duties as the Queens' Chamberlain. I, however, stopped trying to get along with the kitchen many years ago."

Apollon pulled her close. "We burned down her kitchen when we left Tenebra."

"Well," Komnena conceded, "there was a decapitated mage in it."

"We would have burned the place down just for you."

"You showed that war mage some poetic justice," Cassia marveled.

"So they did," Lio agreed.

Cassia could think of some places at Solorum she would like to burn down. What must that feel like, to leave your personal prison in ashes behind you, literally?

"Speaking of when I left Tenebra..." Komnena picked up a small, thick book from the table and ran a hand over it. "Cassia, I would like you to have this as a welcome gift from me. It is the dictionary I learned with during my early nights in Orthros."

Cassia knotted her hands. "That's a treasure you can't replace. Are you sure?"

"Knowledge is meant to be handed on. This book will be a good friend to you, and it will give me joy to see you together."

The book must be a hundred years old. The immortals who had hand-crafted it in their scriptorium were most likely walking around Selas this very night. The Hesperines had showered Cassia in luxuries since her arrival, but this was a book. She had never expected to possess more than the few hoarded volumes her sister had bequeathed her.

Komnena pressed the dictionary into Cassia's hands. "I hope you enjoy it."

There was no way Cassia could refuse. As soon as she opened the book, she didn't want to. "It has all the words in Vulgus *and* Divine!"

"I couldn't have gotten by without it in my early nights here."

"Thank you so much," said Cassia. "This is exactly what I needed. I was just saying to Lio tonight how much I want to learn Divine. Did he tell you?"

"I didn't have a chance." Lio smiled, reading over Cassia's shoulder.

"You told me, Cassia." Komnena tapped her heart. "I remember what it feels like."

"Mind healers must always know how to choose the perfect gift," said Cassia.

"I'm a mind healer now. I have studied under Queen Soteira, written treatises that sit on the shelves of my library next to the works that once taught me, and become a calligrapher by craft. But when I arrived here, I was illiterate." Komnena nodded to the book in Cassia's hands. "You only need two things to make something dangerous happen. A curious mind and one book to get you started."

"Now I have both."

"And I know you like living dangerously."

She and Komnena exchanged a grin. Cassia held the book to her, letting it remind her of all she had to look forward to. That made the past easier to bear.

At that moment, the First Prince stepped into sight at the edge of the Ritual circle, his face drawn. "Sorry I'm late."

Knight leapt to his feet. He bounded toward the prince. Cassia lunged for his ruff and missed. She was about to shout a command when she realized. His tail was wagging.

Her deadly liegehound ran to the warrior prince of the Hesperines and looked up at him with hopeful eyes that begged for attention.

The prince, his gray gaze fearsome, stared down at Knight. "I have never in all my many, many years seen a liegehound respond to me thus."

Apollon had a good laugh at the spectacle.

The prince raised an eyebrow in Apollon's direction. "I shall be disappointed if I discover my aura has grown less threatening with age."

"If it is any comfort," Apollon replied, "the hound has yet to raise his hackles at me, either. I suspect I owe his tolerance to his devotion to my children."

Cassia pressed a hand to her mouth to hide a smile. "Knight has recently become an abject devotee of the Queens. Do you suppose he senses them in you, First Prince?"

Lio chuckled. "Well, Rudhira, I think we can conclude Knight's adoration extends to you as a member of the royal bloodline."

The prince furrowed his brows at Knight. "He looks like he wants something from me."

"Probably a pat on the head," Lio suggested, "or a treat."

The prince shook his head. "With all due respect to your faithful guardian, Cassia, I shall leave the demonstrations of affection to those who have not had my past experiences with liegehounds."

Knight's eyes grew larger and more pitiful.

The prince frowned at her hound for a moment. Then finally he said, "Good dog."

Knight's tail swished furiously.

Cassia called him back to her, and he returned to his post on her feet, drooling and sanguine.

At last the prince took his eyes off of Knight. Lio's Ritual father glanced around their gathering. "I missed Zoe."

Komnena clicked her tongue and poured him a cup of coffee. "Imagine starting your first night here in ages with an apology."

"Nonsense," Apollon agreed. "Sit down. Rest. Eat."

With a sigh, the First Prince took the chair that awaited him. "If I keep on like this, Zoe will forget she has a Ritual father."

"Impossible," Lio scoffed. "Do you know how often she asks me to tell her Rudhira stories? It makes us feel you're with us all the time."

Komnena pressed coffee and mincemeat into the prince's hands. It seemed Hesperines' urge to show care through food was not actually limited to their mortal guests. "She's so proud of her Ritual father. She knows you're helping people like her in Tenebra."

"Even Zoe understands." There was something pointed in Apollon's tone. "Your work is vital. She accepts we must honor your sacrifices by sacrificing our time with you."

The prince turned to Cassia. "Good to see you here, Cassia. You met Zoe?"

"Yes." A smile came over Cassia before she even thought about it.

An answering smile flickered on the prince's face. "The Brave Gardener made her grand entrance, then. I am sure Zoe was too excited to regret my absence."

That the First Prince of Orthros would deem Cassia a welcome substitute for his presence under any circumstances was not something her mind seemed ready to understand. That Zoe might be as happy to see

Cassia as to receive a rare visit from her own Ritual father was just as startling a thought.

"I am sure she missed you terribly," Cassia protested. Which would not reassure him, she realized. "But we did have a wonderful evening, and she was in excellent spirits when we put her to bed."

The prince's smile softened. "I'm glad to hear it. When I do see her next, I am sure she will tell me all about it."

Cassia cleared her throat, thinking of all she had told Zoe about Solia. She should tell the prince she was ready for his questions.

Then he stretched his legs out before him, crossing his ankles, one Tenebran riding boot over the other. Balancing his cup and napkin on his knee, he devoted his attention to the coffee and mincemeat. This was as near to relaxed as Cassia had seen him all night. His body language was easier to read than other Hesperines'. Perhaps that was a result of all the time he spent around mortals in Tenebra, or perhaps concealing his emotions did not come naturally to him.

This was not just a conference between the commander of the Charge and a recent arrival from Tenebra who had information for him. This was time with Lio's family. Cassia did not wish to be the one who disrupted it by pushing herself to attend to her cause. She found she was far more content to leave Tenebra outside the Ritual circle, at least for a little while longer.

The Hesperines spoke of the glass figurines Lio planned to cast as Winter Solstice gifts, of a discussion circle on mind healing that Komnena would soon host, and of what stone Apollon would choose for his next sculpture. The conversation flowed comfortably around Cassia, and she found it surprisingly easy to join in, as long as she did not try to meet Apollon's gaze. No one seemed to mind her starry-eyed questions about their work and life in Orthros. In fact, everyone seemed to enjoy satisfying her curiosity.

After the prince finished his coffee and pie, he reached into a pocket of his short crimson robe and fished out a knot of wood, along with a knife. It was the sharpest implement Cassia had seen in Selas, although she supposed it qualified as a tool, not a weapon. While they all talked, the prince began to whittle.

"Is woodworking your craft?" Cassia asked.

"Yes," the prince answered. "Wood is used sparingly in Orthros, but knowing how to work with it assists me in the field."

Cassia felt the world beyond the Ritual circle pulling at them again. "The demands of living Abroad are very different from life here behind the ward."

Shavings fell away from the palm-sized lump of mottled brown-and-beige wood. The prince's gaze never left his work. "In the field, we live by Charge Law. It is an entirely separate body of laws from the canon that governs us here at home. Of course, the Equinox Oath is the backbone of Charge Law."

"Are you the author of the Charge's laws, First Prince?"

"I am one crafter of them. Charge Law is a living thing, shaped by Hespera's tenets, errant deeds, and raw necessity. Its foremost purpose is to protect. When someone is harmed, the law failed them."

Cassia could almost hear the words the prince wasn't saying. *I failed them.*

"Tenebra has failed everyone," Cassia said. "The lapse of the Oath puts everyone in danger."

"But you have done more than any mortal to shield my people from the consequences." The prince's hands went still, and he met her gaze. "In gratitude for your help, especially with my search for Nike, I swear I will personally help you find your three Hesperine rescuers. I do not take oaths lightly. You can rely on me to keep this promise, no matter the cost."

"You have Rudhira on your side now," Lio said gravely. "You have won yourself the most relentless ally you could ask for."

"Such is my respect for you, Cassia," the prince said.

She put a hand on her heart. "I treasure your respect, and I am grateful for your aid. With your help, I have no doubt the Hesperines who saved me can be found."

"Together, we will see them safely home."

"Lio's father said you had some questions for me. How can I help?"

"I'm afraid I must ask you to think back on difficult memories. I inherited my mother Soteira's affinities; as a mind healer, I know how it can harm a person to relive painful events at the wrong time or in the wrong way. But as the leader of the Charge, it is my responsibility to make use of every possible scrap of information to find my missing people."

"You know I will do anything for them."

"I know. But I am hesitant to ask this of you. Do not mistake me; I do not mean to imply you are fragile. You bear your burdens with great strength. But at what cost to your spirit?" The prince shook his head. "I do not push my patients or my warriors past their breaking points."

Komnena put in, "It is Cassia's decision how much she wishes to say, but I am confident her mind will not suffer from recalling those events for you. In fact, it could do her good."

The prince had yet to return to his carving. "Thank you for your opinion, Komnena. You would deem it safe, then?"

"Cassia told me only tonight that speaking of her sister is now a greater solace than pain."

Now the prince's steel gaze rested on Cassia. "Is that how you feel?"

She nodded. "I never told anyone about that night. Until I told Lio."

Lio rubbed her back, and she felt his reassuring presence on the edges of her mind, within reach, but never intruding.

She went on. "Telling him changed…everything. He helped me through the worst. It only gets easier to be open about what happened. When I talked with Zoe about my sister tonight…it gave me joy."

Lio smiled. "Zoe has a way of healing us without even trying."

"Very well," the prince said. "It sounds as if I can, in good conscience, make this request of you, Cassia. It will by no means be easy, but I believe you are equal to it."

"It doesn't matter how difficult it is," she replied. "I will honor my bond of gratitude with my rescuers."

"I thought that would be your answer." His smile appeared briefly again, and there seemed to be approval in it. Then his gaze settled on Lio. "We will need the assistance of your light magic and mind magic. I trust you are comfortable with an expense of power tonight."

Lio answered immediately. "I will help in any way I can."

He didn't hesitate. It seemed he had left his mistrust of his own power behind on the other side of the sea. Cassia leaned into him, offering her thanks and her support, if he needed it. His arm came around her again, his body relaxed.

The prince turned his carving-in-progress over and over in his palm, studying what was taking shape. "Cassia, may I ask if you are comfortable with Lio's presence in your mind?"

She was sure her face turned as red as Lio's rose window, but she declared, "Entirely."

Lio grinned.

The prince set his knife to the carving again. "In that case, with your permission, I would like Lio to walk through your memories of your rescuers with you. Try to recall every single detail you can, while Lio is present in your thoughts. Then I would like for him to cast an illusion so I can see what you two are seeing. I want to know if I recognize the three Hesperines you met that night. Even if I do not, we may discover details that will help me identify and ultimately locate them."

Lio leaned forward. "Brilliant."

"Ah," said Apollon, "Nike and Methu's old strategy. She would delve into the mind's eye, and he would craft the illusions."

The prince gave a nod and dug his knife into the piece of wood.

Lio took a deep breath. "I am following in great footsteps tonight. I will do my best."

They all knew Lio's magic was more than sufficient for the task, but no one reminded him of how powerful he was. Cassia was happy to see a return of his comfortable humility in place of the agony about his power that had overtaken him after Martyr's Pass.

"If you would prefer not to have an audience," the prince added, "I am sure Lio's parents will understand if we go somewhere more private."

"We can go ahead right here." Cassia felt more and more comfortable with Komnena, and as for Apollon, she had to admit... "Lio's father might be able to help us identify them, if he sees my memories."

"I would value Apollon's observations," the prince agreed.

"Hmm," came Apollon's response. "There may be a few new Hesperines errant I haven't met, but I have watched most of Orthros and Orthros Abroad grow up and welcomed every newcomer who joins our people under my Grace's guidance. I'll see what I can do."

The prince met Cassia's gaze. "Are you ready?"

Lio touched her cheek and turned her to look at him. "We will do this together, Cassia. Every step of the way."

She put a hand over his. She had walked through these memories alone so many times. Even when she had first shared them with him, she had not yet learned to accept all the support he wanted to give her. This time would be different. "I will tread that path again—with you, this time."

ECHOES

$\mathcal{C}$ASSIA TOOK A DEEP breath. "I am ready."

Lio's hand slid under her hair and came to rest at the nape of her neck, his fingers cool and gentle. "Close your eyes."

She exhaled and let her eyes slide shut. As he rubbed his thumb in the groove at the base of her head, she felt his mind enfold hers. This felt like a chaste, reassuring embrace, in contrast to the compelling intimacy of his mind-touch when they were alone.

She recalled the very first time he had wrapped his arms around her, when he had dared to cross her defenses to offer her comfort after she had first told him of the very memories they were about to confront now. As she remembered that moment, she felt his smile in her thoughts.

"Let us begin with that memory," Lio suggested, "and work backward from there."

Cassia reached out and found his free hand, taking it in hers.

Lio holding her for the first time. Lio cupping blood and light in their joined hands, explaining her sister was light now. Lio, grief-stricken and furious for her sake, asking how her own father could have done such a thing.

Lio, listening, understanding, as no one else had, as she told him about the three of his people who had changed her life forever.

He had said then, *I cannot bear to imagine a history in which you did not survive that night to stand here with me.*

He said now, "Sit here in safety at House Komnena and cast your thoughts back to the very first moment you met the Hesperine who saved your life."

Cassia could see the arrow in the ground that had almost struck her.

She could feel her cold feet swinging, feel the Hesperine's strong arms around her. She could feel her fear. But between her and that childhood terror, she now felt a veil that seemed woven of Lio. The fear receded.

"You don't need that," he said quietly. "Information is all we are here for."

"You are making this easy for me."

"As easy as possible."

She squeezed his hand in thanks.

She stopped struggling and let her rescuer carry her away from the threat, away from—no, she did not have to dwell on the fact that her sister's remains were just there, slipping out of sight on the field below the walls of the fortress.

"Easy, little one. You're safe. I'll keep you safe now. Nothing in the world can harm you while I protect you."

When Cassia heard the lady Hesperine's voice for the first time in fifteen years, she gasped and jumped in her seat. She felt Knight rise from her feet, and his toes clicked restlessly on the floor. Lio pressed his hand gently against her neck in reassurance.

"Auditory projection," he murmured. "It's just thelemancy, making all of us think we hear her. I want to know if Rudhira and Father recognize her voice."

"Less thelemancy, please," the prince requested. "I can't hear her natural tones."

"That's not my magic," Lio replied. "That's how she sounds in Cassia's memory."

The prince made a noise of frustration. "Then the distortions we hear are time and pain. Childhood memories are seldom crystal clear, especially difficult ones."

"I'm sorry," Cassia said.

"No, no," the prince reassured her. "No need to apologize for your mind's natural defenses coming to your aid."

"That night is vivid in your memory," said Komnena, "because it was painful. Parts of your memories will be missing for the same reason."

Cassia closed her eyes tighter and focused. Her rescuers' lives might depend on every detail she could manage to recall.

Carefully she reexamined the three Hesperines as she had first seen them. The beautiful female who had saved her life had been shrouded in a black cowl and long black robes. No way to tell what color her hair was, but her face had appeared pale. Her two companions had also worn hoods. The color of their eyes had been obscured by shadow.

She heard exclamations of surprise around her in the Ritual hall and the sound of Knight pacing. She reached out and found his ruff with her hand. He quieted, despite the tide of Lio's magic all around them.

"Directly from Cassia's memory," Lio reiterated.

"Keep going." Now the prince sounded eager. "Could we fill in more details?"

Cassia tried to concentrate on features. Their faces swam before her mind's eye, a blur of beauty, strangeness, and compassion. But she would never forget the lady Hesperine's smile. That had been the first time Cassia had seen fangs.

"That must have been startling," she heard Komnena say.

"Don't be afraid, little one." Her savior's voice echoed about her again. "We would never hurt you."

Cassia could not resist. She wanted to see them, hear them brought to life. She opened her eyes.

She gasped at the sight of Lio's illusion. Three giants of light and darkness towered above the Ritual circle, one on her knees, the other two standing sentinel behind her. Their faces were auras of starlight, their robes spun of shadows.

As Cassia studied them, the images wavered. She concentrated again, holding her memory firmly in her mind, even as she gazed upon the present.

She shook her head. "This is not what I meant to show you."

"This is what they looked like to you as a child." Lio's tone was patient as he explained. "Of course they would seem larger than life."

The prince appeared about to smile. "We may not be able to recognize them, but we have learned a great deal about your first impression of our people. When I do find them, I shall award them Charge honors for representing us so well."

"But I must do better," Cassia said, "if you are to recognize anything about them."

Lio rubbed her neck again. "Let us continue through the memory. Perhaps some details we missed will surface."

Moment by moment, breath by breath, Cassia relived her memories in her mind while she watched Lio bring them to life before her. Her heart pounded and her palms sweated. She felt she held ice and fire, one in each hand, as she sat here in Selas with her heart in the worst night of her life.

But each burn of emotion was easier than the last. Placing that night here inside House Komnena, containing it within the Ritual circle, cooled the memories until she could think and analyze rather than fight the threat of tears.

"What is that bundle on her back?" Cassia wondered aloud. "I don't remember noticing that. At least, not until now."

"Sometimes," Komnena said, "our memories hold details we are not aware of. We think we have forgotten, but our minds hold on to them for us, until we are ready to recall them."

Lio's eyes blazed, and the illusion sharpened. The hazy, dark burden on the lady Hesperine's back took shape. She carried something long and narrow wrapped in black fabric.

The prince frowned at the image. "Whatever she is carrying, it must be of great value, for her not to be parted from it even while performing the Mercy."

"A map?" Komnena wondered aloud.

"Tools," Apollon suggested.

"Her usual travel attire, perhaps," Lio offered, "rolled for ease of transport."

The prince nodded. "It's a feat that they managed to wear formals in the middle of a siege. She would need to change into fighting gear at a moment's notice."

"Let us go through all of it again," Cassia insisted. "Perhaps more details I didn't recall before will come to the surface."

"As you wish," Lio replied.

His only motion was to caress the back of her neck again and shift his hand slightly in hers. The illusion faded seamlessly back into the image of Cassia's first glimpse of the Hesperines errant.

"Don't be afraid, little one," her savior repeated in Vulgus. "We would never hurt you."

The lady Hesperine looked over her shoulder at her companions and exchanged words with them in Divine, which Cassia had not even attempted to understand at that age. Their conversation drifted up to the vaults of the Ritual hall in distant whispers and memorial echoes.

She would always wonder what they had said to each other. She had only known their voices were kind. She considered their concerned tones, straining to recall the sounds she had heard around her.

The whispers grew louder.

Lio sucked in a breath. "I almost understood that. Something about the cold and wool."

They watched one of the illusions take off her mantle and reach toward Cassia.

"Your auditory memories are strong," Komnena said.

"Try to remember more of their conversation," the prince encouraged.

Cassia closed her eyes once more and revisited her memories yet again, this time concentrating on words, not images. She listened to their voices and watched their lips. She couldn't understand what her memories were saying to each other. No one around the Ritual circle spoke. They must be listening carefully.

Divine rose and fell around her, the echoes tangling, until they faded into three distinct voices. A few words kept recurring every time the illusions spoke to each other.

"Alkaios!" the prince exclaimed. "Nephalea."

"Iskhyra?" Cassia opened her eyes.

Her illusory savior looked right at her, tears flowing down her face. Cassia reached out and touched her. Lio's illusion dissolved into bands of light, then disappeared.

"Those are not just words," Lio smiled at her. "They are names. Cassia, you remembered the names your rescuers called each other."

She let out a breath and looked at the prince. "Do you know them?"

He was leaning forward in his chair, his whittling abandoned on the coffee table. "By reputation, yes. They are among the Hesperines errant who take full advantage of the freedom Charge Law affords. They work alone and seldom avail themselves of my aid. But their deeds speak for them. They have been active in Tenebra for at least twenty years. Alkaios is a light mage, known to travel with his Grace, Nephalea, and their comrade Iskhyra, both warders."

Cassia held Lio's hand in her lap. "Then they are still alive."

"When last I heard," the prince answered, "yes."

She braced herself. "When did you most recently hear news of them? Please tell me everything you know. I am accustomed to keeping my expectations realistic."

"Only last night. A Charge scout brought word that Alkaios was sighted near Tenebra's southern border. She is still on his trail."

"Thank the Goddess." Komnena gave voice to all the gratitude Cassia could not find the words to express.

"May the Goddess's Eyes light their path," said Apollon.

"And Her darkness keep them in Sanctuary," Lio added.

"Many factors could cause the Charge to lose Alkaios's trail," the prince cautioned. "If he is unwilling to return to Orthros before his work in Tenebra is done, as seems to be the case, he may use his light magery to hide from his own. Or, if there are war mages on his trail, he may deliberately avoid contact with other Hesperines out of self-sacrifice."

"That would not surprise me," Cassia said, "for I have seen his heroism. But I will hold out hope his reward for it will be a safe return to Orthros."

"I will take my leave and join the search now." The prince got to his feet, looking at Cassia again. "You heard what Iskhyra said about her brother."

She nodded.

"You may wish to know that Alkaios, Nephalea, and Iskhyra have no family left in Orthros."

"Now they do."

"You will be the first to receive any news of them," the prince promised. He was gone before she could say more.

Cassia sank back in her chair, and Lio put an arm around her again.

She swallowed. "I hope they make it home."

ICE AND SNOW

"ARE YOU ALL RIGHT?" Lio asked her quietly.

Cassia nodded. "More than all right. Knowing we have done something to help them is a greater comfort than anything."

Lio's mother pulled her chair closer and took Cassia's hands. "If your memories trouble you, or you simply wish to talk, you can always come to me. Not just as a mind healer, but as a friend."

"Thank you."

Komnena nodded and released her hands with a smile.

Cassia glanced at the now-peaceful Ritual circle, where the stunning vision of her past had come to life just moments ago. Her pulse was calmer now.

Her gaze fell to the carving the prince had left behind on the coffee table. It was an exquisite little goat.

Apollon's hand entered her vision and picked up the carving. He chuckled. "Zoe will wake to a surprise from her Ritual father."

His tone could be so gentle. His deep, gravelly voice reminded Cassia of granite. He wasn't so hard to listen to when she didn't look at him.

When Cassia felt a hand on her head, she started. She could not look up, but she knew whose broad, powerful hand it was. Apollon touched her crown as if granting reassurance. Or a blessing. A sense of safety wrapped around her, just like at the welcoming ceremony. She wanted it so much. But something inside her fought it off with all her might.

She hated how she trembled at his touch. He could feel her trembling. How could she respond to his kindness with fear?

There was a smile in Apollon's voice and his presence above her. "This house is strong enough to weather all your worries and your fears with you. Take as much time as you need letting them run their course."

"Thank you," she managed, although the words were not enough.

"When you are ready for my welcome gift, it will be ready for you."

Komnena's voice eased into the conversation. "Well, I think we elders are past our bedtime now. If you youngbloods will excuse us."

Apollon lifted his hand from Cassia. From the corner of her eye, she glimpsed him take Komnena's arm. He didn't seem offended at all.

"Good veil," Lio told his parents.

"Good veil." Cassia tried looking at his father.

But she was too late. All she saw were his parents' backs as they retreated through an archway and out of sight. Their voices, relaxed and too low to make out words, drifted in their wake. Komnena gave a playful laugh.

"I thought mature Hesperines don't Slumber during polar night."

Lio grinned. "They don't."

"I see. Of course."

"Mother was away for a few nights, and I'm still not sure they had any time between the welcoming ceremony and the circle."

"You mean they haven't…availed themselves of the sideboard either?"

Lio chuckled at her metaphor. "As occupied as they've been, probably not."

Cassia hesitated, glancing at the archway through which his parents had disappeared. "Perhaps it is unseemly of me to pry, but in the spirit of our early conversations about Hesperine life…"

"I am always open to an informative discussion about birds, bees, and Hesperines."

"I know you were the only member of the Hesperine embassy who needed the sustenance of mortal blood. You mentioned once that the others who came to Tenebra need not rely on animals or humans. Although you never specified why, I inferred it was because they are all pairs."

"That's correct. My aunt and uncle provide for one another, as do Javed and Kadi, as well as Basir and Kumeta. That is the nature of Grace."

"So that's true of your parents as well?"

"Graces' fidelity to one another is absolute. They drink from no one but each other, and they give their blood to no one but the children they suckle together. The only exception is what we call the Ritual Drink, when any Hesperine will provide for any other if the need is dire."

Cassia let out a breath. "Then your mother didn't have to hesitate about becoming a Hesperine. I think it would have been much too sad if she faced the choice between remaining a mortal who could sustain your father, or having eternity with him only for him to drink from other humans. What a bittersweet eternity that would be."

Lio leaned nearer, circling his arm closer around her. "That is not a concern for any prospective Hesperine. Hespera does not offer eternity with a catch."

"I didn't know two Hesperines could sustain one another. I thought you always needed mortal blood."

"When two Hesperines are merely sharing, one must seek sustenance from humans to provide for the other. Only Graced pairs are free from that need, and so are children nurtured on their blood. It is the nature of the Grace bond and one of the most powerful magics known to our kind."

Could a Hesperine's immortal mate sustain him even better than a mere human could? Did that mean a mortal could never compare? "So, there *is* one kind of blood that is…superior to a mortal's?"

Lio dawdled his fingers on her shoulder, toying with the neckline of her dress. "You know, I must admit, my first taste of mortal blood was not remarkable, as everyone said it would be. The brief time I spent drinking from the guests before my departure for Tenebra was unimpressive. But then…" He held her gaze, running his hand down her throat. "I tasted you. I think you know how that affected me."

"Perhaps that's because you took more than the Drink from me."

"You know what the first swallow did to me, even before we kissed. A mere drink would never have been enough. You remember what I said to you the night of our first feast." He murmured in her ear, as he had then. "You are the best."

She reached up and brushed a lock of hair back from his forehead, and the warmth within her gave way to alarm. "You're freezing! Hesperines are supposed to be impervious to cold."

"This is a normal hunger chill. I feel like I'm burning up, actually. There's nothing to worry about now. This is no comparison to how I felt before you arrived."

She ran her hands over his shoulders. "But you're shivering. It's as bad as when we were on the ship."

"It has been some time since we made the crossing."

Grace must be a powerful bond indeed. Cassia had not even been able to tell Apollon and Komnena's fast was troubling them. But then, they had only done without one another for a few nights out of a lifetime, Cassia reasoned. Lio had fed on animals for half a year, then had only a few nights with her.

"You also used a great deal of magic tonight," she pointed out. "Do not take this question to mean I doubt you, Lio, but are you all right?"

"More than all right, as you said. Thank you for your concern. I needed to use my power to help. That was...cleansing. In any case, you know I would push my magic to the limit to honor my bond of gratitude with your rescuers."

"And now you need to replenish. I will give you what you need," she assured him. She would. She could.

He brought her hand to his mouth and kissed the inside of her wrist. "You priced your name at a kiss. What shall I pay you for a sip?"

"Nothing, my champion. For you, I will give freely, and more than a sip."

He let out a little groan against her skin. "You sweeten our arrangement indeed, my lady."

He stood, pulling her to her feet with him, then held her close and drew her with him across the Ritual Circle. When their feet left the floor, she couldn't stifle a gasp.

"Should you be levitating in your state?"

"With you here to rescue me from my state, I cannot keep my feet on the floor." He danced with her in the air, spinning them in a turn.

She put her arms around his neck and held on tight. Her stomach dipped, and her head spun, and she treasured the astonishing sensation of standing on nothing but his magic. It wasn't until they reached the double doors at the far end of the Ritual hall that he set her down.

"Allow me to invite you to my residence." His half-grin belied the formality of his words.

"I've looked forward to seeing your rooms," she admitted. And fantasized about them.

He led her through the halls, some softly lit, others shadowed. There were black floors like marble night skies and carpets soft and thick as snow. At every turn, stained glass windows pulled in moonlight and cast translucent, shifting colors under their feet. When a statue emerged suddenly from the darkness, Cassia caught her breath. A face of brilliant crimson stone looked at her with a seductive, laughing smile.

"Who is that?" she asked Lio.

"Hespera. One of Father's visions of her."

"Oh, I see now. She has one white eye of a different stone."

They passed through a courtyard, where there sat cross-legged a rotund, wizened man of dull green stone, his beard and belly overgrown with moss and lichens. Like a delighted child who had just made a discovery, he peered at the weeds before him with one white eye and one red.

"But who could this be?" Cassia wondered aloud.

"Hespera," Lio answered again.

Back into the house, down a staircase, into a long gallery. Here were some of the elusive fountains. They played all around Hespera, who danced through the corridor as a barefoot youth of river stone, whether male or female, Cassia could not tell.

Cassia was glad Lio held her hand, for she soon lost her way in the rambling halls and hidden pockets of courtyards. "The whole house is like a spell. A magical labyrinth, where I expect to stumble upon a goddess around every corner."

His hand tightened on hers. "When you are here long enough, you get to know every twist and turn. It comes to feel like home."

"Does it not still seem magical to you, although it is home? Does the wonder wear off?"

He paused, as if considering his answer. "No. No, it doesn't."

They came to what appeared to be an exit hall with modest double doors flanked by more of Lio's windows. A side table held someone's gloves and a half-open scroll. On the rug in front of the door, a pair of wool slippers of Zoe's size lay cast aside.

"Here we are. The back door." Smiling, Lio retrieved the stray shoes.

Cradling her new betony plant in one arm, Cassia ran her fingers over the two small slippers Lio held in one hand. "You're a wonderful brother."

"Thank you." The sincerity in his voice gave weight to the simple words. "After all she's been through, I just want to shower her with everything good. Can you imagine, before the Prisma's mages rescued the children, they were struggling on their own? In one of the Eriphites' refuges, a cave where they had hidden their little ones and their last surviving elder. But Bosko and Thenie's grandmother died, and with her, much of their cult's stories and traditions. Bosko and Zoe salvaged what they could use from her body and blocked off that part of the cave with stones and branches to deter scavengers and the other children." He gazed down at his sister's shoes with her pain in his eyes. "They foraged as best they knew how for themselves and twenty-two others, but they wouldn't have lasted much longer. They were probably already sick with frost fever before they were discovered. All it might have taken was one more hard freeze, or a lone predator."

"To think, they escaped that only to nearly die because of Tenebran superstition. Nearly. But they didn't."

Their gazes met over the shoes. Neither of them said it, but Cassia knew they didn't need to. He held in his hand the greatest trophy of all their victories.

"How did you resist adopting all of them?" she asked.

Lio grinned. "As my mother is the chamberlain, many new arrivals to Orthros stay right here with us in House Komnena while she helps them find a permanent place, and the children were no exception. We got to enjoy all of them while prospective parents came to visit and discover who was a good match for whom."

"I imagine it helped their adjustment a great deal to remain together at first."

"Certainly. Javed and Kadi even left Bosko and Thenie here while they all became more comfortable with each other. But from the moment I came home with Zoe, Mother and Father's minds were made up she would stay for good. I didn't know they'd already been talking about another child. When they told me they wanted Zoe, it was the best news. The only good news. That last night in Tenebra…" He shook his head. "When the embassy met the Prisma to get the children, we were all just trying to keep the little ones awake and reassured long enough to get them home to Orthros. The scent of your betony charm led me to Zoe's side. And in trying to ease her fears, I found as much comfort as I gave her."

"I understand." Cassia swallowed. "Can you really provide for her better because of my help?"

He gave her another speaking glance, as he had when Zoe had taken the Drink from his blood. From their blood.

"Of course," he answered. "Keeping up with young Hesperines' appetites is a challenge, and usually only Graced pairs have the strength to properly nourish a suckling. It's customary for the whole family to assist. Drawing my nourishment directly from you, I have the strength to lend a hand."

"I am...honored...to help sustain your little sister."

"Thank you for striving to put her at ease. Your acceptance means so much to her."

Cassia searched for words to describe her encounter with the child. The ones she found surprised her. "I..." she tried. "I love her."

Lio's gaze softened. "She is fortunate in your love, Cassia."

"I do know how," she said with all the force of her conviction. "I have not had much in my life to learn from, but what kindness I have known, I hold all the closer. I am capable of love."

"Of course you are."

"Flavian may call me his Lady of Ice, but I'm not cold. I have been so, but I have been warm and giving too. No matter how I harden myself to achieve what I must, it's not at the expense of—of love."

Lio placed the shoes in her hands. "Cassia, love is the very reason you fight."

She held Zoe's slippers to her. "It is."

That power inside her, which she called anger, or a thirst for justice. It was not that. Those were mere signs of what it really was.

It was love.

Lio took her face in his hands and kissed her forehead. "Flavian is a blind fool. Any name he calls you preceded by 'my' is an offense. But as for the 'ice' part, well, ice and snow are home and hearth to Hesperines, aren't they?"

Lio turned Cassia around and stood behind her, wrapping her in his arms once more. The back doors sailed open to reveal what lay beyond.

Ice and snow and green. As far as Cassia could see.

"Shall I show you the garden?" Lio asked.

"Oh, yes."

They put Zoe's shoes away under the side table, and Cassia's cloak appeared in Lio's hand. He bundled her up, stealing kisses in the process, and took her outside.

Cassia came to a standstill on the back steps. "This is the garden?"

"You have discovered the dark secret of House Komnena. We are all useless with a spade."

The garden walls rose tall, their color lost under lichens, mosses, and rime. Enclosed in their imposing embrace was a rampant tangle as untamed as the grounds beyond the house. Tufted flowers Cassia had never seen choked the beds, and every open space was covered in snow-dusted willows no higher than her knees.

From sharp, bare tree branches and twisted thorn bushes hung long icicles, crystalline twins of the spines that armed the thickets. Drops of rich red were bearberries, hanging taut and succulent on their vivid green bushes. The lush, pungent growth and fragrant branches and fresh, chilly scent of snow inebriated her.

"It is beautiful," she said.

Lio huffed a laugh. "I'm afraid we've let it go for ages. Father built the house anticipating a vast bloodline, then had it all to himself for fifteen hundred years. He couldn't bear to set foot in it for a long time, until Mother."

"He gave her name to the house."

"And our bloodline, in defiance of the tradition that elder firstbloods' dynasties bear their names. Such is his love for her. Together they have finally made the house a home. But the truth is, the one thing Mother cannot abide is gardening."

Cassia walked down the steps and waded onto an overgrown path. She ran her hand along the tops of the willows, collecting sparkling, soft snow on her gloves. "I can't even count how many plants there are here that I've never seen. Others I know well from northern Tenebra but have never seen in such abundance. I can just imagine how things I've struggled to grow would run wild here under the ward."

Lio followed her, levitating occasionally to keep his robe from snagging on thorns. Cassia admired spines as long as her fingers, but from a safe distance. Knight stayed close by her, leaving paw prints behind in the snow like markers to point the way back out of the dark wilds. But snowflakes began drifting down from the clouding sky, promising his trail would soon disappear.

Lio pointed ahead through an iron gate. "My residence is this way."

Past the gate, an arbor of intertwined vines swallowed them on all sides. Cassia couldn't see above or below, ahead or behind. Cold and verdure weighed on her chest, and she drank them down in great gulps. She could disappear into this and never be seen again. Let herself get lost in it, never to return.

The arbor ended, and they came out onto a flagstone terrace. Cassia gazed up a flight of stairs to a pair of iron doors, then upward still.

The white marble tower seemed weightless, like an illusion cast by the Light Moon. At the very top, archways stood open to the night, and the polar wind piped through the tower's hollow peak.

"You live in a sorcerer's tower."

"I suppose you could call it that, yes." He wiggled his fingers. "There are even heretical incantations and bloodstained scrolls."

But his teasing did not reach the corners of his mouth and eyes. She took his hands again. His skin was colder than before, but he wasn't looking at her with hunger. He studied the tower with the critical eye of an artist unsure of his creation.

For the first time, something occurred to Cassia. Could Lio be as anxious about her first visit to his home as she was?

She almost laughed. How could he be worried about how his glorious, ancient house seemed to her, a waif from Tenebra who had lain her head in every backwater palace where the king stashed her? How could he ever doubt where he laid his head was more precious to her than any other place in the world?

But this was the earnest young Hesperine who had so carefully explained every detail of his people to her in their long walks at Solorum, clearly hoping his next remark would not be the one that drove her away. As much as he had worked to make her see Hesperine life through his eyes, it had always been the details of his own life he was most hesitant to share—and most relieved to discover did not send her running.

"I love it here," she told him simply, sincerely.

His gaze came back to hers, and his candid face told her everything. That was exactly how he had hoped she would feel. Well, for a mortal with no Blood Union, she was quite the mind mage herself, wasn't she?

He scooped her up in his arms and carried her across the terrace.

MOONFLOWER AND SANDALWOOD

HOW SATISFYING IT WAS to hold Cassia this way, completely in his arms. This time in safety and leisure. She held onto his neck, resting her head on his shoulder.

He took her up the stairs, which climbed past the ground floor to the first floor entrance. He Willed the doors open ahead of them and carried her over the threshold into the warmth of his residence. The doors shut behind them with a gentle clang and closed out the chill of the garden, but not its fragrances, which always seemed to creep into the tower. She would like that.

Lio swept her through the polished entry hall, which was bare but for his Gifting chart and Ritual tapestry. The inner doors let them into his room that occupied the rest of the first floor of the tower. Cassia leaned her head back. Her gaze traveled up the tall windows, bookshelves, and scroll racks to the high ceiling to drift among the ribbed vaults.

"You live here? Lio, it isn't a room, it's—a library. Or a temple." She sighed. "It is you."

It was also where he had slept without her for weeks, and his thoughts at the moment were anything but scholarly or prayerful. He didn't want to put Cassia down. He wanted to carry her right to the bed. But now was the time for a more thorough and seductive invitation into the home he had to offer her.

"I'm very happy it pleases you." He gave her one more squeeze, then set her gently on her feet.

"It is yours. Therefore, it pleases me better than anything."

Yet again she read the worry on his heart and spoke aloud the answer he longed for in his thoughts. She was his Grace. Although still a mortal, she already knew him better than anyone. It shouldn't surprise him.

But it did surprise him. Because it was entirely, wonderfully new. He had spent a lifetime with people who knew and loved him well. But after the short time he and Cassia had been together, no one knew him as she did.

"Is the tower very ancient?" she asked.

"A project of Father's and mine, actually. We started it when I was a student. I needed a place to practice my magic away from the main house, where I wouldn't disturb anyone." He cleared his throat. "If an experiment went wrong, you know."

Cassia's tone was light-hearted. "Were there many explosions?"

She made it so easy to jest about his youthful accidents, as if those were the worst close calls he'd had in his magical career. "Mostly just a lot of shattered glass. We built my glazing workshop on the ground floor. That makes repairs easy."

He took her cloak, letting his hands slide slowly over her shoulders. She tilted her head back, and he almost gave into the temptation to kiss her neck. But he was trying to seduce her, not tempt himself.

He gave her only a smile and sent her cloak to hang on the iron stand by the door. Next he tugged off her gloves. One finger at a time. Then he levitated them away, and they landed on the table by the cloak stand.

"I have a confession," he murmured. "I intend to have my way with you tonight in utterly indecent ways. Do you think we can distract your escort so he is none the wiser?" Lio gestured to the place he had prepared for Knight by the tower's side door, below an empty window seat.

"Let us see how fast I can distract him." Cassia called her dog over to the blanket. "Look at this, Knight! Lio has gone to all this trouble just for you."

Knight sniffed the bowl of fresh water and the promising, empty food dish. He nosed around in the wool blanket, finally discovering the Imperial rubber chew buried in its folds. He gave the unfamiliar material an experimental gnaw and wagged his tail. A few words from Cassia, and he accepted his new place.

"He's not going to sniff my whole room for hidden danger? I do feel appreciated."

Cassia turned back to Lio. "He has learned that your scent means safety. Let me say thank you for both of us."

"I'm glad he approves." Lio gestured at the side door. "Outside in the cold vault, I have much better meat for him than the embassy's provisions. We don't have trouble keeping things fresh here."

She knotted her hands. "You didn't have to do that. How did you bear it?"

"There are a few Hesperines in Orthros who keep cats, dogs, and other animals whose natures have different requirements than our own. Veils go a long way against smells. We trade with the Empire for the meat. They care for their animals well."

"You really did think of everything." She set the potted betony on the window seat Lio had so hastily cleared before her arrival. "The light is certainly good right here."

He went to her side. "You know, the same thought occurred to me. Plants might even do well here. You wouldn't happen to know anyone interested in providing me with some house plants, would you?"

She returned a knowing smile. "You are in luck. I have a gift for you."

With careful, almost reverent fingers, she unfastened a small pouch from her belt. She opened it and showed him the small, golden treasures within.

"Rose seeds," he said in recognition. "There is only one place you could have gotten them. The glyph shard is not the only treasure you brought from the shrine."

"I shall plant these for you if you find me a few pots and some good Orthros soil. I know roses grow on every corner here, but—"

"Not *our* roses. This gift is inimitable. Irreplaceable."

Emotion came to a head inside her, but just as quickly sank back down beyond the reach of his senses. He thought she might speak, but she pulled back with a playful smile. "They're vigorous climbers, I've found. We shall need some strong stakes to encourage them upward and keep them from overgrowing your bookcases."

"I hope they take over the whole room."

"Is there a safe place you can keep the seeds here until we have what we need to plant them?"

From the shelf under the window seat, Lio pulled out a storage basket.

She unfastened the pouch from her belt and tucked the bag of rose seeds inside the basket, eying the rest of the empty shelf. "There's enough room here for potting tools."

"Why yes, there is, isn't there?"

"Thank you for doing all this for me, Lio. If not for polar night, I would ask you when *you* took time to sleep."

"Veil hours without you have been magefire," he admitted. "I've tried to keep myself as occupied as possible. Doing things for you was a way of shaking my fist at despair."

"I felt the same way about caring for our roses." She took his hands. "No more solitary veil hours."

He drew her closer to him. "The guest house will do for keeping up appearances, nothing more. My residence is where you'll actually be staying. I want you to make yourself at home."

Now her feelings were clear in the Union, a bright bloom of happiness, fragile and ready to scatter in a puff of wind. She ran a hand down the front of his robe, as brazen outwardly as she was tentative within. She drifted past him, her silk-shod feet whispering across the marble floor, and he followed her.

She took a step down to the lower center of the room to meander across the rug between the benches and chairs of the sitting area. With one hand, she teased a tasseled pillow. The pillow he had spilled Polar Night Roast on one night when he and Kia had been arguing so long about dung beetles, he'd shaken with laughter.

Cassia passed the seat that was Nodora's favorite, which Lio had moved to the precise spot his Trial sister said made her songs sound best in the room. Cassia studied the low table and the Prince and Diplomat board, the only field where Lio could beat Mak and Lyros two against one.

"This is where you entertain friends?"

"You can join us for music and a game one of these evenings."

She paused to admire the glass coffee service, then opened a jar of fresh grounds and lifted it to her nose. "Mm. This smells like you."

"For my Initiation gift, my uncle generously created a new coffee to my taste and gave it my name, Deukalion's Blend."

"I can't wait to try it."

Lio could hardly believe his eyes. Here was Cassia, in his room. In his life. Meeting with all that was familiar to him, making him see it all anew. He felt he was living a waking dream.

And yet this moment could not be more real, exciting his senses as she left her scent on his things with her exploratory touches and soft breaths, as she filled his space with her aura. Cup and thorns, he had thought a handkerchief stained with her blood arousing. Now traces of her were all over his room, surrounding him everywhere he turned.

He had intended to give her a tour, a carefully planned introduction to the residence that would hopefully make it seem appealing to her. But she seemed to know precisely where she was going, and he followed after her to see what captured her interest.

There was a questing look in her eyes, and it was not with aimless leisure that she put the coffee jar away and turned to face the back of the room. She ascended the step on the other side of the common area and went to stand behind Lio's desk.

She folded her hands in front of her. "This is where you wrote your initiation treatise, which inspired you to first come to Tenebra. And your proposal for the Summit, which made it possible for me to come to Orthros."

"I can't tell you how many times I wanted to ask you your opinion while I was drawing up the proposal." He gave a soft laugh. "I even conjured an illusion of you to recite the wisdom I heard you speak in Tenebra."

She looked at him in surprise, then glanced over the books and scrolls on his desk. "You seem to have plenty of ancient wisdom to see you through."

"Nothing so relevant as yours." At least he'd managed to restore some semblance of order here before she'd arrived. His desk was still cluttered with the sources he'd used for his proposal, but he'd stacked the scrolls and tomes close at hand in case Cassia showed interest in any of them.

But what she picked up was a blank scroll he had set out for whatever he next needed to write down. She sniffed the wooden roller. "I've never smelled this before, either. It's lovely. What wood could this be?"

"Imperial cedar. We use scrap wood or gathered limbs to make things like scroll-ends."

"Coffee and cedar, and…" She scanned the desk, fiddling with a couple of quills, then shook her head. Finally, she uncapped a glass vial and smiled to herself. "Ink." She sniffed again and followed her nose to the candy tin. "A hint of these, too."

"Those are Zoe's sweets. She sat under my desk while I wrote the proposal."

"Then you had the best of company. I'm sure Moonbeam and Aurora were valuable contributors."

"Yes, they volunteered to eat the passages that weren't any good."

Cassia grinned and straightened, then turned in a circle. Her gaze fell to his dressing screen. She continued her mysterious search behind it at his washing area.

"What could a Hesperine need with a wash basin?" she asked. "Aren't cleaning spells more efficient than water, soap, and towels?"

"Ritual ablutions are a surviving tradition from the temples. We still have a custom of washing at the beginning of moon hours."

"This must be it." She picked up his soap and took a deep whiff. "Ohh. Yes, this is definitely it."

"What?" he finally asked, smiling in puzzlement.

"The verdant floral note in your scent. I have never been able to put names to what you smell like."

So this was the tour Cassia had embarked on! A tour of…him. "Well, we draw the scent of our cleaning spells from our favorite things, and things we use often sneak in on accident."

"From what wondrous flora is your soap made?"

"Sandalwood and moonflower."

"There's such a thing as a moonflower?"

"They bloom only at night, big white flowers the size of my hand. They're a symbol of the diplomatic service. You've seen them embroidered on my uncle's tablion. I promise you shall see the real thing when we take our tour of Selas's greenhouses."

"I have never heard of a greenhouse, but it sounds like something lovely."

"It is a building constructed entirely of glass to serve as an indoor garden. Like the courtyard at Rose House, but on a grander scale."

Her face lit up. "A whole tour of these greenhouses?"

"I put it on the Summit itinerary. Interesting the free lords in beneficial agricultural exchanges seemed a good excuse."

"A customary handful of flowers would have been enough, and yet you offer me gardens and greenhouses."

"You have made do with *enough* for too long. I shall see you enjoy plenty."

At that, she slid her arms around him, resting her face against his chest. "I shall forget how to fast."

"I hope you do."

"Where am I to banish the memories of your fast?" She lifted her face to look at him. "I have seen where you relax and work. But where do you sleep?"

He gave her a rueful look and gestured behind her.

She turned around and saw the other window seat, with its blue damask coverlet and pile of cushions.

"I have another confession," he said. "When I turned eighty and moved into the tower, I regarded it as something of a temporary arrangement. I didn't intend to establish a proper residence until after my initiation. By the time I finished Trial this past winter, I still hadn't really settled in here. I'm afraid I don't have a bed yet."

She looked at him again, not with amusement or surprise, but with warmth. Understanding. "You found yourself unexpectedly not needing a bed to share with anyone."

He sighed. "The truth is, I expected to establish my residence with Xandra. Before that, I always went to her family's House, and we didn't require a bed in any case. Need I say how glad I am things didn't turn out the way I expected?"

"So you, suddenly an initiate errant, chose to remain in the tower and establish your residence here..."

"Instead of a cozy wing in the main house, yes. Father was delighted our tower project wouldn't go abandoned, but I think Mother was disappointed."

"...and you decided the window seat would do well enough for just you."

"There you have it. This is my errant Sanctuary."

She slid back his coverlet and hopped up to sit on the edge of the window seat, her purple velvet backside sinking into his black silk sheets and the wool pallet beneath. She swung her feet, which didn't touch the floor by far.

The stained glass panels behind her cast shards of multicolored light around her. Lio watched the vision from his fantasies without breathing, trying to keep his thoughts from plummeting downward with his blood flow.

"It's a very comfortable window seat," she said.

"Not as comfortable as your bed at Rose House."

"My bed at Rose House does not have this." With a fond smile, she tugged at the Tenebran army blanket hidden between the coverlet and the sheets. "You kept it."

"I sleep under it every night."

She patted the pallet. "This is wide enough for your height and deep enough for two. Well, one and a half. Scrap that I am, I fit conveniently anywhere. I should tuck nicely in beside you and you still have room."

He closed the small distance between them and braced his hands on either side of her thighs. She sat there with her hands in her lap and her short nose a finger's breadth away from his, swinging those feet. Her toes brushed his legs through his robes.

"You have no idea," he murmured, "how many times and in how many ways I have imagined this moment."

"Oh, I do. Although your window seat seems a much nicer place to imagine it than my bed back in Tenebra."

He slid his hands up her thighs, crushing layers of violet and lavender skirts so he could ease between her freckled knees. "Would you like to try imagining them again now?"

She coaxed her foot under his robe and along the inside of his leg. "I'll tell you mine if you tell me yours."

A hunger chill made him shake before her. Goddess, but he wanted her slow and satisfying. When would he once again find the strength to go slowly? "I'm at a loss as to where to start. I want you in more ways than there are hours in the night."

"It's a good thing we have many, many nights, isn't it?"

For those words, he gave her a kiss, long and leisurely, to tell her she was right. If she kept slaking him with such words, he would become drunk. Drunk on the antidote to all the nightmares that had haunted him in his empty tower.

He had resolved to seduce her tonight, not lose his head to her seduction. But she kissed him deeper, stroking his tongue with hers as she tightened her knees on either side of him. That was all it took for his purpose to waver and his kiss to turn hungry and eager in answer. She only pulled back to breathe.

He rested his face in the curve of her neck, feeling her pulse against his skin, and his gums throbbed. "I've imagined your heartbeat filling this room until you echo all around me. Illusions don't have heartbeats, Cassia. All I've had of you for months is illusions."

"Then I'm not the only one who's been longing after light and wishing I could touch it."

"The portraits I've conjured of you when I'm alone are anything but innocent bedtime stories. I swear, never a dishonor to you. Only my tribute." He slid to his knees in front of her.

She ran her hands through his hair, flushed and looking pleased. "Actually it is among the most flattering compliments anyone has ever paid me. No one has ever longed for me, and yet now a powerful, immortal blood mage with a dual affinity conjures illusions of me to tide him over."

"Was there anything to tide you over, my rose? Did you ever find some solace in fantasies of me while you slept alone?"

"Well." Her flush deepened. "I don't sleep alone, you know. Knight is just right there. It doesn't make a very inspiring setting for such explorations."

They laughed together, and Lio kissed the inside of her knee. "You needed to use your few hours in bed for sound sleep, in any case."

She frowned in frustration. "Sometimes I was awake all night feeling like I wouldn't last till morning without you. Other times..." She made a noise of disgust. "I hated that exhaustion."

"It's natural to feel less desire when you're that tired."

"Remarkably, I haven't felt tired since I set foot in Orthros."

"You will never need to worry about finding the enthusiasm when you're with me. I will see to that." He slid her skirts still further up her legs.

She tugged on his shoulders. "No. No cold, hard floor for you tonight, my champion. Come up here in this bed with me. It may be a window seat, but it's our bed."

Our bed. Cassia didn't need him to show her in, only to throw open the doors and let her make her way. She didn't need him to seduce her, only to let her seduce him. To feel her power over him.

What better way could there be to bring her into his world than to let her make it her own?

And what a sweet conquest she seemed to have in mind. He got to his feet as she had bade, and she began disrobing him. They helped each other out of their garments, touching, reminding, appreciating with mouths and hands as they went. When she was wearing nothing but her shoes, she pulled him into bed with her.

He braced himself over her on his arms and looked down at her hair tangled across the embroidered pillows and her brown, freckled skin against the black silk sheets. "You are the most beautiful sight I have ever beheld."

She reached up and touched a hand to his cheek, and blue and red moonlight played between her fingers. "So are you to me."

He lowered his head and drank the light from her skin. Crimson on her lips, brilliant white on her throat, silver black on her breast.

She traced her fingers down his back. "Did you and illusory me do very exciting things together?"

"Nothing so exciting as a single kiss from the real you." He lipped her nipple.

"Then doing imaginative things with the real me would surely prove very exiting indeed," she tantalized him.

He devoured her in kisses and nips, long strokes of his tongue and grazes of his teeth, all the way to her lower belly. "The positive side of all this time apart," he said to the inside of her thigh, "is that I had ample opportunity to devise solutions to dilemmas that have troubled me. Such as, how can I best enjoy your feet and your blood at the same time?"

She gave a breathless laugh. "You must show me your answer to this pressing problem."

He knelt between her legs and kissed his way up the inside of her calf, propping her ankles on his shoulders. He undressed each of her feet in turn, caressing and massaging as he freed her from her shoes and stockings. While he paused to admire one of her ankle bones with his tongue, she rubbed the side of his face with her big toe and treated him to one of her hiccuping laughs.

"Mm," he encouraged, nuzzling the bottom of her right foot. Taking it in his hand, he held it to him while he laved his tongue along the sweep of her arch. He slipped his free hand between her thighs again, all the way to her curls.

As he covered her krana with his hand, she hooked her left heel over his shoulder and scooted herself a little closer to him. He murmured another encouragement and began to stroke her krana. She flexed against him, tangling the toes of her left foot in his hair.

He grinned. "Shall we work on your Divine?"

She laughed again. "Of course. We should continue in the setting where we first began."

He dipped a finger into her krana and teased her most sensitive place. "*Kalux.*"

She fisted her hands in the sheets, gazing up at him with boldness in her eyes that answered the fire in his veins. She was here at last, and it was clear she intended to enjoy it to the fullest.

He twirled his finger in circles around that small, responsive spot. "Say it back to me."

She licked her lips and swallowed. "*Kalux.*"

While he pleasured her there with his thumb and forefinger, he tried dipping his tongue between each of her toes. Her breasts rose and fell with her ever-swifter breaths. He proceeded to suck each of her toes in his mouth one by one.

He finished with her smallest toe. "I love watching you. Just the sight of you makes me want to thrust inside you right now."

Her gaze lingered on his rhabdos. "Everything you want is right here. You don't have to wait anymore."

He positioned his mouth upon the arch of her foot and sank his fangs into her with precision. She let out a sound of astonishment and came up off the bed, leveraging herself on his shoulder, her left foot curling against his neck.

He worked his hand on her krana as he sucked her right foot in his mouth. Oh, yes, this had been a fine idea. The tender web of rich veins in her arch pleasured him, while his mouth upon such a sensitive place pleasured her. She panted harder, voicing her enjoyment with each breath, and rubbed herself against his touch in time with his caresses and swallows.

He lifted his mouth from her to lap an escaping trail of blood from her heel. "I love listening to you."

"Ohhh. I don't know what's happened to me. I can't—stop—*ohhhh.*"

"Why should you stop? We're alone behind my veils, with this whole tower to ourselves, hidden by the garden. No one can hear you."

She took deeper, steadier breaths as if to brace herself. "*I* can hear me."

"So can I." He licked his lips before clamping his mouth on her foot again.

She cried out this time, and the sound urged him on as surely as if she had touched him. With her foot secure in the grip of his teeth, he wrapped both hands around her hips. He lifted her and put her on his rhabdos, thrusting hard into her krana as he tugged her onto him. She called out his name. He growled against her foot as the head of his rhabdos lodged deep inside her and her buttocks met his groin.

She stretched and bowed her body in a luxurious, torturous motion. "You can have…everything you want…as much as you want…as long as you want."

He took it. Gave it to her. He held her to him and worked his hips and back, thrusting as hard as he wanted, as deep as he needed. He nudged his face against her foot, working his tongue too, to open her up and slake himself. He tapped her until that moment came once more when she didn't try to stop voicing her pleasure.

He listened to her and watched her undulate on him. She scoured the sheets with her hands, leveraging her leg against his shoulder as she lifted herself off the bed, delivered herself into his hands and onto his rhabdos again and again.

Pushing her away, he drew back, prying their bodies apart. The way her krana sucked at him made him grit his teeth on her foot still harder. With a groan, he let her slide onto his lap, then resettled his grip on her.

"Yes," she breathed. "Again, just as hard—yes—"

They both called out as they thrust their bodies together again. His shout turned into a groan as her tightest depths resisted his erection. They took it hard and slow, bringing themselves completely together once more in a single motion.

He grasped at his self-control fast slipping away in the torrent of pleasure and her blood. The infusion of her into him made his pulse pound in his whole body. He throbbed where their bodies were joined, where her every motion moved him.

She must see and feel how lost he was in her. He knew his fingers were digging into her hips, but she wanted more. She was moving faster, harder on him, her voice pitching up into a keen.

Her cry echoed off the walls of his residence and resounded through her blood, and his whole body jerked. Her climax roared through his veins and dragged him into his own, freeing him from hunger, feeding him ecstasy. His body spasmed against her and drove him deep. The tremors in her krana worked him into satisfaction and ease.

He lifted his mouth from her foot at last, letting his head fall back and the last swallow of her blood slide down his throat. The metallic tang and rich spice of her flavor. The power in his own body. The sensation of her legs relaxing against his shoulders and chest and her hips nestled in his lap where their bodies were still one.

He glanced down to see her spread-eagled and catching her breath in a new blush of moonlight. She looked thoroughly pleasured and utterly shameless.

She found her thoughts and her voice first. "I approve your solution to the dilemma."

Laughter rolled out of him, and no worry or regret was there to stop it.

She propped herself up on her elbows and gave him her secret smile. But not secret from him. He was the one she had given a taste of all her secrets.

"It may take some time to do justice to all our fantasies," she mused, "but I think we now have a head start."

A head start on eternity and his plan to make it hers, one night at a time.

THE ENDLESS SKY

ONLY IN ORTHROS COULD an unlikely seductress such as Cassia luxuriate for hours with someone like Lio in a silk bed under a stained glass window.

She would soon learn to read the grand letters over their heads, but already the images spoke to her. Black wings beneath a double full moon and a deep, dark blue sky glittering with stars.

She touched the hand that had wrought them. "What does this window say?"

"'He who feasts upon Cassia sips from the Goddess's own cup.'"

She elbowed him playfully under the covers. "It does not. I'm sure the Changing Queen was still a maiden when some wise mage of Hespera wrote whatever sacred teachings you have put there."

"The wisdom of martyred elders would dampen the mood over the bed, don't you think?" Lio caught Cassia's elbow in his hand and tweaked the most ticklish spot.

Laughing, she squirmed until they were wrestling in the bedclothes.

With unabashed Hesperine strength and agility, he came out on top. "I chose a quote from the *Discourses on Love*."

"That sounds philosophical."

"It is Orthros's canon of erotic texts."

"Oh."

"This is a passage from the 'Discourse on Sanctuary,' in which the speaker invites her lover to experience the Goddess's realm with her through acts of passion."

"You do have heretical incantations in here."

He touched his forehead to hers, and their hearts beat against one another as he recited:

Awaken unto me,
to my certain embrace
under the wing of darkness,
where together we find shelter.

Against my heart,
you shall find strength.
With your heart against mine,
I shall be strong.

Oh light of my eyes,
let us shine with joy
beneath the endless sky,
where we are free.

What a strange moment for her tears to threaten. Cassia blinked them away, but not before he noticed. He must have seen the gleam in her eyes, for he kissed her eyelids.

"I know," he said. "After everything we've been through, suddenly this."

"Glass is not the rarest luxury in this room."

"No," he agreed.

"There are mornings in Tenebra," she confessed, "when I'm not sure I'm going to make it out of bed. I don't know what comes over me. I try and try, and my body simply lays there. I look ahead into the day, and it's not even that I dread facing it. It's not only that I am weary. It's as if…the day is empty, and so am I." Her voice lowered of its own accord, trying to keep the secret in, but she said it to him, anyway. "It's unforgivable, Lio. Sometimes I don't care anymore. I simply cannot bring myself to care."

"If it is unforgivable, then you and I are both condemned. Only two things have kept me on my feet these past months. The knowledge that Zoe needs me, and the hope of hearing news of you from Tenebra that will reassure me you're safe."

"What if we keep feeling this way? What if it gets worse?"

"Has it gotten worse since you came to Orthros?"

"Of course not. I feel better than I have in…I don't know how long." Never. She had never felt this happy.

"Is that so?" he asked, his body a gentle, irresistible weight upon her. "You wouldn't find it difficult to get out of bed right now?"

"Right now, I never want to move again. But that's because I'm so happy where I am."

His smile told her he had another surprise for her. "There is one place I think I can persuade you to go at the moment."

"Surely nowhere could be more appealing than your bed."

"How about my bath?"

She glanced over at the washbasin not far from the window seat. "I think I can make it there."

"I don't mean the washbasin. I mean my bath downstairs, which is big enough for both of us to get in together."

A bathtub and Lio in the same thought. Cassia swallowed. "You have a tub all to yourself? Surely you don't ever miss an opportunity to use it instead of a washstand."

"I am often too busy to do more than just clean up here, and you are often too busy saving the kingdom for me to attend you at your basin. Tonight you get to enjoy a real bath, and I get to enjoy it with you from start to finish."

They floundered out of the cushions and covers and made it to their feet. Lio summoned his veil hours robe to hand and wrapped it around Cassia.

"The stairs can be drafty," he explained. "Besides, I seem to remember you complaining about me getting to see more of you than you get to see of me."

"Consider the scales of justice balanced." Cassia wrapped his robe close around her, enjoying the intimacy of wearing it. And him wearing nothing, so at ease with himself and her gaze upon him.

The night they had met, the sight of him clothed from head to toe in black silk and darkness had bewitched her. Now his attire of only stubble and moonlight wove the spell ever more irresistibly around her, even as it probed the ache in her heart. His color and his smile might have returned to his face, but he was still gaunt everywhere else.

And yet, it was not only his lack of sustenance that had sharpened his edges. His long runner's legs had always been strong, but there was a hint of new definition in his body everywhere else, too.

"Have you been lifting more than a quill these past months, Sir Scholar?"

He gave her a half-smile. "I've let Mak and Lyros knock me around the training ring on a nightly basis."

She laughed in surprise. "My diplomat has become a warrior?"

"I have made an attempt. I still regard my fists as a last resort, but I deem it wise to know how to use them. My lady might need me to defend her from monsters with more than words."

"No monsters here. You need only slay hunger."

He took her hand and coaxed her around to the other side of his dressing screen. Only when he opened a discreet door did she notice it was there. He pulled her through it into a stairwell.

"A hidden passageway?" she jested. "Where are you leading me, mind mage?"

"Still more secrets lurk in the depths of my tower." He led her all the way down to the bottom of the stairs and opened another door for her.

Cassia stepped into damp, fragrant warmth. Soft spell light seemed to come from everywhere and nowhere. She gasped in the steamy air. The bath was in fact a deep pool the breadth of the room, tiled in geometric patterns of blue-black, cerulean, and pale blue. Except for the walls. Those were covered in enormous mirrors. They showed her every glorious angle of Lio.

Cassia met his gaze in the glass. "And you said you'd neglected your glassmaking craft."

"I've only worked on *private* projects." He slid his robe off of her slowly.

She watched it slide down her skin and pile at her bloodstained feet. "Just standing in this room, I feel more wanton than I ever have in my life."

Lio framed her hips in his hands and licked her shoulder. "Hedon has nothing on Hespera. Shall we turn this night into one of the darkest tales mortals tell of Hesperine seduction?"

"Let us hold a blood ritual in the bath. I want to watch you feast on me."

"Take a deep breath," he said against her vein.

He picked her up in his arms and levitated right past the steps that led down into the bath. He sank them together into the pool, taking them all the way under. The deliciously, intensely warm water made pleasure bloom all over her body. As Lio let them surface, she gasped a breath and found the bottom of the bath with her feet.

He stood before her, water dripping from his hair and trickling along the chiseled features of his face, over his shoulders, and down his chest. She let her hands follow the rivulets of water. Slowly she traced every part of him. His proud brow and long, straight nose. His exquisite lips. The line of his stubbled jaw, which tightened at her touch.

She slid both her hands down his neck and out to his shoulders, then together again upon his chest. Flattening her palms, she rubbed the new contours and tautness in his body all the way down under the surface of the water to his navel. She felt and learned how his body had changed while they'd been apart, trying to show him with her touch how handsome he had always been to her, then as now. How she desired him, always, in fasting and in plenty, at war or at peace.

He tangled his hands in her wet hair, pulling her mouth to his. Slowly he pleasured her in return with his mouth, thrusting with his tongue. She melted against him, trembling between her legs.

He let her come up for air from their kiss, only to duck into the water. She thought to follow him under, but he took her hips in his hands. When she felt his mouth on her krana, she grasped at his shoulders to steady herself on her feet. After four languid strokes of his tongue, it occurred to her he didn't need to breathe, and he was not going to stop.

Her blood would not be the first course of his feast. She leaned on him to keep her knees from buckling.

He kneaded her buttocks, tilting and parting her hips. He devoured her with long, slow motions of his mouth. His tongue probed and laved her as he sucked at the pinpoint of her pleasure.

There was no sound in the bath but the water lapping her body and her breathing echoing around her. Waves of pleasure rippled around and through her, warm water on her skin and his hot mouth on her krana. She relaxed into his kisses and let him pleasure her. It felt wonderful to relax, to open herself to him. To revel in the sensation and the sight of the bodies together in the water.

In the mirrors she saw herself wearing nothing but her dark, wet hair that clung about her body. The looking glasses revealed him beneath the surface of the water with his mouth fastened to her. The bath rippled softly with the motions of his head. The last time she had beheld such a sight was on the floor of their shrine by moonlight and this same spell light. That moment, that night—that place—was not lost.

He glanced up at her, his eyes glowing at her from under the water. Their gazes locked. She looked into his eyes as he heightened her pleasure to an unbearable edge and held her there. He teased her in brief flicks of his tongue, keeping the tide of her pleasure high without letting it break.

She didn't plead, didn't try. She let him draw it out and make this moment last.

When the tears coursed down her cheeks, he took her fully in his mouth again. With three consuming kisses, he dragged her over the edge.

Her climax came at last, hard and harrowing. She dug her fingers into his shoulders, watching her hips convulse against his mouth. He sucked at the raw edge of her pleasure in time to each spasm, until the sensation was so intense the vision before her faded to a steamy blur.

Finally he surfaced with a gasp. She drifted boneless in the water and gazed up at his dilated eyes and unsheathed fangs. His feast had only just begun.

He wrapped an arm around her, supporting her under her backside with one hand, and drew her up close to him. The glass behind him presented her with a view of his broad shoulders, slender waist, and trim buttocks.

There was a mirror reflected within the mirror that showed her the back of her hair and his arm holding her. With his free hand, Lio slid her hair aside, giving her a clear view of her throat.

She watched him lower his head and open his mouth upon her throat. Saw the tip of his fangs come to rest on her. His tongue darted out and flicked over her skin as if her vein also needed foreplay to be ready for him. She stared in fascination. Any moment now, he would bite her. She would get to see his fangs sink into her.

Once more he met her gaze, this time in the reflection of their reflection. She swam in an otherworld of water and light and his gaze all around her. Within the space of one heartbeat, the tips of his fangs pricked her a thousand times over in the endless reflections around them. She watched his ivory lengths sink slowly into her flesh and saw her own jaw drop at the pleasure that drove down through her body.

Lio's lashes dipped, even as his pupils enlarged still more. He let out a long, low moan, grimacing as if in his passion, his eyes rolling back as if in ecstasy. She saw his jaw flex, and she felt his bite tighten.

Twin trails of blood spilled from where he penetrated her, slid down over her shoulder, and caressed her back. Crimson bloomed in the water and drifted in little tendrils and clouds around her hips. The bloodstained bath stirred with the motion of his hands as he took hold of her hips once more, bracing her and holding her closer.

She clutched at his shoulders again and let him guide her krana to his rhabdos. Her gaze went to his hands on her, then to his hips. She watched his buttocks clench, saw his hips flex. Hard, thick flesh thrust into her. His back muscles rippled as her krana filled with him.

"*Lio.* You are..."

She floated, impaled on him. He raked his hand down the length of her back, through her hair and the trail of her blood. His impulsive caress on her hip left behind a bloody hand print on her skin.

She put her arms around his neck and her legs around his waist, drawing him closer. She reveled in the sight of her legs wrapped around him while his body worked. She smiled at the vision of her hands buried in his hair, holding him to her throat while he took his pleasure at her vein. Their bodies were beautiful together, joined fast, rocking in tandem in the water.

"Lio. You are magnificent."

She saw him smile against her skin. His mirrored gaze met hers again, heated with more than she could name, all of it ardent, all of it for her.

Their gluttony of sight and sensation fed her until she moaned, speechless, that she had had her fill. She let her head fall back, only to see another mirror on the ceiling. It showed her Lio supporting her head, biting down and feasting on her throat anew as she tightened her hold around him, bracing herself for release.

She wanted to see him release inside her. She looked over his shoulder again at his back and hips. All his muscles strained with effort.

She managed to find her voice. "Let go. Right now."

He shuddered in her arms, but kept sucking, kept thrusting her toward her own pleasure.

"I want you to. I want to see you climax. If you let go...right now..."

With a rough groan, he surrendered. His body spasmed against her, all around her. She felt his rhabdos pulse and fill her with warmth as she watched his body pump in her arms.

"The goddess outdid herself when she made you," Cassia breathed.

Then the erotic vision surrounding her and the force of his release inside her robbed her of her breath and thrust her into climax again.

Was that woman in his arms *her*? That sensual creature writhing with him, riding him, having her extravagant fill of him?

Yes. This was her. This torrent of gratifying release was all inside of her. She felt her thighs holding him to the last ripple of his climax, her hands upon his skin as his body relaxed at last. It was her heart that thundered in her chest and her blood that gleamed on his mouth when he lifted his head. It was with her own strength and tenderness that she held him close as they both sighed and breathed together.

She didn't want to let him go. She couldn't bear to let him go. Not a second time.

The thought realized in her mind before she could stop it. She had been trying to keep it at bay, to deny it a chance to crystalize and confront her. But she had been under its power all along.

She never wanted to leave Orthros.

She hid her face against his neck to keep from weeping aloud. Not that she could hide her feelings from their Union.

She had sworn she wouldn't let herself get her hopes up. It was too late. Far, far too late. Hope, desire, *need* had already swept her aloft, and she was flying high now.

It had happened when he'd said those words in the courtyard. *We are going to win your fight.* She had meant her answer.

She believed they could.

It actually seemed possible that they could solve this another way than the last resort she dreaded. That would mean she wouldn't need to find the strength to set foot in Tenebra ever again. It would be all right for her to stay. With Lio.

If that was what he wanted.

Lio eased their bodies apart, only to take her in his arms. He settled on a bench built into the side of the bath and gathered her on his lap. He said nothing, just held her close, lounging with her in the lulling warmth of the water.

He might assume her feelings were the afterglow of what they had just shared. Or perhaps the revelation inside her made sense to him already. Perhaps he was thinking the same thing.

Was that not what his welcome here had meant? He had made a place for her in his life, his family, his home. It would take longer than the Solstice Summit for their roses to reach full bloom. That empty window with its perfect light was surely a promise of a future.

How long a future?

How would she know? She had no idea how Hesperines communicated these things to one another. Their language of courtship was utterly unlike heartless bids of bride prices and offers of dowries.

She wanted to learn that language. Let Lio teach it to her. Discover what his messages to her meant.

She had only just arrived, and it was much too soon for them to talk about a future in any case. They were still becoming reacquainted. And that too was wonderful.

She let herself sit on his lap and enjoy every moment of indulging themselves and each other. This was what would keep her motivated not to leave, but to stay. What would give her the strength to keep fighting so they could keep this.

Good things didn't last long in Tenebra. She had lived by that law. But this was Orthros. Good things could last...even forever.

She rested her face against his chest, trying to keep hold of her emotions. But why should she? Not only was it fruitless, it was not in keeping with their Oath.

She didn't know how Hesperine courtship worked, but she knew how things worked between her and Lio.

Yes, they had spent too few nights together again to speak of how many more they would have. But let him feel what these few nights had done for her. Let him feel the first hint of what she wanted. This was her courtship of him, too. It was fitting that it should begin in the Union, which was both secret and honest.

She couldn't feel his response by magic, but she did feel the change in his touch. His arms tightened around her, and he caressed the hair away from her face, tilting her head back to look at him.

There was a new light in his eyes. "There's one more room I want to show you. It is still mostly empty, like the rest of the tower, but it offers an inspiring view."

He carried her out of the bath and into a corner of the room where dry warmth drifted out of the tile. He stood holding her while their skin and hair dried.

At length, he set her on her feet and summoned her cloak. He wrapped her up from head to toe in the bespelled silk. She returned his veil hours robe to him, and as soon as she fastened it up to his waist, he scooped her up against his bare chest again.

She smiled at him, dawdling her legs over his arm. "How long do you plan to hold me?"

"Now that I have you to feast on, I shall never tire. I shall not let you go."

She wrapped her arms around his neck again in agreement. With a laugh, he bounced her in his embrace and carried her out of the bath, taking the steps two at a time all the way back to his room. He crossed the chamber to another door that flew open before them.

He carried her up a larger stairwell, around and around in a spiral toward the top of the tower. No stepping, no levitation, just his preternatural strength carrying them ever upward.

At the top, a yawning opening awaited them. He swept her up into a loft, and polar wind blasted her, ready to snatch her from the warmth of her cloak and his arms. This was the tower's peak she had spotted from the ground.

Lio stood in the very center of the room and turned with her slowly, letting her see all around them. It was indeed an empty chamber with only a bare stone floor. The roof was nothing but rafters, and there were no walls, only eight perfectly matched, floor-to-ceiling window frames. The wind whistled and moaned by turns, gusting through the six empty window frames, tugging at the fabric that covered two.

But Cassia smiled at the unfinished work. "I can imagine what this will look like when you complete it. How beautiful it will be. A room almost entirely of glass."

"It's my next project."

"You're skipping to the very top of the tower?"

"Yes. Do you wonder why?"

He carried her toward the nearest window frame. He kept going, nearer and nearer, until his toes perched on the very edge. On instinct, Cassia clutched more tightly at his neck.

He was holding her over empty space.

Spread out below her was the garden, so lush she thought she might dive into it as into a depthless sea. Above and all around them was the indigo sky, blooming with stars and damp with snow clouds.

"No, I don't wonder," she said. "This view is incredible."

Even as she said it, the clouds shifted and revealed a new and strange light. Cassia gasped at the vivid color that seemed to dance in the sky. A curtain of crimson and scarlet stretched across the horizon.

"Lio, is that the ward?"

"No, that is an entirely natural wonder of the Goddess's. An aurora. But it does not look the same anywhere else, for the ward reacts to its light and enhances it to even more astonishing beauty."

"Do auroras happen often?"

"On nearly any clear night. And you got to see your first one from right here."

"I can understand why you work to capture light in glass. What designs do you have in mind to do this room justice?"

"Something suitable for the bedchamber."

She turned her face to him again. "This is the bedchamber?"

He smiled down at her with his gentle humor at the corners of his mouth and that new heat in his gaze. He stepped back into the room and turned her to face the two shrouded window frames.

The cloth coverings fell away. The wind snatched them and her breath. Lio had already installed two exquisite stained glass windows.

The first portrayed their roses in perfect, tiny petals of crimson and slender panes of green intertwining. Blood ran in rivulets inside the glass. Lio's lifeblood filled the petals of each rose he had wrought there.

The second panel was all vivid hues of purple, a whole garden of betony flowers in full bloom. The glass blossoms emanated spell light and the feeling of Lio's magic, intimate as when his power touched her mind.

They had both saved their roses. They had both triumphed over their nightmares.

"Please accept my welcome gift," Lio said.

Somewhere in the distance, the bells of Selas sounded. High, crystal tones chimed through the clear air, ringing in moon hours.

A fortnight would never have been enough. Neither was one more Summit. Not for her and Lio. Not for Zoe. Not for evenings around the Ritual circle with family or for laughter with brothers like Mak and Lyros. Not for that vast, neglected garden below or all this room would become.

She would not end this fight only to begin another. This Summit, she would not settle for anything less than complete victory. Not just for Orthros and Tenebra, but for them. For her. She wanted triumph... peace...*life*. Here, with Lio.

She reached up and caressed his face. "I accept."

Lio and Cassia's story continues in
Blood Grace Book 3, *Blood Sanctuary Part One*.
Learn more at
vroth.co/sanctuary1

GLOSSARY

Abroad: Hesperine term for lands outside of Orthros where Hesperines errant roam, meaning Tenebra and Cordium. See **Orthros Abroad**

Adelphos: false name assumed by Chrysanthos to hide his identity as a war mage from the Hesperines.

Adrogan: Tenebran lord, once one of Cassia's unwanted suitors, now betrothed to Biata.

affinity: the type of magic for which a person has an aptitude, such as light magic, warding, or healing.

Aithourian Circle: the war mages of the Order of Anthros, sworn enemies of the Hesperines, who have specialized spells for finding and destroying Hespera worshipers. Founded by Aithouros in ancient times, this circle was responsible for most of the destruction of Hespera's temples during the Last War. Oversees the training of all war mages from Tenebra and Cordium to ensure their lifelong loyalty to the Order.

Aithouros: fire mage of the Order of Anthros who personally led the persecution of Hespera worshipers during the Last War. Founder and namesake of the Aithourian Circle, who continue his teachings. Killed by Hippolyta.

Akron: highest-ranking mage in the Order of Anthros, who holds the ultimate authority in the Order that dominates all other mages.

Akron's Altar: the altar in Corona upon which the Order of Anthros executes heretics by immolation, where many Hesperines have met their deaths.

Alatheia: the first mage of Hespera executed on the Akron's Altar by the Order of Anthros. Because she refused to recant, the inquisitors put out one of her eyes before immolating her. Known in Orthros as "the First Heretic," she is celebrated as a martyr and immortalized in a constellation. Hesperines swear sacred oaths on the star that represents her remaining eye, called the Truth Star.

Alea: one of the two Queens of Orthros, who has ruled the Hesperines for nearly sixteen hundred years with her Grace, Queen Soteira. A mage of Hespera in her mortal life, she is the only Prisma of a temple of Hespera who survived the Ordering.

Alexandra: royal firstblood and Eighth Princess of Orthros, the youngest of the

Queens' family. Solaced from Tenebra as a child. She raises silkworms for her craft. Lio's childhood sweetheart.

Amachos: false name assumed by Dalos while he was in disguise as the royal mage of Tenebra.

Anastasios: Ritual firstblood who Gifted Apollon, founder of Lio's bloodline. He was a powerful healer and Prismos of Hagia Boreia, who sacrificed his life to help Alea protect their Great Temple from the Order of Anthros's onslaught.

Andragathos: god of male virtue and righteous warfare in the Tenebran and Cordian pantheon. The seventh scion and youngest son of Kyria and Anthros. A lesser deity alongside his brothers and sisters, the Fourteen Scions. Holy warriors in the Knightly Order of Andragathos adhere to a strict moral code and persecute Hesperines.

Annassa: honorific for the Queens of Orthros.

Anthros: god of war, order, and fire. Supreme deity of the Tenebran and Cordian pantheon and ruler of summer. The sun is said to be Anthros riding his chariot across the sky. According to myth, he is the husband of Kyria and brother of Hypnos and Hespera.

Anthros's fire: a flower commonly grown in Tenebra, used by humans in combination with the herb sunsword to ward off Hesperines.

Anthros's pyre: Anthros's eternal, holy flames, where he punishes those who displease him.

Apollon: Lio's father, an elder firstblood and founder of Orthros. In his mortal life before the Ordering, he was a mage of Demergos. Transformed by Anastasios, he was the first Hesperine ever to receive the Gift from one of the Ritual firstbloods. Renowned for his powerful stone magic and prowess in battle, he once roamed Abroad as one of the Blood Errant. Now retired to live peacefully in Orthros with his Grace, Komnena.

apostate: rogue mage who illegally practices magic outside of the Orders.

Archipelagos: land to the west of the Empire comprising a series of islands, which maintains strict isolation from the rest of the world. See **Nodora** and **Matsu**

Argyros: Lio's uncle and mentor in diplomacy and mind magic. Elder firstblood and founder of Orthros from Hagia Anatela, Gifted by Eidon. Graced to Lyta, father of Nike, Kadi and Mak. An elder firstblood and founder of Orthros like Apollon, his brother by mortal birth. Attended the first Equinox Summit and every one since as the Queens' Master Ambassador. One of the most powerful thelemancers in history, known as Silvertongue for his legendary abilities as a negotiator.

Arkadia: Lio's cousin, daughter of Argyros and Lyta. Solaced from Tenebra as a child. With her mother's affinity for warding and aptitude for the battle arts, she serves as a Master Steward in Hippolyta's Stand.

aromagus: agricultural mage who uses spells to assist farmers.

Athena: two-year-old Eriphite child Solaced by Javed and Kadi. Younger sister of Boskos by birth and blood. The severe case of frost fever she suffered as a mortal damaged her brain. While the Gift has healed her, she is still recovering lost development.

Autumn Greeting: ancient courtship festival of Tenebra. When a woman shares this dance with a man, it is considered a promise of betrothal, after which their fathers will arrange their marriage.

avowal: Hesperine ceremony in which Graces profess their bond before their people; legally binding and an occasion of great celebration.

Basileus: title of the King of Tenebra, appended to the name of every monarch who takes the throne.

Basilis: title of a non-royal female relative of the king, outside of the line of succession.

Basir: Hesperine thelemancer and one of the two spymasters of Orthros, alongside his Grace, Kumeta. From the Empire in his mortal life. His official title is "Queens' Master Envoy" to conceal the nature of their work.

Bellator: Tenebran free lord who kidnapped Solia and held her for ransom inside Castra Roborra before murdering her. Led the short-lived rebellion that ended there with the Siege of Sovereigns.

Benedict: First Knight of Segetia, Flavian's best friend, who harbors unrequited love for Genie. Cassia trusts him and considers him a friend, despite his hostility toward Hesperines as a devotee of Andragathos.

Biata: young Tenebran lady who is one of Lady Hadrian's followers and frequents her weaving room. Prone to gossiping. Betrothed to Lord Tyran.

Blood Errant: group of four ancient and powerful Hesperine warriors who went errant together for eight centuries: Apollon, Nike, Rudhira, and Methu. They performed legendary but controversial deeds in Hespera's name.

blood magic: type of magic practiced by worshipers of Hespera, from which the power of the Gift stems. All Hesperines possess innate blood magic.

Blood Moon: Hesperine name for one of the two moons, which appears red with a liquid texture to the naked eye. Believed to be an eye of the Goddess Hespera, potent with her blood magic.

blood shackles: warding spell cast with blood magic, which compels a person to not take a particular action. Persists until they are released by a key, a magical condition determined by the caster.

Blood Union: magical empathic connection that allows Hesperines to sense the emotions of any living thing that has blood.

bloodborn: Hesperine born with the Gift because their mother was transformed during pregnancy.

bloodless: undead; a corpse reanimated by a necromancer, so called because blood no longer flows through its veins, although it has a semblance of life.

Bosko or Boskos: ten-year-old Eriphite child Solaced by Javed and Kadi. Elder brother of Athena by birth and blood. Harbors anger over what the children suffered and is struggling to adjust to life in Orthros.

Brotherhood of Hedon: secret society of highborn men dedicated to the god Hedon, who engage in indulgences such as gambling, drinking, magical drugs, and sex with prostitutes in their god's temples.

Caelum: Solia and Cassia's thirteen-year-old half-brother, only son of King Lucis, crown prince of Tenebra.

Callen: Perita's loving husband. Once a guard in Lord Hadrian's service, he lost a promising military career due to a leg injury he suffered during his unjust imprisonment. Now serves the royal household of Tenebra as Cassia's trusted bodyguard.

Cassia: Tenebran lady, illegitimate daughter of King Lucis and his concubine, Thalia. Secretly a traitor, she sabotages the king's plots in order to protect his subjects from his cruelty and prevent him from going to war with the Hesperines. Deeply in love with Lio, she remains devoted to him despite the politics keeping them apart.

Castra Justa: the stronghold of the First Prince and base of operations for the Prince's Charge.

Castra Roborra: fortress in Tenebra that belonged to Lord Bellator, where he held Solia captive and ultimately murdered her. Site of the Siege of Sovereigns.

Changing Queen: ancient Queen of Tenebra who reigned during the Last War, the Mage King's wife and co-ruler. As a Silvicultrix, she was a powerful mage in her own right. Her name in Vulgus was Hedera, while her own people knew her as Ebah in an older language. Also known as the Hawk of the Lustra and associated with her plant symbol, ivy.

the Charge: see **Prince's Charge**

Charge Law: legal code of Orthros Abroad, named for the Prince's Charge. An evolving body of laws established and enforced by the First Prince, based on the Equinox Oath and Hespera's sacred tenets.

charm: physical object imbued with a mage's spell, usually crafted of botanicals or other materials with their own magical properties. Offers a mild beneficial effect to an area or the holder of the charm, even if that person is not a mage.

Chera: goddess of rain and spinning in the Tenebran and Cordian pantheon, known as the Mourning Goddess and the Widow. According to myth, she was the Bride of Spring before Anthros destroyed her god-husband, Demergos, for disobedience.

Chrysanthos: war mage from Cordium with an affinity for fire, rival of the late Dalos. As the Dexion of the Aithourian Circle, he is one of the highest-ranking elites in the Order of Anthros. An adroit politician born to an aristocratic family in Corona.

Cordium: land to the south of Tenebra where the Mage Orders hold sway. Its once-mighty principalities and city-states have now lost power to the magical and religious authorities. Wealthy and cultured, but prone to deadly politics. Also known as the Magelands.

Corona: capital city of Cordium and holy seat of the Mage Orders, where the main temples of each god are located, including the Hagion of Anthros.

Council of Free Lords: a body of Tenebran lords who have the hereditary authority to convey or revoke the nobility's mandate upon a reigning monarch. Their rights and privileges were established in the Free Charter.

the Craving: a Hesperine's addiction to their Grace's blood. When deprived of each other, Graces suffer agonizing withdrawal symptoms and fatal illness.

Daedala: Prisma of Hagia Zephyra. Ritual firstblood and Gifter of Timarete.

Dalos: Aithourian war mage who disguised himself as a Tenebran and conspired with King Lucis to assassinate the attendees of the Equinox Summit. When the Hesperines' ward stopped him, his spell rebounded, killing him with his own magic.

Dawn Slumber: deep sleep Hesperines fall into when the sun rises. Although the sunlight causes them no harm, they're unable to awaken until nightfall, leaving them vulnerable during daylight hours.

Demergos: formerly the god of agriculture, now stricken from the Tenebran and Cordian pantheon. His worshipers were disbanded in ancient times when the mages of Anthros seized power. According to myth, he was the husband of Chera, but disobeyed Anthros and brought on his own death and her grief.

Departure: contingency plan that dates from the founding of Orthros, when Hesperines feared the Last War might break out again at any time. If the Queens invoked the Departure, all Hesperines errant would return home, and the border between Orthros and Tenebra would be closed forever.

Deukalion: bloodborn firstgift of Apollon and Komnena, Ambassador in Orthros's diplomatic service who has devoted his career to improving relations between Orthros and Tenebra. Journeyed to Tenebra with the embassy during the Equinox Summit, where he had a secret affair with Cassia and helped her stop Dalos's assassination attempt. Upon his return to Orthros, he discovered she is his Grace and has suffered life-threatening Craving for her blood ever since.

Deutera: respected mage at the Temple of Kyria at Solorum, the Prisma's right hand and trusted confidant.

Deverran: Tenebran free lord who was betrothed to Caelum's mother before Lucis married her. Now betrothed to Nivalis.

Dexion: second highest ranking mage in the Aithourian Circle, second in command to the Synthikos and destined to succeed him.

Discourses on Love: Orthros's canon of erotic texts.

Divine Tongue: language spoken by Hesperines and mages, used for spells, rituals, and magical texts. The common tongue of Orthros, spoken freely by all Hesperines. In Tenebra and Cordium, the mages keep it a secret and disallow non-mages from learning it.

the Drink: when a Hesperine drinks blood from a human or animal; a nonsexual act, considered sacred, which should be carried out with respect for the donor. It's forbidden to take the Drink from an unwilling person. Or Hesperine sacred tenet, the commitment to thriving without the death of other living things.

eastern Tenebrae: wilderness east of the settled regions of Tenebra, sparsely populated by homesteads under the leadership of hold lords. Officially under the king's rule, but prone to lawlessness. Hesperines roam freely here.

Eidon: Prismos of Hagia Anatela. Ritual firstblood and Gifter of Argyros.

elder firstbloods: the ancient Hesperine founders of Orthros. Gifted by the Ritual firstbloods. See **Apollon, Argyros, Hypatia, Kassandra, Kitharos, Timarete**

elder Grace: the Grace of an elder firstblood.

the Empire: vast and prosperous human lands located far to the west, across an ocean from Tenebra. Comprises many different languages and cultures united under the Empress. Allied with Orthros and welcoming to Hesperines, many of whom began their mortal lives as Imperial citizens. Maintains a strict policy of isolation toward Tenebra an Cordium to guard against the Mage Orders.

the Empress: the ruler of the Empire, admired by her citizens. The Imperial throne has passed down through the female line for many generations.

envoy: according to common knowledge, a messenger attached to the Hesperine diplomatic service. In fact, envoys are the Queens' spies who gather information from the mortal world to protect Orthros and Hesperines errant. See **Basir** and **Kumeta**

Equinox Oath: ancient treaty between Orthros and Tenebra, which prescribes the conduct of Hesperines errant and grants them protection from humans.

Equinox Summit: peace talks in which the Hesperines send ambassadors from Orthros to meet with the King of Tenebra and renew the Equinox Oath. Each mortal king is expected to convene it once upon his accession to the throne.

Eriphites: worshipers of the pastoral god Eriphon, branded heretics by the Order of Anthros. The last surviving members of their cult are twenty-four orphaned children recently brought to safety in Orthros thanks to Cassia and Lio. See **Zosime, Boskos, Athena**

errant: a Hesperine who has left Orthros to travel through Tenebra doing good deeds for mortals.

essential affinities: the four types of magic used by the Ritual firstbloods during the spell that transformed them into Hesperines: light magic, warding, healing, and thelemancy. These affinities manifest in Hesperines' innate abilities and run in the bloodlines of Orthros.

essential displacement: process by which necromancers can transfer the magic of one person, the source, into another person, the vessel, through a third person called the channel. The vessel must die for the source to reclaim their power.

Eudias: young war mage from Cordium with an affinity for weather, including lightning. Compelled to join the Aithourian circle due to his magic, he does not relish their murderous plots. Apprenticed to Dalos, he reluctantly assisted his late master in Tenebra and now answers to Chrysanthos.

Eudokia: Hesperine youngblood, one of Lio's Trial sisters in Orthros. Solaced from Tenebra as a child. An initiate mathematician, calligrapher, and accomplished scholar. Daughter of Hypatia.

Eugenia: young Tenebran lady, believed to be Flavian's cousin and daughter of his late uncle, Lord Eugenius. In fact she is his sister, the daughter of Titus and his concubine Risara.

Evander: see **Evandrus the Younger**

Evandrus the Elder: Tenebran free lord who assisted Lord Bellator in kidnapping Solia and joined forces with him at Castra Roborra during their rebellion.

Evandrus the Younger: son and heir of Evandrus the Elder, who died with him at Castra Roborra during the Siege of Sovereigns.

Eye of Light: see **Light Moon**

familiar: the animal companion of a Hesperine, bound to them by blood.

the Feast: Hesperine term for drinking blood while making love.

Ferus: a Tenebran free lord, the most threatening of Cassia's unwanted suitors, until she exposed him as a traitor. Now in exile in the eastern Tenebrae.

First Prince: see **Rudhira**

firstblood: the first Hesperine in a bloodline, who founds the family and passes the Gift to their children.

Firstblood Circle: the governing body of Orthros. Every firstblood has a vote on behalf of their bloodline, while non-voting Hesperines can attempt to influence policy by displays of partisanship. The Queens retain veto power, but use it sparingly.

firstgift: the eldest child of a Hesperine bloodline, first to receive the gift from their parents.

flametongue: rare herb whose oil can be used to fireproof armor or clothing against mundane flame. Offers no protection against magefire, but still prized by the few royals and nobles who can afford it. The Order of Anthros forbids anyone but their mages to grow and prepare it.

Flavian: young Tenebran lord, son of Free Lord Titus and heir to Segetia's seat on the Council. Despite his family's feud with Hadria, he is admired by women on both sides of the conflict as a paragon of manhood.

foregiver: a Hesperine's ancestor who gave the Gift to their bloodline in the past.

the Fourteen Scions: see **Scions**

Free Charter: founding document of the kingdom of Tenebra, an agreement between the Mage King and the lords regarding the rights and privileges of the nobility. Grants the free lords influence over the royal succession.

free lord: highest noble rank in Tenebra. Has a seat on the Council of Free Lords and heredity authority to vote on whether a king should receive the nobility's mandate.

Frigorum: Tenebran fortress in the Umbral Mountains, located on Mount Frigora. The Summit Beacon is kept here.

frost fever: contagious illness that is dangerous for adults but especially deadly to children. Tenebra suffers periodic epidemics of frost fever due to poor sanitation and nutrition.

Gaius: aging Tenebran lord loyal to Free Lord Hadrian.

Galanthian: Tenebran free lord with lands in the cold northern region of the kingdom. Father of Nivalis.

Genie: see **Eugenia**

geomagus: mage with an affinity for geological forces, who can use their magic to conjure heat from the ground or create artifacts like warming plates for heating food and drink.

get one's fangs polished: Hesperine slang for the Feast.

the Gift: Hesperines' immortality and magical abilities, which they regard as a blessing from the goddess Hespera. The practice of offering the Gift to all is a Hesperine sacred tenet.

Gift Collector: mage-assassin and bounty hunter who hunts down Hesperines for the Order of Hypnos using necromancy, alchemy, and fighting tactics. Known for adapting common items into weapons to skirt the Orders' religious laws against mages arming themselves.

Gift Night: the night of a person's transformation into a Hesperine, usually marked by great celebration.

Gifting chart: a star chart drawn up by Orthros's astronomers for each new Hesperine, recording astronomical portents that appeared in the sky on the night of their Gifting.

Glasstongue: see **Lio**

glyph: sacred symbol of a deity. Each god or goddess in the pantheon has a unique glyph. Often used as a pattern in spell casting or carved on shrines and temples.

glyph stone: the capstone of the doorway of a shrine, inscribed with the glyph of the deity worshiped there, where any spells over the structure are usually seated.

the Goddess's Eyes: the two moons, the red Blood Moon and the white Light Moon; associated with Hespera and regarded as her gaze by Hesperines.

Gorgos: master mage from the Sun Temple of Anthros at Solorum who aspires to become royal mage.

Grace: Hesperine sacred tenet, a magical bond between two Hesperine lovers. Frees them from the need for human blood and enables them to sustain each other, but comes at the cost of the Craving. A fated bond that happens when their love is true. It is believed every Hesperine has a Grace just waiting to be found. See **Craving**

Grace braids: thin braids of one another's hair that Graces exchange. They may wear them privately after professing their bond to one another, then exchange them publicly at their avowal and thereafter wear them for all to see to signify their commitment.

Grace-family (Grace-son, Grace-father, Grace-sister, etc.): the family members of a Hesperine's Grace; compare with human in-laws.

Grace Union: the particularly powerful and intimate Blood Union between two Hesperines who are Graced; enables them to communicate telepathically and empathically.

Great Temple Epoch: the historical period when the Great Temples of every cult flourished across Tenebra and Cordium, and all mages cooperated. Came to a cataclysmic end due to the Ordering and the Last War.

Great Temples of Hespera: powerful, thriving temples where mages of Hespera worshiped and worked their magic in peace, before they were branded heretics. Razed during the Last War.

Guardian of Orthros: see **Hippolyta**

Hadria: domain of Free Lord Hadrian, located on Tenebra's rocky western coast, where they seas are treacherous.

Lady Hadrian: Lord Hadrian's wife, a mature lady above reproach in the court of Tenebra, admired for her graces and respected for her political acumen.

Lord Hadrian: one of the two most powerful free lords in Tenebra, who commands the fealty of many other free lords and lesser nobles. His family has been feuding with Segetia for generations. Known for his loyalty to the throne, but also for honor superior to the king's.

Hagia Anatela: one of the four Great Temples of Hespera that flourished during the Great Temple Epoch, located in the eastern part of the continent. See **Eidon, Ourania**

Hagia Boreia: one of the four Great Temples of Hespera that flourished during the Great Temple Epoch, located in the northern part of the continent. See **Alea, Anastatios**

Hagia Zephyra: one of the four Great Temples of Hespera that flourished during the Great Temple Epoch, located in the western part of the continent. See **Daedala, Thelxinos**

Hammer of the Sun: Apollon's famous battle hammer, which he wielded while Abroad with the Blood Errant.

Harbor: bay in Orthros around which Selas was built. The founders landed here when they first escaped Tenebra and found refuge in the unsettled north.

Healing Sanctuary: infirmary in Orthros founded and run by Queen Soteira, where humans are given care and Hesperines are trained in the healing arts.

heart bow: traditional gesture of devotion to the Queens of Orthros, a deep bow with one hand over the heart.

heart hunters: warbands of Tenebrans who hunt down Hesperines, regarded by their countrymen as protectors of humanity. They patrol the northern borders of Tenebra with packs of liegehounds, waiting to attack Hesperines who leave Orthros.

hedge warlocks, hedge witch: practitioner of Tenebran nature arts, including herbalism and remnants of Lustra magic.

Hedon: god of pleasure and chance in the Tenebran and Cordian pantheon, patron of sexual acts and gambling. Styled as the god of fertility and prosperity by the Order of Anthros in their attempts to promote morality. The Orders allow prostitution and gambling within the temples of Hedon, where they can control these activities.

Hespera: goddess of night cast from the Tenebran and Cordian pantheon. The Mage Orders have declared her worship heresy punishable by death. Hesperines keep her cult alive and continue to revere her as the goddess of the moons, Sanctuary, and Mercy. Associated with roses, thorns, and fanged creatures. According to myth, she is the sister of Anthros and Hypnos.

Hespera's Rose: the most sacred symbol of the Hesperines, a rose with five petals and five thorns representing Hespera's sacred tenets. Frequently embroidered on clothing or represented on stained glass windows. Based on real roses, which are the Goddess's sacred flower and beloved by Hesperines. The mages uproot them wherever they're found in Tenebra or Cordium and punish those who grow them for heresy.

Hesperine: nocturnal immortal being with fangs who gains nourishment from drinking blood. Tenebrans and Cordians believe them to be monsters bent on humanity's destruction. In truth, they follow a strict moral code in the name of their goddess, Hespera, and wish only to ease humankind's suffering.

Hesperite: human worshiper of Hespera, persecuted as a heretic by the Orders.

hexmaster: necromancer who leads a hex, or group of six mages of Hypnos.

the Hilt: cliff in the eastern Tenebrae where mortals often expose unwanted infants as sacrifices to the gods. Hesperines stay secretly active in the area to rescue and Solace the children.

Hippolyta: Lio's aunt, Graced to Argyros, mother of Nike, Kadi, and Mak. Greatest and most ancient Hesperine warrior, a founder of Orthros. Known as the Guardian of Orthros for her deeds in Tenebra during the Last War and for establishing the Stand.

Hippolyta's Gymnasium: gymnasium in Orthros founded by Hippolyta, where she trains the Stand and Orthros's athletes compete.

Hippolyta's Stand: Orthros's standing army, founded by Hippolyta. Under her leadership, they patrol the border with Tenebra as Stewards of the Queens' ward. So few of the peaceful Hesperines take up the battle arts that Nike, Kadi, Mak, and Lyros are the only Stewards.

hold lord: Tenebran lord who holds a homestead in the eastern Tenebrae.

hornbearer: the leader of a band of heart hunters, so called for the horn he carries, which is imbued with nature magic.

House Annassa: the residence of the Queens of Orthros, the Hesperine counterpart to a royal palace.

House Komnena: Lio's family home in Orthros, seat of his bloodline, named for his mother.

the Hunger: a combination of sexual desire and the need for blood, which Hesperines experience with their lovers.

Hylonome: bloodborn from Orthros's history who starved herself to death on the top of Hypatia's Observatory after the death of her Grace.

Hypatia: elder firstblood and founder of Orthros from Hagia Anatela, Gifted by Ourania. Grace of Khaldaios and mother of Kia. Orthros's greatest astronomer, who invented the Hesperine calendar.

Hypatia's Observatory: tower in Orthros established by Hypatia, where Hesperine astronomers study the heavens and teach their students. Every Autumn Equinox, Orthros's diplomats watch for the Summit Beacon from here.

Hypnos: god of death and dreams in the Tenebran and Cordian pantheon. Winter is considered his season. Humans unworthy of going to Anthros's Hall are believed to spend the afterlife in Hypnos's realm of the dead. According to myth, he is the brother of Anthros and Hespera.

initiate: Hesperine who has achieved initiate rank in their craft or service, more advanced than a student but not yet of full rank. Attained after the young Hesperine completes a significant crafting project or research treatise that meets with their mentor's approval.

Initiation: see **Trial**

Inner Eyes: the necromancers who hold the highest authority within the Order of Hypnos.

Ioustin or Ioustinianos: First Prince of the Hesperines, eldest child of the Queens of Orthros. Lio's Ritual father. Solaced from Tenebra as a child. Once a warrior in the Blood Errant, he now leads a force of Hesperines errant known as the Charge. Young Hesperines call him Rudhira, an affectionate name given to him by Methu.

Irene: mage expelled from the Temple of Kyria at Solorum after betraying them to Dalos. Sister of Lord Tyran, she looks down on anyone of lesser birth.

Iris: Tenebran lady, Solia's handmaiden and closest companion, who died with her at the Siege of Sovereigns.

ivy pendant: wooden pendant carved with a triquetra of ivy. Secretly passed down from one Tenebran queen to another and finally, from Solia to Cassia. Imbued with Lustra magic and connected to the Changing Queen in some way, it allowed Cassia to access secret passages inside Solorum Palace.

Javed: Lio's Grace-cousin, avowed to Kadi, father of Bosko and Thenie. From the Empire in his mortal life. Has an affinity for healing and now serves in Orthros's Healing Sanctuary.

Justinian: see **Ioustinianos**

Kadi: see **Arkadia**

kaetlii: word in the tongue used by Tenebrans to train liegehounds, meaning the person the dog is bonded to and will protect until death.

kalux: Hesperine word in the Divine Tongue for clitoris.

Kassandra: Lio's Ritual mother, an elder firstblood and founder of Orthros. Ritual sister to the Queens, who Gifted her, and mother of Prometheus. An Imperial princess in her mortal life, she became the first Hesperine from the Empire and secured Orthros's alliance with their Imperial allies. Now the Queens' Master Economist who oversees Orthros's trade. Has the gift of foresight and as Orthros's oracle, guides the Hesperines with her prophecies.

Khaldaios: elder Grace, avowed to Hypatia, father of Kia. From the Empire in his mortal life.

Kia: see **Eudokia**

King of Tenebra: see **Lucis**

Kings and Mages: Tenebran and Cordian name for the game Hesperines call Prince and Diplomat.

Kitharos: elder firstblood and founder of Orthros from Hagia Zephyra, father to Nodora. One of the Hesperines' greatest musicians.

Knight: Cassia's beloved liegehound. Solia gave him to Cassia as a puppy so Cassia would have protection and companionship.

Komnena: Lio's mother, still rather young by Hesperine standards. Fled a life of squalor as a Tenebran farmwife and ran away to Orthros with Apollon, who Gifted her while she was pregnant and raised her son as his own. Now a respected mind healer. As the Queens' Chamberlain, she is responsible for helping newcomers to Orthros settle and adjust.

Konstantina: royal firstblood, Second Princess of Orthros, the second child and eldest daughter of the Queens. From the Empire in her mortal life. As the Royal Master Magistrate, she is the author of Orthros's legal code and an influential politician who oversees the proceedings of the Firstblood Circle.

krana: Hesperine term in the Divine Tongue for vagina.

Kumeta: Hesperine light mage and one of the two spymasters of Orthros, alongside her Grace, Basir. From the Empire in her mortal life. Her official title is "Queens' Master Envoy" to conceal the nature of their work.

Kyria: goddess of weaving and the harvest in the Tenebran and Cordian pantheon, known as the Mother Goddess or the Wife. Her season is autumn. According to myth, she is married to Anthros.

Laskara: Timarete's firstgift, Lyros's elder sister. One of Orthros's most renowned sculptors, know for her contributions to art and mathematics.

Last Call: a powerful magical summons that the Queens of Orthros issue only in times of imminent danger. Calls all Hesperines errant home from Abroad to seek safety in Orthros behind the ward.

the Last War: the cataclysmic violence sparked by the Ordering sixteen hundred years ago. When the Order of Anthros sought to suppress all resistance to their authority, magical and armed conflict ravaged Tenebra and Cordium, destroying the civilization of the Great Temple Epoch. Peace came at the cost of the Hesperines' exile and the Order of Anthros's victory, while the Mage King secured his rule in Tenebra.

Laurentius: favored warrior of the Mage King. Worshiped Anthros, but loved Hesperite mage Makaria. After the Orders martyred her, he sacrificed himself in battle. Went to his funeral pyre with his amulet of Anthros and her votive statue of Hespera.

liegehound: war dogs bred and trained by Tenebrans to track, hunt, and slay Hesperines. Veil spells do not throw them off the scent, and they can leap high enough to pull a levitating Hesperine from the air. The only animals that do not trust Hesperines. They live longer than other canines and can withstand poison and disease.

Light Moon: Hesperine name for one of the two moons, which appears white with a smooth texture. Believed to be an eye of the Goddess Hespera, shining with her light.

Lio: see **Deukalion Komnenos**

Lion of Orthros: see **Apollon**

Lucis: current King of Tenebra, who reigns with ruthlessness and brutality. Born a lord, he secured the crown by might and political schemes, and he upholds his authority by any means necessary. Cassia has never forgiven him for Solia's death.

Lustra magic: Tenebran name referring to old nature magic. Practiced in ancient times by the Changing Queen. The Orders have never been able to understand or control it, and most knowledge of it is now lost.

Lysandros or Lyros: Lio's Trial brother and Grace-cousin, avowed to Mak, Solaced as a child from Tenebra. Also a warder and warrior serving in the Stand.

Lyta: see **Hippolyta**

Mage King: Tenebra's most famous monarch who reigned sixteen hundred years ago, widely considered by Hesperines and mortals alike to have been a just ruler. He and his wife made the original Equinox Oath with the Queens of Orthros. A fire mage and warrior, he ruled before the Mage Orders mandated that men must choose between wielding spells or weapons.

mage of dreams: mage of Hypnos with an affinity for thelemancy.

Mage Orders: the magical and religious authorities in Cordium, which also dictate sacred law to Tenebran temples. Responsible for training and governing mages and punishing heretics.

Mak: see **Telemakhos**

Makaria: Hesperite Sanctuary mage martyred in the Ordering. Lover of Laurentius Centuries later, Lio and Cassia fell in love at the shrine of Hespera she once tended near Solorum.

Martyrs' Pass: the only known passage to Orthros through the Umbral Mountains. Site of Aithouros's last stand against the Hesperines when he and his war mages tried to pursue them into Orthros.

Matsu: Nodora's Ritual mother and the only other Hesperine from the Archipelagos. A beloved thespian and fashion leader in Orthros.

Menodora: Hesperine youngblood, one of Lio's Trial sisters. An initiate musician, admired vocalist, and crafter of musical instruments. She is one of only two Hesperines from the Archipelagos and the immortal expert on the music of her mortal homeland.

Mercy: Hesperine sacred tenet, the practice of caring for dead or dying humans.

Methu: see **Prometheus**

Midnight Moonbeam: a black-and-white dwarf goat kid, one of Zoe's two familiars.

Migration Night: event twice a year when Hesperines travel between hemispheres to avoid longer hours of daylight. The night after Spring Equinox, they vacate Orthros Boreou in the northern hemisphere and migrate to Orthros Notou in the southern hemisphere. The night before Autumn Equinox, they change residence again, leaving Orthros Notou and returning to Orthros Boreou.

mind healer: see **theramancer**

mind mage: see **thelemancer**

moon hours: by the Hesperine clock, the hours corresponding to night, when Hesperines pursue public activities.

Mount Frigora: peak in the Umbral Mountains on Tenebra's northern border, location of the fortress holding their Summit Beacon.

Namenti: Tenebran coastal city on the southern border, near Cordium.

New Guest House: guest house for visiting mortals on the docks of Selas, built four hundred years ago.

newblood: Hesperine youth, no longer a suckling child but not yet an initiated youngblood.

Night Call: magical summons a Hesperine elder can perform on a less powerful Hesperine to prematurely break them out of the Dawn Slumber.

Nike: see **Pherenike**

Nivalis: young Tenebran lady, one of Lady Hadrian's followers who frequents her weaving room. Daughter of Lord and Lady Galanthian. Her three younger siblings died in a past epidemic of frost fever. Betrothed to Deverran.

Nodora: see **Menodora**

the Oath: see **Equinox Oath**

Order of Anthros: Mage Order dedicated to the god Anthros, which holds the ultimate religious and magical authority over all other Orders and temples. Bent on destroying Hesperines. War mages, light mages, and warders serve in this Order, as do agricultural and stone mages.

Order of Hypnos: Mage Order devoted to Hypnos, which holds authority over necromancers, mind mages, and illusionists. Oversees rites for the dead, purportedly to prevent Hesperine grave robbing, but in practice to stop rogue necromancers from raising the dead. The Order of Anthros's closest ally in their effort to destroy Hesperines.

the Orders: see **Mage Orders**

Orthros: homeland of the Hesperines, ruled by the Queens. The Mage Orders describe it as a horrific place where no human can survive, but in reality, it is a land of peace, prosperity, and culture. Located north of Tenebra.

Orthros Abroad: the population of Hesperines who are errant in Tenebra at any given time. Under the jurisdiction of the First Prince, who is the Queens' regent outside their ward.

Orthros Boreou: Hesperine homeland in the northern hemisphere, located north of and sharing a border with Tenebra.

Orthros Notou: Hesperine homeland in the southern hemisphere, near the Empire.

Ourania: Prisma of Hagia Anatela. Ritual firstblood and Gifter of Hypatia.

Perita: Cassia's handmaiden and dearest friend. Wife of Callen. Has assisted Cassia in her schemes ever since Cassia helped her save Callen from prison, and she delivered crucial information that enabled Cassia to save the Hesperine embassy from Dalos's assassination attempt.

Phaedros: the most notorious and only criminal in Orthros's history, who lives in eternal exile under the midnight sun.

Pherenike: Lio's cousin, a warder and warrior second only to her mother Lyta in strength, a thelemancer second only to her father Argyros in power. Solaced from Tenebra as a child. One of the Blood Errant alongside her uncle, Apollon, and her Trial brothers Rudhira and Methu. After the surviving Blood Errant's campaign to avenge Methu, she remained Abroad alone and has now been missing in action for over ninety years.

Prince and Diplomat: board game and beloved Hesperine pastime; requires strategy and practice to master. See **Kings and Mages**

Prince's Charge: the force of Hesperines errant that serve under the First Prince.

Prisma: highest ranking female mage in a temple.

the Prisma of the Temple of Kyria at Solorum: powerful mage who leads the women of her temple with pragmatism and kindness.

Prismos: highest ranking male mage in a temple.

Prometheus: legendary Hesperine warrior and martyr. Bloodborn to Kassandra and descendant of Imperial royalty. As a member of the Blood Errant, he was the close comrade of Nike, Rudhira, and Apollon during their travels Abroad. Captured by the Aithourian Circle before Lio's birth. Orthros still mourns his death.

the Queens: the Hesperine monarchs of Orthros. See **Alea, Soteira**

the Queens' Terrace: a terrace at House Annassa that fulfills the function of a throne room, although the Queens sit together on a modest bench, and their terrace is open to all.

the Queens' ward: the powerful Sanctuary ward cast by the Queens, which spans the borders of Orthros, protecting Hesperines from human threats.

Rainbow Aurora: brown-and-white dwarf goat kid, one of Zoe's two familiars.

revelatory spell: one of the Anthrian mages' specialized spells for revealing hidden Hesperines.

rhabdos: Hesperine term in the Divine Tongue meaning penis.

Riga: most skilled seamstress in the King of Tenebra's household. Once had a grudge against Cassia, but now her ally.

rimelace: flowering herb that requires extremely cold conditions. Difficult to grow in Tenebra, even with the aid of magic, but thrives in Orthros. The only known treatment for frost fever.

Risara: Titus's charismatic, beloved concubine of thirty years, adept at navigating the nobility's personal and political foibles.

Ritual: Hesperine sacred tenet. A ceremony in which Hesperines share blood, but in a broader sense, the whole of their religious beliefs.

Ritual circle: area where Hesperines gather to perform Ritual, usually marked with sacred symbols on the floor.

Ritual Drink: the Drink given by one Hesperine to another for healing or sustenance, without intimacy or invoking a family bond.

Ritual firstbloods: the eight blood mages who performed the Ritual that created Hesperines. As the leaders of the Great Temples of Hespera, all except Alea were martyred during the Ordering. See **Alea, Anastasios, Daedala, Eidon, Ourania, Thelxinos**

Ritual Grace: Soteira, the Grace of the only surviving Ritual firstblood.

Ritual hall: central chamber in Hesperine homes where the bloodline's Ritual circle is located.

Ritual parents: Hesperines who attend a new suckling's first Ritual or who give the Gift to a mortal who becomes a Hesperine as an adult. They remain mentors and trusted guides for eternity. Comparable to Tenebran temple parents.

Ritual Sanctuary: innermost chamber of a shrine or temple of Hespera, where sacred rituals were performed by mages.

Ritual separation: eight nights that Hesperine Graces must spend apart to demonstrate their Craving symptoms and prove their bond to their people; required before avowal.

Ritual tapestry: tapestry crafted by Kassandra for a new Hesperine to commemorate their Gifting, into which she weaves prophecies about their immortal destiny.

Ritual tributary: Hesperine who establishes their own bloodline rather than joining their Gifter's family.

Rose House: the newest guest house on the docks of Selas, built in recent years by Apollon and Lio for Komnena's use.

Rota Overlook: a hidden Hesperine Sanctuary near Solorum, where an old, enduring Sanctuary ward offers protection to Hesperines traveling Abroad in hostile situations.

royal firstbloods: the Queens' children, who are to establish their own bloodlines in order to share the Annassa's power with their people.

Rudhira: see **Ioustinianos**

Sabina: Tenebran lady, eldest daughter of Lord and Lady Hadrian. With no brothers, she is the heir of Hadria and runs the estate while her parents are at court.

Sanctuary: Hesperine sacred tenet, the practice of offering refuge to anyone in need. Or Hesperine refuge in hostile territory, concealed and protected from humans by Sanctuary magic.

Sanctuary mage: a mage with a rare dual affinity for warding and light magic, who can create powerful protections that also conceal. Queen Alea of Orthros is the only mage with this affinity who survived the Orders' persecution of Hespera worshipers.

Scions: lesser deities in the Tenebran and Cordian pantheon, the fourteen children of Anthros and Kyria, comprising seven sons and seven daughters. Each has their own cult and mages.

Segetia: domain of Free Lord Titus, landlocked and known for its gentle hills.

Selas: capital city of Orthros Boreou.

Semna: retired Prisma of the Temple of Kyria at Solorum.

Severin: see **Severinus the Younger**

Severinus the Elder: Tenebran free lord with deeply held prejudices against Hesperines, lord of a domain on Tenebra's northern border with Orthros.

Severinus the Younger: son and heir of Severinus the Elder, who tries to mitigate his father's abuses against their people.

shamisen: long-necked, three-stringed musical instrument from the Archipelagos favored by Nodora.

share: human or immortal with whom a Hesperine is romantically involved, sharing blood and intimacy.

Siege of Sovereigns: King Lucis's assault on Castra Roborra after the murder of Solia. Ended the rebellion of the nobles who styled themselves the sovereign free lords and resulted in the death of every living thing in the fortress. Lucis also sent his own men to certain death in the battle so they could not tell his subjects he had abandoned Solia.

Silvertongue: see **Argyros**

Skleros: master necromancer and Gift Collector who holds the Order of Hypnos's record for completing the most bounties on Hesperines. Expert in essential displacement.

Slumber: see **Dawn Slumber**

Solace: Hesperine sacred tenet, the practice of rescuing and Gifting abandoned children.

Solia: late Princess of Tenebra, King Lucis's legitimate daughter and heir before the birth of his son. When she was seventeen, rebel lords kidnapped her. Lucis refused to ransom her or collect her remains and ensured all witnesses perished in the ensuing Siege of Sovereigns. Nobles and commoners alike still mourn her.

Solorum: ancestral capital of Tenebra, royal seat of the king.

Solorum Fortress: castle built for the defense of the capital by seven successive kings over the course of two hundred years. The Hesperine embassy lodged here during the Equinox Summit due to the humans' fears.

Solorum Palace: oldest palace in Tenebra, built by the Mage King, still the most important royal residence for the King of Tenebra.

sophia: title of a Hesperine whose service is teaching and scholarship.

Soteira: one of the two Queens of Orthros, who has ruled the Hesperines for nearly sixteen hundred years with her Grace, Alea. Originally from the Empire, she was a powerful mortal mage with an affinity for healing before leaving to found Orthros alongside Alea.

speires: symbolic hair ties Lyta gives to trainees when they begin learning the battle arts. Stewards wear them as part of their Stand regalia.

the Stand: see **Hippolyta's Stand**

stepping: innate Hesperine ability to teleport instantly from one place to another with little magical effort.

Steward: see **Hippolyta's Stand**

stinglily: plant that produces a severe skin rash on contact.

Summit Beacon: bonfire on the border between Tenebra and Orthros, which the King of Tenebra lights to announce to the Hesperines he wishes to convene the Equinox Summit.

Sun Temple: see **Temple of Anthros at Solorum**

sunbound: mild Hesperine curse word.

Synthikos: the leader of a mage circle.

Synthikos of the Aithourian Circle: head of the elite war mages of the Order of Anthros, a position their founder Aithouros once held.

Telemakhos: Lio's cousin and best friend. Exposed as a child in Tenebra due to his club foot, Solaced by Argyros and Lyta. A warrior by profession and warder by affinity, he serves in the Stand. He and his Grace, Lyros, are newly avowed.

Temple of Anthros at Namenti: one of the most powerful and influential temples in Tenebra. Conspired with the Aithourian Circle to help Dalos infiltrate Tenebra.

Temple of Anthros at Solorum: temple in Tenebra's capital, once an ancient site of outdoor Anthros worship that was later walled and roofed by kings. The temple of the royal mage, where the king and his court attend rites.

Temple of Kyria at Solorum: most influential and respected temple of Kyria in Tenebra, located near the royal palace. Houses orphans and provides healing services to the surrounding area. Due to their reputation and magical power, the women here enjoy a great degree of autonomy.

Tenebra: human kingdom south of Orthros and north of Cordium. Agrarian, feudal society ruled by a king, prone to instability due to rivalries between lords. Land of the Hesperines' origin, where they are now persecuted.

Thalia: Cassia's mother, King Lucis's concubine. Murdered the day Cassia was born by an apostate fire mage attempting to assassinate Lucis.

thelemancer: a mage with an affinity for thelemancy, or mind magic, which gives them the power to manipulate others' thoughts and control their Wills.

Thelxinos: Prismos of Hagia Zephyra. Ritual firstblood and Gifter of Kitharos.

Thenie: see Athena

theramancer: a person with an affinity for theramancy, or mind healing, who can use magic to treat mental illness.

Timarete: elder firstblood and founder of Orthros from Hagia Zephyra, Gifted by Daedala. Mother of Laskara and Lyros. One of the Hesperines' greatest painters.

Titus: free lord of Segetia, one of the most powerful men in Tenebra, who commands the fealty of many other free lords and lesser nobles. Segetia has been feuding with Hadria for generations.

traversal: teleportation ability of human mages; requires a great expense of magic and usually leaves the mortal mage seriously ill.

Trial circle: age set of Hesperines who go through the Trial of Initiation together. They consider each other Trial sisters and brothers for the rest of their immortal lives. Although not related by birth or blood, they maintain strong bonds of loyalty and friendship for eternity.

Trial of Initiation or Trial: Hesperine rite of passage marking an immortal's transition into adulthood.

Tychon: young war mage with an affinity for fire, Chrysanthos's apprentice. Zealous in his devotion to his master and the Aithourian Circle's cause.

Tyran: ambitious young free lord of Tenebra, loyal to Flavian and eager to stoke Segetia's feud with Hadria. Known for his and his soldiers' misconduct toward commoners, especially women.

Umbral Mountains: mountain range spanning the border between Tenebra and Orthros.

Union: Hesperine sacred tenet, the principle of living with empathy and compassion for all. See **Blood Union**

Valentia: Tenebran lady who fell into disgrace after her family supported Lord Bellator's rebellion. Known for her excellent personal character. Loyal to Flavian's faction, betrothed to Tyran.

veil hours: by the Hesperine clock, the hours corresponding to day, when Hesperines Slumber or devote their private time to friends, family, and lovers.

veil spell: innate Hesperine ability to cast magical concealments that hide their presence and activities from humans or fellow immortals.

Verruc: Tyran's guard who harassed and attempted to assault Perita. Callen killed him in combat to protect her.

war mage: mage with an affinity for fire, lightning, or other type of magic that can be weaponized. The Order of Anthros compels them to dedicate their lives to the Aithourian Circle.

warder: mage with an affinity for warding, the power to create magical protections that block spells or physical attacks.

Waystar: Hesperine fortress, Orthros's first refuge for those crossing the border from Tenebra. Hesperines errant who use weapons must leave their armaments here before crossing the Sea of Komne to Selas.

Will: free will, willpower. Or Hesperine sacred tenet, the principle of guarding the sanctity of each person's freedom of choice.

Xandra: see **Alexandra**

youngblood: young adult Hesperine who has recently reached their majority by passing the Trial of Initiation.

Zoe or Zosime: Lio's little sister, a seven-year-old Eriphite child Solaced by Apollon and Komnena. Loves her new family and idolizes her brother for his role in saving her from Tenebra. Has yet to heal from the emotional wounds she suffered as a mortal.

PART ONE
BLOOD SANCTUARY
BLOOD GRACE BOOK III

**Their love could last forever -
unless the king's assassins cut her life short...**

Cassia has reunited with her beloved Lio in the land of eternal night. She longs to become a Hesperine like him so they can stay together for all time, but she's torn between their happiness and her duty to the kingdom of mortals. To win her freedom, she must convince the humans to ally with the Hesperines, despite centuries of conflict.

Lio won't force her to stay by revealing their blood bond, although certain death awaits him if she leaves. While they negotiate for peace in public, he tempts her in private with the promise of everlasting passion. But the king's agents will block an alliance at any cost. Can Lio protect Cassia when she becomes their target?

Steamy romance meets classic fantasy worldbuilding in Blood Grace. Follow fated mates Cassia and Lio through their epic story of forbidden love for a guaranteed series HEA.

Blood Sanctuary Parts One and Two were previously published as one ebook.

Learn more at
vroth.co/sanctuary1

BLOOD RUSE

A BLOOD ERRANT *Adventure*

Saving damsels is all in a night's work for these four chivalrous Hesperines. Too bad the gutsy women believe they're the enemy.

The Blood Errant are famous heroes. Or infamous monsters, depending on who you ask. When they set out to save a roadside inn from bandits, they can't show their fangs to the charming locals.

In a daring trick, they pose as human guests with the help of Apollon's mortal lover. Alas, Methu cannot woo the vivacious innkeeper while impersonating a cleric. Or can he? Nike pretends to be a lady, but spars with a handsome soldier. Rudhira plays the role of holy knight even as the lovely barmaid stirs his forbidden desires.

If anyone sees through their disguises, their allies will be more dangerous than their enemies.

In this romantic fantasy, join the Blood Errant on their past adventures in battle and misadventures in love.

Get this book for free when you
sign up for my newsletter!
vroth.co/ruse

ACKNOWLEDGEMENTS

THANK YOU to my dad for your unbelievable support. You know I always have to lead with that.

Where do I start thanking the coven, the wonderful word witches of the FaRo Authors group? Harriet, thank you for the incredible amount of work you've poured into making this year's FaRoFeb a bigger success than ever. Thank you to our powerhouse team of organizers for all your contributions to the event: Colleen, Dani, Elsie, Kristina, Lisette, Steph, Trish, and Zoey. Special thanks to Steph, Elsie, Lisette, Kristina, Rae, and Jennie for taking part in my launch!

Patricia, my marvelous illustrator, your artwork brings joy to fans of the series and to me. With every new piece you add to the gallery of Blood Grace covers, you top your last creation, and we fall more in love with your vision of Lio and Cassia.

My Ambassadors for Orthros, what would I do without you? To my faithful beta readers, reviewers, and street team, I'm so glad for your support and friendship. To those of you who have been on the team a long time, thank you for believing in my work before anyone knew who I was. To all the new members who have joined us via an ARC of Blood Mercy, I'm so glad you found us. Thank you all for going the extra mile to become Ambassadors. Special thanks to Alex, Angela, Aurora, Brandy, Bridie, Cheyenne, Erika, Heather, Jessica R., Jordie, Kadie, Kristen, Melissa, Nat, Nicole D., Raley, Samantha, Sasha, Sharon, Sherri, Stephanie D., Tammy, and Tia.

My gratitude to Kaija for stepping forward to become my PA and social media ninja. Thank you for your knowledge, enthusiasm, and energy! I'm so glad someone who actually understands and likes social media is here to rescue this introverted author from herself. I look forward to growing our futures in this business together.

Brittany, you have my gratitude for all the hats you wear - assistant, researcher, editor, train conductor, moral support expert (to name a few). Thank you for loving and believing in these books unconditionally...and for reminding me to sleep.

A huge thank you to Graceley Knox for all your tireless efforts for the community, including organizing my Paper Myths blog tour. Massive appreciation to all the book bloggers who pour passion and time into sharing authors' books with your audiences. I am in awe of how hard you work to build your platforms, produce truly valuable content for readers, and support authors, all purely for the love of books.

To the good souls at my local Postal Annex, thank you for your endless patience with that author who keeps coming in with more batches of ARCs and swag to mail out. I appreciate you helping me get dozens of packages off to all corners of the world for readers and bloggers to enjoy!

And finally, thank you to my feline familiar, Milly, for purring on my lap during long work sessions, posing for Instagram, and rubbing your chin on every book I ship out. I know some extra treats will mean more to you than these silly human words, so I'll give you some tidbits as soon as I finish typing this.

ABOUT THE AUTHOR

VELA ROTH grew up with female-driven fantasy books and classic epics, then grew into romance novels. She set out to write stories that blend the rich worlds of fantasy with the passion of romance.

She has pursued a career in academia, worked as a web designer and book formatter, and stayed home as a full-time caregiver for her loved ones with severe illnesses. Writing through her own grief and trauma, she created the Blood Grace series, which now offers comfort to readers around the world.

She lives in a solar-powered writer's garret in the Southwestern United States, finding inspiration in the mountains and growing roses in the desert. Her feline familiar is a rescue cat named Milly with a missing fang and a big heart.

Vela loves hearing from readers and hopes you'll visit her at velaroth.com.

CPSIA information can be obtained
at www.ICGtesting.com
Printed in the USA
LVHW090832140723
752123LV00021B/572/J

9 781957 040073